The Complete Works of Nathaniel Hawthorne ...

Nathaniel Hawthorne

Wayside Edition

THE COMPLETE WORKS

OF

NATHANIEL HAWTHORNE

IN THIRTEEN VOLUMES

VOLUME III

THE HOUSE OF THE SEVEN GABLES

AND

THE SNOW-IMAGE
AND OTHER TWICE-TOLD TALES

BY

NATHANIEL HAWTHORNE

BOSTON AND NEW YORK

HOUGHTON MIFFLIN COMPANY

The Riverside Press Cambridge

CONTENTS.

———◆———

THE HOUSE OF THE SEVEN GABLES.

THE SNOW-IMAGE AND OTHER TWICE-TOLD TALES.

THE

HOUSE OF THE SEVEN GABLES.

A ROMANCE.

INTRODUCTORY NOTE.

THE HOUSE OF THE SEVEN GABLES.

In September of the year during the February of which Hawthorne had completed "The Scarlet Letter," he began "The House of the Seven Gables." Meanwhile, he had removed from Salem to Lenox, in Berkshire County, Massachusetts, where he occupied with his family a small red wooden house, still standing at the date of this edition, near the Stockbridge Bowl.

"I sha'n't have the new story ready by November," he explained to his publisher, on the 1st of October, "for I am never good for anything in the literary way till after the first autumnal frost, which has somewhat such an effect on my imagination that it does on the foliage here about me — multiplying and brightening its hues." But by vigorous application he was able to complete the new work about the middle of the January following.

Since research has disclosed the manner in which the romance is interwoven with incidents from the history of the Hawthorne family, "The House of the Seven Gables" has acquired an interest apart from that by which it first appealed to the public. John Hathorne (as the name was then spelled), the great-grandfather of Nathaniel Hawthorne, was a magistrate at Salem in the latter part of the seventeenth century, and officiated at the famous trials for witchcraft held there. It is of record that he used peculiar severity towards a certain woman who was among the accused; and the husband of this woman prophesied that God would take revenge upon his wife's persecutors. This circumstance doubtless furnished a hint for that piece of tradition in the book which represents a Pyncheon of a former generation as having persecuted one Maule, who declared that God would give his enemy "blood to drink." It became a conviction with the Hawthorne family that a curse had been pronounced upon its members, which continued in force in the time of the romancer; a conviction perhaps derived from the recorded prophecy of the injured woman's husband, just mentioned; and, here again, we have a correspondence with Maule's malediction in the story. Furthermore, there occurs in the "American Note-Books" (August 27, 1837), a reminiscence of the author's family, to the following effect. Philip English, a character well-known in early Salem annals, was among those who suffered from John Hathorne's magisterial harshness, and he maintained in consequence a lasting feud with the old Puritan official. But at his death English left daughters, one of whom is said to have married the son of Justice John Hathorne, whom English had declared he would never forgive. It is scarcely necessary to point out how clearly this foreshadows the final union of those hereditary foes, the Pyncheons and Maules, through the marriage of Phœbe and Holgrave. The romance, however, describes the Maules as possessing some of the traits known to have been characteristic of the Hawthornes: for example, " so long as any of the race were to be found, they had been marked out from other men — not strikingly, nor as with a sharp line, but with an effect that was felt rather than spoken of — by an hereditary characteristic of reserve." Thus, while the general suggestion of the Hawthorne line and its fortunes was followed in the romance, the Pyncheons taking the place of the author's family, certain distinguishing marks of the Hawthornes were assigned to the imaginary Maule posterity.

There are one or two other points which indicate Hawthorne's method of basing his compositions, the result in the main of pure invention, on the solid ground of particular facts. Allusion is made, in the first chapter of the "Seven Gables," to a grant of lands in Waldo County, Maine, owned by the Pyncheon family. In the "American Note-Books" there is an entry, dated August 12, 1837, which speaks of the Revolutionary general, Knox, and his land-grant in Waldo County, by virtue of which the owner had hoped to establish an estate on the English plan, with a tenantry to make it profitable for him. An incident of much greater importance in the story is the supposed murder of one of the Pyncheons by his nephew, to whom we are introduced as Clifford Pyncheon. In all probability Hawthorne connected with this, in his mind, the murder of Mr. White, a wealthy gentleman of Salem, killed by a man whom his nephew had hired. This took place a few years after Hawthorne's graduation from college, and was one of the celebrated cases of the day, Daniel Webster taking part prominently in the trial. But it should be observed here that such resemblances as these between sundry elements in the work of Hawthorne's fancy and details of reality are only fragmentary, and are rearranged to suit the author's purposes.

In the same way he has made his description of Hepzibah Pyncheon's seven-gabled mansion conform so nearly to several old dwellings formerly or still extant in Salem, that strenuous efforts have been made to fix upon some one of them as the veritable edifice of the romance. A paragraph in the opening chapter has perhaps assisted this delusion that there must have been a single original House of the Seven Gables, framed by flesh-and-blood carpenters; for it runs thus : —

" Familiar as it stands in the writer's recollection — for it has been an object of curiosity with him from boyhood, both as a specimen of the best and stateliest architecture of a long-past epoch, and as the scene of events more full of interest perhaps than those of a gray feudal castle — familiar as it stands, in its rusty old age, it is therefore only the more difficult to imagine the bright novelty with which it first caught the sunshine."

Hundreds of pilgrims annually visit a house in Salem, belonging to one branch of the Ingersoll family of that place, which is stoutly maintained to have been the model for Hawthorne's visionary dwelling. Others have supposed that the now vanished house of the identical Philip English, whose blood, as we have already noticed, became mingled with that of the Hawthornes, supplied the pattern; and still a third building, known as the Curwen mansion, has been declared the only genuine establishment. Notwithstanding persistent popular belief, the authenticity of all these must positively be denied; although it is possible that isolated reminiscences of all three may have blended with the ideal image in the mind of Hawthorne. He, it will be seen, remarks in the Preface, alluding to himself in the third person, that he trusts not to be condemned for "laying out a street that infringes upon nobody's private rights . . . and building *a house of materials long in use for constructing castles in the air.*" More than this, he stated to persons still living that the house of the romance was not copied from any actual edifice, but was simply a general reproduction of a style of architecture belonging to colonial days, examples of which survived into the period of his youth, but have since been radically modified or destroyed. Here, as elsewhere, he exercised the liberty of a creative mind to heighten the probability of his pictures without confining himself to a literal description of something he had seen.

While Hawthorne remained at Lenox, and during the composition of this romance, various other literary personages settled or stayed for a time in the vicinity; among them, Herman Melville, whose intercourse Hawthorne greatly enjoyed, Henry James, Sr., Doctor Holmes, J. T. Headley, James Russell Lowell, Edwin P. Whipple, Frederika Bremer, and J. T. Fields; so that there was no lack of intellectual society in the midst of the beautiful and inspiring mountain scenery of the place. "In the afternoons, nowadays," he records, shortly before beginning the work, "this valley in which I dwell seems like a vast basin filled with golden sunshine as with wine;" and, happy in the companionship of his wife and their three children, he led a simple, refined, idyllic life, despite the restrictions of a scanty and uncertain income. A letter written by Mrs. Hawthorne, at this time, to a member of her family, gives incidentally a glimpse of the scene, which may properly find a place here. She says: "I delight to think that you also can look forth, as I do now, upon a broad valley and a fine amphitheatre of hills, and are about to watch the stately ceremony of the sunset from your piazza. But you have not this lovely lake, nor, I suppose, the delicate purple mist which folds these slumbering mountains in airy veils. Mr. Hawthorne has been lying down in the sunshine, slightly fleckered with the shadows of a tree, and Una and Julian have been making him look like the mighty Pan, by covering his chin and breast with long grass-blades, that looked like a verdant and venerable beard." The pleasantness and peace of his surroundings and of his modest home, in Lenox, may be taken into account as harmonizing with the mellow serenity of the romance then produced. Of the work, when it appeared in the early spring of 1851, he wrote to Horatio Bridge these words, now published for the first time : —

" ' The House of the Seven Gables,' in my opinion, is better than ' The Scarlet Letter ; ' but I should not wonder if I had refined upon the principal character a little too much for popular appreciation, nor if the romance of the book should be somewhat at odds with the humble and familiar scenery in which I invest it. But I feel that portions of it are as good as anything I can hope to write, and the publisher speaks encouragingly of its success."

From England, especially, came many warm expressions of praise, — a fact which Mrs. Hawthorne, in a private letter, commented on as the fulfilment of a possibility which Hawthorne, writing in boyhood to his mother, had looked forward to. He had asked her if she would not like him to become an author and have his books read in England.

G. P. L.

PREFACE.

WHEN a writer calls his work a Romance, it need hardly be observed that he wishes to claim a certain latitude, both as to its fashion and material, which he would not have felt himself entitled to assume had he professed to be writing a Novel. The latter form of composition is presumed to aim at a very minute fidelity, not merely to the possible, but to the probable and ordinary course of man's experience. The former — while, as a work of art, it must rigidly subject itself to laws, and while it sins unpardonably so far as it may swerve aside from the truth of the human heart — has fairly a right to present that truth under circumstances, to a great extent, of the writer's own choosing or creation. If he think fit, also, he may so manage his atmospherical medium as to bring out or mellow the lights and deepen and enrich the shadows of the picture. He will be wise, no doubt, to make a very moderate use of the privileges here stated, and, especially, to mingle the Marvellous rather as a slight, delicate, and evanescent flavor, than as any portion of the actual substance of the dish offered to the public. He can hardly be said, however, to commit a literary crime even if he disregard this caution.

In the present work, the author has proposed to himself — but with what success, fortunately, it is not for him to judge — to keep undeviatingly within his immunities. The point of view in which this tale comes under the Romantic definition lies in the attempt to connect a bygone time with the very present that is flitting away from us. It is a legend prolonging itself, from an epoch now gray in the distance, down into our own broad daylight, and bringing along with it some of its legendary mist, which the reader, according to his pleasure, may either disregard, or allow it to float almost imperceptibly about the characters and events for the sake of a picturesque effect. The narrative, it may be, is woven of so humble a texture as to require this advantage, and, at the same time, to render it the more difficult of attainment.

Many writers lay very great stress upon some definite moral purpose, at which they profess to aim their works. Not to be deficient in this particular, the author has provided himself with a moral, — the truth, namely, that the wrong-doing of one generation lives into the successive ones, and, divesting itself of every temporary advantage, becomes a pure and uncontrollable mischief; and he would feel it a singular gratification if this romance might effectually convince mankind — or, indeed, any one man — of the folly of tumbling down an avalanche of ill-gotten gold, or real estate, on the heads of an unfortunate posterity, thereby to maim and crush them, until the accumulated mass shall be scattered abroad in its original atoms. In good faith, however, he is not sufficiently imaginative to flatter himself with the slightest hope of this kind. When romances do really teach anything, or produce any effective operation, it is usually through a far more subtile process than the ostensible one. The author has considered it hardly worth his while, therefore, relentlessly to impale the story with its

moral as with an iron rod, — or, rather, as by sticking
a pin through a butterfly, — thus at once depriving it
of life, and causing it to stiffen in an ungainly and unnatural attitude.   A high truth, indeed, fairly, finely,
and skilfully wrought out, brightening at every step,
and crowning the final development of a work of fiction, may add an artistic glory, but is never any truer,
and seldom any more evident, at the last page than at
the first.

The reader may perhaps choose to assign an actual
locality to the imaginary events of this narrative.   If
permitted by the historical connection, — which, though
slight, was essential to his plan, — the author would
very willingly have avoided anything of this nature.
Not to speak of other objections, it exposes the romance to an inflexible and exceedingly dangerous species of criticism, by bringing his fancy-pictures almost
into positive contact with the realities of the moment.
It has been no part of his object, however, to describe
local manners, nor in any way to meddle with the
characteristics of a community for whom he cherishes
a proper respect and a natural regard.   He trusts not
to be considered as unpardonably offending by laying
out a street that infringes upon nobody's private rights,
and appropriating a lot of land which had no visible
owner, and building a house of materials long in use
for constructing castles in the air.   The personages of
the tale — though they give themselves out to be of
ancient stability and considerable prominence — are
really of the author's own making, or, at all events, of
his own mixing ; their virtues can shed no lustre, nor
their defects redound, in the remotest degree, to the
discredit of the venerable town of which they profess
to be inhabitants.   He would be glad, therefore, if —

especially in the quarter to which he alludes — the book may be read strictly as a Romance, having a great deal more to do with the clouds overhead than with any portion of the actual soil of the County of Essex.

Lenox, January 27, 1851.

THE
HOUSE OF THE SEVEN GABLES.

I.

THE OLD PYNCHEON FAMILY.

HALF-WAY down a by-street of one of our New England towns stands a rusty wooden house, with seven acutely peaked gables, facing towards various points of the compass, and a huge, clustered chimney in the midst. The street is Pyncheon Street; the house is the old Pyncheon House; and an elm-tree, of wide circumference, rooted before the door, is familiar to every town-born child by the title of the Pyncheon Elm. On my occasional visits to the town aforesaid, I seldom failed to turn down Pyncheon Street, for the sake of passing through the shadow of these two antiquities, — the great elm-tree and the weather-beaten edifice.

The aspect of the venerable mansion has always affected me like a human countenance, bearing the traces not merely of outward storm and sunshine, but expressive, also, of the long lapse of mortal life, and accompanying vicissitudes that have passed within. Were these to be worthily recounted, they would form a narrative of no small interest and instruction, and possessing, moreover, a certain remarkable unity,

which might almost seem the result of artistic arrangement.   But the story would include a chain of events
extending over the better part of two centuries, and,
written out with reasonable amplitude, would fill a
bigger folio volume, or a longer series of duodecimos,
than could prudently be appropriated to the annals of
all New England during a similar period.   It consequently becomes imperative to make short work with
most of the traditionary lore of which the old Pyncheon House, otherwise known as the House of the
Seven Gables, has been the theme.   With a brief
sketch, therefore, of the circumstances amid which the
foundation of the house was laid, and a rapid glimpse
at its quaint exterior, as it grew black in the prevalent
east wind, — pointing, too, here and there, at some
spot of more verdant mossiness on its roof and walls,
— we shall commence the real action of our tale at an
epoch not very remote from the present day.   Still,
there will be a connection with the long past — a reference to forgotten events and personages, and to
manners, feelings, and opinions, almost or wholly ob-
solete — which, if adequately translated to the reader,
would serve to illustrate how much of old material
goes to make up the freshest novelty of human life.
Hence, too, might be drawn a weighty lesson from the
little-regarded truth, that the act of the passing generation is the germ which may and must produce good
or evil fruit in a far-distant time ; that, together with
the seed of the merely temporary crop, which mortals
term expediency, they inevitably sow the acorns of a
more enduring growth, which may darkly overshadow
their posterity.

The House of the Seven Gables, antique as it now
looks, was not the first habitation erected by civilized

man on precisely the same spot of ground. Pyncheon
Street formerly bore the humbler appellation of Maule's
Lane, from the name of the original occupant of the
soil, before whose cottage-door it was a cow-path. A
natural spring of soft and pleasant water — a rare
treasure on the sea-girt peninsula, where the Puritan
settlement was made — had early induced Matthew
Maule to build a hut, shaggy with thatch, at this
point, although somewhat too remote from what was
then the centre of the village. In the growth of the
town, however, after some thirty or forty years, the
site covered by this rude hovel had become exceedingly desirable in the eyes of a prominent and powerful personage, who asserted plausible claims to the
proprietorship of this, and a large adjacent tract of
land, on the strength of a grant from the legislature.
Colonel Pyncheon, the claimant, as we gather from
whatever traits of him are preserved, was characterized by an iron energy of purpose. Matthew Maule,
on the other hand, though an obscure man, was stubborn in the defence of what he considered his right;
and, for several years, he succeeded in protecting the
acre or two of earth, which, with his own toil, he had
hewn out of the primeval forest, to be his garden-
ground and homestead. No written record of this
dispute is known to be in existence. Our acquaintance with the whole subject is derived chiefly from
tradition. It would be bold, therefore, and possibly
unjust, to venture a decisive opinion as to its merits;
although it appears to have been at least a matter of
doubt, whether Colonel Pyncheon's claim were not
unduly stretched, in order to make it cover the small
metes and bounds of Matthew Maule. What greatly
strengthens such a suspicion is the fact that this con-

troversy between two ill-matched antagonists—at a period, moreover, laud it as we may, when personal influence had far more weight than now—remained for years undecided, and came to a close only with the death of the party occupying the disputed soil. The mode of his death, too, affects the mind differently, in our day, from what it did a century and a half ago. It was a death that blasted with strange horror the humble name of the dweller in the cottage, and made 't seem almost a religious act to drive the plough over the little area of his habitation, and obliterate his place and memory from among men.

Old Matthew Maule, in a word, was executed for the crime of witchcraft. He was one of the martyrs to that terrible delusion, which should teach us, among its other morals, that the influential classes, and those who take upon themselves to be leaders of the people, are fully liable to all the passionate error that has ever characterized the maddest mob. Clergymen, judges, statesmen,—the wisest, calmest, holiest persons of their day,—stood in the inner circle round about the gallows, loudest to applaud the work of blood, latest to confess themselves miserably deceived. If any one part of their proceedings can be said to deserve less blame than another, it was the singular indiscrimination with which they persecuted, not merely the poor and aged, as in former judicial massacres, but people of all ranks; their own equals, brethren, and wives. Amid the disorder of such various ruin, it is not strange that a man of inconsiderable note, like Maule, should have trodden the martyr's path to the hill of execution almost unremarked in the throng of his fellow-sufferers. But, in after days, when the frenzy of that hideous epoch had subsided, it was remembered how loudly Colonel Pyncheon had joined in the general cry, to purge the land from witchcraft; nor did it fail to be whispered, that there was an invidious acrimony in the zeal with which he had sought the condemnation of Matthew Maule. It was well known that the victim had recognized the bitterness of personal enmity in his persecutor's conduct towards him, and that he declared himself hunted to death for his spoil. At the moment of execution — with the halter about his neck, and while Colonel Pyncheon sat on horseback, grimly gazing at the scene — Maule had addressed him from the scaffold, and uttered a prophecy, of which history, as well as fireside tradition, has preserved the very words. "God," said the dying man, pointing his finger, with a ghastly look, at the undismayed countenance of his enemy, — "God will give him blood to drink!"

After the reputed wizard's death, his humble homestead had fallen an easy spoil into Colonel Pyncheon's grasp. When it was understood, however, that the Colonel intended to erect a family mansion — spacious, ponderously framed of oaken timber, and calculated to endure for many generations of his posterity — over the spot first covered by the log-built hut of Matthew Maule, there was much shaking of the head among the village gossips. Without absolutely expressing a doubt whether the stalwart Puritan had acted as a man of conscience and integrity throughout the proceedings which have been sketched, they, nevertheless, hinted that he was about to build his house over an unquiet grave. His home would include the home of the dead and buried wizard, and would thus afford the ghost of the latter a kind of privilege to haunt its new apartments, and the chambers into which future bridegrooms were to lead their brides, and where children of the Pyncheon blood were to be born. The terror and ugliness of Maule's crime, and the wretchedness of his punishment, would darken the freshly plastered walls, and infect them early with the scent of an old and melancholy house. Why, then,—while so much of the soil around him was bestrewn with the virgin forest-leaves,—why should Colonel Pyncheon prefer a site that had already been accurst?

But the Puritan soldier and magistrate was not a man to be turned aside from his well-considered scheme, either by dread of the wizard's ghost, or by flimsy sentimentalities of any kind, however specious. Had he been told of a bad air, it might have moved him somewhat; but he was ready to encounter an evil spirit on his own ground. Endowed with common-sense, as massive and hard as blocks of granite, fastened together by stern rigidity of purpose, as with iron clamps, he followed out his original design, probably without so much as imagining an objection to it. On the score of delicacy, or any scrupulousness which a finer sensibility might have taught him, the Colonel, like most of his breed and generation, was impenetrable. He, therefore, dug his cellar, and laid the deep foundations of his mansion, on the square of earth whence Matthew Maule, forty years before, had first swept away the fallen leaves. It was a curious, and, as some people thought, an ominous fact, that, very soon after the workmen began their operations, the spring of water, above mentioned, entirely lost the deliciousness of its pristine quality. Whether its sources were disturbed by the depth of the new cellar, or whatever subtler cause might lurk at the bottom, it is certain that the water of Maule's Well, as it continued to be called, grew hard and brackish. Even such we find it now ; and any old woman of the neighborhood will certify that it is productive of intestinal mischief to those who quench their thirst there.

The reader may deem it singular that the head carpenter of the new edifice was no other than the son of the very man from whose dead gripe the property of the soil had been wrested. Not improbably he was the best workman of his time ; or, perhaps, the Colonel thought it expedient, or was impelled by some better feeling, thus openly to cast aside all animosity against the race of his fallen antagonist. Nor was it out of keeping with the general coarseness and matter-of-fact character of the age, that the son should be willing to earn an honest penny, or, rather, a weighty amount of sterling pounds, from the purse of his father's deadly enemy. At all events, Thomas Maule became the architect of the House of the Seven Gables, and performed his duty so faithfully that the timber framework fastened by his hands still holds together.

Thus the great house was built. Familiar as it stands in the writer's recollection, — for it has been an object of curiosity with him from boyhood, both as a specimen of the best and stateliest architecture of a long-past epoch, and as the scene of events more full of human interest, perhaps, than those of a gray feudal castle, — familiar as it stands, in its rusty old age, it is therefore only the more difficult to imagine the bright novelty with which it first caught the sunshine. The impression of its actual state, at this distance of a hundred and sixty years, darkens inevitably through the picture which we would fain give of its appearance on the morning when the Puritan magnate bade all the town to be his guests. A ceremony of consecration,

festive as well as religious, was now to be performed.
A prayer and discourse from the Rev. Mr. Higginson,
and the outpouring of a psalm from the general throat
of the community, was to be made acceptable to the
grosser sense by ale, cider, wine, and brandy, in copi-
ous effusion, and, as some authorities aver, by an ox,
roasted whole, or at least, by the weight and substance
of an ox, in more manageable joints and sirloins. The
carcass of a deer, shot within twenty miles, had supplied material for the vast circumference of a pasty.
A codfish of sixty pounds, caught in the bay, had
been dissolved into the rich liquid of a chowder. The
chimney of the new house, in short, belching forth
its kitchen-smoke, impregnated the whole air with the
scent of meats, fowls, and fishes, spicily concocted with
odoriferous herbs, and onions in abundance. The
mere smell of such festivity, making its way to everybody's nostrils, was at once an invitation and an appetite.

Maule's Lane, or Pyncheon Street, as it were now
more decorous to call it, was thronged, at the appointed
hour, as with a congregation on its way to church.
All, as they approached, looked upward at the imposing edifice, which was henceforth to assume its rank
among the habitations of mankind. There it rose, a
little withdrawn from the line of the street, but in
pride, not modesty. Its whole visible exterior was ornamented with quaint figures, conceived in the grotesqueness of a Gothic fancy, and drawn or stamped
in the glittering plaster, composed of lime, pebbles,
and bits of glass, with which the woodwork of the
walls was overspread. On every side the seven gables
pointed sharply towards the sky, and presented the
aspect of a whole sisterhood of edifices, breathing

through the spiracles of one great chimney. The many lattices, with their small, diamond-shaped panes, admitted the sunlight into hall and chamber, while, nevertheless, the second story, projecting far over the base, and itself retiring beneath the third, threw a shadowy and thoughtful gloom into the lower rooms. Carved globes of wood were affixed under the jutting stories. Little spiral rods of iron beautified each of the seven peaks. On the triangular portion of the gable, that fronted next the street, was a dial, put up that very morning, and on which the sun was still marking the passage of the first bright hour in a history that was not destined to be all so bright. All around were scattered shavings, chips, shingles, and broken halves of bricks; these, together with the lately turned earth, on which the grass had not begun . to grow, contributed to the impression of strangeness and novelty proper to a house that had yet its place to make among men's daily interests.

The principal entrance, which had almost the breadth of a church-door, was in the angle between the two front gables, and was covered by an open porch, with benches beneath its shelter. Under this arched doorway, scraping their feet on the unworn threshold, now trod the clergymen, the elders, the magistrates, the deacons, and whatever of aristocracy there was in town or county. Thither, too, thronged the plebeian classes as freely as their betters, and in larger number. Just within the entrance, however, stood two serving-men, pointing some of the guests to the neighborhood of the kitchen, and ushering others into the statelier rooms, — hospitable alike to all, but still with a scrutinizing regard to the high or low degree of each. Velvet garments, sombre but rich, stiffly plaited ruffs and bands, embroidered gloves, venerable beards, the mien and countenance of authority, made it easy to distinguish the gentleman of worship, at that period, from the tradesman, with his plodding air, or the laborer, in his leathern jerkin, stealing awe-stricken into the house which he had perhaps helped to build.

One inauspicious circumstance there was, which awakened a hardly concealed displeasure in the breasts of a few of the more punctilious visitors. The founder of this stately mansion — a gentleman noted for the square and ponderous courtesy of his demeanor — ought surely to have stood in his own hall, and to have offered the first welcome to so many eminent personages as here presented themselves in honor of his solemn festival. He was as yet invisible; the most favored of the guests had not beheld him. This sluggishness on Colonel Pyncheon's part became still more unaccountable, when the second dignitary of the province made his appearance, and found no more ceremonious a reception. The lieutenant - governor, although his visit was one of the anticipated glories of the day, had alighted from his horse, and assisted his lady from her side-saddle, and crossed the Colonel's threshold, without other greeting than that of the principal domestic.

This person — a gray - headed man, of quiet and most respectful deportment — found it necessary to explain that his master still remained in his study, or private apartment; on entering which, an hour before, he had expressed a wish on no account to be disturbed.

"Do not you see, fellow," said the high-sheriff of the county, taking the servant aside, "that this is no less a man than the lieutenant-governor? Summon

Colonel Pyncheon at once! I know that he received letters from England this morning; and, in the perusal and consideration of them, an hour may have passed away without his noticing it. But he will be ill-pleased, I judge, if you suffer him to neglect the courtesy due to one of our chief rulers, and who may be said to represent King William, in the absence of the governor himself. Call your master instantly!"

"Nay, please your worship," answered the man, in much perplexity, but with a backwardness that strikingly indicated the hard and severe character of Colonel Pyncheon's domestic rule; "my master's orders were exceeding strict; and, as your worship knows, he permits of no discretion in the obedience of those who owe him service. Let who list open yonder door; I dare not, though the governor's own voice should bid me do it!"

"Pooh, pooh, master high-sheriff!" cried the lieutenant-governor, who had overheard the foregoing discussion, and felt himself high enough in station to play a little with his dignity. "I will take the matter into my own hands. It is time that the good Colonel came forth to greet his friends; else we shall be apt to suspect that he has taken a sip too much of his Canary wine, in his extreme deliberation which cask it were best to broach in honor of the day! But since he is so much behindhand, I will give him a remembrancer myself!"

Accordingly, with such a tramp of his ponderous riding-boots as might of itself have been audible in the remotest of the seven gables, he advanced to the door, which the servant pointed out, and made its new panels reëcho with a loud, free knock. Then, looking round, with a smile, to the spectators, he awaited a response. As none came, however, he knocked again, but with the same unsatisfactory result as at first. And now, being a trifle choleric in his temperament, the lieutenant-governor uplifted the heavy hilt of his sword, wherewith he so beat and banged upon the door, that, as some of the by-standers whispered, the racket might have disturbed the dead. Be that as it might, it seemed to produce no awakening effect on Colonel Pyncheon. When the sound subsided, the silence through the house was deep, dreary, and oppressive, notwithstanding that the tongues of many of the guests had already been loosened by a surreptitious cup or two of wine or spirits.

"Strange, forsooth! — very strange!" cried the lieutenant-governor, whose smile was changed to a frown. "But seeing that our host sets us the good example of forgetting ceremony, I shall likewise throw it aside, and make free to intrude on his privacy!"

He tried the door, which yielded to his hand, and was flung wide open by a sudden gust of wind that passed, as with a loud sigh, from the outermost portal through all the passages and apartments of the new house. It rustled the silken garments of the ladies, and waved the long curls of the gentlemen's wigs, and shook the window-hangings and the curtains of the bedchambers; causing everywhere a singular stir, which yet was more like a hush. A shadow of awe and half-fearful anticipation — nobody knew wherefore, nor of what — had all at once fallen over the company.

They thronged, however, to the now open door, pressing the lieutenant-governor, in the eagerness of their curiosity, into the room in advance of them. At the first glimpse they beheld nothing extraordinary: a handsomely furnished room, of moderate size, some what darkened by curtains; books arranged on shelves; a large map on the wall, and likewise a portrait of Colonel Pyncheon, beneath which sat the original Colonel himself, in an oaken elbow-chair, with a pen in his hand. Letters, parchments, and blank sheets of paper were on the table before him. He appeared to gaze at the curious crowd, in front of which stood the lieutenant-governor; and there was a frown on his dark and massive countenance, as if sternly resentful of the boldness that had impelled them into his private retirement.

A little boy — the Colonel's grandchild, and the only human being that ever dared to be familiar with him — now made his way among the guests, and ran towards the seated figure; then pausing half-way, he began to shriek with terror. The company, tremulous as the leaves of a tree, when all are shaking together, drew nearer, and perceived that there was an unnatural distortion in the fixedness of Colonel Pyncheon's stare; that there was blood on his ruff, and that his hoary beard was saturated with it. It was too late to give assistance. The iron-hearted Puritan, the relentless persecutor, the grasping and strong-willed man, was dead! Dead, in his new house! There is a tradition, only worth alluding to as lending a tinge of superstitious awe to a scene perhaps gloomy enough without it, that a voice spoke loudly among the guests, the tones of which were like those of old Matthew Maule, the executed wizard, — "God hath given him blood to drink!"

Thus early had that one guest, — the only guest who is certain, at one time or another, to find his way into every human dwelling, — thus early had Death stepped across the threshold of the House of the Seven Gables!

Colonel Pyncheon's sudden and mysterious **end** made a vast deal of noise in its day. There were many rumors, some of which have vaguely drifted down to the present time, how that appearances indicated violence; that there were the marks of fingers on his throat, and the print of a bloody hand on his plaited ruff; and that his peaked beard was dishevelled, as if it had been fiercely clutched and pulled. It was averred, likewise, that the lattice window, near the Colonel's chair, was open; and that, only a few minutes before the fatal occurrence, the figure of a man had been seen clambering over the garden-fence, in the rear of the house. But it were folly to lay any stress on stories of this kind, which are sure to spring up around such an event as that now related, and which, as in the present case, sometimes prolong themselves for ages afterwards, like the toadstools that indicate where the fallen and buried trunk of a tree has long since mouldered into the earth. For our own part, we allow them just as little credence as to that other fable of the skeleton hand which the lieutenant-governor was said to have seen at the Colonel's throat, but which vanished away, as he advanced farther into the room. Certain it is, however, that there was a great consultation and dispute of doctors over the dead body. One — John Swinnerton by name — who appears to have been a man of eminence, upheld it, if we have rightly understood his terms of art, to be a case of apoplexy. His professional brethren, each for himself, adopted various hypotheses, more or less plausible, but all dressed out in a perplexing mystery of phrase, which, if it do not show a bewilderment of mind in these erudite physicians, certainly causes it in the unlearned peruser of their opinions. The coroner's jury sat upon the corpse, and, like sensible men, returned an unassailable verdict of " Sudden Death ! "

It is indeed difficult to imagine that there could have been a serious suspicion of murder, or the slightest grounds for implicating any particular individual as the perpetrator. The rank, wealth, and eminent character of the deceased must have insured the strictest scrutiny into every ambiguous circumstance. As none such is on record, it is safe to assume that none existed. Tradition, — which sometimes brings down truth that history has let slip, but is oftener the wild babble of the time, such as was formerly spoken at the fireside and now congeals in newspapers, — tradition is responsible for all contrary averments. In Colonel Pyncheon's funeral sermon, which was printed, and is still extant, the Rev. Mr. Higginson enumerates, among the many felicities of his distinguished parishioner's earthly career, the happy seasonableness of his death. His duties all performed, — the highest prosperity attained, — his race and future generations fixed on a stable basis, and with a stately roof to shelter them, for centuries to come, — what other upward step remained for this good man to take, save the final step from earth to the golden gate of heaven ! The pious clergyman surely would not have uttered words like these had he in the least suspected that the Colonel had been thrust into the other world with the clutch of violence upon his throat.

The family of Colonel Pyncheon, at the epoch of his death, seemed destined to as fortunate a permanence as can anywise consist with the inherent instability of human affairs. It might fairly be anticipated that the progress of time would rather increase and ripen their prosperity, than wear away and destroy it. For, not

only had his son and heir come into immediate enjoyment of a rich estate, but there was a claim through
an Indian deed, confirmed by a subsequent grant of
the General Court, to a vast and as yet unexplored
and unmeasured tract of Eastern lands. These possessions — for as such they might almost certainly be
reckoned — comprised the greater part of what is now
known as Waldo County, in the State of Maine, and
were more extensive than many a dukedom, or even a
reigning prince's territory, on European soil. When
the pathless forest that still covered this wild princi-
pality should give place — as it inevitably must, though
perhaps not till ages hence — to the golden fertility of
human culture, it would be the source of incalculable
wealth to the Pyncheon blood. Had the Colonel survived only a few weeks longer, it is probable that his
great political influence, and powerful connections at
home and abroad, would have consummated all that
was necessary to render the claim available. But, in
spite of good Mr. Higginson's congratulatory eloquence, this appeared to be the one thing which Colonel Pyncheon, provident and sagacious as he was, had
allowed to go at loose ends. So far as the prospective
territory was concerned, he unquestionably died too
soon. His son lacked not merely the father's eminent
position, but the talent and force of character to
achieve it : he could, therefore, effect nothing by dint
of political interest ; and the bare justice or legality
of the claim was not so apparent, after the Colonel's
decease, as it had been pronounced in his lifetime.
Some connecting link had slipped out of the evidence,
and could not anywhere be found.

Efforts, it is true, were made by the Pyncheons,
not only then, but at various periods for nearly a hun-

dred years afterwards, to obtain what they stubbornly
persisted in deeming their right. But, in course of
time, the territory was partly re-granted to more favored individuals, and partly cleared and occupied by
actual settlers. These last, if they ever heard of the
Pyncheon title, would have laughed at the idea of any
man's asserting a right — on the strength of mouldy
parchments, signed with the faded autographs of governors and legislators long dead and forgotten — to
the lands which they or their fathers had wrested from
the wild hand of nature by their own sturdy toil.
This impalpable claim, therefore, resulted in nothing
more solid than to cherish, from generation to generation, an absurd delusion of family importance, which
all along characterized the Pyncheons. It caused the
poorest member of the race to feel as if he inherited a
kind of nobility, and might yet come into the possession of princely wealth to support it. In the better
specimens of the breed, this peculiarity threw an ideal
grace over the hard material of human life, without
stealing away any truly valuable quality. In the
baser sort, its effect was to increase the liability to
sluggishness and dependence, and induce the victim of
a shadowy hope to remit all self-effort, while awaiting the realization of his dreams. Years and years
after their claim had passed out of the public memory,
the Pyncheons were accustomed to consult the Colonel's ancient map, which had been projected while
Waldo County was still an unbroken wilderness.
Where the old land-surveyor had put down woods,
lakes, and rivers, they marked out the cleared spaces,
and dotted the villages and towns, and calculated the
progressively increasing value of the territory, as if

there were yet a prospect of its ultimately forming a princedom for themselves.

In almost every generation, nevertheless, there happened to be some one descendant of the family gifted with a portion of the hard, keen sense, and practical energy, that had so remarkably distinguished the orig inal founder. His character, indeed, might be traced all the way down, as distinctly as if the Colonel himself, a little diluted, had been gifted with a sort of intermittent immortality on earth. At two or three epochs, when the fortunes of the family were low, this representative of hereditary qualities had made his appearance, and caused the traditionary gossips of the town to whisper among themselves, "Here is the old Pyncheon come again! Now the Seven Gables will be new-shingled!" From father to son, they clung to the ancestral house with singular tenacity of home attachment. For various reasons, however, and from impressions often too vaguely founded to be put on paper, the writer cherishes the belief that many, if not most, of the successive proprietors of this estate were troubled with doubts as to their moral right to hold it. Of their legal tenure there could be no question; but old Matthew Maule, it is to be feared, trode downward from his own age to a far later one, planting a heavy footstep, all the way, on the conscience of a Pyncheon. If so, we are left to dispose of the awful query, whether each inheritor of the property — conscious of wrong, and failing to rectify it — did not commit anew the great guilt of his ancestor, and incur all its original responsibilities. And supposing such to be the case, would it not be a far truer mode of expression to say of the Pyncheon family, that they inherited a great misfortune, than the reverse?

We have already hinted that it is not our purpose to trace down the history of the Pyncheon family, in its unbroken connection with the House of the Seven Gables; nor to show, as in a magic picture, how the rustiness and infirmity of age gathered over the venerable house itself. As regards its interior life, a large, dim looking-glass used to hang in one of the rooms, and was fabled to contain within its depths all the shapes that had ever been reflected there, — the old Colonel himself, and his many descendants, some in the garb of antique babyhood, and others in the bloom of feminine beauty or manly prime, or saddened with the wrinkles of frosty age. Had we the secret of that mirror, we would gladly sit down before it, and transfer its revelations to our page. But there was a story, for which it is difficult to conceive any foundation, that the posterity of Matthew Maule had some connection with the mystery of the looking-glass, and that, by what appears to have been a sort of mesmeric process, they could make its inner region all alive with the departed Pyncheons; not as they had shown themselves to the world nor in their better and happier hours, but as doing over again some deed of sin, or in the crisis of life's bitterest sorrow. The popular imagination, indeed, long kept itself busy with the affair of the old Puritan Pyncheon and the wizard Maule; the curse, which the latter flung from his scaffold, was remembered, with the very important addition, that it had become a part of the Pyncheon inheritance. If one of the family did but gurgle in his throat, a bystander would be likely enough to whisper, between jest and earnest, "He has Maule's blood to drink!" The sudden death of a Pyncheon, about a hundred years ago, with circumstances very similar to what have been related of the Colonel's exit, was held as giving additional probability to the received opinion on this topic. It was considered, moreover, an ugly and ominous circumstance, that Colonel Pyncheon's picture — in obedience, it was said, to a provision of his will — remained affixed to the wall of the room in which he died. Those stern, immitigable features seemed to symbolize an evil influence, and so darkly to mingle the shadow of their presence with the sunshine of the passing hour, that no good thoughts or purposes could ever spring up and blossom there. To the thoughtful mind there will be no tinge of superstition in what we figuratively express, by affirming that the ghost of a dead progenitor — perhaps as a portion of his own punishment — is often doomed to become the Evil Genius of his family.

The Pyncheons, in brief, lived along, for the better part of two centuries, with perhaps less of outward vicissitude than has attended most other New England families during the same period of time. Possessing very distinctive traits of their own, they nevertheless took the general characteristics of the little community in which they dwelt; a town noted for its frugal, discreet, well-ordered, and home-loving inhabitants, as well as for the somewhat confined scope of its sympathies; but in which, be it said, there are odder individuals, and, now and then, stranger occurrences, than one meets with almost anywhere else. During the Revolution, the Pyncheon of that epoch, adopting the royal side, became a refugee; but repented, and made his reappearance, just at the point of time to preserve the House of the Seven Gables from confiscation. For the last seventy years the most noted event in the Pyncheon annals had been likewise the heaviest calamity that ever befell the race; no less than the violent death — for so it was adjudged — of one member of the family by the criminal act of another. Certain circumstances attending this fatal occurrence had brought the deed irresistibly home to a nephew of the deceased Pyncheon. The young man was tried and convicted of the crime; but either the circumstantial nature of the evidence, and possibly some lurking doubt in the breast of the executive, or, lastly, — an argument of greater weight in a republic than it could have been under a monarchy, — the high respectability and political influence of the criminal's connections, had availed to mitigate his doom from death to perpetual imprisonment. This sad affair had chanced about thirty years before the action of our story commences. Latterly, there were rumors (which few believed, and only one or two felt greatly interested in) that this long-buried man was likely, for some reason or other, to be summoned forth from his living tomb.

It is essential to say a few words respecting the victim of this now almost forgotten murder. He was an old bachelor, and possessed of great wealth, in addition to the house and real estate which constituted what remained of the ancient Pyncheon property. Being of an eccentric and melancholy turn of mind, and greatly given to rummaging old records and hearkening to old traditions, he had brought himself, it is averred, to the conclusion that Matthew Maule, the wizard, had been foully wronged out of his homestead, if not out of his life. Such being the case, and he, the old bachelor, in possession of the ill-gotten spoil, — with the black stain of blood sunken deep into it, and still to be scented by conscientious nostrils, — the question occurred, whether it were not im-

perative upon him, even at this late hour, to make
restitution to Maule's posterity. To a man living so
much in the past, and so little in the present, as the
secluded and antiquarian old bachelor, a century and
a half seemed not so vast a period as to obviate the
propriety of substituting right for wrong. It was the
belief of those who knew him best, that he would
positively have taken the very singular step of giving
up the House of the Seven Gables to the representative of Matthew Maule, but for the unspeakable tumult which a suspicion of the old gentleman's project
awakened among his Pyncheon relatives. Their exer-
tions had the effect of suspending his purpose; but it
was feared that he would perform, after death, by the
operation of his last will, what he had so hardly been
prevented from doing in his proper lifetime. But
there is no one thing which men so rarely do, whatever the provocation or inducement, as to bequeath
patrimonial property away from their own blood. They
may love other individuals far better than their relatives, — they may even cherish dislike, or positive
hatred, to the latter; but yet, in view of death, the
strong prejudice of propinquity revives, and impels the
testator to send down his estate in the line marked
out by custom so immemorial that it looks like nature.
In all the Pyncheons, this feeling had the energy of
disease. It was too powerful for the conscientious
scruples of the old bachelor; at whose death, accordingly, the mansion-house, together with most of his
other riches, passed into the possession of his next
legal representative.

This was a nephew, the cousin of the miserable
young man who had been convicted of the uncle's
murder. The new heir, up to the period of his acces-

sion, was reckoned rather a dissipated youth, but had at once reformed, and made himself an exceedingly respectable member of society. In fact, he showed more of the Pyncheon quality, and had won higher eminence in the world than any of his race since the time of the original Puritan. Applying himself in earlier manhood to the study of the law, and having a natural tendency towards office, he had attained, many years ago, to a judicial situation in some inferior court, which gave him for life the very desirable and imposing title of judge. Later, he had engaged in politics, and served a part of two terms in Congress, besides making a considerable figure in both branches of the State legislature. Judge Pyncheon was unquestionably an honor to his race. He had built himself a country-seat within a few miles of his native town, and there spent such portions of his time as could be spared from public service in the display of every grace and virtue — as a newspaper phrased it, on the eve of an election — befitting the Christian, the good citizen, the horticulturist, and the gentleman.

There were few of the Pyncheons left to sun themselves in the glow of the Judge's prosperity. In respect to natural increase, the breed had not thriven; it appeared rather to be dying out. The only members of the family known to be extant were, first, the Judge himself, and a single surviving son, who was now travelling in Europe; next, the thirty years' prisoner, already alluded to, and a sister of the latter, who occupied, in an extremely retired manner, the House of the Seven Gables, in which she had a life-estate by the will of the old bachelor. She was understood to be wretchedly poor, and seemed to make it her choice to remain so; inasmuch as her affluent cousin, the Judge, had repeatedly offered her all the comforts of life, either in the old mansion or his own modern residence. The last and youngest Pyncheon was a little country-girl of seventeen, the daughter of another of the Judge's cousins, who had married a young woman of no family or property, and died early and in poor circumstances. His widow had recently taken another husband.

As for Matthew Maule's posterity, it was supposed now to be extinct. For a very long period after the witchcraft delusion, however, the Maules had continued to inhabit the town where their progenitor had suffered so unjust a death. To all appearance, they were a quiet, honest, well-meaning race of people, cherishing no malice against individuals or the public for the wrong which had been done them; or if, at their own fireside, they transmitted, from father to child, any hostile recollection of the wizard's fate and their lost patrimony, it was never acted upon, nor openly expressed. Nor would it have been singular had they ceased to remember that the House of the Seven Gables was resting its heavy framework on a foundation that was rightfully their own. There is something so massive, stable, and almost irresistibly imposing in the exterior presentment of established rank and great possessions, that their very existence seems to give them a right to exist; at least, so excellent a counterfeit of right, that few poor and humble men have moral force enough to question it, even in their secret minds. Such is the case now, after so many ancient prejudices have been overthrown; and it was far more so in ante-Revolutionary days, when the aristocracy could venture to be proud, and the low were content to be abased. Thus the Maules, at all

events, kept their resentments within their own breasts.
They were generally poverty-stricken; always plebeian
and obscure; working with unsuccessful diligence at
handicrafts; laboring on the wharves, or following the
sea, as sailors before the mast; living here and there
about the town, in hired tenements, and coming finally
to the almshouse as the natural home of their old age.
At last, after creeping as it were, for such a length of
time, along the utmost verge of the opaque puddle
of obscurity, they had taken that downright plunge,
which, sooner or later, is the destiny of all families,
whether princely or plebeian. For thirty years past,
neither town-record, nor gravestone, nor the directory,
nor the knowledge or memory of man, bore any trace
of Matthew Maule's descendants. His blood might
possibly exist elsewhere; here, where its lowly current
could be traced so far back, it had ceased to keep an
onward course.

So long as any of the race were to be found, they
had been marked out from other men — not strikingly,
nor as with a sharp line, but with an effect that was
felt rather than spoken of — by an hereditary character of reserve. Their companions, or those who endeavored to become such, grew conscious of a circle
round about the Maules, within the sanctity or the
spell of which, in spite of an exterior of sufficient
frankness and good-fellowship, it was impossible for
any man to step. It was this indefinable peculiarity,
perhaps, that, by insulating them from human aid,
kept them always so unfortunate in life. It certainly
operated to prolong in their case, and to confirm to
them as their only inheritance, those feelings of repugnance and superstitious terror with which the people
of the town, even after awakening from their frenzy,

continued to regard the memory of the reputed witches.
The mantle, or rather the ragged cloak, of old Matthew Maule, had fallen upon his children. They were
half believed to inherit mysterious attributes; the family eye was said to possess strange power. Among
other good-for-nothing properties and privileges, one
was especially assigned them, — that of exercising an
influence over people's dreams. The Pyncheons, if all
stories were true, haughtily as they bore themselves in
the noonday streets of their native town, were no better than bond-servants to these plebeian Maules, on
entering the topsy-turvy commonwealth of sleep. Modern psychology, it may be, will endeavor to reduce
these alleged necromancies within a system, instead
of rejecting them as altogether fabulous.

A descriptive paragraph or two, treating of the
seven-gabled mansion in its more recent aspect, will
bring this preliminary chapter to a close. The street
in which it upreared its venerable peaks has long
ceased to be a fashionable quarter of the town; so
that, though the old edifice was surrounded by habitations of modern date, they were mostly small, built
entirely of wood, and typical of the most plodding
uniformity of common life. Doubtless, however, the
whole story of human existence may be latent in each
of them, but with no picturesqueness, externally, that
can attract the imagination or sympathy to seek it
there. But as for the old structure of our story, its
white-oak frame, and its boards, shingles, and crumbling plaster, and even the huge, clustered chimney
in the midst, seemed to constitute only the least and
meanest part of its reality. So much of mankind's
varied experience had passed there, — so much had
been suffered, and something, too, enjoyed, — that

the very timbers were oozy, as with the moisture of a heart. It was itself like a great human heart, with a life of its own, and full of rich and sombre reminiscences.

The deep projection of the second story gave the house such a meditative look, that you could not pass it without the idea that it had secrets to keep, and an eventful history to moralize upon. In front, just on the edge of the unpaved sidewalk, grew the Pyncheon Elm, which, in reference to such trees as one usually meets with, might well be termed gigantic. It had been planted by a great-grandson of the first Pyncheon, and, though now fourscore years of age, or perhaps nearer a hundred, was still in its strong and broad maturity, throwing its shadow from side to side of the street, overtopping the seven gables, and sweeping the whole black roof with its pendent foliage. It gave beauty to the old edifice, and seemed to make it a part of nature. The street having been widened about forty years ago, the front gable was now precisely on a line with it. On either side extended a ruinous wooden fence of open lattice-work, through which could be seen a grassy yard, and, especially in the angles of the building, an enormous fertility of burdocks, with leaves, it is hardly an exaggeration to say, two or three feet long. Behind the house there appeared to be a garden, which undoubtedly had once been extensive, but was now infringed upon by other enclosures, or shut in by habitations and outbuildings that stood on another street. It would be an omission, trifling, indeed, but unpardonable, were we to forget the green moss that had long since gathered over the projections of the windows, and on the slopes of the roof; nor must we fail to direct the reader's eye to a crop, not of weeds, but flower-shrubs, which were growing aloft in the air, not a great way from the chimney, in the nook between two of the gables. They were called Alice's Posies. The tradition was, that a certain Alice Pyncheon had flung up the seeds, in sport, and that the dust of the street and the decay of the roof gradually formed a kind of soil for them, out of which they grew, when Alice had long been in her grave. However the flowers might have come there, it was both sad and sweet to observe how Nature adopted to herself this desolate, decaying, gusty, rusty old house of the Pyncheon family; and how the ever-returning summer did her best to gladden it with tender beauty, and grew melancholy in the effort.

There is one other feature, very essential to be noticed, but which, we greatly fear, may damage any picturesque and romantic impression which we have been willing to throw over our sketch of this respectable edifice. In the front gable, under the impending brow of the second story, and contiguous to the street, was a shop-door, divided horizontally in the midst, and with a window for its upper segment, such as is often seen in dwellings of a somewhat ancient date. This same shop-door had been a subject of no slight mortification to the present occupant of the august Pyncheon House, as well as to some of her predecessors. The matter is disagreeably delicate to handle; but, since the reader must needs be let into the secret, he will please to understand, that, about a century ago, the head of the Pyncheons found himself involved in serious financial difficulties. The fellow (gentleman, as he styled himself) can hardly have been other than a spurious interloper; for, instead of seeking office from the king or the royal governor, or urging his hereditary claim to Eastern lands, he bethought him-self of no better avenue to wealth than by cutting a shop-door through the side of his ancestral residence. It was the custom of the time, indeed, for merchants to store their goods and transact business in their own dwellings. But there was something pitifully small in this old Pyncheon's mode of setting about his com-mercial operations; it was whispered, that, with his own hands, all beruffled as they were, he used to give change for a shilling, and would turn a half-penny twice over, to make sure that it was a good one. Be-yond all question, he had the blood of a petty huckster in his veins, through whatever channel it may have found its way there.

Immediately on his death, the shop-door had been locked, bolted, and barred, and, down to the period of our story, had probably never once been opened. The old counter, shelves, and other fixtures of the little shop remained just as he had left them. It used to be affirmed, that the dead shop-keeper, in a white wig, a faded velvet coat, an apron at his waist, and his ruffles carefully turned back from his wrists, might be seen through the chinks of the shutters, any night of the year, ransacking his till, or poring over the dingy pages of his day-book. From the look of un-utterable woe upon his face, it appeared to be his doom to spend eternity in a vain effort to make his accounts balance.

And now — in a very humble way, as will be seen — we proceed to open our narrative.

II.

THE LITTLE SHOP-WINDOW.

IT still lacked half an hour of sunrise, when Miss
Hepzibah Pyncheon — we will not say awoke, it being doubtful whether the poor lady had so much as
closed her eyes during the brief night of midsummer
— but, at all events, arose from her solitary pillow,
and began what it would be mockery to term the
adornment of her person. Far from us be the in-
decorum of assisting, even in imagination, at a maiden
lady's toilet! Our story must therefore await Miss
Hepzibah at the threshold of her chamber; only pre-
suming, meanwhile, to note some of the heavy sighs
that labored from her bosom, with little restraint as
to their lugubrious depth and volume of sound, inasmuch as they could be audible to nobody save a disembodied listener like ourself. The Old Maid was
alone in the old house. Alone, except for a certain
respectable and orderly young man, an artist in the
daguerreotype line, who, for about three months back,
had been a lodger in a remote gable, — quite a house
by itself, indeed, — with locks, bolts, and oaken bars
on all the intervening doors. Inaudible, consequently,
were poor Miss Hepzibah's gusty sighs. Inaudible
the creaking joints of her stiffened knees, as she knelt
down by the bedside. And inaudible, too, by mortal
ear, but heard with all-comprehending love and pity in
the farthest heaven, that almost agony of prayer — now

whispered, now a groan, now a struggling silence —
wherewith she besought the Divine assistance through
the day! Evidently, this is to be a day of more than
ordinary trial to Miss Hepzibah, who, for above a
quarter of a century gone by, has dwelt in strict seclusion, taking no part in the business of life, and just as
little in its intercourse and pleasures. Not with such
fervor prays the torpid recluse, looking forward to the
cold, sunless, stagnant calm of a day that is to be like
innumerable yesterdays!

The maiden lady's devotions are concluded. Will
she now issue forth over the threshold of our story?
Not yet, by many moments. First, every drawer in
the tall, old-fashioned bureau is to be opened, with
difficulty, and with a succession of spasmodic jerks;
then, all must close again, with the same fidgety reluctance. There is a rustling of stiff silks; a tread of
backward and forward footsteps to and fro across the
chamber. We suspect Miss Hepzibah, moreover, of
taking a step upward into a chair, in order to give
heedful regard to her appearance on all sides, and at
full length, in the oval, dingy-framed toilet-glass, that
hangs above her table. Truly! well, indeed! who
would have thought it! Is all this precious time to
be lavished on the matutinal repair and beautifying of
an elderly person, who never goes abroad, whom nobody ever visits, and from whom, when she shall have
done her utmost, it were the best charity to turn one's
eyes another way?

Now she is almost ready. Let us pardon her one
other pause; for it is given to the sole sentiment, or,
we might better say, — heightened and rendered intense, as it has been, by sorrow and seclusion, — to the
strong passion of her life. We heard the turning of

a key in a small lock; she has opened a secret drawer of an escritoire, and is probably looking at a certain miniature, done in Malbone's most perfect style, and representing a face worthy of no less delicate a pencil. It was once our good fortune to see this picture. It is a likeness of a young man, in a silken dressing-gown of an old fashion, the soft richness of which is well adapted to the countenance of reverie, with its full, tender lips, and beautiful eyes, that seem to indicate not so much capacity of thought, as gentle and voluptuous emotion. Of the possessor of such features we shall have a right to ask nothing, except that he would take the rude world easily, and make himself happy in it. Can it have been an early lover of Miss Hepzibah? No; she never had a lover — poor thing, how could she? — nor ever knew, by her own experience, what love technically means. And yet, her undying faith and trust, her fresh remembrance, and continual devotedness towards the original of that miniature, have been the only substance for her heart to feed upon.

She seems to have put aside the miniature, and is standing again before the toilet-glass. There are tears to be wiped off. A few more footsteps to and fro; and here, at last, — with another pitiful sigh, like a gust of chill, damp wind out of a long-closed vault, the door of which has accidentally been set ajar, — here comes Miss Hepzibah Pyncheon! Forth she steps into the dusky, time-darkened passage; a tall figure, clad in black silk, with a long and shrunken waist, feeling her way towards the stairs like a near-sighted person, as in truth she is.

The sun, meanwhile, if not already above the horizon, was ascending nearer and nearer to its verge. A few clouds, floating high upward, caught some of the earliest light, and threw down its golden gleam on the windows of all the houses in the street, not forgetting the House of the Seven Gables, which — many such sunrises as it had witnessed — looked cheerfully at the present one. The reflected radiance served to show, pretty distinctly, the aspect and arrangement of the room which Hepzibah entered, after descending the stairs. It was a low-studded room, with a beam across the ceiling, panelled with dark wood, and having a large chimney-piece, set round with pictured tiles, but now closed by an iron fire-board, through which ran the funnel of a modern stove. There was a carpet on the floor, originally of rich texture, but so worn and faded in these latter years that its once brilliant figure had quite vanished into one indistinguishable hue. In the way of furniture, there were two tables : one, constructed with perplexing intricacy and exhibiting as many feet as a centipede ; the other, most delicately wrought, with four long and slender legs, so apparently frail that it was almost incredible what a length of time the ancient tea-table had stood upon them. Half a dozen chairs stood about the room, straight and stiff, and so ingeniously contrived for the discomfort of the human person that they were irksome even to sight, and conveyed the ugliest possible idea of the state of society to which they could have been adapted. One exception there was, however, in a very antique elbow-chair, with a high back, carved elaborately in oak, and a roomy depth within its arms, that made up, by its spacious comprehensiveness, for the lack of any of those artistic curves which abound in a modern chair.

As for ornamental articles of furniture, we recollect but two, if such they may be called. One was a map of the Pyncheon territory at the eastward, not en-

graved, but the handiwork of some skilful old draughts-
man, and grotesquely illuminated with pictures of Indians and wild beasts, among which was seen a lion;
the natural history of the region being as little known
as its geography, which was put down most fantastically awry. The other adornment was the portrait of
old Colonel Pyncheon, at two thirds length, representing the stern features of a Puritanic-looking personage,
in a skull-cap, with a laced band and a grizzly beard;
holding a Bible with one hand, and in the other up-
lifting an iron sword-hilt. The latter object, being
more successfully depicted by the artist, stood out in
far greater prominence than the sacred volume. Face
to face with this picture, on entering the apartment,
Miss Hepzibah Pyncheon came to a pause; regarding
it with a singular scowl, a strange contortion of the
brow, which, by people who did not know her, would
probably have been interpreted as an expression of
bitter anger and ill-will. But it was no such thing.
She, in fact, felt a reverence for the pictured visage,
of which only a far-descended and time-stricken virgin
could be susceptible; and this forbidding scowl was
the innocent result of her near-sightedness, and an
effort so to concentrate her powers of vision as to substitute a firm outline of the object instead of a vague
one.

We must linger a moment on this unfortunate expression of poor Hepzibah's brow. Her scowl, — as
the world, or such part of it as sometimes caught a
transitory glimpse of her at the window, wickedly persisted in calling it, — her scowl had done Miss Hepzibah a very ill office, in establishing her character as
an ill-tempered old maid; nor does it appear improbable that, by often gazing at herself in a dim looking-

glass, and perpetually encountering her own frown within its ghostly sphere, she had been led to interpret the expression almost as unjustly as the world did. "How miserably cross I look!" she must often have whispered to herself; and ultimately have fancied herself so, by a sense of inevitable doom. But her heart never frowned. It was naturally tender, sensitive, and full of little tremors and palpitations; all of which weaknesses it retained, while her visage was growing so perversely stern, and even fierce. Nor had Hepzibah ever any hardihood, except what came from the very warmest nook in her affections.

All this time, however, we are loitering faint-heartedly on the threshold of our story. In very truth, we have an invincible reluctance to disclose what Miss Hepzibah Pyncheon was about to do.

It has already been observed, that, in the basement story of the gable fronting on the street, an unworthy ancestor, nearly a century ago, had fitted up a shop. Ever since the old gentleman retired from trade, and fell asleep under his coffin-lid, not only the shop-door, but the inner arrangements, had been suffered to remain unchanged; while the dust of ages gathered inch-deep over the shelves and counter, and partly filled an old pair of scales, as if it were of value enough to be weighed. It treasured itself up, too, in the half-open till, where there still lingered a base sixpence, worth neither more nor less than the hereditary pride which had here been put to shame. Such had been the state and condition of the little shop in old Hepzibah's childhood, when she and her brother used to play at hide-and-seek in its forsaken precincts. So it had remained, until within a few days past.

But now, though the shop-window was still closely

curtained from the public gaze, a remarkable change
had taken place in its interior. The rich and heavy
festoons of cobweb, which it had cost a long ancestral
succession of spiders their life's labor to spin and
weave, had been carefully brushed away from the ceiling. The counter, shelves, and floor had all been
scoured, and the latter was overstrewn with fresh blue
sand. The brown scales, too, had evidently undergone
rigid discipline, in an unavailing effort to rub off the
rust, which, alas! had eaten through and through
their substance. Neither was the little old shop any
longer empty of merchantable goods. A curious eye,
privileged to take an account of stock, and investi-
gate behind the counter, would have discovered a barrel, — yea, two or three barrels and half ditto, — one
containing flour, another apples, and a third, perhaps,
Indian meal. There was likewise a square box of
pine-wood, full of soap in bars; also, another of the
same size, in which were tallow-candles, ten to the
pound. A small stock of brown sugar, some white
beans and split peas, and a few other commodities of
low price, and such as are constantly in demand, made
up the bulkier portion of the merchandise. It might
have been taken for a ghostly or phantasmagoric reflection of the old shop-keeper Pyncheon's shabbily
provided shelves, save that some of the articles were
of a description and outward form which could hardly
have been known in his day. For instance, there was
a glass pickle-jar, filled with fragments of Gibraltar
rock; not, indeed, splinters of the veritable stone
foundation of the famous fortress, but bits of delectable
candy, neatly done up in white paper. Jim Crow,
moreover, was seen executing his world-renowned
dance, in gingerbread. A party of leaden dragoons

were galloping along one of the shelves, in equipments and uniform of modern cut; and there were some sugar figures, with no strong resemblance to the humanity of any epoch, but less unsatisfactorily representing our own fashions than those of a hundred years ago. Another phenomenon, still more strikingly modern, was a package of lucifer matches, which, in old times, would have been thought actually to borrow their instantaneous flame from the nether fires of Tophet.

In short, to bring the matter at once to a point, it was incontrovertibly evident that somebody had taken the shop and fixtures of the long-retired and forgotten Mr. Pyncheon, and was about to renew the enterprise of that departed worthy, with a different set of customers. Who could this bold adventurer be? And, of all places in the world, why had he chosen the House of the Seven Gables as the scene of his commercial speculations?

We return to the elderly maiden. She at length withdrew her eyes from the dark countenance of the Colonel's portrait, heaved a sigh, — indeed, her breast was a very cave of Æolus that morning, — and stept across the room on tiptoe, as is the customary gait of elderly women. Passing through an intervening passage, she opened a door that communicated with the shop, just now so elaborately described. Owing to the projection of the upper story — and still more to the thick shadow of the Pyncheon Elm, which stood almost directly in front of the gable — the twilight, here, was still as much akin to night as morning. Another heavy sigh from Miss Hepzibah! After a moment's pause on the threshold, peering towards the window with her near-sighted scowl, as if frowning down some bitter enemy, she suddenly projected herself into the shop. The haste, and, as it were, the galvanic impulse of the movement, were really quite startling.

Nervously — in a sort of frenzy, we might almost say — she began to busy herself in arranging some children's playthings, and other little wares, on the shelves and at the shop-window. In the aspect of this dark-arrayed, pale-faced, lady-like old figure there was a deeply tragic character that contrasted irreconcilably with the ludicrous pettiness of her employment. It seemed a queer anomaly, that so gaunt and dismal a personage should take a toy in hand; a miracle, that the toy did not vanish in her grasp; a miserably absurd idea, that she should go on perplexing her stiff and sombre intellect with the question how to tempt little boys into her premises! Yet such is undoubtedly her object. Now she places a gingerbread elephant against the window, but with so tremulous a touch that it tumbles upon the floor, with the dismemberment of three legs and its trunk; it has ceased to be an elephant, and has become a few bits of musty gingerbread. There, again, she has upset a tumbler of marbles, all of which roll different ways, and each individual marble, devil-directed, into the most difficult obscurity that it can find. Heaven help our poor old Hepzibah, and forgive us for taking a ludicrous view of her position! As her rigid and rusty frame goes down upon its hands and knees, in quest of the absconding marbles, we positively feel so much the more inclined to shed tears of sympathy, from the very fact that we must needs turn aside and laugh at her. For here, — and if we fail to impress it suitably upon the reader, it is our own fault, not that of the

theme, — here is one of the truest points of melancholy interest that occur in ordinary life. It was the
final throe of what called itself old gentility. A lady
— who had fed herself from childhood with the shadowy food of aristocratic reminiscences, and whose religion it was that a lady's hand soils itself irremedi-
ably by doing aught for bread — this born lady, after
sixty years of narrowing means, is fain to step down
from her pedestal of imaginary rank. Poverty, treading closely at her heels for a lifetime, has come up
with her at last. She must earn her own food, or
starve! And we have stolen upon Miss Hepzibah
Pyncheon, too irreverently, at the instant of time
when the patrician lady is to be transformed into the
plebeian woman.

In this republican country, amid the fluctuating
waves of our social life, somebody is always at the
drowning-point. The tragedy is enacted with as continual a repetition as that of a popular drama on a
holiday; and, nevertheless, is felt as deeply, perhaps, as when an hereditary noble sinks below his order. More deeply; since, with us, rank is the grosser
substance of wealth and a splendid establishment, and
has no spiritual existence after the death of these, but
dies hopelessly along with them. And, therefore,
since we have been unfortunate enough to introduce
our heroine at so inauspicious a juncture, we would
entreat for a mood of due solemnity in the spectators
of her fate. Let us behold, in poor Hepzibah, the immemorial lady, — two hundred years old, on this side
of the water, and thrice as many on the other, — with
her antique portraits, pedigrees, coats of arms, records
and traditions, and her claim, as joint heiress, to that
princely territory at the eastward, no longer a wilder-

ness, but a populous fertility, — born, too, in Pyncheon Street, under the Pyncheon Elm, and in the Pyncheon House, where she has spent all her days, — reduced now, in that very house, to be the hucksteress of a cent-shop.

This business of setting up a petty shop is almost the only resource of women, in circumstances at all similar to those of our unfortunate recluse. With her near-sightedness, and those tremulous fingers of hers, at once inflexible and delicate, she could not be a seamstress; although her sampler, of fifty years gone by, exhibited some of the most recondite specimens of ornamental needlework. A school for little children had been often in her thoughts; and, at one time, she had begun a review of her early studies in the New England Primer, with a view to prepare herself for the office of instructress. But the love of children had never been quickened in Hepzibah's heart, and was now torpid, if not extinct; she watched the little people of the neighborhood from her chamber-window, and doubted whether she could tolerate a more intimate acquaintance with them. Besides, in our day, the very A B C has become a science greatly too abstruse to be any longer taught by pointing a pin from letter to letter. A modern child could teach old Hepzibah more than old Hepzibah could teach the child. So — with many a cold, deep heart-quake at the idea of at last coming into sordid contact with the world, from which she had so long kept aloof, while every added day of seclusion had rolled another stone against the cavern-door of her hermitage — the poor thing bethought herself of the ancient shop-window, the rusty scales, and dusty till. She might have held back a little longer; but another circumstance, not yet hinted at, had somewhat hastened her decision. Her humble preparations, therefore, were duly made, and the enterprise was now to be commenced. Nor was she entitled to complain of any remarkable singularity in her fate; for, in the town of her nativity, we might point to several little shops of a similar description, some of them in houses as ancient as that of the Seven Gables; and one or two, it may be, where a decayed gentlewoman stands behind the counter, as grim an image of family pride as Miss Hepzibah Pyncheon herself.

It was overpoweringly ridiculous — we must honestly confess it — the deportment of the maiden lady while setting her shop in order for the public eye. She stole on tiptoe to the window, as cautiously as if she conceived some bloody-minded villain to be watching behind the elm-tree, with intent to take her life. Stretching out her long, lank arm, she put a paper of pearl buttons, a jew's-harp, or whatever the small article might be, in its destined place, and straightway vanished back into the dusk, as if the world need never hope for another glimpse of her. It might have been fancied, indeed, that she expected to minister to the wants of the community unseen, like a disembodied divinity or enchantress, holding forth her bargains to the reverential and awe-stricken purchaser in an invisible hand. But Hepzibah had no such flattering dream. She was well aware that she must ultimately come forward, and stand revealed in her proper individuality; but, like other sensitive persons, she could not bear to be observed in the gradual process, and chose rather to flash forth on the world's astonished gaze at once.

The inevitable moment was not much longer to be delayed. The sunshine might now be seen stealing

down the front of the opposite house, from the windows of which came a reflected gleam, struggling
through the boughs of the elm-tree, and enlightening
the interior of the shop more distinctly than heretofore. The town appeared to be waking up. A baker's
cart had already rattled through the street, chasing
away the latest vestige of night's sanctity with the
jingle-jangle of its dissonant bells. A milkman was
distributing the contents of his cans from door to
door; and the harsh peal of a fisherman's conch-shell
was heard far off, around the corner. None of these
tokens escaped Hepzibah's notice. The moment had
arrived. To delay longer would be only to lengthen
out her misery. Nothing remained, except to take
down the bar from the shop-door, leaving the entrance
free — more than free — welcome, as if all were
household friends — to every passer-by, whose eyes
might be attracted by the commodities at the window.
This last act Hepzibah now performed, letting the bar
fall with what smote upon her excited nerves as a
most astounding clatter. Then — as if the only barrier betwixt herself and the world had been thrown
down, and a flood of evil consequences would come
tumbling through the gap — she fled into the inner
parlor, threw herself into the ancestral elbow-chair,
and wept.

Our miserable old Hepzibah! It is a heavy annoyance to a writer, who endeavors to represent nature,
its various attitudes and circumstances, in a reasonably correct outline and true coloring, that so much of
the mean and ludicrous should be hopelessly mixed up
with the purest pathos which life anywhere supplies
to him. What tragic dignity, for example, can be
wrought into a scene like this! How can we elevate

our history of retribution for the sin of long ago, when, as one of our most prominent figures, we are compelled to introduce — not a young and lovely woman, nor even the stately remains of beauty, storm-shattered by affliction — but a gaunt, sallow, rusty-jointed maiden, in a long-waisted silk gown, and with the strange horror of a turban on her head! Her visage is not even ugly. It is redeemed from insignificance only by the contraction of her eyebrows into a near-sighted scowl. And, finally, her great life-trial seems to be, that, after sixty years of idleness, she finds it convenient to earn comfortable bread by setting up a shop in a small way. Nevertheless, if we look through all the heroic fortunes of mankind, we shall find this same entanglement of something mean and trivial with whatever is noblest in joy or sorrow. Life is made up of marble and mud. And, without all the deeper trust in a comprehensive sympathy above us, we might hence be led to suspect the insult of a sneer, as well as an immitigable frown, on the iron countenance of fate. What is called poetic insight is the gift of discerning, in this sphere of strangely mingled elements, the beauty and the majesty which are compelled to assume a garb so sordid.

III.

THE FIRST CUSTOMER.

MISS HEPZIBAH PYNCHEON sat in the oaken elbow-chair, with her hands over her face, giving way to that heavy down-sinking of the heart which most persons have experienced, when the image of hope itself seems ponderously moulded of lead, on the eve of an enterprise at once doubtful and momentous. She was suddenly startled by the tinkling alarum — high, sharp, and irregular — of a little bell. The maiden lady arose upon her feet, as pale as a ghost at cock-crow; for she was an enslaved spirit, and this the talisman to which she owed obedience. This little bell, — to speak in plainer terms, — being fastened over the shop-door, was so contrived as to vibrate by means of a steel spring, and thus convey notice to the inner regions of the house when any customer should cross the threshold. Its ugly and spiteful little din (heard now for the first time, perhaps, since Hepzibah's periwigged predecessor had retired from trade) at once set every nerve of her body in responsive and tumultuous vibration. The crisis was upon her! Her first customer was at the door!

Without giving herself time for a second thought, she rushed into the shop, pale, wild, desperate in gesture and expression, scowling portentously, and looking far better qualified to do fierce battle with a house-breaker than to stand smiling behind the counter, bartering small wares for a copper recompense. Any ordinary customer, indeed, would have turned his back and fled. And yet there was nothing fierce in Hepzibah's poor old heart; nor had she, at the moment, a single bitter thought against the world at large, or one individual man or woman. She wished them all well, but wished, too, that she herself were done with them, and in her quiet grave.

The applicant, by this time, stood within the doorway. Coming freshly, as he did, out of the morning light, he appeared to have brought some of its cheery influences into the shop along with him. It was a slender young man, not more than one or two and twenty years old, with rather a grave and thoughtful expression for his years, but likewise a springy alacrity and vigor. These qualities were not only perceptible, physically, in his make and motions, but made themselves felt almost immediately in his character. A brown beard, not too silken in its texture, fringed his chin, but as yet without completely hiding it; he wore a short mustache, too, and his dark, high-featured countenance looked all the better for these natural ornaments. As for his dress, it was of the simplest kind; a summer sack of cheap and ordinary material, thin checkered pantaloons, and a straw hat, by no means of the finest braid. Oak Hall might have supplied his entire equipment. He was chiefly marked as a gentleman — if such, indeed, he made any claim to be — by the rather remarkable whiteness and nicety of his clean linen.

He met the scowl of old Hepzibah without apparent alarm, as having heretofore encountered it and found it harmless.

"So, my dear Miss Pyncheon," said the daguerreotypist, — for it was that sole other occupant of the seven-gabled mansion, — "I am glad to see that you have not shrunk from your good purpose. I merely look in to offer my best wishes, and to ask if I can assist you any further in your preparations."

People in difficulty and distress, or in any manner at odds with the world, can endure a vast amount of harsh treatment, and perhaps be only the stronger for it; whereas they give way at once before the simplest expression of what they perceive to be genuine sympathy. So it proved with poor Hepzibah; for, when she saw the young man's smile, — looking so much the brighter on a thoughtful face, — and heard his kindly tone, she broke first into a hysteric giggle and then began to sob.

"Ah, Mr. Holgrave," cried she, as soon as she could speak, "I never can go through with it! Never, never, never! I wish I were dead, and in the old family-tomb, with all my forefathers! With my father, and my mother, and my sister! Yes, and with my brother, who had far better find me there than here! The world is too chill and hard, — and I am too old, and too feeble, and too hopeless!"

"Oh, believe me, Miss Hepzibah," said the young man, quietly, "these feelings will not trouble you any longer, after you are once fairly in the midst of your enterprise. They are unavoidable at this moment, standing, as you do, on the outer verge of your long seclusion, and peopling the world with ugly shapes, which you will soon find to be as unreal as the giants and ogres of a child's story-book. I find nothing so singular in life, as that everything appears to lose its substance the instant one actually grapples with it. So it will be with what you think so terrible."

" But I am a woman ! " said Hepzibah, piteously.
" I was going to say, a lady, — but I consider that as
past."

" Well ; no matter if it be past ! " answered the
artist, a strange gleam of half-hidden sarcasm flashing
through the kindliness of his manner. " Let it go !
You are the better without it. I speak frankly, my
dear Miss Pyncheon ! for are we not friends ? I look
upon this as one of the fortunate days of your life.
It ends an epoch and begins one. Hitherto, the life-
blood has been gradually chilling in your veins as you
sat aloof, within your circle of gentility, while the rest
of the world was fighting out its battle with one kind
of necessity or another. Henceforth, you will at least
have the sense of healthy and natural effort for a purpose, and of lending your strength — be it great or
small — to the united struggle of mankind. This is
success, — all the success that anybody meets with ! "

" It is natural enough, Mr. Holgrave, that you
should have ideas like these," rejoined Hepzibah,
drawing up her gaunt figure, with slightly offended
dignity. " You are a man, a young man, and brought
up, I suppose, as almost everybody is nowadays, with
a view to seeking your fortune. But I was born a
lady, and have always lived one ; no matter in what
narrowness of means, always a lady ! "

" But I was not born a gentleman ; neither have I
lived like one," said Holgrave, slightly smiling ; " so,
my dear madam, you will hardly expect me to sympathize with sensibilities of this kind ; though, unless
I deceive myself, I have some imperfect comprehension of them. These names of gentleman and lady
had a meaning, in the past history of the world, and
conferred privileges, desirable or otherwise, on those

entitled to bear them. In the present — and still more in the future condition of society — they imply, not privilege, but restriction!"

"These are new notions," said the old gentlewoman, shaking her head. "I shall never understand them; neither do I wish it."

"We will cease to speak of them, then," replied the artist, with a friendlier smile than his last one, "and I will leave you to feel whether it is not better to be a true woman than a lady. Do you really think, Miss Hepzibah, that any lady of your family has ever done a more heroic thing, since this house was built, than you are performing in it to-day? Never; and if the Pyncheons had always acted so nobly, I doubt whether an old wizard Maule's anathema, of which you told me once, would have had much weight with Providence against them."

"Ah! — no, no!" said Hepzibah, not displeased at this allusion to the sombre dignity of an inherited curse. "If old Maule's ghost, or a descendant of his, could see me behind the counter to-day, he would call it the fulfilment of his worst wishes. But I thank you for your kindness, Mr. Holgrave, and will do my utmost to be a good shop-keeper."

"Pray do," said Holgrave, "and let me have the pleasure of being your first customer. I am about taking a walk to the sea-shore, before going to my rooms, where I misuse Heaven's blessed sunshine by tracing out human features through its agency. A few of those biscuits dipt in sea-water, will be just what I need for breakfast. What is the price of half a dozen?"

"Let me be a lady a moment longer," replied Hepzibah, with a manner of antique stateliness to which a melancholy smile lent a kind of grace. She put the biscuits into his hand, but rejected the compensation. " A Pyncheon must not, at all events under her forefathers' roof, receive money for a morsel of bread from her only friend ! "

Holgrave took his departure, leaving her, for the moment, with spirits not quite so much depressed. Soon, however, they had subsided nearly to their former dead level. With a beating heart, she listened to the footsteps of early passengers, which now began to be frequent along the street. Once or twice they seemed to linger; these strangers, or neighbors, as the case might be, were looking at the display of toys and petty commodities in Hepzibah's shop - window. She was doubly tortured; in part, with a sense of overwhelming shame that strange and unloving eyes should have the privilege of gazing, and partly because the idea occurred to her, with ridiculous importunity, that the window was not arranged so skilfully, nor nearly to so much advantage, as it might have been. It seemed as if the whole fortune or failure of her shop might depend on the display of a different set of articles, or substituting a fairer apple for one which appeared to be specked. So she made the change, and straightway fancied that everything was spoiled by it; not recognizing that it was the nervousness of the juncture, and her own native squeamishness as an old maid, that wrought all the seeming mischief.

Anon, there was an encounter, just at the door-step, betwixt two laboring men, as their rough voices denoted them to be. After some slight talk about their own affairs, one of them chanced to notice the shop-window, and directed the other's attention to it.

" See here ! " cried he; " what do you think of

this? Trade seems to be looking up in Pyncheon Street!"

"Well, well, this is a sight, to be sure!" exclaimed the other. "In the old Pyncheon House, and underneath the Pyncheon Elm! Who would have thought it? Old Maid Pyncheon is setting up a cent-shop!"

"Will she make it go, think you, Dixey?" said his friend. "I don't call it a very good stand. There's another shop just round the corner."

"Make it go!" cried Dixey, with a most contemptuous expression, as if the very idea were impossible to be conceived. "Not a bit of it! Why, her face — I've seen it, for I dug her garden for her one year — her face is enough to frighten the Old Nick himself, if he had ever so great a mind to trade with her. People can't stand it, I tell you! She scowls dreadfully, reason or none, out of pure ugliness of temper!"

"Well, that's not so much matter," remarked the other man. "These sour-tempered folks are mostly handy at business, and know pretty well what they are about. But, as you say, I don't think she'll do much. This business of keeping cent-shops is overdone, like all other kinds of trade, handicraft, and bodily labor. I know it, to my cost! My wife kept a cent-shop three months, and lost five dollars on her outlay!"

"Poor business!" responded Dixey, in a tone as if he were shaking his head, — "poor business!"

For some reason or other, not very easy to analyze, there had hardly been so bitter a pang in all her previous misery about the matter as what thrilled Hepzibah's heart, on overhearing the above conversation. The testimony in regard to her scowl was frightfully important; it seemed to hold up her image wholly re-

lieved from the false light of her self-partialities, and
so hideous that she dared not look at it. She was ab-
surdly hurt, moreover, by the slight and idle effect
that her setting up shop — an event of such breathless
interest to herself — appeared to have upon the public, of which these two men were the nearest representatives. A glance; a passing word or two; a
coarse laugh; and she was doubtless forgotten before
they turned the corner! They cared nothing for her
dignity, and just as little for her degradation. Then,
also, the augury of ill-success, uttered from the sure
wisdom of experience, fell upon her half-dead hope
like a clod into a grave. The man's wife had already
tried the same experiment, and failed! How could
the born lady, — the recluse of half a lifetime, utterly
unpractised in the world, at sixty years of age, — how
could she ever dream of succeeding, when the hard,
vulgar, keen, busy, hackneyed New England woman
had lost five dollars on her little outlay! Success presented itself as an impossibility, and the hope of it as
a wild hallucination.

Some malevolent spirit, doing his utmost to drive
Hepzibah mad, unrolled before her imagination a kind
of panorama, representing the great thoroughfare of a
city all astir with customers. So many and so magnificent shops as there were! Groceries, toy-shops, dry
goods stores, with their immense panes of plate-glass,
their gorgeous fixtures, their vast and complete assort-
ments of merchandise, in which fortunes had been invested; and those noble mirrors at the farther end
of each establishment, doubling all this wealth by a
brightly burnished vista of unrealities! On one side
of the street this splendid bazaar, with a multitude of
perfumed and glossy salesmen, smirking, smiling, bow-

ing, and measuring out the goods. On the other, the dusky old House of the Seven Gables, with the antiquated shop-window under its projecting story, and Hepzibah herself, in a gown of rusty black silk, behind the counter, scowling at the world as it went by! This mighty contrast thrust itself forward as a fair expression of the odds against which she was to begin her struggle for a subsistence. Success? Preposterous! She would never think of it again! The house might just as well be buried in an eternal fog while all other houses had the sunshine on them; for not a foot would ever cross the threshold, nor a hand so much as try the door!

But, at this instant, the shop-bell, right over her head, tinkled as if it were bewitched. The old gentlewoman's heart seemed to be attached to the same steel spring, for it went through a series of sharp jerks, in unison with the sound. The door was thrust open, although no human form was perceptible on the other side of the half-window. Hepzibah, nevertheless, stood at a gaze, with her hands clasped, looking very much as if she had summoned up an evil spirit, and were afraid, yet resolved, to hazard the encounter.

"Heaven help me!" she groaned, mentally. "Now is my hour of need!"

The door, which moved with difficulty on its creaking and rusty hinges, being forced quite open, a square and sturdy little urchin became apparent, with cheeks as red as an apple. He was clad rather shabbily (but, as it seemed, more owing to his mother's carelessness than his father's poverty), in a blue apron, very wide and short trousers, shoes somewhat out at the toes, and a chip-hat, with the frizzles of his curly hair sticking through its crevices. A book and a small slate, under his arm, indicated that he was on his way to school. He stared at Hepzibah a moment, as an elder customer than himself would have been likely enough to do, not knowing what to make of the tragic attitude and queer scowl wherewith she regarded him.

"Well, child," said she, taking heart at sight of a personage so little formidable, — "well, my child, what did you wish for?"

"That Jim Crow there in the window," answered the urchin, holding out a cent, and pointing to the gingerbread figure that had attracted his notice, as he loitered along to school; "the one that has not a broken foot."

So Hepzibah put forth her lank arm, and, taking the effigy from the shop-window, delivered it to her first customer.

"No matter for the money," said she, giving him a little push towards the door; for her old gentility was contumaciously squeamish at sight of the copper coin, and, besides, it seemed such pitiful meanness to take the child's pocket-money in exchange for a bit of stale gingerbread. "No matter for the cent. You are welcome to Jim Crow."

The child, staring with round eyes at this instance of liberality, wholly unprecedented in his large experience of cent-shops, took the man of gingerbread, and quitted the premises. No sooner had he reached the sidewalk (little cannibal that he was!) than Jim Crow's head was in his mouth. As he had not been careful to shut the door, Hepzibah was at the pains of closing it after him, with a pettish ejaculation or two about the troublesomeness of young people, and particularly of small boys. She had just placed another

representative of the renowned Jim Crow at the window, when again the shop-bell tinkled clamorously,
and again the door being thrust open, with its characteristic jerk and jar, disclosed the same sturdy little
urchin who, precisely two minutes ago, had made his
exit. The crumbs and discoloration of the cannibal
feast, as yet hardly consummated, were exceedingly
visible about his mouth.

"What is it now, child?" asked the maiden lady,
rather impatiently; "did you come back to shut the
door?"

"No," answered the urchin, pointing to the figure
that had just been put up; "I want that other Jim
Crow."

"Well, here it is for you," said Hepzibah, reaching it down; but recognizing that this pertinacious
customer would not quit her on any other terms, so
long as she had a gingerbread figure in her shop, she
partly drew back her extended hand, "Where is the
cent?"

The little boy had the cent ready, but, like a true-
born Yankee, would have preferred the better bargain
to the worse. Looking somewhat chagrined, he put
the coin into Hepzibah's hand, and departed, sending
the second Jim Crow in quest of the former one. The
new shopkeeper dropped the first solid result of her
commercial enterprise into the till. It was done!
The sordid stain of that copper coin could never be
washed away from her palm. The little school-boy,
aided by the impish figure of the negro dancer, had
wrought an irreparable ruin. The structure of ancient aristocracy had been demolished by him, even as
if his childish gripe had torn down the seven-gabled
mansion. Now let Hepzibah turn the old Pyncheon

portraits with their faces to the wall, and take the map of her Eastern territory to kindle the kitchen fire, and blow up the flame with the empty breath of her ancestral traditions! What had she to do with ancestry? Nothing; no more than with posterity! No lady, now, but simply Hepzibah Pyncheon, a forlorn old maid, and keeper of a cent-shop!

Nevertheless, even while she paraded these ideas somewhat ostentatiously through her mind, it is altogether surprising what a calmness had come over her. The anxiety and misgivings which had tormented her, whether asleep or in melancholy day-dreams, ever since her project began to take an aspect of solidity, had now vanished quite away. She felt the novelty of her position, indeed, but no longer with disturbance or affright. Now and then, there came a thrill of almost youthful enjoyment. It was the invigorating breath of a fresh outward atmosphere, after the long torpor and monotonous seclusion of her life. So wholesome is effort! So miraculous the strength that we do not know of! The healthiest glow that Hepzibah had known for years had come now in the dreaded crisis, when, for the first time, she had put forth her hand to help herself. The little circlet of the school-boy's copper coin — dim and lustreless though it was, with the small services which it had been doing here and there about the world — had proved a talisman, fragrant with good, and deserving to be set in gold and worn next her heart. It was as potent, and perhaps endowed with the same kind of efficacy, as a galvanic ring! Hepzibah, at all events, was indebted to its subtile operation both in body and spirit; so much the more, as it inspired her with energy to get some breakfast, at which, still the better to keep up her courage, she allowed herself an extra spoonful in her infusion of black tea.

Her introductory day of shop-keeping did not run on, however, without many and serious interruptions of this mood of cheerful vigor. As a general rule, Providence seldom vouchsafes to mortals any more than just that degree of encouragement which suffices to keep them at a reasonably full exertion of their powers. In the case of our old gentlewoman, after the excitement of new effort had subsided, the despondency of her whole life threatened, ever and anon, to return. It was like the heavy mass of clouds which we may often see obscuring the sky, and making a gray twilight everywhere, until, towards nightfall, it yields temporarily to a glimpse of sunshine. But, always, the envious cloud strives to gather again across the streak of celestial azure.

Customers came in, as the forenoon advanced, but rather slowly; in some cases, too, it must be owned, with little satisfaction either to themselves or Miss Hepzibah; nor, on the whole, with an aggregate of very rich emolument to the till. A little girl, sent by her mother to match a skein of cotton thread, of a peculiar hue, took one that the near-sighted old lady pronounced extremely like, but soon came running back, with a blunt and cross message, that it would not do, and, besides, was very rotten! Then, there was a pale, care-wrinkled woman, not old but haggard, and already with streaks of gray among her hair, like silver ribbons; one of those women, naturally delicate, whom you at once recognize as worn to death by a brute — probably a drunken brute — of a husband, and at least nine children. She wanted a few pounds of flour, and offered the money, which the decayed gentlewoman silently rejected, and gave the poor soul better measure than if she had taken it. Shortly afterwards, a man in a blue cotton frock, much soiled, came in and bought a pipe, filling the whole shop, meanwhile, with the hot odor of strong drink, not only exhaled in the torrid atmosphere of his breath, but oozing out of his entire system, like an inflammable gas. It was impressed on Hepzibah's mind that this was the husband of the care-wrinkled woman. He asked for a paper of tobacco; and as she had neglected to provide herself with the article, her brutal customer dashed down his newly-bought pipe and left the shop, muttering some unintelligible words, which had the tone and bitterness of a curse. Hereupon Hepzibah threw up her eyes, unintentionally scowling in the face of Providence!

No less than five persons, during the forenoon, inquired for ginger-beer, or root-beer, or any drink of a similar brewage, and, obtaining nothing of the kind, went off in an exceedingly bad humor. Three of them left the door open, and the other two pulled it so spitefully in going out that the little bell played the very deuce with Hepzibah's nerves. A round, bustling, fire-ruddy housewife of the neighborhood, burst breathless into the shop, fiercely demanding yeast; and when the poor gentlewoman, with her cold shyness of manner, gave her hot customer to understand that she did not keep the article, this very capable housewife took upon herself to administer a regular rebuke.

"A cent-shop, and no yeast!" quoth she; "that will never do! Who ever heard of such a thing? Your loaf will never rise, no more than mine will to day. You had better shut up shop at once."

"Well," said Hepzibah, heaving a deep sigh, "per haps I had!"

Several times, moreover, besides the above instance, her lady-like sensibilities were seriously infringed upon by the familiar, if not rude, tone with which people addressed her. They evidently considered themselves not merely her equals, but her patrons and superiors. Now, Hepzibah had unconsciously flattered herself with the idea that there would be a gleam or halo, of some kind or other, about her person, which would insure an obeisance to her sterling gentility, or, at least, a tacit recognition of it. On the other hand, nothing tortured her more intolerably than when this recognition was too prominently expressed. To one or two rather officious offers of sympathy, her responses were little short of acrimonious; and, we regret to say, Hepzibah was thrown into a positively unchristian state of mind by the suspicion that one of her customers was drawn to the shop, not by any real need of the article which she pretended to seek, but by a wicked wish to stare at her. The vulgar creature was determined to see for herself what sort of a figure a mildewed piece of aristocracy, after wasting all the bloom and much of the decline of her life apart from the world, would cut behind a counter. In this particular case, however mechanical and innocuous it might be at other times, Hepzibah's contortion of brow served her in good stead.

"I never was so frightened in my life!" said the curious customer, in describing the incident to one of her acquaintances. "She's a real old vixen, take my word of it! She says little, to be sure; but if you could only see the mischief in her eye!"

On the whole, therefore, her new experience led our

decayed gentlewoman to very disagreeable conclusions as to the temper and manners of what she termed the lower classes, whom heretofore she had looked down upon with a gentle and pitying complaisance, as herself occupying a sphere of unquestionable superiority. But, unfortunately, she had likewise to struggle against a bitter emotion of a directly opposite kind: a sentiment of virulence, we mean, towards the idle aristocracy to which it had so recently been her pride to belong. When a lady, in a delicate and costly summer garb, with a floating veil and gracefully swaying gown, and, altogether, an etherial lightness that made you look at her beautifully slippered feet, to see whether she trod on the dust or floated in the air, — when such a vision happened to pass through this retired street, leaving it tenderly and delusively fragrant with her passage, as if a bouquet of tea-roses had been borne along, — then again, it is to be feared, old Hepzibah's scowl could no longer vindicate itself entirely on the plea of near-sightedness.

"For what end," thought she, giving vent to that feeling of hostility which is the only real abasement of the poor in presence of the rich, — "for what good end, in the wisdom of Providence, does that woman live? Must the whole world toil, that the palms of her hands may be kept white and delicate?"

Then, ashamed and penitent, she hid her face.

"May God forgive me!" said she.

Doubtless, God did forgive her. But, taking the inward and outward history of the first half-day into consideration, Hepzibah began to fear that the shop would prove her ruin in a moral and religious point of view, without contributing very essentially towards even her temporal welfare.

IV.

A DAY BEHIND THE COUNTER.

TOWARDS noon, Hepzibah saw an elderly gentleman, large and portly, and of remarkably dignified
demeanor, passing slowly along on the opposite side
of the white and dusty street. On coming within the
shadow of the Pyncheon Elm, he stopt, and (taking
off his hat, meanwhile, to wipe the perspiration from
his brow) seemed to scrutinize, with especial interest,
the dilapidated and rusty-visaged House of the Seven
Gables. He himself, in a very different style, was as
well worth looking at as the house. No better model
need be sought, nor could have been found, of a very
high order of respectability, which, by some indescribable magic, not merely expressed itself in his looks
and gestures, but even governed the fashion of his
garments, and rendered them all proper and essential
to the man. Without appearing to differ, in any
tangible way, from other people's clothes, there was
yet a wide and rich gravity about them that must
have been a characteristic of the wearer, since it could
not be defined as pertaining either to the cut or material. His gold-headed cane, too, — a serviceable
staff, of dark polished wood, — had similar traits, and,
had it chosen to take a walk by itself, would have
been recognized anywhere as a tolerably adequate representative of its master. This character — which
showed itself so strikingly in everything about him,

and the effect of which we seek to convey to the reader — went no deeper than his station, habits of life, and external circumstances. One perceived him to be a personage of marked influence and authority; and, especially, you could feel just as certain that he was opulent as if he had exhibited his bank account, or as if you had seen him touching the twigs of the Pyncheon Elm, and, Midas-like, transmuting them to gold.

In his youth, he had probably been considered a handsome man; at his present age, his brow was too heavy, his temples too bare, his remaining hair too gray, his eye too cold, his lips too closely compressed, to bear any relation to mere personal beauty. He would have made a good and massive portrait; better now, perhaps, than at any previous period of his life, although his look might grow positively harsh in the process of being fixed upon the canvas. The artist would have found it desirable to study his face, and prove its capacity for varied expression; to darken it with a frown, — to kindle it up with a smile.

While the elderly gentleman stood looking at the Pyncheon House, both the frown and the smile passed successively over his countenance. His eye rested on the shop-window, and putting up a pair of gold-bowed spectacles, which he held in his hand, he minutely surveyed Hepzibah's little arrangement of toys and commodities. At first it seemed not to please him, — nay, to cause him exceeding displeasure, — and yet, the very next moment, he smiled. While the latter expression was yet on his lips, he caught a glimpse of Hepzibah, who had involuntarily bent forward to the window; and then the smile changed from acrid and disagreeable to the sunniest complacency and benevolence. He bowed, with a happy mixture of dignity and courteous kindliness, and pursued his way.

"There he is!" said Hepzibah to herself, gulping down a very bitter emotion, and, since she could not rid herself of it, trying to drive it back into her heart. "What does he think of it, I wonder? Does it please him? Ah! he is looking back!"

The gentleman had paused in the street, and turned himself half about, still with his eyes fixed on the shop-window. In fact, he wheeled wholly round, and commenced a step or two, as if designing to enter the shop; but, as it chanced, his purpose was anticipated by Hepzibah's first customer, the little cannibal of Jim Crow, who, staring up at the window, was irresistibly attracted by an elephant of gingerbread. What a grand appetite had this small urchin! — Two Jim Crows immediately after breakfast! — and now an elephant, as a preliminary whet before dinner! By the time this latter purchase was completed, the elderly gentleman had resumed his way, and turned the street corner.

"Take it as you like, Cousin Jaffrey!" muttered the maiden lady, as she drew back, after cautiously thrusting out her head, and looking up and down the street, — "take it as you like! You have seen my little shop-window! Well! — what have you to say? — is not the Pyncheon House my own, while I 'm alive?"

After this incident, Hepzibah retreated to the back parlor, where she at first caught up a half-finished stocking, and began knitting at it with nervous and irregular jerks; but quickly finding herself at odds with the stitches, she threw it aside, and walked hurriedly about the room. At length, she paused before the portrait of the stern old Puritan, her ancestor, and the founder of the house. In one sense, this picture had almost faded into the canvas, and hidden itself behind the duskiness of age : in another, she could not but fancy that it had been growing more promi nent, and strikingly expressive, ever since her earliest familiarity with it as a child. For, while the physical outline and substance were darkening away from the beholder's eye, the bold, hard, and, at the same time, indirect character of the man seemed to be brought out in a kind of spiritual relief. Such an effect may occasionally be observed in pictures of antique date. They acquire a look which an artist (if he have anything like the complacency of artists nowadays) would never dream of presenting to a patron as his own characteristic expression, but which, nevertheless, we at once recognize as reflecting the unlovely truth of a human soul. In such cases, the painter's deep conception of his subject's inward traits has wrought itself into the essence of the picture, and is seen after the superficial coloring has been rubbed off by time.

While gazing at the portrait, Hepzibah trembled under its eye. Her hereditary reverence made her afraid to judge the character of the original so harshly as a perception of the truth compelled her to do. But still she gazed, because the face of the picture enabled her — at least, she fancied so — to read more accurately, and to a greater depth, the face which she had just seen in the street.

"This is the very man!" murmured she to herself. "Let Jaffrey Pyncheon smile as he will, there is that look beneath! Put on him a skull-cap, and a band, and a black cloak, and a Bible in one hand and a sword in the other, — then let Jaffrey smile as he might, — nobody would doubt that it was the old Pyn-cheon come again! He has proved himself the very man to build up a new house! Perhaps, too, to draw down a new curse!"

Thus did Hepzibah bewilder herself with these fantasies of the old time. She had dwelt too much alone, — too long in the Pyncheon House, — until her very brain was impregnated with the dry-rot of its timbers. She needed a walk along the noonday street to keep her sane.

By the spell of contrast, another portrait rose up before her, painted with more daring flattery than any artist would have ventured upon, but yet so delicately touched that the likeness remained perfect. Malbone's miniature, though from the same original, was far inferior to Hepzibah's air-drawn picture, at which affection and sorrowful remembrance wrought together. Soft, mildly, and cheerfully contemplative, with full, red lips, just on the verge of a smile, which the eyes seemed to herald by a gentle kindling-up of their orbs! Feminine traits, moulded inseparably with those of the other sex! The miniature, likewise, had this last peculiarity; so that you inevitably thought of the original as resembling his mother, and she a lovely and lovable woman, with perhaps some beautiful infirmity of character, that made it all the pleasanter to know and easier to love her.

"Yes," thought Hepzibah, with grief of which it was only the more tolerable portion that welled up from her heart to her eyelids, "they persecuted his mother in him! He never was a Pyncheon!"

But here the shop-bell rang; it was like a sound from a remote distance, — so far had Hepzibah descended into the sepulchral depths of her reminiscences. On entering the shop, she found an old man there, a humble resident of Pyncheon Street, and

whom, for a great many years past, she had suffered
to be a kind of familiar of the house. He was an immemorial personage, who seemed always to have had
a white head and wrinkles, and never to have possessed but a single tooth, and that a half-decayed one,
in the front of the upper jaw. Well advanced as
Hepzibah was, she could not remember when Uncle
Venner, as the neighborhood called him, had not gone
up and down the street, stooping a little and drawing
his feet heavily over the gravel or pavement. But
still there was something tough and vigorous about
him, that not only kept him in daily breath, but enabled him to fill a place which would else have been
vacant in the apparently crowded world. To go of
errands with his slow and shuffling gait, which made
you doubt how he ever was to arrive anywhere; to
saw a small household's foot or two of firewood, or
knock to pieces an old barrel, or split up a pine board
for kindling-stuff; in summer, to dig the few yards of
garden ground appertaining to a low-rented tenement,
and share the produce of his labor at the halves; in winter, to shovel away the snow from the sidewalk, or open
paths to the woodshed, or along the clothes-line; such
were some of the essential offices which Uncle Venner
performed among at least a score of families. Within
that circle, he claimed the same sort of privilege, and
probably felt as much warmth of interest, as a clergyman does in the range of his parishioners. Not that
he laid claim to the tithe pig; but, as an analogous
mode of reverence, he went his rounds, every morning,
to gather up the crumbs of the table and overflowings
of the dinner-pot, as food for a pig of his own.

In his younger days — for, after all, there was a
dim tradition that he had been, not young, but

younger — Uncle Venner was commonly regarded as rather deficient, than otherwise, in his wits. In truth he had virtually pleaded guilty to the charge, by scarcely aiming at such success as other men seek, and by taking only that humble and modest part in the intercourse of life which belongs to the alleged deficiency. But now, in his extreme old age, — whether it were that his long and hard experience had actually brightened him, or that his decaying judgment rendered him less capable of fairly measuring himself, — the venerable man made pretensions to no little wisdom, and really enjoyed the credit of it. There was likewise, at times, a vein of something like poetry in him; it was the moss or wall-flower of his mind in its small dilapidation, and gave a charm to what might have been vulgar and commonplace in his earlier and middle life. Hepzibah had a regard for him, because his name was ancient in the town and had formerly been respectable. It was a still better reason for awarding him a species of familiar reverence that Uncle Venner was himself the most ancient existence, whether of man or thing, in Pyncheon Street, except the House of the Seven Gables, and perhaps the elm that overshadowed it.

This patriarch now presented himself before Hepzibah, clad in an old blue coat, which had a fashionable air, and must have accrued to him from the cast-off wardrobe of some dashing clerk. As for his trousers, they were of tow-cloth, very short in the legs, and bagging down strangely in the rear, but yet having a suitableness to his figure which his other garment entirely lacked. His hat had relation to no other part of his dress, and but very little to the head that wore it. Thus Uncle Venner was a miscellaneous old gentle-

man, partly himself, but, in good measure, somebody
else; patched together, too, of different epochs; an
epitome of times and fashions.

"So, you have really begun trade," said he, —
"really begun trade! Well, I'm glad to see it.
Young people should never live idle in the world, nor
old ones neither, unless when the rheumatize gets hold
of them. It has given me warning already; and in
two or three years longer, I shall think of putting
aside business and retiring to my farm. That's yonder, — the great brick house, you know, — the workhouse, most folks call it; but I mean to do my work
first, and go there to be idle and enjoy myself. And
I'm glad to see you beginning to do your work, Miss
Hepzibah!"

"Thank you, Uncle Venner," said Hepzibah, smiling; for she always felt kindly towards the simple
and talkative old man. Had he been an old woman,
she might probably have repelled the freedom, which
she now took in good part. "It is time for me to
begin work, indeed! Or, to speak the truth, I have
just begun when I ought to be giving it up."

"Oh, never say that, Miss Hepzibah!" answered
the old man. "You are a young woman yet. Why,
I hardly thought myself younger than I am now, it
seems so little while ago since I used to see you playing about the door of the old house, quite a small
child! Oftener, though, you used to be sitting at the
threshold, and looking gravely into the street; for you
had always a grave kind of way with you, — a grown-
up air, when you were only the height of my knee.
It seems as if I saw you now; and your grandfather
with his red cloak, and his white wig, and his cocked
hat, and his cane, coming out of the house, and step-

ping so grandly up the street! Those old gentlemen that grew up before the Revolution used to put on grand airs. In my young days, the great man of the town was commonly called King; and his wife, not Queen to be sure, but Lady. Nowadays, a man would not dare to be called King; and if he feels himself a little above common folks, he only stoops so much the lower to them. I met your cousin, the Judge, ten minutes ago; and, in my old tow-cloth trousers, as you see, the Judge raised his hat to me, I do believe! At any rate, the Judge bowed and smiled!"

"Yes," said Hepzibah, with something bitter stealing unawares into her tone; "my cousin Jaffrey is thought to have a very pleasant smile!"

"And so he has!" replied Uncle Venner. "And that's rather remarkable in a Pyncheon; for, begging your pardon, Miss Hepzibah, they never had the name of being an easy and agreeable set of folks. There was no getting close to them. But now, Miss Hepzibah, if an old man may be bold to ask, why don't Judge Pyncheon, with his great means, step forward, and tell his cousin to shut up her little shop at once? It's for your credit to be doing something, but it's not for the Judge's credit to let you!"

"We won't talk of this, if you please, Uncle Venner," said Hepzibah, coldly. "I ought to say, however, that, if I choose to earn bread for myself, it is not Judge Pyncheon's fault. Neither will he deserve the blame," added she, more kindly, remembering Uncle Venner's privileges of age and humble familiarity, "if I should, by and by, find it convenient to retire with you to your farm."

"And it's no bad place, either, that farm of mine!" cried the old man, cheerily, as if there were something positively delightful in the prospect. "No bad place is the great brick farm-house, especially for them that will find a good many old cronies there, as will be my case. I quite long to be among them, sometimes, of the winter evenings; for it is but dull business for a lonesome elderly man, like me, to be nodding, by the hour together, with no company but his air-tight stove. Summer or winter, there's a great deal to be said in favor of my farm! And, take it in the autumn, what can be pleasanter than to spend a whole day on the sunny side of a barn or a wood-pile, chatting with somebody as old as one's self; or, perhaps, idling away the time with a natural-born simpleton, who knows how to be idle, because even our busy Yankees never have found out how to put him to any use? Upon my word, Miss Hepzibah, I doubt whether I've ever been so comfortable as I mean to be at my farm, which most folks call the workhouse. But you, — you're a young woman yet, — you never need go there! Something still better will turn up for you. I'm sure of it!"

Hepzibah fancied that there was something peculiar in her venerable friend's look and tone; insomuch, that she gazed into his face with considerable earnestness, endeavoring to discover what secret meaning, if any, might be lurking there. Individuals whose affairs have reached an utterly desperate crisis almost invariably keep themselves alive with hopes, so much the more airily magnificent as they have the less of solid matter within their grasp whereof to mould any judicious and moderate expectation of good. Thus, all the while Hepzibah was perfecting the scheme of her little shop, she had cherished an unacknowledged idea that some harlequin trick of fortune would in-

tervene in her favor. For example, an uncle — who
had sailed for India fifty years before, and never
been heard of since — might yet return, and adopt
her to be the comfort of his very extreme and decrepit
age, and adorn her with pearls, diamonds, and Oriental shawls and turbans, and make her the ultimate
heiress of his unreckonable riches. Or the member
of Parliament, now at the head of the English branch
of the family, — with which the elder stock, on this
side of the Atlantic, had held little or no intercourse
for the last two centuries, — this eminent gentleman
might invite Hepzibah to quit the ruinous House of
the Seven Gables, and come over to dwell with her
kindred at Pyncheon Hall. But, for reasons the most
imperative, she could not yield to his request. It was
more probable, therefore, that the descendants of a
Pyncheon who had emigrated to Virginia, in some
past generation, and became a great planter there, —
hearing of Hepzibah's destitution, and impelled by the
splendid generosity of character with which their Vir-
ginian mixture must have enriched the New England
blood, — would send her a remittance of a thousand
dollars, with a hint of repeating the favor annually.
Or, — and, surely, anything so undeniably just could
not be beyond the limits of reasonable anticipation,
— the great claim to the heritage of Waldo County
might finally be decided in favor of the Pyncheons;
so that, instead of keeping a cent-shop, Hepzibah
would build a palace, and look down from its highest
tower on hill, dale, forest, field, and town, as her own
share of the ancestral territory.

These were some of the fantasies which she had long
dreamed about; and, aided by these, Uncle Venner's
casual attempt at encouragement kindled a strange

festal glory in the poor, bare, melancholy chambers of
her brain, as if that inner world were suddenly lighted
up with gas. But either he knew nothing of her castles in the air — as how should he ? — or else her
earnest scowl disturbed his recollection, as it might
a more courageous man's. Instead of pursuing any
weightier topic, Uncle Venner was pleased to favor
Hepzibah with some sage counsel in her shop-keeping
capacity.

"Give no credit ! " — these were some of his golden
maxims, — " Never take paper-money ! Look well to
your change ! Ring the silver on the four-pound
weight ! Shove back all English half-pence and base
copper tokens, such as are very plenty about town !
At your leisure hours, knit children's woollen socks
and mittens ! Brew your own yeast, and make your
own ginger-beer ! "

And while Hepzibah was doing her utmost to digest
the hard little pellets of his already uttered wisdom,
he gave vent to his final, and what he declared to be
his all-important advice, as follows : —

" Put on a bright face for your customers, and smile
pleasantly as you hand them what they ask for ! A
stale article, if you dip it in a good, warm, sunny smile,
will go off better than a fresh one that you 've scowled
upon."

To this last apothegm poor Hepzibah responded with
a sigh so deep and heavy that it almost rustled Uncle
Venner quite away, like a withered leaf, — as he was,
— before an autumnal gale. Recovering himself, however, he bent forward, and, with a good deal of feeling
in his ancient visage, beckoned her nearer to him.

" When do you expect him home ? " whispered he.

" Whom do you mean ? " asked Hepzibah, turning
pale.

"Ah? you don't love to talk about it," said Uncle Venner. "Well, well! we'll say no more, though there's word of it all over town. I remember him, Miss Hepzibah, before he could run alone!"

During the remainder of the day poor Hepzibah acquitted herself even less creditably, as a shop-keeper, than in her earlier efforts. She appeared to be walking in a dream; or, more truly, the vivid life and reality assumed by her emotions made all outward occurrences unsubstantial, like the teasing phantasms of a half-conscious slumber. She still responded, mechanically, to the frequent summons of the shop-bell, and, at the demand of her customers, went prying with vague eyes about the shop, proffering them one article after another, and thrusting aside — perversely, as most of them supposed — the identical thing they asked for. There is sad confusion, indeed, when the spirit thus flits away into the past, or into the more awful future, or, in any manner, steps across the spaceless boundary betwixt its own region and the actual world; where the body remains to guide itself as best it may, with little more than the mechanism of animal life. It is like death, without death's quiet privilege, — its freedom from mortal care. Worst of all, when the actual duties are comprised in such petty details as now vexed the brooding soul of the old gentlewoman. As the animosity of fate would have it, there was a great influx of custom in the course of the afternoon. Hepzibah blundered to and fro about her small place of business, committing the most unheard-of errors: now stringing up twelve, and now seven, tallow-candles, instead of ten to the pound; selling ginger for Scotch snuff, pins for needles, and needles for pins; misreckoning her change, sometimes to the public detriment, and much oftener to her own; and thus she went on, doing her utmost to bring chaos back again, until, at the close of the day's labor, to her inexplicable astonishment, she found the money-drawer almost destitute of coin. After all her painful traffic, the whole proceeds were perhaps half a dozen coppers, and a questionable ninepence which ultimately proved to be copper likewise.

At this price, or at whatever price, she rejoiced that the day had reached its end. Never before had she had such a sense of the intolerable length of time that creeps between dawn and sunset, and of the miserable irksomeness of having aught to do, and of the better wisdom that it would be to lie down at once, in sullen resignation, and let life, and its toils and vexations, trample over one's prostrate body as they may! Hepzibah's final operation was with the little devourer of Jim Crow and the elephant, who now proposed to eat a camel. In her bewilderment, she offered him first a wooden dragoon, and next a handful of marbles; neither of which being adapted to his else omnivorous appetite, she hastily held out her whole remaining stock of natural history in gingerbread, and huddled the small customer out of the shop. She then muffled the bell in an unfinished stocking, and put up the oaken bar across the door.

During the latter process, an omnibus came to a stand-still under the branches of the elm-tree. Hepzibah's heart was in her mouth. Remote and dusky, and with no sunshine on all the intervening space, was that region of the Past whence her only guest might be expected to arrive! Was she to meet him now?

Somebody, at all events, was passing from the farthest interior of the omnibus towards its entrance.

A gentleman alighted; but it was only to offer his hand to a young girl whose slender figure, nowise needing such assistance, now lightly descended the steps, and made an airy little jump from the final one to the sidewalk. She rewarded her cavalier with a smile, the cheery glow of which was seen reflected on his own face as he reëntered the vehicle. The girl then turned towards the House of the Seven Gables, to the door of which, meanwhile, — not the shop-door, but the antique portal, — the omnibus-man had carried a light trunk and a bandbox. First giving a sharp rap of the old iron knocker, he left his passenger and her luggage at the door-step, and departed.

"Who can it be?" thought Hepzibah, who had been screwing her visual organs into the acutest focus of which they were capable. "The girl must have mistaken the house!"

She stole softly into the hall, and, herself invisible, gazed through the dusty side-lights of the portal at the young, blooming, and very cheerful face, which presented itself for admittance into the gloomy old mansion. It was a face to which almost any door would have opened of its own accord.

The young girl, so fresh, so unconventional, and yet so orderly and obedient to common rules, as you at once recognized her to be, was widely in contrast, at that moment, with everything about her. The sordid and ugly luxuriance of gigantic weeds that grew in the angle of the house, and the heavy projection that overshadowed her, and the time-worn framework of the door, — none of these things belonged to her sphere. But, even as a ray of sunshine, fall into what dismal place it may, instantaneously creates for itself a propriety in being there, so did it seem altogether fit that the girl should be standing at the threshold. It was no less evidently proper that the door should swing open to admit her. The maiden lady, herself, sternly inhospitable in her first purposes, soon began to feel that the door ought to be shoved back, and the rusty key be turned in the reluctant lock.

"Can it be Phœbe?" questioned she within herself. "It must be little Phœbe; for it can be nobody else, — and there is a look of her father about her, too! But what does she want here? And how like a country cousin, to come down upon a poor body in this way, without so much as a day's notice, or asking whether she would be welcome! Well; she must have a night's lodging, I suppose; and to-morrow the child shall go back to her mother!"

Phœbe, it must be understood, was that one little offshoot of the Pyncheon race to whom we have already referred, as a native of a rural part of New England, where the old fashions and feelings of relationship are still partially kept up. In her own circle, it was regarded as by no means improper for kinsfolk to visit one another without invitation, or preliminary and ceremonious warning. Yet, in consideration of Miss Hepzibah's recluse way of life, a letter had actually been written and despatched, conveying information of Phœbe's projected visit. This epistle, for three or four days past, had been in the pocket of the penny-postman, who, happening to have no other business in Pyncheon Street, had not yet made it convenient to call at the House of the Seven Gables.

"No! — she can stay only one night," said Hepzibah, unbolting the door. "If Clifford were to find her here, it might disturb him!"

V.

MAY AND NOVEMBER.

PHŒBE PYNCHEON slept, on the night of her arrival, in a chamber that looked down on the garden of the old house. It fronted towards the east, so that at a very seasonable hour a glow of crimson light came flooding through the window, and bathed the dingy ceiling and paper-hangings in its own hue. There were curtains to Phœbe's bed; a dark, antique canopy, and ponderous festoons of a stuff which had been rich, and even magnificent, in its time; but which now brooded over the girl like a cloud, making a night in that one corner, while elsewhere it was beginning to be day. The morning light, however, soon stole into the aperture at the foot of the bed, betwixt those faded curtains. Finding the new guest there, — with a bloom on her cheeks like the morning's own, and a gentle stir of departing slumber in her limbs, as when an early breeze moves the foliage, — the dawn kissed her brow. It was the caress which a dewy maiden — such as the Dawn is, immortally — gives to her sleeping sister, partly from the impulse of irresistible fondness, and partly as a pretty hint that it is time now to unclose her eyes.

At the touch of those lips of light, Phœbe quietly awoke, and, for a moment, did not recognize where she was, nor how those heavy curtains chanced to be festooned around her. Nothing, indeed, was absolutely plain to her, except that it was now early morning, and that, whatever might happen next, it was proper, first of all, to get up and say her prayers. She was the more inclined to devotion from the grim aspect of the chamber and its furniture, especially the tall, stiff chairs ; one of which stood close by her bedside, and looked as if some old-fashioned personage had been sitting there all night, and had vanished only just in season to escape discovery.

When Phœbe was quite dressed, she peeped out of the window, and saw a rose-bush in the garden. Being a very tall one, and of luxuriant growth, it had been propped up against the side of the house, and was literally covered with a rare and very beautiful species of white rose. A large portion of them, as the girl afterwards discovered, had blight or mildew at their hearts ; but, viewed at a fair distance, the whole rose-bush looked as if it had been brought from Eden that very summer, together with the mould in which it grew. The truth was, nevertheless, that it had been planted by Alice Pyncheon, — she was Phœbe's great-great-grand-aunt, — in soil which, reckoning only its cultivation as a garden-plat, was now unctuous with nearly two hundred years of vegetable decay. Growing as they did, however, out of the old earth, the flowers still sent a fresh and sweet incense up to their Creator ; nor could it have been the less pure and acceptable, because Phœbe's young breath mingled with it, as the fragrance floated past the window. Hastening down the creaking and carpetless staircase, she found her way into the garden, gathered some of the most perfect of the roses, and brought them to her chamber.

Little Phœbe was one of those persons who possess,

as their exclusive patrimony, the gift of practical arrangement. It is a kind of natural magic that enables these favored ones to bring out the hidden capabilities of things around them; and particularly to give a look of comfort and habitableness to any place which, for however brief a period, may happen to be their home. A wild hut of underbrush, tossed together by wayfarers through the primitive forest, would acquire the home aspect by one night's lodging of such a woman, and would retain it long after her quiet figure had disappeared into the surrounding shade. No less a portion of such homely witchcraft was requisite to reclaim, as it were, Phœbe's waste, cheerless, and dusky chamber, which had been untenanted so long — except by spiders, and mice, and rats, and ghosts — that it was all overgrown with the desolation which watches to obliterate every trace of man's happier hours. What was precisely Phœbe's process we find it impossible to say. She appeared to have no preliminary design, but gave a touch here and another there; brought some articles of furniture to light and dragged others into the shadow; looped up or let down a window-curtain; and, in the course of half an hour, had fully succeeded in throwing a kindly and hospitable smile over the apartment. No longer ago than the night before, it had resembled nothing so much as the old maid's heart; for there was neither sunshine nor household fire in one nor the other, and, save for ghosts and ghostly reminiscences, not a guest, for many years gone by, had entered the heart or the chamber.

There was still another peculiarity of this inscrutable charm. The bedchamber, no doubt, was a chamber of very great and varied experience, as a scene of

human life: the joy of bridal nights had throbbed itself away here; new immortals had first drawn earthly
breath here; and here old people had died. But —
whether it were the white roses, or whatever the subtile influence might be — a person of delicate instinct
would have known at once that it was now a maiden's
bedchamber, and had been purified of all former evil
and sorrow by her sweet breath and happy thoughts.
Her dreams of the past night, being such cheerful
ones, had exorcised the gloom, and now haunted the
chamber in its stead.

After arranging matters to her satisfaction, Phœbe
emerged from her chamber, with a purpose to descend
again into the garden. Besides the rose-bush, she had
observed several other species of flowers growing there
in a wilderness of neglect, and obstructing one another's development (as is often the parallel case in
human society) by their uneducated entanglement
and confusion. At the head of the stairs, however,
she met Hepzibah, who, it being still early, invited her
into a room which she would probably have called her
boudoir, had her education embraced any such French
phrase. It was strewn about with a few old books,
and a work-basket, and a dusty writing-desk; and had,
on one side, a large, black article of furniture, of very
strange appearance, which the old gentlewoman told
Phœbe was a harpsichord. It looked more like a
coffin than anything else; and, indeed, — not having
been played upon, or opened, for years, — there must
have been a vast deal of dead music in it, stifled for
want of air. Human finger was hardly known to have
touched its chords since the days of Alice Pyncheon,
who had learned the sweet accomplishment of melody
in Europe.

Hepzibah bade her young guest sit down, and, her-self taking a chair near by, looked as earnestly at Phœbe's trim little figure as if she expected to see right into its springs and motive secrets.

"Cousin Phœbe," said she, at last, "I really can't see my way clear to keep you with me."

These words, however, had not the inhospitable bluntness with which they may strike the reader; for the two relatives, in a talk before bedtime, had arrived at a certain degree of mutual understanding. Hepzi-bah knew enough to enable her to appreciate the cir-cumstances (resulting from the second marriage of the girl's mother) which made it desirable for Phœbe to establish herself in another home. Nor did she misin-terpret Phœbe's character, and the genial activity per-vading it, — one of the most valuable traits of the true New England woman, — which had impelled her forth, as might be said, to seek her fortune, but with a self-respecting purpose to confer as much benefit as she could anywise receive. As one of her nearest kindred, she had naturally betaken herself to Hepzi-bah, with no idea of forcing herself on her cousin's protection, but only for a visit of a week or two, which might be indefinitely extended, should it prove for the happiness of both.

To Hepzibah's blunt observation, therefore, Phœbe replied, as frankly, and more cheerfully.

"Dear cousin, I cannot tell how it will be," said she. "But I really think we may suit one another much better than you suppose."

"You are a nice girl, — I see it plainly," continued Hepzibah; "and it is not any question as to that point which makes me hesitate. But, Phœbe, this house of mine is but a melancholy place for a young person to be in. It lets in the wind and rain, and the snow, too, in the garret and upper chambers, in winter-time, but it never lets in the sunshine! And as for myself, you see what I am, — a dismal and lonesome old woman (for I begin to call myself old, Phœbe), whose temper, I am afraid, is none of the best, and whose spirits are as bad as can be. I cannot make your life pleasant, Cousin Phœbe, neither can I so much as give you bread to eat."

"You will find me a cheerful little body," answered Phœbe, smiling, and yet with a kind of gentle dignity; "and I mean to earn my bread. You know I have not been brought up a Pyncheon. A girl learns many things in a New England village."

"Ah! Phœbe," said Hepzibah, sighing, "your knowledge would do but little for you here! And then it is a wretched thought that you should fling away your young days in a place like this. Those cheeks would not be so rosy after a month or two. Look at my face!" — and, indeed, the contrast was very striking, — "you see how pale I am! It is my idea that the dust and continual decay of these old houses are unwholesome for the lungs."

"There is the garden, — the flowers to be taken care of," observed Phœbe. "I should keep myself healthy with exercise in the open air."

"And, after all, child," exclaimed Hepzibah, suddenly rising, as if to dismiss the subject, "it is not for me to say who shall be a guest or inhabitant of the old Pyncheon House. Its master is coming."

"Do you mean Judge Pyncheon?" asked Phœbe, in surprise.

"Judge Pyncheon!" answered her cousin, angrily. "He will hardly cross the threshold while I live! No, no! But, Phœbe, you shall see the face of him I speak of."

She went in quest of the miniature already described, and returned with it in her hand. Giving it to Phœbe, she watched her features narrowly, and with a certain jealousy as to the mode in which the girl would show herself affected by the picture.

"How do you like the face?" asked Hepzibah.

"It is handsome! — it is very beautiful!" said Phœbe, admiringly. "It is as sweet a face as a man's can be, or ought to be. It has something of a child's expression, — and yet not childish, — only one feels so very kindly towards him! He ought never to suffer anything. One would bear much for the sake of sparing him toil or sorrow. Who is it, Cousin Hepzibah?"

"Did you never hear," whispered her cousin, bending towards her, "of Clifford Pyncheon?"

"Never! I thought there were no Pyncheons left, except yourself and our cousin Jaffrey," answered Phœbe. "And yet I seem to have heard the name of Clifford Pyncheon. Yes! — from my father or my mother; but has he not been a long while dead?"

"Well, well, child, perhaps he has!" said Hepzibah, with a sad, hollow laugh; "but, in old houses like this, you know, dead people are very apt to come back again! We shall see. And, Cousin Phœbe, since, after all that I have said, your courage does not fail you, we will not part so soon. You are welcome, my child, for the present, to such a home as your kinswoman can offer you."

With this measured, but not exactly cold assurance of a hospitable purpose, Hepzibah kissed her cheek.

They now went below stairs, where Phœbe — not so

much assuming the office as attracting it to herself, by the magnetism of innate fitness — took the most active part in preparing breakfast. The mistress of the house, meanwhile, as is usual with persons of her stiff and unmalleable cast, stood mostly aside; willing to lend her aid, yet conscious that her natural inaptitude would be likely to impede the business in hand. Phœbe, and the fire that boiled the teakettle, were equally bright, cheerful, and efficient, in their respective offices. Hepzibah gazed forth from her habitual sluggishness, the necessary result of long solitude, as from another sphere. She could not help being interested, however, and even amused, at the readiness with which her new inmate adapted herself to the circumstances, and brought the house, moreover, and all its rusty old appliances, into a suitableness for her purposes. Whatever she did, too, was done without conscious effort, and with frequent outbreaks of song, which were exceedingly pleasant to the ear. This natural tunefulness made Phœbe seem like a bird in a shadowy tree; or conveyed the idea that the stream of life warbled through her heart as a brook sometimes warbles through a pleasant little dell. It betokened the cheeriness of an active temperament, finding joy in its activity, and, therefore, rendering it beautiful; it was a New England trait, — the stern old stuff of Puritanism with a gold thread in the web.

Hepzibah brought out some old silver spoons with the family crest upon them, and a china tea-set painted over with grotesque figures of man, bird, and beast, in as grotesque a landscape. These pictured people were odd humorists, in a world of their own, — a world of vivid brilliancy, so far as color went, and still unfaded, although the teapot and small cups were as ancient as the custom itself of tea-drinking.

"Your great-great-great-great-grandmother had these cups, when she was married," said Hepzibah to Phœbe. "She was a Davenport, of a good family. They were almost the first teacups ever seen in the colony; and if one of them were to be broken, my heart would break with it. But it is nonsense to speak so about a brittle teacup, when I remember what my heart has gone through without breaking."

The cups — not having been used, perhaps, since Hepzibah's youth — had contracted no small burden of dust, which Phœbe washed away with so much care and delicacy as to satisfy even the proprietor of this invaluable china.

"What a nice little housewife you are!" exclaimed the latter, smiling, and, at the same time, frowning so prodigiously that the smile was sunshine under a thunder-cloud. "Do you do other things as well? Are you as good at your book as you are at washing teacups?"

"Not quite, I am afraid," said Phœbe, laughing at the form of Hepzibah's question. "But I was schoolmistress for the little children in our district last summer, and might have been so still."

"Ah! 't is all very well!" observed the maiden lady, drawing herself up. "But these things must have come to you with your mother's blood. I never knew a Pyncheon that had any turn for them."

It is very queer, but not the less true, that people are generally quite as vain, or even more so, of their deficiencies than of their available gifts; as was Hepzibah of this native inapplicability, so to speak, of the Pyncheons to any useful purpose. She regarded it as an hereditary trait; and so, perhaps, it was, but, unfortunately, a morbid one, such as is often generated

in families that remain long above the surface of society.

Before they left the breakfast-table, the shop-bell
rang sharply, and Hepzibah set down the remnant of
her final cup of tea, with a look of sallow despair that
was truly piteous to behold. In cases of distasteful
occupation, the second day is generally worse than the
first; we return to the rack with all the soreness of
the preceding torture in our limbs. At all events,
Hepzibah had fully satisfied herself of the impossibility of ever becoming wonted to this peevishly obstreperous little bell. Ring as often as it might, the
sound always smote upon her nervous system rudely
and suddenly. And especially now, while, with her
crested teaspoons and antique china, she was flattering
herself with ideas of gentility, she felt an unspeakable
disinclination to confront a customer.

"Do not trouble yourself, dear cousin!" cried Phœbe,
starting lightly up. "I am shop-keeper to-day."

"You, child!" exclaimed Hepzibah. "What can
a little country-girl know of such matters?"

"Oh, I have done all the shopping for the family
at our village store," said Phœbe. "And I have had
a table at a fancy fair, and made better sales than
anybody. These things are not to be learnt; they
depend upon a knack that comes, I suppose," added
she, smiling, "with one's mother's blood. You shall
see that I am as nice a little saleswoman as I am a
housewife!"

The old gentlewoman stole behind Phœbe, and peeped
from the passage-way into the shop, to note how she
would manage her undertaking. It was a case of
some intricacy. A very ancient woman, in a white
short gown and a green petticoat, with a string of gold

beads about her neck, and what looked like a nightcap on her head, had brought a quantity of yarn to barter for the commodities of the shop. She was probably the very last person in town who still kept the time-honored spinning-wheel in constant revolution. It was worth while to hear the croaking and hollow tones of the old lady, and the pleasant voice of Phœbe, mingling in one twisted thread of talk; and still better to contrast their figures, — so light and bloomy, — so decrepit and dusky, — with only the counter betwixt them, in one sense, but more than threescore years, in another. As for the bargain, it was wrinkled slyness and craft pitted against native truth and sagacity.

"Was not that well done?" asked Phœbe, laughing, when the customer was gone.

"Nicely done, indeed, child!" answered Hepzibah. "I could not have gone through with it nearly so well. As you say, it must be a knack that belongs to you on the mother's side."

It is a very genuine admiration, that with which persons too shy or too awkward to take a due part in the bustling world regard the real actors in life's stirring scenes; so genuine, in fact, that the former are usually fain to make it palatable to their self-love, by assuming that these active and forcible qualities are incompatible with others, which they choose to deem higher and more important. Thus, Hepzibah was well content to acknowledge Phœbe's vastly superior gifts as a shop-keeper; she listened, with compliant ear, to her suggestion of various methods whereby the influx of trade might be increased, and rendered profitable, without a hazardous outlay of capital. She consented that the village maiden should manufacture yeast, both liquid and in cakes; and should brew a certain kind of beer, nectareous to the palate, and of rare stomachic virtues; and, moreover, should bake and exhibit for sale some little spice-cakes, which whosoever tasted would longingly desire to taste again. All such proofs of a ready mind and skilful handiwork were highly acceptable to the aristocratic hucksteress, so long as she could murmur to herself with a grim smile, and a half-natural sigh, and a sentiment of mixed wonder, pity, and growing affection, —

"What a nice little body she is! If she could only be a lady, too! — but that's impossible! Phœbe is no Pyncheon. She takes everything from her mother."

As to Phœbe's not being a lady, or whether she were a lady or no, it was a point, perhaps, difficult to decide, but which could hardly have come up for judgment at all in any fair and healthy mind. Out of New England, it would be impossible to meet with a person combining so many lady-like attributes with so many others that form no necessary (if compatible) part of the character. She shocked no canon of taste; she was admirably in keeping with herself, and never jarred against surrounding circumstances. Her figure, to be sure, — so small as to be almost childlike, and so elastic that motion seemed as easy or easier to it than rest, — would hardly have suited one's idea of a countess. Neither did her face — with the brown ringlets on either side, and the slightly piquant nose, and the wholesome bloom, and the clear shade of tan, and the half a dozen freckles, friendly remembrancers of the April sun and breeze — precisely give us a right to call her beautiful. But there was both lustre and depth in her eyes. She was very pretty; as graceful as a bird, and graceful much in the same way; as

pleasant about the house as a gleam of sunshine falling on the floor through a shadow of twinkling leaves,
or as a ray of firelight that dances on the wall while
evening is drawing nigh.   Instead of discussing her
claim to rank among ladies, it would be preferable to
regard Phœbe as the example of feminine grace and
availability combined, in a state of society, if there
were any such, where ladies did not exist.   There it
should be woman's office to move in the midst of practical affairs, and to gild them all, the very homeliest,
— were it even the scouring of pots and kettles, —
with an atmosphere of loveliness and joy.

Such was the sphere of Phœbe.   To find the born
and educated lady, on the other hand, we need look
no farther than Hepzibah, our forlorn old maid, in her
rustling and rusty silks, with her deeply cherished and
ridiculous consciousness of long descent, her shadowy
claims to princely territory, and, in the way of accomplishment, her recollections, it may be, of having formerly thrummed on a harpsichord, and walked a min-
uet, and worked an antique tapestry-stitch on her sampler.   It was a fair parallel between new Plebeianism
and old Gentility.

It really seemed as if the battered visage of the
House of the Seven Gables, black and heavy-browed
as it still certainly looked, must have shown a kind of
cheerfulness glimmering through its dusky windows
as Phœbe passed to and fro in the interior.   Otherwise, it is impossible to explain how the people of the
neighborhood so soon became aware of the girl's presence.   There was a great run of custom, setting steadily in, from about ten o'clock until towards noon, —
relaxing, somewhat, at dinner-time, but recommencing
in the afternoon, and, finally, dying away a half an

hour or so before the long day's sunset. One of the stanchest patrons was little Ned Higgins, the devourer of Jim Crow and the elephant, who to-day had signalized his omnivorous prowess by swallowing two dromedaries and a locomotive. Phœbe laughed, as she summed up her aggregate of sales upon the slate; while Hepzibah, first drawing on a pair of silk gloves, reckoned over the sordid accumulation of copper coin, not without silver intermixed, that had jingled into the till.

"We must renew our stock, Cousin Hepzibah!" cried the little saleswoman. "The gingerbread figures are all gone, and so are those Dutch wooden milk-maids, and most of our other playthings. There has been constant inquiry for cheap raisins, and a great cry for whistles, and trumpets, and jew's-harps; and at least a dozen little boys have asked for molasses-candy. And we must contrive to get a peck of russet apples, late in the season as it is. But, dear cousin, what an enormous heap of copper! Positively a copper mountain!"

"Well done! well done! well done!" quoth Uncle Venner, who had taken occasion to shuffle in and out of the shop several times in the course of the day. "Here's a girl that will never end her days at my farm! Bless my eyes, what a brisk little soul!"

"Yes, Phœbe is a nice girl!" said Hepzibah, with a scowl of austere approbation. "But, Uncle Venner, you have known the family a great many years. Can you tell me whether there ever was a Pyncheon whom she takes after?"

"I don't believe there ever was," answered the venerable man. "At any rate, it never was my luck to see her like among them, nor, for that matter, anywhere else. I've seen a great deal of the world, not only in people's kitchens and back-yards, but at the street-corners, and on the wharves, and in other places where my business calls me; and I'm free to say, Miss Hepzibah, that I never knew a human creature do her work so much like one of God's angels as this child Phœbe does!"

Uncle Venner's eulogium, if it appear rather too high-strained for the person and occasion, had, nevertheless, a sense in which it was both subtile and true. There was a spiritual quality in Phœbe's activity. The life of the long and busy day — spent in occupations that might so easily have taken a squalid and ugly aspect — had been made pleasant, and even lovely, by the spontaneous grace with which these homely duties seemed to bloom out of her character; so that labor, while she dealt with it, had the easy and flexible charm of play. Angels do not toil, but let their good works grow out of them; and so did Phœbe.

The two relatives — the young maid and the old one — found time before nightfall, in the intervals of trade, to make rapid advances towards affection and confidence. A recluse, like Hepzibah, usually displays remarkable frankness, and at least temporary affability, on being absolutely cornered, and brought to the point of personal intercourse; like the angel whom Jacob wrestled with, she is ready to bless you when once overcome.

The old gentlewoman took a dreary and proud satisfaction in leading Phœbe from room to room of the house, and recounting the traditions with which, as we may say, the walls were lugubriously frescoed. She showed the indentations made by the lieutenant-governor's sword-hilt in the door-panels of the apartment where old Colonel Pyncheon, a dead host, had received his affrighted visitors with an awful frown. The dusky terror of that frown, Hepzibah observed, was thought to be lingering ever since in the passage-way. She bade Phœbe step into one of the tall chairs, and inspect the ancient map of the Pyncheon territory at the eastward. In a tract of land on which she laid her finger, there existed a silver-mine, the locality of which was precisely pointed out in some memoranda of Colonel Pyncheon himself, but only to be made known when the family claim should be recognized by government. Thus it was for the interest of all New England that the Pyncheons should have justice done them. She told, too, how that there was undoubtedly an immense treasure of English guineas hidden somewhere about the house, or in the cellar, or possibly in the garden.

"If you should happen to find it, Phœbe," said Hepzibah, glancing aside at her with a grim yet kindly smile, "we will tie up the shop-bell for good and all!"

"Yes, dear cousin," answered Phœbe; "but, in the mean time, I hear somebody ringing it!"

When the customer was gone, Hepzibah talked rather vaguely, and at great length, about a certain Alice Pyncheon, who had been exceedingly beautiful and accomplished in her lifetime, a hundred years ago. The fragrance of her rich and delightful character still lingered about the place where she had lived, as a dried rosebud scents the drawer where it has withered and perished. This lovely Alice had met with some great and mysterious calamity, and had grown thin and white, and gradually faded out of the world. But, even now, she was supposed to haunt the House of the Seven Gables, and, a great many times, — especially

when one of the Pyncheons was to die, — she had been
heard playing sadly and beautifully on the harpsichord.
One of these tunes, just as it had sounded from her
spiritual touch, had been written down by an amateur
of music; it was so exquisitely mournful that nobody,
to this day, could bear to hear it played, unless when a
great sorrow had made them know the still profounder
sweetness of it.

"Was it the same harpsichord that you showed
me?" inquired Phœbe.

"The very same," said Hepzibah. "It was Alice
Pyncheon's harpsichord. When I was learning music,
my father would never let me open it. So, as I could
only play on my teacher's instrument, I have forgotten
all my music long ago."

Leaving these antique themes, the old lady began
to talk about the daguerreotypist, whom, as he seemed
to be a well-meaning and orderly young man, and in
narrow circumstances, she had permitted to take up his
residence in one of the seven gables. But, on seeing
more of Mr. Holgrave, she hardly knew what to make
of him. He had the strangest companions imaginable;
men with long beards, and dressed in linen blouses,
and other such new-fangled and ill-fitting garments;
reformers, temperance lecturers, and all manner of
cross-looking philanthropists; community-men, and
come-outers, as Hepzibah believed, who acknowledged
no law, and ate no solid food, but lived on the scent
of other people's cookery, and turned up their noses
at the fare. As for the daguerreotypist, she had read
a paragraph in a penny paper, the other day, accusing
him of making a speech full of wild and disorganiz-
ing matter, at a meeting of his banditti-like associates.
For her own part, she had reason to believe that he

practised animal magnetism, and, if such things were in fashion nowadays, should be apt to suspect him of studying the Black Art up there in his lonesome chamber.

"But, dear cousin," said Phœbe, "if the young man is so dangerous, why do you let him stay? If he does nothing worse, he may set the house on fire!"

"Why, sometimes," answered Hepzibah, "I have seriously made it a question, whether I ought not to send him away. But, with all his oddities, he is a quiet kind of a person, and has such a way of taking hold of one's mind, that, without exactly liking him (for I don't know enough of the young man), I should be sorry to lose sight of him entirely. A woman clings to slight acquaintances when she lives so much alone as I do."

"But if Mr. Holgrave is a lawless person!" remonstrated Phœbe, a part of whose essence it was to keep within the limits of law.

"Oh!" said Hepzibah, carelessly, — for, formal as she was, still, in her life's experience, she had gnashed her teeth against human law, — "I suppose he has a law of his own!"

VI.

MAULE'S WELL.

AFTER an early tea, the little country-girl strayed into the garden. The enclosure had formerly been very extensive, but was now contracted within small compass, and hemmed about, partly by high wooden fences, and partly by the outbuildings of houses that stood on another street. In its centre was a grass-plat, surrounding a ruinous little structure, which showed just enough of its original design to indicate that it had once been a summer-house. A hop-vine, springing from last year's root, was beginning to clamber over it, but would be long in covering the roof with its green mantle. Three of the seven gables either fronted or looked sideways, with a dark solemnity of aspect, down into the garden.

The black, rich soil had fed itself with the decay of a long period of time; such as fallen leaves, the petals of flowers, and the stalks and seed-vessels of vagrant and lawless plants, more useful after their death than ever while flaunting in the sun. The evil of these departed years would naturally have sprung up again, in such rank weeds (symbolic of the transmitted vices of society) as are always prone to root themselves about human dwellings. Phœbe saw, however, that their growth must have been checked by a degree of careful labor, bestowed daily and systematically on the garden. The white double rose-bush had evidently been propped up anew against the house since the commencement of the season; and a pear-tree and three damson-trees, which, except a row of currant-bushes, constituted the only varieties of fruit, bore marks of the recent amputation of several superfluous or defective limbs. There were also a few species of antique and hereditary flowers, in no very flourishing condition, but scrupulously weeded; as if some person, either out of love or curiosity, had been anxious to bring them to such perfection as they were capable of attaining. The remainder of the garden presented a well-selected assortment of esculent vegetables, in a praiseworthy state of advancement. Summer squashes, almost in their golden blossom; cucumbers, now evincing a tendency to spread away from the main stock, and ramble far and wide; two or three rows of string-beans, and as many more that were about to festoon themselves on poles; tomatoes, occupying a site so sheltered and sunny that the plants were already gigantic, and promised an early and abundant harvest.

Phœbe wondered whose care and toil it could have been that had planted these vegetables, and kept the soil so clean and orderly. Not surely her cousin Hepzibah's, who had no taste nor spirits for the lady-like employment of cultivating flowers, and — with her recluse habits, and tendency to shelter herself within the dismal shadow of the house — would hardly have come forth under the speck of open sky to weed and hoe among the fraternity of beans and squashes.

It being her first day of complete estrangement from rural objects. Phœbe found an unexpected charm in this little nook of grass, and foliage, and aristocratic flowers, and plebeian vegetables. The eye of Heaven seemed to look down into it pleasantly, and with a pe-

culiar smile, as if glad to perceive that nature, elsewhere overwhelmed, and driven out of the dusty town,
had here been able to retain a breathing-place.   The
spot acquired a somewhat wilder grace, and yet a very
gentle one, from the fact that a pair of robins had built
their nest in the pear-tree, and were making themselves
exceedingly busy and happy in the dark intricacy of its
boughs.   Bees, too, — strange, to say, — had thought it
worth their while to come hither, possibly from the
range of hives beside some farm-house miles away.
How many aerial voyages might they have made, in
quest of honey, or honey-laden, betwixt dawn and sunset!   Yet, late as it now was, there still arose a pleasant hum out of one or two of the squash-blossoms, in
the depths of which these bees were plying their golden
labor.   There was one other object in the garden which
Nature might fairly claim as her inalienable property,
in spite of whatever man could do to render it his own.
This was a fountain, set round with a rim of old mossy
stones, and paved, in its bed, with what appeared to
be a sort of mosaic-work of variously colored pebbles.
The play and slight agitation of the water, in its upward gush, wrought magically with these variegated
pebbles, and made a continually shifting apparition of
quaint figures, vanishing too suddenly to be definable.
Thence, swelling over the rim of moss-grown stones,
the water stole away under the fence, through what we
regret to call a gutter, rather than a channel.

Nor must we forget to mention a hen-coop of very
reverend antiquity that stood in the farther corner of
the garden, not a great way from the fountain.   It now
contained only Chanticleer, his two wives, and a solitary chicken.   All of them were pure specimens of a
breed which had been transmitted down as an heirloom

In the Pyncheon family, and were said, while in their prime, to have attained almost the size of turkeys, and, on the score of delicate flesh, to be fit for a prince's table. In proof of the authenticity of this legendary renown, Hepzibah could have exhibited the shell of a great egg, which an ostrich need hardly have been ashamed of. Be that as it might, the hens were now scarcely larger than pigeons, and had a queer, rusty, withered aspect, and a gouty kind of movement, and a sleepy and melancholy tone throughout all the variations of their clucking and cackling. It was evident that the race had degenerated, like many a noble race besides, in consequence of too strict a watchfulness to keep it pure. These feathered people had existed too long in their distinct variety; a fact of which the present representatives, judging by their lugubrious deportment, seemed to be aware. They kept themselves alive, unquestionably, and laid now and then an egg, and hatched a chicken; not for any pleasure of their own, but that the world might not absolutely lose what had once been so admirable a breed of fowls. The distinguishing mark of the hens was a crest of lamentably scanty growth, in these latter days, but so oddly and wickedly analogous to Hepzibah's turban, that Phœbe — to the poignant distress of her conscience, but inevitably — was led to fancy a general resemblance betwixt these forlorn bipeds and her respectable relative.

The girl ran into the house to get some crumbs of bread, cold potatoes, and other such scraps as were suitable to the accommodating appetite of fowls. Returning, she gave a peculiar call, which they seemed to recognize. The chicken crept through the pales of the coop and ran, with some show of liveliness, to her feet;

while Chanticleer and the ladies of his household regarded her with queer, sidelong glances, and then
croaked one to another, as if communicating their sage
opinions of her character.   So wise, as well as antique,
was their aspect, as to give color to the idea, not merely
that they were the descendants of a time-honored race,
but that they had existed, in their individual capacity,
ever since the House of the Seven Gables was founded,
and were somehow mixed up with its destiny.   They
were a species of tutelary sprite, or Banshee; although
winged and feathered differently from most other
guardian angels.

"Here, you odd little chicken!" said Phœbe; "here
are some nice crumbs for you!"

The chicken, hereupon, though almost as venerable
in appearance as its mother, — possessing, indeed, the
whole antiquity of its progenitors in miniature, — mustered vivacity enough to flutter upward and alight on
Phœbe's shoulder.

"That little fowl pays you a high compliment!"
said a voice behind Phœbe.

Turning quickly, she was surprised at sight of a
young man, who had found access into the garden by
a door opening out of another gable than that whence
she had emerged.   He held a hoe in his hand, and,
while Phœbe was gone in quest of the crumbs, had begun to busy himself with drawing up fresh earth about
the roots of the tomatoes.

"The chicken really treats you like an old acquaintance," continued he, in a quiet way, while a smile
made his face pleasanter than Phœbe at first fancied
it. ` "Those venerable personages in the coop, too,
seem very affably disposed.   You are lucky to be in
their good graces so soon!   They have known me

much longer, but never honor me with any familiarity, though hardly a day passes without my bringing them food. Miss Hepzibah, I suppose, will interweave the fact with her other traditions, and set it down that the fowls know you to be a Pyncheon!"

"The secret is," said Phœbe, smiling, "that I have learned how to talk with hens and chickens."

"Ah, but these hens," answered the young man, — "these hens of aristocratic lineage would scorn to understand the vulgar language of a barn-yard fowl. I prefer to think — and so would Miss Hepzibah — that they recognize the family tone. For you are a Pyncheon?"

"My name is Phœbe Pyncheon," said the girl, with a manner of some reserve; for she was aware that her new acquaintance could be no other than the daguerreotypist, of whose lawless propensities the old maid had given her a disagreeable idea. "I did not know that my cousin Hepzibah's garden was under another person's care."

"Yes," said Holgrave, "I dig, and hoe, and weed, in this black old earth, for the sake of refreshing myself with what little nature and simplicity may be left in it, after men have so long sown and reaped here. I turn up the earth by way of pastime. My sober occupation, so far as I have any, is with a lighter material. In short, I make pictures out of sunshine; and, not to be too much dazzled with my own trade, I have prevailed with Miss Hepzibah to let me lodge in one of these dusky gables. It is like a bandage over one's eyes, to come into it. But would you like to see a specimen of my productions?"

"A daguerreotype likeness, do you mean?" asked Phœbe, with less reserve; for, in spite of prejudice, her own youthfulness sprang forward to meet his. "I don't much like pictures of that sort, — they are so hard and stern; besides dodging away from the eye, and trying to escape altogether. They are conscious of looking very unamiable, I suppose, and therefore hate to be seen."

"If you would permit me," said the artist, looking at Phœbe, "I should like to try whether the daguerreotype can bring out disagreeable traits on a perfectly amiable face. But there certainly is truth in what you have said. Most of my likenesses do look unamiable; but the very sufficient reason, I fancy, is, because the originals are so. There is a wonderful insight in Heaven's broad and simple sunshine. While we give it credit only for depicting the merest surface, it actually brings out the secret character with a truth that no painter would ever venture upon, even could he detect it. There is, at least, no flattery in my humble line of art. Now, here is a likeness which I have taken over and over again, and still with no better result. Yet the original wears, to common eyes, a very different expression. It would gratify me to have your judgment on this character."

He exhibited a daguerreotype miniature in a morocco case. Phœbe merely glanced at it, and gave it back.

"I know the face," she replied; "for its stern eye has been following me about all day. It is my Puritan ancestor, who hangs yonder in the parlor. To be sure, you have found some way of copying the portrait without its black velvet cap and gray beard, and have given him a modern coat and satin cravat, instead of his cloak and band. I don't think him improved by your alterations."

"You would have seen other differences had you looked a little longer," said Holgrave, laughing, yet apparently much struck. "I can assure you that this is a modern face, and one which you will very probably meet. Now, the remarkable point is, that the original wears, to the world's eye, — and, for aught I know, to his most intimate friends, — an exceedingly pleasant countenance, indicative of benevolence, openness of heart, sunny good-humor, and other praiseworthy qualities of that cast. The sun, as you see, tells quite another story, and will not be coaxed out of it, after half a dozen patient attempts on my part. Here we have the man, sly, subtle, hard, imperious, and, withal, cold as ice. Look at that eye! Would you like to be at its mercy? At that mouth! Could it ever smile? And yet, if you could only see the benign smile of the original! It is so much the more unfortunate, as he is a public character of some eminence, and the likeness was intended to be engraved."

"Well, I don't wish to see it any more," observed Phœbe, turning away her eyes. "It is certainly very like the old portrait. But my cousin Hepzibah has another picture, — a miniature. If the original is still in the world, I think he might defy the sun to make him look stern and hard."

"You have seen that picture, then!" exclaimed the artist, with an expression of much interest. "I never did, but have a great curiosity to do so. And you judge favorably of the face?"

"There never was a sweeter one," said Phœbe. "It is almost too soft and gentle for a man's."

"Is there nothing wild in the eye?" continued Holgrave, so earnestly that it embarrassed Phœbe, as did also the quiet freedom with which he presumed on their so recent acquaintance. " Is there nothing dark or sinister anywhere ? Could you not conceive the original to have been guilty of a great crime ? "

" It is nonsense," said Phœbe, a little impatiently, " for us to talk about a picture which you have never seen. You mistake it for some other. A crime, indeed ! Since you are a friend of my cousin Hepzi bah's, you should ask her to show you the picture."

" It will suit my purpose still better to see the original," replied the daguerreotypist coolly. " As to his character, we need not discuss its points ; they have already been settled by a competent tribunal, or one which called itself competent. But, stay ! Do not go yet, if you please ! I have a proposition to make you."

Phœbe was on the point of retreating, but turned back, with some hesitation ; for she did not exactly comprehend his manner, although, on better observation, its feature seemed rather to be lack of ceremony than any approach to offensive rudeness. There was an odd kind of authority, too, in what he now proceeded to say, rather as if the garden were his own than a place to which he was admitted merely by Hepzibah's courtesy.

" If agreeable to you," he observed, " it would give me pleasure to turn over these flowers, and those ancient and respectable fowls, to your care. Coming fresh from country air and occupations, you will soon feel the need of some such out-of-door employment. My own sphere does not so much lie among flowers. You can trim and tend them, therefore, as you please ; and I will ask only the least trifle of a blossom, now and then, in exchange for all the good, honest kitchen-vegetables with which I propose to enrich Miss Hepzibah's table. So we will be fellow-laborers, somewhat on the community system."

Silently, and rather surprised at her own compliance, Phœbe accordingly betook herself to weeding a flower-bed, but busied herself still more with cogitations respecting this young man, with whom she so unexpectedly found herself on terms approaching to familiarity. She did not altogether like him. His character perplexed the little country-girl, as it might a more practised observer; for, while the tone of his conversation had generally been playful, the impression left on her mind was that of gravity, and, except as his youth modified it, almost sternness. She rebelled, as it were, against a certain magnetic element in the artist's nature, which he exercised towards her, possibly without being conscious of it.

After a little while, the twilight, deepened by the shadows of the fruit-trees and the surrounding buildings, threw an obscurity over the garden.

"There," said Holgrave, "it is time to give over work! That last stroke of the hoe has cut off a beanstalk. Good-night, Miss Phœbe Pyncheon! Any bright day, if you will put one of those rosebuds in your hair, and come to my rooms in Central Street, I will seize the purest ray of sunshine, and make a picture of the flower and its wearer."

He retired towards his own solitary gable, but turned his head, on reaching the door, and called to Phœbe, with a tone which certainly had laughter in it, yet which seemed to be more than half in earnest.

"Be careful not to drink at Maule's well!" said he. "Neither drink nor bathe your face in it!"

"Maule's well!" answered Phœbe. "Is that it with the rim of mossy stones? I have no thought of drinking there, — but why not?"

" Oh," rejoined the daguerreotypist, "because, like an old lady's cup of tea, it is water bewitched!"

He vanished; and Phœbe, lingering a moment, saw a glimmering light, and then the steady beam of a lamp, in a chamber of the gable. On returning into Hepzibah's apartment of the house, she found the low-studded parlor so dim and dusky that her eyes could not penetrate the interior. She was indistinctly aware, however, that the gaunt figure of the old gentlewoman was sitting in one of the straight-backed chairs, a little withdrawn from the window, the faint gleam of which showed the blanched paleness of her cheek, turned sideway towards a corner.

" Shall I light a lamp, Cousin Hepzibah?" she asked.

" Do, if you please, my dear child," answered Hepzibah. " But put it on the table in the corner of the passage. My eyes are weak; and I can seldom bear the lamplight on them."

What an instrument is the human voice! How wonderfully responsive to every emotion of the human soul! In Hepzibah's tone, at that moment, there was a certain rich depth and moisture, as if the words, commonplace as they were, had been steeped in the warmth of her heart. Again, while lighting the lamp in the kitchen, Phœbe fancied that her cousin spoke to her.

" In a moment, cousin!" answered the girl. "These matches just glimmer, and go out."

But, instead of a response from Hepzibah, she seemed to hear the murmur of an unknown voice. It was strangely indistinct, however, and less like articulate words than an unshaped sound, such as would be the utterance of feeling and sympathy, rather than of the

intellect. So vague was it, that its impression or echo
in Phœbe's mind was that of unreality. She concluded that she must have mistaken some other sound
for that of the human voice; or else that it was altogether in her fancy.

She set the lighted lamp in the passage, and again
entered the parlor. Hepzibah's form, though its sable
outline mingled with the dusk, was now less imperfectly visible. In the remoter parts of the room, however, its walls being so ill adapted to reflect light, there
was nearly the same obscurity as before.

"Cousin," said Phœbe, "did you speak to me just
now?"

"No, child!" replied Hepzibah.

Fewer words than before, but with the same mysterious music in them! Mellow, melancholy, yet not
mournful, the tone seemed to gush up out of the deep
well of Hepzibah's heart, all steeped in its profoundest
emotion. There was a tremor in it, too, that — as all
strong feeling is electric — partly communicated itself
to Phœbe. The girl sat silently for a moment. But
soon, her senses being very acute, she became conscious
of an irregular respiration in an obscure corner of
the room. Her physical organization, moreover, being
at once delicate and healthy, gave her a perception,
operating with almost the effect of a spiritual medium,
that somebody was near at hand.

"My dear cousin," asked she, overcoming an indefinable reluctance, "is there not some one in the room
with us?"

"Phœbe, my dear little girl," said Hepzibah, after
a moment's pause, "you were up betimes, and have
been busy all day. Pray go to bed; for I am sure
you must need rest. I will sit in the parlor awhile,

and collect my thoughts. It has been my custom for more years, child, than you have lived!"

While thus dismissing her, the maiden lady stept forward, kissed Phœbe, and pressed her to her heart, which beat against the girl's bosom with a strong, high, and tumultuous swell. How came there to be so much love in this desolate old heart, that it could afford to well over thus abundantly?

"Good night, cousin," said Phœbe, strangely affected by Hepzibah's manner. "If you begin to love me, I am glad!"

She retired to her chamber, but did not soon fall asleep, nor then very profoundly. At some uncertain period in the depths of night, and, as it were, through the thin veil of a dream, she was conscious of a footstep mounting the stairs heavily, but not with force and decision. The voice of Hepzibah, with a hush through it, was going up along with the footsteps; and, again, responsive to her cousin's voice, Phœbe heard that strange, vague murmur, which might be likened to an indistinct shadow of human utterance.

VII.

THE GUEST.

WHEN Phœbe awoke, — which she did with the early twittering of the conjugal couple of robins in the pear-tree, — she heard movements below stairs, and, hastening down, found Hepzibah already in the kitchen. She stood by a window, holding a book in close contiguity to her nose, as if with the hope of gaining an olfactory acquaintance with its contents, since her imperfect vision made it not very easy to read them. If any volume could have manifested its essential wisdom in the mode suggested, it would certainly have been the one now in Hepzibah's hand; and the kitchen, in such an event, would forthwith have steamed with the fragrance of venison, turkeys, capons, larded partridges, puddings, cakes, and Christmas pies, in all manner of elaborate mixture and concoction. It was a cookery book, full of innumerable old fashions of English dishes, and illustrated with engravings, which represented the arrangements of the table at such banquets as it might have befitted a nobleman to give in the great hall of his castle. And, amid these rich and potent devices of the culinary art (not one of which, probably, had been tested, within the memory of any man's grandfather), poor Hepzibah was seeking for some nimble little titbit, which, with what skill she had, and such materials as were at hand, she might toss up for breakfast.

Soon, with a deep sigh, she put aside the savory volume, and inquired of Phœbe whether old Speckle, as she called one of the hens, had laid an egg the preceding day. Phœbe ran to see, but returned without the expected treasure in her hand. At that instant, however, the blast of a fish-dealer's conch was heard, announcing his approach along the street. With energetic raps at the shop-window, Hepzibah summoned the man in, and made purchase of what he warranted as the finest mackerel in his cart, and as fat a one as ever he felt with his finger so early in the season. Requesting Phœbe to roast some coffee, — which she casually observed was the real Mocha, and so long kept that each of the small berries ought to be worth its weight in gold, — the maiden lady heaped fuel into the vast receptacle of the ancient fireplace in such quantity as soon to drive the lingering dusk out of the kitchen. The country-girl, willing to give her utmost assistance, proposed to make an Indian cake, after her mother's peculiar method, of easy manufacture, and which she could vouch for as possessing a richness, and, if rightly prepared, a delicacy, unequalled by any other mode of breakfast-cake. Hepzibah gladly assenting, the kitchen was soon the scene of savory preparation. Perchance, amid their proper element of smoke, which eddied forth from the ill-constructed chimney, the ghosts of departed cook-maids looked wonderingly on, or peeped down the great breadth of the flue, despising the simplicity of the projected meal, yet ineffectually pining to thrust their shadowy hands into each inchoate dish. The half-starved rats, at any rate, stole visibly out of their hiding-places, and sat on their hind-legs, snuffing the fumy atmosphere, and wistfully awaiting an opportunity to nibble.

Hepzibah had no natural turn for cookery, and, to say the truth, had fairly incurred her present meagreness by often choosing to go without her dinner rather than be attendant on the rotation of the spit, or ebullition of the pot. Her zeal over the fire, therefore, was quite an heroic test of sentiment. It was touching, and positively worthy of tears (if Phœbe, the only spectator, except the rats and ghosts aforesaid, had not been better employed than in shedding them), to see her rake out a bed of fresh and glowing coals, and proceed to broil the mackerel. Her usually pale cheeks were all ablaze with heat and hurry. She watched the fish with as much tender care and minuteness of attention as if, — we know not how to express it otherwise, — as if her own heart were on the gridiron, and her immortal happiness were involved in its being done precisely to a turn !

Life, within doors, has few pleasanter prospects than a neatly arranged and well-provisioned breakfast-table. We come to it freshly, in the dewy youth of the day, and when our spiritual and sensual elements are in better accord than at a later period ; so that the material delights of the morning meal are capable of being fully enjoyed, without any very grievous reproaches, whether gastric or conscientious, for yielding even a trifle overmuch to the animal department of our nature. The thoughts, too, that run around the ring of familiar guests have a piquancy and mirthfulness, and oftentimes a vivid truth, which more rarely find their way into the elaborate intercourse of dinner. Hepzibah's small and ancient table, supported on its slender and graceful legs, and covered with a cloth of the richest damask, looked worthy to be the scene and centre of one of the cheerfullest of parties. The vapor of the broiled fish arose like incense from the shrine of a barbarian idol, while the fragrance of the Mocha might have gratified the nostrils of a tutelary Lar, or whatever power has scope over a modern breakfast-table. Phœbe's Indian cakes were the sweetest offering of all, — in their hue befitting the rustic altars of the innocent and golden age, — or, so brightly yellow were they, resembling some of the bread which was changed to glistening gold when Midas tried to eat it. The butter must not be forgotten, — butter which Phœbe herself had churned, in her own rural home, and brought it to her cousin as a propitiatory gift, — smelling of clover-blossoms, and diffusing the charm of pastoral scenery through the dark-panelled parlor. All this, with the quaint gorgeousness of the old china cups and saucers, and the crested spoons, and a silver cream-jug (Hepzibah's only other article of plate, and shaped like the rudest porringer), set out a board at which the stateliest of old Colonel Pyncheon's guests need not have scorned to take his place. But the Puritan's face scowled down out of the picture, as if nothing on the table pleased his appetite.

By way of contributing what grace she could, Phœbe gathered some roses and a few other flowers, possessing either scent or beauty, and arranged them in a glass pitcher, which, having long ago lost its handle, was so much the fitter for a flower-vase. The early sunshine — as fresh as that which peeped into Eve's bower while she and Adam sat at breakfast there — came twinkling through the branches of the pear-tree, and fell quite across the table. All was now ready. There were chairs and plates for three. A chair and plate for Hepzibah, — the same for Phœbe, — but what other guest did her cousin look for?

Throughout this preparation there had been a constant tremor in Hepzibah's frame; an agitation so powerful that Phœbe could see the quivering of her gaunt shadow, as thrown by the firelight on the kitchen wall, or by the sunshine on the parlor floor. Its manifestations were so various, and agreed so little with one another, that the girl knew not what to make of it. Sometimes it seemed an ecstasy of delight and happiness. At such moments, Hepzibah would fling out her arms, and infold Phœbe in them, and kiss her cheek as tenderly as ever her mother had; she appeared to do so by an inevitable impulse, and as if her bosom were oppressed with tenderness, of which she must needs pour out a little, in order to gain breathing-room. The next moment, without any visible cause for the change, her unwonted joy shrank back, appalled, as it were, and clothed itself in mourning; or it ran and hid itself, so to speak, in the dungeon of her heart, where it had long lain chained, while a cold, spectral sorrow took the place of the imprisoned joy, that was afraid to be enfranchised, — a sorrow as black as that was bright. She often broke into a little, nervous, hysteric laugh, more touching than any tears could be; and forthwith, as if to try which was the most touching, a gush of tears would follow; or perhaps the laughter and tears came both at once, and surrounded our poor Hepzibah, in a moral sense, with a kind of pale, dim rainbow. Towards Phœbe, as we have said, she was affectionate, — far tenderer than ever before, in their brief acquaintance, except for that one kiss on the preceding night, — yet with a continually recurring pettishness and irritability. She would speak sharply to her; then, throwing aside all the starched reserve of her ordinary manner, ask pardon, and the next instant renew the just-forgiven injury.

At last, when their mutual labor was all finished, she took Phœbe's hand in her own trembling one.

"Bear with me, my dear child," she cried; "for truly my heart is full to the brim! Bear with me; for I love you, Phœbe, though I speak so roughly! Think nothing of it, dearest child! By and by, I shall be kind, and only kind!"

"My dearest cousin, cannot you tell me what has happened?" asked Phœbe, with a sunny and tearful sympathy. "What is it that moves you so?"

"Hush! hush! He is coming!" whispered Hepzibah, hastily wiping her eyes. "Let him see you first, Phœbe; for you are young and rosy, and cannot help letting a smile break out whether or no. He always liked bright faces! And mine is old now, and the tears are hardly dry on it. He never could abide tears. There; draw the curtain a little, so that the shadow may fall across his side of the table! But let there be a good deal of sunshine, too; for he never was fond of gloom, as some people are. He has had but little sunshine in his life, — poor Clifford, — and, oh, what a black shadow! Poor, poor Clifford!"

Thus murmuring in an undertone, as if speaking rather to her own heart than to Phœbe, the old gentlewoman stepped on tiptoe about the room, making such arrangements as suggested themselves at the crisis.

Meanwhile there was a step in the passage-way, above stairs. Phœbe recognized it as the same which had passed upward, as through her dream, in the night-time. The approaching guest, whoever it might be, appeared to pause at the head of the staircase; he paused twice or thrice in the descent; he paused again at the foot. Each time, the delay seemed to be without purpose, but rather from a forgetfulness of the purpose which had set him in motion, or as if the person's feet came involuntarily to a stand-still because the motive-power was too feeble to sustain his progress. Finally, he made a long pause at the threshold of the parlor. He took hold of the knob of the door; then loosened his grasp without opening it. Hepzibah, her hands convulsively clasped, stood gazing at the entrance.

"Dear Cousin Hepzibah, pray don't look so!" said Phœbe, trembling; for her cousin's emotion, and this mysteriously reluctant step, made her feel as if a ghost were coming into the room. "You really frighten me! Is something awful going to happen?"

"Hush!" whispered Hepzibah. "Be cheerful! whatever may happen, be nothing but cheerful!"

The final pause at the threshold proved so long, that Hepzibah, unable to endure the suspense, rushed forward, threw open the door, and led in the stranger by the hand. At the first glance, Phœbe saw an elderly personage, in an old-fashioned dressing-gown of faded damask, and wearing his gray or almost white hair of an unusual length. It quite overshadowed his forehead, except when he thrust it back, and stared vaguely about the room. After a very brief inspection of his face, it was easy to conceive that his footstep must necessarily be such an one as that which, slowly, and with as indefinite an aim as a child's first journey across a floor, had just brought him hitherward. Yet there were no tokens that his physical strength might not have sufficed for a free and determined gait. It was the spirit of the man that could not walk. The expression of his countenance — while, notwithstanding, it had the light of reason in it — seemed to waver, and glimmer, and nearly to die away, and feebly to recover itself again. It was like a flame which we see twinkling among half-extinguished embers; we gaze at it more intently than if it were a positive blaze, gushing vividly upward, — more intently, but with a certain impatience, as if it ought either to kindle it self into satisfactory splendor, or be at once extinguished.

For an instant after entering the room, the guest stood still, retaining Hepzibah's hand, instinctively, as a child does that of the grown person who guides it. He saw Phœbe, however, and caught an illumination from her youthful and pleasant aspect, which, indeed, threw a cheerfulness about the parlor, like the circle of reflected brilliancy around the glass vase of flowers that was standing in the sunshine. He made a salutation, or, to speak nearer the truth, an ill-defined, abortive attempt at courtesy. Imperfect as it was, however, it conveyed an idea, or, at least, gave a hint, of indescribable grace, such as no practised art of external manners could have attained. It was too slight to seize upon at the instant; yet, as recollected afterwards, seemed to transfigure the whole man.

"Dear Clifford," said Hepzibah, in the tone with which one soothes a wayward infant, "this is our cousin Phœbe, — little Phœbe Pyncheon, — Arthur's only child, you know. She has come from the country to stay with us awhile; for our old house has grown to be very lonely now."

"Phœbe? — Phœbe Pyncheon? — Phœbe?" repeated the guest, with a strange, sluggish, ill-defined utterance. "Arthur's child! Ah, I forget! No matter! She is very welcome!"

" Come, dear Clifford, take this chair," said Hepzibah, leading him to his place. " Pray, Phœbe, lower the curtain a very little more. Now let us begin breakfast."

The guest seated himself in the place assigned him, and looked strangely around. He was evidently trying to grapple with the present scene, and bring it home to his mind with a more satisfactory distinctness. He desired to be certain, at least, that he was here, in the low-studded, cross-beamed, oaken-panelled parlor, and not in some other spot, which had stereotyped itself into his senses. But the effort was too great to be sustained with more than a fragmentary success. Continually, as we may express it, he faded away out of his place ; or, in other words, his mind and consciousness took their departure, leaving his wasted, gray, and melancholy figure — a substantial emptiness, a material ghost — to occupy his seat at table. Again, after a blank moment, there would be a flickering taper-gleam in his eyeballs. It betokened that his spiritual part had returned, and was doing its best to kindle the heart's household fire, and light up intellectual lamps in the dark and ruinous mansion, where it was doomed to be a forlorn inhabitant.

At one of these moments of less torpid, yet still imperfect animation, Phœbe became convinced of what she had at first rejected as too extravagant and startling an idea. She saw that the person before her must have been the original of the beautiful miniature in her cousin Hepzibah's possession. Indeed, with a feminine eye for costume, she had at once identified the damask dressing-gown, which enveloped him, as the same in figure, material, and fashion, with that so elaborately represented in the picture. This old, faded garment, with all its pristine brilliancy extinct, seemed, in some indescribable way, to translate the wearer's untold misfortune, and make it perceptible to the beholder's eye. It was the better to be discerned, by this exterior type, how worn and old were the soul's more immediate garments; that form and countenance, the beauty and grace of which had almost transcended the skill of the most exquisite of artists. It could the more adequately be known that the soul of the man must have suffered some miserable wrong, from its earthly experience. There he seemed to sit, with a dim veil of decay and ruin betwixt him and the world, but through which, at flitting intervals, might be caught the same expression, so refined, so softly imaginative, which Malbone — venturing a happy touch, with suspended breath — had imparted to the miniature! There had been something so innately characteristic in this look, that all the dusky years, and the burden of unfit calamity which had fallen upon him, did not suffice utterly to destroy it.

Hepzibah had now poured out a cup of deliciously fragrant coffee, and presented it to her guest. As his eyes met hers, he seemed bewildered and disquieted.

"Is this you, Hepzibah?" he murmured, sadly; then, more apart, and perhaps unconscious that he was overheard, "How changed! how changed! And is she angry with me? Why does she bend her brow so?"

Poor Hepzibah! It was that wretched scowl which time and her near-sightedness, and the fret of inward discomfort, had rendered so habitual that any vehemence of mood invariably evoked it. But at the indistinct murmur of his words her whole face grew tender, and even lovely, with sorrowful affection; the harsh ness of her features disappeared, as it were, behind the warm and misty glow.

"Angry!" she repeated; "angry with you, Clifford!"

Her tone, as she uttered the exclamation, had a plaintive and really exquisite melody thrilling through it, yet without subduing a certain something which an obtuse auditor might still have mistaken for asperity. It was as if some transcendent musician should draw a soul-thrilling sweetness out of a cracked instrument, which makes its physical imperfection heard in the midst of ethereal harmony, — so deep was the sensibility that found an organ in Hepzibah's voice!

"There is nothing but love, here, Clifford," she added, — "nothing but love! You are at home!"

The guest responded to her tone by a smile, which did not half light up his face. Feeble as it was, however, and gone in a moment, it had a charm of wonderful beauty. It was followed by a coarser expression; or one that had the effect of coarseness on the fine mould and outline of his countenance, because there was nothing intellectual to temper it. It was a look of appetite. He ate food with what might almost be termed voracity; and seemed to forget himself, Hepzibah, the young girl, and everything else around him, in the sensual enjoyment which the bountifully spread table afforded. In his natural system, though high-wrought and delicately refined, a sensibility to the delights of the palate was probably inherent. It would have been kept in check, however, and even converted into an accomplishment, and one of the thousand modes of intellectual culture, had his more ethereal characteristics retained their vigor. But as it existed now, the effect was painful and made Phœbe droop her eyes.

In a little while the guest became sensible of the fragrance of the yet untasted coffee. He quaffed it eagerly. The subtle essence acted on him like a charmed draught, and caused the opaque substance of his animal being to grow transparent, or, at least, translucent; so that a spiritual gleam was transmitted through it, with a clearer lustre than hitherto.

"More, more!" he cried, with nervous haste in his utterance, as if anxious to retain his grasp of what sought to escape him. "This is what I need! Give me more!"

Under this delicate and powerful influence he sat more erect, and looked out from his eyes with a glance that took note of what it rested on. It was not so much that his expression grew more intellectual; this, though it had its share, was not the most peculiar effect. Neither was what we call the moral nature so forcibly awakened as to present itself in remarkable prominence. But a certain fine temper of being was now not brought out in full relief, but changeably and imperfectly betrayed, of which it was the function to deal with all beautiful and enjoyable things. In a character where it should exist as the chief attribute, it would bestow on its possessor an exquisite taste, and an enviable susceptibility of happiness. Beauty would be his life; his aspirations would all tend toward it; and, allowing his frame and physical organs to be in consonance, his own developments would likewise be beautiful. Such a man should have nothing to do with sorrow; nothing with strife; nothing with the martyrdom which, in an infinite variety of shapes, awaits those who have the heart, and will, and conscience, to fight a battle with the world. To these heroic tempers, such martyrdom is the richest

meed in the world's gift. To the individual before
us, it could only be a grief, intense in due proportion
with the severity of the infliction. He had no right
to be a martyr; and, beholding him so fit to be happy
and so feeble for all other purposes, a generous, strong,
and noble spirit would, methinks, have been ready to
sacrifice what little enjoyment it might have planned
for itself, — it would have flung down the hopes, so
paltry in its regard, — if thereby the wintry blasts of
our rude sphere might come tempered to such a man.

Not to speak it harshly or scornfully, it seemed Clifford's nature to be a Sybarite. It was perceptible,
even there, in the dark old parlor, in the inevitable
polarity with which his eyes were attracted towards
the quivering play of sunbeams through the shadowy
foliage. It was seen in his appreciating notice of the
vase of flowers, the scent of which he inhaled with a
zest almost peculiar to a physical organization so refined that spiritual ingredients are moulded in with it.
It was betrayed in the unconscious smile with which
he regarded Phœbe, whose fresh and maidenly figure
was both sunshine and flowers, — their essence, in a
prettier and more agreeable mode of manifestation.
Not less evident was this love and necessity for the
Beautiful, in the instinctive caution with which, even
so soon, his eyes turned away from his hostess, and
wandered to any quarter rather than come back. It
was Hepzibah's misfortune, — not Clifford's fault.
How could he, — so yellow as she was, so wrinkled,
so sad of mien, with that odd uncouthness of a turban
on her head, and that most perverse of scowls contort-
ing her brow, — how could he love to gaze at her?
But, did he owe her no affection for so much as she
had silently given? He owed her nothing. A nature

like Clifford's can contract no debts of that kind. It is — we say it without censure, nor in diminution of the claim which it indefeasibly possesses on beings of another mould — it is always selfish in its essence; and we must give it leave to be so, and heap up our heroic and disinterested love upon it so much the more, without a recompense. Poor Hepzibah knew this truth, or, at least, acted on the instinct of it. So long estranged from what was lovely as Clifford had been, she rejoiced — rejoiced, though with a present sigh, and a secret purpose to shed tears in her own chamber — that he had brighter objects now before his eyes than her aged and uncomely features. They never possessed a charm; and if they had, the canker of her grief for him would long since have destroyed it.

The guest leaned back in his chair. Mingled in his countenance with a dreamy delight, there was a troubled look of effort and unrest. He was seeking to make himself more fully sensible of the scene around him; or, perhaps, dreading it to be a dream, or a play of imagination, was vexing the fair moment with a struggle for some added brilliancy and more durable illusion.

"How pleasant! — How delightful!" he murmured, but not as if addressing any one. "Will it last? How balmy the atmosphere through that open window! An open window! How beautiful that play of sunshine! Those flowers, how very fragrant! That young girl's face, how cheerful, how blooming! — a flower with the dew on it, and sunbeams in the dew-drops! Ah! this must be all a dream! A dream! A dream! But it has quite hidden the four stone walls!"

Then his face darkened, as if the shadow of a cavern or a dungeon had come over it; there was no more light in its expression than might have come through the iron grates of a prison window, — still lessening, too, as if he were sinking farther into the depths. Phœbe (being of that quickness and activity of temperament that she seldom long refrained from taking a part, and generally a good one, in what was going forward) now felt herself moved to address the stranger.

"Here is a new kind of rose, which I found this morning in the garden." said she, choosing a small crimson one from among the flowers in the vase. "There will be but five or six on the bush this season. This is the most perfect of them all; not a speck of blight or mildew in it. And how sweet it is! — sweet like no other rose! One can never forget that scent!"

"Ah! — let me see! — let me hold it!" cried the guest, eagerly seizing the flower, which, by the spell peculiar to remembered odors, brought innumerable associations along with the fragrance that it exhaled. "Thank you! This has done me good. I remember how I used to prize this flower, — long ago, I suppose, very long ago! — or was it only yesterday? It makes me feel young again! Am I young? Either this remembrance is singularly distinct, or this consciousness strangely dim! But how kind of the fair young girl! Thank you! Thank you!"

The favorable excitement derived from this little crimson rose afforded Clifford the brightest moment which he enjoyed at the breakfast-table. It might have lasted longer, but that his eyes happened, soon afterwards, to rest on the face of the old Puritan, who, out of his dingy frame and lustreless canvas, was looking down on the scene like a ghost, and a most ill-tempered and ungenial one. The guest made an impatient gesture of the hand, and addressed Hepzibah with what might easily be recognized as the licensed irritability of a petted member of the family.

"Hepzibah!—Hepzibah!" cried he with no little force and distinctness, "why do you keep that odious picture on the wall? Yes, yes!—that is precisely your taste! I have told you, a thousand times, that it was the evil genius of the house!—my evil genius particularly! Take it down, at once!"

"Dear Clifford," said Hepzibah, sadly, "you know it cannot be!"

"Then, at all events," continued he, still speaking with some energy, "pray cover it with a crimson curtain, broad enough to hang in folds, and with a golden border and tassels. I cannot bear it! It must not stare me in the face!"

"Yes, dear Clifford, the picture shall be covered," said Hepzibah, soothingly. "There is a crimson curtain in a trunk above stairs,—a little faded and moth-eaten, I'm afraid,—but Phœbe and I will do wonders with it."

"This very day, remember!" said he; and then added, in a low, self-communing voice, "Why should we live in this dismal house at all? Why not go to the South of France?—to Italy?—Paris, Naples, Venice, Rome? Hepzibah will say we have not the means. A droll idea that!"

He smiled to himself, and threw a glance of fine sarcastic meaning towards Hepzibah.

But the several moods of feeling, faintly as they were marked, through which he had passed, occurring in so brief an interval of time, had evidently wearied the stranger. He was probably accustomed to a sad monotony of life, not so much flowing in a stream, however sluggish, as stagnating in a pool around his feet. A slumberous veil diffused itself over his countenance, and had an effect, morally speaking, on its naturally delicate and elegant outline, like that which a brooding mist, with no sunshine in it, throws over the features of a landscape. He appeared to become grosser, — almost cloddish. If aught of interest or beauty — even ruined beauty — had heretofore been visible in this man, the beholder might now begin to doubt it, and to accuse his own imagination of deluding him, with whatever grace had flickered over that visage, and whatever exquisite lustre had gleamed in those filmy eyes.

Before he had quite sunken away, however, the sharp and peevish tinkle of the shop-bell made itself audible. Striking most disagreeably on Clifford's auditory organs and the characteristic sensibility of his nerves, it caused him to start upright out of his chair.

"Good heavens, Hepzibah! what horrible disturbance have we now in the house?" cried he, wreaking his resentful impatience — as a matter of course, and a custom of old — on the one person in the world that loved him. "I have never heard such a hateful clamor! Why do you permit it? In the name of all dissonance, what can it be?"

It was very remarkable into what prominent relief — even as if a dim picture should leap suddenly from its canvas — Clifford's character was thrown by this apparently trifling annoyance. The secret was, that an individual of his temper can always be pricked more acutely through his sense of the beautiful and harmonious than through his heart. It is even possible — for similar cases have often happened — that if

Clifford, in his foregoing life, had enjoyed the means of cultivating his taste to its utmost perfectibility, that subtile attribute might, before this period, have completely eaten out or filed away his affections. Shall we venture to pronounce, therefore, that his long and black calamity may not have had a redeeming drop of mercy at the bottom?

"Dear Clifford, I wish I could keep the sound from your ears," said Hepzibah, patiently, but reddening with a painful suffusion of shame. "It is very disagreeable even to me. But, do you know, Clifford, I have something to tell you? This ugly noise, — pray run, Phœbe, and see who is there! — this naughty little tinkle is nothing but our shop-bell!"

"Shop-bell!" repeated Clifford, with a bewildered stare.

"Yes, our shop-bell," said Hepzibah, a certain natural dignity, mingled with deep emotion, now asserting itself in her manner. "For you must know, dearest Clifford, that we are very poor. And there was no other resource, but either to accept assistance from a hand that I would push aside (and so would you!) were it to offer bread when we were dying for it, — no help, save from him, or else to earn our subsistence with my own hands! Alone, I might have been content to starve. But you were to be given back to me! Do you think, then, dear Clifford," added she, with a wretched smile, "that I have brought an irretrievable disgrace on the old house, by opening a little shop in the front gable? Our great-great-grandfather did the same, when there was far less need! Are you ashamed of me?"

"Shame! Disgrace! Do you speak these words to me, Hepzibah?" said Clifford, — not angrily, how ever; for when a man's spirit has been thoroughly crushed, he may be peevish at small offences, but never resentful of great ones. So he spoke with only a grieved emotion. " It was not kind to say so, Hepzibah! What shame can befall me now?"

. And then the unnerved man — he that had been born for enjoyment, but had met a doom so very wretched — burst into a woman's passion of tears. It was but of brief continuance, however; soon leaving him in a quiescent, and, to judge by his countenance, not an uncomfortable state. From this mood, too, he partially rallied for an instant, and looked at Hepzibah with a smile, the keen, half-derisory purport of which was a puzzle to her.

" Are we so very poor, Hepzibah? " said he.

Finally, his chair being deep and softly cushioned, Clifford fell asleep. Hearing the more regular rise and fall of his breath (which, however, even then, instead of being strong and full, had a feeble kind of tremor, corresponding with the lack of vigor in his character), — hearing these tokens of settled slumber, Hepzibah seized the opportunity to peruse his face more attentively than she had yet dared to do. Her heart melted away in tears; her profoundest spirit sent forth a moaning voice, low, gentle, but inexpressibly sad. In this depth of grief and pity she felt that there was no irreverence in gazing at his altered, aged, faded, ruined face. But no sooner was she a little relieved than her conscience smote her for gazing curiously at him, now that he was so changed; and, turning hastily away, Hepzibah let down the curtain over the sunny window, and left Clifford to slumber there.

VIII.

THE PYNCHEON OF TO-DAY.

PHŒBE, on entering the shop, beheld there the already familiar face of the little devourer — if we can reckon his mighty deeds aright — of Jim Crow, the elephant, the camel, the dromedaries, and the locomotive. Having expended his private fortune, on the two preceding days, in the purchase of the above unheard-of luxuries, the young gentleman's present errand was on the part of his mother, in quest of three eggs and half a pound of raisins. These articles Phœbe accordingly supplied, and, as a mark of gratitude for his previous patronage, and a slight superadded morsel after breakfast, put likewise into his hand a whale! The great fish, reversing his experience with the prophet of Nineveh, immediately began his progress down the same red pathway of fate whither so varied a caravan had preceded him. This remarkable urchin, in truth, was the very emblem of old Father Time, both in respect of his all-devouring appetite for men and things, and because he, as well as Time, after ingulfing thus much of creation, looked almost as youthful as if he had been just that moment made.

After partly closing the door, the child turned back, and mumbled something to Phœbe, which, as the whale was but half disposed of, she could not perfectly understand.

"What did you say, my little fellow?" asked she.

"Mother wants to know," repeated Ned Higgins, more distinctly, "how Old Maid Pyncheon's brother does? Folks say he has got home."

"My cousin Hepzibah's brother!" exclaimed Phœbe, surprised at this sudden explanation of the relationship between Hepzibah and her guest. "Her brother! And where can he have been?"

The little boy only put his thumb to his broad snubnose, with that look of shrewdness which a child, spending much of his time in the street, so soon learns to throw over his features, however unintelligent in themselves. Then as Phœbe continued to gaze at him, without answering his mother's message, he took his departure.

As the child went down the steps, a gentleman ascended them, and made his entrance into the shop. It was the portly, and, had it possessed the advantage of a little more height, would have been the stately figure of a man considerably in the decline of life, dressed in a black suit of some thin stuff, resembling broadcloth as closely as possible. A gold-headed cane, of rare Oriental wood, added materially to the high respectability of his aspect, as did also a neckcloth of the utmost snowy purity, and the conscientious polish of his boots. His dark, square countenance, with its almost shaggy depth of eyebrows, was naturally impressive, and would, perhaps, have been rather stern, had not the gentleman considerately taken upon himself to mitigate the harsh effect by a look of exceeding good-humor and benevolence. Owing, however, to a somewhat massive accumulation of animal substance about the lower region of his face, the look was, perhaps, unctuous, rather than spiritual, and had, so to speak,

a kind of fleshly effulgence, not altogether so satisfactory as he doubtless intended it to be.   A susceptible
observer, at any rate, might have regarded it as affording very little evidence of the general benignity of
soul whereof it purported to be the outward reflection.
And if the observer chanced to be ill-natured, as well
as acute and susceptible, he would probably suspect
that the smile on the gentleman's face was a good deal
akin to the shine on his boots, and that each must have
cost him and his boot-black, respectively, a good deal
of hard labor to bring out and preserve them.

As the stranger entered the little shop, where the
projection of the second story and the thick foliage
of the elm-tree, as well as the commodities at the window, created a sort of gray medium, his smile grew as
intense as if he had set his heart on counteracting
the whole gloom of the atmosphere (besides any moral
gloom pertaining to Hepzibah and her inmates) by the
unassisted light of his countenance.   On perceiving a
young rose-bud of a girl, instead of the gaunt presence of the old maid, a look of surprise was manifest.
He at first knit his brows ; then smiled with more unctuous benignity than ever.

"Ah, I see how it is ! " said he, in a deep voice, —
a voice which, had it come from the throat of an uncultivated man, would have been gruff, but, by dint of
careful training, was now sufficiently agreeable, — " I
was not aware that Miss Hepzibah Pyncheon had commenced business under such favorable auspices.   You
are her assistant, I suppose ? "

" I certainly am," answered Phœbe, and added, with
a little air of lady-like assumption (for, civil as the
gentleman was, he evidently took her to be a young
person serving for wages), " I am a cousin of Miss
Hepzibah, on a visit to her."

" Her cousin ? —and from the country ? Pray par.
don me, then," said the gentleman, bowing and smil.
ing, as Phœbe never had been bowed to nor smiled on
before ; " in that case, we must be better acquainted ;
for, unless I am sadly mistaken, you are my own little
kinswoman likewise ! Let me see, — Mary ? — Dolly?
— Phœbe ? — yes, Phœbe is the name ! Is it possible
that you are Phœbe Pyncheon, only child of my dear
cousin and classmate, Arthur ? Ah, I see your father
now, about your mouth ! Yes, yes ! we must be better
acquainted ! I am your kinsman, my dear. Surely
you must have heard of Judge Pyncheon ? "

As Phœbe courtesied in reply, the Judge bent forward, with the pardonable and even praiseworthy purpose — considering the nearness of blood, and the difference of age —of bestowing on his young relative a
kiss of acknowledged kindred and natural affection.
Unfortunately (without design, or only with such instinctive design as gives no account of itself to the
intellect) Phœbe, just at the critical moment, drew
back ; so that her highly respectable kinsman, with his
body bent over the counter, and his lips protruded,
was betrayed into the rather absurd predicament of
kissing the empty air. It was a modern parallel to
the case of Ixion embracing a cloud, and was so much
the more ridiculous, as the Judge prided himself on
eschewing all airy matter, and never mistaking a
shadow for a substance. The truth was, — and it is
Phœbe's only excuse, — that, although Judge Pyncheon's glowing benignity might not be absolutely unpleasant to the feminine beholder, with the width of a
street, or even an ordinary-sized room, interposed between, yet it became quite too intense, when this dark,
full-fed physiognomy (so roughly bearded, too, that

no razor could ever make it smooth) sought to bring it-self into actual contact with the object of its regards. The man, the sex, somehow or other, was entirely too prominent in the Judge's demonstrations of that sort. Phœbe's eyes sank, and, without knowing why, she felt herself blushing deeply under his look. Yet she had been kissed before, and without any particular squeamishness, by perhaps half a dozen different cousins, younger as well as older than this dark-browed, grisly-bearded, white-neck-clothed, and unctuously-benevolent Judge! Then, why not by him?

On raising her eyes, Phœbe was startled by the change in Judge Pyncheon's face. It was quite as striking, allowing for the difference of scale, as that betwixt a landscape under a broad sunshine and just before a thunder-storm; not that it had the passionate intensity of the latter aspect, but was cold, hard, immitigable, like a day-long brooding cloud.

"Dear me! what is to be done now?" thought the country-girl to herself. "He looks as if there were nothing softer in him than a rock, nor milder than the east wind! I meant no harm! Since he is really my cousin, I would have let him kiss me, if I could!"

Then, all at once, it struck Phœbe that this very Judge Pyncheon was the original of the miniature which the daguerreotypist had shown her in the garden, and that the hard, stern, relentless look, now on his face, was the same that the sun had so inflexibly persisted in bringing out. Was it, therefore, no momentary mood, but, however skilfully concealed, the settled temper of his life? And not merely so, but was it hereditary in him, and transmitted down, as a precious heirloom, from that bearded ancestor, in whose picture both the expression, and, to a singular degree, the features of the modern Judge were shown as by a kind of prophecy? A deeper philosopher than Phœbe might have found something very terrible in this idea. It implied that the weaknesses and defects, the bad passions, the mean tendencies, and the moral diseases which lead to crime are handed down from one generation to another, by a far surer process of transmission than human law has been able to establish in respect to the riches and honors which it seeks to entail upon posterity.

But, as it happened, scarcely had Phœbe's eyes rested again on the Judge's countenance than all its ugly sternness vanished; and she found herself quite overpowered by the sultry, dog-day heat, as it were, of benevolence, which this excellent man diffused out of his great heart into the surrounding atmosphere, — very much like a serpent, which, as a preliminary to fascination, is said to fill the air with his peculiar odor.

"I like that, Cousin Phœbe!" cried he, with an emphatic nod of approbation. "I like it much, my little cousin! You are a good child, and know how to take care of yourself. A young girl — especially if she be a very pretty one — can never be too chary of her lips."

"Indeed, sir," said Phœbe, trying to laugh the matter off, "I did not mean to be unkind."

Nevertheless, whether or no it were entirely owing to the inauspicious commencement of their acquaintance, she still acted under a certain reserve, which was by no means customary to her frank and genial nature. The fantasy would not quit her, that the original Puritan, of whom she had heard so many sombre traditions, — the progenitor of the whole race of New England Pyncheons, the founder of the House of the Seven Gables, and who had died so strangely in it, — had now stept into the shop. In these days of off-hand equipment, the matter was easily enough arranged. On his arrival from the other world, he had merely found it necessary to spend a quarter of an hour at a barber's, who had trimmed down the Puritan's full beard into a pair of grizzled whiskers, then, patronizing a ready-made clothing establishment, he had exchanged his velvet doublet and sable cloak, with the richly worked band under his chin, for a white collar and cravat, coat, vest, and pantaloons; and lastly, putting aside his steel-hilted broadsword to take up a gold-headed cane, the Colonel Pyncheon of two centuries ago steps forward as the Judge of the passing moment!

Of course, Phœbe was far too sensible a girl to entertain this idea in any other way than as matter for a smile. Possibly, also, could the two personages have stood together before her eye, many points of difference would have been perceptible, and perhaps only a general resemblance. The long lapse of intervening years, in a climate so unlike that which had fostered the ancestral Englishman, must inevitably have wrought important changes in the physical system of his descendant. The Judge's volume of muscle could hardly be the same as the Colonel's; there was undoubtedly less beef in him. Though looked upon as a weighty man among his contemporaries in respect of animal substance, and as favored with a remarkable degree of fundamental development, well adapting him for the judicial bench, we conceive that the modern Judge Pyncheon, if weighed in the same balance with his ancestor, would have required at least an old-fashioned fifty-six to keep the scale in equilibrio. Then the Judge's face had lost the ruddy English hue that showed its warmth through all the duskiness of the Colonel's weather-beaten cheek, and had taken a sallow shade, the established complexion of his countrymen. If we mistake not, moreover, a certain quality of nervousness had become more or less manifest, even in so solid a specimen of Puritan descent as the gentleman now under discussion. As one of its effects, it bestowed on his countenance a quicker mobility than the old Englishman's had possessed, and keener vivacity, but at the expense of a sturdier something, on which these acute endowments seemed to act like dissolving acids. This process, for aught we know, may belong to the great system of human progress, which, with every ascending footstep, as it diminishes the necessity for animal force, may be destined gradually to spiritualize us, by refining away our grosser attributes of body. If so, Judge Pyncheon could endure a century or two more of such refinement as well as most other men.

The similarity, intellectual and moral, between the Judge and his ancestor appears to have been at least as strong as the resemblance of mien and feature would afford reason to anticipate. In old Colonel Pyncheon's funeral discourse the clergyman absolutely canonized his deceased parishioner, and opening, as it were, a vista through the roof of the church, and thence through the firmament above, showed him seated, harp in hand, among the crowned choristers of the spiritual world. On his tombstone, too, the record is highly eulogistic; nor does history, so far as he holds a place upon its page, assail the consistency and uprightness of his character. So also, as regards the Judge Pyncheon of to-day, neither clergy-man, nor legal critic, nor inscriber of tombstones, nor historian of general or local politics, would venture a word against this eminent person's sincerity as a Christian, or respectability as a man, or integrity as a judge, or courage and faithfulness as the often-tried representative of his political party. But, besides these cold, formal, and empty words of the chisel that inscribes, the voice that speaks, and the pen that writes, for the public eye and for distant time, — and which inevitably lose much of their truth and freedom by the fatal consciousness of so doing, — there were traditions about the ancestor, and private diurnal gos-sip about the Judge, remarkably accordant in their testimony. It is often instructive to take the wom-an's, the private and domestic, view of a public man; nor can anything be more curious than the vast dis-crepancy between portraits intended for engraving and the pencil-sketches that pass from hand to hand be-hind the original's back.

For example : tradition affirmed that the Puritan had been greedy of wealth; the Judge, too, with all the show of liberal expenditure, was said to be as close-fisted as if his gripe were of iron. The ancestor had clothed himself in a grim assumption of kindliness, a rough heartiness of word and manner, which most people took to be the genuine warmth of nature, making its way through the thick and inflexible hide of a manly character. His descendant, in compliance with the requirements of a nicer age, had etherealized this rude benevolence into that broad benignity of smile, wherewith he shone like a noonday sun along the streets, or glowed like a household fire in the drawing-rooms of his private acquaintance. The Puritan — if not belied by some singular stories, murmured, even at this day, under the narrator's breath — had fallen into certain transgressions to which men of his great animal development, whatever their faith or principles, must continue liable, until they put off impurity, along with the gross earthly substance that involves it. We must not stain our page with any contemporary scandal, to a similar purport, that may have been whispered against the Judge. The Puritan, again, an autocrat in his own household, had worn out three wives, and, merely by the remorseless weight and hardness of his character in the conjugal relation, had sent them, one after another, broken-hearted, to their graves. Here the parallel, in some sort, fails. The Judge had wedded but a single wife, and lost her in the third or fourth year of their marriage. There was a fable, however, — for such we choose to consider it, though, not impossibly, typical of Judge Pyncheon's marital deportment, — that the lady got her death-blow in the honeymoon, and never smiled again, because her husband compelled her to serve him with coffee every morning at his bedside, in token of fealty to her liege-lord and master.

But it is too fruitful a subject, this of hereditary resemblances, — the frequent recurrence of which, in a direct line, is truly unaccountable, when we consider how large an accumulation of ancestry lies behind every man at the distance of one or two centuries. We shall only add, therefore, that the Puritan — so, at least, says chimney-corner tradition, which often preserves traits of character with marvellous fidelity — was bold, imperious, relentless, crafty ; laying his purposes deep, and following them out with an inveteracy of pursuit that knew neither rest nor conscience ;

trampling on the weak, and, when essential to his ends, doing his utmost to beat down the strong. Whether the Judge in any degree resembled him the further progress of our narrative may show.

Scarcely any of the items in the above-drawn parallel occurred to Phœbe, whose country birth and residence, in truth, had left her pitifully ignorant of most of the family traditions, which lingered, like cobwebs and incrustations of smoke, about the rooms and chimney-corners of the House of the Seven Gables. Yet there was a circumstance, very trifling in itself, which impressed her with an odd degree of horror. She had heard of the anathema flung by Maule, the executed wizard, against Colonel Pyncheon and his posterity, — that God would give them blood to drink, — and likewise of the popular notion, that this miraculous blood might now and then be heard gurgling in their throats. The latter scandal — as became a person of sense, and, more especially, a member of the Pyncheon family — Phœbe had set down for the absurdity which it unquestionably was. But ancient superstitions, after being steeped in human hearts and embodied in human breath, and passing from lip to ear in manifold repetition, through a series of generations, become imbued with an effect of homely truth. The smoke of the domestic hearth has scented them through and through. By long transmission among household facts, they grow to look like them, and have such a familiar way of making themselves at home that their influence is usually greater than we suspect. Thus it happened, that when Phœbe heard a certain noise in Judge Pyncheon's throat, — rather habitual with him, not altogether voluntary, yet indicative of nothing, unless it were a slight bronchial complaint, or, as some people hinted, an apoplectic symptom, — when the girl heard this queer and awkward ingurgitation (which the writer never did hear, and therefore cannot describe), she, very foolishly, started, and clasped her hands.

Of course, it was exceedingly ridiculous in Phœbe to be discomposed by such a trifle, and still more unpardonable to show her discomposure to the individual most concerned in it. But the incident chimed in so oddly with her previous fancies about the Colonel and the Judge, that, for the moment, it seemed quite to mingle their identity.

"What is the matter with you, young woman?" said Judge Pyncheon, giving her one of his harsh looks. "Are you afraid of anything?"

"Oh, nothing, sir, — nothing in the world!" answered Phœbe, with a little laugh of vexation at herself. "But perhaps you wish to speak with my cousin Hepzibah. Shall I call her?"

"Stay a moment, if you please," said the Judge, again beaming sunshine out of his face. "You seem to be a little nervous this morning. The town air, Cousin Phœbe, does not agree with your good, wholesome country habits. Or has anything happened to disturb you? — anything remarkable in Cousin Hepzibah's family? — An arrival, eh? I thought so! No wonder you are out of sorts, my little cousin. To be an inmate with such a guest may well startle an innocent young girl!"

"You quite puzzle me, sir," replied Phœbe, gazing inquiringly at the Judge. "There is no frightful guest in the house, but only a poor, gentle, childlike man, whom I believe to be Cousin Hepzibah's brother. I am afraid (but you, sir, will know better than I) that he is not quite in his sound senses; but so mild and quiet he seems to be, that a mother might trust her baby with him; and I think he would play with the baby as if he were only a few years older than itself. He startle me! — Oh, no indeed!"

"I rejoice to hear so favorable and so ingenuous an account of my cousin Clifford," said the benevolent Judge. "Many years ago, when we were boys and young men together, I had a great affection for him, and still feel a tender interest in all his concerns. You, say, Cousin Phœbe, he appears to be weak-minded. Heaven grant him at least enough of intellect to repent of his past sins!"

"Nobody, I fancy," observed Phœbe, "can have fewer to repent of."

"And is it possible, my dear," rejoined the Judge, with a commiserating look, "that you have never heard of Clifford Pyncheon? — that you know nothing of his history? Well, it is all right; and your mother has shown a very proper regard for the good name of the family with which she connected herself. Believe the best you can of this unfortunate person, and hope the best! It is a rule which Christians should always follow, in their judgments of one another; and especially is it right and wise among near relatives, whose characters have necessarily a degree of mutual dependence. But is Clifford in the parlor? I will just step in and see."

"Perhaps, sir, I had better call my cousin Hepzibah," said Phœbe; hardly knowing, however, whether she ought to obstruct the entrance of so affectionate a kinsman into the private regions of the house. "Her brother seemed to be just falling asleep after breakfast; and I am sure she would not like him to be disturbed. Pray sir, let me give her notice!"

But the Judge showed a singular determination to enter unannounced; and as Phœbe, with the vivacity of a person whose movements unconsciously answer to her thoughts, had stepped towards the door, he used little or no ceremony in putting her aside.

" No, no, Miss Phœbe ! " said Judge Pyncheon, in a voice as deep as a thunder-growl, and with a frown as black as the cloud whence it issues. " Stay you here ! I know the house, and know my cousin Hepzibah, and know her brother Clifford likewise ! — nor need my little country cousin put herself to the trouble of announcing me ! " — in these latter words, by the by, there were symptoms of a change from his sudden harshness into his previous benignity of manner. " I am at home here, Phœbe, you must recollect, and you are the stranger. I will just step in, therefore, and see for myself how Clifford is, and assure him and Hepzibah of my kindly feelings and best wishes. It is right, at this juncture, that they should both hear from my own lips how much I desire to serve them. Ha ! here is Hepzibah herself ! "

Such was the case. The vibrations of the Judge's voice had reached the old gentlewoman in the parlor, where she sat, with face averted, waiting on her brother's slumber. She now issued forth, as would appear, to defend the entrance, looking, we must needs say, amazingly like the dragon which, in fairy tales, is wont to be the guardian over an enchanted beauty. The habitual scowl of her brow was, undeniably, too fierce, at this moment, to pass itself off on the innocent score of near-sightedness; and it was bent on Judge Pyncheon in a way that seemed to confound, if not alarm him, so inadequately had he estimated the moral force of a deeply grounded antipathy.

She made a repelling gesture with her hand, and stood a perfect picture of prohibition, at full length, in the dark frame of the doorway. But we must betray Hepzibah's secret, and confess that the native timorousness of her character even now developed itself in a quick tremor, which, to her own perception, set each of her joints at variance with its fellows.

Possibly, the Judge was aware how little true hardihood lay behind Hepzibah's formidable front. At any rate, being a gentleman of steady nerves, he soon recovered himself, and failed not to approach his cousin with outstretched hand; adopting the sensible precaution, however, to cover his advance with a smile, so broad and sultry, that, had it been only half as warm as it looked, a trellis of grapes might at once have turned purple under its summer-like exposure. It may have been his purpose, indeed, to melt poor Hepzibah on the spot, as if she were a figure of yellow wax.

"Hepzibah, my beloved cousin, I am rejoiced!" exclaimed the Judge, most emphatically. "Now, at length, you have something to live for. Yes, and all of us, let me say, your friends and kindred, have more to live for than we had yesterday. I have lost no time in hastening to offer any assistance in my power towards making Clifford comfortable. He belongs to us all. I know how much he requires,—how much he used to require,—with his delicate taste, and his love of the beautiful. Anything in my house,—pictures, books, wine, luxuries of the table,—he may command them all! It would afford me most heartfelt gratification to see him! Shall I step in, this moment?"

"No," replied Hepzibah, her voice quivering too

painfully to allow of many words. "He cannot see visitors!"

"A visitor, my dear cousin!—do you call me so?" cried the Judge, whose sensibility, it seems, was hurt by the coldness of the phrase. "Nay, then, let me be Clifford's host, and your own likewise. Come at once to my house. The country air, and all the conveniences—I may say luxuries—that I have gathered about me, will do wonders for him. And you and I, dear Hepzibah, will consult together, and watch together, and labor together, to make our dear Clifford happy. Come! why should we make more words about what is both a duty and a pleasure on my part? Come to me at once!"

On hearing these so hospitable offers, and such generous recognition of the claims of kindred, Phœbe felt very much in the mood of running up to Judge Pyncheon, and giving him, of her own accord, the kiss from which she had so recently shrunk away. It was quite otherwise with Hepzibah; the Judge's smile seemed to operate on her acerbity of heart like sunshine upon vinegar, making it ten times sourer than ever.

"Clifford," said she,—still too agitated to utter more than an abrupt sentence,—"Clifford has a home here!"

"May Heaven forgive you, Hepzibah," said Judge Pyncheon,—reverently lifting his eyes towards that high court of equity to which he appealed,—"if you suffer any ancient prejudice or animosity to weigh with you in this matter! I stand here with an open heart, willing and anxious to receive yourself and Clifford into it. Do not refuse my good offices,—my earnest propositions for your welfare! They are such, in all respects, as it behooves your nearest kinsman to make. It will be a heavy responsibility, cousin, if you confine your brother to this dismal house and stifled air, when the delightful freedom of my country-seat is at his command."

"It would never suit Clifford," said Hepzibah, as briefly as before.

"Woman!" broke forth the Judge, giving way to his resentment, "what is the meaning of all this? Have you other resources? Nay, I suspected as much! Take care, Hepzibah, take care! Clifford is on the brink of as black a ruin as ever befell him yet! But why do I talk with you, woman as you are? Make way! — I must see Clifford!"

Hepzibah spread out her gaunt figure across the door, and seemed really to increase in bulk; looking the more terrible, also, because there was so much terror and agitation in her heart. But Judge Pyncheon's evident purpose of forcing a passage was interrupted by a voice from the inner room; a weak, tremulous, wailing voice, indicating helpless alarm, with no more energy for self-defence than belongs to a frightened infant.

"Hepzibah, Hepzibah!" cried the voice; "go down on your knees to him! Kiss his feet! Entreat him not to come in! Oh, let him have mercy on me! Mercy! — mercy!"

For the instant, it appeared doubtful whether it were not the Judge's resolute purpose to set Hepzibah aside, and step across the threshold into the parlor, whence issued that broken and miserable murmur of entreaty. It was not pity that restrained him, for, at the first sound of the enfeebled voice, a red fire kindled in his eyes, and he made a quick pace forward.

with something inexpressibly fierce and grim darkening forth, as it were, out of the whole man. To know
Judge Pyncheon, was to see him at that moment.
After such a revelation, let him smile with what sultriness he would, he could much sooner turn grapes
purple, or pumpkins yellow, than melt the iron-
branded impression out of the beholder's memory.
And it rendered his aspect not the less, but more
frightful, that it seemed not to express wrath or
hatred, but a certain hot fellness of purpose, which
annihilated everything but itself.

Yet, after all, are we not slandering an excellent
and amiable man? Look at the Judge now! He is
apparently conscious of having erred, in too energetically pressing his deeds of loving-kindness on persons
unable to appreciate them. He will await their better
mood, and hold himself as ready to assist them then
as at this moment. As he draws back from the door,
an all-comprehensive benignity blazes from his visage,
indicating that he gathers Hepzibah, little Phœbe, and
the invisible Clifford, all three, together with the
whole world besides, into his immense heart, and
gives them a warm bath in its flood of affection.

" You do me great wrong, dear Cousin Hepzibah!"
said he, first kindly offering her his hand, and then
drawing on his glove preparatory to departure. " Very
great wrong! But I forgive it, and will study to make
you think better of me. Of course, our poor Clifford
being in so unhappy a state of mind, I cannot think
of urging an interview at present. But I shall watch
over his welfare as if he were my own beloved brother;
nor do I at all despair, my dear cousin, of constrain-
ing both him and you to acknowledge your injustice.
When that shall happen, I desire no other revenge

than your acceptance of the best offices in my power to do you."

With a bow to Hepzibah, and a degree of paternal benevolence in his parting nod to Phœbe, the Judge left the shop, and went smiling along the street. As is customary with the rich, when they aim at the honors of a republic, he apologized, as it were, to the people, for his wealth, prosperity, and elevated station, by a free and hearty manner towards those who knew him; putting off the more of his dignity in due proportion with the humbleness of the man whom he saluted, and thereby proving a haughty consciousness of his advantages as irrefragably as if he had marched forth preceded by a troop of lackeys to clear the way. On this particular forenoon so excessive was the warmth of Judge Pyncheon's kindly aspect, that (such, at least, was the rumor about town) an extra passage of the water-carts was found essential, in order to lay the dust occasioned by so much extra sunshine!

No sooner had he disappeared than Hepzibah grew deadly white, and, staggering towards Phœbe, let her head fall on the young girl's shoulder.

"O Phœbe!" murmured she, "that man has been the horror of my life! Shall I never, never have the courage, — will my voice never cease from trembling long enough to let me tell him what he is?"

"Is he so very wicked?" asked Phœbe. "Yet his offers were surely kind!"

"Do not speak of them, — he has a heart of iron!" rejoined Hepzibah. "Go, now, and talk to Clifford! Amuse and keep him quiet! It would disturb him wretchedly to see me so agitated as I am. There, go, dear child, and I will try to look after the shop."

Phœbe went, accordingly, but perplexed herself,

meanwhile, with queries as to the purport of the scene which she had just witnessed, and also whether judges, clergymen, and other characters of that eminent stamp and respectability, could really, in any single instance, be otherwise than just and upright men. A doubt of this nature has a most disturbing influence, and, if shown to be a fact, comes with fearful and startling effect on minds of the trim, orderly, and limit-loving class, in which we find our little country-girl. Dispositions more boldly speculative may derive a stern enjoyment from the discovery, since there must be evil in the world, that a high man is as likely to grasp his share of it as a low one. A wider scope of view, and a deeper insight, may see rank, dignity, and station, all proved illusory, so far as regards their claim to human reverence, and yet not feel as if the universe were thereby tumbled headlong into chaos. But Phœbe, in order to keep the universe in its old place, was fain to smother, in some degree, her own intuitions as to Judge Pyncheon's character. And as for her cousin's testimony in disparagement of it, she concluded that Hepzibah's judgment was imbittered by one of those family feuds, which render hatred the more deadly by the dead and corrupted love that they intermingle with its native poison.

IX.

CLIFFORD AND PHŒBE.

TRULY was there something high, generous, and noble in the native composition of our poor old Hepzibah! Or else, — and it was quite as probably the case, — she had been enriched by poverty, developed by sorrow, elevated by the strong and solitary affection of her life, and thus endowed with heroism, which never could have characterized her in what are called happier circumstances. Through dreary years Hepzibah had looked forward — for the most part despairingly, never with any confidence of hope, but always with the feeling that it was her brightest possibility — to the very position in which she now found herself. In her own behalf, she had asked nothing of Providence but the opportunity of devoting herself to this brother, whom she had so loved, — so admired for what he was, or might have been, — and to whom she had kept her faith, alone of all the world, wholly, unfalteringly, at every instant, and throughout life. And here, in his late decline, the lost one had come back out of his long and strange misfortune, and was thrown on her sympathy, as it seemed, not merely for the bread of his physical existence, but for everything that should keep him morally alive. She had responded to the call. She had come forward, — our poor, gaunt Hepzibah, in her rusty silks, with her rigid joints, and the sad perversity of her scowl, —

ready to do her utmost; and with affection enough, if that were all, to do a hundred times as much! There could be few more tearful sights, — and Heaven forgive us if a smile insist on mingling with our conception of it! — few sights with truer pathos in them, than Hepzibah presented on that first afternoon.

How patiently did she endeavor to wrap Clifford up in her great, warm love, and make it all the world to him, so that he should retain no torturing sense of the coldness and dreariness without! Her little efforts to amuse him! How pitiful, yet magnanimous, they were!

Remembering his early love of poetry and fiction, she unlocked a bookcase, and took down several books that had been excellent reading in their day. There was a volume of Pope, with the Rape of the Lock in it, and another of the Tatler, and an odd one of Dryden's Miscellanies, all with tarnished gilding on their covers, and thoughts of tarnished brilliancy inside. They had no success with Clifford. These, and all such writers of society, whose new works glow like the rich texture of a just-woven carpet, must be content to relinquish their charm, for every reader, after an age or two, and could hardly be supposed to retain any portion of it for a mind that had utterly lost its estimate of modes and manners. Hepzibah then took up Rasselas, and began to read of the Happy Valley, with a vague idea that some secret of a contented life had there been elaborated, which might at least serve Clifford and herself for this one day. But the Happy Valley had a cloud over it. Hepzibah troubled her auditor, moreover, by innumerable sins of emphasis, which he seemed to detect, without any reference to the meaning; nor, in fact, did he appear to take much note of the sense of what she read, but evidently felt the tedium of the lecture, without harvesting its profit. His sister's voice, too, naturally harsh, had, in the course of her sorrowful lifetime, contracted a kind of croak, which, when it once gets into the human throat, is as ineradicable as sin. In both sexes, occasionally, this life-long croak, accompanying each word of joy or sorrow, is one of the symptoms of a settled melancholy; and wherever it occurs, the whole history of misfortune is conveyed in its slightest accent. The effect is as if the voice had been dyed black; or, — if we must use a more moderate simile, — this miserable croak, running through all the variations of the voice, is like a black silken thread, on which the crystal beads of speech are strung, and whence they take their hue. Such voices have put on mourning for dead hopes; and they ought to die and be buried along with them!

Discerning that Clifford was not gladdened by her efforts, Hepzibah searched about the house for the means of more exhilarating pastime. At one time, her eyes chanced to rest on Alice Pyncheon's harpsichord. It was a moment of great peril; for, — despite the traditionary awe that had gathered over this instrument of music, and the dirges which spiritual fingers were said to play on it, — the devoted sister had solemn thoughts of thrumming on its chords for Clifford's benefit, and accompanying the performance with her voice. Poor Clifford! Poor Hepzibah! Poor harpsichord! All three would have been miserable together. By some good agency, — possibly, by the unrecognized interposition of the long-buried Alice herself, — the threatening calamity was averted.

But the worst of all — the hardest stroke of fate for Hepzibah to endure, and perhaps for Clifford too — was his invincible distaste for her appearance. Her features, never the most agreeable, and now harsh with age and grief, and resentment against the world for his sake ; her dress, and especially her turban ; the queer and quaint manners, which had unconsciously grown upon her in solitude, — such being the poor gentlewoman's outward characteristics, it is no great marvel, although the mournfullest of pities, that the instinctive lover of the Beautiful was fain to turn away his eyes. There was no help for it. It would be the latest impulse to die within him. In his last extremity, the expiring breath stealing faintly through Clifford's lips, he would doubtless press Hepzibah's hand, in fervent recognition of all her lavished love, and close his eyes, — but not so much to die, as to be constrained to look no longer on her face! Poor Hepzibah! She took counsel with herself what might be done, and thought of putting ribbons on her turban ; but, by the instant rush of several guardian angels, was withheld from an experiment that could hardly have proved less than fatal to the beloved object of her anxiety.

To be brief, besides Hepzibah's disadvantages of person, there was an uncouthness pervading all her deeds ; a clumsy something, that could but ill adapt itself for use, and not at all for ornament. She was a grief to Clifford, and she knew it. In this extremity, the antiquated virgin turned to Phœbe. No grovelling jealousy was in her heart. Had it pleased Heaven to crown the heroic fidelity of her life by making her personally the medium of Clifford's happiness, it would have rewarded her for all the past, by a joy with no bright tints, indeed, but deep and true, and worth a thousand gayer ecstasies. This could not be. She therefore turned to Phœbe, and resigned the task into the young girl's hands. The latter took it up cheerfully, as she did everything, but with no sense of a mission to perform, and succeeding all the better for that same simplicity.

By the involuntary effect of a genial temperament, Phœbe soon grew to be absolutely essential to the daily comfort, if not the daily life, of her two forlorn companions. The grime and sordidness of the House of the Seven Gables seemed to have vanished since her appearance there; the gnawing tooth of the dry-rot was stayed among the old timbers of its skeleton frame; the dust had ceased to settle down so densely, from the antique ceilings, upon the floors and furniture of the rooms below, — or, at any rate, there was a little housewife, as light-footed as the breeze that sweeps a garden walk, gliding hither and thither to brush it all away. The shadows of gloomy events that haunted the else lonely and desolate apartments; the heavy, breathless scent which death had left in more than one of the bedchambers, ever since his visits of long ago, — these were less powerful than the purifying influence scattered throughout the atmosphere of the household by the presence of one youthful, fresh, and thoroughly wholesome heart. There was no morbidness in Phœbe; if there had been, the old Pyncheon House was the very locality to ripen it into incurable disease. But now her spirit resembled, in its potency, a minute quantity of ottar of rose in one of Hepzibah's huge, iron-bound trunks, diffusing its fragrance through the various articles of linen and wrought-lace, kerchiefs, caps, stockings, folded dresses, gloves, and whatever else was treasured there. As every article in the great trunk was the sweeter for the rose-scent, so did all the thoughts and emotions of Hepzibah and Clifford, sombre as they might seem, acquire a subtle attribute of happiness from Phœbe's intermixture with them. Her activity of body, intellect, and heart impelled her continually to perform the ordinary little toils that offered themselves around her, and to think the thought proper for the moment, and to sympathize, — now with the twittering gayety of the robins in the pear-tree, and now to such a depth as she could with Hepzibah's dark anxiety, or the vague moan of her brother. This facile adaptation was at once the symptom of perfect health and its best preservative.

A nature like Phœbe's has invariably its due influence, but is seldom regarded with due honor. Its spiritual force, however, may be partially estimated by the fact of her having found a place for herself, amid circumstances so stern as those which surrounded the mistress of the house ; and also by the effect which she produced on a character of so much more mass than her own. For the gaunt, bony frame and limbs of Hepzibah, as compared with the tiny lightsomeness of Phœbe's figure, were perhaps in some fit proportion with the moral weight and substance, respectively, of the woman and the girl.

To the guest, — to Hepzibah's brother, — or Cousin Clifford, as Phœbe now began to call him, — she was especially necessary. Not that he could ever be said to converse with her, or often manifest, in any other very definite mode, his sense of a charm in her society. But if she were a long while absent he became pettish and nervously restless, pacing the room to and fro with the uncertainty that characterized all his movements ; or else would sit broodingly in his great chair, resting his head on his hands, and evincing life only by an electric sparkle of ill-humor, whenever Hepzibah endeavored to arouse him. Phœbe's presence, and the contiguity of her fresh life to his blighted one, was usually all that he required. Indeed, such was the native gush and play of her spirit, that she was seldom perfectly quiet and undemonstrative, any more than a fountain ever ceases to dimple and warble with its flow. She possessed the gift of song, and that, too, so naturally, that you would as little think of inquiring whence she had caught it, or what master had taught her, as of asking the same questions about a bird, in whose small strain of music we recognize the voice of the Creator as distinctly as in the loudest accents of his thunder. So long as Phœbe sang, she might stray at her own will about the house. Clifford was content, whether the sweet, airy homeliness of her tones came down from the upper chambers, or along the passage-way from the shop, or was sprinkled through the foliage of the pear-tree, inward from the garden, with the twinkling sunbeams. He would sit quietly, with a gentle pleasure gleaming over his face, brighter now, and now a little dimmer, as the song happened to float near him, or was more remotely heard. It pleased him best, however, when she sat on a low footstool at his knee.

It is perhaps remarkable, considering her temperament, that Phœbe oftener chose a strain of pathos than of gayety. But the young and happy are not ill pleased to temper their life with a transparent shadow. The deepest pathos of Phœbe's voice and song, moreover, came sifted through the golden texture of a cheery spirit, and was somehow so interfused with the quality thence acquired, that one's heart felt all the lighter for having wept at it. Broad mirth, in the sacred presence of dark misfortune, would have jarred harshly and irreverently with the solemn symphony that rolled its undertone through Hepzibah's and her brother's life. Therefore, it was well that Phœbe so often chose sad themes, and not amiss that they ceased to be so sad while she was singing them.

Becoming habituated to her companionship, Clifford readily showed how capable of imbibing pleasant tints and gleams of cheerful light from all quarters his nature must originally have been. He grew youthful while she sat by him. A beauty, — not precisely real, even in its utmost manifestation, and which a painter would have watched long to seize and fix upon his canvas, and, after all, in vain, — beauty, nevertheless, that was not a mere dream, would sometimes play upon and illuminate his face. It did more than to illuminate; it transfigured him with an expression that could only be interpreted as the glow of an exquisite and happy spirit. That gray hair, and those furrows, — with their record of infinite sorrow so deeply written across his brow, and so compressed, as with a futile effort to crowd in all the tale, that the whole inscription was made illegible, — these, for the moment, vanished. An eye, at once tender and acute, might have beheld in the man some shadow of what he was meant to be. Anon, as age came stealing, like a sad twilight, back over his figure, you would have felt tempted to hold an argument with Destiny, and affirm, that either this being should not have been made mortal, or mortal existence should have been tempered to his qualities. There seemed no necessity for his having drawn breath at all; the world never wanted him; but, as he had breathed, it ought always to have been the balmiest of summer air. The same perplexity will invariably haunt us with regard to natures that tend to feed exclusively upon the Beautiful, let their earthly fate be as lenient as it may.

Phœbe, it is probable, had but a very imperfect comprehension of the character over which she had thrown so beneficent a spell. Nor was it necessary. The fire upon the hearth can gladden a whole semicircle of faces round about it, but need not know the individuality of one among them all. Indeed, there was something too fine and delicate in Clifford's traits to be perfectly appreciated by one whose sphere lay so much in the Actual as Phœbe's did. For Clifford, however, the reality, and simplicity, and thorough homeliness of the girl's nature, were as powerful a charm as any that she possessed. Beauty, it is true, and beauty almost perfect in its own style, was indispensable. Had Phœbe been coarse in feature, shaped clumsily, of a harsh voice, and uncouthly mannered, she might have been rich with all good gifts, beneath this unfortunate exterior, and still, so long as she wore the guise of woman, she would have shocked Clifford, and depressed him by her lack of beauty. But nothing more beautiful — nothing prettier, at least — was ever made than Phœbe. And, therefore, to this man, — whose whole poor and impalpable enjoyment of existence heretofore, and until both his heart and fancy died within him, had been a dream, — whose images of women had more and more lost their warmth and substance, and been frozen, like the pictures of secluded artists, into the chillest ideality, — to him, this little figure of the cheeriest household life was just what he required to bring him back into the breathing world. Persons who have wandered, or been expelled, out of the common track of things, even were it for a better system, desire nothing so much as to be led back. They shiver in their loneliness, be it on a mountain-top or in a dungeon. Now, Phœbe's presence made a home about her, — that very sphere which the outcast, the prisoner, the potentate, — the wretch beneath mankind, the wretch aside from it, or the wretch above it, — instinctively pines after, — a home! She was real! Holding her hand, you felt something; a tender something; a substance, and a warm one: and so long as you should feel its grasp, soft as it was, you might be certain that your place was good in the whole sympathetic chain of human nature. The world was no longer a delusion.

By looking a little further in this direction, we might suggest an explanation of an often-suggested mystery. Why are poets so apt to choose their mates, not for any similarity of poetic endowment, but for qualities which might make the happiness of the rudest handicraftsman as well as that of the ideal craftsman of the spirit? Because, probably, at his highest elevation, the poet needs no human intercourse; but he finds it dreary to descend, and be a stranger.

There was something very beautiful in the relation that grew up between this pair, so closely and constantly linked together, yet with such a waste of gloomy and mysterious years from his birthday to hers. On Clifford's part it was the feeling of a man naturally endowed with the liveliest sensibility to feminine influence, but who had never quaffed the cup of passionate love, and knew that it was now too late. He knew it, with the instinctive delicacy that had survived his intellectual decay. Thus, his sentiment for Phœbe, without being paternal, was not less chaste than if she had been his daughter. He was a man, it is true, and recognized her as a woman. She was his only representative of womankind. He took unfailing note of every charm that appertained to her sex, and saw the ripeness of her lips, and the virginal development of her bosom. All her little womanly ways, budding out of her like blossoms on a young fruit-tree, had their effect on him, and sometimes caused his very heart to tingle with the keenest thrills of pleasure. At such moments, — for the effect was seldom more than momentary, — the half-torpid man would be full of harmonious life, just as a long-silent harp is full of sound, when the musician's fingers sweep across it. But, after all, it seemed rather a perception, or a sympathy, than a sentiment belonging to himself as an individual. He read Phœbe, as he would a sweet and simple story; he listened to her, as if she were a verse of household poetry, which God, in requital of his bleak and dismal lot, had permitted some angel, that most pitied him, to warble through the house. She was not an actual fact for him, but the interpretation of all that he had lacked on earth brought warmly home to his conception; so that this mere symbol, or lifelike picture, had almost the comfort of reality.

But we strive in vain to put the idea into words. No adequate expression of the beauty and profound pathos with which it impresses us is attainable. This being, made only for happiness, and heretofore so miserably failing to be happy, — his tendencies so hideously thwarted, that, some unknown time ago, the delicate springs of his character, never morally or intellectually strong, had given way, and he was now imbecile, — this poor, forlorn, voyager from the Islands of the Blest, in a frail bark, on a tempestuous sea, had been flung, by the last mountain-wave of his shipwreck, into a quiet harbor. There, as he lay more than half lifeless on the strand, the fragrance of an earthly rose-bud had come to his nostrils, and, as odors will, had summoned up reminiscences or visions of all the living and breathing beauty amid which he should have had his home. With his native susceptibility of happy influences, he inhales the slight, ethereal rapture into his soul, and expires!

And how did Phœbe regard Clifford? The girl's was not one of those natures which are most attracted by what is strange and exceptional in human character. The path which would best have suited her was the well-worn track of ordinary life; the companions in whom she would most have delighted were such as one encounters at every turn. The mystery which enveloped Clifford, so far as it affected her at all, was an annoyance, rather than the piquant charm which many women might have found in it. Still, her native kindliness was brought strongly into play, not by what was darkly picturesque in his situation, nor so much, even, by the finer graces of his character, as by the simple appeal of a heart so forlorn as his to one so full of genuine sympathy as hers. She gave him an affectionate regard, because he needed so much love, and seemed to have received so little. With a ready tact, the result of ever-active and wholesome sensibility, she discerned what was good for him, and did it. Whatever was morbid in his mind and experience she ignored; and thereby kept their intercourse healthy, by the incautious, but, as it were, heaven-directed freedom of her whole conduct. The sick in mind, and, perhaps, in body, are rendered more darkly and hopelessly so by the manifold reflection of their disease, mirrored back from all quarters in the deportment of those about them; they are compelled to inhale the poison of their own breath, in infinite repetition. But Phœbe afforded her poor patient a supply of purer air. She impregnated it, too, not with a wild-flower scent, — for wildness was no trait of hers, — but with the perfume of garden-roses, pinks, and other blossoms of much sweetness, which nature and man have consented together in making grow from summer to summer, and from century to century. Such a flower was Phœbe, in her relation with Clifford, and such the delight that he inhaled from her.

Yet, it must be said, her petals sometimes drooped a little, in consequence of the heavy atmosphere about her. She grew more thoughtful than heretofore. Looking aside at Clifford's face, and seeing the dim, unsatisfactory elegance and the intellect almost quenched, she would try to inquire what had been his life. Was he always thus? Had this veil been over him from his birth? — this veil, under which far more of his spirit was hidden than revealed, and through which he so imperfectly discerned the actual world, — or was its gray texture woven of some dark calamity? Phœbe loved no riddles, and would have been glad to escape the perplexity of this one. Nevertheless, there was so far a good result of her meditations on Clifford's character, that, when her involuntary conjectures, together with the tendency of every strange circumstance to tell its own story, had gradually taught her the fact, it had no terrible effect upon her. Let the world have done him what vast wrong it might, she knew Cousin Clifford too well — or fancied so — ever to shudder at the touch of his thin delicate fingers.

Within a few days after the appearance of this remarkable inmate, the routine of life had established itself with a good deal of uniformity in the old house of our narrative. In the morning, very shortly after breakfast, it was Clifford's custom to fall asleep in his chair; nor, unless accidentally disturbed, would he emerge from a dense cloud of slumber or the thinner mists that flitted to and fro, until well towards noonday. These hours of drowsihead were the season of the old gentlewoman's attendance on her brother, while Phœbe took charge of the shop; an arrangement which the public speedily understood, and evinced their decided preference of the younger shopwoman by the multiplicity of their calls during her administration of affairs. Dinner over, Hepzibah took her knitting-work, — a long stocking of gray yarn, for her brother's winter-wear, — and with a sigh, and a scowl of affectionate farewell to Clifford, and a gesture enjoining watchfulness on Phœbe, went to take her seat behind the counter. It was now the young girl's turn to be the nurse, — the guardian, the playmate, — or whatever is the fitter phrase, — of the gray-haired man.

X.

THE PYNCHEON GARDEN.

CLIFFORD, except for Phœbe's more active instigation, would ordinarily have yielded to the torpor which had crept through all his modes of being, and which sluggishly counselled him to sit in his morning chair till eventide. But the girl seldom failed to propose a removal to the garden, where Uncle Venner and the daguerreotypist had made such repairs on the roof of the ruinous arbor, or summer-house, that it was now a sufficient shelter from sunshine and casual showers. The hop-vine, too, had begun to grow luxuriantly over the sides of the little edifice, and made an interior of verdant seclusion, with innumerable peeps and glimpses into the wider solitude of the garden.

Here, sometimes, in this green play-place of flickering light, Phœbe read to Clifford. Her acquaintance, the artist, who appeared to have a literary turn, had supplied her with works of fiction, in pamphlet-form, and a few volumes of poetry, in altogether a different style and taste from those which Hepzibah selected for his amusement. Small thanks were due to the books, however, if the girl's readings were in any degree more successful than her elderly cousin's. Phœbe's voice had always a pretty music in it, and could either enliven Clifford by its sparkle and gayety of tone, or soothe him by a continued flow of pebbly and brook-like cadences. But the fictions — in which the country-girl, unused to works of that nature, often became deeply absorbed — interested her strange auditor very little, or not at all. Pictures of life, scenes of passion or sentiment, wit, humor, and pathos, were all thrown away, or worse than thrown away, on Clifford; either because he lacked an experience by which to test their truth, or because his own griefs were a touch-stone of reality that few feigned emotions could withstand. When Phœbe broke into a peal of merry laughter at what she read, he would now and then laugh for sympathy, but oftener respond with a troubled, questioning look. If a tear — a maiden's sunshiny tear over imaginary woe — dropped upon some melancholy page, Clifford either took it as a token of actual calamity, or else grew peevish, and angrily motioned her to close the volume. And wisely too! Is not the world sad enough, in genuine earnest, without making a pastime of mock-sorrows?

With poetry it was rather better. He delighted in the swell and subsidence of the rhythm, and the happily recurring rhyme. Nor was Clifford incapable of feeling the sentiment of poetry, — not, perhaps, where it was highest or deepest, but where it was most flitting and ethereal. It was impossible to foretell in what exquisite verse the awakening spell might lurk; but, on raising her eyes from the page to Clifford's face, Phœbe would be made aware, by the light breaking through it, that a more delicate intelligence than her own had caught a lambent flame from what she read. One glow of this kind, however, was often the precursor of gloom for many hours afterward; because, when the glow left him, he seemed conscious of a missing sense and power, and groped about for them, as if a blind man should go seeking his lost eyesight.

It pleased him more, and was better for his **inward** welfare, that Phœbe should talk, and make passing occurrences vivid to his mind by her accompanying description and remarks. The life of the garden offered topics enough for such discourse as suited Clifford best. He never failed to inquire what flowers had bloomed since yesterday. His feeling for flowers was very exquisite, and seemed not so much a taste as an emotion; he was fond of sitting with one in his hand, intently observing it, and looking from its petals into Phœbe's face, as if the garden flower were the sister of the household maiden. Not merely was there a delight in the flower's perfume, or pleasure in its beautiful form, and the delicacy or brightness of its hue; but Clifford's enjoyment was accompanied with a perception of life, character, and individuality, that made him love these blossoms of the garden, as if they were endowed with sentiment and intelligence. This affection and sympathy for flowers is almost exclusively a woman's trait. Men, if endowed with it by nature, soon lose, forget, and learn to despise it, in their contact with coarser things than flowers. Clifford, too, had long forgotten it; but found it again now, as he slowly revived from the chill torpor of his life.

It is wonderful how many pleasant incidents continually came to pass in that secluded garden-spot when once Phœbe had set herself to look for them. She had seen or heard a bee there, on the first day of her acquaintance with the place. And often, — almost continually, indeed, — since then, the bees kept coming thither, Heaven knows why, or by what pertinacious desire, for far-fetched sweets, when, no doubt, there were broad clover-fields, and all kinds of garden growth, much nearer home than this. Thither the bees came, however, and plunged into the squash-blossoms, as if there were no other squash-vines within a long day's flight, or as if the soil of Hepzibah's garden gave its productions just the very quality which these laborious little wizards wanted, in order to impart the Hymettus odor to their whole hive of New England honey. When Clifford heard their sunny, buzzing murmur, in the heart of the great yellow blossoms, he looked about him with a joyful sense of warmth, and blue sky, and green grass, and of God's free air in the whole height from earth to heaven. After all, there need be no question why the bees came to that one green nook in the dusty town. God sent them thither to gladden our poor Clifford. They brought the rich summer with them, in requital of a little honey.

When the bean-vines began to flower on the poles, there was one particular variety which bore a vivid scarlet blossom. The daguerreotypist had found these beans in a garret, over one of the seven gables, treasured up in an old chest of drawers, by some horticultural Pyncheon of days gone by, who, doubtless, meant to sow them the next summer, but was himself first sown in Death's garden-ground. By way of testing whether there were still a living germ in such ancient seeds, Holgrave had planted some of them; and the result of his experiment was a splendid row of bean-vines, clambering, early, to the full height of the poles, and arraying them, from top to bottom, in a spiral profusion of red blossoms. And, ever since the unfolding of the first bud, a multitude of humming-birds had been attracted thither. At times, it seemed as if for every one of the hundred blossoms there was one of these tiniest fowls of the air, — a thumb's bigness of burnished plumage, hovering and vibrating about the bean-poles. It was with indescribable interest, and even more than childish delight, that Clifford watched the humming-birds. He used to thrust his head softly out of the arbor to see them the better; all the while, too, motioning Phœbe to be quiet, and snatching glimpses of the smile upon her face, so as to heap his enjoyment up the higher with her sympathy. He had not merely grown young; — he was a child again.

Hepzibah, whenever she happened to witness one of these fits of miniature enthusiasm, would shake her head, with a strange mingling of the mother and sister, and of pleasure and sadness, in her aspect. She said that it had always been thus with Clifford when the humming-birds came, — always, from his babyhood, — and that his delight in them had been one of the earliest tokens by which he showed his love for beautiful things. And it was a wonderful coincidence, the good lady thought, that the artist should have planted these scarlet-flowering beans — which the humming-birds sought far and wide, and which had not grown in the Pyncheon garden before for forty years — on the very summer of Clifford's return.

Then would the tears stand in poor Hepzibah's eyes, or overflow them with a too abundant gush, so that she was fain to betake herself into some corner lest Clifford should espy her agitation. Indeed, all the enjoyments of this period were provocative of tears. Coming so late as it did, it was a kind of Indian summer, with a mist in its balmiest sunshine, and decay and death in its gaudiest delight. The more Clifford seemed to taste the happiness of a child, the sadder was the difference to be recognized. With a mysterious and terrible Past, which had annihilated his memory, and a blank Future before him, he had only this visionary and impalpable Now, which, if you once look closely at it, is nothing. He himself, as was perceptible by many symptoms, lay darkly behind his pleasure, and knew it to be a baby-play, which he was to toy and trifle with, instead of thoroughly believing. Clifford saw, it may be, in the mirror of his deeper consciousness, that he was an example and representative of that great class of people whom an inexplicable Providence is continually putting at cross-purposes with the world : breaking what seems its own promise in their nature ; withholding their proper food, and setting poison before them for a banquet : and thus — when it might so easily, as one would think, have been adjusted otherwise — making their existence a strangeness, a solitude, and torment. All his life long, he had been learning how to be wretched, as one learns a foreign tongue ; and now, with the lesson thoroughly by heart, he could with difficulty comprehend his little airy happiness. Frequently there was a dim shadow of doubt in his eyes. "Take my hand, Phœbe," he would say, "and pinch it hard with your little fingers ! Give me a rose, that I may press its thorns, and prove myself awake by the sharp touch of pain !" Evidently, he desired this prick of a trifling anguish, in order to assure himself, by that quality which he best knew to be real, that the garden, and the seven weather-beaten gables, and Hepzibah's scowl, and Phœbe's smile, were real likewise. Without this signet in his flesh, he could have attributed no more substance to them than to the empty confusion of imaginary scenes with which he had fed his spirit, until even that poor sustenance was exhausted.

The author needs great faith in his reader's sympathy; else he must hesitate to give details so minute, and incidents apparently so trifling, as are essential to make up the idea of this garden-life. It was the Eden of a thunder-smitten Adam, who had fled for refuge thither out of the same dreary and perilous wilderness into which the original Adam was expelled.

One of the available means of amusement, of which Phœbe made the most in Clifford's behalf, was that feathered society, the hens, a breed of whom, as we have already said, was an immemorial heirloom in the Pyncheon family. In compliance with a whim of Clifford, as it troubled him to see them in confinement, they had been set at liberty, and now roamed at will about the garden; doing some little mischief but hindered from escape by buildings on three sides, and the difficult peaks of a wooden fence on the other. They spent much of their abundant leisure on the margin of Maule's well, which was haunted by a kind of snail, evidently a titbit to their palates; and the brackish water itself, however nauseous to the rest of the world, was so greatly esteemed by these fowls, that they might be seen tasting, turning up their heads, and smacking their bills, with precisely the air of wine-bibbers round a probationary cask. Their generally quiet, yet often brisk, and constantly diversified talk, one to another, or sometimes in soliloquy, — as they scratched worms out of the rich, black soil, or pecked at such plants as suited their taste, — had such a domestic tone, that it was almost a wonder why you could not establish a regular interchange of ideas about household matters, human and gallinaceous. All hens are well worth studying for the piquancy and rich variety of their manners; but by no possibility can there have been other fowls of such odd appearance and deportment as these ancestral ones. They probably embodied the traditionary peculiarities of their whole line of progenitors, derived through an unbroken succession of eggs; or else this individual Chanticleer and his two wives had grown to be humorists, and a little crack-brained withal, on account of their solitary way of life, and out of sympathy for Hepzibah, their lady-patroness.

Queer, indeed, they looked! Chanticleer himself, though stalking on two stilt-like legs, with the dignity of interminable descent in all his gestures, was hardly bigger than an ordinary partridge; his two wives were about the size of quails; and as for the one chicken, it looked small enough to be still in the egg, and, at the same time, sufficiently old, withered, wizened, and experienced, to have been the founder of the antiquated race. Instead of being the youngest of the family, it rather seemed to have aggregated into itself the ages, not only of these living specimens of the breed, but of all its forefathers and foremothers, whose united excellences and oddities were squeezed into its little body. Its mother evidently regarded it as the one chicken of the world, and as necessary, in fact, to the world's continuance, or, at any rate, to the equilibrium of the present system of affairs, whether in church or state. No lesser sense of the infant fowl's importance could have justified, even in a mother's eyes, the perseverance with which she watched over its safety, ruffling her small person to twice its proper size, and flying in everybody's face that so much as looked towards her hopeful progeny. No lower estimate could have vindicated the indefatigable zeal with which she scratched, and her unscrupulousness in digging up the

choicest flower or vegetable, for the sake of the fat
earthworm at its root. Her nervous cluck, when the
chicken happened to be hidden in the long grass or
under the squash-leaves; her gentle croak of satisfaction,
while sure of it beneath her wing; her note of
ill-concealed fear and obstreperous defiance, when she
saw her arch-enemy, a neighbor's cat, on the top of
the high fence, — one or other of these sounds was
to be heard at almost every moment of the day. By
degrees, the observer came to feel nearly as much interest in this chicken of illustrious race as the mother-
hen did.

Phœbe, after getting well acquainted with the old
hen, was sometimes permitted to take the chicken in
her hand, which was quite capable of grasping its cu-
bic inch or two of body. While she curiously examined
its hereditary marks, — the peculiar speckle of its
plumage, the funny tuft on its head, and a knob on
each of its legs, — the little biped, as she insisted, kept
giving her a sagacious wink. The daguerreotypist
once whispered her that these marks betokened the
oddities of the Pyncheon family, and that the chicken
itself was a symbol of the life of the old house, embodying its interpretation, likewise, although an unintelligible one, as such clews generally are. It was a
feathered riddle; a mystery hatched out of an egg,
and just as mysterious as if the egg had been addle!

The second of Chanticleer's two wives, ever since
Phœbe's arrival, had been in a state of heavy despondency, caused, as it afterwards appeared, by her
inability to lay an egg. One day, however, by her
self-important gait, the sideway turn of her head, and
the cock of her eye, as she pried into one and another
nook of the garden, — croaking to herself, all the

while, with inexpressible complacency, — it was made evident that this identical hen, much as mankind undervalued her, carried something about her person the worth of which was not to be estimated either in gold or precious stones. Shortly after there was a prodigious cackling and gratulation of Chanticleer and all his family, including the wizened chicken, who appeared to understand the matter quite as well as did his sire, his mother, or his aunt. That afternoon Phœbe found a diminutive egg, — not in the regular nest, it was far too precious to be trusted there, — but cunningly hidden under the currant-bushes, on some dry stalks of last year's grass. Hepzibah, on learning the fact, took possession of the egg and appropriated it to Clifford's breakfast, on account of a certain delicacy of flavor, for which, as she affirmed, these eggs had always been famous. Thus unscrupulously did the old gentlewoman sacrifice the continuance, perhaps, of an ancient feathered race, with no better end than to supply her brother with a dainty that hardly filled the bowl of a tea-spoon! It must have been in reference to this outrage that Chanticleer, the next day, accompanied by the bereaved mother of the egg, took his post in front of Phœbe and Clifford, and delivered himself of a harangue that might have proved as long as his own pedigree, but for a fit of merriment on Phœbe's part. Hereupon, the offended fowl stalked away on his long stilts, and utterly withdrew his notice from Phœbe and the rest of human nature, until she made her peace with an offering of spice-cake, which, next to snails, was the delicacy most in favor with his aristocratic taste.

We linger too long, no doubt, beside this paltry rivulet of life that flowed through the garden of the

Pyncheon House. But we deem it pardonable to record these mean incidents and poor delights, because
they proved so greatly to Clifford's benefit. They
had the earth-smell in them, and contributed to give
him health and substance. Some of his occupations
wrought less desirably upon him. He had a singular
propensity, for example, to hang over Maule's well,
and look at the constantly shifting phantasmagoria of
figures produced by the agitation of the water over
the mosaic-work of colored pebbles at the bottom. He
said that faces looked upward to him there,— beautiful
faces, arrayed in bewitching smiles, — each momentary face so fair and rosy, and every smile so sunny,
that he felt wronged at its departure, until the same
flitting witchcraft made a new one. But sometimes he
would suddenly cry out, " The dark face gazes at me!"
and be miserable the whole day afterwards. Phœbe,
when she hung over the fountain by Clifford's side,
could see nothing of all this, — neither the beauty nor
the ugliness, — but only the colored pebbles, looking
as if the gush of the waters shook and disarranged
them. And the dark face, that so troubled Clifford,
was no more than the shadow thrown from a branch
of one of the damson-trees, and breaking the inner
light of Maule's well. The truth was, however, that
his fancy — reviving faster than his will and judgment, and always stronger than they — created shapes
of loveliness that were symbolic of his native character, and now and then a stern and dreadful shape that
typified his fate.

On Sundays, after Phœbe had been at church, —
for the girl had a church-going conscience, and would
hardly have been at ease had she missed either prayer,
singing, sermon, or benediction, — after church-time,

therefore, there was, ordinarily, a sober little festival in the garden. In addition to Clifford, Hepzibah, and Phœbe, two guests made up the company. One was the artist, Holgrave, who, in spite of his consociation with reformers, and his other queer and questionable traits, continued to hold an elevated place in Hepzibah's regard. The other, we are almost ashamed to say, was the venerable Uncle Venner, in a clean shirt, and a broadcloth coat, more respectable than his ordinary wear, inasmuch as it was neatly patched on each elbow, and might be called an entire garment, except for a slight inequality in the length of its skirts. Clifford, on several occasions, had seemed to enjoy the old man's intercourse, for the sake of his mellow, cheerful vein, which was like the sweet flavor of a frost-bitten apple, such as one picks up under the tree in December. A man at the very lowest point of the social scale was easier and more agreeable for the fallen gentleman to encounter than a person at any of the intermediate degrees; and, moreover, as Clifford's young manhood had been lost, he was fond of feeling himself comparatively youthful, now, in apposition with the patriarchal age of Uncle Venner. In fact, it was sometimes observable that Clifford half wilfully hid from himself the consciousness of being stricken in years, and cherished visions of an earthly future still before him; visions, however, too indistinctly drawn to be followed by disappointment — though, doubtless, by depression — when any casual incident or recollection made him sensible of the withered leaf.

So this oddly composed little social party used to assemble under the ruinous arbor. Hepzibah — stately as ever at heart, and yielding not an inch of her old

gentility, but resting upon it so much the more, as jus-
tifying a princess-like condescension — exhibited a not
ungraceful hospitality. She talked kindly to the vagrant artist, and took sage counsel — lady as she was
— with the wood-sawyer, the messenger of everybody's
petty errands, the patched philosopher. And Uncle
Venner, who had studied the world at street-corners,
and other posts equally well adapted for just observation, was as ready to give out his wisdom as a town-
pump to give water.

"Miss Hepzibah, ma'am," said he once, after they
had all been cheerful together, "I really enjoy these
quiet little meetings of a Sabbath afternoon. They
are very much like what I expect to have after I retire
to my farm!"

"Uncle Venner," observed Clifford, in a drowsy, inward tone, "is always talking about his farm. But I
have a better scheme for him, by and by. We shall
see!"

"Ah, Mr. Clifford Pyncheon!" said the man of
patches, "you may scheme for me as much as you
please; but I'm not going to give up this one scheme
of my own, even if I never bring it really to pass. It
does seem to me that men make a wonderful mistake
in trying to heap up property upon property. If I had
done so, I should feel as if Providence was not bound
to take care of me; and, at all events, the city wouldn't
be! I'm one of those people who think that infinity
is big enough for us all — and eternity long enough."

"Why, so they are, Uncle Venner," remarked
Phœbe, after a pause; for she had been trying to
fathom the profundity and appositeness of this concluding apothegm. "But for this short life of ours,
one would like a house and a moderate garden-spot of
one's own."

"It appears to me," said the daguerreotypist, smiling, " that Uncle Venner has the principles of Fourier at the bottom of his wisdom ; only they have not quite so much distinctness, in his mind as in that of the systematizing Frenchman."

"Come, Phœbe," said Hepzibah, "it is time to bring the currants."

And then, while the yellow richness of the declining sunshine still fell into the open space of the garden, Phœbe brought out a loaf of bread and a china bowl of currants, freshly gathered from the bushes, and crushed with sugar. These, with water, — but not from the fountain of ill omen, close at hand, — constituted all the entertainment. Meanwhile, Holgrave took some pains to establish an intercourse with Clifford, actuated it might seem, entirely by an impulse of kindliness, in order that the present hour might be cheerfuller than most which the poor recluse had spent, or was destined yet to spend. Nevertheless, in the artist's deep, thoughtful, all-observant eyes, there was, now and then, an expression, not sinister, but questionable ; as if he had some other interest in the scene than a stranger, a youthful and unconnected adventurer, might be supposed to have. With great mobility of outward mood, however, he applied himself to the task of enlivening the party; and with so much success, that even dark-hued Hepzibah threw off one tint of melancholy, and made what shift she could with the remaining portion. Phœbe said to herself, — " How pleasant he can be ! " As for Uncle Venner, as a mark of friendship and approbation, he readily consented to afford the young man his countenance in the way of his profession, — not metaphorically, be it understood, but literally, by allowing a daguerreotype of his face, so familiar to the town, to be exhibited at the entrance of Holgrave's studio.

Clifford, as the company partook of their little banquet, grew to be the gayest of them all. Either it was one of those up-quivering flashes of the spirit, to which minds in an abnormal state are liable, or else the artist had subtly touched some chord that made musical vibration. Indeed, what with the pleasant summer evening, and the sympathy of this little circle of not unkindly souls, it was perhaps natural that a character so susceptible as Clifford's should become animated, and show itself readily responsive to what was said around him. But he gave out his own thoughts, likewise, with an airy and fanciful glow; so that they glistened, as it were, through the arbor, and made their escape among the interstices of the foliage. He had been as cheerful, no doubt, while alone with Phœbe, but never with such tokens of acute, although partial intelligence.

But, as the sunlight left the peaks of the Seven Gables, so did the excitement fade out of Clifford's eyes. He gazed vaguely and mournfully about him, as if he missed something precious, and missed it the more drearily for not knowing precisely what it was.

" I want my happiness ! " at last he murmured, hoarsely and indistinctly, hardly shaping out the words. " Many, many years have I waited for it ! It is late ! It is late ! I want my happiness ! "

Alas, poor Clifford ! You are old, and worn with troubles that ought never to have befallen you. You are partly crazy and partly imbecile ; a ruin, a failure, as almost everybody is, — though some in less degree, or less perceptibly, than their fellows. Fate has no happiness in store for you ; unless your quiet home in

the old family residence with the faithful Hepzibah,
and your long summer afternoons with Phœbe, and
these Sabbath festivals with Uncle Venner and the
daguerreotypist, deserve to be called happiness! Why
not? If not the thing itself, it is marvellously like it,
and the more so for that ethereal and intangible quality which causes it all to vanish at too close an intro-
spection. Take it, therefore, while you may! Murmur not, — question not, — but make the most of it!

XI.

THE ARCHED WINDOW.

FROM the inertness, or what we may term the vege-
tative character, of his ordinary mood, Clifford would
perhaps have been content to spend one day after another, interminably, — or, at least, throughout the
summer-time, — in just the kind of life described in
the preceding pages. Fancying, however, that it might
be for his benefit occasionally to diversify the scene,
Phœbe sometimes suggested that he should look out
upon the life of the street. For this purpose, they
used to mount the staircase together, to the second
story of the house, where, at the termination of a wide
entry, there was an arched window of uncommonly
large dimensions, shaded by a pair of curtains. It
opened above the porch, where there had formerly
been a balcony, the balustrade of which had long since
gone to decay, and been removed. At this arched
window, throwing it open, but keeping himself in com-
parative obscurity by means of the curtain, Clifford
had an opportunity of witnessing such a portion of the
great world's movement as might be supposed to roll
through one of the retired streets of a not very populous city. But he and Phœbe made a sight as well
worth seeing as any that the city could exhibit. The
pale, gray, childish, aged, melancholy, yet often simply
cheerful, and sometimes delicately intelligent aspect
of Clifford, peering from behind the faded crimson of

the curtain, — watching the monotony of every-day occurrences with a kind of inconsequential interest and earnestness, and, at every petty throb of his sensibility, turning for sympathy to the eyes of the bright young girl!

If once he were fairly seated at the window, even Pyncheon Street would hardly be so dull and lonely but that, somewhere or other along its extent, Clifford might discover matter to occupy his eye, and titillate, if not engross, his observation. Things familiar to the youngest child that had begun its outlook at existence seemed strange to him. A cab; an omnibus, with its populous interior, dropping here and there a passenger, and picking up another, and thus typifying that vast rolling vehicle, the world, the end of whose journey is everywhere and nowhere; these objects he followed eagerly with his eyes, but forgot them before the dust raised by the horses and wheels had settled along their track. As regarded novelties (among which cabs and omnibuses were to be reckoned), his mind appeared to have lost its proper gripe and retentiveness. Twice or thrice, for example, during the sunny hours of the day, a water-cart went along by the Pyncheon House, leaving a broad wake of moistened earth, instead of the white dust that had risen at a lady's lightest footfall; it was like a summer shower, which the city authorities had caught and tamed, and compelled it into the commonest routine of their convenience. With the water-cart Clifford could never grow familiar; it always affected him with just the same surprise as at first. His mind took an apparently sharp impression from it, but lost the recollection of this perambulatory shower, before its next reappearance, as completely as did the street itself, along which the heat so quickly strewed white dust again. It was the same with the railroad. Clifford could hear the obstreperous howl of the steam-devil, and, by leaning a little way from the arched window, could catch a glimpse of the trains of cars, flashing a brief transit across the extremity of the street. The idea of terrible energy thus forced upon him was new at every recurrence, and seemed to affect him as disagreeably, and with almost as much surprise, the hundredth time as the first.

Nothing gives a sadder sense of decay than this loss or suspension of the power to deal with unaccustomed things, and to keep up with the swiftness of the passing moment. It can merely be a suspended animation; for, were the power actually to perish, there would be little use of immortality. We are less than ghosts, for the time being, whenever this calamity befalls us.

Clifford was indeed the most inveterate of conservatives. All the antique fashions of the street were dear to him; even such as were characterized by a rudeness that would naturally have annoyed his fastidious senses. He loved the old rumbling and jolting carts, the former track of which he still found in his long-buried remembrance, as the observer of to-day finds the wheel-tracks of ancient vehicles in Herculaneum. The butcher's cart, with its snowy canopy, was an acceptable object; so was the fish-cart, heralded by its horn; so, likewise, was the countryman's cart of vegetables, plodding from door to door, with long pauses of the patient horse, while his owner drove a trade in turnips, carrots, summer-squashes, string-beans, green peas, and new potatoes, with half the housewives of the neighborhood. The baker's cart, with the harsh

music of its bells, had a pleasant effect on Clifford, because, as few things else did, it jingled the very dissonance of yore. One afternoon a scissor - grinder
chanced to set his wheel a-going under the Pyncheon
Elm, and just in front of the arched window. Children
came running with their mothers' scissors, or the carv-
ing-knife, or the paternal razor, or anything else that
lacked an edge (except, indeed, poor Clifford's wits),
that the grinder might apply the article to his magic
wheel, and give it back as good as new. Round went
the busily revolving machinery, kept in motion by the
scissor - grinder's foot, and wore away the hard steel
against the hard stone, whence issued an intense and
spiteful prolongation of a hiss as fierce as those emitted
by Satan and his compeers in Pandemonium, though
squeezed into smaller compass. It was an ugly, little,
venomous serpent of a noise, as ever did petty violence
to human ears. But Clifford listened with rapturous
delight. The sound, however disagreeable, had very
brisk life in it, and, together with the circle of curious
children watching the revolutions of the wheel, appeared to give him a more vivid sense of active, bustling, and sunshiny existence than he had attained in
almost any other way. Nevertheless, its charm lay
chiefly in the past; for the scissor-grinder's wheel had
hissed in his childish ears.

He sometimes made doleful complaint that there
were no stage-coaches nowadays. And he asked in an
injured tone what had become of all those old square-
top chaises, with wings sticking out on either side,
that used to be drawn by a plough-horse, and driven
by a farmer's wife and daughter, peddling whortle-
berries and blackberries about the town. Their disappearance made him doubt, he said, whether the ber-

ries had not left off growing in the broad pastures and along the shady country lanes.

But anything that appealed to the sense of beauty, in however humble a way, did not require to be recommended by these old associations. This was observable when one of those Italian boys (who are rather a modern feature of our streets) came along with his barrel-organ, and stopped under the wide and cool shadows of the elm. With his quick professional eye he took note of the two faces watching him from the arched window, and, opening his instrument, began to scatter its melodies abroad. He had a monkey on his shoulder, dressed in a Highland plaid; and, to complete the sum of splendid attractions wherewith he presented himself to the public, there was a company of little figures, whose sphere and habitation was in the mahogany case of his organ, and whose principle of life was the music which the Italian made it his business to grind out. In all their variety of occupation,—the cobbler, the blacksmith, the soldier, the lady with her fan, the toper with his bottle, the milkmaid sitting by her cow,—this fortunate little society might truly be said to enjoy a harmonious existence, and to make life literally a dance. The Italian turned a crank; and, behold! every one of these small individuals started into the most curious vivacity. The cobbler wrought upon a shoe; the blacksmith hammered his iron; the soldier waved his glittering blade; the lady raised a tiny breeze with her fan; the jolly toper swigged lustily at his bottle; a scholar opened his book with eager thirst for knowledge, and turned his head to and fro along the page; the milkmaid energetically drained her cow; and a miser counted gold into his strong-box,—all at the same turning of a crank. Yes; and, moved by the self-same impulse, a lover saluted his mistress on her lips! Possibly some cynic, at once merry and bitter, had desired to signify, in this pantomimic scene, that we mortals, whatever our business or amusement, — however serious, however trifling, — all dance to one identical tune, and, in spite of our ridiculous activity, bring nothing finally to pass. For the most remarkable aspect of the affair was, that, at the cessation of the music, everybody was petrified, at once, from the most extravagant life into a dead torpor. Neither was the cobbler's shoe finished, nor the blacksmith's iron shaped out; nor was there a drop less of brandy in the toper's bottle, nor a drop more of milk in the milkmaid's pail, nor one additional coin in the miser's strong-box, nor was the scholar a page deeper in his book. All were precisely in the same condition as before they made themselves so ridiculous by their haste to toil, to enjoy, to accumulate gold, and to become wise. Saddest of all, moreover, the lover was none the happier for the maiden's granted kiss! But, rather than swallow this last too acrid ingredient, we reject the whole moral of the show.

The monkey, meanwhile, with a thick tail curling out into preposterous prolixity from beneath his tartans, took his station at the Italian's feet. He turned a wrinkled and abominable little visage to every passer-by, and to the circle of children that soon gathered round, and to Hepzibah's shop-door, and upward to the arched window, whence Phœbe and Clifford were looking down. Every moment, also, he took off his Highland bonnet, and performed a bow and scrape. Sometimes, moreover, he made personal application to individuals, holding out his small black palm, and otherwise plainly signifying his excessive desire for whatever filthy lucre might happen to be in anybody's pocket. The mean and low, yet strangely man-like expression of his wilted countenance; the prying and crafty glance, that showed him ready to gripe at every miserable advantage; his enormous tail (too enormous to be decently concealed under his gabardine), and the deviltry of nature which it betokened, — take this monkey just as he was, in short, and you could desire no better image of the Mammon of copper coin, symbolizing the grossest form of the love of money. Neither was there any possibility of satisfying the covetous little devil. Phœbe threw down a whole handful of cents, which he picked up with joyless eagerness, handed them over to the Italian for safe-keeping, and immediately recommenced a series of pantomimic petitions for more.

Doubtless, more than one New-Englander — or, let him be of what country he might, it is as likely to be the case — passed by, and threw a look at the monkey, and went on, without imagining how nearly his own moral condition was here exemplified. Clifford, however, was a being of another order. He had taken childish delight in the music, and smiled, too, at the figures which it set in motion. But, after looking a while at the long-tailed imp, he was so shocked by his horrible ugliness, spiritual as well as physical, that he actually began to shed tears; a weakness which men of merely delicate endowments, and destitute of the fiercer, deeper, and more tragic power of laughter, can hardly avoid, when the worst and meanest aspect of life happens to be presented to them.

Pyncheon Street was sometimes enlivened by spectacles of more imposing pretensions than the above, and which brought the multitude along with them. With a shivering repugnance at the idea of personal contact with the world, a powerful impulse still seized on Clifford, whenever the rush and roar of the human tide grew strongly audible to him. This was made evident, one day, when a political procession, with hundreds of flaunting banners, and drums, fifes, clarions, and cymbals, reverberating between the rows of buildings, marched all through town, and trailed its length of trampling footsteps, and most infrequent uproar, past the ordinarily quiet House of the Seven Gables. As a mere object of sight, nothing is more deficient in picturesque features than a procession seen in its passage through narrow streets. The spectator feels it to be fool's play, when he can distinguish the tedious commonplace of each man's visage, with the perspiration and weary self-importance on it, and the very cut of his pantaloons, and the stiffness or laxity of his shirt-collar, and the dust on the back of his black coat. In order to become majestic, it should be viewed from some vantage point, as it rolls its slow and long array through the centre of a wide plain, or the stateliest public square of a city; for then, by its remoteness, it melts all the petty personalities, of which it is made up, into one broad mass of existence, — one great life, — one collected body of mankind, with a vast, homogeneous spirit animating it. But, on the other hand, if an impressible person, standing alone over the brink of one of these processions, should behold it, not in its atoms, but in its aggregate, — as a mighty river of life, massive in its tide, and black with mystery, and, out of its depths, calling to the kindred depth within him, — then the contiguity would add to the effect. It might so fascinate him that he would hardly be restrained from plunging into the surging stream of human sympathies.

So it proved with Clifford. He shuddered; he grew pale; he threw an appealing look at Hepzibah and Phœbe, who were with him at the window. They comprehended nothing of his emotions, and supposed him merely disturbed by the unaccustomed tumult. At last, with tremulous limbs, he started up, set his foot on the window-sill, and in an instant more would have been in the unguarded balcony. As it was, the whole procession might have seen him, a wild, haggard figure, his gray locks floating in the wind that waved their banners; a lonely being, estranged from his race, but now feeling himself man again, by virtue of the irrepressible instinct that possessed him. Had Clifford attained the balcony, he would probably have leaped into the street; but whether impelled by the species of terror that sometimes urges its victim over the very precipice which he shrinks from, or by a natural magnetism, tending towards the great centre of humanity, it were not easy to decide. Both impulses might have wrought on him at once.

But his companions, affrighted by his gesture, — which was that of a man hurried away in spite of himself, — seized Clifford's garment and held him back. Hepzibah shrieked. Phœbe, to whom all extravagance was a horror, burst into sobs and tears.

"Clifford, Clifford! are you crazy?" cried his sister.

"I hardly know, Hepzibah," said Clifford, drawing a long breath. "Fear nothing, — it is over now, — but had I taken that plunge, and survived it, methinks it would have made me another man!"

Possibly, in some sense, Clifford may have been

right. He needed a shock; or perhaps he required to take a deep, deep plunge into the ocean of human life, and to sink down and be covered by its profoundness, and then to emerge, sobered, invigorated, restored to the world and to himself. Perhaps, again, he required nothing less than the great final remedy — death!

A similar yearning to renew the broken links of brotherhood with his kind sometimes showed itself in a milder form; and once it was made beautiful by the religion that lay even deeper than itself. In the incident now to be sketched, there was a touching recognition, on Clifford's part, of God's care and love towards him, — towards this poor, forsaken man, who, if any mortal could, might have been pardoned for regarding himself as thrown aside, forgotten, and left to be the sport of some fiend, whose playfulness was an ecstasy of mischief.

It was the Sabbath morning; one of those bright, calm Sabbaths, with its own hallowed atmosphere, when Heaven seems to diffuse itself over the earth's face in a solemn smile, no less sweet than solemn. On such a Sabbath morn, were we pure enough to be its medium, we should be conscious of the earth's natural worship ascending through our frames, on whatever spot of ground we stood. The church-bells, with various tones, but all in harmony, were calling out, and responding to one another, — "It is the Sabbath! —The Sabbath! — Yea; the Sabbath!" — and over the whole city the bells scattered the blessed sounds, now slowly, now with livelier joy, now one bell alone, now all the bells together, crying earnestly, — "It is the Sabbath!" and flinging their accents afar off, to melt into the air, and pervade it with the holy word. The air, with God's sweetest and tenderest sunshine in it, was meet for mankind to breathe into their hearts, and send it forth again as the utterance of prayer.

Clifford sat at the window with Hepzibah, watching the neighbors as they stepped into the street. All of them, however unspiritual on other days, were transfigured by the Sabbath influence ; so that their very garments — whether it were an old man's decent coat well brushed for the thousandth time, or a little boy's first sack and trousers finished yesterday by his mother's needle — had somewhat of the quality of ascension-robes. Forth, likewise, from the portal of the old house, stepped Phœbe, putting up her small green sunshade, and throwing upward a glance and smile of parting kindness to the faces at the arched window. In her aspect there was a familiar gladness, and a holiness that you could play with, and yet reverence it as much as ever. She was like a prayer, offered up in the homeliest beauty of one's mother-tongue. Fresh was Phœbe, moreover, and airy and sweet in her apparel ; as if nothing that she wore — neither her gown, nor her small straw bonnet, nor her little kerchief, any more than her snowy stockings — had ever been put on before ; or, if worn, were all the fresher for it, and with a fragrance as if they had lain among the rose-buds.

The girl waved her hand to Hepzibah and Clifford, and went up the street ; a religion in herself, warm, simple, true, with a substance that could walk on earth, and a spirit that was capable of heaven.

" Hepzibah," asked Clifford, after watching Phœbe to the corner, " do you never go to church ? "

" No, Clifford ! " she replied, — " not these many, many years ! "

" Were I to be there," he rejoined, " it seems to me that I could pray once more, when so many human souls were praying all around me! "

She looked into Clifford's face, and beheld there a soft natural effusion; for his heart gushed out, as it were, and ran over at his eyes, in delightful reverence for God, and kindly affection for his human brethren. The emotion communicated itself to Hepzibah. She yearned to take him by the hand, and go and kneel down, they two together, — both so long separate from the world, and, as she now recognized, scarcely friends with Him above, — to kneel down among the people, and be reconciled to God and man at once.

" Dear brother," said she, earnestly, " let us go! We belong nowhere. We have not a foot of space in any church to kneel upon; but let us go to some place of worship, even if we stand in the broad aisle. Poor and forsaken as we are, some pew-door will be opened to us! "

So Hepzibah and her brother made themselves ready, — as ready as they could in the best of their old-fashioned garments, which had hung on pegs, or been laid away in trunks, so long that the dampness and mouldy smell of the past was on them, — made themselves ready, in their faded bettermost, to go to church. They descended the staircase together, — gaunt, sallow Hepzibah, and pale, emaciated, age-stricken Clifford! They pulled open the front door, and stepped across the threshold, and felt, both of them, as if they were standing in the presence of the whole world, and with mankind's great and terrible eye on them alone. The eye of their Father seemed to be withdrawn, and gave them no encouragement. The warm sunny air of the street made them shiver

Their hearts quaked within them at the idea of taking one step farther.

"It cannot be, Hepzibah!—it is too late," said Clifford, with deep sadness. "We are ghosts! We have no right among human beings,—no right any-where but in this old house, which has a curse on it, and which, therefore, we are doomed to haunt! And, besides," he continued, with a fastidious sensibility, inalienably characteristic of the man, "it would not be fit nor beautiful to go! It is an ugly thought that I should be frightful to my fellow-beings, and that children would cling to their mothers' gowns at sight of me!"

They shrank back into the dusky passage-way, and closed the door. But, going up the staircase again, they found the whole interior of the house tenfold more dismal, and the air closer and heavier, for the glimpse and breath of freedom which they had just snatched. They could not flee; their jailer had but left the door ajar in mockery, and stood behind it to watch them stealing out. At the threshold, they felt his pitiless gripe upon them. For, what other dungeon is so dark as one's own heart! What jailer so inexorable as one's self!

But it would be no fair picture of Clifford's state of mind were we to represent him as continually or prevailingly wretched. On the contrary, there was no other man in the city, we are bold to affirm, of so much as half his years, who enjoyed so many lightsome and griefless moments as himself. He had no burden of care upon him; there were none of those questions and contingencies with the future to be settled which wear away all other lives, and render them not worth having by the very process of providing for their support. In

this respect he was a child, — a child for the whole
term of his existence, be it long or short.   Indeed, his
life seemed to be standing still at a period little in advance of childhood, and to cluster all his reminiscences
about that epoch ; just as, after the torpor of a heavy
blow, the sufferer's reviving consciousness goes back to
a moment considerably behind the accident that stupefied him.   He sometimes told Phœbe and Hepzibah
his dreams, in which he invariably played the part of
a child, or a very young man.   So vivid were they, in
his relation of them, that he once held a dispute with
his sister as to the particular figure or print of a chintz
morning-dress, which he had seen their mother wear,
in the dream of the preceding night.   Hepzibah, piqu-
ing herself on a woman's accuracy in such matters,
held it to be slightly different from what Clifford described ; but, producing the very gown from an old
trunk, it proved to be identical with his remembrance
of it.   Had Clifford, every time that he emerged out
of dreams so lifelike, undergone the torture of transformation from a boy into an old and broken man, the
daily recurrence of the shock would have been too
much to bear.   It would have caused an acute agony
to thrill from the morning twilight, all the day through,
until bedtime ; and even then would have mingled a
dull, inscrutable pain, and pallid hue of misfortune,
with the visionary bloom and adolescence of his slumber.   But the nightly moonshine interwove itself with
the morning mist, and enveloped him as in a robe,
which he hugged about his person, and seldom let realities pierce through ; he was not often quite awake,
but slept open-eyed, and perhaps fancied himself most
dreaming then.

Thus, lingering always so near his childhood, he

had sympathies with children, and kept his heart the fresher thereby, like a reservoir into which rivulets were pouring not far from the fountain-head. Though prevented, by a subtile sense of propriety, from desiring to associate with them, he loved few things better than to look out of the arched window, and see a little girl driving her hoop along the sidewalk, or schoolboys at a game of ball. Their voices, also, were very pleasant to him, heard at a distance, all swarming and intermingling together as flies do in a sunny room.

Clifford would, doubtless, have been glad to share their sports. One afternoon he was seized with an irresistible desire to blow soap-bubbles; an amusement, as Hepzibah told Phœbe apart, that had been a favorite one with her brother when they were both children. Behold him, therefore, at the arched window, with an earthen pipe in his mouth! Behold him, with his gray hair, and a wan, unreal smile over his countenance, where still hovered a beautiful grace, which his worst enemy must have acknowledged to be spiritual and immortal, since it had survived so long! Behold him, scattering airy spheres abroad, from the window into the street! Little impalpable worlds were those soap-bubbles, with the big world depicted, in hues bright as imagination, on the nothing of their surface. It was curious to see how the passers-by regarded these brilliant fantasies, as they came floating down, and made the dull atmosphere imaginative about them. Some stopped to gaze, and, perhaps, carried a pleasant recollection of the bubbles onward as far as the street-corner; some looked angrily upward, as if poor Clifford wronged them by setting an image of beauty afloat so near their dusty pathway. A great many put out their fingers or their walking-sticks to touch, withal;

and were perversely gratified, no doubt, when the bubble, with all its pictured earth and sky scene, vanished as if it had never been.

At length, just as an elderly gentleman of very dignified presence happened to be passing, a large bubble sailed majestically down, and burst right against his nose! He looked up, — at first with a stern, keen glance, which penetrated at once into the obscurity behind the arched window, — then with a smile which might be conceived as diffusing a dog-day sultriness for the space of several yards about him.

"Aha, Cousin Clifford!" cried Judge Pyncheon. "What! still blowing soap-bubbles!"

The tone seemed as if meant to be kind and soothing, but yet had a bitterness of sarcasm in it. As for Clifford, an absolute palsy of fear came over him. Apart from any definite cause of dread which his past experience might have given him, he felt that native and original horror of the excellent Judge which is proper to a weak, delicate, and apprehensive character in the presence of massive strength. Strength is incomprehensible by weakness, and, therefore, the more terrible. There is no greater bugbear than a strong-willed relative in the circle of his own connections.

XII

THE DAGUERREOTYPIST.

IT must not be supposed that the life of a personage naturally so active as Phœbe could be wholly confined within the precincts of the old Pyncheon House. Clifford's demands upon her time were usually satisfied, in those long days, considerably earlier than sunset. Quiet as his daily existence seemed, it nevertheless drained all the resources by which he lived. It was not physical exercise that overwearied him, — for except that he sometimes wrought a little with a hoe, or paced the garden-walk, or, in rainy weather, traversed a large unoccupied room, — it was his tendency to remain only too quiescent, as regarded any toil of the limbs and muscles. But, either there was a smouldering fire within him that consumed his vital energy, or the monotony that would have dragged itself with benumbing effect over a mind differently situated was no monotony to Clifford. Possibly, he was in a state of second growth and recovery, and was constantly assimilating nutriment for his spirit and intellect from sights, sounds, and events, which passed as a perfect void to persons more practised with the world. As all is activity and vicissitude to the new mind of a child, so might it be, likewise, to a mind that had undergone a kind of new creation, after its long-suspended life.

Be the cause what it might, Clifford commonly retired to rest, thoroughly exhausted, while the sunbeams were still melting through his window-curtains, or were thrown with late lustre on the chamber wall. And while he thus slept early, as other children do, and dreamed of childhood, Phœbe was free to follow her own tastes for the remainder of the day and evening.

This was a freedom essential to the health even of a character so little susceptible of morbid influences as that of Phœbe. The old house, as we have already said, had both the dry-rot and the damp-rot in its walls; it was not good to breathe no other atmosphere than that. Hepzibah, though she had her valuable and redeeming traits, had grown to be a kind of lunatic, by imprisoning herself so long in one place, with no other company than a single series of ideas, and but one affection, and one bitter sense of wrong. Clifford, the reader may perhaps imagine, was too inert to operate morally on his fellow-creatures, however intimate and exclusive their relations with him. But the sympathy or magnetism among human beings is more subtile and universal than we think; it exists, indeed, among different classes of organized life, and vibrates from one to another. A flower, for instance, as Phœbe herself observed, always began to droop sooner in Clifford's hand, or Hepzibah's, than in her own; and by the same law, converting her whole daily life into a flower-fragrance for these two sickly spirits, the blooming girl must inevitably droop and fade much sooner than if worn on a younger and happier breast. Unless she had now and then indulged her brisk impulses, and breathed rural air in a suburban walk, or ocean breezes along the shore, — had occasionally obeyed the impulse of Nature, in New England girls, by attending a metaphysical or philosophical lecture, or viewing a seven-mile panorama, or listening to a concert, — had gone shopping about the city, ransacking entire depots of splendid merchandise, and bringing home a ribbon, — had employed, likewise, a little time to read the Bible in her chamber, and had stolen a little more to think of her mother and her native place, — unless for such moral medicines as the above, we should soon have beheld our poor Phœbe grow thin and put on a bleached unwholesome aspect, and assume strange, shy ways, prophetic of old-maidenhood and a cheerless future.

Even as it was, a change grew visible; a change partly to be regretted, although whatever charm it infringed upon was repaired by another, perhaps more precious. She was not so constantly gay, but had her moods of thought, which Clifford, on the whole, liked better than her former phase of unmingled cheerfulness; because now she understood him better and more delicately, and sometimes even interpreted him to himself. Her eyes looked larger, and darker, and deeper; so deep, at some silent moments, that they seemed like Artesian wells, down, down, into the infinite. She was less girlish than when we first beheld her alighting from the omnibus; less girlish, but more a woman.

The only youthful mind with which Phœbe had an opportunity of frequent intercourse was that of the daguerreotypist. Inevitably, by the pressure of the seclusion about them, they had been brought into habits of some familiarity. Had they met under different circumstances, neither of these young persons would have been likely to bestow much thought upon the other, unless, indeed, their extreme dissimilarity should have proved a principle of mutual attraction. Both, it is true, were characters proper to New England life and possessing a common ground, therefore, in their more external developments; but as unlike, in their respective interiors, as if their native climes had been at world-wide distance. During the early part of their acquaintance, Phœbe had held back rather more than was customary with her frank and simple manners from Holgrave's not very marked advances. Nor was she yet satisfied that she knew him well, although they almost daily met and talked together, in a kind, friendly, and what seemed to be a familiar way.

The artist, in a desultory manner, had imparted to Phœbe something of his history. Young as he was, and had his career terminated at the point already attained, there had been enough of incident to fill, very creditably, an autobiographic volume. A romance on the plan of Gil Blas, adapted to American society and manners, would cease to be a romance. The experience of many individuals among us, who think it hardly worth the telling, would equal the vicissitudes of the Spaniard's earlier life; while their ultimate success, or the point whither they tend, may be incomparably higher than any that a novelist would imagine for his hero. Holgrave, as he told Phœbe, somewhat proudly, could not boast of his origin, unless as being exceedingly humble, nor of his education, except that it had been the scantiest possible, and obtained by a few winter-months' attendance at a district school. Left early to his own guidance, he had begun to be self-dependent while yet a boy; and it was a condition aptly suited to his natural force of will. Though now but twenty-two years old (lacking some months, which are years in such a life), he had already been, first, a country schoolmaster; next, a salesman in a country store; and, either at the same time or afterwards, the political editor of a country newspaper. He had subsequently travelled New England and the Middle States, as a pedlar, in the employment of a Connecticut manufactory of cologne-water and other essences. In an episodical way he had studied and practised dentistry, and with very flattering success, especially in many of the factory-towns along our inland streams. As a supernumerary official, of some kind or other, aboard a packet-ship, he had visited Europe, and found means, before his return, to see Italy, and part of France and Germany. At a later period he had spent some months in a community of Fourierists. Still more recently he had been a public lecturer on Mesmerism, for which science (as he assured Phœbe, and, indeed, satisfactorily proved, by putting Chanticleer, who happened to be scratching near by, to sleep) he had very remarkable endowments.

His present phase, as a daguerreotypist, was of no more importance in his own view, nor likely to be more permanent, than any of the preceding ones. It had been taken up with the careless alacrity of an adventurer, who had his bread to earn. It would be thrown aside as carelessly, whenever he should choose to earn his bread by some other equally digressive means. But what was most remarkable, and, perhaps, showed a more than common poise in the young man, was the fact that, amid all these personal vicissitudes, he had never lost his identity. Homeless as he had been, — continually changing his whereabout, and, therefore, responsible neither to public opinion nor to individuals, — putting off one exterior, and snatching up another, to be soon shifted for a third, — he had never violated the innermost man, but had carried his conscience along with him. It was impossible to know Holgrave without recognizing this to be the fact. Hepzibah had seen it. Phœbe soon saw it, likewise, and gave him the sort of confidence which such a certainty inspires. She was startled, however, and sometimes repelled, — not by any doubt of his integrity to whatever law he acknowledged, but by a sense that his law differed from her own. He made her uneasy, and seemed to unsettle everything around her, by his lack of reverence for what was fixed, unless, at a moment's warning, it could establish its right to hold its ground.

Then, moreover, she scarcely thought him affectionate in his nature. He was too calm and cool an observer. Phœbe felt his eye, often; his heart, seldom or never. He took a certain kind of interest in Hepzibah and her brother, and Phœbe herself. He studied them attentively, and allowed no slightest circumstance of their individualities to escape him. He was ready to do them whatever good he might; but, after all, he never exactly made common cause with them, nor gave any reliable evidence that he loved them better in proportion as he knew them more. In his relations with them, he seemed to be in quest of mental food, not heart-sustenance. Phœbe could not conceive what interested him so much in her friends and herself, intellectually, since he cared nothing for them, or, comparatively, so little, as objects of human affection.

Always, in his interviews with Phœbe, the artist made especial inquiry as to the welfare of Clifford, whom, except at the Sunday festival, he seldom saw.

"Does he still seem happy?" he asked one day.

"As happy as a child," answered Phœbe; "but like a child, too — very easily disturbed."

"How disturbed?" inquired Holgrave. "By things without, or by thoughts within?"

"I cannot see his thoughts! How should I?" replied Phœbe, with simple piquancy. "Very often his humor changes without any reason that can be guessed at, just as a cloud comes over the sun. Latterly, since I have begun to know him better, I feel it to be not quite right to look closely into his moods. He has had such a great sorrow, that his heart is made all solemn and sacred by it. When he is cheerful, — when the sun shines into his mind, — then I venture to peep in, just as far as the light reaches, but no further. It is holy ground where the shadow falls!"

"How prettily you express this sentiment!" said the artist. "I can understand the feeling, without possessing it. Had I your opportunities, no scruples would prevent me from fathoming Clifford to the full depth of my plummet-line!"

"How strange that you should wish it!" remarked Phœbe, involuntarily. "What is Cousin Clifford to you?"

"Oh, nothing, — of course, nothing!" answered Holgrave, with a smile. "Only this is such an odd and incomprehensible world! The more I look at it the more it puzzles me, and I begin to suspect that a man's bewilderment is the measure of his wisdom. Men and women, and children, too, are such strange creatures, that one never can be certain that he really knows them; nor ever guess what they have been, from what he sees them to be now. Judge Pyncheon! Clifford! What a complex riddle — a complexity of complexities — do they present! It requires intuitive sympathy, like a young girl's, to solve it. A mere observer, like myself (who never have any intuitions, and am, at best, only subtile and acute), is pretty certain to go astray."

The artist now turned the conversation to themes less dark than that which they had touched upon. Phœbe and he were young together; nor had Holgrave, in his premature experience of life, wasted entirely that beautiful spirit of youth, which, gushing forth from one small heart and fancy, may diffuse itself over the universe, making it all as bright as on the first day of creation. Man's own youth is the world's youth; at least, he feels as if it were, and imagines that the earth's granite substance is something not yet hardened, and which he can mould into whatever shape he likes. So it was with Holgrave. He could talk sagely about the world's old age, but never actually believed what he said; he was a young man still, and therefore looked upon the world — that gray-bearded and wrinkled profligate, decrepit, without being venerable — as a tender stripling, capable of being improved into all that it ought to be, but scarcely yet had shown the remotest promise of becoming. He had that sense, or inward prophecy, — which a young man had better never have been born than not to have, and a mature man had better die at once than utterly to relinquish, — that we are not doomed to creep on forever in the old bad way, but that, this very now, there are the harbingers abroad of a golden era, to be accomplished in his own lifetime. It seemed to Holgrave — as doubtless it has seemed to the hopeful of every century since the epoch of Adam's grandchildren — that in this age, more than ever before, the moss-grown and rotten Past is to be torn down, and lifeless institutions to be thrust out of the way, and their dead corpses buried, and everything to begin anew.

As to the main point, — may we never live to doubt it! — as to the better centuries that are coming, the artist was surely right. His error lay in supposing that this age, more than any past or future one, is destined to see the tattered garments of Antiquity exchanged for a new suit, instead of gradually renewing themselves by patchwork; in applying his own little life-span as the measure of an interminable achievement; and, more than all, in fancying that it mattered anything to the great end in view whether he himself should contend for it or against it. Yet it was well for him to think so. This enthusiasm, infusing itself through the calmness of his character, and thus taking an aspect of settled thought and wisdom, would serve to keep his youth pure, and make his aspirations high. And when, with the years settling down more weightily upon him, his early faith should be modified by inevitable experience, it would be with no harsh and sudden revolution of his sentiments. He would still have faith in man's brightening destiny, and perhaps love him all the better, as he should recognize his helplessness in his own behalf; and the haughty faith, with which he began life, would be well bartered for a far humbler one at its close, in discerning that man's best directed effort accomplishes a kind of dream, while God is the sole worker of realities.

Holgrave had read very little, and that little in passing through the thoroughfare of life, where the mystic language of his books was necessarily mixed up with the babble of the multitude, so that both one and the other were apt to lose any sense that might have been properly their own. He considered himself a thinker, and was certainly of a thoughtful turn, but, with his own path to discover, had perhaps hardly yet reached the point where an educated man begins to think. The true value of his character lay in that deep consciousness of inward strength, which made all his past vicissitudes seem merely like a change of garments; in that enthusiasm, so quiet that he scarcely knew of its existence, but which gave a warmth to everything that he laid his hand on; in that personal ambition, hidden — from his own as well as other eyes — among his more generous impulses, but in which lurked a certain efficacy, that might solidify him from a theorist into the champion of some practicable cause. Altogether in his culture and want of culture, — in his crude, wild, and misty philosophy, and the practical experience that counteracted some of its tendencies; in his magnanimous zeal for man's welfare, and his recklessness of whatever the ages had established in man's behalf; in his faith, and in his infidelity; in what he had, and in what he lacked, — the artist might fitly enough stand forth as the representative of many compeers in his native land.

His career it would be difficult to prefigure. There appeared to be qualities in Holgrave, such as, in a country where everything is free to the hand that can grasp it, could hardly fail to put some of the world's prizes within his reach. But these matters are delightfully uncertain. At almost every step in life, we meet with young men of just about Holgrave's age, for whom we anticipate wonderful things, but of whom, even after much and careful inquiry, we never happen to hear another word. The effervescence of youth and passion, and the fresh gloss of the intellect and imagination, endow them with a false brilliancy, which makes fools of themselves and other people.   Like certain chintzes, calicoes, and ginghams, they show finely in their first newness, but cannot stand the sun and rain, and assume a very sober aspect after washing-day.

But our business is with Holgrave as we find him on this particular afternoon, and in the arbor of the Pyncheon garden.   In that point of view, it was a pleasant sight to behold this young man, with so much faith in himself, and so fair an appearance of admirable powers, — so little harmed, too, by the many tests that had tried his metal, — it was pleasant to see him in his kindly intercourse with Phœbe.   Her thought had scarcely done him justice when it pronounced him cold; or, if so, he had grown warmer now.   Without such purpose on her part, and unconsciously on his, she made the House of the Seven Gables like a home to him, and the garden a familiar precinct. With the insight on which he prided himself, he fancied that he could look through Phœbe, and all around her, and could read her off like a page of a child's story-book.   But these transparent natures are often deceptive in their depth; those pebbles at the bottom of the fountain are farther from us than we think. Thus the artist, whatever he might judge of Phœbe's capacity, was beguiled, by some silent charm of hers, to talk freely of what he dreamed of doing in the world.   He poured himself out as to another self. Very possibly, he forgot Phœbe while he talked to her, and was moved only by the inevitable tendency of thought, when rendered sympathetic by enthusiasm and emotion, to flow into the first safe reservoir which it finds.   But, had you peeped at them through the chinks of the garden-fence, the young man's earnest ness and heightened color might have led you to suppose that he was making love to the young girl!

At length, something was said by Holgrave that made it apposite for Phœbe to inquire what had first brought him acquainted with her cousin Hepzibah, and why he now chose to lodge in the desolate old Pyncheon House. Without directly answering her, he turned from the Future, which had heretofore been the theme of his discourse, and began to speak of the influences of the Past. One subject, indeed, is but the reverberation of the other.

" Shall we never, never get rid of this Past ? " cried he, keeping up the earnest tone of his preceding conversation. " It lies upon the Present like a giant's dead body! In fact, the case is just as if a young giant were compelled to waste all his strength in carrying about the corpse of the old giant, his grandfather, who died a long while ago, and only needs to be decently buried. Just think a moment, and it will startle you to see what slaves we are to bygone times, — to Death, if we give the matter the right word ! "

" But I do not see it," observed Phœbe.

" For example, then," continued Holgrave : "a dead man, if he happen to have made a will, disposes of wealth no longer his own ; or, if he die intestate, it is distributed in accordance with the notions of men much longer dead than he. A dead man sits on all our judgment-seats ; and living judges do but search out and repeat his decisions. We read in dead men's books! We laugh at dead men's jokes, and cry at dead men's pathos! We are sick of dead men's diseases, physical and moral, and die of the same remedies with which dead doctors killed their patients! We worship the living Deity according to dead men's forms and creeds. Whatever we seek to do, of our own free motion, a dead man's icy hand obstructs us! Turn our eyes to what point we may, a dead man's white, immitigable face encounters them, and freezes our very heart! And we must be dead ourselves before we can begin to have our proper influence on our own world, which will then be no longer our world, but the world of another generation, with which we shall have no shadow of a right to interfere. I ought to have said, too, that we live in dead men's houses; as, for instance, in this of the Seven Gables!"

"And why not," said Phœbe, "so long as we can be comfortable in them?"

"But we shall live to see the day, I trust," went on the artist, "when no man shall build his house for posterity. Why should he? He might just as reasonably order a durable suit of clothes, — leather, or gutta-percha, or whatever else lasts longest, — so that his great-grandchildren should have the benefit of them, and cut precisely the same figure in the world that he himself does. If each generation were allowed and expected to build its own houses, that single change, comparatively unimportant in itself, would imply almost every reform which society is now suffering for. I doubt whether even our public edifices — our capitols, state-houses, court-houses, city-hall, and churches — ought to be built of such permanent materials as stone or brick. It were better that they should crumble to ruin once in twenty years, or thereabouts, as a hint to the people to examine into and reform the institutions which they symbolize."

"How you hate everything old!" said Phœbe, in dismay. "It makes me dizzy to think of such a shifting world!"

"I certainly love nothing mouldy," answered Holgrave. "Now, this old Pyncheon House! Is it a wholesome place to live in, with its black shingles, and the green moss that shows how damp they are? — its dark, low-studded rooms? — its grime and sordidness, which are the crystallization on its walls of the human breath, that has been drawn and exhaled here in discontent and anguish? The house ought to be purified with fire, — purified till only its ashes remain!"

"Then why do you live in it?" asked Phœbe, a little piqued.

"Oh, I am pursuing my studies here; not in books, however," replied Holgrave. "The house, in my view, is expressive of that odious and abominable Past, with all its bad influences, against which I have just been declaiming. I dwell in it for a while, that I may know the better how to hate it. By the by, did you ever hear the story of Maule, the wizard, and what happened between him and your immeasurably great-grandfather?"

"Yes, indeed!" said Phœbe; "I heard it long ago, from my father, and two or three times from my cousin Hepzibah, in the month that I have been here. She seems to think that all the calamities of the Pyncheons began from that quarrel with the wizard, as you call him. And you, Mr. Holgrave, look as if you thought so too! How singular, that you should believe what is so very absurd, when you reject many things that are a great deal worthier of credit!"

"I do believe it," said the artist, seriously; "not as a superstition, however, but as proved by unquestionable facts, and as exemplifying a theory. Now, see: under those seven gables, at which we now look up,

—and which old Colonel Pyncheon meant to be the house of his descendants, in prosperity and happiness, down to an epoch far beyond the present, — under that roof, through a portion of three centuries, there has been perpetual remorse of conscience, a constantly defeated hope, strife amongst kindred, various misery, a strange form of death, dark suspicion, unspeakable disgrace, — all, or most of which calamity I have the means of tracing to the old Puritan's inordinate desire to plant and endow a family. To plant a family! This idea is at the bottom of most of the wrong and mischief which men do. The truth is, that, once in every half-century, at longest, a family should be merged into the great, obscure mass of humanity, and forget all about its ancestors. Human blood, in order to keep its freshness, should run in hidden streams, as the water of an aqueduct is conveyed in subterranean pipes. In the family existence of these Pyncheons, for instance, — forgive me, Phœbe; but I cannot think of you as one of them, — in their brief New England pedigree, there has been time enough to infect them all with one kind of lunacy or another!"

"You speak very unceremoniously of my kindred," said Phœbe, debating with herself whether she ought to take offence.

"I speak true thoughts to a true mind!" answered Holgrave, with a vehemence which Phœbe had not before witnessed in him. "The truth is as I say! Furthermore, the original perpetrator and father of this mischief appears to have perpetuated himself, and still walks the street, — at least, his very image, in mind and body, — with the fairest prospect of transmitting to posterity as rich and as wretched an inheritance as he has received! Do you remember the daguerreotype, and its resemblance to the old portrait?"

"How strangely in earnest you are!" exclaimed Phœbe, looking at him with surprise and perplexity; half alarmed and partly inclined to laugh. "You talk of the lunacy of the Pyncheons; is it contagious?"

"I understand you!" said the artist, coloring and laughing. "I believe I am a little mad. This subject has taken hold of my mind with the strangest tenacity of clutch since I have lodged in yonder old gable. As one method of throwing it off, I have put an incident of the Pyncheon family history, with which I happen to be acquainted, into the form of a legend, and mean to publish it in a magazine."

"Do you write for the magazines?" inquired Phœbe.

"Is it possible you did not know it?" cried Holgrave. "Well, such is literary fame! Yes, Miss Phœbe Pyncheon, among the multitude of my marvellous gifts I have that of writing stories; and my name has figured, I can assure you, on the covers of Graham and Godey, making as respectable an appearance, for aught I could see, as any of the canonized bead-roll with which it was associated. In the humorous line, I am thought to have a very pretty way with me; and as for pathos, I am as provocative of tears as an onion. But shall I read you my story?"

"Yes, if it is not very long," said Phœbe, — and added laughingly, — "nor very dull."

As this latter point was one which the daguerreotypist could not decide for himself, he forthwith produced his roll of manuscript, and, while the late sunbeams gilded the seven gables, began to read.

XIII.

ALICE PYNCHEON.

THERE was a message brought, one day, from the worshipful Gervayse Pyncheon to young Matthew Maule, the carpenter, desiring his immediate presence at the House of the Seven Gables.

"And what does your master want with me?" said the carpenter to Mr. Pyncheon's black servant. "Does the house need any repair? Well it may, by this time; and no blame to my father who built it, neither! I was reading the old Colonel's tombstone, no longer ago than last Sabbath; and, reckoning from that date, the house has stood seven-and-thirty years. No wonder if there should be a job to do on the roof."

"Don't know what massa wants," answered Scipio. "The house is a berry good house, and old Colonel Pyncheon think so too, I reckon;—else why the old man haunt it so, and frighten a poor nigga, as he does?"

"Well, well, friend Scipio; let your master know that I'm coming," said the carpenter, with a laugh. "For a fair, workmanlike job, he'll find me his man. And so the house is haunted, is it? It will take a tighter workman than I am to keep the spirits out of the Seven Gables. Even if the Colonel would be quiet," he added, muttering to himself, "my old grandfather, the wizard, will be pretty sure to stick to the Pyncheons as long as their walls hold together."

"What 's that you mutter to yourself, Matthew Maule?" asked Scipio. "And what for do you look so black at me?"

"No matter, darky!" said the carpenter. "Do you think nobody is to look black but yourself? Go tell your master I 'm coming; and if you happen to see Mistress Alice, his daughter, give Matthew Maule's humble respects to her. She has brought a fair face from Italy, — fair, and gentle, and proud, — has that same Alice Pyncheon!"

"He talk of Mistress Alice!" cried Scipio, as he returned from his errand. "The low carpenter-man! He no business so much as to look at her a great way off!"

This young Matthew Maule, the carpenter, it must be observed, was a person little understood, and not very generally liked, in the town where he resided; not that anything could be alleged against his integrity, or his skill and diligence in the handicraft which he exercised. The aversion (as it might justly be called) with which many persons regarded him was partly the result of his own character and deportment, and partly an inheritance.

He was the grandson of a former Matthew Maule, one of the early settlers of the town, and who had been a famous and terrible wizard in his day. This old reprobate was one of the sufferers when Cotton Mather, and his brother ministers, and the learned judges, and other wise men, and Sir William Phipps, the sagacious governor, made such laudable efforts to weaken the great enemy of souls, by sending a multitude of his adherents up the rocky pathway of Gallows Hill. Since those days, no doubt, it had grown to be suspected that, in consequence of an unfortunate overdoing of a work praiseworthy in itself, the proceedings against the witches had proved far less acceptable to the Beneficent Father than to that very Arch Enemy whom they were intended to distress and utterly overwhelm. It is not the less certain, however, that awe and terror brooded over the memories of those who died for this horrible crime of witchcraft. Their graves, in the crevices of the rocks, were supposed to be incapable of retaining the occupants who had been so hastily thrust into them. Old Matthew Maule, especially, was known to have as little hesitation or difficulty in rising out of his grave as an ordinary man in getting out of bed, and was as often seen at midnight as living people at noonday. This pestilent wizard (in whom his just punishment seemed to have wrought no manner of amendment) had an inveterate habit of haunting a certain mansion, styled the House of the Seven Gables, against the owner of which he pretended to hold an unsettled claim for ground-rent. The ghost, it appears, — with the pertinacity which was one of his distinguishing characteristics while alive, — insisted that he was the rightful proprietor of the site upon which the house stood. His terms were, that either the aforesaid ground-rent, from the day when the cellar began to be dug, should be paid down, or the mansion itself given up; else he, the ghostly creditor, would have his finger in all the affairs of the Pyncheons, and make everything go wrong with them, though it should be a thousand years after his death. It was a wild story, perhaps, but seemed not altogether so incredible to those who could remember what an inflexibly obstinate old fellow this wizard Maule had been.

Now, the wizard's grandson, the young Matthew

Maule of our story, was popularly supposed to have inherited some of his ancestor's questionable traits. It is wonderful how many absurdities were promulgated in reference to the young man. He was fabled, for example, to have a strange power of getting into people's dreams, and regulating matters there according to his own fancy, pretty much like the stage-manager of a theatre. There was a great deal of talk among the neighbors, particularly the petticoated ones, about what they called the witchcraft of Maule's eye. Some said that he could look into people's minds; others, that, by the marvellous power of this eye, he could draw people into his own mind, or send them, if he pleased, to do errands to his grandfather, in the spiritual world; others, again, that it was what is termed an Evil Eye, and possessed the valuable faculty of blighting corn, and drying children into mummies with the heartburn. But, after all, what worked most to the young carpenter's disadvantage was, first, the reserve and sternness of his natural disposition, and next, the fact of his not being a church-communicant, and the suspicion of his holding heretical tenets in matters of religion and polity.

After receiving Mr. Pyncheon's message, the carpenter merely tarried to finish a small job, which he happened to have in hand, and then took his way towards the House of the Seven Gables. This noted edifice, though its style might be getting a little out of fashion, was still as respectable a family residence as that of any gentleman in town. The present owner, Gervayse Pyncheon, was said to have contracted a dislike to the house, in consequence of a shock to his sensibility, in early childhood, from the sudden death of his grandfather. In the very act of running to climb

Colonel Pyncheon's knee, the boy had discovered the old Puritan to be a corpse! On arriving at manhood, Mr. Pyncheon had visited England, where he married a lady of fortune, and had subsequently spent many years, partly in the mother country, and partly in various cities on the continent of Europe. During this period, the family mansion had been consigned to the charge of a kinsman, who was allowed to make it his home for the time being, in consideration of keeping the premises in thorough repair. So faithfully had this contract been fulfilled, that now, as the carpenter approached the house, his practised eye could detect nothing to criticise in its condition. The peaks of the seven gables rose up sharply; the shingled roof looked thoroughly water-tight; and the glittering plaster-work entirely covered the exterior walls, and sparkled in the October sun, as if it had been new only a week ago.

The house had that pleasant aspect of life which is like the cheery expression of comfortable activity in the human countenance. You could see, at once, that there was the stir of a large family within it. A huge load of oak-wood was passing through the gateway, towards the outbuildings in the rear; the fat cook — or probably it might be the housekeeper — stood at the side door, bargaining for some turkeys and poultry, which a countryman had brought for sale. Now and then a maid-servant, neatly dressed, and now the shining sable face of a slave, might be seen bustling across the windows, in the lower part of the house. At an open window of a room in the second story, hanging over some pots of beautiful and delicate flowers, — exotics, but which had never known a more genial sunshine than that of the New England autumn,

— was the figure of a young lady, an exotic, like the flowers, and beautiful and delicate as they. Her presence imparted an indescribable grace and faint witchery to the whole edifice. In other respects, it was a substantial, jolly-looking mansion, and seemed fit to be the residence of a patriarch, who might establish his own headquarters in the front gable and assign one of the remainder to each of his six children, while the great chimney in the centre should symbolize the old fellow's hospitable heart, which kept them all warm, and made a great whole of the seven smaller ones.

There was a vertical sundial on the front gable; and as the carpenter passed beneath it, he looked up and noted the hour.

"Three o'clock!" said he to himself. "My father told me that dial was put up only an hour before the old Colonel's death. How truly it has kept time these seven-and-thirty years past! The shadow creeps and creeps, and is always looking over the shoulder of the sunshine!"

It might have befitted a craftsman, like Matthew Maule, on being sent for to a gentleman's house, to go to the back door, where servants and work-people were usually admitted; or at least to the side entrance, where the better class of tradesmen made application. But the carpenter had a great deal of pride and stiffness in his nature; and, at this moment, moreover, his heart was bitter with the sense of hereditary wrong, because he considered the great Pyncheon House to be standing on soil which should have been his own. On this very site, beside a spring of delicious water, his grandfather had felled the pine-trees and built a cottage, in which children had been born to him; and it was only from a dead man's stiffened fingers that Colonel Pyncheon had wrested away the title-deeds.   So young Maule went straight to the principal entrance, beneath a portal of carved oak, and gave such a peal of the iron knocker that you would have imagined the stern old wizard himself to be standing at the threshold.

Black Scipio answered the summons in a prodigious hurry; but showed the whites of his eyes, in amazement on beholding only the carpenter.

"Lord-a-mercy! what a great man he be, this carpenter fellow!" mumbled Scipio, down in his throat. "Anybody think he beat on the door with his biggest hammer!"

"Here I am!" said Maule, sternly. "Show me the way to your master's parlor!"

As he stept into the house, a note of sweet and melancholy music thrilled and vibrated along the passage-way, proceeding from one of the rooms above stairs. It was the harpsichord which Alice Pyncheon had brought with her from beyond the sea. The fair Alice bestowed most of her maiden leisure between flowers and music, although the former were apt to droop, and the melodies were often sad. She was of foreign education, and could not take kindly to the New England modes of life, in which nothing beautiful had ever been developed.

As Mr. Pyncheon had been impatiently awaiting Maule's arrival, black Scipio, of course, lost no time in ushering the carpenter into his master's presence. The room in which this gentleman sat was a parlor of moderate size, looking out upon the garden of the house, and having its windows partly shadowed by the foliage of fruit-trees. It was Mr. Pyncheon's peculiar apartment, and was provided with furniture, in an elegant and costly style, principally from Paris; the floor (which was unusual at that day) being covered with a carpet, so skilfully and richly wrought that it seemed to glow as with living flowers. In one corner stood a marble woman, to whom her own beauty was the sole and sufficient garment. Some pictures — that looked old, and had a mellow tinge diffused through all their artful splendor — hung on the walls. Near the fireplace was a large and very beautiful cabinet of ebony, inlaid with ivory; a piece of antique furniture, which Mr. Pyncheon had bought in Venice, and which he used as the treasure-place for medals, ancient coins, and whatever small and valuable curiosities he had picked up on his travels. Through all this variety of decoration, however, the room showed its original characteristics; its low stud, its cross-beam, its chimney-piece, with the old-fashioned Dutch tiles; so that it was the emblem of a mind industriously stored with foreign ideas, and elaborated into artificial refinement, but neither larger, nor, in its proper self, more elegant than before.

There were two objects that appeared rather out of place in this very handsomely furnished room. One was a large map, or surveyor's plan, of a tract of land, which looked as if it had been drawn a good many years ago, and was now dingy with smoke, and soiled, here and there, with the touch of fingers. The other was a portrait of a stern old man, in a Puritan garb, painted roughly, but with a bold effect, and a remarkably strong expression of character.

At a small table, before a fire of English sea-coal, sat Mr. Pyncheon, sipping coffee, which had grown to be a very favorite beverage with him in France. He was a middle-aged and really handsome man, with a wig flowing down upon his shoulders; his coat was of blue velvet, with lace on the borders and at the button-holes; and the firelight glistened on the spacious breadth of his waistcoat, which was flowered all over with gold. On the entrance of Scipio, ushering in the carpenter, Mr. Pyncheon turned partly round, but re-sumed his former position, and proceeded deliberately to finish his cup of coffee, without immediate notice of the guest whom he had summoned to his presence. It was not that he intended any rudeness or improper neglect, — which, indeed, he would have blushed to be guilty of, — but it never occurred to him that a person in Maule's station had a claim on his courtesy, or would trouble himself about it one way or the other.

The carpenter, however, stepped at once to the hearth, and turned himself about, so as to look Mr. Pyncheon in the face.

"You sent for me," said he. "Be pleased to ex-plain your business, that I may go back to my own af-fairs."

"Ah! excuse me," said Mr. Pyncheon, quietly. "I did not mean to tax your time without a recompense. Your name, I think, is Maule, — Thomas or Matthew Maule, — a son or grandson of the builder of this house?"

"Matthew Maule," replied the carpenter, — "son of him who built the house, — grandson of the right-ful proprietor of the soil."

"I know the dispute to which you allude," observed Mr. Pyncheon with undisturbed equanimity. "I am well aware that my grandfather was compelled to re-sort to a suit at law, in order to establish his claim to the foundation-site of this edifice. We will not, if you please, renew the discussion. The matter was settled at the time, and by the competent authorities, — equitably, it is to be presumed, — and, at all events, irrevocably. Yet, singularly enough, there is an incidental reference to this very subject in what I am now about to say to you. And this same inveterate grudge, — excuse me, I mean no offence, — this irritability, which you have just shown, is not entirely aside from the matter."

"If you can find anything for your purpose, Mr. Pyncheon," said the carpenter, "in a man's natural resentment for the wrongs done to his blood, you are welcome to it!"

"I take you at your word, Goodman Maule," said the owner of the Seven Gables, with a smile, "and will proceed to suggest a mode in which your hereditary resentments — justifiable, or otherwise — may have had a bearing on my affairs. You have heard, I suppose, that the Pyncheon family, ever since my grandfather's days, have been prosecuting a still unsettled claim to a very large extent of territory at the Eastward?"

"Often," replied Maule, — and it is said that a smile came over his face, — "very often, — from my father!"

"This claim," continued Mr. Pyncheon, after pausing a moment, as if to consider what the carpenter's smile might mean, "appeared to be on the very verge of a settlement and full allowance, at the period of my grandfather's decease. It was well known, to those in his confidence, that he anticipated neither difficulty nor delay. Now, Colonel Pyncheon, I need hardly say, was a practical man, well acquainted with public and private business, and not at all the person to cherish ill-founded hopes, or to attempt the following out of an impracticable scheme. It is obvious to conclude, therefore, that he had grounds, not apparent to his heirs, for his confident anticipation of success in the matter of this Eastern claim. In a word, I believe, — and my legal advisers coincide in the belief, which moreover, is authorized, to a certain extent, by the family traditions, — that my grandfather was in possession of some deed, or other document, essential to this claim, but which has since disappeared."

"Very likely," said Matthew Maule, — and again, it is said, there was a dark smile on his face, — "but what can a poor carpenter have to do with the grand affairs of the Pyncheon family?"

"Perhaps nothing," returned Mr. Pyncheon, — "possibly, much!"

Here ensued a great many words between Matthew Maule and the proprietor of the Seven Gables, on the subject which the latter had thus broached. It seems (although Mr. Pyncheon had some hesitation in referring to stories so exceedingly absurd in their aspect) that the popular belief pointed to some mysterious connection and dependence, existing between the family of the Maules and these vast unrealized possessions of the Pyncheons. It was an ordinary saying that the old wizard, hanged though he was, had obtained the best end of the bargain in his contest with Colonel Pyncheon; inasmuch as he had got possession of the great Eastern claim, in exchange for an acre or two of garden-ground. A very aged woman, recently dead, had often used the metaphorical expression, in her fireside talk, that miles and miles of the Pyncheon lands had been shovelled into Maule's grave; which, by the by, was but a very shallow nook, between two rocks, near the summit of Gallows Hill. Again, when the lawyers were making inquiry for the missing document, it was a by-word that it would never be found, unless in the wizard's skeleton hand. So much weight had the shrewd lawyers assigned to these fables, that (but Mr. Pyncheon did not see fit to inform the carpenter of the fact) they had secretly caused the wizard's grave to be searched. Nothing was discovered, however, except that, unaccountably, the right hand of the skeleton was gone.

Now, what was unquestionably important, a portion of these popular rumors could be traced, though rather doubtfully and indistinctly, to chance words and obscure hints of the executed wizard's son, and the father of this present Matthew Maule. And here Mr. Pyncheon could bring an item of his own personal evidence into play. Though but a child at the time, he either remembered or fancied that Matthew's father had had some job to perform, on the day before, or possibly the very morning of the Colonel's decease, in the private room where he and the carpenter were at this moment talking. Certain papers belonging to Colonel Pyncheon, as his grandson distinctly recollected, had been spread out on the table.

Matthew Maule understood the insinuated suspicion.

"My father," he said, — but still there was that dark smile, making a riddle of his countenance, — "my father was an honester man than the bloody old Colonel! Not to get his rights back again would he have carried off one of those papers!"

"I shall not bandy words with you," observed the foreign-bred Mr. Pyncheon, with haughty composure. "Nor will it become me to resent any rudeness towards either my grandfather or myself. A gentleman,

before seeking intercourse with a person of your station and habits, will first consider whether the urgency
of the end may compensate for the disagreeableness of
the means. It does so in the present instance."

He then renewed the conversation, and made great
pecuniary offers to the carpenter, in case the latter
should give information leading to the discovery of the
lost document, and the consequent success of the
Eastern claim. For a long time Matthew Maule is
said to have turned a cold ear to these propositions.
At last, however, with a strange kind of laugh, he inquired whether Mr. Pyncheon would make over to him
the old wizard's homestead-ground, together with the
House of the Seven Gables, now standing on it, in
requital of the documentary evidence so urgently required.

The wild, chimney-corner legend (which, without
copying all its extravagances, my narrative essentially
follows) here gives an account of some very strange
behavior on the part of Colonel Pyncheon's portrait.
This picture, it must be understood, was supposed to
be so intimately connected with the fate of the house,
and so magically built into its walls, that, if once it
should be removed, that very instant the whole edifice
would come thundering down in a heap of dusty ruin.
All through the foregoing conversation between Mr.
Pyncheon and the carpenter, the portrait had been
frowning, clenching its fist, and giving many such
proofs of excessive discomposure, but without attracting the notice of either of the two colloquists. And
finally, at Matthew Maule's audacious suggestion of a
transfer of the seven-gabled structure, the ghostly portrait is averred to have lost all patience, and to have
shown itself on the point of descending bodily from

its frame. But such incredible incidents are merely to be mentioned aside.

"Give up this house!" exclaimed Mr. Pyncheon, in amazement at the proposal. "Were I to do so, my grandfather would not rest quiet in his grave!"

"He never has, if all stories are true," remarked the carpenter, composedly. "But that matter concerns his grandson more than it does Matthew Maule. I have no other terms to propose."

Impossible as he at first thought it to comply with Maule's conditions, still, on a second glance, Mr. Pyncheon was of opinion that they might at least be made matter of discussion. He himself had no personal attachment for the house, nor any pleasant associations connected with his childish residence in it. On the contrary, after seven-and-thirty years, the presence of his dead grandfather seemed still to pervade it, as on that morning when the affrighted boy had beheld him, with so ghastly an aspect, stiffening in his chair. His long abode in foreign parts, moreover, and familiarity with many of the castles and ancestral halls of England, and the marble palaces of Italy, had caused him to look contemptuously at the House of the Seven Gables, whether in point of splendor or convenience. It was a mansion exceedingly inadequate to the style of living which it would be incumbent on Mr. Pyncheon to support, after realizing his territorial rights. His steward might deign to occupy it, but never, certainly, the great landed proprietor himself. In the event of success, indeed, it was his purpose to return to England; nor, to say the truth, would he recently have quitted that more congenial home, had not his own fortune, as well as his deceased wife's, begun to give symptoms of exhaustion. The Eastern claim once fairly settled, and put upon the firm basis of actual possession, Mr. Pyncheon's property — to be measured by miles, not acres — would be worth an earldom, and would reasonably entitle him to solicit, or enable him to purchase, that elevated dignity from the British monarch. Lord Pyncheon! — or the Earl of Waldo! — how could such a magnate be expected to contract his grandeur within the pitiful compass of seven shingled gables?

In short, on an enlarged view of the business, the carpenter's terms appeared so ridiculously easy that Mr. Pyncheon could scarcely forbear laughing in his face. He was quite ashamed, after the foregoing reflections, to propose any diminution of so moderate a recompense for the immense service to be rendered.

"I consent to your proposition, Maule," cried he. "Put me in possession of the document essential to establish my rights, and the House of the Seven Gables is your own!"

According to some versions of the story, a regular contract to the above effect was drawn up by a lawyer, and signed and sealed in the presence of witnesses. Others say that Matthew Maule was contented with a private written agreement, in which Mr. Pyncheon pledged his honor and integrity to the fulfilment of the terms concluded upon. The gentleman then ordered wine, which he and the carpenter drank together, in confirmation of their bargain. During the whole preceding discussion and subsequent formalities, the old Puritan's portrait seems to have persisted in its shadowy gestures of disapproval; but without effect, except that, as Mr. Pyncheon set down the emptied glass, he thought he beheld his grandfather frown.

" This sherry is too potent a wine for me; it has af-

fected my brain already," he observed, after a somewhat startled look at the picture. "On returning to
Europe, I shall confine myself to the more delicate vintages of Italy and France, the best of which will not
bear transportation."

"My Lord Pyncheon may drink what wine he will,
and wherever he pleases," replied the carpenter, as if
he had been privy to Mr. Pyncheon's ambitious projects. "But first, sir, if you desire tidings of this lost
document, I must crave the favor of a little talk with
your fair daughter Alice."

"You are mad, Maule!" exclaimed Mr. Pyncheon,
haughtily; and now, at last, there was anger mixed
up with his pride. "What can my daughter have to
do with a business like this?"

Indeed, at this new demand on the carpenter's part,
the proprietor of the Seven Gables was even more
thunder-struck than at the cool proposition to surrender his house. There was, at least, an assignable
motive for the first stipulation; there appeared to be
none whatever for the last. Nevertheless, Matthew
Maule sturdily insisted on the young lady being summoned, and even gave her father to understand, in a
mysterious kind of explanation, — which made the
matter considerably darker than it looked before, —
that the only chance of acquiring the requisite knowledge was through the clear, crystal medium of a pure
and virgin intelligence, like that of the fair Alice.
Not to encumber our story with Mr. Pyncheon's scruples, whether of conscience, pride, or fatherly affection, he at length ordered his daughter to be called.
He well knew that she was in her chamber, and engaged in no occupation that could not readily be laid
aside; for, as it happened, ever since Alice's name

had been spoken, both her father and the carpenter had heard the sad and sweet music of her harpsichord, and the airier melancholy of her accompanying voice.

So Alice Pyncheon was summoned and appeared. A portrait of this young lady, painted by a Venetian artist, and left by her father in England, is said to have fallen into the hands of the present Duke of Devonshire, and to be now preserved at Chatsworth; not on account of any associations with the original, but for its value as a picture, and the high character of beauty in the countenance. If ever there was a lady born, and set apart from the world's vulgar mass by a certain gentle and cold stateliness, it was this very Alice Pyncheon. Yet there was the womanly mixture in her; the tenderness, or, at least, the tender capabilities. For the sake of that redeeming quality, a man of generous nature would have forgiven all her pride, and have been content, almost, to lie down in her path, and let Alice set her slender foot upon his heart. All that he would have required was simply the acknowledgment that he was indeed a man, and a fellow-being, moulded of the same elements as she.

As Alice came into the room, her eyes fell upon the carpenter, who was standing near its centre, clad in a green woollen jacket, a pair of loose breeches, open at the knees, and with a long pocket for his rule, the end of which protruded; it was as proper a mark of the artisan's calling, as Mr. Pyncheon's full-dress sword of that gentleman's aristocratic pretensions. A glow of artistic approval brightened over Alice Pyncheon's face; she was struck with admiration — which she made no attempt to conceal — of the remarkable comeiness, strength, and energy of Maule's figure. But that admiring glance (which most other men, perhaps, would have cherished as a sweet recollection, all through life) the carpenter never forgave. It must have been the devil himself that made Maule so subtile in his perception.

"Does the girl look at me as if I were a brute beast?" thought he, setting his teeth. "She shall know whether I have a human spirit; and the worse for her, if it prove stronger than her own!"

"My father, you sent for me," said Alice, in her sweet and harp-like voice. "But, if you have business with this young man, pray let me go again. You know I do not love this room, in spite of that Claude, with which you try to bring back sunny recollections."

"Stay a moment, young lady, if you please!" said Matthew Maule. "My business with your father is over. With yourself, it is now to begin!"

Alice looked towards her father, in surprise and inquiry.

"Yes, Alice," said Mr. Pyncheon, with some disturbance and confusion. "This young man — his name is Matthew Maule — professes, so far as I can understand him, to be able to discover, through your means, a certain paper or parchment, which was missing long before your birth. The importance of the document in question renders it advisable to neglect no possible, even if improbable, method of regaining it. You will therefore oblige me, my dear Alice, by answering this person's inquiries, and complying with his lawful and reasonable requests, so far as they may appear to have the aforesaid object in view. As I shall remain in the room, you need apprehend no rude nor unbecoming deportment, on the young man's part; and, at your slightest wish, of course, the investigation, or whatever we may call it, shall immediately be broken off.

"Mistress Alice Pyncheon," remarked Matthew Maule, with the utmost deference, but yet a half-hidden sarcasm in his look and tone, "will no doubt feel herself quite safe in her father's presence, and under his all-sufficient protection."

"I certainly shall entertain no manner of apprehension, with my father at hand," said Alice, with maidenly dignity. "Neither do I conceive that a lady, while true to herself, can have aught to fear from whomsoever, or in any circumstances!"

Poor Alice! By what unhappy impulse did she thus put herself at once on terms of defiance against a strength which she could not estimate?

"Then, Mistress Alice," said Matthew Maule, handing a chair, — gracefully enough, for a craftsman, — "will it please you only to sit down, and do me the favor (though altogether beyond a poor carpenter's deserts) to fix your eyes on mine!"

Alice complied. She was very proud. Setting aside all advantages of rank, this fair girl deemed herself conscious of a power — combined of beauty, high, unsullied purity, and the preservative force of womanhood — that could make her sphere impenetrable, unless betrayed by treachery within. She instinctively knew, it may be, that some sinister or evil potency was now striving to pass her barriers; nor would she decline the contest. So Alice put woman's might against man's might; a match not often equal on the part of woman.

Her father meanwhile had turned away, and seemed absorbed in the contemplation of a landscape by Claude, where a shadowy and sun-streaked vista penetrated so remotely into an ancient wood, that it would have been no wonder if his fancy had lost itself in the picture's bewildering depths. But, in truth, the picture was no more to him at that moment than the blank wall against which it hung. His mind was haunted with the many and strange tales which he had heard, attributing mysterious if not supernatural endowments to these Maules, as well the grandson here present as his two immediate ancestors. Mr. Pyncheon's long residence abroad, and intercourse with men of wit and fashion, — courtiers, worldlings, and free-thinkers, — had done much towards obliterating the grim Puritan superstitions, which no man of New England birth at that early period could entirely escape. But, on the other hand, had not a whole community believed Maule's grandfather to be a wizard? Had not the crime been proved? Had not the wizard died for it? Had he not bequeathed a legacy of hatred against the Pyncheons to this only grandson, who, as it appeared, was now about to exercise a subtle influence over the daughter of his enemy's house? Might not this influence be the same that was called witchcraft?

Turning half around, he caught a glimpse of Maule's figure in the looking-glass. At some paces from Alice, with his arms uplifted in the air, the carpenter made a gesture as if directing downward a slow, ponderous, and invisible weight upon the maiden.

"Stay, Maule!" exclaimed Mr. Pyncheon, stepping forward. "I forbid your proceeding further!"

"Pray, my dear father, do not interrupt the young man," said Alice, without changing her position. "His efforts, I assure you, will prove very harmless."

Again Mr. Pyncheon turned his eyes towards the Claude. It was then his daughter's will, in opposition to his own, that the experiment should be fully tried. Henceforth, therefore, he did but consent, not urge it. And was it not for her sake far more than for his own that he desired its success? That lost parchment once restored, the beautiful Alice Pyncheon, with the rich dowry which he could then bestow, might wed an English duke or a German reigning-prince, instead of some New England clergyman or lawyer! At the thought, the ambitious father almost consented, in his heart, that, if the devil's power were needed to the accomplishment of this great object, Maule might evoke him. Alice's own purity would be her safeguard.

With his mind full of imaginary magnificence, Mr. Pyncheon heard a half-uttered exclamation from his daughter. It was very faint and low; so indistinct that there seemed but half a will to shape out the words, and too undefined a purport to be intelligible. Yet it was a call for help! — his conscience never doubted it; — and, little more than a whisper to his ear, it was a dismal shriek, and long reëchoed so, in the region round his heart! But this time the father did not turn.

After a further interval, Maule spoke.

"Behold your daughter!" said he.

Mr. Pyncheon came hastily forward. The carpenter was standing erect in front of Alice's chair, and pointing his finger towards the maiden with an expression of triumphant power the limits of which could not be defined, as, indeed, its scope stretched vaguely towards the unseen and the infinite. Alice sat in an attitude of profound repose, with the long brown lashes drooping over her eyes.

"There she is!" said the carpenter. "Speak to her!"

"Alice! My daughter!" exclaimed Mr. Pyncheon. "My own Alice!"

She did not stir.

"Louder!" said Maule, smiling.

"Alice! Awake!" cried her father. "It troubles me to see you thus! Awake!"

He spoke loudly, with terror in his voice, and close to that delicate ear which had always been so sensitive to every discord. But the sound evidently reached her not. It is indescribable what a sense of remote, dim, unattainable distance, betwixt himself and Alice, was impressed on the father by this impossibility of reaching her with his voice.

"Best touch her!" said Matthew Maule. "Shake the girl, and roughly too! My hands are hardened with too much use of axe, saw, and plane, — else I might help you!"

Mr. Pyncheon took her hand, and pressed it with the earnestness of startled emotion. He kissed her, with so great a heart-throb in the kiss, that he thought she must needs feel it. Then, in a gust of anger at her insensibility, he shook her maiden form with a violence which, the next moment, it affrighted him to remember. He withdrew his encircling arms, and Alice — whose figure, though flexible, had been wholly impassive — relapsed into the same attitude as before these attempts to arouse her. Maule having shifted his position, her face was turned towards him slightly, but with what seemed to be a reference of her very slumber to his guidance.

Then it was a strange sight to behold how the man of conventionalities shook the powder out of his periwig; how the reserved and stately gentleman forgot his dignity; how the gold-embroidered waistcoat flickered and glistened in the firelight with the convulsion of rage, terror, and sorrow in the human heart that was beating under it.

"Villain!" cried Mr. Pyncheon, shaking his clenched fist at Maule. "You and the fiend together have robbed me of my daughter! Give her back, spawn of the old wizard, or you shall climb Gallows Hill in your grandfather's footsteps!"

"Softly, Mr. Pyncheon!" said the carpenter, with scornful composure. "Softly, an it please your worship, else you will spoil those rich lace ruffles at your wrists! Is it my crime if you have sold your daughter for the mere hope of getting a sheet of yellow parchment into your clutch? There sits Mistress Alice quietly asleep! Now let Matthew Maule try whether she be as proud as the carpenter found her awhile since."

He spoke, and Alice responded, with a soft, subdued, inward acquiescence, and a bending of her form towards him, like the flame of a torch when it indicates a gentle draught of air. He beckoned with his hand, and, rising from her chair, — blindly, but undoubtingly, as tending to her sure and inevitable centre, — the proud Alice approached him. He waved her back, and, retreating, Alice sank again into her seat.

"She is mine!" said Matthew Maule. "Mine, by the right of the strongest spirit!"

In the further progress of the legend, there is a long, grotesque, and occasionally awe-striking account of the carpenter's incantations (if so they are to be called), with a view of discovering the lost document. It appears to have been his object to convert the mind of Alice into a kind of telescopic medium, through which Mr. Pyncheon and himself might obtain a glimpse into the spiritual world. He succeeded, accordingly, in holding an imperfect sort of intercourse, at one remove, with the departed personages, in whose custody the so much valued secret had been carried beyond the precincts of earth. During her trance, Alice described three figures as being present to her spiritualized perception. One was an aged, dignified, stern-looking gentleman, clad as for a solemn festival in grave and costly attire, but with a great bloodstain on his richly wrought band; the second, an aged man, meanly dressed, with a dark and malign countenance, and a broken halter about his neck; the third, a person not so advanced in life as the former two, but beyond the middle age, wearing a coarse woollen tunic and leather breeches, and with a carpenter's rule sticking out of his side pocket. These three visionary characters possessed a mutual knowledge of the missing document. One of them, in truth, — it was he with the blood-stain on his band, — seemed, unless his gestures were misunderstood, to hold the parchment in his immediate keeping, but was prevented, by his two partners in the mystery, from disburdening himself of the trust. Finally, when he showed a purpose of shouting forth the secret, loudly enough to be heard from his own sphere into that of mortals, his companions struggled with him, and pressed their hands over his mouth; and forthwith — whether that he were choked by it, or that the secret itself was of a crimson hue — there was a fresh flow of blood upon his band. Upon this, the two meanly dressed figures mocked and jeered at the much-abashed old dignitary, and pointed their fingers at the stain.

At this juncture, Maule turned to Mr. Pyncheon.

"It will never be allowed," said he. "The custody of this secret, that would so enrich his heirs, makes part of your grandfather's retribution. He must choke with it until it is no longer of any value. And keep you the House of the Seven Gables! It is too dear bought an inheritance, and too heavy with the curse upon it, to be shifted yet awhile from the Colonel's posterity!"

Mr. Pyncheon tried to speak, but — what with fear and passion — could make only a gurgling murmur in his throat. The carpenter smiled.

"Aha, worshipful sir! — so, you have old Maule's blood to drink!" said he, jeeringly.

"Fiend in man's shape! why dost thou keep dominion over my child?" cried Mr. Pyncheon, when his choked utterance could make way. "Give me back my daughter! Then go thy ways; and may we never meet again!"

"Your daughter!" said Matthew Maule. "Why, she is fairly mine! Nevertheless, not to be too hard with fair Mistress Alice, I will leave her in your keeping; but I do not warrant you that she shall never have occasion to remember Maule, the carpenter."

He waved his hands with an upward motion; and, after a few repetitions of similar gestures, the beautiful Alice Pyncheon awoke from her strange trance. She awoke, without the slightest recollection of her visionary experience; but as one losing herself in a momentary reverie, and returning to the consciousness of actual life, in almost as brief an interval as the down-sinking flame of the hearth should quiver again up the chimney. On recognizing Matthew Maule, she assumed an air of somewhat cold but gentle dignity, the rather, as there was a certain peculiar smile on the carpenter's visage that stirred the native pride of the fair Alice. So ended, for that time, the quest for the lost title-deed of the Pyncheon territory at the East-ward; nor, though often subsequently renewed, has it ever yet befallen a Pyncheon to set his eye upon that parchment.

But, alas for the beautiful, the gentle, yet too haughty Alice! A power that she little dreamed of had laid its grasp upon her maiden soul. A will, most unlike her own, constrained her to do its grotesque and fantastic bidding. Her father, as it proved, had martyred his poor child to an inordinate desire for measuring his land by miles instead of acres. And, therefore, while Alice Pyncheon lived, she was Maule's slave, in a bondage more humiliating, a thousand-fold, than that which binds its chain around the body. Seated by his humble fireside, Maule had but to wave his hand; and, wherever the proud lady chanced to be, — whether in her chamber, or entertaining her father's stately guests, or worshipping at church, — whatever her place or occupation, her spirit passed from beneath her own control, and bowed itself to Maule. "Alice, laugh!" — the carpenter, beside his hearth, would say; or perhaps intensely will it, with-out a spoken word. And, even were it prayer-time, or at a funeral, Alice must break into wild laughter. "Alice, be sad!" — and, at the instant, down would come her tears, quenching all the mirth of those around her like sudden rain upon a bonfire. "Alice, dance!" — and dance she would, not in such court-like measures as she had learned abroad, but some high-paced jig, or hop-skip rigadoon, befitting the brisk lasses at a rustic merry-making. It seemed to be Maule's impulse, not to ruin Alice, nor to visit her with any black or gigantic mischief, which would have crowned her sorrows with the grace of tragedy, but to wreak a low, ungenerous scorn upon her. Thus all the dignity of life was lost. She felt herself too much abased, and longed to change natures with some worm!

One evening, at a bridal-party (but not her own; for, so lost from self-control, she would have deemed it sin to marry), poor Alice was beckoned forth by her unseen despot, and constrained, in her gossamer white dress and satin slippers, to hasten along the street to the mean dwelling of a laboring-man. There was laughter and good cheer within; for Matthew Maule, that night, was to wed the laborer's daughter, and had summoned proud Alice Pyncheon to wait upon his bride. And so she did; and when the twain were one, Alice awoke out of her enchanted sleep. Yet, no longer proud, — humbly, and with a smile all steeped in sadness, — she kissed Maule's wife, and went her way. It was an inclement night; the southeast wind drove the mingled snow and rain into her thinly sheltered bosom; her satin slippers were wet through and through, as she trod the muddy sidewalks. The next day a cold; soon, a settled cough; anon, a hectic cheek, a wasted form, that sat beside the harpsichord, and filled the house with music! Music, in which a strain of the heavenly choristers was echoed! Oh, joy! For Alice had borne her last humiliation! Oh, greater joy! For Alice was penitent of her one earthly sin, and proud no more!

The Pyncheons made a great funeral for Alice. The kith and kin were there, and the whole respectability of the town besides. But, last in the procession, came Matthew Maule, gnashing his teeth, as if he would have bitten his own heart in twain, — the darkest and wofullest man that ever walked behind a corpse! He meant to humble Alice, not to kill her; but he had taken a woman's delicate soul into his rude gripe, to play with — and she was dead!

XIV.

PHŒBE'S GOOD-BY.

HOLGRAVE, plunging into his tale with the energy and absorption natural to a young author, had given a good deal of action to the parts capable of being developed and exemplified in that manner. He now observed that a certain remarkable drowsiness (wholly unlike that with which the reader possibly feels himself affected) had been flung over the senses of his auditress. It was the effect, unquestionably, of the mystic gesticulations by which he had sought to bring bodily before Phœbe's perception the figure of the mesmerizing carpenter. With the lids drooping over her eyes, — now lifted for an instant, and drawn down again as with leaden weights, — she leaned slightly towards him, and seemed almost to regulate her breath by his. Holgrave gazed at her, as he rolled up his manuscript, and recognized an incipient stage of that curious psychological condition, which, as he had himself told Phœbe, he possessed more than an ordinary faculty of producing. A veil was beginning to be muffled about her, in which she could behold only him, and live only in his thoughts and emotions. His glance, as he fastened it on the young girl, grew involuntarily more concentrated; in his attitude there was the consciousness of power, investing his hardly mature figure with a dignity that did not belong to its physical manifestation. It was evident, that, with but one wave of his hand and a corresponding effort of his will, he could complete his mastery over Phœbe's yet free and virgin spirit: he could establish an influence over this good, pure, and simple child, as dangerous, and perhaps as disastrous, as that which the carpenter of his legend had acquired and exercised over the ill-fated Alice.

To a disposition like Holgrave's, at once speculative and active, there is no temptation so great as the opportunity of acquiring empire over the human spirit; nor any idea more seductive to a young man than to become the arbiter of a young girl's destiny. Let us, therefore,— whatever his defects of nature and education, and in spite of his scorn for creeds and institutions,— concede to the daguerreotypist the rare and high quality of reverence for another's individuality. Let us allow him integrity, also, forever after to be confided in; since he forbade himself to twine that one link more which might have rendered his spell over Phœbe indissoluble.

He made a slight gesture upward with his hand.

"You really mortify me, my dear Miss Phœbe!" he exclaimed, smiling half-sarcastically at her. "My poor story, it is but too evident, will never do for Godey or Graham! Only think of your falling asleep at what I hoped the newspaper critics would pronounce a most brilliant, powerful, imaginative, pathetic, and original winding up! Well, the manuscript must serve to light lamps with; — if, indeed, being so imbued with my gentle dulness, it is any longer capable of flame!"

"Me asleep! How can you say so?" answered Phœbe, as unconscious of the crisis through which she had passed as an infant of the precipice to the verge of which it has rolled. " No, no! I consider myself as having been very attentive ; and, though I don't re-member the incidents quite distinctly, yet I have an impression of a vast deal of trouble and calamity, — so, no doubt, the story will prove exceedingly attrac-tive."

By this time the sun had gone down, and was tint-ing the clouds towards the zenith with those bright hues which are not seen there until some time after sunset, and when the horizon has quite lost its richer brilliancy. The moon, too, which had long been climb-ing overhead, and unobtrusively melting its disk into the azure, — like an ambitious demagogue, who hides his aspiring purpose by assuming the prevalent hue of popular sentiment, — now began to shine out, broad and oval, in its middle pathway. These silvery beams were already powerful enough to change the character of the lingering daylight. They softened and embel-lished the aspect of the old house ; although the shad-ows fell deeper into the angles of its many gables, and lay brooding under the projecting story, and within the half-open door. With the lapse of every moment, the garden grew more picturesque ; the fruit-trees, shrubbery, and flower-bushes had a dark obscurity among them. The commonplace characteristics — which, at noontide, it seemed to have taken a century of sordid life to accumulate — were now transfigured by a charm of romance. A hundred mysterious years were whispering among the leaves, whenever the slight sea-breeze found its way thither and stirred them. Through the foliage that roofed the little summer-house the moonlight flickered to and fro, and fell silvery white on the dark floor, the table, and the circular bench, with a continual shift and play, according as the chinks and wayward crevices among the twigs admitted or shut out the glimmer.

So sweetly cool was the atmosphere, after all the feverish day, that the summer eve might be fancied as sprinkling dews and liquid moonlight, with a dash of icy temper in them, out of a silver vase. Here and there, a few drops of this freshness were scattered on a human heart, and gave it youth again, and sympathy with the eternal youth of nature. The artist chanced to be one on whom the reviving influence fell. It made him feel — what he sometimes almost forgot, thrust so early as he had been into the rude struggle of man with man — how youthful he still was.

"It seems to me," he observed, "that I never watched the coming of so beautiful an eve, and never felt anything so very much like happiness as at this moment. After all, what a good world we live in ! How good, and beautiful ! How young it is, too, with nothing really rotten or age-worn in it ! This old house, for example, which sometimes has positively oppressed my breath with its smell of decaying timber ! And this garden, where the black mould always clings to my spade, as if I were a sexton delving in a grave-yard ! Could I keep the feeling that now possesses me, the garden would every day be virgin soil, with the earth's first freshness in the flavor of its beans and squashes ; and the house ! — it would be like a bower in Eden, blossoming with the earliest roses that God ever made. Moonlight, and the sentiment in man's heart responsive to it, are the greatest of renovators and reformers. And all other reform and renovation, I suppose, will prove to be no better than moon-shine ! "

"I have been happier than I am now ; at least,

much gayer," said Phœbe, thoughtfully. "Yet I am sensible of a great charm in this brightening moon-light; and I love to watch how the day, tired as it is, lags away reluctantly, and hates to be called yester-day so soon. I never cared much about moonlight before. What is there, I wonder, so beautiful in it, to-night?"

"And you have never felt it before?" inquired the artist, looking earnestly at the girl through the twi-light.

"Never," answered Phœbe; "and life does not look the same, now that I have felt it so. It seems as if I had looked at everything, hitherto, in broad daylight, or else in the ruddy light of a cheerful fire, glimmer-ing and dancing through a room. Ah, poor me!" she added, with a half-melancholy laugh. "I shall never be so merry as before I knew Cousin Hepzibah and poor Cousin Clifford. I have grown a great deal older, in this little time. Older, and, I hope, wiser, and, — not exactly sadder, — but, certainly, with not half so much lightness in my spirits! I have given them my sunshine, and have been glad to give it; but, of course, I cannot both give and keep it. They are welcome, notwithstanding!"

"You have lost nothing, Phœbe, worth keeping, nor which it was possible to keep," said Holgrave, after a pause. "Our first youth is of no value; for we are never conscious of it until after it is gone. But sometimes — always, I suspect, unless one is exceed-ingly unfortunate — there comes a sense of second youth, gushing out of the heart's joy at being in love; or, possibly, it may come to crown some other grand festival in life, if any other such there be. This be-moaning of one's self (as you do now) over the first, careless, shallow gayety of youth departed, and this profound happiness at youth regained, — so much deeper and richer than that we lost, — are essential to the soul's development. In some cases, the two states come almost simultaneously, and mingle the sadness and the rapture in one mysterious emotion."

"I hardly think I understand you," said Phœbe.

"No wonder," replied Holgrave, smiling; "for I have told you a secret which I hardly began to know before I found myself giving it utterance. Remember it, however; and when the truth becomes clear to you, then think of this moonlight scene!"

"It is entirely moonlight now, except only a little flush of faint crimson, upward from the west, between those buildings," remarked Phœbe. "I must go in. Cousin Hepzibah is not quick at figures, and will give herself a headache over the day's accounts, unless I help her."

But Holgrave detained her a little longer.

"Miss Hepzibah tells me," observed he, "that you return to the country in a few days."

"Yes, but only for a little while," answered Phœbe; "for I look upon this as my present home. I go to make a few arrangements, and to take a more deliberate leave of my mother and friends. It is pleasant to live where one is much desired and very useful; and I think I may have the satisfaction of feeling myself so here."

"You surely may, and more than you imagine," said the artist. "Whatever health, comfort, and natural life exists in the house, is embodied in your person. These blessings came along with you, and will vanish when you leave the threshold. Miss Hepzibah, by secluding herself from society, has lost all true relation with it, and is, in fact, dead; although she galvanizes herself into a semblance of life, and stands behind her counter, afflicting the world with a greatly-to-be-deprecated scowl. Your poor cousin Clifford is another dead and long-buried person, on whom the governor and council have wrought a necromantic miracle. I should not wonder if he were to crumble away, some morning, after you are gone, and nothing be seen of him more, except a heap of dust. Miss Hepzibah, at any rate, will lose what little flexibility she has. They both exist by you."

"I should be very sorry to think so," answered Phœbe, gravely. "But it is true that my small abilities were precisely what they needed; and I have a real interest in their welfare, — an odd kind of motherly sentiment, — which I wish you would not laugh at! And let me tell you frankly, Mr. Holgrave, I am sometimes puzzled to know whether you wish them well or ill."

"Undoubtedly," said the daguerreotypist, "I do feel an interest in this antiquated, poverty-stricken old maiden lady, and this degraded and shattered gentleman, — this abortive lover of the beautiful. A kindly interest, too, helpless old children that they are! But you have no conception what a different kind of heart mine is from your own. It is not my impulse, as regards these two individuals, either to help or hinder; but to look on, to analyze, to explain matters to myself, and to comprehend the drama which, for almost two hundred years, has been dragging its slow length over the ground where you and I now tread. If permitted to witness the close, I doubt not to derive a moral satisfaction from it, go matters how they may. There is a conviction within me that the end draws nigh. But, though Providence sent you hither to help, and sends me only as a privileged and meet spectator, I pledge myself to lend these unfortunate beings whatever aid I can!"

"I wish you would speak more plainly," cried Phœbe, perplexed and displeased; "and, above all, that you would feel more like a Christian and a human being! How is it possible to see people in distress, without desiring, more than anything else, to help and comfort them? You talk as if this old house were a theatre; and you seem to look at Hepzibah's and Clifford's misfortunes, and those of generations before them, as a tragedy, such as I have seen acted in the hall of a country hotel, only the present one appears to be played exclusively for your amusement. I do not like this. The play costs the performers too much, and the audience is too cold-hearted."

"You are severe," said Holgrave, compelled to recognize a degree of truth in this piquant sketch of his own mood.

"And then," continued Phœbe, "what can you mean by your conviction, which you tell me of, that the end is drawing near? Do you know of any new trouble hanging over my poor relatives? If so, tell me at once, and I will not leave them!"

"Forgive me, Phœbe!" said the daguerreotypist, holding out his hand, to which the girl was constrained to yield her own. "I am somewhat of a mystic, it must be confessed. The tendency is in my blood, together with the faculty of mesmerism, which might have brought me to Gallows Hill, in the good old times of witchcraft. Believe me, if I were really aware of any secret, the disclosure of which would benefit your friends, — who are my own friends, likewise,—you should learn it before we part. But I have no such knowledge."

"You hold something back!" said Phœbe.

"Nothing,—no secrets but my own," answered Holgrave. "I can perceive, indeed, that Judge Pyncheon still keeps his eye on Clifford, in whose ruin he had so large a share. His motives and intentions, however, are a mystery to me. He is a determined and relentless man, with the genuine character of an inquisitor; and had he any object to gain by putting Clifford to the rack, I verily believe that he would wrench his joints from their sockets, in order to accomplish it. But, so wealthy and eminent as he is,— so powerful in his own strength, and in the support of society on all sides,—what can Judge Pyncheon have to hope or fear from the imbecile, branded, half-torpid Clifford?"

"Yet," urged Phœbe, "you did speak as if misfortune were impending!"

"Oh, that was because I am morbid!" replied the artist. "My mind has a twist aside, like almost everybody's mind, except your own. Moreover, it is so strange to find myself an inmate of this old Pyncheon House, and sitting in this old garden—(hark, how Maule's well is murmuring!)—that, were it only for this one circumstance, I cannot help fancying that Destiny is arranging its fifth act for a catastrophe."

"There!" cried Phœbe with renewed vexation; for she was by nature as hostile to mystery as the sunshine to a dark corner. "You puzzle me more than ever!"

"Then let us part friends!" said Holgrave, pressing her hand. "Or, if not friends, let us part before you entirely hate me. You, who love everybody else in the world!"

"Good-by, then," said Phœbe, frankly. "I do not mean to be angry a great while, and should be sorry to have you think so. There has Cousin Hepzibah been standing in the shadow of the doorway, this quarter of an hour past! She thinks I stay too long in the damp garden. So, good-night, and good-by!"

On the second morning thereafter, Phœbe might have been seen, in her straw bonnet, with a shawl on one arm and a little carpet-bag on the other, bidding adieu to Hepzibah and Cousin Clifford. She was to take a seat in the next train of cars, which would transport her to within half a dozen miles of her country village.

The tears were in Phœbe's eyes; a smile, dewy with affectionate regret, was glimmering around her pleasant mouth. She wondered how it came to pass, that her life of a few weeks, here in this heavy-hearted old mansion, had taken such hold of her, and so melted into her associations, as now to seem a more important centre-point of remembrance than all which had gone before. How had Hepzibah — grim, silent, and irresponsive to her overflow of cordial sentiment — contrived to win so much love? And Clifford, — in his abortive decay, with the mystery of fearful crime upon him, and the close prison-atmosphere yet lurking in his breath, — how had he transformed himself into the simplest child, whom Phœbe felt bound to watch over, and be, as it were, the providence of his unconsidered hours! Everything, at that instant of farewell, stood out prominently to her view. Look where she would, lay her hand on what she might, the object responded to her consciousness, as if a moist human heart were in it.

She peeped from the window into the garden, and felt herself more regretful at leaving this spot of black earth, vitiated with such an age-long growth of weeds, than joyful at the idea of again scenting her pine forests and fresh clover-fields. She called Chanticleer, his two wives, and the venerable chicken, and threw them some crumbs of bread from the breakfast-table. These being hastily gobbled up, the chicken spread its wings, and alighted close by Phœbe on the window-sill, where it looked gravely into her face and vented its emotions in a croak. Phœbe bade it be a good old chicken during her absence, and promised to bring it a little bag of buckwheat.

"Ah, Phœbe!" remarked Hepzibah, "you do not smile so naturally as when you came to us! Then, the smile chose to shine out; now, you choose it should. It is well that you are going back, for a little while, into your native air. There has been too much weight on your spirits. The house is too gloomy and lone-some; the shop is full of vexations; and as for me, I have no faculty of making things look brighter than they are. Dear Clifford has been your only comfort!"

"Come hither, Phœbe," suddenly cried her cousin Clifford, who had said very little all the morning. "Close!—closer!—and look me in the face!"

Phœbe put one of her small hands on each elbow of his chair, and leaned her face towards him, so that he might peruse it as carefully as he would. It is prob-able that the latent emotions of this parting hour had revived, in some degree, his bedimmed and enfeebled faculties. At any rate, Phœbe soon felt that, if not the profound insight of a seer, yet a more than fem-

inine delicacy of appreciation, was making her heart
the subject of its regard. A moment before, she had
known nothing which she would have sought to hide.
Now, as if some secret were hinted to her own consciousness through the medium of another's perception,
she was fain to let her eyelids droop beneath Clifford's
gaze. A blush, too, — the redder, because she strove
hard to keep it down, — ascended higher and higher,
in a tide of fitful progress, until even her brow was all
suffused with it.

" It is enough, Phœbe," said Clifford, with a melancholy smile. " When I first saw you, you were the
prettiest little maiden in the world ; and now you have
deepened into beauty ! Girlhood has passed into
womanhood ; the bud is a bloom ! Go, now ! — I feel
lonelier than I did."

Phœbe took leave of the desolate couple, and passed
through the shop, twinkling her eyelids to shake off a
dew-drop ; for — considering how brief her absence
was to be, and therefore the folly of being cast down
about it — she would not so far acknowledge her tears
as to dry them with her handkerchief. On the doorstep, she met the little urchin whose marvellous feats
of gastronomy have been recorded in the earlier pages
of our narrative. She took from the window some
specimen or other of natural history, — her eyes being too dim with moisture to inform her accurately
whether it was a rabbit or a hippopotamus, — put it
into the child's hand, as a parting gift, and went her
way. Old Uncle Venner was just coming out of his
door, with a wood-horse and saw on his shoulder ; and,
trudging along the street, he scrupled not to keep
company with Phœbe. so far as their paths lay together ; nor, in spite of his patched coat and rusty

beaver, and the curious fashion of his tow-cloth trousers, could she find it in her heart to outwalk him.

"We shall miss you, next Sabbath afternoon," observed the street philosopher. "It is unaccountable
how little while it takes some folks to grow just as
natural to a man as his own breath; and, begging
your pardon, Miss Phœbe (though there can be no
offence in an old man's saying it), that's just what
you've grown to me! My years have been a great
many, and your life is but just beginning; and yet,
you are somehow as familiar to me as if I had found
you at my mother's door, and you had blossomed, like
a running vine, all along my pathway since. Come
back soon, or I shall be gone to my farm; for I begin
to find these wood-sawing jobs a little too tough for
my back-ache."

"Very soon, Uncle Venner," replied Phœbe.

"And let it be all the sooner, Phœbe, for the sake
of those poor souls yonder," continued her companion. "They can never do without you, now, — never,
Phœbe, never! — no more than if one of God's angels
had been living with them, and making their dismal
house pleasant and comfortable! Don't it seem to
you they'd be in a sad case, if, some pleasant summer
morning like this, the angel should spread his wings,
and fly to the place he came from? Well, just so they
feel, now that you're going home by the railroad!
They can't bear it, Miss Phœbe; so be sure to come
back!"

"I am no angel, Uncle Venner," said Phœbe, smiling, as she offered him her hand at the street-corner.
"But, I suppose, people never feel so much like angels as when they are doing what little good they may.
So I shall certainly come back!"

Thus parted the old man and the rosy girl ; and Phœbe took the wings of the morning, and was soon flitting almost as rapidly away as if endowed with the aerial locomotion of the angels to whom Uncle Venner had so graciously compared her.

XV.

THE SCOWL AND SMILE.

SEVERAL days passed over the Seven Gables, heavily and drearily enough. In fact (not to attribute the whole gloom of sky and earth to the one inauspicious circumstance of Phœbe's departure), an easterly storm had set in, and indefatigably applied itself to the task of making the black roof and walls of the old house look more cheerless than ever before. Yet was the outside not half so cheerless as the interior. Poor Clifford was cut off, at once, from all his scanty resources of enjoyment. Phœbe was not there; nor did the sunshine fall upon the floor. The garden, with its muddy walks, and the chill, dripping foliage of its summer-house, was an image to be shuddered at. Nothing flourished in the cold, moist, pitiless atmosphere, drifting with the brackish scud of sea-breezes, except the moss along the joints of the shingle-roof, and the great bunch of weeds, that had lately been suffering from drought, in the angle between the two front gables.

As for Hepzibah, she seemed not merely possessed with the east wind, but to be, in her very person, only another phase of this gray and sullen spell of weather; the east wind itself, grim and disconsolate, in a rusty black silk gown, and with a turban of cloud-wreaths on its head. The custom of the shop fell off, because a story got abroad that she soured her small beer and other damageable commodities, by scowling on them. It is, perhaps, true that the public had something reasonably to complain of in her deportment; but towards Clifford she was neither ill-tempered nor unkind, nor felt less warmth of heart than always, had it been possible to make it reach him. The inutility of her best efforts, however, palsied the poor old gentlewoman. She could do little else than sit silently in a corner of the room, when the wet pear-tree branches, sweeping across the small windows, created a noon-day dusk, which Hepzibah unconsciously darkened with her woe-begone aspect. It was no fault of Hepzibah's. Everything — even the old chairs and tables, that had known what weather was for three or four such lifetimes as her own — looked as damp and chill as if the present were their worst experience. The picture of the Puritan Colonel shivered on the wall. The house itself shivered, from every attic of its seven gables, down to the great kitchen fireplace, which served all the better as an emblem of the mansion's heart, because, though built for warmth, it was now so comfortless and empty.

Hepzibah attempted to enliven matters by a fire in the parlor. But the storm-demon kept watch above, and, whenever a flame was kindled, drove the smoke back again, choking the chimney's sooty throat with its own breath. Nevertheless, during four days of this miserable storm, Clifford wrapt himself in an old cloak, and occupied his customary chair. On the morning of the fifth, when summoned to breakfast, he responded only by a broken-hearted murmur, expressive of a determination not to leave his bed. His sister made no attempt to change his purpose. In fact, entirely as she loved him, Hepzibah could hardly have

borne any longer the wretched duty — so impracticable by her few and rigid faculties — of seeking pastime for a still sensitive, but ruined mind, critical and
fastidious, without force or volition. It was, at least,
something short of positive despair, that, to-day, she
might sit shivering alone, and not suffer continually a
new grief, and unreasonable pang of remorse, at every
fitful sigh of her fellow-sufferer.

But Clifford, it seemed, though he did not make his
appearance below stairs, had, after all, bestirred himself in quest of amusement. In the course of the forenoon, Hepzibah heard a note of music, which (there
being no other tuneful contrivance in the House of
the Seven Gables) she knew must proceed from Alice
Pyncheon's harpsichord. She was aware that Clifford, in his youth, had possessed a cultivated taste for
music, and a considerable degree of skill in its prac-
tice. It was difficult, however, to conceive of his retaining an accomplishment to which daily exercise is
so essential, in the measure indicated by the sweet,
airy, and delicate, though most melancholy strain,
that now stole upon her ear. Nor was it less marvellous that the long-silent instrument should be capable
of so much melody. Hepzibah involuntarily thought
of the ghostly harmonies, prelusive of death in the
family, which were attributed to the legendary Alice.
But it was, perhaps, proof of the agency of other than
spiritual fingers, that, after a few touches, the chords
seemed to snap asunder with their own vibrations, and
the music ceased.

But a harsher sound succeeded to the mysterious
notes ; nor was the easterly day fated to pass without
an event sufficient in itself to poison, for Hepzibah
and Clifford, the balmiest air that ever brought the

humming-birds along with it. The final echoes of Alice Pyncheon's performance (or Clifford's, if his we must consider it) were driven away by no less vulgar a dissonance than the ringing of the shop-bell. A foot was heard scraping itself on the threshold, and thence somewhat ponderously stepping on the floor. Hepzibah delayed a moment, while muffling herself in a faded shawl, which had been her defensive armor in a forty years' warfare against the east wind. A characteristic sound, however, — neither a cough nor a hem, but a kind of rumbling and reverberating spasm in somebody's capacious depth of chest, — impelled her to hurry forward, with that aspect of fierce faint-heartedness so common to women in cases of perilous emergency. Few of her sex, on such occasions, have ever looked so terrible as our poor scowling Hepzibah. But the visitor quietly closed the shop-door behind him, stood up his umbrella against the counter, and turned a visage of composed benignity, to meet the alarm and anger which his appearance had excited.

Hepzibah's presentiment had not deceived her. It was no other than Judge Pyncheon, who, after in vain trying the front door, had now effected his entrance into the shop.

"How do you do, Cousin Hepzibah? — and how does this most inclement weather affect our poor Clifford?" began the Judge; and wonderful it seemed, indeed, that the easterly storm was not put to shame, or, at any rate, a little mollified, by the genial benevolence of his smile. "I could not rest without calling to ask, once more, whether I can in any manner promote his comfort, or your own."

"You can do nothing," said Hepzibah, controlling her agitation as well as she could. "I devote myself to Clifford.   He has every comfort which his situation admits of."

"But allow me to suggest, dear cousin," rejoined the Judge, " you err, — in all affection and kindness, no doubt, and with the very best intentions, — but you do err, nevertheless, in keeping your brother so se- cluded.   Why insulate him thus from all sympathy and kindness?   Clifford, alas! has had too much of solitude.   Now let him try society, — the society, that is to say, of kindred and old friends.   Let me, for in- stance, but see Clifford, and I will answer for the good effect of the interview."

"You cannot see him," answered Hepzibah.   "Clif- ford has kept his bed since yesterday."

"What!   How!   Is he ill?" exclaimed Judge Pyn- cheon, starting with what seemed to be angry alarm; for the very frown of the old Puritan darkened through the room as he spoke.   "Nay, then, I must and will see him!   What if he should die?"

"He is in no danger of death," said Hepzibah, — and added, with bitterness that she could repress no longer, "none; unless he shall be persecuted to death, now, by the same man who long ago attempted it!"

"Cousin Hepzibah," said the Judge, with an im- pressive earnestness of manner, which grew even to tearful pathos as he proceeded, "is it possible that you do not perceive how unjust, how unkind, how unchris- tian, is this constant, this long - continued bitterness against me, for a part which I was constrained by duty and conscience, by the force of law, and at my own peril, to act?   What did I do, in detriment to Clifford, which it was possible to leave undone?   How could you, his sister, — if, for your never-ending sorrow, as it has been for mine, you had known what I did, — have shown greater tenderness?   And do you think, cousin, that it has cost me no pang? — that it has left no anguish in my bosom, from that day to this, amidst all the prosperity with which Heaven has blessed me? — or that I do not now rejoice, when it is deemed consistent with the dues of public justice and the welfare of society that this dear kinsman, this early friend, this nature so delicately and beautifully constituted, — so unfortunate, let us pronounce him, and forbear to say, so guilty, — that our own Clifford, in fine, should be given back to life, and its possibilities of enjoyment? Ah, you little know me, Cousin Hepzibah!   You little know this heart!   It now throbs at the thought of meeting him!   There lives not the human being (except yourself, — and you not more than I) who has shed so many tears for Clifford's calamity!   You behold some of them now.   There is none who would so delight to promote his happiness!   Try me, Hepzibah! — try me, cousin! — try the man whom you have treated as your enemy and Clifford's! — try Jaffrey Pyncheon, and you shall find him true, to the heart's core!"

"In the name of Heaven," cried Hepzibah, provoked only to intenser indignation by this outgush of the inestimable tenderness of a stern nature, — "in God's name, whom you insult, and whose power I could almost question, since he hears you utter so many false words without palsying your tongue, — give over, I beseech you, this loathsome pretence of affection for your victim!   You hate him!   Say so, like a man! You cherish, at this moment, some black purpose against him in your heart!   Speak it out, at once! — or, if you hope so to promote it better, hide it till you can triumph in its success! But never speak again of your love for my poor brother! I cannot bear it! It will drive me beyond a woman's decency! It will drive me mad! Forbear! Not another word! It will make me spurn you!"

For once, Hepzibah's wrath had given her courage. She had spoken. But, after all, was this unconquerable distrust of Judge Pyncheon's integrity, and this utter denial, apparently, of his claim to stand in the ring of human sympathies, — were they founded in any just perception of his character, or merely the offspring of a woman's unreasonable prejudice, deduced from nothing?

The Judge, beyond all question, was a man of eminent respectability. The church acknowledged it; the state acknowledged it. It was denied by nobody. In all the very extensive sphere of those who knew him, whether in his public or private capacities, there was not an individual — except Hepzibah, and some lawless mystic, like the daguerreotypist, and, possibly, a few political opponents — who would have dreamed of seriously disputing his claim to a high and honorable place in the world's regard. Nor (we must do him the further justice to say) did Judge Pyncheon himself, probably, entertain many or very frequent doubts, that his enviable reputation accorded with his deserts. His conscience, therefore, usually considered the surest witness to a man's integrity, — his conscience, unless it might be for the little space of five minutes in the twenty-four hours, or, now and then, some black day in the whole year's circle, — his conscience bore an accordant testimony with the world's laudatory voice. And yet, strong as this evidence may seem to be, we should hesitate to peril our own conscience on the assertion, that the Judge and the con-senting world were right, and that poor Hepzibah, with her solitary prejudice was wrong. Hidden from mankind, — forgotten by himself, or buried so deeply under a sculptured and ornamented pile of ostenta-tious deeds that his daily life could take no note of it, — there may have lurked some evil and unsightly thing. Nay, we could almost venture to say, further, that a daily guilt might have been acted by him, con-tinually renewed, and reddening forth afresh, like the miraculous blood-stain of a murder, without his necessarily and at every moment being aware of it.

Men of strong minds, great force of character, and a hard texture of the sensibilities, are very capable of falling into mistakes of this kind. They are ordinarily men to whom forms are of paramount importance. Their field of action lies among the external phenom-ena of life. They possess vast ability in grasping, and arranging, and appropriating to themselves, the big, heavy, solid unrealities, such as gold, landed es-tate, offices of trust and emolument, and public honors. With these materials, and with deeds of goodly as-pect, done in the public eye, an individual of this class builds up, as it were, a tall and stately edifice, which, in the view of other people, and ultimately in his own view, is no other than the man's character, or the man himself. Behold, therefore, a palace! Its splendid halls, and suites of spacious apartments, are floored with a mosaic-work of costly marbles; its windows, the whole height of each room, admit the sunshine through the most transparent of plate-glass; its high cornices are gilded, and its ceilings gorgeously painted; and a lofty dome — through which, from the central pavement, you may gaze up to the sky, as with no obstructing medium between — surmounts the whole. With what fairer and nobler emblem could any man desire to shadow forth his character? Ah! but in some low and obscure nook, — some narrow closet on the ground-floor, shut, locked and bolted, and the key flung away, — or beneath the marble pavement, in a stagnant water-puddle, with the richest pattern of mosaic-work above, — may lie a corpse, half decayed, and still decaying, and diffusing its death-scent all through the palace! The inhabitant will not be conscious of it, for it has long been his daily breath! Neither will the visitors, for they smell only the rich odors which the master sedulously scatters through the palace, and the incense which they bring, and delight to burn before him! Now and then, perchance, comes in a seer, before whose sadly gifted eye the whole structure melts into thin air, leaving only the hidden nook, the bolted closet, with the cobwebs festooned over its forgotten door, or the deadly hole under the pavement, and the decaying corpse within. Here, then, we are to seek the true emblem of the man's character, and of the deed that gives whatever reality it possesses to his life. And, beneath the show of a marble palace, that pool of stagnant water, foul with many impurities, and, perhaps, tinged with blood, — that secret abomination, above which, possibly, he may say his prayers, without remembering it, — is this man's miserable soul!

To apply this train of remark somewhat more closely to Judge Pyncheon. We might say (without in the least imputing crime to a personage of his eminent respectability) that there was enough of splendid rubbish in his life to cover up and paralyze a more active and subtile conscience than the Judge was ever troubled

with. The purity of his judicial character, while on
the bench; the faithfulness of his public service in
subsequent capacities; his devotedness to his party,
and the rigid consistency with which he had adhered
to its principles, or, at all events, kept pace with its
organized movements; his remarkable zeal as president of a Bible society; his unimpeachable integrity
as treasurer of a widow's and orphan's fund; his
benefits to horticulture, by producing two much-es-
teemed varieties of the pear, and to agriculture, through
the agency of the famous Pyncheon bull; the cleanli-
ness of his moral deportment, for a great many years
past; the severity with which he had frowned upon,
and finally cast off, an expensive and dissipated son,
delaying forgiveness until within the final quarter
of an hour of the young man's life; his prayers at
morning and eventide, and graces at meal-time; his
efforts in furtherance of the temperance cause; his
confining himself, since the last attack of the gout, to
five diurnal glasses of old sherry wine; the snowy
whiteness of his linen, the polish of his boots, the hand-
someness of his gold-headed cane, the square and roomy
fashion of his coat, and the fineness of its material,
and, in general, the studied propriety of his dress and
equipment; the scrupulousness with which he paid
public notice, in the street, by a bow, a lifting of the
hat, a nod, or a motion of the hand, to all and sundry
of his acquaintances, rich or poor; the smile of broad
benevolence wherewith he made it a point to gladden
the whole world, — what room could possibly be found
for darker traits in a portrait made up of lineaments
like these? This proper face was what he beheld in
the looking-glass. This admirably arranged life was
what he was conscious of in the progress of every day.

Then, might not he claim to be its result and sum, and say to himself and the community, " Behold Judge Pyncheon there " ?

And allowing that, many, many years ago, in his early and reckless youth, he had committed some one wrong act, — or that, even now, the inevitable force of circumstances should occasionally make him do one questionable deed among a thousand praiseworthy, or, at least, blameless ones, — would you characterize the Judge by that one necessary deed, and that half-forgotten act, and let it overshadow the fair aspect of a lifetime ? What is there so ponderous in evil, that a thumb's bigness of it should outweigh the mass of things not evil which were heaped into the other scale ! This scale and balance system is a favorite one with people of Judge Pyncheon's brotherhood. A hard, cold man, thus unfortunately situated, seldom or never looking inward, and resolutely taking his idea of himself from what purports to be his image as reflected in the mirror of public opinion, can scarcely arrive at true self-knowledge, except through loss of property and reputation. Sickness will not always help him do it ; not always the death-hour !

But our affair now is with Judge Pyncheon as he stood confronting the fierce outbreak of Hepzibah's wrath. Without premeditation, to her own surprise, and indeed terror, she had given vent, for once, to the inveteracy of her resentment, cherished against this kinsman for thirty years.

Thus far the Judge's countenance had expressed mild forbearance, — grave and almost gentle deprecation of his cousin's unbecoming violence, — free and Christian-like forgiveness of the wrong inflicted by her words. But when those words were irrevocably spoken his look assumed sternness, the sense of power, and immitigable resolve ; and this with so natural and imperceptible a change, that it seemed as if the iron man had stood there from the first, and the meek man not at all. The effect was as when the light, vapory clouds, with their soft coloring, suddenly vanish from the stony brow of a precipitous mountain, and leave there the frown which you at once feel to be eternal. Hepzibah almost adopted the insane belief that it was her old Puritan ancestor, and not the modern Judge, on whom she had just been wreaking the bitterness of her heart. Never did a man show stronger proof of the lineage attributed to him than Judge Pyncheon, at this crisis, by his unmistakable resemblance to the picture in the inner room.

"Cousin Hepzibah," said he, very calmly, "it is time to have done with this."

"With all my heart!" answered she. "Then, why do you persecute us any longer? Leave poor Clifford and me in peace. Neither of us desires anything better!"

"It is my purpose to see Clifford before I leave this house," continued the Judge. "Do not act like a mad-woman, Hepzibah! I am his only friend, and an all-powerful one. Has it never occurred to you, — are you so blind as not to have seen, — that, without not merely my consent, but my efforts, my representations, the exertion of my whole influence, political, official, personal, Clifford would never have been what you call free? Did you think his release a triumph over me? Not so, my good cousin ; not so, by any means! The furthest possible from that! No ; but it was the accomplishment of a purpose long entertained on my part. I set him free!"

"You!" answered Hepzibah. "I never will be-lieve it! He owed his dungeon to you; his freedom to God's providence!"

"I set him free!" reaffirmed Judge Pyncheon, with the calmest composure. "And I came hither now to decide whether he shall retain his freedom. It will depend upon himself. For this purpose, I must see him."

"Never!—it would drive him mad!" exclaimed Hepzibah, but with an irresoluteness sufficiently per-ceptible to the keen eye of the Judge; for, without the slightest faith in his good intentions, she knew not whether there was most to dread in yielding or re-sistance. "And why should you wish to see this wretched, broken man, who retains hardly a fraction of his intellect, and will hide even that from an eye which has no love in it?"

"He shall see love enough in mine, if that be all!" said the Judge, with well-grounded confidence in the benignity of his aspect. "But, Cousin Hepzibah, you confess a great deal, and very much to the purpose. Now, listen, and I will frankly explain my reasons for insisting on this interview. At the death, thirty years since, of our uncle Jaffrey, it was found,—I know not whether the circumstance ever attracted much of your attention, among the sadder interests that clus-tered round that event,—but it was found that his visible estate, of every kind, fell far short of any es-timate ever made of it. He was supposed to be im-mensely rich. Nobody doubted that he stood among the weightiest men of his day. It was one of his eccen-tricities, however,—and not altogether a folly, neither, —to conceal the amount of his property by making distant and foreign investments, perhaps under other names than his own, and by various means, familiar enough to capitalists, but unnecessary here to be specified. By Uncle Jaffrey's last will and testament, as you are aware, his entire property was bequeathed to me, with the single exception of a life interest to yourself in this old family mansion, and the strip of patrimonial estate remaining attached to it."

"And do you seek to deprive us of that?" asked Hepzibah, unable to restrain her bitter contempt. "Is this your price for ceasing to persecute poor Clifford?"

"Certainly not, my dear cousin!" answered the Judge, smiling benevolently. "On the contrary, as you must do me the justice to own, I have constantly expressed my readiness to double or treble your resources, whenever you should make up your mind to accept any kindness of that nature at the hands of your kinsman. No, no! But here lies the gist of the matter. Of my uncle's unquestionably great estate, as I have said, not the half — no, not one third, as I am fully convinced — was apparent after his death. Now, I have the best possible reasons for believing that your brother Clifford can give me a clew to the recovery of the remainder."

"Clifford! — Clifford know of any hidden wealth? — Clifford have it in his power to make you rich?" cried the old gentlewoman, affected with a sense of something like ridicule, at the idea. "Impossible! You deceive yourself! It is really a thing to laugh at!"

"It is as certain as that I stand here!" said Judge Pyncheon, striking his gold-headed cane on the floor, and at the same time stamping his foot, as if to express his conviction the more forcibly by the whole emphasis of his substantial person. "Clifford told me so himself!"

"No, no!" exclaimed Hepzibah, incredulously. "You are dreaming, Cousin Jaffrey!"

"I do not belong to the dreaming class of men," said the Judge, quietly. "Some months before my uncle's death, Clifford boasted to me of the possession of the secret of incalculable wealth. His purpose was to taunt me, and excite my curiosity. I know it well. But, from a pretty distinct recollection of the particulars of our conversation, I am thoroughly convinced that there was truth in what he said. Clifford, at this moment, if he chooses, — and choose he must! — can inform me where to find the schedule, the documents, the evidences, in whatever shape they exist, of the vast amount of Uncle Jaffrey's missing property. He has the secret. His boast was no idle word. It had a directness, an emphasis, a particularity, that showed a backbone of solid meaning within the mystery of his expression."

"But what could have been Clifford's object," asked Hepzibah, "in concealing it so long?"

"It was one of the bad impulses of our fallen nature," replied the Judge, turning up his eyes. "He looked upon me as his enemy. He considered me as the cause of his overwhelming disgrace, his imminent peril of death, his irretrievable ruin. There was no great probability, therefore, of his volunteering information, out of his dungeon, that should elevate me still higher on the ladder of prosperity. But the moment has now come when he must give up his secret."

"And what if he should refuse?" inquired Hepzibah. "Or, — as I steadfastly believe, — what if he has no knowledge of this wealth?"

"My dear cousin," said Judge Pyncheon, with a quietude which he had the power of making more formidable than any violence, "since your brother's return, I have taken the precaution (a highly proper one in the near kinsman and natural guardian of an individual so situated) to have his deportment and habits constantly and carefully overlooked. Your neighbors have been eye-witnesses to whatever has passed in the garden. The butcher, the baker, the fish-monger, some of the customers of your shop, and many a prying old woman, have told me several of the secrets of your interior. A still larger circle — I myself, among the rest — can testify to his extravagances at the arched window. Thousands beheld him, a week or two ago, on the point of flinging himself thence into the street. From all this testimony, I am led to apprehend — reluctantly, and with deep grief — that Clifford's misfortunes have so affected his intellect, never very strong, that he cannot safely remain at large. The alternative, you must be aware, — and its adoption will depend entirely on the decision which I am now about to make, — the alternative is his confinement, probably for the remainder of his life, in a public asylum for persons in his unfortunate state of mind."

"You cannot mean it!" shrieked Hepzibah.

"Should my cousin Clifford," continued Judge Pyncheon, wholly undisturbed, "from mere malice, and hatred of one whose interests ought naturally to be dear to him, — a mode of passion that, as often as any other, indicates mental disease, — should he refuse me the information so important to myself, and which he assuredly possesses, I shall consider it the one needed jot of evidence to satisfy my mind of his insanity. And, once sure of the course pointed out by conscience, you know me too well, Cousin Hepzibah, to entertain a doubt that I shall pursue it."

"O, Jaffrey, — Cousin Jaffrey!" cried Hepzibah, mournfully, not passionately, "it is you that are diseased in mind, not Clifford! You have forgotten that a woman was your mother! — that you have had sisters, brothers, children of your own! — or that there ever was affection between man and man, or pity from one man to another, in this miserable world! Else, how could you have dreamed of this? You are not young, Cousin Jaffrey! — no, nor middle-aged, — but already an old man! The hair is white upon your head! How many years have you to live? Are you not rich enough for that little time? Shall you be hungry, — shall you lack clothes, or a roof to shelter you, — between this point and the grave? No! but, with the half of what you now possess, you could revel in costly food and wines, and build a house twice as splendid as you now inhabit, and make a far greater show to the world, — and yet leave riches to your only son, to make him bless the hour of your death! Then, why should you do this cruel, cruel thing? — so mad a thing, that I know not whether to call it wicked! Alas, Cousin Jaffrey, this hard and grasping spirit has run in our blood these two hundred years. You are but doing over again, in another shape, what your ancestor before you did, and sending down to your posterity the curse inherited from him!"

"Talk sense, Hepzibah, for Heaven's sake!" exclaimed the Judge, with the impatience natural to a reasonable man, on hearing anything so utterly absurd as the above, in a discussion about matters of business. "I have told you my determination. I am not apt to change. Clifford must give up his secret or take the consequences. And let him decide quickly; for I have several affairs to attend to this morning, and an important dinner engagement with some polit. ical friends."

" Clifford has no secret ! " answered Hepzibah. " And God will not let you do the thing you medi- tate ! "

" We shall see," said the unmoved Judge. "Mean- while, choose whether you will summon Clifford, and allow this business to be amicably settled by an inter- view between two kinsmen, or drive me to harsher measures, which I should be most happy to feel my- self justified in avoiding. The responsibility is alto- gether on your part."

" You are stronger than I," said Hepzibah, after a brief consideration; " and you have no pity in your strength ! Clifford is not now insane ; but the inter- view which you insist upon may go far to make him so. Nevertheless, knowing you as I do, I believe it to be my best course to allow you to judge for your- self as to the improbability of his possessing any valu- able secret. I will call Clifford. Be merciful in your dealings with him ! — be far more merciful than your heart bids you be ! — for God is looking at you, Jaf- frey Pyncheon ! "

The Judge followed his cousin from the shop, where the foregoing conversation had passed, into the par- lor, and flung himself heavily into the great ances- tral chair. Many a former Pyncheon had found re- pose in its capacious arms : rosy children, after their sports ; young men, dreamy with love ; grown men, weary with cares ; old men, burdened with winters,

— they had mused, and slumbered, and departed to a yet profounder sleep. It had been a long tradition, though a doubtful one, that this was the very chair, seated in which, the earliest of the Judge's New England forefathers — he whose picture still hung upon the wall — had given a dead man's silent and stern reception to the throng of distinguished guests. From that hour of evil omen until the present, it may be, — though we know not the secret of his heart, — but it may be that no wearier and sadder man had ever sunk into the chair than this same Judge Pyncheon, whom we have just beheld so immitigably hard and resolute. Surely, it must have been at no slight cost that he had thus fortified his soul with iron. Such calmness is a mightier effort than the violence of weaker men. And there was yet a heavy task for him to do. Was it a little matter, — a trifle to be prepared for in a single moment, and to be rested from in another moment, — that he must now, after thirty years, encounter a kinsman risen from a living tomb, and wrench a secret from him, or else consign him to a living tomb again?

"Did you speak?" asked Hepzibah, looking in from the threshold of the parlor; for she imagined that the Judge had uttered some sound which she was anxious to interpret as a relenting impulse. "I thought you called me back."

"No, no!" gruffly answered Judge Pyncheon, with a harsh frown, while his brow grew almost a black purple, in the shadow of the room. "Why should I call you back? Time flies! Bid Clifford come to me!"

The Judge had taken his watch from his vest-pocket and now held it in his hand, measuring the interval which was to ensue before the appearance of Clifford.

XVI.

CLIFFORD'S CHAMBER.

NEVER had the old house appeared so dismal to poor Hepzibah as when she departed on that wretched errand. There was a strange aspect in it. As she trode along the foot-worn passages, and opened one crazy door after another, and ascended the creaking staircase, she gazed wistfully and fearfully around. It would have been no marvel, to her excited mind, if, behind or beside her, there had been the rustle of dead people's garments, or pale visages awaiting her on the landing-place above. Her nerves were set all ajar by the scene of passion and terror through which she had just struggled. Her colloquy with Judge Pyncheon, who so perfectly represented the person and attributes of the founder of the family, had called back the dreary past. It weighed upon her heart. Whatever she had heard, from legendary aunts and grandmothers, concerning the good or evil fortunes of the Pyncheons, — stories which had heretofore been kept warm in her remembrance by the chimney-corner glow that was associated with them, — now recurred to her, sombre, ghastly, cold, like most passages of family history, when brooded over in melancholy mood. The whole seemed little else but a series of calamity, reproducing itself in successive generations, with one general hue, and varying in little, save the outline. But Hepzibah now felt as if the Judge, and Clifford, and herself, —

they three together, — were on the point of adding another incident to the annals of the house, with a bolder relief of wrong and sorrow, which would cause it to stand out from all the rest. Thus it is that the grief of the passing moment takes upon itself an individuality, and a character of climax, which it is destined to lose after a while, and to fade into the dark gray tissue common to the grave or glad events of many years ago. It is but for a moment, comparatively, that anything looks strange or startling, — a truth that has the bitter and the sweet in it.

But Hepzibah could not rid herself of the sense of something unprecedented at that instant passing and soon to be accomplished. Her nerves were in a shake. Instinctively she paused before the arched window, and looked out upon the street, in order to seize its permanent objects with her mental grasp, and thus to steady herself from the reel and vibration which affected her more immediate sphere. It brought her up, as we may say, with a kind of shock, when she beheld everything under the same appearance as the day before, and numberless preceding days, except for the difference between sunshine and sullen storm. Her eyes travelled along the street, from doorstep to doorstep, noting the wet sidewalks, with here and there a puddle in hollows that had been imperceptible until filled with water. She screwed her dim optics to their acutest point, in the hope of making out, with greater distinctness, a certain window, where she half saw, half guessed, that a tailor's seamstress was sitting at her work. Hepzibah flung herself upon that unknown woman's companionship, even thus far off. Then she was attracted by a chaise rapidly passing, and watched its moist and glistening top, and its splashing wheels, until it had turned the corner, and refused to carry any further her idly trifling, because appalled and overburdened, mind. When the vehicle had disappeared, she allowed herself still another loitering moment; for the patched figure of good Uncle Venner was now visible, coming slowly from the head of the street downward, with a rheumatic limp, because the east wind had got into his joints. Hepzibah wished that he would pass yet more slowly, and befriend her shivering solitude a little longer. Anything that would take her out of the grievous present, and interpose human beings betwixt herself and what was nearest to her, — whatever would defer for an instant, the inevitable errand on which she was bound, — all such impediments were welcome. Next to the lightest heart, the heaviest is apt to be most playful.

Hepzibah had little hardihood for her own proper pain and far less for what she must inflict on Clifford. Of so slight a nature, and so shattered by his previous calamities, it could not well be short of utter ruin to bring him face to face with the hard, relentless man, who had been his evil destiny through life. Even had there been no bitter recollections, nor any hostile interest now at stake between them, the mere natural repugnance of the more sensitive system to the massive, weighty, and unimpressible one, must, in itself, have been disastrous to the former. It would be like flinging a porcelain vase, with already a crack in it, against a granite column. Never before had Hepzibah so adequately estimated the powerful character of her cousin Jaffrey, — powerful by intellect, energy of will, the long habit of acting among men, and, as she believed, by his unscrupulous pursuit of selfish ends through evil means. It did but increase the difficulty that Judge Pyncheon was under a delusion as to the secret which he supposed Clifford to possess. Men of his strength of purpose, and customary sagacity, if they chance to adopt a mistaken opinion in practical matters, so wedge it and fasten it among things known to be true, that to wrench it out of their minds is hardly less difficult than pulling up an oak. Thus, as the Judge required an impossibility of Clifford, the latter, as he could not perform it, must needs perish. For what, in the grasp of a man like this, was to become of Clifford's soft poetic nature, that never should have had a task more stubborn than to set a life of beautiful enjoyment to the flow and rhythm of musical cadences! Indeed, what had become of it already? Broken! Blighted! All but annihilated! Soon to be wholly so!

For a moment, the thought crossed Hepzibah's mind, whether Clifford might not really have such knowledge of their deceased uncle's vanished estate as the Judge imputed to him. She remembered some vague intimations, on her brother's part, which — if the supposition were not essentially preposterous — might have been so interpreted. There had been schemes of travel and residence abroad, day-dreams of brilliant life at home, and splendid castles in the air, which it would have required boundless wealth to build and realize. Had this wealth been in her power, how gladly would Hepzibah have bestowed it all upon her iron-hearted kinsman, to buy for Clifford the freedom and seclusion of the desolate old house! But she believed that her brother's schemes were as destitute of actual substance and purpose as a child's pictures of its future life, while sitting in a little chair by its mother's knee. Clifford had none but shadowy gold

at his command; and it was not the stuff to satisfy
Judge Pyncheon!

Was there no help, in their extremity? It seemed
strange that there should be none, with a city round
about her. It would be so easy to throw up the window, and send forth a shriek, at the strange agony of
which everybody would come hastening to the rescue,
well understanding it to be the cry of a human soul,
at some dreadful crisis! But how wild, how almost
laughable, the fatality, — and yet how continually it
comes to pass, thought Hepzibah, in this dull delirium
of a world, — that whosoever, and with however kindly
a purpose, should come to help, they would be sure to
help the strongest side! Might and wrong combined,
like iron magnetized, are endowed with irresistible attraction. There would be Judge Pyncheon, — a person eminent in the public view, of high station and
great wealth, a philanthropist, a member of Congress
and of the church, and intimately associated with
whatever else bestows good name, — so imposing, in
these advantageous lights, that Hepzibah herself could
hardly help shrinking from her own conclusions as to
his hollow integrity. The Judge, on one side! And
who, on the other? The guilty Clifford! Once a by-
word! Now, an indistinctly remembered ignominy!

Nevertheless, in spite of this perception that the
Judge would draw all human aid to his own behalf,
Hepzibah was so unaccustomed to act for herself, that
the least word of counsel would have swayed her to
any mode of action. Little Phœbe Pyncheon would
at once have lighted up the whole scene, if not by any
available suggestion, yet simply by the warm vivacity
of her character. The idea of the artist occurred to
Hepzibah. Young and unknown, mere vagrant ad-

venturer as he was, she had been conscious of a force in Holgrave which might well adapt him to be the champion of a crisis.   With this thought in her mind, she unbolted a door, cobwebbed and long disused, but which had served as a former medium of communication between her own part of the house and the gable where the wandering daguerreotypist had now established his temporary home.   He was not there.   A book, face downward, on the table, a roll of manuscript, a half-written sheet, a newspaper, some tools of his present occupation, and several rejected daguerreotypes, conveyed an impression as if he were close at hand.   But, at this period of the day, as Hepzibah might have anticipated, the artist was at his public rooms.   With an impulse of idle curiosity, that flickered among her heavy thoughts, she looked at one of the daguerreotypes, and beheld Judge Pyncheon frowning at her.   Fate stared her in the face.   She turned back from her fruitless quest, with a heart-sinking sense of disappointment.   In all her years of seclusion, she had never felt, as now, what it was to be alone.   It seemed as if the house stood in a desert, or, by some spell, was made invisible to those who dwelt around, or passed beside it; so that any mode of misfortune, miserable accident, or crime might happen in it without the possibility of aid.   In her grief and wounded pride, Hepzibah had spent her life in divesting herself of friends; she had wilfully cast off the support which God has ordained his creatures to need from one another; and it was now her punishment, that Clifford and herself would fall the easier victims to their kindred enemy.

Returning to the arched window, she lifted her eyes, -- scowling, poor, dim-sighted Hepzibah, in the face of Heaven!—and strove hard to send up a prayer through the dense gray pavement of clouds. Those mists had gathered, as if to symbolize a great, brooding mass of human trouble, doubt, confusion, and chill indifference, between earth and the better regions. Her faith was too weak; the prayer too heavy to be thus uplifted. It fell back, a lump of lead, upon her heart. It smote her with the wretched conviction that Providence intermeddled not in these petty wrongs of one individual to his fellow, nor had any balm for these little agonies of a solitary soul; but shed its justice, and its mercy, in a broad, sunlike sweep, over half the universe at once. Its vastness made it nothing. But Hepzibah did not see that, just as there comes a warm sunbeam into every cottage window, so comes a love-beam of God's care and pity for every separate need.

At last, finding no other pretext for deferring the torture that she was to inflict on Clifford,—her reluctance to which was the true cause of her loitering at the window, her search for the artist, and even her abortive prayer,—dreading, also, to hear the stern voice of Judge Pyncheon from below stairs, chiding her delay,—she crept slowly, a pale, grief-stricken figure, a dismal shape of woman, with almost torpid limbs, slowly to her brother's door, and knocked!

There was no reply!

And how should there have been? Her hand, tremulous with the shrinking purpose which directed it, had smitten so feebly against the door that the sound could hardly have gone inward. She knocked again. Still, no response! Nor was it to be wondered at. She had struck with the entire force of her heart's vibration, communicating, by some subtile magnetism, her own terror to the summons. Clifford would turn his face to the pillow, and cover his head beneath the bedclothes, like a startled child at midnight. She knocked a third time, three regular strokes, gentle, but perfectly distinct, and with meaning in them; for, modulate it with what cautious art we will, the hand cannot help playing some tune of what we feel, upon the senseless wood.

Clifford returned no answer.

"Clifford! dear brother!" said Hepzibah. "Shall I come in?"

A silence.

Two or three times, and more, Hepzibah repeated his name, without result; till, thinking her brother's sleep unwontedly profound, she undid the door, and entering, found the chamber vacant. How could he have come forth, and when, without her knowledge? Was it possible that, in spite of the stormy day, and worn out with the irksomeness within doors, he had betaken himself to his customary haunt in the garden, and was now shivering under the cheerless shelter of the summer-house? She hastily threw up a window, thrust forth her turbaned head and the half of her gaunt figure, and searched the whole garden through, as completely as her dim vision would allow. She could see the interior of the summer-house, and its circular seat, kept moist by the droppings of the roof. It had no occupant. Clifford was not thereabouts; unless, indeed, he had crept for concealment (as, for a moment, Hepzibah fancied might be the case) into a great, wet mass of tangled and broad-leaved shadow, where the squash-vines were clambering tumultuously upon an old wooden framework, set casually aslant against the fence. This could not be, however; he was not there; for, while Hepzibah was looking, a strange grimalkin stole forth from the very spot, and picked his way across the garden. Twice he paused to snuff the air, and then anew directed his course towards the parlor window. Whether it was only on account of the stealthy, prying manner common to the race, or that this cat seemed to have more than ordinary mischief in his thoughts, the old gentlewoman, in spite of her much perplexity, felt an impulse to drive the animal away, and accordingly flung down a window-stick. The cat stared up at her, like a detected thief or murderer, and, the next instant, took to flight. No other living creature was visible in the garden. Chanticleer and his family had either not left their roost, disheartened by the interminable rain, or had done the next wisest thing, by seasonably returning to it. Hepzibah closed the window.

But where was Clifford? Could it be that, aware of the presence of his Evil Destiny, he had crept silently down the staircase, while the Judge and Hepzibah stood talking in the shop, and had softly undone the fastenings of the outer door, and made his escape into the street? With that thought, she seemed to behold his gray, wrinkled, yet childlike aspect, in the old-fashioned garments which he wore about the house; a figure such as one sometimes imagines himself to be, with the world's eye upon him, in a troubled dream. This figure of her wretched brother would go wandering through the city, attracting all eyes, and everybody's wonder and repugnance, like a ghost, the more to be shuddered at because visible at noontide. To incur the ridicule of the younger crowd, that knew him not, — the harsher scorn and indignation of a few old men, who might recall his once familiar features! To be the sport of boys, who, when old enough to run about the streets, have no more reverence for what is beautiful and holy, nor pity for what is sad, — no more sense of sacred misery, sanctifying the human shape in which it embodies itself, — than if Satan were the father of them all! Goaded by their taunts, their loud, shrill cries, and cruel laughter, — insulted by the filth of the public ways, which they would fling upon him, — or, as it might well be, distracted by the mere strangeness of his situation, though nobody should afflict him with so much as a thoughtless word, — what wonder if Clifford were to break into some wild extravagance which was certain to be interpreted as lunacy? Thus Judge Pyncheon's fiendish scheme would be ready accomplished to his hands!

Then Hepzibah reflected that the town was almost completely water-girdled. The wharves stretched out towards the centre of the harbor, and, in this inclement weather, were deserted by the ordinary throng of merchants, laborers, and sea-faring men; each wharf a solitude, with the vessels moored stem and stern, along its misty length. Should her brother's aimless footsteps stray thitherward, and he but bend, one moment, over the deep, black tide, would he not bethink himself that here was the sure refuge within his reach, and that, with a single step, or the slightest overbalance of his body, he might be forever beyond his kinsman's gripe? Oh, the temptation! To make of his ponderous sorrow a security! To sink, with its leaden weight upon him, and never rise again!

The horror of this last conception was too much for Hepzibah. Even Jaffrey Pyncheon must help her now! She hastened down the staircase, shrieking as she went.

"Clifford is gone!" she cried. "I cannot find my

brother! Help, Jaffrey Pyncheon! Some harm will happen to him!"

She threw open the parlor-door. But, what with the shade of branches across the windows, and the smoke-blackened ceiling, and the dark oak-panelling of the walls, there was hardly so much daylight in the room that Hepzibah's imperfect sight could accurately distinguish the Judge's figure. She was certain, however, that she saw him sitting in the ancestral arm-chair, near the centre of the floor, with his face somewhat averted, and looking towards a window. So firm and quiet is the nervous system of such men as Judge Pyncheon, that he had perhaps stirred not more than once since her departure, but, in the hard composure of his temperament, retained the position into which accident had thrown him.

"I tell you, Jaffrey," cried Hepzibah, impatiently, as she turned from the parlor-door to search other rooms, "my brother is not in his chamber! You must help me seek him!"

But Judge Pyncheon was not the man to let himself be startled from an easy-chair with haste ill-befitting either the dignity of his character or his broad personal basis, by the alarm of an hysteric woman. Yet, considering his own interest in the matter, he might have bestirred himself with a little more alacrity.

"Do you hear me, Jaffrey Pyncheon?" screamed Hepzibah, as she again approached the parlor-door, after an ineffectual search elsewhere. "Clifford is gone!"

At this instant, on the threshold of the parlor, emerging from within, appeared Clifford himself! His face was preternaturally pale; so deadly white, indeed, that, through all the glimmering indistinctness of the passage-way, Hepzibah could discern his features, as if a light fell on them alone. Their vivid and wild expression seemed likewise sufficient to illuminate them; it was an expression of scorn and mockery, coinciding with the emotions indicated by his gesture. As Clifford stood on the threshold, partly turning back, he pointed his finger within the parlor, and shook it slowly as though he would have summoned, not Hepzibah alone, but the whole world, to gaze at some object inconceivably ridiculous. This action, so ill-timed and extravagant, — accompanied, too, with a look that showed more like joy than any other kind of excitement, — compelled Hepzibah to dread that her stern kinsman's ominous visit had driven her poor brother to absolute insanity. Nor could she otherwise account for the Judge's quiescent mood than by supposing him craftily on the watch, while Clifford developed these symptoms of a distracted mind.

"Be quiet, Clifford!" whispered his sister, raising her hand to impress caution. "Oh, for Heaven's sake, be quiet!"

"Let him be quiet! What can he do better?" answered Clifford, with a still wilder gesture, pointing into the room which he had just quitted. "As for us, Hepzibah, we can dance now! — we can sing, laugh, play, do what we will! The weight is gone, Hepzibah! it is gone off this weary old world, and we may be as light-hearted as little Phœbe herself!"

And, in accordance with his words, he began to laugh, still pointing his finger at the object, invisible to Hepzibah, within the parlor. She was seized with a sudden intuition of some horrible thing. She thrust herself past Clifford, and disappeared into the room; but almost immediately returned, with a cry choking in her throat. Gazing at her brother with an affrighted glance of inquiry, she beheld him all in a tremor and a quake, from head to foot, while, amid these commoted elements of passion or alarm, still flickered his gusty mirth.

"My God! what is to become of us?" gasped Hepzibah.

"Come!" said Clifford, in a tone of brief decision, most unlike what was usual with him. "We stay here too long! Let us leave the old house to our cousin Jaffrey! He will take good care of it!"

Hepzibah now noticed that Clifford had on a cloak, — a garment of long ago, — in which he had constantly muffled himself during these days of easterly storm. He beckoned with his hand, and intimated, so far as she could comprehend him, his purpose that they should go together from the house. There are chaotic, blind, or drunken moments, in the lives of persons who lack real force of character, — moments of test, in which courage would most assert itself, — but where these individuals, if left to themselves, stagger aimlessly along, or follow implicitly whatever guidance may befall them, even if it be a child's. No matter how preposterous or insane, a purpose is a God-send to them. Hepzibah had reached this point. Unaccustomed to action or responsibility, — full of horror at what she had seen, and afraid to inquire, or almost to imagine, how it had come to pass, — affrighted at the fatality which seemed to pursue her brother, — stupefied by the dim, thick, stifling atmosphere of dread, which filled the house as with a death-smell, and obliterated all definiteness of thought, —

she yielded without a question, and on the instant, to the will which Clifford expressed. For herself, she was like a person in a dream, when the will always sleeps. Clifford, ordinarily so destitute of this faculty, had found it in the tension of the crisis.

"Why do you delay so?" cried he, sharply. "Put on your cloak and hood, or whatever it pleases you to wear! No matter what; you cannot look beautiful nor brilliant, my poor Hepzibah! Take your purse, with money in it, and come along!"

Hepzibah obeyed these instructions, as if nothing else were to be done or thought of. She began to wonder, it is true, why she did not wake up, and at what still more intolerable pitch of dizzy trouble her spirit would struggle out of the maze, and make her conscious that nothing of all this had actually happened. Of course it was not real; no such black, easterly day as this had yet begun to be; Judge Pyncheon had not talked with her; Clifford had not laughed, pointed, beckoned her away with him; but she had merely been afflicted — as lonely sleepers often are — with a great deal of unreasonable misery, in a morning dream!

"Now — now — I shall certainly awake!" thought Hepzibah, as she went to and fro, making her little preparations. "I can bear it no longer! I must wake up now!"

But it came not, that awakening moment! It came not, even when, just before they left the house, Clifford stole to the parlor-door, and made a parting obeisance to the sole occupant of the room.

"What an absurd figure the old fellow cuts now!" whispered he to Hepzibah. "Just when he fancied he had me completely under his thumb! Come,

come; make haste! or he will start up, like Giant Despair in pursuit of Christian and Hopeful, and catch us yet!"

As they passed into the street, Clifford directed Hepzibah's attention to something on one of the posts of the front door. It was merely the initials of his own name, which. with somewhat of his characteristic grace about the forms of the letters, he had cut there when a boy. The brother and sister departed, and left Judge Pyncheon sitting in the old home of his forefathers, all by himself; so heavy and lumpish that we can liken him to nothing better than a defunct nightmare, which had perished in the midst of its wickedness, and left its flabby corpse on the breast of the tormented one, to be gotten rid of as it might!

XVII.

THE FLIGHT OF TWO OWLS.

SUMMER as it was, the east wind set poor Hepzibah's few remaining teeth chattering in her head, as she and Clifford faced it, on their way up Pyncheon Street, and towards the centre of the town. Not merely was it the shiver which this pitiless blast brought to her frame (although her feet and hands, especially, had never seemed so death-a-cold as now), but there was a moral sensation, mingling itself with the physical chill, and causing her to shake more in spirit than in body. The world's broad, bleak atmosphere was all so comfortless! Such, indeed, is the impression which it makes on every new adventurer, even if he plunge into it while the warmest tide of life is bubbling through his veins. What, then, must it have been to Hepzibah and Clifford, — so time-stricken as they were, yet so like children in their inexperience, — as they left the doorstep, and passed from beneath the wide shelter of the Pyncheon Elm! They were wandering all abroad, on precisely such a pilgrimage as a child often meditates, to the world's end, with perhaps a sixpence and a biscuit in his pocket. In Hepzibah's mind, there was the wretched consciousness of being adrift. She had lost the faculty of self-guidance; but, in view of the difficulties around her, felt it hardly worth an effort to regain it, and was, moreover, incapable of making one.

As they proceeded on their strange expedition she now and then cast a look sidelong at Clifford, and could not but observe that he was possessed and swayed by a powerful excitement. It was this, indeed, that gave him the control which he had at once, and so irresistibly, established over his movements. It not a little resembled the exhilaration of wine. Or, it might more fancifully be compared to a joyous piece of music, played with wild vivacity, but upon a disordered instrument. As the cracked jarring note might always be heard, and as it jarred loudest amid the loftiest exultation of the melody, so was there a continual quake through Clifford, causing him most to quiver while he wore a triumphant smile, and seemed almost under a necessity to skip in his gait.

They met few people abroad, even on passing from the retired neighborhood of the House of the Seven Gables into what was ordinarily the more thronged and busier portion of the town. Glistening sidewalks, with little pools of rain, here and there, along their unequal surface; umbrellas displayed ostentatiously in the shop-windows, as if the life of trade had concentred itself in that one article; wet leaves of the horse-chestnut or elm-trees, torn off untimely by the blast and scattered along the public way; an unsightly accumulation of mud in the middle of the street, which perversely grew the more unclean for its long and laborious washing, — these were the more definable points of a very sombre picture. In the way of movement, and human life, there was the hasty rattle of a cab or coach, its driver protected by a water-proof cap over his head and shoulders; the forlorn figure of an old man, who seemed to have crept out of some subterranean sewer, and was stooping along the kennel, and poking the wet rubbish with a stick, in quest of rusty nails; a merchant or two, at the door of the post-office, together with an editor, and a miscellaneous politician, awaiting a dilatory mail; a few visages of retired sea-captains at the window of an insurance office, looking out vacantly at the vacant street, blaspheming at the weather, and fretting at the dearth as well of public news as local gossip. What a treasure-trove to these venerable quidnuncs, could they have guessed the secret which Hepzibah and Clifford were carrying along with them! But their two figures attracted hardly so much notice as that of a young girl, who passed at the same instant, and happened to raise her skirt a trifle too high above her ankles. Had it been a sunny and cheerful day, they could hardly have gone through the streets without making themselves obnoxious to remark. Now, probably, they were felt to be in keeping with the dismal and bitter weather, and therefore did not stand out in strong relief; as if the sun were shining on them, but melted into the gray gloom and were forgotten as soon as gone.

Poor Hepzibah! Could she have understood this fact, it would have brought her some little comfort; for, to all her other troubles, — strange to say! — there was added the womanish and old-maiden-like misery arising from a sense of unseemliness in her attire. Thus, she was fain to shrink deeper into herself, as it were, as if in the hope of making people suppose that here was only a cloak and hood, threadbare and wofully faded, taking an airing in the midst of the storm, without any wearer!

As they went on, the feeling of indistinctness and unreality kept dimly hovering round about her, and so diffusing itself into her system that one of her hands was hardly palpable to the touch of the other. Any certainty would have been preferable to this. She whispered to herself, again and again, " Am I awake ? — Am I awake ? " and sometimes exposed her face to the chill spatter of the wind, for the sake of its rude assurance that she was. Whether it was Clifford's purpose, or only chance, had led them thither, they now found themselves passing beneath the arched entrance of a large structure of gray stone. Within, there was a spacious breadth, and an airy height from floor to roof, now partially filled with smoke and steam, which eddied voluminously upward and formed a mimic cloud - region over their heads. A train of cars was just ready for a start; the loco-motive was fretting and fuming, like a steed impa-tient for a headlong rush; and the bell rang out its hasty peal, so well expressing the brief summons which life vouchsafes to us in its hurried career. Without question or delay, — with the irresistible decision, if not rather to be called recklessness, which had so strangely taken possession of him, and through him of Hepzibah, — Clifford impelled her towards the cars, and assisted her to enter. The signal was given; the engine puffed forth its short, quick breaths; the train began its movement; and, along with a hundred other passengers, these two unwonted travellers sped onward like the wind.

At last, therefore, and after so long estrangement from everything that the world acted or enjoyed, they had been drawn into the great current of human life, and were swept away with it, as by the suction of fate itself.

Still haunted with the idea that not one of the past incidents, inclusive of Judge Pyncheon's visit, could be real, the recluse of the Seven Gables murmured in her brother's ear, —

"Clifford! Clifford! Is not this a dream?"

"A dream, Hepzibah!" repeated he, almost laughing in her face. "On the contrary, I have never been awake before!"

Meanwhile, looking from the window, they could see the world racing past them. At one moment, they were rattling through a solitude; the next, a village had grown up around them; a few breaths more, and it had vanished, as if swallowed by an earthquake. The spires of meeting-houses seemed set adrift from their foundations; the broad-based hills glided away. Everything was unfixed from its age-long rest, and moving at whirlwind speed in a direction opposite to their own.

Within the car there was the usual interior life of the railroad, offering little to the observation of other passengers, but full of novelty for this pair of strangely enfranchised prisoners. It was novelty enough, indeed, that there were fifty human beings in close relation with them, under one long and narrow roof, and drawn onward by the same mighty influence that had taken their two selves into its grasp. It seemed marvellous how all these people could remain so quietly in their seats, while so much noisy strength was at work in their behalf. Some, with tickets in their hats (long travellers these, before whom lay a hundred miles of railroad), had plunged into the English scenery and adventures of pamphlet novels, and were keeping company with dukes and earls. Others, whose briefer span forbade their devoting themselves to studies so abstruse, beguiled the little tedium of the way with penny-papers. A party of girls, and one young man, on opposite sides of the car, found huge amusement in a game of ball. They tossed it to and fro, with peals of laughter that might be measured by mile-lengths; for, faster than the nimble ball could fly, the merry players fled unconsciously along, leaving the trail of their mirth afar behind, and ending their game under another sky than had witnessed its commencement. Boys, with apples, cakes, candy, and rolls of variously tinctured lozenges, — merchandise that reminded Hepzibah of her deserted shop, — appeared at each momentary stopping-place, doing up their business in a hurry, or breaking it short off, lest the market should ravish them away with it. New people continually entered. Old acquaintances — for such they soon grew to be, in this rapid current of affairs — continually departed. Here and there, amid the rumble and the tumult sat one asleep. Sleep; sport; business; graver or lighter study; and the common and inevitable movement onward! It was life itself!

Clifford's naturally poignant sympathies were all aroused. He caught the color of what was passing about him, and threw it back more vividly than he received it, but mixed, nevertheless, with a lurid and portentous hue. Hepzibah, on the other hand, felt herself more apart from human kind than even in the seclusion which she had just quitted.

"You are not happy, Hepzibah!" said Clifford, apart, in a tone of reproach. "You are thinking of that dismal old house, and of Cousin Jaffrey," — here came the quake through him, — "and of Cousin Jaffrey sitting there, all by himself! Take my advice, — follow my example, — and let such things slip aside. Here we are, in the world, Hepzibah! — in the midst of life! — in the throng of our fellow-beings!

Let you and I be happy! As happy as that youth, and those pretty girls, at their game of ball!"

"Happy!" thought Hepzibah, bitterly conscious, at the word, of her dull and heavy heart, with the frozen pain in it, — "happy! He is mad already; and, if I could once feel myself broad awake, I should go mad too!"

If a fixed idea be madness, she was perhaps not remote from it. Fast and far as they had rattled and clattered along the iron track, they might just as well, as regarded Hepzibah's mental images, have been passing up and down Pyncheon Street. With miles and miles of varied scenery between, there was no scene for her, save the seven old gable-peaks, with their moss, and the tuft of weeds in one of the angles, and the shop-window, and a customer shaking the door, and compelling the little bell to jingle fiercely, but without disturbing Judge Pyncheon! This one old house was everywhere! It transported its great, lumbering bulk with more than railroad speed, and set itself phlegmatically down on whatever spot she glanced at. The quality of Hepzibah's mind was too unmalleable to take new impressions so readily as Clifford's. He had a winged nature; she was rather of the vegetable kind, and could hardly be kept long alive, if drawn up by the roots. Thus it happened that the relation heretofore existing between her brother and herself was changed. At home, she was his guardian; here, Clifford had become hers, and seemed to comprehend whatever belonged to their new position with a singular rapidity of intelligence. He had been startled into manhood and intellectual vigor; or, at least, into a condition that resembled them, though it might be both diseased and transitory.

The conductor now applied for their tickets; and Clifford, who had made himself the purse-bearer, put a bank-note into his hand, as he had observed others do.

" For the lady and yourself ? " asked the conductor. " And how far ? "

" As far as that will carry us," said Clifford. " It is no great matter. We are riding for pleasure merely ! "

" You choose a strange day for it, sir ! " remarked a gimlet-eyed old gentleman, on the other side of the car, looking at Clifford and his companion, as if curious to make them out. " The best chance of pleasure, in an easterly rain, I take it, is in a man's own house, with a nice little fire in the chimney."

" I cannot precisely agree with you," said Clifford, courteously bowing to the old gentleman, and at once taking up the clew of conversation which the latter had proffered. " It had just occurred to me, on the contrary, that this admirable invention of the railroad — with the vast and inevitable improvements to be looked for, both as to speed and convenience — is destined to do away with those stale ideas of home and fireside, and substitute something better."

" In the name of common - sense," asked the old gentleman, rather testily, " what can be better for a man than his own parlor and chimney-corner ? "

" These things have not the merit which many good people attribute to them," replied Clifford. " They may be said, in few and pithy words, to have ill served a poor purpose. My impression is, that our wonderfully increased and still increasing facilities of locomotion are destined to bring us round again to the nomadic state. You are aware, my dear sir, -- you must have observed it in your own experience, — that all human progress is in a circle; or, to use a more accurate and beautiful figure, in an ascending spiral curve. While we fancy ourselves going straight forward, and attaining, at every step, an entirely new position of affairs, we do actually return to something long ago tried and abandoned, but which we now find etherealized, refined, and perfected to its ideal. The past is but a coarse and sensual prophecy of the present and the future. To apply this truth to the topic now under discussion. In the early epochs of our race, men dwelt in temporary huts, of bowers of branches, as easily constructed as a bird's-nest, and which they built, — if it should be called building, when such sweet homes of a summer solstice rather grew than were made with hands, — which Nature, we will say, assisted them to rear where fruit abounded, where fish and game were plentiful, or, most especially, where the sense of beauty was to be gratified by a lovelier shade than elsewhere, and a more exquisite arrangement of lake, wood, and hill. This life possessed a charm, which, ever since man quitted it, has vanished from existence. And it typified something better than itself. It had its drawbacks; such as hunger and thirst, inclement weather, hot sunshine, and weary and foot-blistering marches over barren and ugly tracts, that lay between the sites desirable for their fertility and beauty. But in our ascending spiral, we escape all this. These railroads — could but the whistle be made musical, and the rumble and the jar got rid of — are positively the greatest blessing that the ages have wrought out for us. They give us wings; they annihilate the toil and dust of pilgrimage; they spiritualize travel! Transition being so facile, what can be any man's inducement to tarry in one spot? Why, therefore, should he build a more cumbrous habitation than can readily be carried off with him? Why should he make himself a prisoner for life in brick, and stone, and old worm-eaten timber, when he may just as easily dwell, in one sense, nowhere, — in a better sense, wher ever the fit and beautiful shall offer him a home?"

Clifford's countenance glowed, as he divulged this theory; a youthful character shone out from within, converting the wrinkles and pallid duskiness of age into an almost transparent mask. The merry girls let their ball drop upon the floor, and gazed at him. They said to themselves, perhaps, that, before his hair was gray and the crow's-feet tracked his temples, this now decaying man must have stamped the impress of his features on many a woman's heart. But, alas! no woman's eye had seen his face while it was beautiful.

"I should scarcely call it an improved state of things," observed Clifford's new acquaintance, "to live everywhere and nowhere!"

"Would you not?" exclaimed Clifford, with singular energy. "It is as clear to me as sunshine, — were there any in the sky, — that the greatest possible stumbling-blocks in the path of human happiness and improvement are these heaps of bricks and stones, consolidated with mortar, or hewn timber, fastened together with spike-nails, which men painfully contrive for their own torment, and call them house and home! The soul needs air; a wide sweep and frequent change of it. Morbid influences, in a thousand-fold variety, gather about hearths, and pollute the life of households. There is no such unwholesome atmosphere as that of an old home, rendered poisonous by one's defunct forefathers and relatives. I speak of what I know. There is a certain house within my familiar recollection, — one of those peaked-gable (there are seven of them), projecting-storied edifices, such as you occasionally see in our older towns, — a rusty, crazy, creaky, dry-rotted, damp-rotted, dingy, dark, and miserable old dungeon, with an arched window over the porch, and a little shop-door on one side, and a great, melancholy elm before it! Now, sir, whenever my thoughts recur to this seven-gabled mansion (the fact is so very curious that I must needs mention it), immediately I have a vision or image of an elderly man, of remarkably stern countenance, sitting in an oaken elbow-chair, dead, stone-dead, with an ugly flow of blood upon his shirt-bosom! Dead, but with open eyes! He taints the whole house, as I remember it. I could never flourish there, nor be happy, nor do nor enjoy what God meant me to do and enjoy!"

His face darkened, and seemed to contract, and shrivel itself up, and wither into age.

"Never, sir!" he repeated. "I could never draw cheerful breath there!"

"I should think not," said the old gentleman, eying Clifford earnestly, and rather apprehensively. "I should conceive not, sir, with that notion in your head!"

"Surely not," continued Clifford; "and it were a relief to me if that house could be torn down, or burnt up, and so the earth be rid of it, and grass be sown abundantly over its foundation. Not that I should ever visit its site again! for, sir, the farther I get away from it, the more does the joy, the lightsome freshness, the heart-leap, the intellectual dance, the youth, in short, — yes, my youth, my youth! — the more does it come back to me. No longer ago than this morning, I was old. I remember looking in the glass, and wondering at my own gray hair, and the wrinkles, many and deep, right across my brow, and the furrows down my cheeks, and the prodigious trampling of crow's-feet about my temples! It was too soon! I could not bear it! Age had no right to come! 'I had not lived! But now do I look old? If so, my aspect belies me strangely; for — a great weight being off my mind — I feel in the very heyday of my youth, with the world and my best days before me!"

"I trust you may find it so," said the old gentleman, who seemed rather embarrassed, and desirous of avoiding the observation which Clifford's wild talk drew on them both. "You have my best wishes for it."

"For Heaven's sake, dear Clifford, be quiet!" whispered his sister. "They think you mad."

"Be quiet yourself, Hepzibah!" returned her brother. "No matter what they think! I am not mad. For the first time in thirty years my thoughts gush up and find words ready for them. I must talk, and I will!"

He turned again towards the old gentleman, and renewed the conversation.

"Yes, my dear sir," said he, "it is my firm belief and hope that these terms of roof and hearth-stone, which have so long been held to embody something sacred, are soon to pass out of men's daily use, and be forgotten. Just imagine, for a moment, how much of human evil will crumble away, with this one change! What we call real estate — the solid ground to build a house on — is the broad foundation on which nearly all the guilt of this world rests. A man will commit almost any wrong, — he will heap up an immense pile of wickedness, as hard as granite, and which will weigh as heavily upon his soul, to eternal ages, — only to build a great, gloomy, dark-chambered mansion, for himself to die in, and for his posterity to be miserable in. He lays his own dead corpse beneath the underpinning, as one may say, and hangs his frowning picture on the wall, and, after thus converting himself into an evil destiny, expects his remotest great-grandchildren to be happy there! I do not speak wildly. I have just such a house in my mind's eye!"

"Then, sir," said the old gentleman, getting anxious to drop the subject, "you are not to blame for leaving it."

"Within the lifetime of the child already born," Clifford went on, "all this will be done away. The world is growing too ethereal and spiritual to bear these enormities a great while longer. To me, — though, for a considerable period of time, I have lived chiefly in retirement, and know less of such things than most men, — even to me, the harbingers of a better era are unmistakable. Mesmerism, now! Will that effect nothing, think you, towards purging away the grossness out of human life?"

"All a humbug!" growled the old gentleman.

"These rapping spirits, that little Phœbe told us of, the other day," said Clifford, — "what are these but the messengers of the spiritual world, knocking at the door of substance? And it shall be flung wide open!"

"A humbug, again!" cried the old gentleman, growing more and more testy, at these glimpses of Clifford's metaphysics. "I should like to rap with a good stick on the empty pates of the dolts who circulate such nonsense!"

"Then there is electricity, — the demon, the angel, the mighty physical power, the all-pervading intelligence!" exclaimed Clifford. "Is that a humbug, too? Is it a fact — or have I dreamt it — that, by means of electricity, the world of matter has become a great nerve, vibrating thousands of miles in a breathless point of time? Rather, the round globe is a vast head, a brain, instinct with intelligence! Or, shall we say, it is itself a thought, nothing but thought, and no longer the substance which we deemed it!"

"If you mean the telegraph," said the old gentleman, glancing his eye toward its wire, alongside the rail-track, "it is an excellent thing, — that is, of course, if the speculators in cotton and politics don't get possession of it. A great thing, indeed, sir, particularly as regards the detection of bank-robbers and murderers."

"I don't quite like it, in that point of view," replied Clifford. "A bank-robber, and what you call a murderer, likewise, has his rights, which men of enlightened humanity and conscience should regard in so much the more liberal spirit, because the bulk of society is prone to controvert their existence.. An almost spiritual medium, like the electric telegraph, should be consecrated to high, deep, joyful, and holy missions. Lovers, day by day, — hour by hour, if so often moved to do it, — might send their heart-throbs from Maine to Florida, with some such words as these, 'I love you forever!' — 'My heart runs over with love!' — 'I love you more than I can!' and, again, at the next message, 'I have lived an hour longer, and love you twice as much!' Or, when a good man has departed, his distant friend should be conscious of an electric thrill, as from the world of happy spirits, telling him, 'Your dear friend is in bliss!' Or, to an absent husband, should come tidings thus, 'An immortal being, of whom you are the father, has this moment come from God!' and immediately its little voice would seem to have reached so far, and to be echoing in his heart. But for these poor rogues, the bank-robbers, — who after all, are about as honest as nine people in ten, except that they disregard certain formalities, and prefer to transact business at midnight rather than 'Change-hours, — and for these murderers, as you phrase it, who are often excusable in the motives of their deed, and deserve to be ranked among public benefactors, if we consider only its result, — for unfortunate individuals like these, I really cannot applaud the enlistment of an immaterial and miraculous power in the universal world-hunt at their heels!"

"You can't, hey?" cried the old gentleman, with a hard look.

"Positively, no!" answered Clifford. "It puts them too miserably at disadvantage. For example, sir, in a dark, low, cross-beamed, panelled room of an old house, let us suppose a dead man, sitting in an arm-chair, with a blood-stain on his shirt-bosom, — and let us add to our hypothesis another man, issuing from the house, which he feels to be over-filled with the dead man's presence, — and let us lastly imagine him fleeing, Heaven knows whither, at the speed of a hurricane, by railroad! Now, sir, if the fugitive alight in some distant town, and find all the people babbling about that self-same dead man, whom he has fled so far to avoid the sight and thought of, will you not allow that his natural rights have been infringed? He has been deprived of his city of refuge, and, in my humble opinion, has suffered infinite wrong!"

" You are a strange man, sir ! " said the old gentleman, bringing his gimlet-eye to a point on Clifford, as
if determined to bore right into him. " I can't see
through you ! "

" No, I 'll be bound you can't ! " cried Clifford,
laughing. " And yet, my dear sir, I am as transparent as the water of Maule's well ! But come, Hepzibah ! We have flown far enough for once. Let us
alight, as the birds do, and perch ourselves on the
nearest twig, and consult whither we shall fly next ! "

Just then, as it happened, the train reached a solitary way - station. Taking advantage of the brief
pause, Clifford left the car, and drew Hepzibah along
with him. A moment afterwards, the train — with
all the life of its interior, amid which Clifford had
made himself so conspicuous an object — was gliding
away in the distance, and rapidly lessening to a point,
which, in another moment, vanished. The world had
fled away from these two wanderers. They gazed
drearily about them. At a little distance stood a
wooden church, black with age, and in a dismal state
of ruin and decay, with broken windows, a great rift
through the main body of the edifice, and a rafter
dangling from the top of the square tower. Farther
off was a farm-house, in the old style, as venerably
black as the church, with a roof sloping downward
from the three-story peak, to within a man's height of
the ground. It seemed uninhabited. There were the
relics of a wood-pile, indeed, near the door, but with
grass sprouting up among the chips and scattered logs.
The small rain-drops came down aslant ; the wind was
not turbulent, but sullen, and full of chilly moisture.

Clifford shivered from head to foot. The wild effervescence of his mood — which had so readily supplied

thoughts, fantasies, and a strange aptitude of words, and impelled him to talk from the mere necessity of giving vent to this bubbling-up gush of ideas — had entirely subsided. A powerful excitement had given him energy and vivacity. Its operation over, he forthwith began to sink.

"You must take the lead now, Hepzibah!" murmured he, with a torpid and reluctant utterance. "Do with me as you will!"

She knelt down upon the platform where they were standing and lifted her clasped hands to the sky. The dull, gray weight of clouds made it invisible; but it was no hour for disbelief, — no juncture this to question that there was a sky above, and an Almighty Father looking from it!

"O God!" — ejaculated poor, gaunt Hepzibah, — then paused a moment, to consider what her prayer should be, — "O God. — our Father, — are we not thy children? Have mercy on us!"

XVIII.

GOVERNOR ·PYNCHEON.

JUDGE PYNCHEON, while his two relatives have fled away with such ill-considered haste, still sits in the old parlor, keeping house, as the familiar phrase is, in the absence of its ordinary occupants. To him, and to the venerable House of the Seven Gables, does our story now betake itself, like an owl, bewildered in the daylight, and hastening back to his hollow tree.

The Judge has not shifted his position for a long while now. He has not stirred hand or foot, nor withdrawn his eyes so much as a hair's-breadth from their fixed gaze towards the corner of the room, since the footsteps of Hepzibah and Clifford creaked along the passage, and the outer door was closed cautiously behind their exit. He holds his watch in his left hand, but clutched in such a manner that you cannot see the dial-plate. How profound a fit of meditation! Or, supposing him asleep, how infantile a quietude of conscience, and what wholesome order in the gastric region, are betokened by slumber so entirely undisturbed with starts, cramp, twitches, muttered dream-talk, trumpet-blasts through the nasal organ, or any the slightest irregularity of breath! You must hold your own breath, to satisfy yourself whether he breathes at all. It is quite inaudible. You hear the ticking of his watch; his breath you do not hear. A most refreshing slumber, doubtless! And yet, the Judge can-

not be asleep. His eyes are open! A veteran politician, such as he, would never fall asleep with wide-
open eyes, lest some enemy or mischief-maker, taking
him thus at unawares, should peep through these windows into his consciousness, and make strange discov-
eries among the reminiscences, projects, hopes, apprehensions, weaknesses, and strong points, which he has
heretofore shared with nobody. A cautious man is
proverbially said to sleep with one eye open. That
may be wisdom. But not with both; for this were
heedlessness! No, no! Judge Pyncheon cannot be
asleep.

It is odd, however, that a gentleman so burdened
with engagements, — and noted, too, for punctuality,
— should linger thus in an old lonely mansion, which
he has never seemed very fond of visiting. The oaken
chair, to be sure, may tempt him with its roominess.
It is, indeed, a spacious, and, allowing for the rude
age that fashioned it, a moderately easy seat, with capacity enough, at all events, and offering no restraint
to the Judge's breadth of beam. A bigger man might
find ample accommodation in it. His ancestor, now
pictured upon the wall, with all his English beef about
him, used hardly to present a front extending from
elbow to elbow of this chair, or a base that would
cover its whole cushion. But there are better chairs
than this, — mahogany, black-walnut, rosewood, spring-
seated and damask-cushioned, with varied slopes, and
innumerable artifices to make them easy, and obviate
the irksomeness of too tame an ease, — a score of
such might be at Judge Pyncheon's service. Yes!
in a score of drawing-rooms he would be more than
welcome. Mamma would advance to meet him, with
outstretched hand; the virgin daughter, elderly as he

has now got to be, — an old widower, as he smilingly describes himself, — would shake up the cushion for the Judge, and do her pretty little utmost to make him comfortable. For the Judge is a prosperous man. He cherishes his schemes, moreover, like other people, and reasonably brighter than most others ; or did so, at least, as he lay abed this morning, in an agreeable half-drowse, planning the business of the day, and speculating on the probabilities of the next fifteen years. With his firm health, and the little inroad that age has made upon him, fifteen years or twenty — yes, or perhaps five-and-twenty ! — are no more than he may fairly call his own. Five-and-twenty years for the enjoyment of his real estate in town and country, his railroad, bank, and insurance shares, his United States stock, — his wealth, in short, however invested, now in possession, or soon to be acquired ; together with the public honors that have fallen upon him, and the weightier ones that are yet to fall ! It is good ! It is excellent ! It is enough !

Still lingering in the old chair ! If the Judge has a little time to throw away, why does not he visit the insurance office, as is his frequent custom, and sit awhile in one of their leathern-cushioned arm-chairs, listening to the gossip of the day, and dropping some deeply designed chance-word, which will be certain to become the gossip of to-morrow ! And have not the bank directors a meeting at which it was the Judge's purpose to be present, and his office to preside ? Indeed they have ; and the hour is noted on a card, which is, or ought to be, in Judge Pyncheon's right vest-pocket. Let him go thither, and loll at ease upon his money-bags ! He has lounged long enough in the old chair !

This was to have been such a busy day ! In the

first place, the interview with Clifford. Half an hour, by the Judge's reckoning, was to suffice for that; it would probably be less, but — taking into consideraation that Hepzibah was first to be dealt with, and that these women are apt to make many words where a few would do much better — it might be safest to allow half an hour. Half an hour? Why, Judge, it is already two hours, by your own undeviatingly accurate chronometer! Glance your eye down at it and see! Ah! he will not give himself the trouble either to bend his head, or elevate his hand, so as to bring the faithful time-keeper within his range of vision! Time, all at once, appears to have become a matter of no moment with the Judge!

And has he forgotten all the other items of his memoranda? Clifford's affair arranged, he was to meet a State Street broker, who has undertaken to procure a heavy percentage, and the best of paper, for a few loose thousands which the Judge happens to have by him, uninvested. The wrinkled note-shaver will have taken his railroad trip in vain. Half an hour later, in the street next to this, there was to be an auction of real estate, including a portion of the old Pyncheon property, originally belonging to Maule's gardenground. It has been alienated from the Pyncheons these four-score years; but the Judge had kept it in his eye, and had set his heart on reannexing it to the small demesne still left around the Seven Gables; and now, during this odd fit of oblivion, the fatal hammer must have fallen, and transferred our ancient patrimony to some alien possessor! Possibly, indeed, the sale may have been postponed till fairer weather. If so, will the Judge make it convenient to be present, and favor the auctioneer with his bid, on the proximate occasion?

The next affair was to buy a horse for his own driv. ing. The one heretofore his favorite stumbled, this very morning, on the road to town, and must be at once discarded. Judge Pyncheon's neck is too precious to be risked on such a contingency as a stumbling steed. Should all the above business be seasonably got through with, he might attend the meeting of a charitable society; the very name of which, however, in the multiplicity of his benevolence, is quite forgotten; so that this engagement may pass unfulfilled, and no great harm done. And if he have time, amid the press of more urgent matters, he must take measures for the renewal of Mrs. Pyncheon's tombstone, which, the sexton tells him, has fallen on its marble face, and is cracked quite in twain. She was a praiseworthy woman enough, thinks the Judge, in spite of her nervousness, and the tears that she was so oozy with, and her foolish behavior about the coffee; and as she took her departure so seasonably, he will not grudge the second tombstone. It is better, at least, than if she had never needed any! The next item on his list was to give orders for some fruit-trees, of a rare variety, to be deliverable at his country-seat, in the ensuing autumn. Yes, buy them, by all means; and may the peaches be luscious in your mouth, Judge Pyncheon! After this comes something more important. A committee of his political party has besought him for a hundred or two of dollars, in addition to his previous disbursements, towards carrying on the fall campaign. The Judge is a patriot; the fate of the country is staked on the November election; and besides, as will be shadowed forth in another paragraph, he has no trifling stake of his own in the same great game. He will do what the committee asks;

nay, he will be liberal beyond their expectations; they shall have a check for five hundred dollars, and more anon, if it be needed. What next? A decayed widow, whose husband was Judge Pyncheon's early friend, has laid her case of destitution before him, in a very moving letter. She and her fair daughter have scarcely bread to eat. He partly intends to call on her, to-day,—perhaps so—perhaps not,—accordingly as he may happen to have leisure, and a small bank-note.

Another business, which, however, he puts no great weight on (it is well, you know, to be heedful, but not over-anxious, as respects one's personal health),—another business, then, was to consult his family physician. About what, for Heaven's sake? Why, it is rather difficult to describe the symptoms. A mere dimness of sight and dizziness of brain, was it?—or a disagreeable choking, or stifling, or gurgling, or bubbling, in the region of the thorax, as the anatomists say?—or was it a pretty severe throbbing and kicking of the heart, rather creditable to him than otherwise, as showing that the organ had not been left out of the Judge's physical contrivance? No matter what it was. The doctor, probably, would smile at the statement of such trifles to his professional ear; the Judge would smile in his turn; and meeting one another's eyes, they would enjoy a hearty laugh together! But a fig for medical advice! The Judge will never need it.

Pray, pray, Judge Pyncheon, look at your watch, now! What—not a glance! It is within ten minutes of the dinner-hour! It surely cannot have slipped your memory that the dinner of to-day is to be the most important, in its consequences, of all the dinners you ever ate. Yes, precisely the most important; although, in the course of your somewhat eminent career, you have been placed high towards the head of the table, at splendid banquets, and have poured out your festive eloquence to ears yet echoing with Webster's mighty organ - tones. No public dinner this, however. It is merely a gathering of some dozen or so of friends from several districts of the State; men of distinguished character and influence, assembling, almost casually, at the house of a common friend, likewise distinguished, who will make them welcome to a little better than his ordinary fare. Nothing in the way of French cookery, but an excellent dinner nevertheless. Real turtle, we understand, and salmon, tautog, canvas-backs, pig, English mutton, good roast-beef, or dainties of that serious kind, fit for substantial country gentlemen, as these honorable persons mostly are. The delicacies of the season, in short, and flavored by a brand of old Madeira which has been the pride of many seasons. It is the Juno brand; a glorious wine, fragrant, and full of gentle might; a bottled - up happiness, put by for use; a golden liquid, worth more than liquid gold; so rare and admirable, that veteran wine-bibbers count it among their epochs to have tasted it! It drives away the heart-ache, and substitutes no head-ache! Could the Judge but quaff a glass, it might enable him to shake off the unaccountable lethargy which (for the ten intervening minutes, and five to boot, are already past) has made him such a laggard at this momentous dinner. It would all but revive a dead man! Would you like to sip it now, Judge Pyncheon?

Alas, this dinner! Have you really forgotten its true object? Then let us whisper it, that you may start at once out of the oaken chair, which really seems to be enchanted, like the one in Comus, or that in which Moll Pitcher imprisoned your own grand-father. But ambition is a talisman more powerful than witchcraft. Start up, then, and, hurrying through the streets, burst in upon the company, that they may begin before the fish is spoiled! They wait for you; and it is little for your interest that they should wait. These gentlemen — need you be told it? — have as-sembled, not without purpose, from every quarter of the State. They are practised politicians, every man of them, and skilled to adjust those preliminary measures which steal from the people, without its knowledge, the power of choosing its own rulers. The popular voice, at the next gubernatorial election, though loud as thunder, will be really but an echo of what these gentlemen shall speak, under their breath, at your friend's festive board. They meet to decide upon their candidate. This little knot of subtle schemers will control the convention, and, through it, dictate to the party. And what worthier candidate, — more wise and learned, more noted for philan-thropic liberality, truer to safe principles, tried oftener by public trusts, more spotless in private character, with a larger stake in the common welfare, and deeper grounded, by hereditary descent, in the faith and prac-tice of the Puritans, — what man can be presented for the suffrage of the people, so eminently combining all these claims to the chief-rulership as Judge Pyncheon here before us?

Make haste, then! Do your part! The meed for which you have toiled, and fought, and climbed, and crept, is ready for your grasp! Be present at this dinner! — drink a glass or two of that noble wine! —

make your pledges in as low a whisper as you will!—
and you rise up from table virtually governor of the
glorious old State! Governor Pyncheon of Massachusetts!

And is there no potent and exhilarating cordial in
a certainty like this? It has been the grand purpose
of half your lifetime to obtain it. Now, when there
needs little more than to signify your acceptance, why
do you sit so lumpishly in your great-great-grandfather's oaken chair, as if preferring it to the gubernatorial one? We have all heard of King Log; but,
in these jostling times, one of that royal kindred will
hardly win the race for an elective chief-magistracy.

Well! it is absolutely too late for dinner! Turtle,
salmon, tautog, woodcock, boiled turkey, South-Down
mutton, pig, roast-beef, have vanished, or exist only
in fragments, with lukewarm potatoes, and gravies
crusted over with cold fat. The Judge, had he done
nothing else, would have achieved wonders with his
knife and fork. It was he, you know, of whom it
used to be said, in reference to his ogre-like appetite,
that his Creator made him a great animal, but that
the dinner-hour made him a great beast. Persons
of his large sensual endowments must claim indulgence, at their feeding-time. But, for once, the Judge
is entirely too late for dinner! Too late, we fear, even
to join the party at their wine! The guests are warm
and merry; they have given up the Judge; and, concluding that the Free-Soilers have him, they will fix
upon another candidate. Were our friend now to
stalk in among them, with that wide-open stare, at
once wild and stolid, his ungenial presence would be
apt to change their cheer. Neither would it be seemly
in Judge Pyncheon, generally so scrupulous in his

attire, to show himself at a dinner-table with that crimson stain upon his shirt-bosom. By the by, how came it there? It is an ugly sight, at any rate; and the wisest way for the Judge is to button his coat closely over his breast, and, taking his horse and chaise from the livery-stable, to make all speed to his own house. There, after a glass of brandy and water, and a mutton-chop, a beefsteak, a broiled fowl, or some such hasty little dinner and supper all in one, he had better spend the evening by the fireside. He must toast his slippers a long while, in order to get rid of the chilliness which the air of this vile old house has sent curdling through his veins.

Up, therefore, Judge Pyncheon, up! You have lost a day. But to-morrow will be here anon. Will you rise, betimes, and make the most of it? To-morrow! To-morrow! 'To-morrow! We, that are alive, may rise betimes to-morrow. As for him that has died to-day, his morrow will be the resurrection morn.

Meanwhile the twilight is glooming upward out of the corners of the room. The shadows of the tall furniture grow deeper, and at first become more definite; then, spreading wider, they lose their distinctness of outline in the dark gray tide of oblivion, as it were, that creeps slowly over the various objects, and the one human figure sitting in the midst of them. The gloom has not entered from without; it has brooded here all day, and now, taking its own inevitable time, will possess itself of everything. The Judge's face, indeed, rigid, and singularly white, refuses to melt into this universal solvent. Fainter and fainter grows the light. It is as if another double-handful of darkness had been scattered through the air. Now it is no longer gray, but sable. There is still a faint appearance at the window; neither a glow, nor a gleam, nor a glimmer, — any phrase of light would express something far brighter than this doubtful perception, or sense, rather, that there is a window there. Has it yet vanished? No! — yes! — not quite! And there is still the swarthy whiteness, — we shall venture to marry these ill-agreeing words, — the swarthy whiteness of Judge Pyncheon's face. The features are all gone: there is only the paleness of them left. And how looks it now? There is no window! There is no face! An infinite, inscrutable blackness has annihilated sight! Where is our universe? All crumbled away from us; and we, adrift in chaos, may hearken to the gusts of homeless wind, that go sighing and murmuring about, in quest of what was once a world!

Is there no other sound? One other, and a fearful one. It is the ticking of the Judge's watch, which, ever since Hepzibah left the room in search of Clifford, he has been holding in his hand. Be the cause what it may, this little, quiet, never-ceasing throb of Time's pulse, repeating its small strokes with such busy regularity, in Judge Pyncheon's motionless hand, has an effect of terror, which we do not find in any other accompaniment of the scene.

But, listen! That puff of the breeze was louder; it had a tone unlike the dreary and sullen one which has bemoaned itself, and afflicted all mankind with miserable sympathy, for five days past. The wind has veered about! It now comes boisterously from the northwest, and, taking hold of the aged framework of the Seven Gables, gives it a shake, like a wrestler that would try strength with his antagonist. Another and another sturdy tussle with the blast! The old house creaks again, and makes a vociferous but somewhat unintelligible bellowing in its sooty throat (the big flue, we mean, of its wide chimney), partly in complaint at the rude wind, but rather, as befits their century and a half of hostile intimacy, in tough defiance. A rumbling kind of a bluster roars behind the fire-board. A door has slammed above stairs. A window, perhaps, has been left open, or else is driven in by an unruly gust. It is not to be conceived, beforehand, what wonderful wind-instruments are these old timber mansions, and how haunted with the strangest noises, which immediately begin to sing, and sigh, and sob, and shriek, — and to smite with sledge-hammers, airy but ponderous, in some distant chamber, — and to tread along the entries as with stately footsteps, and rustle up and down the staircase, as with silks miraculously stiff, — whenever the gale catches the house with a window open, and gets fairly into it. Would that we were not an attendant spirit here! It is too awful! This clamor of the wind through the lonely house; the Judge's quietude, as he sits invisible; and that pertinacious ticking of his watch!

As regards Judge Pyncheon's invisibility, however, that matter will soon be remedied. The northwest wind has swept the sky clear. The window is distinctly seen. Through its panes, moreover, we dimly catch the sweep of the dark, clustering foliage, outside, fluttering with a constant irregularity of movement, and letting in a peep of starlight, now here, now there. Oftener than any other object, these glimpses illuminate the Judge's face. But here comes more effectual light. Observe that silvery dance upon the upper branches of the pear-tree, and now a little lower, and now on the whole mass of boughs, while, through their shifting intricacies, the moonbeams fall aslant into the room. They play over the Judge's figure and show that he has not stirred throughout the hours of darkness. They follow the shadows, in changeful sport, across his unchanging features. They gleam upon his watch. His grasp conceals the dial-plate; but we know that the faithful hands have met; for one of the city clocks tells midnight.

A man of sturdy understanding, like Judge Pyncheon, cares no more for twelve o'clock at night than for the corresponding hour of noon. However just the parallel drawn, in some of the preceding pages, between his Puritan ancestor and himself, it fails in this point. The Pyncheon of two centuries ago, in common with most of his contemporaries, professed his full belief in spiritual ministrations, although reckoning them chiefly of a malignant character. The Pyncheon of to-night, who sits in yonder arm-chair, believes in no such nonsense. Such, at least, was his creed, some few hours since. His hair will not bristle, therefore, at the stories which — in times when chimney-corners had benches in them, where old people sat poking into the ashes of the past, and raking out traditions like live coals — used to be told about this very room of his ancestral house. In fact, these tales are too absurd to bristle even childhood's hair. What sense, meaning, or moral, for example, such as even ghost-stories should be susceptible of, can be traced in the ridiculous legend, that, at midnight, all the dead Pyncheons are bound to assemble in this parlor? And, pray, for what? Why, to see whether the portrait of their ancestor still keeps its place upon the wall, in compliance with his testamentary directions! Is it worth while to come out of their graves for that?

We are tempted to make a little sport with the idea. Ghost-stories are hardly to be treated seriously, any longer. The family-party of the defunct Pyncheons, we presume, goes off in this wise.

First comes the ancestor himself, in his black cloak, steeple-hat, and trunk-breeches, girt about the waist with a leathern belt, in which hangs his steel-hilted sword ; he has a long staff in his hand, such as gentlemen in advanced life used to carry, as much for the dignity of the thing as for the support to be derived from it. He looks up at the portrait ; a thing of no substance, gazing at its own painted image ! All is safe. The picture is still there. The purpose of his brain has been kept sacred thus long after the man himself has sprouted up in graveyard grass. See! he lifts his ineffectual hand, and tries the frame. All safe ! But is that a smile ? — is it not, rather, a frown of deadly import, that darkens over the shadow of his features ? The stout Colonel is dissatisfied ! So decided is his look of discontent as to impart additional distinctness to his features ; through which, nevertheless, the moonlight passes, and flickers on the wall beyond. Something has strangely vexed the ancestor ! With a grim shake of the head, he turns away. Here come other Pyncheons, the whole tribe, in their half a dozen generations, jostling and elbowing one another, to reach the picture. We behold aged men and grandames, a clergyman with the Puritanic stiffness still in his garb and mien, and a red-coated officer of the old French war ; and there comes the shop-keeping Pyncheon of a century ago, with the ruffles turned back from his wrists ; and there the periwigged and brocaded gentleman of the artist's legend, with the beautiful and pensive Alice, who brings no pride out of her virgin grave. All try the picture-frame. What do these ghostly people seek? A mother lifts her child, that his little hands may touch it! There is evidently a mystery about the picture, that perplexes these poor Pyncheons when they ought to be at rest. In a corner, meanwhile, stands the figure of an elderly man, in a leather jerkin and breeches, with a carpenter's rule sticking out of his side pocket; he points his finger at the bearded Colonel and his descendants, nodding, jeering, mocking, and finally bursting into obstreperous, though inaudible laughter.

Indulging our fancy in this freak, we have partly lost the power of restraint and guidance. We distinguish an unlooked-for figure in our visionary scene. Among those ancestral people there is a young man, dressed in the very fashion of to-day: he wears a dark frock-coat, almost destitute of skirts, gray pantaloons, gaiter boots of patent leather, and has a finely wrought gold chain across his breast, and a little silver-headed whalebone stick in his hand. Were we to meet this figure at noonday, we should greet him as young Jaffrey Pyncheon, the Judge's only surviving child, who has been spending the last two years in foreign travel. If still in life, how comes his shadow hither? If dead, what a misfortune! The old Pyncheon property, together with the great estate acquired by the young man's father, would devolve on whom? On poor, foolish Clifford, gaunt Hepzibah, and rustic little Phœbe! But another and a greater marvel greets us! Can we believe our eyes? A stout, elderly gentleman has made his appearance; he has an aspect of eminent respectability, wears a black coat and pantaloons, of roomy width, and might be pronounced scrupulously neat in his attire, but for a broad crimson stain across his snowy neckcloth and down his shirt-bosom. Is it the Judge, or no? How can it be Judge Pyncheon? We discern his figure, as plainly as the flickering moonbeams can show us anything, still seated in the oaken chair! Be the apparition whose it may, it advances to the picture, seems to seize the frame, tries to peep behind it, and turns away, with a frown as black as the ancestral one.

The fantastic scene just hinted at must by no means be considered as forming an actual portion of our story. We were betrayed into this brief extravagance by the quiver of the moonbeams; they dance hand-in-hand with shadows, and are reflected in the looking-glass, which, you are aware, is always a kind of window or doorway into the spiritual world. We needed relief, moreover, from our too long and exclusive contemplation of that figure in the chair. This wild wind, too, has tossed our thoughts into strange confusion, but without tearing them away from their one determined centre. Yonder leaden Judge sits immovably upon our soul. Will he never stir again? We shall go mad unless he stirs! You may the better estimate his quietude by the fearlessness of a little mouse, which sits on its hind legs, in a streak of moonlight, close by Judge Pyncheon's foot, and seems to meditate a journey of exploration over this great black bulk. Ha! what has startled the nimble little mouse? It is the visage of grimalkin, outside of the window, where he appears to have posted himself for a deliberate watch. This grimalkin has a very ugly look. Is it a cat watching for a mouse, or the devil for a human soul? Would we could scare him from the window!

Thank Heaven, the night is wellnigh past! The moonbeams have no longer so silvery a gleam, nor contrast so strongly with the blackness of the shadows among which they fall. They are paler, now; the shadows look gray, not black. The boisterous wind is hushed. What is the hour? Ah! the watch has at last ceased to tick; for the Judge's forgetful fingers neglected to wind it up, as usual, at ten o'clock, being half an hour or so before his ordinary bedtime, — and it has run down, for the first time in five years. But the great world-clock of Time still keeps its beat. The dreary night — for, oh, how dreary seems its haunted waste, behind us! — gives place to a fresh, transparent cloudless morn. Blessed, blessed radiance! The day-beam — even what little of it finds its way into this always dusky parlor — seems part of the universal benediction, annulling evil, and rendering all goodness possible, and happiness attainable. Will Judge Pyncheon now rise up from his chair? Will he go forth, and receive the early sunbeams on his brow? Will he begin this new day, — which God has smiled upon, and blessed, and given to mankind, — will he begin it with better purposes than the many that have been spent amiss? Or are all the deep-laid schemes of yesterday as stubborn in his heart, and as busy in his brain, as ever?

In this latter case, there is much to do. Will the Judge still insist with Hepzibah on the interview with Clifford? Will he buy a safe, elderly gentleman's horse? Will he persuade the purchaser of the old Pyncheon property to relinquish the bargain, in his favor? Will he see his family physician, and obtain a medicine that shall preserve him, to be an honor and blessing to his race, until the utmost term of patri-archal longevity? Will Judge Pyncheon, above all, make due apologies to that company of honorable friends, and satisfy them that his absence from the festive board was unavoidable, and so fully retrieve himself in their good opinion that he shall yet be Governor of Massachusetts? And all these great purposes accomplished, will he walk the streets again, with that dog-day smile of elaborate benevolence, sultry enough to tempt flies to come and buzz in it? Or will he, after the tomb-like seclusion of the past day and night, go forth a humbled and repentant man, sorrowful, gentle, seeking no profit, shrinking from worldly honor, hardly daring to love God, but bold to love his fellow-man, and to do him what good he may? Will he bear about with him, — no odious grin of feigned benignity, insolent in its pretence, and loathsome in its falsehood, — but the tender sadness of a contrite heart, broken, at last, beneath its own weight of sin? For it is our belief, whatever show of honor he may have piled upon it, that there was heavy sin at the base of this man's being.

Rise up, Judge Pyncheon! The morning sunshine glimmers through the foliage, and, beautiful and holy as it is, shuns not to kindle up your face. Rise up, thou subtle, worldly, selfish, iron-hearted hypocrite, and make thy choice whether still to be subtle, worldly, selfish, iron-hearted, and hypocritical, or to tear these sins out of thy nature, though they bring the life-blood with them! The Avenger is upon thee! Rise up, before it be too late!

What! Thou art not stirred by this last appeal? No, not a jot! And there we see a fly, — one of your common house-flies, such as are always buzzing on the window-pane, — which has smelt out Governor Pyncheon, and alights, now on his forehead, now on his chin, and now, Heaven help us! is creeping over the bridge of his nose, towards the would-be chief-magistrate's wide-open eyes! Canst thou not brush the fly away? Art thou too sluggish? Thou man, that hadst so many busy projects yesterday! Art thou too weak, that wast so powerful? Not brush away a fly? Nay, then, we give thee up!

And hark! the shop-bell rings. After hours like these latter ones, through which we have borne our heavy tale, it is good to be made sensible that there is a living world, and that even this old, lonely mansion retains some manner of connection with it. We breathe more freely, emerging from Judge Pyncheon's presence into the street before the Seven Gables.

XIX.

ALICE'S POSIES.

UNCLE VENNER, trundling a wheelbarrow, was the earliest person stirring in the neighborhood the day after the storm.

Pyncheon Street, in front of the House of the Seven Gables, was a far pleasanter scene than a by-lane, confined by shabby fences, and bordered with wooden dwellings of the meaner class, could reasonably be expected to present. Nature made sweet amends, that morning, for the five unkindly days which had preceded it. It would have been enough to live for, merely to look up at the wide benediction of the sky, or as much of it as was visible between the houses, genial once more with sunshine. Every object was agreeable, whether to be gazed at in the breadth, or examined more minutely. Such, for example, were the well-washed pebbles and gravel of the sidewalk; even the sky-reflecting pools in the centre of the street; and the grass, now freshly verdant, that crept along the base of the fences, on the other side of which, if one peeped over, was seen the multifarious growth of gardens. Vegetable productions, of whatever kind, seemed more than negatively happy, in the juicy warmth and abundance of their life. The Pyncheon Elm, throughout its great circumference, was all alive, and full of the morning sun and a sweet-tempered little breeze, which lingered within this verdant sphere, and set a thousand leafy tongues a-whispering all at once. This aged tree appeared to have suffered nothing from the gale. It had kept its boughs unshattered, and its full complement of leaves; and the whole in perfect verdure, except a single branch, that, by the earlier change with which the elm-tree sometimes prophesies the autumn, had been transmuted to bright gold. It was like the golden branch that gained Æneas and the Sibyl admittance into Hades.

This one mystic branch hung down before the main entrance of the Seven Gables, so nigh the ground that any passer-by might have stood on tiptoe and plucked it off. Presented at the door, it would have been a symbol of his right to enter, and be made acquainted with all the secrets of the house. So little faith is due to external appearance, that there was really an inviting aspect over the venerable edifice, conveying an idea that its history must be a decorous and happy one, and such as would be delightful for a fireside tale. Its windows gleamed cheerfully in the slanting sunlight. The lines and tufts of green moss, here and there, seemed pledges of familiarity and sisterhood with Nature; as if this human dwelling-place, being of such old date, had established its prescriptive title among primeval oaks and whatever other objects, by virtue of their long continuance, have acquired a gracious right to be. A person of imaginative temperament, while passing by the house, would turn, once and again, and peruse it well: its many peaks, consenting together in the clustered chimney; the deep projection over its basement-story; the arched window, imparting a look, if not of grandeur, yet of antique gentility, to the broken portal over which it opened; the luxuriance of gigantic burdocks, near the threshold; he would note all these characteristics, and be conscious of some-thing deeper than he saw. He would conceive the mansion to have been the residence of the stubborn old Puritan, Integrity, who, dying in some forgotten generation, had left a blessing in all its rooms and chambers, the efficacy of which was to be seen in the religion, honesty, moderate competence, or upright poverty and solid happiness, of his descendants, to this day.

One object, above all others, would take root in the imaginative observer's memory. It was the great tuft of flowers, — weeds, you would have called them, only a week ago, — the tuft of crimson-spotted flowers, in the angle between the two front gables. The old people used to give them the name of Alice's Posies, in remembrance of fair Alice Pyncheon, who was believed to have brought their seeds from Italy. They were flaunting in rich beauty and full bloom to-day, and seemed, as it were, a mystic expression that something within the house was consummated.

It was but little after sunrise, when Uncle Venner made his appearance, as aforesaid, impelling a wheelbarrow along the street. He was going his matutinal rounds to collect cabbage-leaves, turnip-tops, potato-skins, and the miscellaneous refuse of the dinner-pot, which the thrifty housewives of the neighborhood were accustomed to put aside, as fit only to feed a pig. Uncle Venner's pig was fed entirely, and kept in prime order, on these eleemosynary contributions; insomuch that the patched philosopher used to promise that, before retiring to his farm, he would make a feast of the portly grunter, and invite all his neighbors to partake of the joints and spare-ribs which they had helped to fatten. Miss Hepzibah Pyncheon's housekeeping had so greatly improved, since Clifford became a member of the family, that her share of the banquet would have been no lean one; and Uncle Venner, accordingly, was a good deal disappointed not to find the large earthen pan, full of fragmentary eatables, that ordinarily awaited his coming at the back doorstep of the Seven Gables.

"I never knew Miss Hepzibah so forgetful before," said the patriarch to himself. "She must have had a dinner yesterday, — no question of that! She always has one, nowadays. So where's the pot-liquor and potato-skins, I ask? Shall I knock, and see if she's stirring yet? No, no, — 't won't do! If little Phœbe was about the house, I should not mind knocking; but Miss Hepzibah, likely as not, would scowl down at me out of the window, and look cross, even if she felt pleasantly. So, I 'll come back at noon."

With these reflections, the old man was shutting the gate of the little back-yard. Creaking on its hinges, however, like every other gate and door about the premises, the sound reached the ears of the occupant of the northern gable, one of the windows of which had a side-view towards the gate.

"Good morning, Uncle Venner!" said the daguerreotypist, leaning out of the window. "Do you hear nobody stirring?"

"Not a soul," said the man of patches. "But that's no wonder. 'T is barely half an hour past sunrise, yet. But I 'm really glad to see you, Mr. Holgrave! There's a strange, lonesome look about this side of the house; so that my heart misgave me, somehow or other, and I felt as if there was nobody alive in it. The front of the house looks a good deal cheerier; and Alice's Posies are blooming there beautifully;

and if I were a young man, Mr. Holgrave, my sweet heart should have one of those flowers in her bosom, though I risked my neck climbing for it! Well, and did the wind keep you awake last night?"

"It did, indeed!" answered the artist, smiling. "If I were a believer in ghosts, — and I don't quite know whether I am or not, — I should have concluded that all the old Pyncheons were running riot in the lower rooms, especially in Miss Hepzibah's part of the house. But it is very quiet now."

"Yes, Miss Hepzibah will be apt to over-sleep herself, after being disturbed, all night, with the racket," said Uncle Venner. "But it would be odd, now, would n't it, if the Judge had taken both his cousins into the country along with him? I saw him go into the shop yesterday."

"At what hour?" inquired Holgrave.

"Oh, along in the forenoon," said the old man. "Well, well! I must go my rounds, and so must my wheelbarrow. But I 'll be back here at dinner-time; for my pig likes a dinner as well as a breakfast. No meal-time, and no sort of victuals, ever seems to come amiss to my pig. Good morning to you! And, Mr. Holgrave, if I were a young man, like you, I 'd get one of Alice's Posies, and keep it in water till Phœbe comes back."

"I have heard," said the daguerreotypist, as he drew in his head, "that the water of Maule's well suits those flowers best."

Here the conversation ceased, and Uncle Venner went on his way. For half an hour longer, nothing disturbed the repose of the Seven Gables; nor was there any visitor, except a carrier-boy, who, as he passed the front doorstep, threw down one of his newspapers; for Hepzibah, of late, had regularly taken it in. After a while, there came a fat woman, making prodigious speed, and stumbling as she ran up the steps of the shop-door. Her face glowed with fire-heat, and, it being a pretty warm morning, she bubbled and hissed, as it were, as if all a-fry with chimney-warmth, and summer-warmth, and the warmth of her own corpulent velocity. She tried the shop-door; it was fast. She tried it again, with so angry a jar that the bell tinkled angrily back at her.

"The deuce take Old Maid Pyncheon!" muttered the irascible housewife. "Think of her pretending to set up a cent-shop, and then lying abed till noon! These are what she calls gentlefolk's airs, I suppose! But I'll either start her ladyship, or break the door down!"

She shook it accordingly, and the bell, having a spiteful little temper of its own, rang obstreperously, making its remonstrances heard, — not, indeed, by the ears for which they were intended, — but by a good lady on the opposite side of the street. She opened her window, and addressed the impatient applicant.

"You'll find nobody there, Mrs. Gubbins."

"But I must and will find somebody here!" cried Mrs. Gubbins, inflicting another outrage on the bell. "I want a half-pound of pork, to fry some first-rate flounders, for Mr. Gubbins's breakfast; and, lady or not, Old Maid Pyncheon shall get up and serve me with it!"

"But do hear reason, Mrs. Gubbins!" responded the lady opposite. "She, and her brother too, have both gone to their cousin, Judge Pyncheon's at his country-seat. There's not a soul in the house, but that young daguerreotype-man that sleeps in the north gable. I saw old Hepzibah and Clifford go away yesterday; and a queer couple of ducks they were, paddling through the mud-puddles! They 're gone, I 'll assure you."

"And how do you know they 're gone to the Judge's?" asked Mrs. Gubbins. "He 's a rich man; and there 's been a quarrel between him and Hepzibah, this many a day because he won't give her a living. That 's the main reason of her setting up a cent-shop."

"I know that well enough," said the neighbor. "But they 're gone, — that 's one thing certain. And who but a blood relation, that could n't help himself, I ask you, would take in that awful-tempered old maid, and that dreadful Clifford? That 's it, you may be sure."

Mrs. Gubbins took her departure, still brimming over with hot wrath against the absent Hepzibah. For another half-hour, or, perhaps, considerably more, there was almost as much quiet on the outside of the house as within. The elm, however, made a pleasant, cheerful, sunny sigh, responsive to the breeze that was elsewhere imperceptible; a swarm of insects buzzed merrily under its drooping shadow, and became specks of light whenever they darted into the sunshine; a locust sang, once or twice, in some inscrutable seclusion of the tree; and a solitary little bird, with plumage of pale gold, came and hovered about Alice's Posies.

At last our small acquaintance, Ned Higgins, trudged up the street, on his way to school; and happening, for the first time in a fortnight, to be the possessor of a cent, he could by no means get past the shop-door of the Seven Gables. But it would not open. Again and again, however, and half a dozen other agains, with the inexorable pertinacity of a child intent upon some object important to itself, did he renew his efforts for ad

mittance. He had, doubtless, set his heart upon an elephant; or, possibly, with Hamlet, he meant to eat a
crocodile. In response to his more violent attacks, the
bell gave, now and then, a moderate tinkle, but could
not be stirred into clamor by any exertion of the little
fellow's childish and tiptoe strength. Holding by the
door-handle, he peeped through a crevice of the curtain, and saw that the inner door, communicating with
the passage towards the parlor, was closed.

"Miss Pyncheon!" screamed the child, rapping on
the window-pane, "I want an elephant!"

There being no answer to several repetitions of the
summons, Ned began to grow impatient; and his little
pot of passion quickly boiling over, he picked up a
stone, with a naughty purpose to fling it through the
window; at the same time blubbering and sputtering
with wrath. A man — one of two who happened to
be passing by — caught the urchin's arm.

"What's the trouble, old gentleman?" he asked.

"I want old Hepzibah, or Phœbe, or any of them!"
answered Ned, sobbing. "They won't open the door;
and I can't get my elephant!"

"Go to school, you little scamp!" said the man.
"There's another cent-shop round the corner. 'T is
very strange, Dixey," added he to his companion,
"what's become of all these Pyncheons! Smith, the
livery-stable keeper, tells me Judge Pyncheon put his
horse up yesterday, to stand till after dinner, and has
not taken him away yet. And one of the Judge's hired
men has been in, this morning, to make inquiry about
him. He's a kind of person, they say, that seldom
breaks his habits, or stays out o' nights."

"Oh, he'll turn up safe enough!" said Dixey. "And
as for Old Maid Pyncheon, take my word for it, she

has run in debt, and gone off from her creditors. I foretold, you remember, the first morning she set up shop, that her devilish scowl would frighten away customers. They could n't stand it!"

"I never thought she 'd make it go," remarked his friend. "This business of cent-shops is overdone among the womenfolks. My wife tried it, and lost five dollars on her outlay!"

"Poor business!" said Dixey, shaking his head. "Poor business!"

In the course of the morning, there were various other attempts to open a communication with the supposed inhabitants of this silent and impenetrable mansion. The man of root-beer came, in his neatly painted wagon, with a couple of dozen full bottles, to be exchanged for empty ones; the baker, with a lot of crackers which Hepzibah had ordered for her retail custom; the butcher, with a nice titbit which he fancied she would be eager to secure for Clifford. Had any observer of these proceedings been aware of the fearful secret hidden within the house, it would have affected him with a singular shape and modification of horror, to see the current of human life making this small eddy hereabouts, — whirling sticks, straws, and all such trifles, round and round, right over the black depth where a dead corpse lay unseen!

The butcher was so much in earnest with his sweet-bread of lamb, or whatever the dainty might be, that he tried every accessible door of the Seven Gables, and at length came round again to the shop, where he ordinarily found admittance.

"It 's a nice article, and I know the old lady would jump at it," said he to himself. "She can't be gone away! In fifteen years that I have driven my cart through Pyncheon Street, I've never known her to be away from home; though often enough, to be sure, a man might knock all day without bringing her to the door. But that was when she'd only herself to provide for."

Peeping through the same crevice of the curtain where, only a little while before, the urchin of elephantine appetite had peeped, the butcher beheld the inner door, not closed, as the child had seen it, but ajar, and almost wide open. However it might have happened, it was the fact. Through the passage-way there was a dark vista into the lighter but still obscure interior of the parlor. It appeared to the butcher that he could pretty clearly discern what seemed to be the stalwart legs, clad in black pantaloons, of a man sitting in a large oaken chair, the back of which concealed all the remainder of his figure. This contemptuous tranquillity on the part of an occupant of the house, in response to the butcher's indefatigable efforts to attract notice, so piqued the man of flesh that he determined to withdraw.

" So," thought he, " there sits Old Maid Pyncheon's bloody brother, while I've been giving myself all this trouble! Why, if a hog had n't more manners, I'd stick him! I call it demeaning a man's business to trade with such people; and from this time forth, if they want a sausage or an ounce of liver, they shall run after the cart for it! "

He tossed the titbit angrily into his cart, and drove off in a pet.

Not a great while afterwards there was a sound of music turning the corner, and approaching down the street, with several intervals of silence, and then a renewed and nearer outbreak of brisk melody. A mob of children was seen moving onward, or stopping, in unison with the sound, which appeared to proceed from the centre of the throng; so that they were loosely bound together by slender strains of harmony, and drawn along captive; with ever and anon an accession of some little fellow in an apron and straw-hat, capering forth from door or gateway. Arriving under the shadow of the Pyncheon Elm, it proved to be the Italian boy, who, with his monkey and show of puppets, had once before played his hurdy-gurdy beneath the arched window. The pleasant face of Phœbe — and doubtless, too, the liberal recompense which she had flung him — still dwelt in his remembrance. His expressive features kindled up, as he recognized the spot where this trifling incident of his erratic life had chanced. He entered the neglected yard (now wilder than ever, with its growth of hog-weed and burdock), stationed himself on the doorstep of the main entrance, and, opening his show-box, began to play. Each individual of the automatic community forthwith set to work, according to his or her proper vocation: the monkey, taking off his Highland bonnet, bowed and scraped to the by-standers most obsequiously, with ever an observant eye to pick up a stray cent; and the young foreigner himself, as he turned the crank of his machine, glanced upward to the arched window, expectant of a presence that would make his music the livelier and sweeter. The throng of children stood near; some on the sidewalk; some within the yard; two or three establishing themselves on the very door-step; and one squatting on the threshold. Meanwhile, the locust kept singing in the great old Pyncheon Elm.

"I don't hear anybody in the house," said one of the children to another. "The monkey won't pick up anything here."

"There is somebody at home," affirmed the urchin on the threshold. "I heard a step!"

Still the young Italian's eye turned sidelong up. ward; and it really seemed as if the touch of genuine, though slight and almost playful, emotion communicated a juicier sweetness to the dry, mechanical process of his minstrelsy. These wanderers are readily responsive to any natural kindness — be it no more than a smile, or a word itself not understood, but only a warmth in it — which befalls them on the roadside of life. They remember these things, because they are the little enchantments which, for the instant, — for the space that reflects a landscape in a soap-bubble, — build up a home about them. Therefore, the Italian boy would not be discouraged by the heavy silence with which the old house seemed resolute to clog the vivacity of his instrument. He persisted in his melodious appeals; he still looked upward, trusting that his dark, alien countenance would soon be brightened by Phœbe's sunny aspect. Neither could he be willing to depart without again beholding Clifford, whose sensibility, like Phœbe's smile, had talked a kind of heart's language to the foreigner. He repeated all his music over and over again, until his auditors were getting weary. So were the little wooden people in his show-box, and the monkey most of all. There was no response, save the singing of the locust.

"No children live in this house," said a school-boy, at last. "Nobody lives here but an old maid and an old man. You'll get nothing here! Why don't you go along?"

"You fool, you, why do you tell him?" whispered a shrewd little Yankee, caring nothing for the music, but a good deal for the cheap rate at which it was had

" Let him play as long as he likes ! If there 's nobody
to pay him, that 's his own lookout ! "

Once more, however, the Italian ran over his round
of melodies. To the common observer — who could
understand nothing of the case, except the music and
the sunshine on the hither side of the door — it might
have been amusing to watch the pertinacity of the
street-performer. Will he succeed at last ? Will that
stubborn door be suddenly flung open ? Will a group
of joyous children, the young ones of the house, come
dancing, shouting, laughing, into the open air, and
cluster round the show-box, looking with eager merriment at the puppets, and tossing each a copper for
long-tailed Mammon, the monkey, to pick up ?

But to us, who know the inner heart of the Seven
Gables as well as its exterior face, there is a ghastly
effect in this repetition of light popular tunes at its
door-step. It would be an ugly business, indeed, if
Judge Pyncheon (who would not have cared a fig for
Paganini's fiddle in his most harmonious mood) should
make his appearance at the door, with a bloody shirt-
bosom, and a grim frown on his swarthily white visage,
and motion the foreign vagabond away ! Was ever
before such a grinding out of jigs and waltzes, where
nobody was in the cue to dance ? Yes, very often.
This contrast, or intermingling of tragedy with mirth,
happens daily, hourly, momently. The gloomy and
desolate old house, deserted of life, and with awful
Death sitting sternly in its solitude, was the emblem
of many a human heart, which, nevertheless, is compelled to hear the thrill and echo of the world's gayety
around it.

Before the conclusion of the Italian's performance,
a couple of men happened to be passing, on their way
to dinner.

"I say, you young French fellow!" called out one of them, — "come away from that doorstep, and go somewhere else with your nonsense! The Pyncheon family live there; and they are in great trouble, just about this time. They don't feel musical to-day. It is reported all over town that Judge Pyncheon, who owns the house, has been murdered; and the city marshal is going to look into the matter. So be off with you, at once!"

As the Italian shouldered his hurdy-gurdy, he saw on the doorstep a card, which had been covered, all the morning, by the newspaper that the carrier had flung upon it, but was now shuffled into sight. He picked it up, and perceiving something written in pencil, gave it to the man to read. In fact, it was an engraved card of Judge Pyncheon's with certain pencilled memoranda on the back, referring to various businesses which it had been his purpose to transact during the preceding day. It formed a prospective epitome of the day's history; only that affairs had not turned out altogether in accordance with the programme. The card must have been lost from the Judge's vest-pocket, in his preliminary attempt to gain access by the main entrance of the house. Though well soaked with rain, it was still partially legible.

"Look here, Dixey!" cried the man. "This has something to do with Judge Pyncheon. See! — here's his name printed on it; and here, I suppose, is some of his handwriting."

"Let's go to the city marshal with it!" said Dixey. "It may give him just the view he wants. After all," whispered he in his companion's ear, "it would be no wonder if the Judge has gone into that door and never come out again! A certain cousin of his may have been at his old tricks. And Old Maid Pyncheon having got herself in debt by the cent-shop, — and the Judge's pocket-book being well filled, — and bad blood amongst them already! Put all these things together and see what they make!"

"Hush, hush!" whispered the other. "It seems like a sin to be the first to speak of such a thing. But I think, with you, that we had better go to the city marshal."

"Yes, yes!" said Dixey. "Well! — I always said there was something devilish in that woman's scowl!"

The men wheeled about, accordingly, and retraced their steps up the street. The Italian, also, made the best of his way off, with a parting glance up at the arched window. As for the children, they took to their heels, with one accord, and scampered as if some giant or ogre were in pursuit, until, at a good distance from the house, they stopped as suddenly and simultaneously as they had set out. Their susceptible nerves took an indefinite alarm from what they had overheard. Looking back at the grotesque peaks and shadowy angles of the old mansion, they fancied a gloom diffused about it which no brightness of the sunshine could dispel. An imaginary Hepzibah scowled and shook her finger at them, from several windows at the same moment. An imaginary Clifford — for (and it would have deeply wounded him to know it) he had always been a horror to these small people — stood behind the unreal Hepzibah, making awful gestures, in a faded dressing-gown. Children are even more apt, if possible, than grown people, to catch the contagion of a panic terror. For the rest of the day, the more timid went whole streets about, for the sake of avoiding the Seven Gables; while the bolder signalized their hardihood by challenging their comrades to race past the mansion at full speed.

It could not have been more than half an hour after the disappearance of the Italian boy, with his unseasonable melodies, when a cab drove down the street. It stopped beneath the Pyncheon Elm; the cabman took a trunk, a canvas bag, and a bandbox, from the top of his vehicle, and deposited them on the doorstep of the old house; a straw bonnet, and then the pretty figure of a young girl, came into view from the interior of the cab. It was Phœbe! Though not altogether so blooming as when she first tripped into our story, — for, in the few intervening weeks, her experiences had made her graver, more womanly, and deeper-eyed, in token of a heart that had begun to suspect its depths, — still there was the quiet glow of natural sunshine over her. Neither had she forfeited her proper gift of making things look real, rather than fantastic, within her sphere. Yet we feel it to be a questionable venture, even for Phœbe, at this juncture, to cross the threshold of the Seven Gables. Is her healthful presence potent enough to chase away the crowd of pale, hideous, and sinful phantoms, that have gained admittance there since her departure? Or will she, likewise, fade, sicken, sadden, and grow into deformity, and be only another pallid phantom, to glide noiselessly up and down the stairs, and affright children as she pauses at the window?

At least, we would gladly forewarn the unsuspecting girl that there is nothing in human shape or substance to receive her, unless it be the figure of Judge Pyncheon, who — wretched spectacle that he is, and frightful in our remembrance, since our night-long vigil with him! — still keeps his place in the oaken chair.

Phœbe first tried the shop-door. It did not yield to her hand; and the white curtain, drawn across the window which formed the upper section of the door, struck her quick perceptive faculty as something unusual. Without making another effort to enter here, she betook herself to the great portal, under the arched window. Finding it fastened, she knocked. A reverberation came from the emptiness within. She knocked again, and a third time; and, listening intently, fancied that the floor creaked, as if Hepzibah were coming, with her ordinary tiptoe movement, to admit her. But so dead a silence ensued upon this imaginary sound, that she began to question whether she might not have mistaken the house, familiar as she thought herself with its exterior.

Her notice was now attracted by a child's voice, at some distance. It appeared to call her name. Looking in the direction whence it proceeded, Phœbe saw little Ned Higgins, a good way down the street, stamping, shaking his head violently, making deprecatory gestures with both hands, and shouting to her at mouth-wide screech.

"No, no, Phœbe?" he screamed. "Don't you go in! There's something wicked there! Don't—don't—don't go in!"

But, as the little personage could not be induced to approach near enough to explain himself, Phœbe concluded that he had been frightened, on some of his visits to the shop, by her cousin Hepzibah; for the good lady's manifestations, in truth, ran about an equal chance of scaring children out of their wits, or compelling them to unseemly laughter. Still, she felt the more, for this incident, how unaccountably silent and impenetrable the house had become. As her next

resort, Phœbe made her way into the garden, where
on so warm and bright a day as the present, she had
little doubt of finding Clifford, and perhaps Hepzibah
also, idling away the noontide in the shadow of the
arbor.   Immediately on her entering the garden-gate,
the family of hens half ran, half flew, to meet her;
while a strange grimalkin, which was prowling under
the parlor window, took to his heels, clambered hastily
over the fence, and vanished.   The arbor was vacant,
and its floor, table, and circular bench were still damp,
and bestrewn with twigs, and the disarray of the past
storm.   The growth of the garden seemed to have got
quite out of bounds; the weeds had taken advantage
of Phœbe's absence, and the long-continued rain, to
run rampant over the flowers and kitchen-vegetables.
Maule's well had overflowed its stone border, and
made a pool of formidable breadth in that corner of
the garden.

The impression of the whole scene was that of a
spot where no human foot had left its print for many
preceding days, — probably not since Phœbe's departure, — for she saw a side-comb of her own under the
table of the arbor, where it must have fallen on the
last afternoon when she and Clifford sat there.

The girl knew that her two relatives were capable
of far greater oddities than that of shutting themselves up in their old house, as they appeared now to
have done.   Nevertheless, with indistinct misgivings
of something amiss, and apprehensions to which she
could not give shape, she approached the door that
formed the customary communication between the
house and garden.   It was secured within, like the
two which she had already tried.   She knocked, however; and immediately, as if the application had been

expected, the door was drawn open, by a considerable exertion of some unseen person's strength, not wide, but far enough to afford her a side-long entrance. As Hepzibah, in order not to expose herself to inspection from without, invariably opened a door in this manner, Phœbe necessarily concluded that it was her cousin who now admitted her.

Without hesitation, therefore, she stepped across the threshold, and had no sooner entered than the door closed behind her.

XX.

THE FLOWER OF EDEN.

PHŒBE, coming so suddenly from the sunny daylight, was altogether bedimmed in such density of shadow as lurked in most of the passages of the old house. She was not at first aware by whom she had been admitted. Before her eyes had adapted themselves to the obscurity, a hand grasped her own, with a firm but gentle and warm pressure, thus imparting a welcome which caused her heart to leap and thrill with an indefinable shiver of enjoyment. She felt herself drawn along, not towards the parlor, but into a large and unoccupied apartment, which had formerly been the grand reception-room of the Seven Gables. The sunshine came freely into all the uncurtained windows of this room, and fell upon the dusty floor; so that Phœbe now clearly saw — what, indeed, had been no secret, after the encounter of a warm hand with hers — that it was not Hepzibah nor Clifford, but Holgrave, to whom she owed her reception. The subtile, intuitive communication, or, rather, the vague and formless impression of something to be told, had made her yield unresistingly to his impulse. Without taking away her hand, she looked eagerly in his face, not quick to forebode evil, but unavoidably conscious that the state of the family had changed since her departure, and therefore anxious for an explanation.

The artist looked paler than ordinary; there was a

thoughtful and severe contraction of his forehead, tracing a deep, vertical line between the eyebrows. His smile, however, was full of genuine warmth, and had in it a joy, by far the most vivid expression that Phœbe had ever witnessed, shining out of the New England reserve with which Holgrave habitually masked whatever lay near his heart. It was the look wherewith a man, brooding alone over some fearful object, in a dreary forest, or illimitable desert, would recognize the familiar aspect of his dearest friend, bringing up all the peaceful ideas that belong to home, and the gentle current of every-day affairs. And yet, as he felt the necessity of responding to her look of inquiry, the smile disappeared.

"I ought not to rejoice that you have come, Phœbe," said he. "We meet at a strange moment!"

"What has happened?" she exclaimed. "Why is the house so deserted? Where are Hepzibah and Clifford?"

"Gone! I cannot imagine where they are!" answered Holgrave. "We are alone in the house!"

"Hepzibah and Clifford gone?" cried Phœbe. "It is not possible! And why have you brought me into this room, instead of the parlor? Ah, something terrible has happened! I must run and see!"

"No, no, Phœbe!" said Holgrave, holding her back. "It is as I have told you. They are gone, and I know not whither. A terrible event has, indeed, happened, but not to them, nor, as I undoubtingly believe, through any agency of theirs. If I read your character rightly, Phœbe," he continued, fixing his eyes on hers, with stern anxiety, intermixed with tenderness, "gentle as you are, and seeming to have your sphere among common things, you yet possess re markable strength. You have wonderful poise, and a faculty which, when tested, will prove itself capable of dealing with matters that fall far out of the ordinary rule."

"Oh no, I am very weak!" replied Phœbe, trembling. "But tell me what has happened!"

"You are strong!" persisted Holgrave. "You must be both strong and wise; for I am all astray, and need your counsel. It may be you can suggest the one right thing to do!"

"Tell me! — tell me!" said Phœbe, all in a tremble. "It oppresses, — it terrifies me, — this mystery! Anything else I can bear!"

The artist hesitated. Notwithstanding what he had just said, and most sincerely, in regard to the self-balancing power with which Phœbe impressed him, it still seemed almost wicked to bring the awful secret of yesterday to her knowledge. It was like dragging a hideous shape of death into the cleanly and cheerful space before a household fire, where it would present all the uglier aspect, amid the decorousness of everything about it. Yet it could not be concealed from her; she must needs know it.

"Phœbe," said he, "do you remember this?"

He put into her hand a daguerreotype; the same that he had shown her at their first interview in the garden, and which so strikingly brought out the hard and relentless traits of the original.

"What has this to do with Hepzibah and Clifford?" asked Phœbe, with impatient surprise that Holgrave should so trifle with her at such a moment. "It is Judge Pyncheon! You have shown it to me before!"

"But here is the same face, taken within this half

hour," said the artist, presenting her with another miniature. "I had just finished it, when I heard you at the door."

"This is death!" shuddered Phœbe, turning very pale. "Judge Pyncheon dead!"

"Such as there represented," said Holgrave, "he sits in the next room. The Judge is dead, and Clifford and Hepzibah have vanished! I know no more. All beyond is conjecture. On returning to my solitary chamber, last evening, I noticed no light, either in the parlor, or Hepzibah's room, or Clifford's; no stir nor footstep about the house. This morning, there was the same death-like quiet. From my window, I overheard the testimony of a neighbor, that your relatives were seen leaving the house, in the midst of yesterday's storm. A rumor reached me, too, of Judge Pyncheon being missed. A feeling which I cannot describe — an indefinite sense of some catastrophe, or consummation — impelled me to make my way into this part of the house, where I discovered what you see. As a point of evidence that may be useful to Clifford, and also as a memorial valuable to myself, — for, Phœbe, there are hereditary reasons that connect me strangely with that man's fate, — I used the means at my disposal to preserve this pictorial record of Judge Pyncheon's death."

Even in her agitation, Phœbe could not help remarking the calmness of Holgrave's demeanor. He appeared, it is true, to feel the whole awfulness of the Judge's death, yet had received the fact into his mind without any mixture of surprise, but as an event preordained, happening inevitably, and so fitting itself into past occurrences that it could almost have been prophesied.

"Why have you not thrown open the doors, and called in witnesses?" inquired she, with a painful shudder. "It is terrible to be here alone!"

"But Clifford!" suggested the artist. "Clifford and Hepzibah! We must consider what is best to be done in their behalf. It is a wretched fatality that they should have disappeared! Their flight will throw the worst coloring over this event of which it is susceptible. Yet how easy is the explanation, to those who know them! Bewildered and terror-stricken by the similarity of this death to a former one, which was attended with such disastrous consequences to Clifford, they have had no idea but of removing themselves from the scene. How miserably unfortunate! Had Hepzibah but shrieked aloud, — had Clifford flung wide the door, and proclaimed Judge Pyncheon's death, — it would have been, however awful in itself, an event fruitful of good consequences to them. As I view it, it would have gone far towards obliterating the black stain on Clifford's character."

"And how," asked Phœbe, "could any good come from what is so very dreadful?"

"Because," said the artist, "if the matter can be fairly considered and candidly interpreted, it must be evident that Judge Pyncheon could not have come unfairly to his end. This mode of death has been an idiosyncrasy with his family, for generations past; not often occurring, indeed, but, when it does occur, usually attacking individuals about the Judge's time of life, and generally in the tension of some mental crisis, or, perhaps, in an access of wrath. Old Maule's prophecy was probably founded on a knowledge of this physical predisposition in the Pyncheon race. Now, there is a minute and almost exact similarity in the appearances connected with the death that occurred yesterday and those recorded of the death of Clifford's uncle thirty years ago. It is true, there was a certain arrangement of circumstances, unnecessary to be recounted, which made it possible — nay, as men look at these things, probable, or even certain — that old Jaffrey Pyncheon came to a violent death, and by Clifford's hands."

"Whence came those circumstances?" exclaimed Phœbe; "he being innocent, as we know him to be!"

"They were arranged," said Holgrave, — "at least such has long been my conviction, — they were arranged after the uncle's death, and before it was made public, by the man who sits in yonder parlor. His own death, so like that former one, yet attended by none of those suspicious circumstances, seems the stroke of God upon him, at once a punishment for his wickedness, and making plain the innocence of Clifford. But this flight, — it distorts everything! He may be in concealment, near at hand. Could we but bring him back before the discovery of the Judge's death the evil might be rectified."

"We must not hide this thing a moment longer!" said Phœbe. "It is dreadful to keep it so closely in our hearts. Clifford is innocent. God will make it manifest! Let us throw open the doors, and call all the neighborhood to see the truth!"

"You are right, Phœbe," rejoined Holgrave. "Doubtless you are right."

Yet the artist did not feel the horror, which was proper to Phœbe's sweet and order-loving character, at thus finding herself at issue with society, and brought in contact with an event that transcended ordinary rules. Neither was he in haste, like her, to betake himself within the precincts of common life. On the contrary, he gathered a wild enjoyment, — as it were, a flower of strange beauty, growing in a desolate spot, and blossoming in the wind, — such a flower of momentary happiness he gathered from his present position. It separated Phœbe and himself from the world, and bound them to each other, by their exclusive knowledge of Judge Pyncheon's mysterious death, and the counsel which they were forced to hold respecting it. The secret, so long as it should continue such, kept them within the circle of a spell, a solitude in the midst of men, a remoteness as entire as that of an island in mid-ocean; once divulged, the ocean would flow betwixt them, standing on its widely sundered shores. Meanwhile, all the circumstances of their situation seemed to draw them together; they were like two children who go hand in hand, pressing closely to one another's side, through a shadow-haunted passage. The image of awful Death, which filled the house, held them united by his stiffened grasp.

These influences hastened the development of emotions that might not otherwise have flowered so. Possibly, indeed, it had been Holgrave's purpose to let them die in their undeveloped germs.

" Why do we delay so ? " asked Phœbe. " This secret takes away my breath! Let us throw open the doors ! "

" In all our lives there can never come another moment like this ! " said Holgrave. " Phœbe, is it all terror ? — nothing but terror ? Are you conscious of no joy, as I am, that has made this the only point of life worth living for ? "

" It seems a sin," replied Phœbe, trembling, "to think of joy at such a time ! "

"Could you but know, Phœbe, how it was with me the hour before you came!" exclaimed the artist. "A dark, cold, miserable hour! The presence of yonder dead man threw a great black shadow over everything; he made the universe, so far as my perception could reach, a scene of guilt and of retribution more dreadful than the guilt. The sense of it took away my youth. I never hoped to feel young again! The world looked strange, wild, evil, hostile; my past life, so lonesome and dreary; my future, a shapeless gloom, which I must mould into gloomy shapes! But, Phœbe, you crossed the threshold; and hope, warmth, and joy came in with you! The black moment became at once a blissful one. It must not pass without the spoken word. I love you!"

"How can you love a simple girl like me?" asked Phœbe, compelled by his earnestness to speak. "You have many, many thoughts, with which I should try in vain to sympathize. And I, — I, too, — I have tendencies with which you would sympathize as little. That is less matter. But I have not scope enough to make you happy."

"You are my only possibility of happiness!" answered Holgrave. "I have no faith in it, except as you bestow it on me!"

"And then — I am afraid!" continued Phœbe, shrinking towards Holgrave, even while she told him so frankly the doubts with which he affected her. "You will lead me out of my own quiet path. You will make me strive to follow you where it is pathless. I cannot do so. It is not my nature. I shall sink down and perish!"

"Ah, Phœbe!" exclaimed Holgrave, with almost a sigh, and a smile that was burdened with thought.

" It will be far otherwise than as you forebode. The world owes all its onward impulses to men ill at ease. The happy man inevitably confines himself within ancient limits. I have a presentiment that, hereafter, it will be my lot to set out trees, to make fences, — perhaps, even, in due time, to build a house for another generation, — in a word, to conform myself to laws, and the peaceful practice of society. Your poise will be more powerful than any oscillating tendency of mine."

" I would not have it so ! " said Phœbe, earnestly.

" Do you love me ? " asked Holgrave. " If we love one another, the moment has room for nothing more. Let us pause upon it, and be satisfied. Do you love me, Phœbe ? "

" You look into my heart," said she, letting her eyes drop. " You know I love you ! "

And it was in this hour, so full of doubt and awe, that the one miracle was wrought, without which every human existence is a blank. The bliss which makes all things true, beautiful, and holy shone around this youth and maiden. They were conscious of nothing sad nor old. They transfigured the earth, and made it Eden again, and themselves the two first dwellers in it. The dead man, so close beside them, was forgotten. At such a crisis, there is no death ; for immortality is revealed anew, and embraces everything in its hallowed atmosphere.

But how soon the heavy earth-dream settled down again !

" Hark ! " whispered Phœbe. " Somebody is at the street-door ! "

" Now let us meet the world ! " said Holgrave. " No doubt, the rumor of Judge Pyncheon's visit to this house, and the flight of Hepzibah and Clifford, is about to lead to the investigation of the premises. We have no way but to meet it. Let us open the door at once."

But, to their surprise, before they could reach the street-door, — even before they quitted the room in which the foregoing interview had passed,—they heard footsteps in the farther passage. The door, therefore, which they supposed to be securely locked, — which Holgrave, indeed, had seen to be so, and at which Phœbe had vainly tried to enter, — must have been opened from without. The sound of footsteps was not harsh, bold, decided, and intrusive, as the gait of strangers would naturally be, making authoritative entrance into a dwelling where they knew themselves unwelcome. It was feeble, as of persons either weak or weary; there was the mingled murmur of two voices, familiar to both the listeners.

"Can it be?" whispered Holgrave.

"It is they!" answered Phœbe. "Thank God! — thank God!"

And then, as if in sympathy with Phœbe's whispered ejaculation, they heard Hepzibah's voice, more distinctly.

"Thank God, my brother, we are at home!"

"Well! — Yes! — thank God!" responded Clifford. "A dreary home, Hepzibah! But you have done well to bring me hither! Stay! That parlor door is open. I cannot pass by it! Let me go and rest me in the arbor, where I used, — oh, very long ago, it seems to me, after what has befallen us, — where I used to be so happy with little Phœbe!"

But the house was not altogether so dreary as Clifford imagined it. They had not made many steps, —

In truth, they were lingering in the entry, with the list-lessness of an accomplished purpose, uncertain what to do next, — when Phœbe ran to meet them. On beholding her, Hepzibah burst into tears. With all her might, she had staggered onward beneath the burden of grief and responsibility, until now that it was safe to fling it down. Indeed, she had not energy to fling it down, but had ceased to uphold it, and suffered it to press her to the earth. Clifford appeared the stronger of the two.

"It is our own little Phœbe ! — Ah ! and Holgrave with her," exclaimed he, with a glance of keen and delicate insight, and a smile, beautiful, kind, but melancholy. "I thought of you both, as we came down the street, and beheld Alice's Posies in full bloom. And so the flower of Eden has bloomed, likewise, in this old, darksome house to-day."

XXI.

THE DEPARTURE.

THE sudden death of so prominent a member of the social world as the Honorable Judge Jaffrey Pyncheon created a sensation (at least, in the circles more immediately connected with the deceased) which had hardly quite subsided in a fortnight.

It may be remarked, however, that, of all the events which constitute a person's biography, there is scarcely one — none, certainly, of anything like a similar importance — to which the world so easily reconciles itself as to his death. In most other cases and contingencies, the individual is present among us, mixed up with the daily revolution of affairs, and affording a definite point for observation. At his decease, there is only a vacancy, and a momentary eddy, — very small, as compared with the apparent magnitude of the ingurgitated object, — and a bubble or two, ascending out of the black depth and bursting at the surface. As regarded Judge Pyncheon, it seemed probable, at first blush, that the mode of his final departure might give him a larger and longer posthumous vogue than ordinarily attends the memory of a distinguished man. But when it came to be understood, on the highest professional authority, that the event was a natural, and — except for some unimportant particulars, denoting a slight idiosyncrasy — by no means an unusual form of death, the public, with its customary alacrity, proceeded to forget that he had ever lived. In short, the honorable Judge was beginning to be a stale subject before half the county newspapers had found time to put their columns in mourning, and publish his exceedingly eulogistic obituary.

Nevertheless, creeping darkly through the places which this excellent person had haunted in his lifetime, there was a hidden stream of private talk, such as it would have shocked all decency to speak loudly at the street-corners. It is very singular, how the fact of a man's death often seems to give people a truer idea of his character, whether for good or evil, than they have ever possessed while he was living and acting among them. Death is so genuine a fact that it excludes falsehood, or betrays its emptiness; it is a touchstone that proves the gold, and dishonors the baser metal. Could the departed, whoever he may be, return in a week after his decease, he would almost invariably find himself at a higher or lower point than he had formerly occupied, on the scale of public appreciation. But the talk, or scandal, to which we now allude, had reference to matters of no less old a date than the supposed murder, thirty or forty years ago, of the late Judge Pyncheon's uncle. The medical opinion, with regard to his own recent and regretted decease, had almost entirely obviated the idea that a murder was committed in the former case. Yet, as the record showed, there were circumstances irrefragably indicating that some person had gained access to old Jaffrey Pyncheon's private apartments, at or near the moment of his death. His desk and private drawers, in a room contiguous to his bedchamber, had been ransacked; money and valuable articles were missing; there was a bloody hand-print on the old man's linen;

and, by a powerfully welded chain of deductive evidence, the guilt of the robbery and apparent murder had been fixed on Clifford, then residing with his uncle in the House of the Seven Gables.

Whencesoever originating, there now arose a theory that undertook so to account for these circumstances as to exclude the idea of Clifford's agency. Many persons affirmed that the history and elucidation of the facts, long so mysterious, had been obtained by the daguerreotypist from one of those mesmerical seers, who, nowadays, so strangely perplex the aspect of human affairs, and put everybody's natural vision to the blush, by the marvels which they see with their eyes shut.

According to this version of the story, Judge Pyncheon, exemplary as we have portrayed him in our narrative, was, in his youth, an apparently irreclaimable scapegrace. The brutish, the animal instincts, as is often the case, had been developed earlier than the intellectual qualities, and the force of character, for which he was afterwards remarkable. He had shown himself wild, dissipated, addicted to low pleasures, little short of ruffianly in his propensities, and recklessly expensive, with no other resources than the bounty of his uncle. This course of conduct had alienated the old bachelor's affection, once strongly fixed upon him. Now it is averred, — but whether on authority available in a court of justice, we do not pretend to have investigated, — that the young man was tempted by the devil, one night, to search his uncle's private drawers, to which he had unsuspected means of access. While thus criminally occupied, he was startled by the opening of the chamber-door. There stood old Jaffrey Pyncheon, in his nightclothes! The surprise of such a discovery, his agitation, alarm, and horror, brought on the crisis of a disorder to which the old bachelor had an hereditary liability; he seemed to choke with blood, and fell upon the floor, striking his temple a heavy blow against the corner of a table. What was to be done? The old man was surely dead! Assistance would come too late! What a misfortune, indeed, should it come too soon, since his reviving consciousness would bring the recollection of the ignominious offence which he had beheld his nephew in the very act of committing!

But he never did revive. With the cool hardihood that always pertained to him, the young man continued his search of the drawers, and found a will, of recent date, in favor of Clifford, — which he destroyed, — and an older one, in his own favor, which he suffered to remain. But before retiring, Jaffrey bethought himself of the evidence, in these ransacked drawers, that some one had visited the chamber with sinister purposes. Suspicion, unless averted, might fix upon the real offender. In the very presence of the dead man, therefore, he laid a scheme that should free himself at the expense of Clifford, his rival, for whose character he had at once a contempt and a repugnance. It is not probable, be it said, that he acted with any set purpose of involving Clifford in a charge of murder. Knowing that his uncle did not die by violence, it may not have occurred to him, in the hurry of the crisis, that such an inference might be drawn. But, when the affair took this darker aspect, Jaffrey's previous steps had already pledged him to those which remained. So craftily had he arranged the circumstances, that, at Clifford's trial, his cousin hardly found it necessary to swear to anything false, but only to withhold the one decisive explanation, by refraining to state what he had himself done and witnessed.

Thus Jaffrey Pyncheon's inward criminality, as regarded Clifford, was, indeed, black and damnable; while its mere outward show and positive commission was the smallest that could possibly consist with so great a sin. This is just the sort of guilt that a man of eminent respectability finds it easiest to dispose of. It was suffered to fade out of sight or be reckoned a venial matter, in the Honorable Judge Pyncheon's long subsequent survey of his own life. He shuffled it aside, among the forgotten and forgiven frailties of his youth, and seldom thought of it again.

We leave the Judge to his repose. He could not be styled fortunate at the hour of death. Unknowingly, he was a childless man, while striving to add more wealth to his only child's inheritance. Hardly a week after his decease, one of the Cunard steamers brought intelligence of the death, by cholera, of Judge Pyncheon's son, just at the point of embarkation for his native land. By this misfortune Clifford became rich; so did Hepzibah; so did our little village maiden, and, through her, that sworn foe of wealth and all manner of conservatism, — the wild reformer, — Holgrave!

It was now far too late in Clifford's life for the good opinion of society to be worth the trouble and anguish of a formal vindication. What he needed was the love of a very few; not the admiration, or even the respect, of the unknown many. The latter might probably have been won for him, had those on whom the guardianship of his welfare had fallen deemed it advisable to expose Clifford to a miserable resuscitation of past ideas, when the condition of whatever comfort he might expect lay in the calm of forgetfulness. After such wrong as he had suffered, there is no reparation. The pitiable mockery of it, which the world might have been ready enough to offer, coming so long after the agony had done its utmost work, would have been fit only to provoke bitterer laughter than poor Clifford was ever capable of. It is a truth (and it would be a very sad one but for the higher hopes which it suggests) that no great mistake, whether acted or endured, in our mortal sphere, is ever really set right. Time, the continual vicissitude of circumstances, and the invariable inopportunity of death, render it impossible. If, after long lapse of years, the right seems to be in our power, we find no niche to set it in. The better remedy is for the sufferer to pass on, and leave what he once thought his irreparable ruin far behind him.

The shock of Judge Pyncheon's death had a permanently invigorating and ultimately beneficial effect on Clifford. That strong and ponderous man had been Clifford's nightmare. There was no free breath to be drawn, within the sphere of so malevolent an influence. The first effect of freedom, as we have witnessed in Clifford's aimless flight, was a tremulous exhilaration. Subsiding from it, he did not sink into his former intellectual apathy. He never, it is true, attained to nearly the full measure of what might have been his faculties. But he recovered enough of them partially to light up his character, to display some outline of the marvellous grace that was abortive in it, and to make him the object of no less deep, although less melancholy interest than heretofore. He was evidently happy. Could we pause to give another picture of his daily life, with all the appliances now at command to gratify his instinct for the Beautiful, the garden scenes, that seemed so sweet to him, would look mean and trivial in comparison.

Very soon after their change of fortune, Clifford, Hepzibah, and little Phœbe, with the approval of the artist, concluded to remove from the dismal old House of the Seven Gables, and take up their abode, for the present, at the elegant country-seat of the late Judge Pyncheon. Chanticleer and his family had already been transported thither, where the two hens had forthwith begun an indefatigable process of egg-laying, with an evident design, as a matter of duty and conscience, to continue their illustrious breed under better auspices than for a century past. On the day set for their departure, the principal personages of our story, including good Uncle Venner, were assembled in the parlor.

" The country-house is certainly a very fine one, so far as the plan goes," observed Holgrave, as the party were discussing their future arrangements. " But I wonder that the late Judge — being so opulent, and with a reasonable prospect of transmitting his wealth to descendants of his own — should not have felt the propriety of embodying so excellent a piece of domestic architecture in stone, rather than in wood. Then, every generation of the family might have altered the interior, to suit its own taste and convenience ; while the exterior, through the lapse of years, might have been adding venerableness to its original beauty, and thus giving that impression of permanence which I consider essential to the happiness of any one moment."

" Why," cried Phœbe, gazing into the artist's face

with infinite amazement, "how wonderfully your ideas
are changed! A house of stone, indeed! It is but
two or three weeks ago that you seemed to wish people to live in something as fragile and temporary as a
bird's-nest!"

"Ah, Phœbe, I told you how it would be!" said
the artist, with a half-melancholy laugh. "You find
me a conservative already! Little did I think ever to
become one. It is especially unpardonable in this
dwelling of so much hereditary misfortune, and under
the eye of yonder portrait of a model conservative,
who, in that very character, rendered himself so long
the evil destiny of his race."

"That picture!" said Clifford, seeming to shrink
from its stern glance. "Whenever I look at it, there
is an old dreamy recollection haunting me, but keeping just beyond the grasp of my mind. Wealth it
seems to say! — boundless wealth! — unimaginable
wealth! I could fancy that, when I was a child, or a
youth, that portrait had spoken, and told me a rich
secret, or had held forth its hand, with the written
record of hidden opulence. But those old matters are
so dim with me, nowadays! What could this dream
have been?"

"Perhaps I can recall it," answered Holgrave.
"See! There are a hundred chances to one that no
person, unacquainted with the secret, would ever touch
this spring."

"A secret spring!" cried Clifford. "Ah, I remember now! I did discover it, one summer afternoon,
when I was idling and dreaming about the house, long
long ago. But the mystery escapes me."

The artist put his finger on the contrivance to which
he had referred. In former days, the effect would

probably have been to cause the picture to start forward. But, in so long a period of concealment, the machinery had been eaten through with rust; so that at Holgrave's pressure, the portrait, frame and all, tumbled suddenly from its position, and lay face downward on the floor. A recess in the wall was thus brought to light, in which lay an object so covered with a century's dust that it could not immediately be recognized as a folded sheet of parchment. Holgrave opened it, and displayed an ancient deed, signed with the hieroglyphics of several Indian sagamores, and conveying to Colonel Pyncheon and his heirs, forever, a vast extent of territory at the Eastward.

"This is the very parchment the attempt to recover which cost the beautiful Alice Pyncheon her happiness and life," said the artist, alluding to his legend. "It is what the Pyncheons sought in vain, while it was valuable; and now that they find the treasure, it has long been worthless."

"Poor Cousin Jaffrey! This is what deceived him," exclaimed Hepzibah. "When they were young together, Clifford probably made a kind of fairy-tale of this discovery. He was always dreaming hither and thither about the house, and lighting up its dark corners with beautiful stories. And poor Jaffrey, who took hold of everything as if it were real, thought my brother had found out his uncle's wealth. He died with this delusion in his mind!"

"But," said Phœbe, apart to Holgrave, "how came you to know the secret?"

"My dearest Phœbe," said Holgrave, "how will it please you to assume the name of Maule? As for the secret, it is the only inheritance that has come down to me from my ancestors. You should have known sooner (only that I was afraid of frightening you away) that, in this long drama of wrong and retribution, I represent the old wizard, and am probably as much a wizard as ever he was. The son of the executed Matthew Maule, while building this house, took the opportunity to construct that recess, and hide away the Indian deed, on which depended the immense land-claim of the Pyncheons. Thus they bartered their Eastern territory for Maule's garden-ground."

"And now," said Uncle Venner, "I suppose their whole claim is not worth one man's share in my farm yonder ! "

"Uncle Venner," cried Phœbe, taking the patched philosopher's hand, " you must never talk any more about your farm ! You shall never go there, as long as you live ! There is a cottage in our new garden, — the prettiest little yellowish-brown cottage you ever saw ; and the sweetest-looking place, for it looks just as if it were made of gingerbread, — and we are going to fit it up and furnish it, on purpose for you. And you shall do nothing but what you choose, and shall be as happy as the day is long, and shall keep Cousin Clifford in spirits with the wisdom and pleasantness which is always dropping from your lips ! "

"Ah ! my dear child," quoth good Uncle Venner, quite overcome, "if you were to speak to a young man as you do to an old one, his chance of keeping his heart another minute would not be worth one of the buttons on my waistcoat ! And — soul alive ! — that great sigh, which you made me heave, has burst off the very last of them ! But, never mind ! It was the happiest sigh I ever did heave ; and it seems as if I must have drawn in a gulp of heavenly breath, to make it with. Well, well Miss Phœbe ! They 'll miss me in the gardens hereabouts, and round by the back doors; and Pyncheon Street, I'm afraid, will hardly look the same without old Uncle Venner, who remembers it with a mowing field on one side, and the garden of the Seven Gables on the other. But either I must go to your country-seat, or you must come to my farm, — that's one of two things certain; and I leave you to choose which!"

"Oh, come with us, by all means, Uncle Venner!" said Clifford, who had a remarkable enjoyment of the old man's mellow, quiet, and simple spirit. " I want you always to be within five minutes' saunter of my chair. You are the only philosopher I ever knew of whose wisdom has not a drop of bitter essence at the bottom!"

"Dear me!" cried Uncle Venner, beginning partly to realize what manner of man he was. "And yet folks used to set me down among the simple ones, in my younger days! But I suppose I am like a Roxbury russet, — a great deal the better, the longer I can be kept. Yes; and my words of wisdom, that you and Phœbe tell me of, are like the golden dandelions, which never grow in the hot months, but may be seen glistening among the withered grass, and under the dry leaves, sometimes as late as December. And you are welcome, friends, to my mess of dandelions, if there were twice as many!"

A plain, but handsome, dark-green barouche had now drawn up in front of the ruinous portal of the old mansion-house. The party came forth, and (with the exception of good Uncle Venner, who was to follow in a few days) proceeded to take their places. They were chatting and laughing very pleasantly together; and — as proves to be often the case, at mo

ments when we ought to palpitate with sensibility —
Clifford and Hepzibah bade a final farewell to the
abode of their forefathers, with hardly more emotion
than if they had made it their arrangement to return
thither at tea-time. Several children were drawn to
the spot by so unusual a spectacle as the barouche and
pair of gray horses. Recognizing little Ned Higgins
among them, Hepzibah put her hand into her pocket,
and presented the urchin, her earliest and staunchest
customer, with silver enough to people the Domdaniel
cavern of his interior with as various a procession of
quadrupeds as passed into the ark.

Two men were passing, just as the barouche drove
off.

"Well, Dixey," said one of them, "what do you
think of this? My wife kept a cent-shop three months,
and lost five dollars on her outlay. Old Maid Pyncheon has been in trade just about as long, and rides
off in her carriage with a couple of hundred thousand,
— reckoning her share, and Clifford's, and Phœbe's,
— and some say twice as much! If you choose to
call it luck, it is all very well; but if we are to take it
as the will of Providence, why, I can't exactly fathom
it!"

"Pretty good business!" quoth the sagacious Dixey,
— "pretty good business!"

Maule's well, all this time, though left in solitude,
was throwing up a succession of kaleidoscopic pictures,
in which a gifted eye might have seen foreshadowed
the coming fortunes of Hepzibah and Clifford, and the
descendant of the legendary wizard, and the village
maiden, over whom he had thrown Love's web of sor-
cery. The Pyncheon Elm, moreover, with what foliage the September gale had spared to it, whispered

unintelligible prophecies.   And wise Uncle Venner, passing slowly from the ruinous porch, seemed to hear a strain of music, and fancied that sweet Alice Pyncheon — after witnessing these deeds, this bygone woe and this present happiness, of her kindred mortals — had given one farewell touch of a spirit's joy upon her harpsichord, as she floated heavenward from the HOUSE OF THE SEVEN GABLES!

THE SNOW-IMAGE,

AND

OTHER TWICE-TOLD TALES.

INTRODUCTORY NOTE.

THE SNOW-IMAGE.

THE summer of 1851, spent at Lenox, was a busy one for Hawthorne; and he closed it by bringing out "The Snow-Image, and Other Twice-Told Tales," in the autumn. The tale which gave this volume its name most probably sprang from some simple episode in the life of his two elder children, then at the ages of about six and eight; and there plays over its pages a soft light of domesticity, transient as the flicker of an open wood-fire, — like all the irradiations of actuality upon Hawthorne's fiction, — but characteristic of its origin. One little coincidence I observe which, though trifling, it is perhaps worth while to mention. When the supposed child playmate, whom Violet and Peony have brought into the house, melts away before the fire by which the matter-of-fact Mr. Lindsey has placed her, he exclaims: "Look what a quantity of snow the children have brought in on their feet! It has made quite a puddle here before the stove. Pray tell Dora to bring some towels and sop it up!" Dora was the name of a woman of rather remarkable character, who had been the attendant of Hawthorne's children in Salem. Far back in 1836, too, the "American Note-Books" show that he entertained the scheme of writing a story about boys battling with snowballs, and the victorious leader being honored with a statue of himself in snow; the purpose, to satirize fame.

This interesting key also gives approximately the date when Hawthorne formed his design for "The Great Stone Face," which comes second in the present volume. Between January 4, 1839, and the year 1840, there occurs this paragraph: —

" The semblance of a human face to be formed on the side of a mountain, or in the fracture of a small stone, by a *lusus naturæ*. The face is an object of curiosity for years or for centuries, and by and by a boy is born, whose features gradually assume the aspect of that portrait. At some critical juncture, the resemblance is found to be perfect. A prophecy might be connected."

A curious incident in the later history of " The Great Stone Face " is that, a few years ago, it was found by some one in a German translation, re-translated into English of an inferior sort, and published in an American periodical of good standing before the mistake or imposition, whichever it may have been, was detected. This spurious version served as indirect testimony to the extreme importance of style, and in especial the subtlety with which Hawthorne's peculiar genius penetrated and impressed itself upon his language; for here the story was the same, yet, by the use of a commonplace style, the beauty of the original was destroyed, and its force lost.

" The Canterbury Pilgrims " was derived from Hawthorne's impressions of the Shaker community at Canterbury, N. H., which he visited in 1830; writing thence to one of his sisters: " I spoke to them about becoming a member of their community, but have come to no decision on that point." Later, in 1838, he took a trip through western Massachusetts, by way of enlarging his horizon. In the Note-Books are somewhat extended accounts of the people he encountered there, or of other matters which struck him; and it is very instructive to notice how he has transferred sundry objects and persons bodily — with but few changes from the wording of his journals — into the romantic fabric of "Ethan Brand" (in the Snow-Image volume). Such are the broken-down and crippled lawyer who has taken to soap-boiling; the travelling German peep-show proprietor; and even an old dog who had a whimsical habit of pursuing his own tail. He had seen them in the neighborhood of Pittsfield, only a few miles from Lenox; and on coming to Lenox, after an interval of thirteen years since his former stay in the Berkshire Valley, his interest in this old "material" may have been revived.

The circumstance that Hawthorne was known in college as "Oberon," and that he burned the manuscript of his first book, indicate clearly on what foundation the sketch entitled "The Devil In Manuscript," in the present series, was based. It refers, obviously, to his own experience.

G. P. L.

PREFACE.

———◆———

TO HORATIO BRIDGE, ESQ., U. S. N.

MY DEAR BRIDGE, — Some of the more crabbed of my critics, I understand, have pronounced your friend egotistical, indiscreet, and even impertinent, on account of the Prefaces and Introductions with which, on several occasions, he has seen fit to pave the reader's way into the interior edifice of a book. In the justice of this censure I do not exactly concur, for the reasons, on the one hand, that the public generally has negatived the idea of undue freedom on the author's part by evincing, it seems to me, rather more interest in those aforesaid Introductions than in the stories which followed; and that, on the other hand, with whatever appearance of confidential intimacy, I have been especially careful to make no disclosures respecting myself which the most indifferent observer might not have been acquainted with, and which I was not perfectly willing my worst enemy should know. I might further justify myself, on the plea that ever since my youth, I have been addressing a very limited circle of friendly readers, without much danger of being overheard by the public at large; and that the habits thus acquired might pardonably continue, although strangers may have begun to mingle with my audience.

But the charge, I am bold to say, is not a reasonable one, in any view which we can fairly take of it. There is no harm, but, on the contrary, good, in arraying some of the ordinary facts of life in a slightly idealized and artistic guise. I have taken facts which relate to myself, because they chance to be nearest at hand, and likewise are my own property. And, as for egotism, a person, who has been burrowing, to his utmost ability, into the depths of our common nature, for the purposes of psychological romance, — and who pursues his researches in that dusky region, as he needs must, as well by the tact of sympathy as by the light of observation, — will smile at incurring such an imputation in virtue of a little preliminary talk about his external habits, his abode, his casual associates, and other matters entirely upon the surface. These things hide the man, instead of displaying him. You must make quite another kind of inquest, and look through the whole range of his fictitious characters, good and evil, in order to detect any of his essential traits.

Be all this as it may, there can be no question as to the propriety of my inscribing this volume of earlier and later sketches to you, and pausing here, a few moments, to speak of them, as friend speaks to friend; still being cautious, however, that the public and the critics shall overhear nothing which we care about concealing. On you, if on no other person, I am entitled to rely, to sustain the position of my Dedicatee. If anybody is responsible for my being at this day an author, it is yourself. I know not whence your faith came; but, while we were lads together at a country college, — gathering blueberries, in study-hours, under those tall academic pines; or watching the great logs, as they tumbled along the current of the Androscoggin; or shooting pigeons and gray squirrels in the woods; or bat-fowling in the summer twilight; or catching trouts in that shadowy little stream which, I suppose, is still wandering river-ward through the forest, — though you and I will never cast a line in it again, — two idle lads, in short (as we need not fear to acknowledge now), doing a hundred things that the Faculty never heard of, or else it had been the worse for us, — still it was your prognostic of your friend's destiny, that he was to be a writer of fiction.

And a fiction-monger, in due season, he became. But was there ever such a weary delay in obtaining the slightest recognition from the public, as in my case? I sat down by the wayside of life, like a man under enchantment, and a shrubbery sprung up around me, and the bushes grew to be saplings, and the saplings became trees, until no exit appeared possible, through the entangling depths of my obscurity. And there, perhaps, I should be sitting at this moment, with the moss on the imprisoning tree-trunks, and the yellow leaves of more than a score of autumns piled above me, if it had not been for you. For it was through your interposition — and that, moreover, unknown to himself — that your early friend was brought before the public, somewhat more prominently than theretofore, in the first volume of "Twice-told Tales." Not a publisher in America, I presume, would have thought well enough of my forgotten or never-noticed stories to risk the expense of print and paper; nor do I say this with any purpose of casting odium on the respectable fraternity of booksellers, for their blindness to my wonderful merit. To confess the truth, I doubted of the public recognition quite as much as they could do. So much the more generous was your confidence; and knowing, as I do, that it was founded on old friendship rather than cold criticism, I value it only the more for that.

So, now, when I turn back upon my path, lighted by a transitory gleam of public favor, to pick up a few articles which were left out of my former collections, I take pleasure in making them the memorial of our very long and unbroken connection. Some of these sketches were among the earliest that I wrote, and, after lying for years in manuscript, they at last skulked into the Annuals or Magazines, and have hidden themselves there ever since. Others were the productions of a later period; others, again, were written recently. The comparison of these various trifles — the indices of intellectual conditions at far separate epochs — affects me with a singular complexity of regrets. I am disposed to quarrel with the earlier sketches, both because a mature judgment discerns so many faults, and still more because they come so nearly up to the standard of the best that I can achieve now. The ripened autumnal fruit tastes but little better than the early windfalls. It would, indeed, be mortifying to believe that the summer-time of life has passed away, without any greater progress and improvement than is indicated here. But — at least so I would fain hope — these things are scarcely to be depended upon, as measures of the intellectual and moral man. In youth, men are apt to write more wisely than they really know or feel; and the remainder of life may be not idly spent in realizing and convincing themselves of the wisdom which they uttered long ago. The truth that was only in the fancy then may have since become a substance in the mind and heart.

I have nothing further, I think, to say; unless it be that the public need not dread my again trespassing on its kindness, with any more of these musty and mouse-nibbled leaves of old periodicals, transformed, by the magic arts of my friendly publishers, into a new book. These are the last. Or, if a few still remain, they are either such as no paternal partiality could induce the author to think worth preserving, or else they have got into some very dark and dusty hiding-place, quite out of my own remembrance, and whence no researches can avail to unearth them. So there let them rest.

Very sincerely yours,

N. H.

Lenox, *November* 1, 1851.

THE SNOW-IMAGE:

A CHILDISH MIRACLE.

ONE afternoon of a cold winter's day, when the sun shone forth with chilly brightness, after a long storm, two children asked leave of their mother to run out and play in the new-fallen snow. The elder child was a little girl, whom, because she was of a tender and modest disposition, and was thought to be very beautiful, her parents, and other people who were familiar with her, used to call Violet. But her brother was known by the style and title of Peony, on account of the ruddiness of his broad and round little phiz, which made everybody think of sunshine and great scarlet flowers. The father of these two children, a certain Mr. Lindsey, it is important to say, was an excellent but exceedingly matter-of-fact sort of man, a dealer in hardware, and was sturdily accustomed to take what is called the common-sense view of all matters that came under his consideration. With a heart about as tender as other people's, he had a head as hard and impenetrable, and therefore, perhaps, as empty, as one of the iron pots which it was a part of his business to sell. The mother's character, on the other hand, had a strain of poetry in it, a trait of unworldly beauty, — a delicate and dewy flower, as it were, that had survived out of her imaginative youth, and still kept itself alive amid the dusty realities of matrimony and motherhood.

So, Violet and Peony, as I began with saying, besought their mother to let them run out and play in the new snow; for, though it had looked so dreary and dismal, drifting downward out of the gray sky, it had a very cheerful aspect, now that the sun was shining on it.   The children dwelt in a city, and had no wider play-place than a little garden before the house, divided by a white fence from the street, and with a pear-tree and two or three plum-trees overshadowing it, and some rose-bushes just in front of the parlor-windows.   The trees and shrubs, however, were now leafless, and their twigs were enveloped in the light snow, which thus made a kind of wintry foliage, with here and there a pendent icicle for the fruit.

"Yes, Violet, — yes, my little Peony," said their kind mother, "you may go out and play in the new snow."

Accordingly, the good lady bundled up her darlings in woollen jackets and wadded sacks, and put comforters round their necks, and a pair of striped gaiters on each little pair of legs, and worsted mittens on their hands, and gave them a kiss apiece, by way of a spell to keep away Jack Frost.   Forth sallied the two children, with a hop-skip-and-jump, that carried them at once into the very heart of a huge snow-drift, whence Violet emerged like a snow-bunting, while little Peony floundered out with his round face in full bloom.   Then what a merry time had they!   To look at them, frolicking in the wintry garden, you would have thought that the dark and pitiless storm had been sent for no other purpose but to provide a new plaything for Violet and Peony; and that they themselves had been created, as the snow-birds were, to take delight only in the tempest, and in the white mantle which it spread over the earth.

At last, when they had frosted one another all over with handfuls of snow, Violet, after laughing heartily at little Peony's figure, was struck with a new idea.

"You look exactly like a snow-image, Peony," said she, "if your cheeks were not so red. And that puts me in mind! Let us make an image out of snow, — an image of a little girl, — and it shall be our sister, and shall run about and play with us all winter long. Won't it be nice?"

"Oh yes!" cried Peony, as plainly as he could speak, for he was but a little boy. "That will be nice! And mamma shall see it!"

"Yes," answered Violet; "mamma shall see the new little girl. But she must not make her come into the warm parlor; for, you know, our little snow-sister will not love the warmth."

And forthwith the children began this great business of making a snow-image that should run about; while their mother, who was sitting at the window and overheard some of their talk, could not help smiling at the gravity with which they set about it. They really seemed to imagine that there would be no difficulty whatever in creating a live little girl out of the snow. And, to say the truth, if miracles are ever to be wrought, it will be by putting our hands to the work in precisely such a simple and undoubting frame of mind as that in which Violet and Peony now undertook to perform one, without so much as knowing that it was a miracle. So thought the mother; and thought, likewise, that the new snow, just fallen from heaven, would be excellent material to make new beings of, if it were not so very cold. She gazed at the children a moment longer, delighting to watch their little figures, — the girl, tall for her age, graceful and agile, and so delicately colored that she looked like a cheerful thought more than a physical reality; while Peony expanded in breadth rather than height, and rolled along on his short and sturdy legs as substantial as an elephant, though not quite so big. Then the mother resumed her work. What it was I forget but she was either trimming a silken bonnet for Violet, or darning a pair of stockings for little Peony's short legs. Again, however, and again, and yet other agains, she could not help turning her head to the window to see how the children got on with their snow-image.

Indeed, it was an exceedingly pleasant sight, those bright little souls at their task! Moreover, it was really wonderful to observe how knowingly and skilfully they managed the matter. Violet assumed the chief direction, and told Peony what to do, while, with her own delicate fingers, she shaped out all the nicer parts of the snow-figure. It seemed, in fact, not so much to be made by the children, as to grow up under their hands, while they were playing and prattling about it. Their mother was quite surprised at this; and the longer she looked, the more and more surprised she grew.

"What remarkable children mine are!" thought she, smiling with a mother's pride; and, smiling at herself, too, for being so proud of them. "What other children could have made anything so like a little girl's figure out of snow at the first trial? Well; but now I must finish Peony's new frock, for his grandfather is coming to-morrow, and I want the little fellow to look handsome."

So she took up the frock, and was soon as busily at work again with her needle as the two children with their snow-image. But still, as the needle travelled hither and thither through the seams of the dress, the mother made her toil light and happy by listening to the airy voices of Violet and Peony. They kept talking to one another all the time, their tongues being quite as active as their feet and hands. Except at intervals, she could not distinctly hear what was said, but had merely a sweet impression that they were in a most loving mood, and were enjoying themselves highly, and that the business of making the snow-image went prosperously on. Now and then, however, when Violet and Peony happened to raise their voices, the words were as audible as if they had been spoken in the very parlor where the mother sat. Oh how delightfully those words echoed in her heart, even though they meant nothing so very wise or wonderful, after all!

But you must know a mother listens with her heart much more than with her ears; and thus she is often delighted with the trills of celestial music, when other people can hear nothing of the kind.

"Peony, Peony!" cried Violet to her brother, who had gone to another part of the garden, "bring me some of that fresh snow, Peony, from the very farthest corner, where we have not been trampling. I want it to shape our little snow-sister's bosom with. You know that part must be quite pure, just as it came out of the sky!"

"Here it is, Violet!" answered Peony, in his bluff tone, — but a very sweet tone, too, — as he came floundering through the half-trodden drifts. "Here is the snow for her little bosom. O Violet, how beau-ti-ful she begins to look!"

"Yes," said Violet, thoughtfully and quietly; "our

snow-sister does look very lovely. I did not quite
know, Peony, that we could make such a sweet little
girl as this."

The mother, as she listened, thought how fit and
delightful an incident it would be, if fairies, or still
better, if angel-children were to come from paradise,
and play invisibly with her own darlings, and help
them to make their snow-image, giving it the features
of celestial babyhood! Violet and Peony would not
be aware of their immortal playmates, — only they
would see that the image grew very beautiful while
they worked at it, and would think that they themselves had done it all.

"My little girl and boy deserve such playmates, if
mortal children ever did!" said the mother to herself; and then she smiled again at her own motherly
pride.

Nevertheless, the idea seized upon her imagination;
and, ever and anon, she took a glimpse out of the window, half dreaming that she might see the golden-
haired children of paradise sporting with her own
golden-haired Violet and bright-cheeked Peony.

Now, for a few moments, there was a busy and earnest, but indistinct hum of the two children's voices,
as Violet and Peony wrought together with one happy
consent. Violet still seemed to be the guiding spirit,
while Peony acted rather as a laborer, and brought
her the snow from far and near. And yet the little
urchin evidently had a proper understanding of the
matter, too!

"Peony, Peony!" cried Violet; for her brother
was again at the other side of the garden. "Bring me
those light wreaths of snow that have rested on the
lower branches of the pear-tree. You can clamber on

the snow-drift, Peony, and reach them easily. I must have them to make some ringlets for our snow-sister's head!"

"Here they are, Violet!" answered the little boy. "Take care you do not break them. Well done! Well done! How pretty!"

"Does she not look sweetly?" said Violet, with a very satisfied tone; "and now we must have some little shining bits of ice, to make the brightness of her eyes. She is not finished yet. Mamma will see how very beautiful she is; but papa will say, 'Tush! nonsense! — come in out of the cold!'"

"Let us call mamma to look out," said Peony; and then he shouted lustily, "Mamma! mamma!! mamma!!! Look out, and see what a nice 'ittle girl we are making!"

The mother put down her work for an instant, and looked out of the window. But it so happened that the sun — for this was one of the shortest days of the whole year — had sunken so nearly to the edge of the world that his setting shine came obliquely into the lady's eyes. So she was dazzled, you must understand, and could not very distinctly observe what was in the garden. Still, however, through all that bright, blinding dazzle of the sun and the new snow, she beheld a small white figure in the garden, that seemed to have a wonderful deal of human likeness about it. And she saw Violet and Peony, — indeed, she looked more at them than at the image, — she saw the two children still at work; Peony bringing fresh snow, and Violet applying it to the figure as scientifically as a sculptor adds clay to his model. Indistinctly as she discerned the snow - child, the mother thought to herself that never before was there a snow-figure so cunningly made, nor ever such a dear little girl and boy to make it.

"They do everything better than other children," said she, very complacently. "No wonder they make better snow-images!"

She sat down again to her work, and made as much haste with it as possible; because twilight would soon come, and Peony's frock was not yet finished, and grandfather was expected, by railroad, pretty early in the morning. Faster and faster, therefore, went her flying fingers. The children, likewise, kept busily at work in the garden, and still the mother listened, whenever she could catch a word. She was amused to observe how their little imaginations had got mixed up with what they were doing, and carried away by it. They seemed positively to think that the snow-child would run about and play with them.

"What a nice playmate she will be for us, all winter long!" said Violet. "I hope papa will not be afraid of her giving us a cold! Sha'n't you love her dearly, Peony?"

"Oh yes!" cried Peony. "And I will hug her, and she shall sit down close by me, and drink some of my warm milk!"

"Oh no, Peony!" answered Violet, with grave wisdom. "That will not do at all. Warm milk will not be wholesome for our little snow-sister. Little snow people, like her, eat nothing but icicles. No, no, Peony; we must not give her anything warm to drink!"

There was a minute or two of silence; for Peony, whose short legs were never weary, had gone on a pilgrimage again to the other side of the garden. All of a sudden, Violet cried out, loudly and joyfully, —

"Look here, Peony! Come quickly! A light has been shining on her cheek out of that rose-colored cloud! and the color does not go away! Is not that beautiful!"

"Yes; it is beau-ti-ful," answered Peony, pronouncing the three syllables with deliberate accuracy. "O Violet, only look at her hair! It is all like gold!"

"Oh certainly," said Violet, with tranquillity, as if it were very much a matter of course. "That color, you know, comes from the golden clouds, that we see up there in the sky. She is almost finished now. But her lips must be made very red,—redder than her cheeks. Perhaps, Peony, it will make them red if we both kiss them!"

Accordingly, the mother heard two smart little smacks, as if both her children were kissing the snow-image on its frozen mouth. But, as this did not seem to make the lips quite red enough, Violet next proposed that the snow-child should be invited to kiss Peony's scarlet cheek.

"Come, 'ittle snow-sister, kiss me!" cried Peony.

"There! she has kissed you," added Violet, "and now her lips are very red. And she blushed a little, too!"

"Oh, what a cold kiss!" cried Peony.

Just then, there came a breeze of the pure west-wind, sweeping through the garden and rattling the parlor-windows. It sounded so wintry cold, that the mother was about to tap on the window-pane with her thimbled finger, to summon the two children in, when they both cried out to her with one voice. The tone was not a tone of surprise, although they were evidently a good deal excited; it appeared rather as if they were very much rejoiced at some event that had now happened, but which they had been looking for, and had reckoned upon all along.

"Mamma! mamma! We have finished our little snow-sister, and she is running about the garden with us!"

"What imaginative little beings my children are!" thought the mother, putting the last few stitches into Peony's frock. "And it is strange, too, that they make me almost as much a child as they themselves are! I can hardly help believing, now, that the snow-image has really come to life!"

"Dear mamma!" cried Violet, "pray look out and see what a sweet playmate we have!"

The mother, being thus entreated, could no longer delay to look forth from the window. The sun was now gone out of the sky, leaving, however, a rich inheritance of his brightness among those purple and golden clouds which make the sunsets of winter so magnificent. But there was not the slightest gleam or dazzle, either on the window or on the snow; so that the good lady could look all over the garden, and see everything and everybody in it. And what do you think she saw there? Violet and Peony, of course, her own two darling children. Ah, but whom or what did she see besides? Why, if you will believe me, there was a small figure of a girl, dressed all in white, with rose-tinged cheeks and ringlets of golden hue, playing about the garden with the two children! A stranger though she was, the child seemed to be on as familiar terms with Violet and Peony, and they with her, as if all the three had been playmates during the whole of their little lives. The mother thought to herself that it must certainly be the daughter of one of the neighbors, and that, seeing Violet and Peony in the garden, the child had run across the street to play with them. So this kind lady went to the door, intending to invite the little runaway into her comfortable parlor; for, now that the sunshine was withdrawn, the atmosphere, out of doors, was already growing very cold.

But, after opening the house-door, she stood an instant on the threshold, hesitating whether she ought to ask the child to come in, or whether she should even speak to her. Indeed, she almost doubted whether it were a real child after all, or only a light wreath of the new-fallen snow, blown hither and thither about the garden by the intensely cold west-wind. There was certainly something very singular in the aspect of the little stranger. Among all the children of the neighborhood, the lady could remember no such face, with its pure white, and delicate rose-color, and the golden ringlets tossing about the forehead and cheeks. And as for her dress, which was entirely of white, and fluttering in the breeze, it was such as no reasonable woman would put upon a little girl, when sending her out to play, in the depth of winter. It made this kind and careful mother shiver only to look at those small feet, with nothing in the world on them, except a very thin pair of white slippers. Nevertheless, airily as she was clad, the child seemed to feel not the slightest inconvenience from the cold, but danced so lightly over the snow that the tips of her toes left hardly a print in its surface; while Violet could but just keep pace with her, and Peony's short legs compelled him to lag behind.

Once, in the course of their play, the strange child placed herself between Violet and Peony, and taking a hand of each, skipped merrily forward, and they along with her. Almost immediately, however, Peony pulled away his little fist, and began to rub it as if the fingers were tingling with cold ; while Violet also released herself, though with less abruptness, gravely remarking that it was better not to take hold of hands. The white-robed damsel said not a word, but danced about, just as merrily as before. If Violet and Peony did not choose to play with her, she could make just as good a playmate of the brisk and cold west-wind, which kept blowing her all about the garden, and took such liberties with her, that they seemed to have been friends for a long time. All this while, the mother stood on the threshold, wondering how a little girl could look so much like a flying snow-drift, or how a snow-drift could look so very like a little girl.

She called Violet, and whispered to her.

"Violet my darling, what is this child's name?" asked she. "Does she live near us?"

"Why, dearest mamma," answered Violet, laughing to think that her mother did not comprehend so very plain an affair, "this is our little snow-sister whom we have just been making!"

"Yes, dear mamma," cried Peony, running to his mother, and looking up simply into her face. "This is our snow-image! Is it not a nice 'ittle child?"

At this instant a flock of snow-birds came flitting through the air. As was very natural, they avoided Violet and Peony. But — and this looked strange — they flew at once to the white-robed child, fluttered eagerly about her head, alighted on her shoulders, and seemed to claim her as an old acquaintance. She, on her part, was evidently as glad to see these little birds, old Winter's grandchildren, as they were to see her, and welcomed them by holding out both her hands.

Hereupon, they each and all tried to alight on her two palms and ten small fingers and thumbs, crowding one another off, with an immense fluttering of their tiny wings. One dear little bird nestled tenderly in her bosom; another put its bill to her lips. They were as joyous, all the while, and seemed as much in their element, as you may have seen them when sporting with a snow-storm.

Violet and Peony stood laughing at this pretty sight; for they enjoyed the merry time which their new playmate was having with these small - winged visitants, almost as much as if they themselves took part in it.

"Violet," said her mother, greatly perplexed, "tell me the truth, without any jest. Who is this little girl?"

"My darling mamma," answered Violet, looking seriously into her mother's face, and apparently surprised that she should need any further explanation, "I have told you truly who she is. It is our little snow-image, which Peony and I have been making. Peony will tell you so, as well as I."

"Yes, mamma," asseverated Peony, with much gravity in his crimson little phiz; "this is 'ittle snow-child. Is not she a nice one? But, mamma, her hand is, oh, so very cold!"

While mamma still hesitated what to think and what to do, the street-gate was thrown open, and the father of Violet and Peony appeared, wrapped in a pilot-cloth sack, with a fur cap drawn down over his ears, and the thickest of gloves upon his hands. Mr. Lindsey was a middle-aged man, with a weary and yet a happy look in his wind-flushed and frost-pinched face, as if he had been busy all the day long, and was

glad to get back to his quiet home. His eyes brightened at the sight of his wife and children, although he
could not help uttering a word or two of surprise, at
finding the whole family in the open air, on so bleak
a day, and after sunset too. He soon perceived the
little white stranger sporting to and fro in the garden,
like a dancing snow-wreath, and the flock of snow-
birds fluttering about her head.

"Pray, what little girl may that be?" inquired this
very sensible man. "Surely her mother must be
crazy to let her go out in such bitter weather as it has
been to-day, with only that flimsy white gown and
those thin slippers!"

"My dear husband," said his wife, "I know no
more about the little thing than you do. Some neighbor's child, I suppose. Our Violet and Peony," she
added, laughing at herself for repeating so absurd a
story, "insist that she is nothing but a snow-image,
which they have been busy about in the garden, almost all the afternoon."

As she said this, the mother glanced her eyes toward
the spot where the children's snow-image had been
made. What was her surprise, on perceiving that
there was not the slightest trace of so much labor! —
no image at all! — no piled up heap of snow! — nothing whatever, save the prints of little footsteps around
a vacant space!

"This is very strange!" said she.

"What is strange, dear mother?" asked Violet.
"Dear father, do not you see how it is? This is our
snow-image, which Peony and I have made, because
we wanted another playmate. Did not we, Peony?"

"Yes, papa," said crimson Peony. "This be our
'ittle snow-sister. Is she not beau-ti-ful? But she
gave me such a cold kiss!"

"Poh, nonsense, children!" cried their good, honest father, who, as we have already intimated, had an exceedingly common-sensible way of looking at matters. "Do not tell me of making live figures out of snow. Come, wife; this little stranger must not stay out in the bleak air a moment longer. We will bring her into the parlor; and you shall give her a supper of warm bread and milk, and make her as comfortable as you can. Meanwhile, I will inquire among the neighbors; or, if necessary, send the city-crier about the streets, to give notice of a lost child."

So saying, this honest and very kind-hearted man was going toward the little white damsel, with the best intentions in the world. But Violet and Peony, each seizing their father by the hand, earnestly besought him not to make her come in.

"Dear father," cried Violet, putting herself before him, "it is true what I have been telling you! This is our little snow-girl, and she cannot live any longer than while she breathes the cold west-wind. Do not make her come into the hot room!"

"Yes, father," shouted Peony, stamping his little foot, so mightily was he in earnest, "this be nothing but our 'ittle snow-child! She will not love the hot fire!"

"Nonsense, children, nonsense, nonsense!" cried the father, half vexed, half laughing at what he considered their foolish obstinacy. "Run into the house, this moment! It is too late to play any longer, now. I must take care of this little girl immediately, or she will catch her death-a-cold!"

"Husband! dear husband!" said his wife, in a low voice, — for she had been looking narrowly at the snow-child, and was more perplexed than ever, —

" there is something very singular in all this. You will think me foolish, — but — but — may it not be that some invisible angel has been attracted by the simplicity and good faith with which our children set about their undertaking? May he not have spent an hour of his immortality in playing with those dear little souls? and so the result is what we call a miracle. No, no! Do not laugh at me; I see what a foolish thought it is ! "

" My dear wife," replied the husband, laughing heartily, " you are as much a child as Violet and Peony."

And in one sense so she was, for all through life she had kept her heart full of childlike simplicity and faith, which was as pure and clear as crystal; and, looking at all matters through this transparent medium, she sometimes saw truths so profound that other people laughed at them as nonsense and absurdity.

But now kind Mr. Lindsey had entered the garden, breaking away from his two children, who still sent their shrill voices after him, beseeching him to let the snow-child stay and enjoy herself in the cold west-wind. As he approached, the snow-birds took to flight. The little white damsel, also, fled backward, shaking her head, as if to say, " Pray, do not touch me ! " and roguishly, as it appeared, leading him through the deepest of the snow. Once, the good man stumbled, and floundered down upon his face, so that, gathering himself up again, with the snow sticking to his rough pilot-cloth sack, he looked as white and wintry as a snow-image of the largest size. Some of the neighbors, meanwhile, seeing him from their windows, wondered what could possess poor Mr. Lindsey to be running about his garden in pursuit of a snow-drift, which the west-wind was driving hither and thither! At length, after a vast deal of trouble, he chased the little stranger into a corner, where she could not possibly escape him. His wife had been looking on, and, it being nearly twilight, was wonder-struck to observe how the snow-child gleamed and sparkled, and how she seemed to shed a glow all round about her; and when driven into the corner, she positively glistened like a star! It was a frosty kind of brightness, too, like that of an icicle in the moonlight. The wife thought it strange that good Mr. Lindsey should see nothing remarkable in the snow-child's appearance.

"Come, you odd little thing!" cried the honest man, seizing her by the hand, "I have caught you at last, and will make you comfortable in spite of yourself. We will put a nice warm pair of worsted stockings on your frozen little feet, and you shall have a good thick shawl to wrap yourself in. Your poor white nose, I am afraid, is actually frost-bitten. But we will make it all right. Come along in."

And so, with a most benevolent smile on his sagacious visage, all purple as it was with the cold, this very well-meaning gentleman took the snow-child by the hand and led her towards the house. She followed him, droopingly and reluctant; for all the glow and sparkle was gone out of her figure; and whereas just before she had resembled a bright, frosty, star-gemmed evening, with a crimson gleam on the cold horizon, she now looked as dull and languid as a thaw. As kind Mr. Lindsey led her up the steps of the door, Violet and Peony looked into his face, — their eyes full of tears, which froze before they could run down their cheeks, — and again entreated him not to bring their snow-image into the house.

"Not bring her in!" exclaimed the kind-hearted
man. "Why, you are crazy, my little Violet!—quite
crazy, my small Peony! She is so cold, already, that
her hand has almost frozen mine, in spite of my thick
gloves. Would you have her freeze to death?"

His wife, as he came up the steps, had been taking
another long, earnest, almost awe-stricken gaze at the
little white stranger. She hardly knew whether it
was a dream or no; but she could not help fancying
that she saw the delicate print of Violet's fingers on
the child's neck. It looked just as if, while Violet was
shaping out the image, she had given it a gentle pat
with her hand, and had neglected to smooth the impression quite away.

"After all, husband," said the mother, recurring to
her idea that the angels would be as much delighted
to play with Violet and Peony as she herself was,—
"after all, she does look strangely like a snow-image!
I do believe she is made of snow!"

A puff of the west-wind blew against the snow-child,
and again she sparkled like a star.

"Snow!" repeated good Mr. Lindsey, drawing the
reluctant guest over his hospitable threshold. "No
wonder she looks like snow. She is half frozen, poor
little thing! But a good fire will put everything to
rights!"

Without further talk, and always with the same best
intentions, this highly benevolent and common-sensible individual led the little white damsel—drooping,
drooping, drooping, more and more—out of the frosty
air, and into his comfortable parlor. A Heidenberg
stove, filled to the brim with intensely burning anthra-
cite, was sending a bright gleam through the isinglass
of its iron door, and causing the vase of water on its top

to fume and bubble with excitement. A warm, sultry smell was diffused throughout the room. A thermometer on the wall farthest from the stove stood at eighty degrees. The parlor was hung with red curtains, and covered with a red carpet, and looked just as warm as it felt. The difference betwixt the atmosphere here and the cold, wintry twilight out of doors, was like stepping at once from Nova Zembla to the hottest part of India, or from the North Pole into an oven. Oh, this was a fine place for the little white stranger!

The common-sensible man placed the snow-child on the hearth-rug, right in front of the hissing and fuming stove.

"Now she will be comfortable!" cried Mr. Lindsey, rubbing his hands and looking about him, with the pleasantest smile you ever saw. "Make yourself at home, my child."

Sad, sad and drooping, looked the little white maiden, as she stood on the hearth-rug, with the hot blast of the stove striking through her like a pestilence. Once, she threw a glance wistfully toward the windows, and caught a glimpse, through its red curtains, of the snow-covered roofs, and the stars glimmering frostily, and all the delicious intensity of the cold night. The bleak wind rattled the window-panes, as if it were summoning her to come forth. But there stood the snow-child, drooping, before the hot stove!

But the common-sensible man saw nothing amiss.

"Come wife," said he, "let her have a pair of thick stockings and a woollen shawl or blanket directly; and tell Dora to give her some warm supper as soon as the milk boils. You, Violet and Peony, amuse your little friend. She is out of spirits, you see, at finding herself in a strange place. For my part, I will go around among the neighbors, and find out where she belongs."

The mother, meanwhile, had gone in search of the shawl and stockings; for her own view of the matter, however subtle and delicate, had given way, as it always did, to the stubborn materialism of her husband. Without heeding the remonstrances of his two children, who still kept murmuring that their little snow-sister did not love the warmth, good Mr. Lindsey took his departure, shutting the parlor-door carefully behind him. Turning up the collar of his sack over his ears, he emerged from the house, and had barely reached the street-gate, when he was recalled by the screams of Violet and Peony, and the rapping of a thimbled finger against the parlor window.

"Husband! husband!" cried his wife, showing her horror-stricken face through the window-panes. "There is no need of going for the child's parents!"

"We told you so, father!" screamed Violet and Peony, as he re-entered the parlor. "You would bring her in; and now our poor — dear — beau-ti-ful little snow-sister is thawed!"

And their own sweet little faces were already dissolved in tears; so that their father, seeing what strange things occasionally happen in this every-day world, felt not a little anxious lest his children might be going to thaw too! In the utmost perplexity, he demanded an explanation of his wife. She could only reply, that, being summoned to the parlor by the cries of Violet and Peony, she found no trace of the little white maiden, unless it were the remains of a heap of snow, which, while she was gazing at it, melted quite away upon the hearth-rug.

"And there you see all that is left of it!" added she, pointing to a pool of water in front of the stove.

"Yes, father," said Violet looking reproachfully at him, through her tears, "there is all that is left of our dear little snow-sister!"

"Naughty father!" cried Peony, stamping his foot, and — I shudder to say — shaking his little fist at the common-sensible man. "We told you how it would be! What for did you bring her in?"

And the Heidenberg stove, through the isinglass of its door, seemed to glare at good Mr. Lindsey, like a red-eyed demon, triumphing in the mischief which it had done!

This, you will observe, was one of those rare cases, which yet will occasionally happen, where common-sense finds itself at fault. The remarkable story of the snow-image, though to that sagacious class of people to whom good Mr. Lindsey belongs it may seem but a childish affair, is, nevertheless, capable of being moralized in various methods, greatly for their edification. One of its lessons, for instance, might be, that it behooves men, and especially men of benevolence, to consider well what they are about, and, before acting on their philanthropic purposes, to be quite sure that they comprehend the nature and all the relations of the business in hand. What has been established as an element of good to one being may prove absolute mischief to another; even as the warmth of the parlor was proper enough for children of flesh and blood, like Violet and Peony, — though by no means very wholesome, even for them, — but involved nothing short of annihilation to the unfortunate snow-image.

But, after all, there is no teaching anything to wise men of good Mr. Lindsey's stamp. They know everything, — oh, to be sure! — everything that has been, and everything that is, and everything that, by any future possibility, can be. And, should some phenomenon of nature or providence transcend their system, they will not recognize it, even if it come to pass under their very noses.

"Wife," said Mr. Lindsey, after a fit of silence, "see what a quantity of snow the children have brought in on their feet! It has made quite a puddle here before the stove. Pray tell Dora to bring some towels and sop it up!"

THE GREAT STONE FACE.

ONE afternoon, when the sun was going down, a mother and her little boy sat at the door of their cottage, talking about the Great Stone Face. They had but to lift their eyes, and there it was plainly to be seen, though miles away, with the sunshine brightening all its features.

And what was the Great Stone Face?

Embosomed amongst a family of lofty mountains, there was a valley so spacious that it contained many thousand inhabitants. Some of these good people dwelt in log-huts, with the black forest all around them, on the steep and difficult hill-sides. Others had their homes in comfortable farm-houses, and cultivated the rich soil on the gentle slopes or level surfaces of the valley. Others, again, were congregated into populous villages, where some wild, highland rivulet, tumbling down from its birthplace in the upper mountain region, had been caught and tamed by human cunning, and compelled to turn the machinery of cotton-factories. The inhabitants of this valley, in short, were numerous, and of many modes of life. But all of them, grown people and children, had a kind of familiarity with the Great Stone Face, although some possessed the gift of distinguishing this grand natural phenomenon more perfectly than many of their neighbors.

The Great Stone Face, then, was a work of Nature in her mood of majestic playfulness, formed on the perpendicular side of a mountain by some immense rocks, which had been thrown together in such a position as, when viewed at a proper distance, precisely to resemble the features of the human countenance. It seemed as if an enormous giant, or a Titan, had sculptured his own likeness on the precipice. There was the broad arch of the forehead, a hundred feet in height; the nose, with its long bridge; and the vast lips, which, if they could have spoken, would have rolled their thunder accents from one end of the valley to the other. True it is, that if the spectator approached too near, he lost the outline of the gigantic visage, and could discern only a heap of ponderous and gigantic rocks, piled in chaotic ruin one upon another. Retracing his steps, however, the wondrous features would again be seen; and the farther he withdrew from them, the more like a human face, with all its original divinity intact, did they appear; until, as it grew dim in the distance, with the clouds and glorified vapor of the mountains clustering about it, the Great Stone Face seemed positively to be alive.

It was a happy lot for children to grow up to manhood or womanhood with the Great Stone Face before their eyes, for all the features were noble, and the expression was at once grand and sweet, as if it were the glow of a vast, warm heart, that embraced all mankind in its affections, and had room for more. It was an education only to look at it. According to the belief of many people, the valley owed much of its fertility to this benign aspect that was continually beaming over it, illuminating the clouds, and infusing its tenderness into the sunshine.

As we began with saying, a mother and her little boy sat at their cottage-door, gazing at the Great Stone

Face, and talking about it. The child's name was Ernest.

"Mother," said he, while the Titanic visage smiled on him, "I wish that it could speak, for it looks so very kindly that its voice must needs be pleasant. If I were to see a man with such a face, I should love him dearly."

"If an old prophecy should come to pass," answered his mother, "we may see a man, some time or other, with exactly such a face as that."

"What prophecy do you mean, dear mother?" eagerly inquired Ernest. "Pray tell me all about it!"

So his mother told him a story that her own mother had told to her, when she herself was younger than little Ernest; a story, not of things that were past, but of what was yet to come; a story, nevertheless, so very old, that even the Indians, who formerly inhabited this valley, had heard it from their forefathers, to whom, as they affirmed, it had been murmured by the mountain streams, and whispered by the wind among the tree-tops. The purport was, that, at some future day, a child should be born hereabouts, who was destined to become the greatest and noblest personage of his time, and whose countenance, in manhood, should bear an exact resemblance to the Great Stone Face. Not a few old-fashioned people, and young ones likewise, in the ardor of their hopes, still cherished an enduring faith in this old prophecy. But others, who had seen more of the world, had watched and waited till they were weary, and had beheld no man with such a face, nor any man that proved to be much greater or nobler than his neighbors, concluded it to be nothing but an idle tale. At all events, the great man of the prophecy had not yet appeared.

"O mother, dear mother!" cried Ernest, clapping his hands above his head, "I do hope that I shall live to see him!"

His mother was an affectionate and thoughtful woman, and felt that it was wisest not to discourage the generous hopes of her little boy. So she only said to him, "Perhaps you may."

And Ernest never forgot the story that his mother told him. It was always in his mind, whenever he looked upon the Great Stone Face. He spent his childhood in the log-cottage where he was born, and was dutiful to his mother, and helpful to her in many things, assisting her much with his little hands, and more with his loving heart. In this manner, from a happy yet often pensive child, he grew up to be a mild, quiet, unobtrusive boy, and sun-browned with labor in the fields, but with more intelligence brightening his aspect than is seen in many lads who have been taught at famous schools. Yet Ernest had had no teacher, save only that the Great Stone Face became one to him. When the toil of the day was over, he would gaze at it for hours, until he began to imagine that those vast features recognized him, and gave him a smile of kindness and encouragement, responsive to his own look of veneration. We must not take upon us to affirm that this was a mistake, although the Face may have looked no more kindly at Ernest than at all the world besides. But the secret was that the boy's tender and confiding simplicity discerned what other people could not see; and thus the love, which was meant for all, became his peculiar portion.

About this time there went a rumor throughout the valley, that the great man, foretold from ages long ago, who was to bear a resemblance to the Great Stone Face, had appeared at last. It seems that, many years before, a young man had migrated from the valley and settled at a distant seaport, where, after getting together a little money, he had set up as a shopkeeper. His name — but I could never learn whether it was his real one, or a nickname that had grown out of his habits and success in life — was Gathergold. Being shrewd and active, and endowed by Providence with that inscrutable faculty which develops itself in what the world calls luck, he became an exceedingly rich merchant, and owner of a whole fleet of bulky-bottomed ships. All the countries of the globe appeared to join hands for the mere purpose of adding heap after heap to the mountainous accumulation of this one man's wealth. The cold regions of the north, almost within the gloom and shadow of the Arctic Circle, sent him their tribute in the shape of furs; hot Africa sifted for him the golden sands of her rivers, and gathered up the ivory tusks of her great elephants out of the forests; the East came bringing him the rich shawls, and spices, and teas, and the effulgence of diamonds, and the gleaming purity of large pearls. The ocean, not to be behindhand with the earth, yielded up her mighty whales, that Mr. Gathergold might sell their oil, and make a profit on it. Be the original commodity what it might, it was gold within his grasp. It might be said of him, as of Midas in the fable, that whatever he touched with his finger immediately glistened, and grew yellow, and was changed at once into sterling metal, or, which suited him still better, into piles of coin. And, when Mr. Gathergold had become so very rich that it would have taken him a hundred years only to count his wealth, he bethought himself of his native valley, and resolved to go back thither, and end his days where he was born. With this purpose in view, he sent a skilful architect to build him such a palace as should be fit for a man of his vast wealth to live in.

As I have said above, it had already been rumored in the valley that Mr. Gathergold had turned out to be the prophetic personage so long and vainly looked for, and that his visage was the perfect and undeniable similitude of the Great Stone Face. People were the more ready to believe that this must needs be the fact, when they beheld the splendid edifice that rose, as if by enchantment, on the site of his father's old weather-beaten farm-house. The exterior was of marble, so dazzlingly white that it seemed as though the whole structure might melt away in the sunshine, like those humbler ones which Mr. Gathergold, in his young play-days, before his fingers were gifted with the touch of transmutation, had been accustomed to build of snow. It had a richly ornamented portico, supported by tall pillars, beneath which was a lofty door, studded with silver knobs, and made of a kind of variegated wood that had been brought from beyond the sea. The windows, from the floor to the ceiling of each stately apartment, were composed, respectively, of but one enormous pane of glass, so transparently pure that it was said to be a finer medium than even the vacant atmosphere. Hardly anybody had been permitted to see the interior of this palace; but it was reported, and with good semblance of truth, to be far more gorgeous than the outside, insomuch that whatever was iron or brass in other houses was silver or gold in this; and Mr. Gathergold's bedchamber, especially, made such a glittering appearance that no ordinary man would have been able to close his eyes there. But, on the other hand, Mr. Gathergold was now so inured to wealth, that perhaps he could not have closed his eyes unless where the gleam of it was certain to find its way beneath his eyelids.

In due time, the mansion was finished; next came the upholsterers, with magnificent furniture; then, a whole troop of black and white servants, the harbingers of Mr. Gathergold, who, in his own majestic person, was expected to arrive at sunset. Our friend Ernest, meanwhile, had been deeply stirred by the idea that the great man, the noble man, the man of prophecy, after so many ages of delay, was at length to be made manifest to his native valley. He knew, boy as he was, that there were a thousand ways in which Mr. Gathergold, with his vast wealth, might transform himself into an angel of beneficence, and assume a control over human affairs as wide and benignant as the smile of the Great Stone Face. Full of faith and hope, Ernest doubted not that what the people said was true, and that now he was to behold the living likeness of those wondrous features on the mountain-side. While the boy was still gazing up the valley, and fancying, as he always did, that the Great Stone Face returned his gaze and looked kindly at him, the rumbling of wheels was heard, approaching swiftly along the winding road.

"Here he comes!" cried a group of people who were assembled to witness the arrival. "Here comes the great Mr. Gathergold!"

A carriage, drawn by four horses, dashed round the turn of the road. Within it, thrust partly out of the window, appeared the physiognomy of the old man, with a skin as yellow as if his own Midas-hand had transmuted it. He had a low forehead, small, sharp eyes, puckered about with innumerable wrinkles, and very thin lips, which he made still thinner by pressing them forcibly together.

"The very image of the Great Stone Face!" shouted the people. "Sure enough, the old prophecy is true; and here we have the great man come, at last!"

And, what greatly perplexed Ernest, they seemed actually to believe that here was the likeness which they spoke of. By the roadside there chanced to be an old beggar-woman and two little beggar-children, stragglers from some far-off region, who, as the carriage rolled onward, held out their hands and lifted up their doleful voices, most piteously beseeching charity. A yellow claw — the very same that had clawed together so much wealth — poked itself out of the coach-window, and dropt some copper coins upon the ground; so that, though the great man's name seems to have been Gathergold, he might just as suitably have been nicknamed Scattercopper. Still, nevertheless, with an earnest shout, and evidently with as much good faith as ever, the people bellowed, —

"He is the very image of the Great Stone Face!"

But Ernest turned sadly from the wrinkled shrewdness of that sordid visage, and gazed up the valley, where, amid a gathering mist, gilded by the last sunbeams, he could still distinguish those glorious features which had impressed themselves into his soul. Their aspect cheered him. What did the benign lips seem to say?

"He will come! Fear not, Ernest; the man will come!"

The years went on, and Ernest ceased to be a boy.

He had grown to be a young man now. He attracted little notice from the other inhabitants of the valley; for they saw nothing remarkable in his way of life, save that, when the labor of the day was over, he still loved to go apart and gaze and meditate upon the Great Stone Face. According to their idea of the matter, it was a folly, indeed, but pardonable, inasmuch as Ernest was industrious, kind, and neighborly, and neglected no duty for the sake of indulging this idle habit. They knew not that the Great Stone Face had become a teacher to him, and that the sentiment which was expressed in it would enlarge the young man's heart, and fill it with wider and deeper sympathies than other hearts. They knew not that thence would come a better wisdom than could be learned from books, and a better life than could be moulded on the defaced example of other human lives. Neither did Ernest know that the thoughts and affections which came to him so naturally, in the fields and at the fireside, and wherever he communed with himself, were of a higher tone than those which all men shared with him. A simple soul, — simple as when his mother first taught him the old prophecy, — he beheld the marvellous features beaming adown the valley, and still wondered that their human counterpart was so long in making his appearance.

By this time poor Mr. Gathergold was dead and buried; and the oddest part of the matter was, that his wealth, which was the body and spirit of his existence, had disappeared before his death, leaving nothing of him but a living skeleton, covered over with a wrinkled, yellow skin. Since the melting away of his gold, it had been very generally conceded that there was no such striking resemblance, after all, betwixt the ignoble features of the ruined merchant and that majestic face upon the mountain-side. So the people ceased to honor him during his lifetime, and quietly consigned him to forgetfulness after his decease. Once in a while, it is true, his memory was brought up in connection·with the magnificent palace which he had built, and which had long ago been turned into a hotel for the accommodation of strangers, multitudes of whom came, every summer, to visit that famous natural curiosity, the Great Stone Face. Thus, Mr. Gathergold being discredited and thrown into the shade, the man of prophecy was yet to come.

It so happened that a native-born son of the valley, many years before, had enlisted as a soldier, and, after a great deal of hard fighting, had now become an illustrious commander. Whatever he may be called in history, he was known in camps and on the battle-field under the nickname of Old Blood-and-Thunder. This war-worn veteran, being now infirm with age and wounds, and weary of the turmoil of a military life, and of the roll of the drum and the clangor of the trumpet, that had so long been ringing in his ears, had lately signified a purpose of returning to his native valley, hoping to find repose where he remembered to have left it. The inhabitants, his old neighbors and their grown-up children, were resolved to welcome the renowned warrior with a salute of cannon and a public dinner; and all the more enthusiastically, it being affirmed that now, at last, the likeness of the Great Stone Face had actually appeared. An aid-de-camp of Old Blood-and-Thunder, travelling through the valley, was said to have been struck with the resemblance. Moreover the schoolmates and early acquaintances of the general were ready to testify, on oath, that, to the best of their recollection, the afore-said general had been exceedingly like the majestic image, even when a boy, only that the idea had never occurred to them at that period. Great, therefore, was the excitement throughout the valley; and many peo-ple, who had never once thought of glancing at the Great Stone Face for years before, now spent their time in gazing at it, for the sake of knowing exactly how General Blood-and-Thunder looked.

On the day of the great festival, Ernest, with all the other people of the valley, left their work, and proceeded to the spot where the sylvan banquet was prepared. As he approached, the loud voice of the Rev. Dr. Battleblast was heard, beseeching a blessing on the good things set before them, and on the dis-tinguished friend of peace in whose honor they were assembled. The tables were arranged in a cleared space of the woods, shut in by the surrounding trees, except where a vista opened eastward, and afforded a distant view of the Great Stone Face. Over the gen-eral's chair, which was a relic from the home of Wash-ington, there was an arch of verdant boughs, with the laurel profusely intermixed, and surmounted by his country's banner, beneath which he had won his victo-ries. Our friend Ernest raised himself on his tiptoes, in hopes to get a glimpse of the celebrated guest; but there was a mighty crowd about the tables anxious to hear the toasts and speeches, and to catch any word that might fall from the general in reply; and a vol-unteer company, doing duty as a guard, pricked ruth-lessly with their bayonets at any particularly quiet person among the throng. So Ernest, being of an unobtrusive character, was thrust quite into the back-ground, where he could see no more of Old Blood-

and-Thunder's physiognomy than if it had been still blazing on the battle-field. To console himself, he turned towards the Great Stone Face, which, like a faithful and long-remembered friend, looked back and smiled upon him through the vista of the forest. Meantime, however, he could overhear the remarks of various individuals, who were comparing the features of the hero with the face on the distant mountain-side.

" 'T is the same face, to a hair!" cried one man, cutting a caper for joy.

" Wonderfully like, that's a fact!" responded another.

" Like! why, I call it Old Blood-and-Thunder himself, in a monstrous looking-glass!" cried a third. " And why not? He's the greatest man of this or any other age, beyond a doubt."

And then all three of the speakers gave a great shout, which communicated electricity to the crowd, and called forth a roar from a thousand voices, that went reverberating for miles among the mountains, until you might have supposed that the Great Stone Face had poured its thunder-breath into the cry. All these comments, and this vast enthusiasm, served the more to interest our friend; nor did he think of questioning that now, at length, the mountain-visage had found its human counterpart. It is true, Ernest had imagined that this long-looked-for personage would appear in the character of a man of peace, uttering wisdom, and doing good, and making people happy. But, taking an habitual breadth of view, with all his simplicity, he contended that Providence should choose its own method of blessing mankind, and could conceive that this great end might be effected even by a warrior and a bloody sword, should inscrutable wisdom see fit to order matters so.

"The general! the general!" was now the cry. "Hush! silence! Old Blood-and-Thunder's going to make a speech."

Even so; for, the cloth being removed, the general's health had been drunk, amid shouts of applause, and he now stood upon his feet to thank the company. Ernest saw him. There he was, over the shoulders of the crowd, from the two glittering epaulets and embroidered collar upward, beneath the arch of green boughs with intertwined laurel, and the banner drooping as if to shade his brow! And there, too, visible in the same glance, through the vista of the forest, appeared the Great Stone Face! And was there, indeed, such a resemblance as the crowd had testified? Alas, Ernest could not recognize it! He beheld a war-worn and weather-beaten countenance, full of energy, and expressive of an iron will; but the gentle wisdom, the deep, broad, tender sympathies, were altogether wanting in Old Blood-and-Thunder's visage; and even if the Great Stone Face had assumed his look of stern command, the milder traits would still have tempered it.

"This is not the man of prophecy," sighed Ernest to himself, as he made his way out of the throng. "And must the world wait longer yet?"

The mists had congregated about the distant mountain-side, and there were seen the grand and awful features of the Great Stone Face, awful but benignant, as if a mighty angel were sitting among the hills, and enrobing himself in a cloud-vesture of gold and purple. As he looked, Ernest could hardly believe but that a smile beamed over the whole visage, with a radiance still brightening, although without motion of the lips. It was probably the effect of the western sunshine, melting through the thinly diffused vapors that had swept between him and the object that he gazed at. But — as it always did — the aspect of his marvellous friend made Ernest as hopeful as if he had never hoped in vain.

" Fear not, Ernest," said his heart, even as if the Great Face were whispering him, — " fear not, Ernest; he will come."

More years sped swiftly and tranquilly away. Ernest still dwelt in his native valley, and was now a man of middle age. By imperceptible degrees, he had become known among the people. Now, as heretofore, he labored for his bread, and was the same simple-hearted man that he had always been. But he had thought and felt so much, he had given so many of the best hours of his life to unworldly hopes for some great good to mankind, that it seemed as though he had been talking with the angels, and had imbibed a portion of their wisdom unawares. It was visible in the calm and well-considered beneficence of his daily life, the quiet stream of which had made a wide green margin all along its course. Not a day passed by, that the world was not the better because this man, humble as he was, had lived. He never stepped aside from his own path, yet would always reach a blessing to his neighbor. Almost involuntarily, too, he had become a preacher. The pure and high simplicity of his thought, which, as one of its manifestations, took shape in the good deeds that dropped silently from his hand, flowed also forth in speech. He uttered truths that wrought upon and moulded the lives of those who heard him. His auditors, it may be, never suspected that Ernest, their own neighbor and familiar friend, was more than an ordinary man; least of all did En nest himself suspect it; but, inevitably as the murmur of a rivulet, came thoughts out of his mouth that no other human lips had spoken.

When the people's minds had had a little time to cool, they were ready enough to acknowledge their mistake in imagining a similarity between General Blood-and-Thunder's truculent physiognomy and the benign visage on the mountain-side. But now, again, there were reports and many paragraphs in the newspapers, affirming that the likeness of the Great Stone Face had appeared upon the broad shoulders of a certain eminent statesman. He, like Mr. Gathergold and Old Blood-and-Thunder, was a native of the valley, but had left it in his early days, and taken up the trades of law and politics. Instead of the rich man's wealth and the warrior's sword, he had but a tongue, and it was mightier than both together. So wonderfully eloquent was he, that whatever he might choose to say, his auditors had no choice but to believe him; wrong looked like right, and right like wrong; for when it pleased him, he could make a kind of illuminated fog with his mere breath, and obscure the natural daylight with it. His tongue, indeed, was a magic instrument: sometimes it rumbled like the thunder; sometimes it warbled like the sweetest music. It was the blast of war, — the song of peace; and it seemed to have a heart in it, when there was no such matter. In good truth, he was a wondrous man; and when his tongue had acquired him all other imaginable success, — when it had been heard in halls of state, and in the courts of princes and potentates, — after it had made him known all over the world, even as a voice crying from shore to shore, — it finally persuaded his countrymen to select him for the Presi-

dency.   Before this time, — indeed, as soon as he began to grow celebrated, — his admirers had found out
the resemblance between him and the Great Stone
Face; and so much were they struck by it, that
throughout the country this distinguished gentleman
was known by the name of Old Stony Phiz.   The
phrase was considered as giving a highly favorable aspect to his political prospects; for, as is likewise the
case with the Popedom, nobody ever becomes President without taking a name other than his own.

While his friends were doing their best to make
him President, Old Stony Phiz, as he was called, set
out on a visit to the valley where he was born.   Of
course, he had no other object than to shake hands
with his fellow-citizens, and neither thought nor cared
about any effect which his progress through the country might have upon the election.   Magnificent preparations were made to receive the illustrious statesman; a cavalcade of horsemen set forth to meet him
at the boundary line of the State, and all the people
left their business and gathered along the wayside to
see him pass.   Among these was Ernest.   Though
more than once disappointed, as we have seen, he had
such a hopeful and confiding nature, that he was always ready to believe in whatever seemed beautiful
and good.   He kept his heart continually open, and
thus was sure to catch the blessing from on high when
it should come.   So now again, as buoyantly as ever,
he went forth to behold the likeness of the Great
Stone Face.

The cavalcade came prancing along the road, with a
great clattering of hoofs and a mighty cloud of dust,
which rose up so dense and high that the visage of the
mountain - side was completely hidden from Ernest's

eyes. All the great men of the neighborhood were there on horseback; militia officers, in uniform; the member of Congress; the sheriff of the county; the editors of newspapers; and many a farmer, too, had mounted his patient steed, with his Sunday coat upon his back. It really was a very brilliant spectacle, especially as there were numerous banners flaunting over the cavalcade, on some of which were gorgeous portraits of the illustrious statesman and the Great Stone Face, smiling familiarly at one another, like two brothers. If the pictures were to be trusted, the mutual resemblance, it must be confessed, was marvellous. We must not forget to mention that there was a band of music, which made the echoes of the mountains ring and reverberate with the loud triumph of its strains; so that airy and soul-thrilling melodies broke out among all the heights and hollows, as if every nook of his native valley had found a voice, to welcome the distinguished guest. But the grandest effect was when the far-off mountain precipice flung back the music; for then the Great Stone Face itself seemed to be swelling the triumphant chorus, in acknowledgment that, at length, the man of prophecy was come.

All this while the people were throwing up their hats and shouting, with enthusiasm so contagious that the heart of Ernest kindled up, and he likewise threw up his hat, and shouted, as loudly as the loudest, "Huzza for the great man! Huzza for Old Stony Phiz!" But as yet he had not seen him.

"Here he is, now!" cried those who stood near Ernest. "There! There! Look at Old Stony Phiz and then at the Old Man of the Mountain, and see if they are not as like as two twin-brothers!"

In the midst of all this gallant array came an open

barouche, drawn by four white horses ; and in the barouche, with his massive head uncovered, sat the illustrious statesman, Old Stony Phiz himself.

"Confess it," said one of Ernest's neighbors to him,
"the Great Stone Face has met its match at last!"

Now, it must be owned that, at his first glimpse of
the countenance which was bowing and smiling from
the barouche, Ernest did fancy that there was a resemblance between it and the old familiar face upon
the mountain-side. The brow, with its massive depth
and loftiness, and all the other features, indeed, were
boldly and strongly hewn, as if in emulation of a more
than heroic, of a Titanic model. But the sublimity
and stateliness, the grand expression of a divine sympathy, that illuminated the mountain visage and etherealized its ponderous granite substance into spirit,
might here be sought in vain. Something had been
originally left out, or had departed. And therefore
the marvellously gifted statesman had always a weary
gloom in the deep caverns of his eyes, as of a child
that has outgrown its playthings or a man of mighty
faculties and little aims, whose life, with all its high
performances, was vague and empty, because no high
purpose had endowed it with reality.

Still, Ernest's neighbor was thrusting his elbow into
his side, and pressing him for an answer.

"Confess! confess! Is not he the very picture of
your Old Man of the Mountain?"

"No!" said Ernest, bluntly, "I see little or no likeness."

"Then so much the worse for the Great Stone
Face!" answered his neighbor; and again he set up
a shout for Old Stony Phiz.

But Ernest turned away, melancholy, and almost

despondent : for this was the saddest of his disappointments, to behold a man who might have fulfilled the prophecy, and had not willed to do so. Meantime, the cavalcade, the banners, the music, and the barouches swept past him, with the vociferous crowd in the rear, leaving the dust to settle down, and the Great Stone Face to be revealed again, with the grandeur that it had worn for untold centuries.

"Lo, here I am, Ernest!" the benign lips seemed to say. "I have waited longer than thou, and am not yet weary. Fear not; the man will come."

The years hurried onward, treading in their haste on one another's heels. And now they began to bring white hairs, and scatter them over the head of Ernest; they made reverend wrinkles across his forehead, and furrows in his cheeks. He was an aged man. But not in vain had he grown old: more than the white hairs on his head were the sage thoughts in his mind; his wrinkles and furrows were inscriptions that Time had graved, and in which he had written legends of wisdom that had been tested by the tenor of a life. And Ernest had ceased to be obscure. Unsought for, undesired, had come the fame which so many seek, and made him known in the great world, beyond the limits of the valley in which he had dwelt so quietly. College professors, and even the active men of cities, came from far to see and converse with Ernest; for the report had gone abroad that this simple husbandman had ideas unlike those of other men, not gained from books, but of a higher tone, — a tranquil and familiar majesty, as if he had been talking with the angels as his daily friends. Whether it were sage, statesman, or philanthropist, Ernest received these visitors with the gentle sincerity that had characterized him from boyhood, and spoke freely with them of whatever came uppermost, or lay deepest in his heart or their own. While they talked together, his face would kindle, unawares, and shine upon them, as with a mild evening light. Pensive with the fulness of such discourse, his guests took leave and went their way ; and passing up the valley, paused to look at the Great Stone Face, imagining that they had seen its likeness in a human countenance, but could not remember where.

While Ernest had been growing up and growing old, a bountiful Providence had granted a new poet to this earth. He, likewise, was a native of the valley, but had spent the greater part of his life at a distance from that romantic region, pouring out his sweet music amid the bustle and din of cities. Often, however, did the mountains which had been familiar to him in his childhood lift their snowy peaks into the clear atmosphere of his poetry. Neither was the Great Stone Face forgotten, for the poet had celebrated it in an ode, which was grand enough to have been uttered by its own majestic lips. This man of genius, we may say, had come down from heaven with wonderful endowments. If he sang of a mountain, the eyes of all mankind beheld a mightier grandeur reposing on its breast, or soaring to its summit, than had before been seen there. If his theme were a lovely lake, a celestial smile had now been thrown over it, to gleam forever on its surface. If it were the vast old sea, even the deep immensity of its dread bosom seemed to swell the higher, as if moved by the emotions of the song. Thus the world assumed another and a better aspect from the hour that the poet blessed it with his happy eyes. The Creator had bestowed him, as the last best touch to his own handiwork.

Creation was not finished till the poet came to inter.
pret, and so complete it.

The effect was no less high and beautiful, when his
human brethren were the subject of his verse. The
man or woman, sordid with the common dust of life,
who crossed his daily path, and the little child who
played in it, were glorified if he beheld them in his
mood of poetic faith. He showed the golden links of
the great chain that intertwined them with an angelic
kindred ; he brought out the hidden traits of a celestial birth that made them worthy of such kin. Some,
indeed, there were, who thought to show the soundness
of their judgment by affirming that all the beauty and
dignity of the natural world existed only in the poet's
fancy. Let such men speak for themselves, who undoubtedly appear to have been spawned forth by Nature with a contemptuous bitterness ; she having plastered them up out of her refuse stuff, after all the swine
were made. As respects all things else, the poet's
ideal was the truest truth.

The songs of this poet found their way to Ernest.
He read them after his customary toil, seated on the
bench before his cottage-door, where for such a length
of time he had filled his repose with thought, by gazing at the Great Stone Face. And now as he read
stanzas that caused the soul to thrill within him, he
lifted his eyes to the vast countenance beaming on him
so benignantly.

" O majestic friend," he murmured, addressing the
Great Stone Face, " is not this man worthy to resemble thee ? "

The Face seemed to smile, but answered not a word.

Now it happened that the poet, though he dwelt
so far away, had not only heard of Ernest, but had

meditated much upon his character, until he deemed nothing so desirable as to meet this man, whose un-taught wisdom walked hand in hand with the noble simplicity of his life. One summer morning, there-fore, he took passage by the railroad, and, in the de-cline of the afternoon, alighted from the cars at no great distance from Ernest's cottage. The great hotel, which had formerly been the palace of Mr. Gather-gold, was close at hand, but the poet, with his carpet-bag on his arm, inquired at once where Ernest dwelt, and was resolved to be accepted as his guest.

Approaching the door, he there found the good old man, holding a volume in his hand, which alternately he read, and then, with a finger between the leaves, looked lovingly at the Great Stone Face.

"Good evening," said the poet. "Can you give a traveller a night's lodging?"

"Willingly," answered Ernest; and then he added, smiling, "Methinks I never saw the Great Stone Face look so hospitably at a stranger."

The poet sat down on the bench beside him, and he and Ernest talked together. Often had the poet held intercourse with the wittiest and the wisest, but never before with a man like Ernest, whose thoughts and feel-ings gushed up with such a natural freedom, and who made great truths so familiar by his simple utterance of them. Angels, as had been so often said, seemed to have wrought with him at his labor in the fields; angels seemed to have sat with him by the fireside; and, dwelling with angels as friend with friends, he had imbibed the sublimity of their ideas, and imbued it with the sweet and lowly charm of household words. So thought the poet. And Ernest, on the other hand, was moved and agitated by the living images which the poet flung out of his mind, and which peopled all the air about the cottage-door with shapes of beauty, both gay and pensive. The sympathies of these two men instructed them with a profounder sense than either could have attained alone. Their minds accorded into one strain, and made delightful music which neither of them could have claimed as all his own, nor distinguished his own share from the other's. They led one another, as it were, into a high pavilion of their thoughts, so remote, and hitherto so dim, that they had never entered it before, and so beautiful that they desired to be there always.

As Ernest listened to the poet, he imagined that the Great Stone Face was bending forward to listen too. He gazed earnestly into the poet's glowing eyes.

"Who are you, my strangely gifted guest?" he said.

The poet laid his finger on the volume that Ernest had been reading.

"You have read these poems," said he. "You know me, then, — for I wrote them."

Again, and still more earnestly than before, Ernest examined the poet's features; then turned towards the Great Stone Face; then back, with an uncertain aspect, to his guest. But his countenance fell; he shook his head, and sighed.

"Wherefore are you sad?" inquired the poet.

"Because," replied Ernest, "all through life I have awaited the fulfilment of a prophecy; and, when I read these poems, I hoped that it might be fulfilled in you."

"You hoped," answered the poet, faintly smiling, "to find in me the likeness of the Great Stone Face. And you are disappointed, as formerly with Mr. Gather

gold, and Old Blood-and-Thunder, and Old Stony
Phiz. Yes Ernest, it is my doom. You must add my
name to the illustrious three, and record another failure of your hopes. For — in shame and sadness do I
speak it, Ernest — I am not worthy to be typified by
yonder benign and majestic image."

" And why ? " asked Ernest. He pointed to the
volume. " Are not those thoughts divine ? "

"They have a strain of the Divinity," replied the
poet. " You can hear in them the far-off echo of a
heavenly song. But my life, dear Ernest, has not corresponded with my thought. I have had grand dreams,
but they have been only dreams, because I have lived
— and that, too, by my own choice — among poor and
mean realities. Sometimes even — shall I dare to say
it ? — I lack faith in the grandeur, the beauty, and the
goodness, which my own works are said to have made
more evident in nature and in human life. Why, then,
pure seeker of the good and true, shouldst thou hope
to find me, in yonder image of the divine ? "

The poet spoke sadly, and his eyes were dim with
tears. So, likewise, were those of Ernest.

At the hour of sunset, as had long been his frequent
custom, Ernest was to discourse to an assemblage of
the neighboring inhabitants in the open air. He and
the poet, arm in arm, still talking together as they
went along, proceeded to the spot. It was a small
nook among the hills, with a gray precipice behind,
the stern front of which was relieved by the pleasant
foliage of many creeping plants that made a tapestry
for the naked rock, by hanging their festoons from all
its rugged angles. At a small elevation above the
ground, set in a rich framework of verdure, there appeared a niche, spacious enough to admit a human

figure, with freedom for such gestures as spontaneously accompany earnest thought and genuine emotion. Into this natural pulpit Ernest ascended, and threw a look of familiar kindness around upon his audience. They stood, or sat, or reclined upon the grass, as seemed good to each, with the departing sunshine falling obliquely over them, and mingling its subdued cheerfulness with the solemnity of a grove of ancient trees, beneath and amid the boughs of which the golden rays were constrained to pass. In another direction was seen the Great Stone Face, with the same cheer, combined with the same solemnity, in its benignant aspect.

Ernest began to speak, giving to the people of what was in his heart and mind. His words had power, because they accorded with his thoughts; and his thoughts had reality and depth, because they harmonized with the life which he had always lived. It was not mere breath that this preacher uttered; they were the words of life, because a life of good deeds and holy love was melted into them. Pearls, pure and rich, had been dissolved into this precious draught. The poet, as he listened, felt that the being and character of Ernest were a nobler strain of poetry than he had ever written. His eyes glistening with tears, he gazed reverentially at the venerable man, and said within himself that never was there an aspect so worthy of a prophet and a sage as that mild, sweet, thoughtful countenance, with the glory of white hair diffused about it. At a distance, but distinctly to be seen, high up in the golden light of the setting sun, appeared the Great Stone Face, with hoary mists around it, like the white hairs around the brow of Ernest. Its look of grand beneficence seemed to embrace the world.

At that moment, in sympathy with a thought which he was about to utter, the face of Ernest assumed a grandeur of expression, so imbued with benevolence, that the poet, by an irresistible impulse, threw his arms aloft, and shouted, —

"Behold! Behold! Ernest is himself the likeness of the Great Stone Face!"

Then all the people looked, and saw that what the deep-sighted poet said was true. The prophecy was fulfilled. But Ernest, having finished what he had to say, took the poet's arm, and walked slowly homeward, still hoping that some wiser and better man than himself would by and by appear, bearing a resemblance to the GREAT STONE FACE.

MAIN STREET.

A RESPECTABLE-LOOKING individual makes his bow and addresses the public. In my daily walks along the principal street of my native town, it has often occurred to me, that, if its growth from infancy upward, and the vicissitude of characteristic scénes that have passed along this thoroughfare during the more than two centuries of its existence, could be presented to the eye in a shifting panorama, it would be an exceedingly effective method of illustrating the march of time. Acting on this idea, I have contrived a certain pictorial exhibition, somewhat in the nature of a puppet-show, by means of which I propose to call up the multiform and many-colored Past before the spectator, and show him the ghosts of his forefathers, amid a succession of historic incidents, with no greater trouble than the turning of a crank. Be pleased, therefore, my indulgent patrons, to walk into the show-room, and take your seats before yonder mysterious curtain. The little wheels and springs of my machinery have been well oiled; a multitude of puppets are dressed in character, representing all varieties of fashion, from the Puritan cloak and jerkin to the latest Oak Hall coat; the lamps are trimmed, and shall brighten into noontide sunshine, or fade away in moonlight, or muffle their brilliancy in a November cloud, as the nature of the scene may require; and, in short, the exhibition is just ready to commence. Unless something should go wrong, — as, for instance, the misplacing of a picture,

whereby the people and events of one century might
be thrust into the middle of another ; or the breaking
of a wire, which would bring the course of time to
a sudden period, — barring, I say, the casualties to
which such a complicated piece of mechanism is liable,
— I flatter myself, ladies and gentlemen, that the per.
formance will elicit your generous approbation.

Ting-a-ting-ting ! goes the bell ; the curtain rises ;
and we behold — not, indeed, the Main Street — but
the track of leaf-strewn forest-land over which its dusty
pavement is hereafter to extend.

You perceive, at a glance, that this is the ancient
and primitive wood, — the ever-youthful and venerably
old, — verdant with new twigs, yet hoary, as it were,
with the snowfall of innumerable years, that have accumulated upon its intermingled branches. The white
man's axe has never smitten a single tree ; his footstep
has never crumpled a single one of the withered leaves,
which all the autumns since the flood have been harvesting beneath. Yet, see ! along through the vista of
impending boughs, there is already a faintly traced
path, running nearly east and west, as if a prophecy
or foreboding of the future street had stolen into the
heart of the solemn old wood. Onward goes this
hardly perceptible track, now ascending over a natural
swell of land, now subsiding gently into a hollow ;
traversed here by a little streamlet, which glitters like
a snake through the gleam of sunshine, and quickly
hides itself among the underbrush, in its quest for the
neighboring cove ; and impeded there by the massy
corpse of a giant of the forest, which had lived out its
incalculable term of life, and been overthrown by mere
old age, and lies buried in the new vegetation that is
born of its decay. What footsteps can have worn this

half-seen path? Hark! Do we not hear them now rustling softly over the leaves? We discern an Indian woman, — a majestic and queenly woman, or else her spectral image does not represent her truly, — for this is the great Squaw Sachem, whose rule, with that of her sons, extends from Mystic to Agawam. That red chief, who stalks by her side, is Wappacowet, her second husband, the priest and magician, whose incantations shall hereafter affright the pale-faced settlers with grisly phantoms, dancing and shrieking in the woods at midnight. But greater would be the affright of the Indian necromancer, if, mirrored in the pool of water at his feet, he could catch a prophetic glimpse of the noonday marvels which the white man is destined to achieve; if he could see, as in a dream, the stone front of the stately hall, which will cast its shadow over this very spot; if he could be aware that the future edifice will contain a noble Museum, where, among countless curiosities of earth and sea, a few Indian arrow-heads shall be treasured up as memorials of a vanished race!

No such forebodings disturb the Squaw Sachem and Wappacowet. They pass on, beneath the tangled shade, holding high talk on matters of state and religion, and imagine, doubtless, that their own system of affairs will endure forever. Meanwhile, how full of its own proper life is the scene that lies around them! The gray squirrel runs up the trees, and rustles among the upper branches. Was not that the leap of a deer? And there is the whirr of a partridge! Methinks, too, I catch the cruel and stealthy eye of a wolf, as he draws back into yonder impervious density of underbrush. So, there, amid the murmur of boughs, go the Indian queen and the Indian priest; while the gloom of the broad wilderness impends over them, and its sombre mystery invests them as with something preternatural; and only momentary streaks of quivering sunlight, once in a great while, find their way down, and glimmer among the feathers in their dusky hair. Can it be that the thronged street of a city will ever pass into this twilight solitude, — over those soft heaps of the decaying tree-trunks, and through the swampy places, green with water-moss, and penetrate that hopeless entanglement of great trees, which have been uprooted and tossed together by a whirlwind? It has been a wilderness from the creation. Must it not be a wilderness forever?

Here an acidulous-looking gentleman in blue glasses, with bows of Berlin steel, who has taken a seat at the extremity of the front row, begins, at this early stage of the exhibition, to criticise.

"The whole affair is a manifest catchpenny!" observes he, scarcely under his breath. "The trees look more like weeds in a garden than a primitive forest; the Squaw Sachem and Wappacowet are stiff in their pasteboard joints; and the squirrels, the deer, and the wolf move with all the grace of a child's wooden monkey, sliding up and down a stick."

"I am obliged to you, sir, for the candor of your remarks," replies the showman, with a bow. "Perhaps they are just. Human art has its limits, and we must now and then ask a little aid from the spectator's imagination."

"You will get no such aid from mine," responds the critic. "I make it a point to see things precisely as they are. But come! go ahead! the stage is waiting!"

The showman proceeds.

Casting our eyes again over the scene, we perceive that strangers have found their way into the solitary place. In more than one spot, among the trees, an upheaved axe is glittering in the sunshine. Roger Conant, the first settler in Naumkeag, has built his dwelling, months ago, on the border of the forest-path; and at this moment he comes eastward through the vista of woods, with his gun over his shoulder, bringing home the choice portions of a deer. His stalwart figure, clad in a leathern jerkin and breeches of the same, strides sturdily onward, with such an air of physical force and energy that we might almost expect the very trees to stand aside and give him room to pass. And so, indeed, they must; for, humble as is his name in history, Roger Conant still is of that class of men who do not merely find, but make, their place in the system of human affairs; a man of thoughtful strength, he has planted the germ of a city. There stands his habitation, showing in its rough architecture some features of the Indian wigwam, and some of the log-cabin, and somewhat, too, of the straw-thatched cottage in Old England, where this good yeoman had his birth and breeding. The dwelling is surrounded by a cleared space of a few acres, where Indian corn grows thrivingly among the stumps of the trees; while the dark forest hems it in, and seems to gaze silently and solemnly, as if wondering at the breadth of sunshine which the white man spreads around him. An Indian, half hidden in the dusky shade, is gazing and wondering too.

Within the door of the cottage you discern the wife, with her ruddy English cheek. She is singing, doubtless, a psalm tune, at her household work; or, perhaps, she sighs at the remembrance of the cheerful gossip,

and all the merry social life, of her native village beyond the vast and melancholy sea. Yet the next moment she laughs, with sympathetic glee, at the sports
of her little tribe of children; and soon turns round,
with the homelook in her face, as her husband's foot
is heard approaching the rough-hewn threshold. How
sweet must it be for those who have an Eden in their
hearts, like Roger Conant and his wife, to find a new
world to project it into, as they have, instead of dwelling among old haunts of men, where so many household fires have been kindled and burnt out, that the
very glow of happiness has something dreary in it!
Not that this pair are alone in their wild Eden, for
here comes Goodwife Massey, the young spouse of
Jeffrey Massey, from her home hard by, with an infant
at her breast. Dame Conant has another of like age;
and it shall hereafter be one of the disputed points of
history which of these two babies was the first town-
born child.

But see! Roger Conant has other neighbors within
view. Peter Palfrey, likewise, has built himself a
house, and so has Balch, and Norman, and Woodbury.
Their dwellings, indeed, — such is the ingenious contrivance of this piece of pictorial mechanism, — seem
to have arisen, at various points of the scene, even
while we have been looking at it. The forest-track,
trodden more and more by the hobnailed shoes of these
sturdy and ponderous Englishmen, has now a distinctness which it never could have acquired from the light
tread of a hundred times as many Indian moccasins.
It will be a street, anon. As we observe it now, it goes
onward from one clearing to another, here plunging
into a shadowy strip of woods, there open to the sunshine, but everywhere showing a decided line, along

which human interests have begun to hold their career. Over yonder swampy spot, two trees have been felled, and laid side by side to make a causeway. In another place, the axe has cleared away a confused intricacy of fallen trees and clustered boughs, which had been tossed together by a hurricane. So now the little children, just beginning to run alone, may trip along the path, and not often stumble over an impediment, unless they stray from it to gather wood-berries beneath the trees. And, besides the feet of grown people and children, there are the cloven hoofs of a small herd of cows, who seek their subsistence from the native grasses, and help to deepen the track of the future thoroughfare. Goats also browse along it, and nibble at the twigs that thrust themselves across the way. Not seldom, in its more secluded portions, where the black shadow of the forest strives to hide the trace of human footsteps, stalks a gaunt wolf, on the watch for a kid or a young calf; or fixes his hungry gaze on the group of children gathering berries, and can hardly forbear to rush upon them. And the Indians, coming from their distant wigwams to view the white man's settlement, marvel at the deep track which he makes, and perhaps are saddened by a flitting presentiment that this heavy tread will find its way over all the land; and that the wild woods, the wild wolf, and the wild Indian will be alike trampled beneath it. Even so shall it be. The pavements of the Main Street must be laid over the red man's grave.

Behold! here is a spectacle which should be ushered in by the peal of trumpets, if Naumkeag had ever yet heard that cheery music, and by the roar of cannon, echoing among the woods. A procession, — for, by its dignity, as marking an epoch in the history of the street, it deserves that name, — a procession advances along the pathway. The good ship Abigail has arrived from England, bringing wares and merchandise, for the comfort of the inhabitants and traffic with the Indians; bringing passengers too, and, more important than all, a governor for the new settlement. Roger Conant and Peter Palfrey, with their companions, have been to the shore to welcome him; and now, with such honor and triumph as their rude way of life permits, are escorting the sea-flushed voyagers to their habitations. At the point where Endicott enters upon the scene, two venerable trees unite their branches high above his head; thus forming a triumphal arch of living verdure, beneath which he pauses, with his wife leaning on his arm, to catch the first impression of their new-found home. The old settlers gaze not less earnestly at him, than he at the hoary woods and the rough surface of the clearings. They like his bearded face, under the shadow of the broad-brimmed and steeple-crowned Puritan hat, — a visage resolute, grave, and thoughtful, yet apt to kindle with that glow of a cheerful spirit by which men of strong character are enabled to go joyfully on their proper tasks. His form, too, as you see it, in a doublet and hose of sad-colored cloth, is of a manly make, fit for toil and hardship, and fit to wield the heavy sword that hangs from his leathern belt. His aspect is a better warrant for the ruler's office than the parchment commission which he bears, however fortified it may be with the broad seal of the London council. Peter Palfrey nods to Roger Conant. " The worshipful Court of Assistants have done wisely," say they between themselves. " They have chosen for our governor a man out of a thousand." Then they toss up their hats, ·— they, and all the uncouth figures of their company, most of whom are clad in skins, inasmuch as their old kersey and linsey-woolsey garments have been torn and tattered by many a long month's wear, — they all toss up their hats, and salute their new governor and captain with a hearty English shout of welcome. We seem to hear it with our own ears, so perfectly is the action represented in this life-like, this almost magic, picture!

But have you observed the lady who leans upon the arm of Endicott? — a rose of beauty from an English garden, now to be transplanted to a fresher soil. It may be that, long years — centuries indeed — after this fair flower shall have decayed, other flowers of the same race will appear in the same soil, and gladden other generations with hereditary beauty. Does not the vision haunt us yet? Has not Nature kept the mould unbroken, deeming it a pity that the idea should vanish from mortal sight forever, after only once assuming earthly substance? Do we not recognize, in that fair woman's face, the model of features which still beam, at happy moments, on what was then the woodland pathway, but has long since grown into a busy street?

"This is too ridiculous! — positively insufferable!" mutters the same critic who had before expressed his disapprobation. "Here is a pasteboard figure, such as a child would cut out of a card, with a pair of very dull scissors; and the fellow modestly requests us to see in it the prototype of hereditary beauty!"

"But, sir, you have not the proper point of view," remarks the showman. "You sit altogether too near to get the best effect of my pictorial exhibition. Pray, oblige me by removing to this other bench, and I venture to assure you the proper light and shadow will transform the spectacle into quite another thing."

"Pshaw!" replies the critic; "I want no other light and shade. I have already told you that it is my business to see things just as they are."

"I would suggest to the author of this ingenious exhibition," observes a gentlemanly person, who has shown signs of being much interested, — "I would suggest that Anna Gower, the first wife of Governor Endicott, and who came with him from England, left no posterity; and that, consequently, we cannot be indebted to that honorable lady for any specimens of feminine loveliness now extant among us."

Having nothing to allege against this genealogical objection, the showman points again to the scene.

During this little interruption, you perceive that the Anglo-Saxon energy — as the phrase now goes — has been at work in the spectacle before us. So many chimneys now send up their smoke, that it begins to have the aspect of a village street; although everything is so inartificial and inceptive, that it seems as if one returning wave of the wild nature might overwhelm it all. But the one edifice which gives the pledge of permanence to this bold enterprise is seen at the central point of the picture. There stands the meeting-house, a small structure, low-roofed, without a spire, and built of rough timber, newly hewn, with the sap still in the logs, and here and there a strip of bark adhering to them. A meaner temple was never consecrated to the worship of the Deity. With the alternative of kneeling beneath the awful vault of the firmament, it is strange that men should creep into this pent-up nook, and expect God's presence there. Such, at least, one would imagine, might be the feeling of these forest-settlers, accustomed, as they had been, to stand under the dim arches of vast cathedrals, and to offer up their hereditary worship in the old ivy-covered churches of rural England, around which lay the bones of many generations of their forefathers. How could they dispense with the carved altar-work? — how, with the pictured windows, where the light of common day was hallowed by being transmitted through the glorified figures of saints? — how, with the lofty roof, imbued, as it must have been, with the prayers that had gone upward for centuries? — how, with the rich peal of the solemn organ, rolling along the aisles, pervading the whole church, and sweeping the soul away on a flood of audible religion? They needed nothing of all this. Their house of worship, like their ceremonial, was naked, simple, and severe. But the zeal of a recovered faith burned like a lamp within their hearts, enriching everything around them with its radiance; making of these new walls, and this narrow compass, its own cathedral; and being, in itself, that spiritual mystery and experience, of which sacred architecture, pictured windows, and the organ's grand solemnity are remote and imperfect symbols. All was well, so long as their lamps were freshly kindled at the heavenly flame. After a while, however, whether in their time or their children's, these lamps began to burn more dimly, or with a less genuine lustre; and then it might be seen how hard, cold, and confined was their system, — how like an iron cage was that which they called Liberty.

Too much of this. Look again at the picture, and observe how the aforesaid Anglo-Saxon energy is now trampling along the street, and raising a positive cloud of dust beneath its sturdy footsteps. For there the carpenters are building a new house, the frame of which was hewn and fitted in England, of English oak, and sent hither on shipboard; and here a blacksmith makes huge clang and clatter on his anvil, shaping out tools and weapons; and yonder a wheelwright, who boasts himself a London workman, regularly bred to his handicraft, is fashioning a set of wagon-wheels, the track of which shall soon be visible. The wild forest is shrinking back; the street has lost the aromatic odor of the pine-trees, and of the sweet-fern that grew beneath them. The tender and modest wild-flowers, those gentle children of savage nature that grew pale beneath the ever-brooding shade, have shrunk away and disappeared, like stars that vanish in the breadth of light. Gardens are fenced in, and display pumpkin-beds and rows of cabbages and beans; and, though the governor and the minister both view them with a disapproving eye, plants of broad-leaved tobacco, which the cultivators are enjoined to use privily, or not at all. No wolf, for a year past, has been heard to bark, or known to range among the dwellings, except that single one, whose grisly head, with a plash of blood beneath it, is now affixed to the portal of the meeting-house. The partridge has ceased to run across the too-frequented path. Of all the wild life that used to throng here, only the Indians still come into the settlement, bringing the skins of beaver and otter, bear and elk, which they sell to Endicott for the wares of England. And there is little John Massey, the son of Jeffrey Massey and first-born of Naumkeag, playing beside his father's threshold, a child of six or seven years old. Which is the better grown infant, — the town or the boy?

The red men have become aware that the street is

no longer free to them, save by the sufferance and permission of the settlers. Often, to impress them with an awe of English power, there is a muster and training of the town-forces, and a stately march of the mail-clad band, like this which we now see advancing up the street. There they come, fifty of them or more; all with their iron breastplates and steel caps well burnished, and glimmering bravely against the sun; their ponderous muskets on their shoulders, their bandoliers about their waists, their lighted matches in their hands, and the drum and fife playing cheerily before them. See! do they not step like martial men? Do they not manœuvre like soldiers who have seen stricken fields? And well they may; for this band is composed of precisely such materials as those with which Cromwell is preparing to beat down the strength of a kingdom; and his famous regiment of Ironsides might be recruited from just such men. In everything at this period, New England was the essential spirit and flower of that which was about to become uppermost in the mother-country. Many a bold and wise man lost the fame which would have accrued to him in English history, by crossing the Atlantic with our forefathers. Many a valiant captain, who might have been foremost at Marston Moor or Naseby, exhausted his martial ardor in the command of a log-built fortress, like that which you observe on the gently rising ground at the right of the pathway, — its banner fluttering in the breeze, and the culverins and sakers showing their deadly muzzles over the rampart.

A multitude of people were now thronging to New England: some, because the ancient and ponderous framework of Church and State threatened to crumble down upon their heads; others, because they de-

spaired of such a downfall. Among those who came to
Naumkeag were men of history and legend, whose feet
leave a track of brightness along any pathway which
they have trodden.   You shall behold their life-like images — their spectres, if you choose so to call them —
passing, encountering with a familiar nod, stopping to
converse together, praying, bearing weapons, laboring,
or resting from their labors, in the Main Street.   Here,
now, comes Hugh Peters, an earnest, restless man,
walking swiftly, as being impelled by that fiery activity of nature which shall hereafter thrust him into the
conflict of dangerous affairs, make him the chaplain
and counsellor of Cromwell, and finally bring him to
a bloody end.   He pauses, by the meeting-house, to
exchange a greeting with Roger Williams, whose face
indicates, methinks, a gentler spirit, kinder and more
expansive, than that of Peters ; yet not less active for
what he discerns to be the will of God, or the welfare
of mankind.   And look ! here is a guest for Endicott,
coming forth out of the forest, through which he has
been journeying from Boston, and which, with its rude
branches, has caught hold of his attire, and has wet his
feet with its swamps and streams.   Still there is something in his mild and venerable, though not aged presence — a propriety, an equilibrium, in Governor Win-
throp's nature — that causes the disarray of his costume to be unnoticed, and gives us the same impression as if he were clad in such grave and rich attire as
we may suppose him to have worn in the Council Chamber of the colony.   Is not this characteristic wonderfully perceptible in our spectral representative of his
person ?   But what dignitary is this crossing from the
other side to greet the governor ?   A stately personage,
in a dark velvet cloak, with a hoary beard, and a gold

chain across his breast; he has the authoritative port of one who has filled the highest civic station in the first of cities. Of all men in the world, we should least expect to meet the Lord Mayor of London — as Sir Richard Saltonstall has been, once and again — in a forest-bordered settlement of the western wilderness.

Farther down the street, we see Emanuel Downing, a grave and worthy citizen, with his son George, a stripling who has a career before him; his shrewd and quick capacity and pliant conscience shall not only exalt him high, but secure him from a downfall. Here is another figure, on whose characteristic make and expressive action I will stake the credit of my pictorial puppet-show. Have you not already detected a quaint, sly humor in that face, — an eccentricity in the manner, — a certain indescribable waywardness, — all the marks, in short, of an original man, unmistakably impressed, yet kept down by a sense of clerical restraint? That is Nathaniel Ward, the minister of Ipswich, but better remembered as the simple cobbler of Agawam. He hammered his sole so faithfully, and stitched his upper-leather so well, that the shoe is hardly yet worn out, though thrown aside for some two centuries past. And next, among these Puritans and Roundheads, we observe the very model of a Cavalier, with the curling lovelock, the fantastically trimmed beard, the embroidery, the ornamented rapier, the gilded dagger, and all other foppishnesses that distinguished the wild gallants who rode headlong to their overthrow in the cause of King Charles. This is Morton of Merry Mount, who has come hither to hold a council with Endicott, but will shortly be his prisoner. Yonder pale, decaying figure of a white-robed woman, who glides slowly along the street, is the Lady Arabella, looking for her own grave in the virgin soil. That other female form, who seems to be talking — we might almost say preaching or expounding — in the centre of a group of profoundly attentive auditors, is Ann Hutchinson. And here comes Vane —

 " But, my dear sir," interrupts the same gentleman who before questioned the showman's genealogical accuracy, "allow me to observe that these historical personages could not possibly have met together in the Main Street. They might, and probably did, all visit our old town, at one time or another, but not simultaneously; and you have fallen into anachronisms that I positively shudder to think of ! "

 "The fellow," adds the scarcely civil critic, "has learned a bead-roll of historic names, whom he lugs into his pictorial puppet-show, as he calls it, helter-skelter, without caring whether they were contemporaries or not, — and sets them all by the ears together. But was there ever such a fund of impudence? To hear his running commentary, you would suppose that these miserable slips of painted pasteboard, with hardly the remotest outlines of the human figure, had all the character and expression of Michael Angelo's pictures. Well ! go on, sir ! "

 " Sir, you break the illusion of the scene," mildly remonstrates the showman.

 " Illusion ! What illusion ? " rejoins the critic, with a contemptuous snort. " On the word of a gentleman, I see nothing illusive in the wretchedly bedaubed sheet of canvas that forms your background, or in these pasteboard slips that hitch and jerk along the front. The only illusion, permit me to say, is in the puppet-showman's tongue, — and that but a wretched one, into the bargain ! "

"We public men," replies the showman, meekly, "must lay our account, sometimes, to meet an uncandid severity of criticism. But — merely for your own pleasure, sir — let me entreat you to take another point of view. Sit farther back, by that young lady, in whose face I have watched the reflection of every changing scene ; only oblige me by sitting there ; and, take my word for it, the slips of pasteboard shall assume spiritual life, and the bedaubed canvas become an airy and changeable reflex of what it purports to represent."

"I know better," retorts the critic, settling himself in his seat, with sullen but self-complacent immovableness. "And, as for my own pleasure, I shall best consult it by remaining precisely where I am."

The showman bows, and waves his hand ; and, at the signal, as if time and vicissitude had been awaiting his permission to move onward, the mimic street becomes alive again.

Years have rolled over our scene, and converted the forest-track into a dusty thoroughfare, which, being intersected with lanes and cross-paths, may fairly be designated as the Main Street. On the ground-sites of many of the log-built sheds, into which the first settlers crept for shelter, houses of quaint architecture have now risen. These later edifices are built, as you see, in one generally accordant style, though with such subordinate variety as keeps the beholder's curiosity excited, and causes each structure, like its owner's character, to produce its own peculiar impression. Most of them have one huge chimney in the centre, with flues so vast that it must have been easy for the witches to fly out of them, as they were wont to do, when bound on an aerial visit to the Black Man in the forest. Around this great chimney the wooden house clusters itself in a whole community of gable-ends, each ascending into its own separate peak; the second story, with its lattice-windows, projecting over the first; and the door, which is perhaps arched, provided on the outside with an iron hammer, wherewith the visitor's hand may give a thundering rat-a-tat. The timber framework of these houses, as compared with those of recent date, is like the skeleton of an old giant, beside the frail bones of a modern man of fashion. Many of them, by the vast strength and soundness of their oaken substance, have been preserved through a length of time which would have tried the stability of brick and stone; so that, in all the progressive decay and continual reconstruction of the street, down to our own days, we shall still behold these old edifices occupying their long-accustomed sites. For instance, on the upper corner of that green lane, which shall hereafter be North Street, we see the Curwen House, newly built, with the carpenters still at work on the roof nailing down the last sheaf of shingles. On the lower corner stands another dwelling, — destined, at some period of its existence, to be the abode of an unsuccessful alchemist, — which shall likewise survive to our own generation, and perhaps long outlive it. Thus, through the medium of these patriarchal edifices, we have now established a sort of kindred and hereditary acquaintance with the Main Street.

Great as is the transformation produced by a short term of years, each single day creeps through the Puritan settlement sluggishly enough. It shall pass before your eyes, condensed into the space of a few moments. The gray light of early morning is slowly diffusing itself over the scene; and the bellman, whose office it is to cry the hour at the street-corners, rings the last peal upon his hand-bell, and goes wearily homewards, with the owls, the bats, and other creatures of the night. Lattices are thrust back on their hinges, as if the town were opening its eyes, in the summer morning. Forth stumbles the still drowsy cowherd, with his horn; putting which to his lips, it emits a bellowing bray, impossible to be represented in the picture, but which reaches the pricked-up ears of every cow in the settlement, and tells her that the dewy pasture-hour is come. House after house awakes, and sends the smoke up curling from its chimney, like frosty breath from living nostrils; and as those white wreaths of smoke, though impregnated with earthy admixtures, climb skyward, so, from each dwelling, does the morning worship — its spiritual essence bearing up its human imperfection — find its way to the heavenly Father's throne.

The breakfast-hour being passed, the inhabitants do not, as usual, go to their fields or workshops, but remain within doors; or perhaps walk the street, with a grave sobriety, yet a disengaged and unburdened aspect, that belongs neither to a holiday nor a Sabbath. And, indeed, this passing day is neither, nor is it a common week-day, although partaking of all the three. It is the Thursday Lecture; an institution which New England has long ago relinquished, and almost forgotten, yet which it would have been better to retain, as bearing relations to both the spiritual and ordinary life, and bringing each acquainted with the other. The tokens of its observance, however, which here meet our eyes, are of rather a questionable cast. It is, in one sense, a day of public shame; the day on which transgressors, who have made themselves liable to the minor severities of the Puritan law, receive their reward of ignominy. At this very moment, the constable has bound an idle fellow to the whipping-post, and is giving him his deserts with a cat-o'-nine-tails. Ever since sunrise, Daniel Fairfield has been standing on the steps of the meeting-house, with a halter about his neck, which he is condemned to wear visibly throughout his lifetime; Dorothy Talby is chained to a post at the corner of Prison Lane, with the hot sun blazing on her matronly face, and all for no other offence than lifting her hand against her husband; while, through the bars of that great wooden cage, in the centre of the scene, we discern either a human being or a wild beast, or both in one, whom this public infamy causes to roar, and gnash his teeth, and shake the strong oaken bars, as if he would break forth, and tear in pieces the little children who have been peeping at him. Such are the profitable sights that serve the good people to while away the earlier part of lecture-day. Betimes in the forenoon, a traveller — the first traveller that has come hitherward this morning — rides slowly into the street on his patient steed. He seems a clergyman; and, as he draws near, we recognize the minister of Lynn, who was pre-engaged to lecture here, and has been revolving his discourse as he rode through the hoary wilderness. Behold, now, the whole town thronging into the meeting-house, mostly with such sombre visages that the sunshine becomes little better than a shadow when it falls upon them. There go the Thirteen Men, grim rulers of a grim community. There goes John Massey, the first town-born child, now a youth of twenty, whose eye wanders with peculiar interest towards that buxom damsel who comes up the

steps at the same instant. There hobbles Goody Fos-
ter, a sour and bitter old beldam, looking as if she
went to curse and not to pray, and whom many of her
neighbors suspect of taking an occasional airing on a
broomstick. There, too, slinking shamefacedly in, you
observe that same poor do-nothing and good-for-nothing whom we saw castigated just now at the whipping-
post. Last of all, there goes the tithing-man, lugging
in a couple of small boys, whom he has caught at play
beneath God's blessed sunshine, in a back lane. What
native of Naumkeag, whose recollections go back more
than thirty years, does not still shudder at that dark
ogre of his infancy, who perhaps had long ceased to
have an actual existence, but still lived in his childish
belief, in a horrible idea, and in the nurse's threat, as
the Tidy Man !

It will be hardly worth our while to wait two, or it
may be three, turnings of the hour-glass, for the conclusion of the lecture. Therefore, by my control over
light and darkness, I cause the dusk, and then the
starless night, to brood over the street ; and summon
forth again the bellman, with his lantern casting a
gleam about his footsteps, to pace wearily from corner
to corner, and shout drowsily the hour to drowsy or
dreaming ears. Happy are we, if for nothing else,
yet because we did not live in those days. In truth,
when the first novelty and stir of spirit had subsided,
— when the new settlement, between the forest-border
and the sea, had become actually a little town, — its
daily life must have trudged onward with hardly anything to diversify and enliven it, while also its rigidity could not fail to cause miserable distortions of the
moral nature. Such a life was sinister to the intellect, and sinister to the heart ; especially when one

generation had bequeathed its religious gloom, and the counterfeit of its religious ardor, to the next; for these characteristics, as was inevitable, assumed the form both of hypocrisy and exaggeration, by being inherited from the example and precept of other human beings, and not from an original and spiritual source. The sons and grandchildren of the first settlers were a race of lower and narrower souls than their progenitors had been. The latter were stern, severe, intolerant, but not superstitious, not even fanatical; and endowed, if any men of that age were, with a far-seeing worldly sagacity. But it was impossible for the succeeding race to grow up, in heaven's freedom, beneath the discipline which their gloomy energy of character had established; nor, it may be, have we even yet thrown off all the unfavorable influences, which, among many good ones, were bequeathed to us by our Puritan forefathers. Let us thank God for having given us such ancestors; and let each successive generation thank Him, not less fervently, for being one step further from them in the march of ages.

"What is all this?" cries the critic. "A sermon? If so, it is not in the bill."

"Very true," replies the showman; "and I ask pardon of the audience."

Look now at the street, and observe a strange people entering it. Their garments are torn and disordered, their faces haggard, their figures emaciated; for they have made their way hither through pathless deserts, suffering hunger and hardship, with no other shelter than a hollow tree, the lair of a wild beast, or an Indian wigwam. Nor, in the most inhospitable and dangerous of such lodging-places, was there half the peril that awaits them in this thoroughfare of

Christian men, with those secure dwellings and warm hearths on either side of it, and yonder meeting-house as the central object of the scene. These wanderers have received from Heaven a gift that, in all epochs of the world, has brought with it the penalties of mortal suffering and persecution, scorn, enmity, and death itself, — a gift that, thus terrible to its possessors, has ever been most hateful to all other men, since its very existence seems to threaten the overthrow of whatever else the toilsome ages have built up, — the gift of a new idea. You can discern it in them, illuminating their faces — their whole persons, indeed, however earthly and cloddish — with a light that inevitably shines through, and makes the startled community aware that these men are not as they themselves are, — not brethren nor neighbors of their thought. Forthwith, it is as if an earthquake rumbled through the town, making its vibrations felt at every hearthstone, and especially causing the spire of the meeting-house to totter. The Quakers have come. We are in peril! See! they trample upon our wise and well-established laws in the person of our chief magistrate; for Governor Endicott is passing, now an aged man, and dignified with long habits of authority, — and not one of the irreverent vagabonds has moved his hat. Did you note the ominous frown of the white-bearded Puritan governor, as he turned himself about, and, in his anger, half uplifted the staff that has become a needful support to his old age? Here comes old Mr. Norris, our venerable minister. Will they doff their hats, and pay reverence to him? No: their hats stick fast to their ungracious heads, as if they grew there; and — impious varlets that they are, and worse than the heathen Indians! — they eye our reverend pastor with a peculiar scorn, distrust, unbelief, and utter denial of his sanctified pretensions, of which he himself immediately becomes conscious; the more bitterly conscious, as he never knew nor dreamed of the like before.

But look yonder! Can we believe our eyes? A Quaker woman, clad in sackcloth, and with ashes on her head, has mounted the steps of the meeting-house. She addresses the people in a wild, shrill voice, — wild and shrill it must be to suit such a figure, — which makes them tremble and turn pale, although they crowd open-mouthed to hear her. She is bold against established authority; she denounces the priest and his steeple-house. Many of her hearers are appalled; some weep; and others listen with a rapt attention, as if a living truth had now, for the first time, forced its way through the crust of habit, reached their hearts, and awakened them to life. This matter must be looked to; else we have brought our faith across the seas with us in vain; and it had been better that the old forest were still standing here, waving its tangled boughs and murmuring to the sky out of its desolate recesses, instead of this goodly street, if such blasphemies be spoken in it.

So thought the old Puritans. What was their mode of action may be partly judged from the spectacles which now pass before your eyes. Joshua Buffum is standing in the pillory. Cassandra Southwick is led to prison. And there a woman, — it is Ann Coleman, — naked from the waist upward, and bound to the tail of a cart, is dragged through the Main Street at the pace of a brisk walk, while the constable follows with a whip of knotted cords. A strong-armed fellow is that constable; and each time that he flourishes his lash in the air, you see a frown wrinkling and twisting his brow, and, at the same instant, a smile upon his lips. He loves his business, faithful officer that he is, and puts his soul into every stroke, zealous to fulfil the injunction of Major Hawthorne's warrant, in the spirit and to the letter. There came down a stroke that has drawn blood! Ten such stripes are to be given in Salem, ten in Boston, and ten in Dedham; and, with those thirty stripes of blood upon her, she is to be driven into the forest. The crimson trail goes wavering along the Main Street; but Heaven grant that, as the rain of so many years has wept upon it, time after time, and washed it all away, so there may have been a dew of mercy to cleanse this cruel blood-stain out of the record of the persecutor's life!

Pass on, thou spectral constable, and betake thee to thine own place of torment. Meanwhile, by the silent operation of the mechanism behind the scenes, a considerable space of time would seem to have lapsed over the street. The older dwellings now begin to look weather-beaten, through the effect of the many eastern storms that have moistened their unpainted shingles and clapboards, for not less than forty years. Such is the age we would assign to the town, judging by the aspect of John Massey, the first town-born child, whom his neighbors now call Goodman Massey, and whom we see yonder, a grave, almost autumnal-looking man, with children of his own about him. To the patriarchs of the settlement, no doubt, the Main Street is still but an affair of yesterday, hardly more antique, even if destined to be more permanent, than a path shovelled through the snow. But to the middle-aged and elderly men who came hither in childhood or early youth, it presents the aspect of a long and well-established work, on which they have expended the strength and ardor of their life. And the younger people, native to the street, whose earliest recollections are of creeping over the paternal threshold, and rolling on the grassy margin of the track, look at it as one of the perdurable things of our mortal state, — as old as the hills of the great pasture, or the headland at the harbor's mouth. Their fathers and grandsires tell them how, within a few years past, the forest stood here with but a lonely track beneath its tangled shade. Vain legend! They cannot make it true and real to their conceptions. With them, moreover, the Main Street is a street indeed, worthy to hold its way with the thronged and stately avenues of cities beyond the sea. The old Puritans tell them of the crowds that hurry along Cheapside and Fleet Street and the Strand, and of the rush of tumultuous life at Temple Bar. They describe London Bridge, itself a street, with a row of houses on each side. They speak of the vast structure of the Tower, and the solemn grandeur of Westminster Abbey. The children listen, and still inquire if the streets of London are longer and broader than the one before their father's door; if the Tower is bigger than the jail in Prison Lane; if the old Abbey will hold a larger congregation than our meeting-house. Nothing impresses them, except their own experience.

It seems all a fable, too, that wolves have ever prowled here; and not less so that the Squaw Sachem, and the Sagamore her son, once ruled over this region, and treated as sovereign potentates with the English settlers, then so few and storm-beaten, now so powerful. There stand some school-boys, you observe, in a little group around a drunken Indian, himself a prince of the Squaw Sachem's lineage. He brought hither some beaver-skins for sale, and has already swallowed the larger portion of their price, in deadly draughts of fire-water. Is there not a touch of pathos in that picture? and does it not go far towards telling the whole story of the vast growth and prosperity of one race, and the fated decay of another? — the children of the stranger making game of the great Squaw Sachem's grandson!

But the whole race of red men have not vanished with that wild princess and her posterity. This march of soldiers along the street betokens the breaking out of King Philip's war; and these young men, the flower of Essex, are on their way to defend the villages on the Connecticut; where, at Bloody Brook, a terrible blow shall be smitten, and hardly one of that gallant band be left alive. And there, at that stately mansion, with its three peaks in front, and its two little peaked towers, one on either side of the door, we see brave Captain Gardner issuing forth, clad in his embroidered buff-coat, and his plumed cap upon his head. His trusty sword, in its steel scabbard, strikes clanking on the doorstep. See how the people throng to their doors and windows, as the cavalier rides past, reining his mettled steed so gallantly, and looking so like the very soul and emblem of martial achievement, — destined, too, to meet a warrior's fate, at the desperate assault on the fortress of the Narragansetts!

"The mettled steed looks like a pig," interrupts the critic, "and Captain Gardner himself like the Devil, though a very tame one, and on a most diminutive scale."

"Sir, sir!" cries the persecuted showman, losing all patience, — for, indeed, he had particularly prided himself on these figures of Captain Gardner and his horse, — "I see that there is no hope of pleasing you. Pray, sir, do me the favor to take back your money, and withdraw!"

"Not I!" answers the unconscionable critic. "I am just beginning to get interested in the matter. Come! turn your crank, and grind out a few more of these fooleries!"

The showman rubs his brow impulsively, whisks the little rod with which he points out the notabilities of the scene, but, finally, with the inevitable acquiescence of all public servants, resumes his composure and goes on.

Pass onward, onward, Time! Build up new houses here, and tear down thy works of yesterday, that have already the rusty moss upon them! Summon forth the minister to the abode of the young maiden, and bid him unite her to the joyful bridegroom! Let the youthful parents carry their first-born to the meeting-house, to receive the baptismal rite! Knock at the door, whence the sable line of the funeral is next to issue! Provide other successive generations of men, to trade, talk, quarrel, or walk in friendly intercourse along the street, as their fathers did before them! Do all thy daily and accustomed business, Father Time, in this thoroughfare, which thy footsteps, for so many years, have now made dusty! But here, at last, thou leadest along a procession which, once witnessed, shall appear no more, and be remembered only as a hideous dream of thine, or a frenzy of thy old brain.

"Turn your crank, I say," bellows the remorseless critic, "and grind it out, whatever it be, without further preface!"

The showman deems it best to comply.

Then, here comes the worshipful Captain Curwen,

sheriff of Essex, on horseback, at the head of an armed guard, escorting a company of condemned prisoners from the jail to their place of execution on Gallows Hill. The witches! There is no mistaking them! The witches! As they approach up Prison Lane, and turn into the Main Street, let us watch their faces, as if we made a part of the pale crowd that presses so eagerly about them, yet shrinks back with such shuddering dread, leaving an open passage betwixt a dense throng on either side. Listen to what the people say.

There is old George Jacobs, known hereabouts, these sixty years, as a man whom we thought upright in all his way of life, quiet, blameless, a good husband before his pious wife was summoned from the evil to come, and a good father to the children whom she left him. Ah! but when that blessed woman went to heaven, George Jacobs's heart was empty, his hearth lonely, his life broken up; his children were married, and betook themselves to habitations of their own; and Satan, in his wanderings up and down, beheld this forlorn old man, to whom life was a sameness and a weariness, and found the way to tempt him. So the miserable sinner was prevailed with to mount into the air, and career among the clouds; and he is proved to have been present at a witch-meeting as far off as Falmouth, on the very same night that his next neighbors saw him, with his rheumatic stoop, going in at his own door. There is John Willard, too; an honest man we thought him, and so shrewd and active in his business, so practical, so intent on every-day affairs, so constant at his little place of trade, where he bartered English goods for Indian corn and all kinds of country produce! How could such a man find time, or what could put it into his mind, to leave his proper calling, and become a wizard? It is a mystery, unless the Black Man tempted him with great heaps of gold. See that aged couple, — a sad sight, truly, — John Proctor, and his wife Elizabeth. If there were two old people in all the county of Essex who seemed to have led a true Christian life, and to be treading hopefully the little remnant of their earthly path, it was this very pair. Yet have we heard it sworn, to the satisfaction of the worshipful Chief-Justice Sewell, and all the court and jury, that Proctor and his wife have shown their withered faces at children's bedsides, mocking, making mouths, and affrighting the poor little innocents in the night-time. They, or their spectral appearances, have stuck pins into the Afflicted Ones, and thrown them into deadly fainting-fits with a touch or but a look. And, while we supposed the old man to be reading the Bible to his old wife, — she meanwhile knitting in the chimney-corner, — the pair of hoary reprobates have whisked up the chimney, both on one broomstick, and flown away to a witch-communion, far into the depths of the chill, dark forest. How foolish! Were it only for fear of rheumatic pains in their old bones, they had better have stayed at home. But away they went; and the laughter of their decayed, cackling voices has been heard at midnight, aloft in the air. Now, in the sunny noontide, as they go tottering to the gallows, it is the Devil's turn to laugh.

Behind these two, — who help one another along, and seem to be comforting and encouraging each other, in a manner truly pitiful, if it were not a sin to pity the old witch and wizard, — behind them comes a woman, with a dark proud face that has been beautiful, and a figure that is still majestic. Do you know her? It is Martha Carrier, whom the Devil found in a humble cottage, and looked into her discontented heart, and saw pride there, and tempted her with his promise that she should be Queen of Hell. And now, with that lofty demeanor, she is passing to her kingdom, and, by her unquenchable pride, transforms this escort of shame into a triumphal procession, that shall attend her to the gates of her infernal palace, and seat her upon the fiery throne. Within this hour, she shall assume her royal dignity.

Last of the miserable train comes a man clad in black, of small stature and a dark complexion, with a clerical band about his neck. Many a time, in the years gone by, that face has been uplifted heavenward from the pulpit of the East Meeting-House, when the Rev. Mr. Burroughs seemed to worship God. What! — he? The holy man! — the learned! — the wise! How has the Devil tempted him? His fellow-criminals, for the most part, are obtuse, uncultivated creatures, some of them scarcely half-witted by nature, and others greatly decayed in their intellects through age. They were an easy prey for the destroyer. Not so with this George Burroughs, as we judge by the inward light which glows through his dark countenance, and, we might almost say, glorifies his figure, in spite of the soil and haggardness of long imprisonment, — in spite of the heavy shadow that must fall on him, while death is walking by his side. What bribe could Satan offer, rich enough to tempt and overcome this man? Alas! it may have been in the very strength of his high and searching intellect that the Tempter found the weakness which betrayed him. He yearned for knowledge; he went groping onward into a world of mystery; at first, as the witnesses have sworn, he summoned up the ghosts of his two dead wives, and talked with them of matters beyond the grave; and, when their responses failed to satisfy the intense and sinful craving of his spirit, he called on Satan, and was heard. Yet — to look at him — who, that had not known the proof, could believe him guilty? Who would not say, while we see him offering comfort to the weak and aged partners of his horrible crime, — while we hear his ejaculations of prayer, that seem to bubble up out of the depths of his heart, and fly heavenward, unawares, — while we behold a radiance brightening on his features as from the other world, which is but a few steps off, — who would not say, that, over the dusty track of the Main Street, a Christian saint is now going to a martyr's death? May not the Arch-Fiend have been too subtle for the court and jury, and betrayed them — laughing in his sleeve the while — into the awful error of pouring out sanctified blood as an acceptable sacrifice upon God's altar? Ah! no; for listen to wise Cotton Mather, who, as he sits there on his horse, speaks comfortably to the perplexed multitude, and tells them that all has been religiously and justly done, and that Satan's power shall this day receive its death-blow in New England.

Heaven grant it be so! — the great scholar must be right; so lead the poor creatures to their death! Do you see that group of children and half-grown girls, and, among them, an old, hag-like Indian woman, Tituba by name? Those are the Afflicted Ones. Behold, at this very instant, a proof of Satan's power and malice! Mercy Parris, the minister's daughter, has been smitten by a flash of Martha Carrier's eye, and falls down in the street, writhing with horrible spasms and foaming at the mouth, like the possessed one spoken of in Scripture. Hurry on the accursed witches to the gallows, ere they do more mischief! — ere they fling out their withered arms, and scatter pestilence by handfuls among the crowd! — ere, as their parting legacy, they cast a blight over the land, so that henceforth it may bear no fruit nor blade of grass, and be fit for nothing but a sepulchre for their unhallowed carcasses! So on they go; and old George Jacobs has stumbled, by reason of his infirmity; but Goodman Proctor and his wife lean on one another, and walk at a reasonably steady pace, considering their age. Mr. Burroughs seems to administer counsel to Martha Carrier, whose face and mien, methinks, are milder and humbler than they were. Among the multitude, meanwhile, there is horror, fear, and distrust; and friend looks askance at friend, and the husband at his wife, and the wife at him, and even the mother at her little child; as if, in every creature that God has made, they suspected a witch, or dreaded an accuser. Never, never again, whether in this or any other shape, may Universal Madness riot in the Main Street!

I perceive in your eyes, my indulgent spectators, the criticism which you are too kind to utter. These scenes, you think, are all too sombre. So, indeed, they are; but the blame must rest on the sombre spirit of our forefathers, who wove their web of life with hardly a single thread of rose-color or gold, and not on me, who have a tropic-love of sunshine, and would gladly gild all the world with it, if I knew where to find so much. That you may believe me, I will exhibit one of the only class of scenes, so far as my investigation has taught me, in which our ancestors were wont to steep their tough old hearts in wine and strong drink, and indulge an outbreak of grisly jollity.

Here it comes, out of the same house whence we saw brave Captain Gardner go forth to the wars. What! A coffin, borne on men's shoulders, and six aged gentlemen as pall-bearers, and a long train of mourners, with black gloves and black hat-bands, and everything black, save a white handkerchief in each mourner's hand, to wipe away his tears withal. Now, my kind patrons, you are angry with me. You were bidden to a bridal-dance, and find yourselves walking in a funeral procession. Even so; but look back through all the social customs of New England, in the first century of her existence, and read all her traits of character; and if you find one occasion, other than a funeral feast, where jollity was sanctioned by universal practice, I will set fire to my puppet-show without another word. These are the obsequies of old Governor Bradstreet, the patriarch and survivor of the first settlers, who, having intermarried with the Widow Gardner, is now resting from his labors, at the great age of ninety-four. The white-bearded corpse, which was his spirit's earthly garniture, now lies beneath yonder coffin-lid. Many a cask of ale and cider is on tap, and many a draught of spiced wine and aqua-vitæ has been quaffed. Else why should the bearers stagger, as they tremulously uphold the coffin? — and the aged pall-bearers, too, as they strive to walk solemnly beside it? — and wherefore do the mourners tread on one another's heels? — and why, if we may ask without offence, should the nose of the Rev. Mr. Noyes, through which he has just been delivering the funeral discourse, glow, like a ruddy coal of fire? Well, well, old friends! Pass on, with your burden of mortality, and lay it in the tomb with jolly hearts. People should be permitted to enjoy themselves in their own fashion; every man to his taste; but New England must have been a dismal abode for the man of pleasure, when the only boon-companion was Death!

Under cover of a mist that has settled over the scene, a few years flit by, and escape our notice. As the atmosphere becomes transparent, we perceive a decrepit grandsire, hobbling along the street. Do you recognize him? We saw him, first, as the baby in Goodwife Massey's arms, when the primeval trees were flinging their shadow over Roger Conant's cabin; we have seen him, as the boy, the youth, the man, bearing his humble part in all the successive scenes, and forming the index-figure whereby to note the age of his coeval town. And here he is, old Goodman Massey, taking his last walk, — often pausing, — often leaning over his staff, — and calling to mind whose dwelling stood at such and such a spot, and whose field or garden occupied the site of those more recent houses. He can render a reason for all the bends and deviations of the thoroughfare, which, in its flexible and plastic infancy, was made to swerve aside from a straight line, in order to visit every settler's door. The Main Street is still youthful; the coeval man is in his latest age. Soon he will be gone, a patriarch of four-score, yet shall retain a sort of infantine life in our local history, as the first town-born child.

Behold here a change, wrought in the twinkling of an eye, like an incident in a tale of magic, even while your observation has been fixed upon the scene. The Main Street has vanished out of sight. In its stead appears a wintry waste of snow, with the sun just peeping over it, cold and bright, and tingeing the white expanse with the faintest and most ethereal rose-color. This is the Great Snow of 1717, famous for the mountain-drifts in which it buried the whole country. It would seem as if the street, the growth of which we have noted so attentively, following it from its first phase, as an Indian track, until it reached the dignity of sidewalks, were all at once obliterated, and resolved into a drearier pathlessness than when the forest covered it. The gigantic swells and billows of the snow have swept over each man's metes and bounds, and annihilated all the visible distinctions of human property. So that now the traces of former times and hitherto accomplished deeds being done away, mankind should be at liberty to enter on new paths, and guide themselves by other laws than heretofore; if, indeed, the race be not extinct, and it be worth our while to go on with the march of life, over the cold and desolate expanse that lies before us. It may be, however, that matters are not so desperate as they appear. That vast icicle, glittering so cheerlessly in the sunshine, must be the spire of the meeting-house, incrusted with frozen sleet. Those great heaps, too, which we mistook for drifts, are houses, buried up to their eaves, and with their peaked roofs rounded by the depth of snow upon them. There, now, comes a gush of smoke from what I judge to be the chimney of the Ship Tavern; and another — another — and another — from the chimneys of other dwellings, where fireside comfort, domestic peace, the sports of children, and the quietude of age are living yet, in spite of the frozen crust above them.

But it is time to change the scene. Its dreary monotony shall not test your fortitude like one of our

actual New England winters, which leaves so large a
blank — so melancholy a death-spot — in lives so
brief that they ought to be all summer-time. Here,
at least, I may claim to be ruler of the seasons. One
turn of the crank shall melt away the snow from the
Main Street, and show the trees in their full foliage,
the rose-bushes in bloom, and a border of green grass
along the sidewalk. There! But what! How! The
scene will not move. A wire is broken. The street
continues buried beneath the snow, and the fate of
Herculaneum and Pompeii has its parallel in this catastrophe.

Alas! my kind and gentle audience, you know not
the extent of your misfortune. The scenes to come
were far better than the past. The street itself would
have been more worthy of pictorial exhibition; the
deeds of its inhabitants not less so. And how would
your interest have deepened, as, passing out of the
cold shadow of antiquity, in my long and weary course,
I should arrive within the limits of man's memory,
and, leading you at last into the sunshine of the present, should give a reflex of the very life that is flitting past us! Your own beauty, my fair townswomen,
would have beamed upon you out of my scene. Not
a gentleman that walks the street but should have beheld his own face and figure, his gait, the peculiar
swing of his arm, and the coat that he put on yesterday. Then, too, — and it is what I chiefly regret, —
I had expended a vast deal of light and brilliancy on
a representation of the street in its whole length, from
Buffum's Corner downward, on the night of the grand
illumination for General Taylor's triumph. Lastly, I
should have given the crank one other turn, and have
brought out the future, showing you who shall walk

the Main Street to-morrow, and, perchance, whose funeral shall pass through it!

But these, like most other human purposes, lie unaccomplished; and I have only further to say, that any lady or gentleman who may feel dissatisfied with the evening's entertainment shall receive back the admission fee at the door.

" Then give me mine," cries the critic, stretching out his palm. " I said that your exhibition would prove a humbug, and so it has turned out. So hand over my quarter!"

ETHAN BRAND:

A CHAPTER FROM AN ABORTIVE ROMANCE.

BARTRAM the lime-burner, a rough, heavy-looking man, begrimed with charcoal, sat watching his kiln at nightfall, while his little son played at building houses with the scattered fragments of marble, when, on the hill-side below them, they heard a roar of laughter, not mirthful, but slow, and even solemn, like a wind shaking the boughs of the forest.

"Father, what is that?" asked the little boy, leaving his play, and pressing betwixt his father's knees.

"Oh, some drunken man, I suppose," answered the lime-burner; "some merry fellow from the bar-room in the village, who dared not laugh loud enough within doors lest he should blow the roof of the house off. So here he is, shaking his jolly sides at the foot of Graylock."

"But, father," said the child, more sensitive than the obtuse, middle-aged clown, "he does not laugh like a man that is glad. So the noise frightens me!"

"Don't be a fool, child!" cried his father, gruffly. "You will never make a man, I do believe; there is too much of your mother in you. I have known the rustling of a leaf startle you. Hark! Here comes the merry fellow now. You shall see that there is no harm in him."

Bartram and his little son, while they were talking thus, sat watching the same lime-kiln that had been

the scene of Ethan Brand's solitary and meditative
life, before he began his search for the Unpardonable
Sin. Many years, as we have seen, had now elapsed,
since that portentous night when the IDEA was first
developed. The kiln, however, on the mountain-side,
stood unimpaired, and was in nothing changed since
he had thrown his dark thoughts into the intense glow
of its furnace, and melted them, as it were, into the
one thought that took possession of his life. It was a
rude, round, tower-like structure about twenty feet
high, heavily built of rough stones, and with a hillock
of earth heaped about the larger part of its circumference; so that the blocks and fragments of marble
might be drawn by cart-loads, and thrown in at the
top. There was an opening at the bottom of the tower,
like an oven-mouth, but large enough to admit a man
in a stooping posture, and provided with a massive
iron door. With the smoke and jets of flame issuing from the chinks and crevices of this door, which
seemed to give admittance into the hill-side, it resembled nothing so much as the private entrance to the
infernal regions, which the shepherds of the Delectable Mountains were accustomed to show to pilgrims.

There are many such lime-kilns in that tract of
country, for the purpose of burning the white marble
which composes a large part of the substance of the
hills. Some of them, built years ago, and long deserted, with weeds growing in the vacant round of the
interior, which is open to the sky, and grass and wild-
flowers rooting themselves into the chinks of the
stones, look already like relics of antiquity, and may
yet be overspread with the lichens of centuries to come.
Others, where the lime-burner still feeds his daily and
night-long fire, afford points of interest to the wan-

derer among the hills, who seats himself on a log of wood or a fragment of marble, to hold a chat with the solitary man. It is a lonesome, and, when the character is inclined to thought, may be an intensely thoughtful occupation; as it proved in the case of Ethan Brand, who had mused to such strange purpose, in days gone by, while the fire in this very kiln was burning.

The man who now watched the fire was of a different order, and troubled himself with no thoughts save the very few that were requisite to his business. At frequent intervals, he flung back the clashing weight of the iron door, and, turning his face from the insufferable glare, thrust in huge logs of oak, or stirred the immense brands with a long pole. Within the furnace were seen the curling and riotous flames, and the burning marble, almost molten with the intensity of heat; while without, the reflection of the fire quivered on the dark intricacy of the surrounding forest, and showed in the foreground a bright and ruddy little picture of the hut, the spring beside its door, the athletic and coal-begrimed figure of the lime-burner, and the half-frightened child, shrinking into the protection of his father's shadow. And when, again, the iron door was closed, then reappeared the tender light of the half-full moon, which vainly strove to trace out the indistinct shapes of the neighboring mountains; and, in the upper sky, there was a flitting congregation of clouds, still faintly tinged with the rosy sunset, though thus far down into the valley the sunshine had vanished long and long ago.

The little boy now crept still closer to his father, as footsteps were heard ascending the hill-side, and a human form thrust aside the bushes that clustered beneath the trees.

"Halloo! who is it?" cried the lime-burner, vexed at his son's timidity, yet half infected by it. "Come forward, and show yourself, like a man, or I'll fling this chunk of marble at your head!"

"You offer me a rough welcome," said a gloomy voice, as the unknown man drew nigh. "Yet I neither claim nor desire a kinder one, even at my own fireside."

To obtain a distincter view, Bartram threw open the iron door of the kiln, whence immediately issued a gush of fierce light, that smote full upon the stranger's face and figure. To a careless eye there appeared nothing very remarkable in his aspect, which was that of a man in a coarse, brown, country-made suit of clothes, tall and thin, with the staff and heavy shoes of a wayfarer. As he advanced, he fixed his eyes — which were very bright — intently upon the brightness of the furnace, as if he beheld, or expected to behold, some object worthy of note within it.

"Good evening, stranger," said the lime-burner; "whence come you, so late in the day?"

"I come from my search," answered the wayfarer; "for, at last, it is finished."

"Drunk! — or crazy!" muttered Bartram to himself. "I shall have trouble with the fellow. The sooner I drive him away, the better."

The little boy, all in a tremble, whispered to his father, and begged him to shut the door of the kiln, so that there might not be so much light; for that there was something in the man's face which he was afraid to look at, yet could not look away from. And, indeed, even the lime-burner's dull and torpid sense began to be impressed by an indescribable something in that thin, rugged, thoughtful visage, with the grizzled hair hanging wildly about it, and those deeply sunken eyes, which gleamed like fires within the entrance of a mysterious cavern. But, as he closed the door, the stranger turned towards him, and spoke in a quiet, familiar way, that made Bartram feel as if he were a sane and sensible man, after all.

"Your task draws to an end, I see," said he. "This marble has already been burning three days. A few hours more will convert the stone to lime."

"Why, who are you?" exclaimed the lime-burner. "You seem as well acquainted with my business as I am myself."

"And well I may be," said the stranger; "for I followed the same craft many a long year, and here, too, on this very spot. But you are a new-comer in these parts. Did you never hear of Ethan Brand?"

"The man that went in search of the Unpardonable Sin?" asked Bartram, with a laugh.

"The same," answered the stranger. "He has found what he sought, and therefore he comes back again."

"What! then you are Ethan Brand himself?" cried the lime-burner, in amazement. "I am a new-comer here, as you say, and they call it eighteen years since you left the foot of Graylock. But, I can tell you, the good folks still talk about Ethan Brand, in the village yonder, and what a strange errand took him away from his lime-kiln. Well, and so you have found the Unpardonable Sin?"

"Even so!" said the stranger, calmly.

"If the question is a fair one," proceeded Bartram, "where might it be?"

Ethan Brand laid his finger on his own heart.

"Here!" replied he.

And then, without mirth in his countenance, but as if moved by an involuntary recognition of the infinite absurdity of seeking throughout the world for what was the closest of all things to himself, and looking into every heart, save his own, for what was hidden in no other breast, he broke into a laugh of scorn. It was the same slow, heavy laugh, that had almost appalled the lime-burner when it heralded the wayfarer's approach.

The solitary mountain-side was made dismal by it. Laughter, when out of place, mistimed, or bursting forth from a disordered state of feeling, may be the most terrible modulation of the human voice. The laughter of one asleep, even if it be a little child, — the madman's laugh, — the wild, screaming laugh of a born idiot, — are sounds that we sometimes tremble to hear, and would always willingly forget. Poets have imagined no utterance of fiends or hobgoblins so fearfully appropriate as a laugh. And even the obtuse lime-burner felt his nerves shaken, as this strange man looked inward at his own heart, and burst into laughter that rolled away into the night, and was indistinctly reverberated among the hills.

"Joe," said he to his little son, "scamper down to the tavern in the village, and tell the jolly fellows there that Ethan Brand has come back, and that he has found the Unpardonable Sin!"

The boy darted away on his errand, to which Ethan Brand made no objection, nor seemed hardly to notice it. He sat on a log of wood, looking steadfastly at the iron door of the kiln. When the child was out of sight, and his swift and light footsteps ceased to be heard treading first on the fallen leaves and then on the rocky mountain-path, the lime-burner began to re gret his departure. He felt that the little fellow's presence had been a barrier between his guest and himself, and that he must now deal, heart to heart, with a man who, on his own confession, had committed the one only crime for which Heaven could afford no mercy. That crime, in its indistinct blackness, seemed to overshadow him. The lime-burner's own sins rose up within him, and made his memory riotous with a throng of evil shapes that asserted their kindred with the Master Sin, whatever it might be, which it was within the scope of man's corrupted nature to conceive and cherish. They were all of one family; they went to and fro between his breast and Ethan Brand's, and carried dark greetings from one to the other.

Then Bartram remembered the stories which had grown traditionary in reference to this strange man, who had come upon him like a shadow of the night, and was making himself at home in his old place, after so long absence, that the dead people, dead and buried for years, would have had more right to be at home, in any familiar spot, than he. Ethan Brand, it was said, had conversed with Satan himself in the lurid blaze of this very kiln. The legend had been matter of mirth heretofore, but looked grisly now. According to this tale, before Ethan Brand departed on his search, he had been accustomed to evoke a fiend from the hot furnace of the lime-kiln, night after night, in order to confer with him about the Unpardonable Sin; the man and the fiend each laboring to frame the image of some mode of guilt which could neither be atoned for nor forgiven. And, with the first gleam of light upon the mountain-top, the fiend crept in at the iron door, there to abide the intensest element of fire until again summoned forth to share in the dreadful task of extending man's possible guilt beyond the scope of Heaven's else infinite mercy.

While the lime-burner was struggling with the horror of these thoughts, Ethan Brand rose from the log, and flung open the door of the kiln. The action was in such accordance with the idea in Bartram's mind, that he almost expected to see the Evil One issue forth, red-hot, from the raging furnace.

"Hold! hold!" cried he, with a tremulous attempt to laugh; for he was ashamed of his fears, although they overmastered him. "Don't, for mercy's sake, bring out your Devil now!"

"Man!" sternly replied Ethan Brand, "what need have I of the Devil? I have left him behind me, on my track. It is with such half-way sinners as you that he busies himself. Fear not, because I open the door. I do but act by old custom, and am going to trim your fire, like a lime-burner, as I was once."

He stirred the vast coals, thrust in more wood, and bent forward to gaze into the hollow prison-house of the fire, regardless of the fierce glow that reddened upon his face. The lime-burner sat watching him, and half suspected this strange guest of a purpose, if not to evoke a fiend, at least to plunge bodily into the flames, and thus vanish from the sight of man. Ethan Brand, however, drew quietly back, and closed the door of the kiln.

"I have looked," said he, "into many a human heart that was seven times hotter with sinful passions than yonder furnace is with fire. But I found not there what I sought. No, not the Unpardonable Sin!"

"What is the Unpardonable Sin?" asked the lime-burner; and then he shrank farther from his companion, trembling lest his question should be answered.

"It is a sin that grew within my own breast," replied Ethan Brand, standing erect, with a pride that distinguishes all enthusiasts of his stamp. "A sin that grew nowhere else! The sin of an intellect that triumphed over the sense of brotherhood with man and reverence for God, and sacrificed everything to its own mighty claims! The only sin that deserves a recompense of immortal agony! Freely, were it to do again, would I incur the guilt. Unshrinkingly I accept the retribution!"

"The man's head is turned," muttered the lime-burner to himself. "He may be a sinner like the rest of us, — nothing more likely, — but, I 'll be sworn, he is a madman too."

Nevertheless, he felt uncomfortable at his situation, alone with Ethan Brand on the wild mountain-side, and was right glad to hear the rough murmur of tongues, and the footsteps of what seemed a pretty numerous party, stumbling over the stones and rustling through the underbrush. Soon appeared the whole lazy regiment that was wont to infest the village tavern, comprehending three or four individuals who had drunk flip beside the bar-room fire through all the winters, and smoked their pipes beneath the stoop through all the summers, since Ethan Brand's departure. Laughing boisterously, and mingling all their voices together in unceremonious talk, they now burst into the moonshine and narrow streaks of firelight that illuminated the open space before the lime-kiln. Bartram set the door ajar again, flooding the spot with light, that the whole company might get a fair view of Ethan Brand, and he of them.

There, among other old acquaintances, was a once ubiquitous man, now almost extinct, but whom we were formerly sure to encounter at the hotel of every thriving village throughout the country. It was the stage-agent. The present specimen of the genus was a wilted and smoke-dried man, wrinkled and red-nosed, in a smartly cut, brown, bobtailed coat, with brass buttons, who, for a length of time unknown, had kept his desk and corner in the bar-room, and was still puffing what seemed to be the same cigar that he had lighted twenty years before. He had great fame as a dry joker, though, perhaps, less on account of any intrinsic humor than from a certain flavor of brandy-toddy and tobacco-smoke, which impregnated all his ideas and expressions, as well as his person. Another well-remembered, though strangely altered, face was that of Lawyer Giles, as people still called him in courtesy; an elderly ragamuffin, in his soiled shirt-sleeves and tow-cloth trousers. This poor fellow had been an attorney, in what he called his better days, a sharp practitioner, and in great vogue among the village litigants; but flip, and sling, and toddy, and cocktails, imbibed at all hours, morning, noon, and night, had caused him to slide from intellectual to various kinds and degrees of bodily labor, till at last, to adopt his own phrase, he slid into a soap-vat. In other words, Giles was now a soap-boiler, in a small way. He had come to be but the fragment of a human being, a part of one foot having been chopped off by an axe, and an entire hand torn away by the devilish grip of a steam-engine. Yet, though the corporeal hand was gone, a spiritual member remained; for, stretching forth the stump, Giles steadfastly averred that he felt an invisible thumb and fingers with as vivid a sensation as before the real ones were amputated. A maimed and miserable wretch he was; but one, nevertheless, whom the world could not trample on, and had no right to scorn, either in this or any previous stage of his misfortunes, since he had still kept up the courage and spirit of a man, asked nothing in charity, and with his one hand — and that the left one — fought a stern battle against want and hostile circumstances.

Among the throng, too, came another personage, who, with certain points of similarity to Lawyer Giles, had many more of difference. It was the village doctor; a man of some fifty years, whom, at an earlier period of his life, we introduced as paying a professional visit to Ethan Brand during the latter's supposed insanity. He was now a purple-visaged, rude, and brutal, yet half-gentlemanly figure, with something wild, ruined, and desperate in his talk, and in all the details of his gesture and manners. Brandy possessed this man like an evil spirit, and made him as surly and savage as a wild beast, and as miserable as a lost soul; but there was supposed to be in him such wonderful skill, such native gifts of healing, beyond any which medical science could impart, that society caught hold of him, and would not let him sink out of its reach. So, swaying to and fro upon his horse, and grumbling thick accents at the bedside, he visited all the sick-chambers for miles about among the mountain towns, and sometimes raised a dying man, as it were, by miracle, or quite as often, no doubt, sent his patient to a grave that was dug many a year too soon. The doctor had an everlasting pipe in his mouth, and, as somebody said, in allusion to his habit of swearing, it was always alight with hell-fire.

These three worthies pressed forward, and greeted Ethan Brand each after his own fashion, earnestly inviting him to partake of the contents of a certain black bottle, in which, as they averred, he would find something far better worth seeking for than the Un-pardonable Sin. No mind, which has wrought itself by intense and solitary meditation into a high state of enthusiasm, can endure the kind of contact with low and vulgar modes of thought and feeling to which Ethan Brand was now subjected. It made him doubt. —and, strange to say, it was a painful doubt—whether he had indeed found the Unpardonable Sin, and found it within himself. The whole question on which he had exhausted life, and more than life, looked like a delusion.

"Leave me," he said bitterly, "ye brute beasts. that have made yourselves so, shrivelling up your souls with fiery liquors! I have done with you. Years and years ago, I groped into your hearts and found noth-ing there for my purpose. Get ye gone!"

"Why, you uncivil scoundrel," cried the fierce doc-tor, "is that the way you respond to the kindness of your best friends? Then let me tell you the truth. You have no more found the Unpardonable Sin than yonder boy Joe has. You are but a crazy fellow,— I told you so twenty years ago,—neither better nor worse than a crazy fellow, and the fit companion of old Humphrey, here!"

He pointed to an old man, shabbily dressed, with long white hair, thin visage, and unsteady eyes. For some years past this aged person had been wandering about among the hills, inquiring of all travellers whom he met for his daughter. The girl, it seemed, had gone off with a company of circus-performers, and oc-casionally tidings of her came to the village, and fine stories were told of her glittering appearance as she rode on horseback in the ring, or performed marvellous feats on the tight-rope.

The white-haired father now approached Ethan Brand, and gazed unsteadily into his face.

"They tell me you have been all over the earth," said he, wringing his hands with earnestness. "You must have seen my daughter, for she makes a grand figure in the world, and everybody goes to see her. Did she send any word to her old father, or say when she was coming back?"

Ethan Brand's eye quailed beneath the old man's. That daughter, from whom he so earnestly desired a word of greeting, was the Esther of our tale, the very girl whom, with such cold and remorseless purpose, Ethan Brand had made the subject of a psychological experiment, and wasted, absorbed, and perhaps annihilated her soul, in the process.

"Yes," murmured he, turning away from the hoary wanderer, "it is no delusion. There is an Unpardonable Sin!"

While these things were passing, a merry scene was going forward in the area of cheerful light, beside the spring and before the door of the hut. A number of the youth of the village, young men and girls, had hurried up the hill-side, impelled by curiosity to see Ethan Brand, the hero of so many a legend familiar to their childhood. Finding nothing, however, very remarkable in his aspect, — nothing but a sunburnt wayfarer, in plain garb and dusty shoes, who sat looking into the fire as if he fancied pictures among the coals, — these young people speedily grew tired of observing him. As it happened, there was other amusement at hand. An old German Jew travelling with a diorama on his back, was passing down the mountain-road towards the village just as the party turned aside from it, and, in hopes of eking out the profits of the day, the showman had kept them company to the lime-kiln.

" Come, old Dutchman," cried one of the young men, " let us see your pictures, if you can swear they are worth looking at ! "

" Oh yes, Captain," answered the Jew, — whether as a matter of courtesy or craft, he styled everybody Captain, — " I shall show you, indeed, some very superb pictures ! "

So, placing his box in a proper position, he invited the young men and girls to look through the glass orifices of the machine, and proceeded to exhibit a series of the most outrageous scratchings and daubings, as specimens of the fine arts, that ever an itinerant showman had the face to impose upon his circle of spectators. The pictures were worn out, moreover, tattered, full of cracks and wrinkles, dingy with tobacco-smoke, and otherwise in a most pitiable condition. Some purported to be cities, public edifices, and ruined castles in Europe ; others represented Napoleon's battles and Nelson's sea-fights ; and in the midst of these would be seen a gigantic, brown, hairy hand, — which might have been mistaken for the Hand of Destiny, though, in truth, it was only the showman's, — pointing its forefinger to various scenes of the conflict, while its owner gave historical illustrations. When, with much merriment at its abominable deficiency of merit, the exhibition was concluded, the German bade little Joe put his head into the box. Viewed through the magnifying-glasses, the boy's round, rosy visage assumed the strangest imaginable aspect of an immense Titanic child, the mouth

grinning broadly, and the eyes and every other fea
ture overflowing with fun at the joke. Suddenly,
however, that merry face turned pale, and its expression changed to horror, for this easily impressed
and excitable child had become sensible that the eye
of Ethan Brand was fixed upon him through the
glass.

"You make the little man to be afraid, Captain,"
said the German Jew, turning up the dark and strong
outline of his visage from his stooping posture. "But
look again, and, by chance, I shall cause you to see
somewhat that is very fine, upon my word!"

Ethan Brand gazed into the box for an instant,
and then starting back, looked fixedly at the German.
What had he seen? Nothing, apparently; for a curious youth, who had peeped in almost at the same moment, beheld only a vacant space of canvas.

"I remember you now," muttered Ethan Brand to
the showman.

"Ah, Captain, whispered the Jew of Nuremburg,
with a dark smile, "I find it to be a heavy matter in
my show - box, — this Unpardonable Sin! By my
faith, Captain, it has wearied my shoulders, this long
day, to carry it over the mountain."

"Peace," answered Ethan Brand, sternly, "or get
thee into the furnace yonder!"

The Jew's exhibition had scarcely concluded, when
a great, elderly dog — who seemed to be his own master, as no person in the company laid claim to him —
saw fit to render himself the object of public notice.
Hitherto, he had shown himself a very quiet, well-dis-
posed old dog, going round from one to another, and,
by way of being sociable, offering his rough head to
be patted by any kindly hand that would take so much

trouble. But now, all of a sudden, this grave and venerable quadruped, of his own mere motion, and without the slightest suggestion from anybody else, began to run round after his tail, which, to heighten the absurdity of the proceeding, was a great deal shorter than it should have been. Never was seen such headlong eagerness in pursuit of an object that could not possibly be attained ; never was heard such a tremendous outbreak of growling, snarling, barking, and snapping, — as if one end of the ridiculous brute's body were at deadly and most unforgivable enmity with the other. Faster and faster, round about went the cur ; and faster and still faster fled the unapproachable brevity of his tail ; and louder and fiercer grew his yells of rage and animosity ; until, utterly exhausted, and as far from the goal as ever, the foolish old dog ceased his performance as suddenly as he had begun it. The next moment he was as mild, quiet, sensible, and respectable in his deportment, as when he first scraped acquaintance with the company.

As may be supposed, the exhibition was greeted with universal laughter, clapping of hands, and shouts of encore, to which the canine performer responded by wagging all that there was to wag of his tail, but appeared totally unable to repeat his very successful effort to amuse the spectators.

Meanwhile, Ethan Brand had resumed his seat upon the log, and moved, it might be, by a perception of some remote analogy between his own case and that of this self-pursuing cur, he broke into the awful laugh, which, more than any other token, expressed the condition of his inward being. From that moment, the merriment of the party was at an end ; they stood aghast, dreading lest the inauspicious sound should be reverberated around the horizon, and that mountain would thunder it to mountain, and so the horror be prolonged upon their ears. Then, whispering one to another that it was late, — that the moon was almost down, — that the August night was growing chill, — they hurried homewards, leaving the lime-burner and little Joe to deal as they might with their unwelcome guest. Save for these three human beings, the open space on the hill-side was a solitude, set in a vast gloom of forest. Beyond that darksome verge, the firelight glimmered on the stately trunks and almost black foliage of pines, intermixed with the lighter verdure of sapling oaks, maples, and poplars, while here and there lay the gigantic corpses of dead trees, decaying on the leaf-strewn soil. And it seemed to little Joe — a timorous and imaginative child — that the silent forest was holding its breath until some fearful thing should happen.

Ethan Brand thrust more wood into the fire, and closed the door of the kiln ; then looking over his shoulder at the lime-burner and his son, he bade, rather than advised, them to retire to rest.

"For myself, I cannot sleep," said he. "I have matters that it concerns me to meditate upon. I will watch the fire, as I used to do in the old time."

"And call the Devil out of the furnace to keep you company, I suppose," muttered Bartram, who had been making intimate acquaintance with the black bottle above mentioned. "But watch, if you like, and call as many devils as you like ! For my part, I shall be all the better for a snooze. Come, Joe !"

As the boy followed his father into the hut, he looked back at the wayfarer, and the tears came into his eyes, for his tender spirit had an intuition of the

bleak and terrible loneliness in which this man had enveloped himself.

When they had gone, Ethan Brand sat listening to
the crackling of the kindled wood, and looking at the
little spirts of fire that issued through the chinks of
the door. These trifles, however, once so familiar, had
but the slightest hold of his attention, while deep within his mind he was reviewing the gradual but marvellous change that had been wrought upon him by the
search to which he had devoted himself. He remembered how the night dew had fallen upon him, — how
the dark forest had whispered to him, — how the stars
had gleamed upon him, — a simple and loving man,
watching his fire in the years gone by, and ever musing as it burned. He remembered with what tenderness, with what love and sympathy for mankind, and
what pity for human guilt and woe, he had first begun
to contemplate those ideas which afterwards became
the inspiration of his life ; with what reverence he had
then looked into the heart of man, viewing it as a
temple originally divine, and, however desecrated, still
to be held sacred by a brother ; with what awful fear
he had deprecated the success of his pursuit, and
prayed that the Unpardonable Sin might never be revealed to him. Then ensued that vast intellectual development, which, in its progress, disturbed the coun-
terpoise between his mind and heart. The Idea that
possessed his life had operated as a means of education ; it had gone on cultivating his powers to the
highest point of which they were susceptible ; it had
raised him from the level of an unlettered laborer to
stand on a star-lit eminence, whither the philosophers
of the earth, laden with the lore of universities, might
vainly strive to clamber after him. So much for the

intellect! But where was the heart? That, indeed, had withered, — had contracted, — had hardened, — had perished! It had ceased to partake of the universal throb. He had lost his hold of the magnetic chain of humanity. He was no longer a brother-man, opening the chambers or the dungeons of our common nature by the key of holy sympathy, which gave him a right to share in all its secrets; he was now a cold observer, looking on mankind as the subject of his experiment, and, at length, converting man and woman to be his puppets, and pulling the wires that moved them to such degrees of crime as were demanded for his study.

Thus Ethan Brand became a fiend. He began to be so from the moment that his moral nature had ceased to keep the pace of improvement with his intellect. And now, as his highest effort and inevitable development, — as the bright and gorgeous flower, and rich, delicious fruit of his life's labor, — he had produced the Unpardonable Sin!

"What more have I to seek? what more to achieve?" said Ethan Brand to himself. "My task is done, and well done!"

Starting from the log with a certain alacrity in his gait and ascending the hillock of earth that was raised against the stone circumference of the lime-kiln, he thus reached the top of the structure. It was a space of perhaps ten feet across, from edge to edge, presenting a view of the upper surface of the immense mass of broken marble with which the kiln was heaped. All these innumerable blocks and fragments of marble were red-hot and vividly on fire, sending up great spouts of blue flame, which quivered aloft and danced madly, as within a magic circle, and sank and rose again, with continual and multitudinous activity. As the lonely man bent forward over this terrible body of fire, the blasting heat smote up against his person with a breath that, it might be supposed, would have scorched and shrivelled him up in a moment.

Ethan Brand stood erect, and raised his arms on high. The blue flames played upon his face, and imparted the wild and ghastly light which alone could have suited its expression; it was that of a fiend on the verge of plunging into his gulf of intensest torment.

"O Mother Earth," cried he, "who art no more my Mother, and into whose bosom this frame shall never be resolved! O mankind, whose brotherhood I have cast off, and trampled thy great heart beneath my feet! O stars of heaven, that shone on me of old, as if to light me onward and upward!—farewell all, and forever. Come, deadly element of Fire,—henceforth my familiar friend! Embrace me, as I do thee!"

That night the sound of a fearful peal of laughter rolled heavily through the sleep of the lime-burner and his little son; dim shapes of horror and anguish haunted their dreams, and seemed still present in the rude hovel, when they opened their eyes to the daylight.

"Up, boy, up!" cried the lime-burner, staring about him. "Thank Heaven, the night is gone, at last; and rather than pass such another, I would watch my lime-kiln, wide awake, for a twelvemonth. This Ethan Brand, with his humbug of an Unpardonable Sin, has done me no such mighty favor, in taking my place!"

He issued from the hut, followed by little Joe, who kept fast hold of his father's hand. The early sunshine was already pouring its gold upon the mountain-tops, and though the valleys were still in shadow, they smiled cheerfully in the promise of the bright day that was hastening onward. The village, completely shut in by hills, which swelled away gently about it, looked as if it had rested peacefully in the hollow of the great hand of Providence. Every dwelling was distinctly visible; the little spires of the two churches pointed upwards, and caught a fore-glimmering of brightness from the sun-gilt skies upon their gilded weather-cocks. The tavern was astir, and the figure of the old, smoke-dried stage-agent, cigar in mouth, was seen beneath the stoop. Old Graylock was glorified with a golden cloud upon his head. Scattered likewise over the breasts of the surrounding mountains, there were heaps of hoary mist, in fantastic shapes, some of them far down into the valley, others high up towards the summits, and still others, of the same family of mist or cloud, hovering in the gold radiance of the upper atmosphere. Stepping from one to another of the clouds that rested on the hills, and thence to the loftier brotherhood that sailed in air, it seemed almost as if a mortal man might thus ascend into the heavenly regions. Earth was so mingled with sky that it was a day-dream to look at it.

To supply that charm of the familiar and homely, which Nature so readily adopts into a scene like this, the stage-coach was rattling down the mountain-road, and the driver sounded his horn, while Echo caught up the notes, and intertwined them into a rich and varied and elaborate harmony, of which the original performer could lay claim to little share. The great hills played a concert among themselves, each contributing a strain of airy sweetness.

Little Joe's face brightened at once.

"Dear father," cried he, skipping cheerily to and fro, "that strange man is gone, and the sky and the mountains all seem glad of it!"

"Yes," growled the lime-burner, with an oath, "but he has let the fire go down, and no thanks to him if five hundred bushels of lime are not spoiled. If I catch the fellow hereabouts again, I shall feel like tossing him into the furnace!"

With his long pole in his hand, he ascended to the top of the kiln. After a moment's pause, he called to his son.

"Come up here, Joe!" said he.

So little Joe ran up the hillock, and stood by his father's side. The marble was all burnt into perfect, snow-white lime. But on its surface, in the midst of the circle, — snow-white too, and thoroughly converted into lime, — lay a human skeleton, in the attitude of a person who, after long toil, lies down to long repose. Within the ribs — strange to say — was the shape of a human heart.

"Was the fellow's heart made of marble?" cried Bartram, in some perplexity at this phenomenon. "At any rate, it is burnt into what looks like special good lime; and, taking all the bones together, my kiln is half a bushel the richer for him."

So saying, the rude lime-burner lifted his pole, and, letting it fall upon the skeleton, the relics of Ethan Brand were crumbled into fragments.

A BELL'S BIOGRAPHY.

HEARKEN to our neighbor with the iron tongue.
While I sit musing over my sheet of foolscap, he emphatically tells the hour, in tones loud enough for all
the town to hear, though doubtless intended only as a
gentle hint to myself, that I may begin his biography
before the evening shall be further wasted. Unquestionably a personage in such an elevated position, and
making so great a noise in the world, has a fair claim
to the services of a biographer. He is the representative and most illustrious member of that innumerable
class, whose characteristic feature is the tongue, and
whose sole business, to clamor for the public good. If
any of his noisy brethren, in our tongue-governed democracy, be envious of the superiority which I have
assigned him, they have my free consent to hang themselves as high as he. And, for his history, let not the
reader apprehend an empty repetition of ding-dong-
bell. He has been the passive hero of wonderful vicissitudes, with which I have chanced to become acquainted, possibly from his own mouth; while the
careless multitude supposed him to be talking merely
of the time of day, or calling them to dinner or to
church, or bidding drowsy people go bedward, or the
dead to their graves. Many a revolution has it been
his fate to go through, and invariably with a prodigious uproar. And whether or no he have told me his
reminiscences, this at least is true, that the more I
study his deep-toned language, the more sense, and
sentiment, and soul, do I discover in it.

This bell — for we may as well drop our quaint personification — is of antique French manufacture, and the symbol of the cross betokens that it was meant to be suspended in the belfry of a Romish place of worship. The old people hereabout have a tradition, that a considerable part of the metal was supplied by a brass cannon, captured in one of the victories of Louis the Fourteenth over the Spaniards, and that a Bourbon princess threw her golden crucifix into the molten mass. It is said, likewise, that a bishop baptized and blessed the bell, and prayed that a heavenly influence might mingle with its tones. When all due ceremonies had been performed, the Grand Monarque bestowed the gift — than which none could resound his beneficence more loudly — on the Jesuits, who were then converting the American Indians to the spiritual dominion of the Pope. So the bell, — our self-same bell, whose familiar voice we may hear at all hours, in the streets, — this very bell sent forth its first-born accents from the tower of a log-built chapel, westward of Lake Champlain, and near the mighty stream of the St. Lawrence. It was called Our Lady's Chapel of the Forest. The peal went forth as if to redeem and consecrate the heathen wilderness. The wolf growled at the sound, as he prowled stealthily through the underbrush; the grim bear turned his back, and stalked sullenly away; the startled doe leaped up, and led her fawn into a deeper solitude. The red men wondered what awful voice was speaking amid the wind that roared through the tree-tops; and, following reverentially its summons, the dark-robed fathers blessed them as they drew near the cross-crowned chapel. In a little time, there was a crucifix on every dusky bosom. The Indians knelt beneath the lowly roof, worshipping in the same forms that were observed under the vast dome of St. Peter's, when the Pope performed high mass in the presence of kneeling princes. All the religious festivals, that awoke the chiming bells of lofty cathedrals, called forth a peal from Our Lady's Chapel of the Forest. Loudly rang the bell of the wilderness while the streets of Paris echoed with rejoicings for the birth-day of the Bourbon, or whenever France had tri-umphed on some European battle-field. And the solemn woods were saddened with a melancholy knell, as often as the thick-strewn leaves were swept away from the virgin soil, for the burial of an Indian chief.

Meantime, the bells of a hostile people and a hostile faith were ringing on Sabbaths and lecture-days, at Boston and other Puritan towns. Their echoes died away hundreds of miles southeastward of Our Lady's Chapel. But scouts had threaded the pathless desert that lay between, and, from behind the huge tree-trunks, perceived the Indians assembling at the sum-mons of the bell. Some bore flaxen-haired scalps at their girdles, as if to lay those bloody trophies on Our Lady's altar. It was reported, and believed, all through New England, that the Pope of Rome, and the King of France, had established this little chapel in the forest, for the purpose of stirring up the red men to a crusade against the English settlers. The latter took energetic measures to secure their religion and their lives. On the eve of an especial fast of the Romish Church, while the bell tolled dismally, and the priests were chanting a doleful stave, a band of New England rangers rushed from the surrounding woods. Fierce shouts, and the report of musketry, pealed sud-denly within the chapel. The ministering priests threw themselves before the altar, and were slain even on its steps.   If, as antique traditions tell us, no grass will grow where the blood of martyrs has been shed, there should be a barren spot, to this very day, on the site of that desecrated altar.

While the blood was still plashing from step to step, the leader of the rangers seized a torch, and applied it to the drapery of the shrine.   The flame and smoke arose, as from a burnt-sacrifice, at once illuminating and obscuring the whole interior of the chapel, — now hiding the dead priests in a sable shroud, now revealing them and their slayers in one terrific glare.   Some already wished that the altar-smoke could cover the deed from the sight of Heaven.   But one of the rangers — a man of sanctified aspect, though his hands were bloody — approached the captain.

"Sir," said he, " our village meeting-house lacks a bell, and hitherto we have been fain to summon the good people to worship by beat of drum.   Give me, I pray you, the bell of this popish chapel, for the sake of the godly Mr. Rogers, who doubtless hath remembered us in the prayers of the congregation ever since we began our march.   Who can tell what share of this night's good success we owe to that holy man's wrestling with the Lord?"

" Nay, then," answered the captain, " if good Mr. Rogers hath holpen our enterprise, it is right that he should share the spoil.   Take the bell and welcome, Deacon Lawson, if you will be at the trouble of carrying it home.   Hitherto it hath spoken nothing but papistry, and that too in the French or Indian gibberish ; but I warrant me, if Mr. Rogers consecrate it anew, it will talk like a good English and Protestant bell."

So Deacon Lawson and half a score of his townsmen took down the bell, suspended it on a pole, and bore it away on their sturdy shoulders, meaning to carry it to the shore of Lake Champlain, and thence homeward by water. Far through the woods gleamed the flames of Our Lady's Chapel, flinging fantastic shadows from the clustered foliage, and glancing on brooks that had never caught the sunlight. As the rangers traversed the midnight forest, staggering under their heavy burden, the tongue of the bell gave many a tremendous stroke, — clang, clang, clang ! — a most doleful sound, as if it were tolling for the slaughter of the priests and the ruin of the chapel. Little dreamed Deacon Lawson and his townsmen that it was their own funeral knell. A war - party of Indians had heard the report of musketry, and seen the blaze of the chapel, and now were on the track of the rangers, summoned to vengeance by the bell's dismal murmurs. In the midst of a deep swamp, they made a sudden onset on the retreating foe. Good Deacon Lawson battled stoutly, but had his skull cloven by a tomahawk, and sank into the depths of the morass, with the ponderous bell above him. And, for many a year thereafter, our hero's voice was heard no more on earth, neither at the hour of worship, nor at festivals nor funerals.

And is he still buried in that unknown grave? Scarcely so, dear reader. Hark! How plainly we hear him at this moment, the spokesman of Time, proclaiming that it is nine o'clock at night! We may therefore safely conclude that some happy chance has restored him to upper air.

But there lay the bell, for many silent years; and the wonder is that he did not lie silent there a century, or perhaps a dozen centuries, till the world should have forgotten not only his voice, but the voices of the whole brotherhood of bells. How would the first accent of his iron tongue have startled his resurrectionists! But he was not fated to be a subject of discussion among the antiquaries of far posterity. Near the close of the Old French War, a party of New England axe-men, who preceded the march of Colonel Bradstreet toward Lake Ontario, were building a bridge of logs through a swamp. Plunging down a stake, one of these pioneers felt it graze against some hard, smooth substance. He called his comrades, and, by their united efforts, the top of the bell was raised to the surface, a rope made fast to it, and thence passed over the horizontal limb of a tree. Heave-ho! up they hoisted their prize, dripping with moisture, and festooned with verdant water-moss. As the base of the bell emerged from the swamp, the pioneers perceived that a skeleton was clinging with its bony fingers to the clapper, but immediately relaxing its nerveless grasp, sank back into the stagnant water. The bell then gave forth a sullen clang. No wonder that he was in haste to speak, after holding his tongue for such a length of time! The pioneers shoved the bell to and fro, thus ringing a loud and heavy peal, which echoed widely through the forest, and reached the ears of Colonel Bradstreet, and his three thousand men. The soldiers paused on their march; a feeling of religion, mingled with home-tenderness, overpowered their rude hearts; each seemed to hear the clangor of the old church-bell, which had been familiar to him from infancy, and had tolled at the funerals of all his forefathers. By what magic had that holy sound strayed over the wide-murmuring ocean, and become audible amid the clash of arms, the loud crashing of the artillery over the rough wilderness-path, and the melancholy roar of the wind among the boughs?

The New-Englanders hid their prize in a shadowy nook, betwixt a large gray stone and the earthy roots of an overthrown tree; and when the campaign was ended, they conveyed our friend to Boston, and put him up at auction on the sidewalk of King Street. He was suspended, for the nonce, by a block and tackle, and, being swung backward and forward, gave such loud and clear testimony to his own merits that the auctioneer had no need to say a word. The highest bidder was a rich old representative from our town, who piously bestowed the bell on the meeting-house where he had been a worshipper for half a century. The good man had his reward. By a strange coincidence, the very first duty of the sexton, after the bell had been hoisted into the belfry, was to toll the funeral knell of the donor. Soon, however, those doleful echoes were drowned by a triumphant peal for the surrender of Quebec.

Ever since that period, our hero has occupied the same elevated station, and has put in his word on all matters of public importance, civil, military, or religious. On the day when Independence was first proclaimed in the street beneath, he uttered a peal which many deemed ominous and fearful, rather than triumphant. But he has told the same story these sixty years, and none mistake his meaning now. When Washington, in the fulness of his glory, rode through our flower-strewn streets, this was the tongue that bade the Father of his Country welcome! Again the same voice was heard, when Lafayette came to gather in his half-century's harvest of gratitude. Meantime, vast changes have been going on below. His voice, which once floated over a little provincial seaport, is now reverberated between brick edifices, and strikes the ear amid the buzz and tumult of a city. On the Sabbaths of olden time, the summons of the bell was obeyed by a picturesque and varied throng; stately gentlemen in purple velvet coats, embroidered waistcoats, white wigs, and gold-laced hats, stepping with grave courtesy beside ladies in flowered satin gowns, and hoop-petticoats of majestic circumference; while behind followed a liveried slave or bondsman, bearing the psalm-book, and a stove for his mistress's feet. The commonalty, clad in homely garb, gave precedence to their betters at the door of the meeting-house, as if admitting that there were distinctions between them, even in the sight of God. Yet, as their coffins were borne one after another through the street, the bell has tolled a requiem for all alike. What mattered it whether or no there were a silver scutcheon on the coffin-lid? "Open thy bosom, Mother Earth!" Thus spake the bell. "Another of thy children is coming to his long rest. Take him to thy bosom, and let him slumber in peace." Thus spake the bell, and Mother Earth received her child. With the self-same tones will the present generation be ushered to the embraces of their mother; and Mother Earth will still receive her children. Is not thy tongue a-weary, mournful talker of two centuries? O funeral bell! wilt thou never be shattered with thine own melancholy strokes? Yea, and a trumpet-call shall arouse the sleepers whom thy heavy clang could awake no more!

Again — again thy voice, reminding me that I am wasting the "midnight oil." In my lonely fantasy, I can scarce believe that other mortals have caught the sound, or that it vibrates elsewhere than in my secret soul. But to many hast thou spoken. Anxious men have heard thee on their sleepless pillows, and bethought themselves anew of to-morrow's care. In a brief interval of wakefulness, the sons of toil have heard thee, and say, " Is so much of our quiet slumber spent? — is the morning so near at hand?" Crime has heard thee, and mutters, " Now is the very hour!" Despair answers thee, "Thus much of this weary life is gone!" The young mother, on her bed of pain and ecstasy, has counted thy echoing strokes, and dates from them her first-born's share of life and immortality. The bridegroom and the bride have listened, and feel that their night of rapture flits like a dream away. Thine accents have fallen faintly on the ear of the dying man, and warned him that, ere thou speakest again, his spirit shall have passed whither no voice of time can ever reach. Alas for the departing traveller, if thy voice — the voice of fleeting time — have taught him no lessons for Eternity !

SYLPH ETHEREGE.

ON a bright summer evening, two persons stood among the shrubbery of a garden, stealthily watching a young girl who sat in the window-seat of a neighboring mansion. One of these unseen observers, a gentleman, was youthful, and had an air of high breeding and refinement, and a face marked with intellect, though otherwise of unprepossessing aspect. His features wore even an ominous, though somewhat mirthful expression, while he pointed his long forefinger at the girl, and seemed to regard her as a creature completely within the scope of his influence.

"The charm works!" said he, in a low, but emphatic whisper.

"Do you know, Edward Hamilton, — since so you choose to be named, — do you know," said the lady beside him, "that I have almost a mind to break the spell at once? What if the lesson should prove too severe! True, if my ward could be thus laughed out of her fantastic nonsense, she might be the better for it through life. But then, she is such a delicate creature! And, besides, are you not ruining your own chance by putting forward this shadow of a rival?"

"But will he not vanish into thin air, at my bidding?" rejoined Edward Hamilton. "Let the charm work!"

The girl's slender and sylph-like figure, tinged with radiance from the sunset clouds, and overhung with the rich drapery of the silken curtains, and set within the deep frame of the window, was a perfect picture; or, rather, it was like the original loveliness in a painter's fancy, from which the most finished picture is but an imperfect copy. Though her occupation excited so much interest in the two spectators, she was merely gazing at a miniature which she held in her hand, encased in white satin and red morocco; nor did there appear to be any other cause for the smile of mockery and malice with which Hamilton regarded her.

"The charm works!" muttered he, again. "Our pretty Sylvia's scorn will have a dear retribution!"

At this moment the girl raised her eyes, and, instead of a life-like semblance of the miniature, beheld the ill-omened shape of Edward Hamilton, who now stepped forth from his concealment in the shrubbery.

Sylvia Etherege was an orphan girl, who had spent her life, till within a few months past, under the guardianship, and in the secluded dwelling, of an old bachelor uncle. While yet in her cradle, she had been the destined bride of a cousin, who was no less passive in the betrothal than herself. Their future union had been projected, as the means of uniting two rich estates, and was rendered highly expedient, if not indispensable, by the testamentary dispositions of the parents on both sides. Edgar Vaughan, the promised bridegroom, had been bred from infancy in Europe, and had never seen the beautiful girl whose heart he was to claim as his inheritance. But already, for several years, a correspondence had been kept up between the cousins, and had produced an intellectual intimacy, though it could but imperfectly acquaint them with each other's character.

Sylvia was shy, sensitive, and fanciful; and her

guardian's secluded habits had shut her out from even so much of the world as is generally open to maidens of her age. She had been left to seek associates and friends for herself in the haunts of imagination, and to converse with them, sometimes in the language of dead poets, oftener in the poetry of her own mind. The companion whom she chiefly summoned up was the cousin with whose idea her earliest thoughts had been connected. She made a vision of Edgar Vaughan, and tinted it with stronger hues than a mere fancy-picture, yet graced it with so many bright and delicate perfections, that her cousin could nowhere have encountered so dangerous a rival. To this shadow she cherished a romantic fidelity. With its airy presence sitting by her side, or gliding along her favorite paths, the loneliness of her young life was blissful; her heart was satisfied with love, while yet its virgin purity was untainted by the earthliness that the touch of a real lover would have left there. Edgar Vaughan seemed to be conscious of her character; for, in his letters, he gave her a name that was happily appropriate to the sensitiveness of her disposition, the delicate peculiarity of her manners, and the ethereal beauty both of her mind and person. Instead of Sylvia, he called her Sylph, — with the prerogative of a cousin and a lover, — his dear Sylph Etherege.

When Sylvia was seventeen, her guardian died, and she passed under the care of Mrs. Grosvenor, a lady of wealth and fashion, and Sylvia's nearest relative, though a distant one. While an inmate of Mrs. Grosvenor's family, she still preserved somewhat of her life-long habits of seclusion, and shrank from a too familiar intercourse with those around her. Still, too, she was faithful to her cousin, or to the shadow which bore his name.

The time now drew near when Edgar Vaughan, whose education had been completed by an extensive range of travel, was to revisit the soil of his nativity. Edward Hamilton, a young gentleman who had been Vaughan's companion, both in his studies and rambles, had already recrossed the Atlantic, bringing letters to Mrs. Grosvenor and Sylvia Etherege. These credentials insured him an earnest welcome, which, however, on Sylvia's part, was not followed by personal partiality, or even the regard that seemed due to her cousin's most intimate friend. As she herself could have assigned no cause for her repugnance, it might be termed instinctive. Hamilton's person, it is true, was the reverse of attractive, especially when beheld for the first time. Yet, in the eyes of the most fastidious judges, the defect of natural grace was compensated by the polish of his manners, and by the intellect which so often gleamed through his dark features. Mrs. Grosvenor, with whom he immediately became a prodigious favorite, exerted herself to overcome Sylvia's dislike. But, in this matter, her ward could neither be reasoned with nor persuaded. The presence of Edward Hamilton was sure to render her cold, shy, and distant, abstracting all the vivacity from her deportment, as if a cloud had come betwixt her and the sunshine.

The simplicity of Sylvia's demeanor rendered it easy for so keen an observer as Hamilton to detect her feelings. Whenever any slight circumstance made him sensible of them, a smile might be seen to flit over the young man's sallow visage. None, that had once beheld this smile, were in any danger of forgetting it; whenever they recalled to memory the features of Edward Hamilton, they were always duskily illuminated by this expression of mockery and malice.

In a few weeks after Hamilton's arrival, he presented to Sylvia Etherege a miniature of her cousin, which, as he informed her, would have been delivered sconer, but was detained with a portion of his baggage. This was the miniature in the contemplation of which we beheld Sylvia so absorbed, at the commencement of our story. Such, in truth, was too often the habit of the shy and musing girl. The beauty of the pictured countenance was almost too perfect to represent a human creature, that had been born of a fallen and world-worn race, and had lived to manhood amid ordinary troubles and enjoyments, and must become wrinkled with age and care. It seemed too bright for a thing formed of dust, and doomed to crumble into dust again. Sylvia feared that such a being would be too refined and delicate to love a simple girl like her. Yet, even while her spirit drooped with that apprehension, the picture was but the masculine counterpart of Sylph Etherege's sylph-like beauty. There was that resemblance between her own face and the miniature which is said often to exist between lovers whom Heaven has destined for each other, and which, in this instance, might be owing to the kindred blood of the two parties. Sylvia felt, indeed, that there was something familiar in the countenance, so like a friend did the eyes smile upon her, and seem to imply a knowledge of her thoughts. She could account for this impression only by supposing that, in some of her day-dreams, imagination had conjured up the true similitude of her distant and unseen lover.

But now could Sylvia give a brighter semblance of reality to those day-dreams. Clasping the miniature to her heart, she could summon forth, from that haunted cell of pure and blissful fantasies, the life-like shadow, to roam with her in the moonlight garden. Even at noontide it sat with her in the arbor, when the sunshine threw its broken flakes of gold into the clustering shade. The effect upon her mind was hardly less powerful than if she had actually listened to, and reciprocated, the vows of Edgar Vaughan; for, though the illusion never quite deceived her, yet the remembrance was as distinct as of a remembered interview. Those heavenly eyes gazed forever into her soul, which drank at them as at a fountain, and was disquieted if reality threw a momentary cloud between. She heard the melody of a voice breathing sentiments with which her own chimed in like music. O happy, yet hapless girl! Thus to create the being whom she loves, to endow him with all the attributes that were most fascinating to her heart, and then to flit with the airy creature into the realm of fantasy and moonlight where dwelt his dreamy kindred! For her lover wiled Sylvia away from earth, which seemed strange, and dull, and darksome, and lured her to a country where her spirit roamed in peaceful rapture, deeming that it had found its home. Many, in their youth, have visited that land of dreams, and wandered so long in its enchanted groves that, when banished thence, they feel like exiles everywhere.

The dark-browed Edward Hamilton, like the villain of a tale, would often glide through the romance wherein poor Sylvia walked. Sometimes, at the most blissful moment of her ecstasy, when the features of the miniature were pictured brightest in the air, they would suddenly change, and darken, and be transformed into his visage. And always, when such change occurred, the intrusive visage wore that pe-

culiar smile with which Hamilton had glanced at
Sylvia.

Before the close of summer, it was told Sylvia Etherege that Vaughan had arrived from France, and
that she would meet him — would meet, for the first
time, the loved of years — that very evening. We will
not tell how often and how earnestly she gazed upon
the miniature, thus endeavoring to prepare herself
for the approaching interview, lest the throbbing of
her timorous heart should stifle the words of welcome.
While the twilight grew deeper and duskier, she sat
with Mrs. Grosvenor in an inner apartment, lighted
only by the softened gleam from an alabaster lamp,
which was burning at a distance on the centre-table of
the drawing-room. Never before had Sylph Etherege
looked so sylph-like. She had communed with a creature of imagination, till her own loveliness seemed but
the creation of a delicate and dreamy fancy. Every
vibration of her spirit was visible in her frame, as she
listened to the rattling of wheels and the tramp upon
the pavement, and deemed that even the breeze bore
the sound of her lover's footsteps, as if he trode
upon the viewless air. Mrs. Grosvenor, too, while she
watched the tremulous flow of Sylvia's feelings, was
deeply moved; she looked uneasily at the agitated
girl, and was about to speak, when the opening of the
street-door arrested the words upon her lips.

Footsteps ascended the staircase, with a confident
and familiar tread, and some one entered the drawing-
room. From the sofa where they sat, in the inner
apartment, Mrs. Grosvenor and Sylvia could not discern the visitor.

"Sylph!" cried a voice. "Dearest Sylph! Where
are you, sweet Sylph Etherege? Here is your Edgar
Vaughan!"

But instead of answering, or rising to meet her lover, — who had greeted her by the sweet and fanciful name, which, appropriate as it was to her character, was known only to him, — Sylvia grasped Mrs. Grosvenor's arm, while her whole frame shook with the throbbing of her heart.

"Who is it?" gasped she. "Who calls me Sylph?"

Before Mrs. Grosvenor could reply, the stranger entered the room, bearing the lamp in his hand. Approaching the sofa, he displayed to Sylvia the features of Edward Hamilton, illuminated by that evil smile, from which his face derived so marked an individuality.

"Is not the miniature an admirable likeness?" inquired he.

Sylvia shuddered, but had not power to turn away her white face from his gaze. The miniature, which she had been holding in her hand, fell down upon the floor, where Hamilton, or Vaughan, set his foot upon it, and crushed the ivory counterfeit to fragments.

"There, my sweet Sylph," he exclaimed. "It was I that created your phantom-lover, and now I annihilate him! Your dream is rudely broken. Awake, Sylph Etherege, awake to truth! I am the only Edgar Vaughan!"

"We have gone too far, Edgar Vaughan," said Mrs. Grosvenor, catching Sylvia in her arms. The revengeful freak, which Vaughan's wounded vanity had suggested, had been countenanced by this lady, in the hope of curing Sylvia of her romantic notions, and reconciling her to the truths and realities of life. "Look at the poor child!" she continued. "I protest I tremble for the consequences!"

"Indeed, madam!" replied Vaughan, sneeringly, as he threw the light of the lamp on Sylvia's closed eyes and marble features. "Well, my conscience is clear. I did but look into this delicate creature's heart; and with the pure fantasies that I found there, I made what seemed a man, — and the delusive shadow has wiled her away to Shadow-land, and vanished there! It is no new tale. Many a sweet maid has shared the lot of poor Sylph Etherege!"

"And now, Edgar Vaughan," said Mrs. Grosvenor, as Sylvia's heart began faintly to throb again, "now try, in good earnest, to win back her love from the phantom which you conjured up. If you succeed, she will be the better, her whole life long, for the lesson we have given her."

Whether the result of the lesson corresponded with Mrs. Grosvenor's hopes may be gathered from the closing scene of our story. It had been made known to the fashionable world that Edgar Vaughan had returned from France, and, under the assumed name of Edward Hamilton, had won the affections of the lovely girl to whom he had been affianced in his boyhood. The nuptials were to take place at an early date. One evening, before the day of anticipated bliss arrived, Edgar Vaughan entered Mrs. Grosvenor's drawing-room, where he found that lady and Sylph Etherege.

"Only that Sylvia makes no complaint," remarked Mrs. Grosvenor, "I should apprehend that the town air is ill-suited to her constitution. She was always, indeed, a delicate creature; but now she is a mere gossamer. Do but look at her! Did you ever imagine anything so fragile?"

Vaughan was already attentively observing his mistress, who sat in a shadowy and moonlighted recess of the room, with her dreamy eyes fixed steadfastly upon his own. The bough of a tree was waving before the window, and sometimes enveloped her in the gloom of its shadow, into which she seemed to vanish.

"Yes," he said, to Mrs. Grosvenor. "I can scarcely deem her 'of the earth, earthy.' No wonder that I call her Sylph! Methinks she will fade into the moonlight, which falls upon her through the window. Or, in the open air, she might flit away upon the breeze, like a wreath of mist!"

Sylvia's eyes grew yet brighter. She waved her hand to Edgar Vaughan, with a gesture of ethereal triumph.

"Farewell!" she said. "I will neither fade into the moonlight, nor flit away upon the breeze. Yet you cannot keep me here!"

There was something in Sylvia's look and tones that startled Mrs. Grosvenor with a terrible apprehension. But, as she was rushing towards the girl, Vaughan held her back.

"Stay!" cried he, with a strange smile of mockery and anguish. "Can our sweet Sylph be going to heaven, to seek the original of the miniature?"

THE CANTERBURY PILGRIMS.

THE summer moon, which shines in so many a tale, was beaming over a broad extent of uneven country. Some of its brightest rays were flung into a spring of water, where no traveller, toiling, as the writer has, up the hilly road beside which it gushes, ever failed to quench his thirst. The work of neat hands and considerate art was visible about this blessed fountain. An open cistern, hewn and hollowed out of solid stone, was placed above the waters, which filled it to the brim, but by some invisible outlet were conveyed away without dripping down its sides. Though the basin had not room for another drop, and the continual gush of water made a tremor on the surface, there was a secret charm that forbade it to overflow. I remember, that when I had slaked my summer thirst, and sat panting by the cistern, it was my fanciful theory that Nature could not afford to lavish so pure a liquid, as she does the waters of all meaner fountains.

While the moon was hanging almost perpendicularly over this spot, two figures appeared on the summit of the hill, and came with noiseless footsteps down towards the spring. They were then in the first freshness of youth; nor is there a wrinkle now on either of their brows, and yet they wore a strange, old-fashioned garb. One, a young man with ruddy cheeks, walked beneath the canopy of a broad-brimmed gray hat; he seemed to have inherited his great-grandsire's square-skirted coat, and a waistcoat that extended its immense flaps to his knees; his brown locks, also, hung down behind, in a mode unknown to our times. By his side was a sweet young damsel, her fair features sheltered by a prim little bonnet, within which appeared the vestal muslin of a cap; her close, long-waisted gown, and indeed her whole attire, might have been worn by some rustic beauty who had faded half a century before. But that there was something too warm and life-like in them, I would here have compared this couple to the ghosts of two young lovers who had died long since in the glow of passion, and now were straying out of their graves, to renew the old vows, and shadow forth the unforgotten kiss of their earthly lips, beside the moonlit spring.

"Thee and I will rest here a moment, Miriam," said the young man, as they drew near the stone cistern, "for there is no fear that the elders know what we have done; and this may be the last time we shall ever taste this water."

Thus speaking, with a little sadness in his face, which was also visible in that of his companion, he made her sit down on a stone, and was about to place himself very close to her side; she, however, repelled him, though not unkindly.

"Nay, Josiah," said she, giving him a timid push with her maiden hand, "thee must sit farther off, on that other stone, with the spring between us. What would the sisters say, if thee were to sit so close to me?"

"But we are of the world's people now, Miriam," answered Josiah.

The girl persisted in her prudery, nor did the youth, in fact, seem altogether free from a similar sort of shyness; so they sat apart from each other, gazing up the hill, where the moonlight discovered the tops of a group of buildings. While their attention was thus occupied, a party of travellers, who had come wearily up the long ascent, made a halt to refresh themselves at the spring. There were three men, a woman, and a little girl and boy. Their attire was mean, covered with the dust of the summer's day, and damp with the night-dew; they all looked woebegone, as if the cares and sorrows of the world had made their steps heavier as they climbed the hill; even the two little children appeared older in evil days than the young man and maiden who had first approached the spring.

"Good evening to you, young folks," was the salutation of the travellers; and "Good evening, friends," replied the youth and damsel.

"Is that white building the Shaker meeting-house?" asked one of the strangers. "And are those the red roofs of the Shaker village?"

"Friend, it is the Shaker village," answered Josiah, after some hesitation.

The travellers, who, from the first, had looked suspiciously at the garb of these young people, now taxed them with an intention which all the circumstances, indeed, rendered too obvious to be mistaken.

"It is true, friends," replied the young man, summoning up his courage. "Miriam and I have a gift to love each other, and we are going among the world's people, to live after their fashion. And ye know that we do not transgress the law of the land; and neither ye, nor the elders themselves, have a right to hinder us."

"Yet you think it expedient to depart without leave-taking," remarked one of the travellers.

"Yea, ye-a," said Josiah, reluctantly, "because father Job is a very awful man to speak with; and being aged himself, he has but little charity for what he calls the iniquities of the flesh."

"Well," said the stranger, "we will neither use force to bring you back to the village, nor will we betray you to the elders. But sit you here awhile, and when you have heard what we shall tell you of the world which we have left, and into which you are going, perhaps you will turn back with us of your own accord. What say you?" added he, turning to his companions. "We have travelled thus far without becoming known to each other. Shall we tell our stories, here by this pleasant spring, for our own pastime, and the benefit of these misguided young lovers?"

In accordance with this proposal, the whole party stationed themselves round the stone cistern; the two children, being very weary, fell asleep upon the damp earth, and the pretty Shaker girl, whose feelings were those of a nun or a Turkish lady, crept as close as possible to the female traveller, and as far as she well could from the unknown men. The same person who had hitherto been the chief spokesman now stood up, waving his hat in his hand, and suffered the moonlight to fall full upon his front.

"In me," said he, with a certain majesty of utterance, — "in me, you behold a poet."

Though a lithographic print of this gentleman is extant, it may be well to notice that he was now nearly forty, a thin and stooping figure, in a black coat, out at elbows; notwithstanding the ill condition of his attire, there were about him several tokens of a peculiar sort of foppery, unworthy of a mature man, par ticularly in the arrangement of his hair, which was so disposed as to give all possible loftiness and breadth to his forehead. However, he had an intelligent eye, and, on the whole, a marked countenance.

"A poet!" repeated the young Shaker, a little puzzled how to understand such a designation, seldom heard in the utilitarian community where he had spent his life. "Oh, ay, Miriam, he means a varse-maker, thee must know."

This remark jarred upon the susceptible nerves of the poet; nor could he help wondering what strange fatality had put into this young man's mouth an epithet, which ill-natured people had affirmed to be more proper to his merit than the one assumed by himself.

"True, I am a verse-maker," he resumed, "but my verse is no more than the material body into which I breathe the celestial soul of thought. Alas! how many a pang has it cost me, this same insensibility to the ethereal essence of poetry, with which you have here tortured me again, at the moment when I am to relinquish my profession forever! O Fate! why hast thou warred with Nature, turning all her higher and more perfect gifts to the ruin of me, their possessor? What is the voice of song, when the world lacks the ear of taste? How can I rejoice in my strength and delicacy of feeling, when they have but made great sorrows out of little ones? Have I dreaded scorn like death, and yearned for fame as others pant for vital air, only to find myself in a middle state between obscurity and infamy? But I have my revenge! I could have given existence to a thousand bright creations. I crush them into my heart, and there let them putrefy! I shake off the dust of my feet against my countrymen! But posterity, tracing my footsteps up this weary hill, will cry shame upon the unworthy age that drove one of the fathers of American song to end his days in a Shaker village!"

During this harangue, the speaker gesticulated with great energy, and, as poetry is the natural language of passion, there appeared reason to apprehend his final explosion into an ode extempore. The reader must understand that, for all these bitter words, he was a kind, gentle, harmless, poor fellow enough, whom Nature, tossing her ingredients together without looking at her recipe, had sent into the world with too much of one sort of brain, and hardly any of another.

"Friend," said the young Shaker, in some perplexity, "thee seemest to have met with great troubles; and, doubtless, I should pity them, if — if I could but understand what they were."

"Happy in your ignorance!" replied the poet, with an air of sublime superiority. "To your coarser mind, perhaps, I may seem to speak of more important griefs when I add, what I had wellnigh forgotten, that I am out at elbows, and almost starved to death. At any rate, you have the advice and example of one individual to warn you back; for I am come hither, a disappointed man, flinging aside the fragments of my hopes, and seeking shelter in the calm retreat which you are so anxious to leave."

"I thank thee, friend," rejoined the youth, "but I do not mean to be a poet, nor, Heaven be praised! do I think Miriam ever made a varse in her life. So we need not fear thy disappointments. But, Miriam," he added, with real concern, "thee knowest that the elders admit nobody that has not a gift to be useful. Now, what under the sun can they do with this poor varse-maker?"

"Nay, Josiah, do not thee discourage the poor man," said the girl, in all simplicity and kindness. "Our hymns are very rough, and perhaps they may trust him to smooth them."

Without noticing this hint of professional employ-ment, the poet turned away, and gave himself up to a sort of vague reverie, which he called thought. Some-times he watched the moon, pouring a silvery liquid on the clouds, through which it slowly melted till they became all bright; then he saw the same sweet radi-ance dancing on the leafy trees which rustled as if to shake it off, or sleeping on the high tops of hills, or hovering down in distant valleys, like the material of unshaped dreams; lastly, he looked into the spring, and there the light was mingling with the water. In its crystal bosom, too, beholding all heaven reflected there, he found an emblem of a pure and tranquil breast. He listened to that most ethereal of all sounds, the song of crickets, coming in full choir upon the wind, and fancied that, if moonlight could be heard, it would sound just like that. Finally, he took a draught at the Shaker spring, and, as if it were the true Castalia, was forthwith moved to compose a lyric, a Farewell to his Harp, which he swore should be its closing strain, the last verse that an ungrateful world should have from him. This effusion, with two or three other little pieces, subsequently written, he took the first oppor-tunity to send, by one of the Shaker brethren, to Con-cord, where they were published in the New Hamp-shire Patriot.

Meantime, another of the Canterbury pilgrims, one so different from the poet that the delicate fancy of the latter could hardly have conceived of him, began to relate his sad experience. He was a small man, of quick and unquiet gestures, about fifty years old, with a narrow forehead, all wrinkled and drawn together. He held in his hand a pencil, and a card of some commission - merchant in foreign parts, on the back of which, for there was light enough to read or write by, he seemed ready to figure out a calculation.

" Young man," said he, abruptly, " what quantity of land do the Shakers own here, in Canterbury?"

" That is more than I can tell thee, friend," answered Josiah, "but it is a very rich establishment, and for a long way by the roadside thee may guess the land to be ours, by the neatness of the fences."

" And what may be the value of the whole," continued the stranger, " with all the buildings and improvements, pretty nearly, in round numbers?"

" Oh, a monstrous sum, — more than I can reckon," replied the young Shaker.

" Well, sir," said the pilgrim, " there was a day, and not very long ago, neither, when I stood at my counting-room window, and watched the signal flags of three of my own ships entering the harbor, from the East Indies, from Liverpool, and from up the Straits, and I would not have given the invoice of the least of them for the title-deeds of this whole Shaker settlement. You stare. Perhaps, now, you won't believe that I could have put more value on a little piece of paper, no bigger than the palm of your hand, than all these solid acres of grain, grass, and pasture-land would sell for?"

" I won't dispute it, friend," answered Josiah, " but I know I had rather have fifty acres of this good land than a whole sheet of thy paper."

" You may say so now," said the ruined merchant, bitterly, " for my name would not be worth the paper

I should write it on. Of course, you must have heard of my failure?"

And the stranger mentioned his name, which, however mighty it might have been in the commercial world, the young Shaker had never heard of among the Canterbury hills.

"Not heard of my failure!" exclaimed the merchant, considerably piqued. "Why, it was spoken of on 'Change in London, and from Boston to New Orleans men trembled in their shoes. At all events, I did fail, and you see me here on my road to the Shaker village, where, doubtless (for the Shakers are a shrewd sect), they will have a due respect for my experience, and give me the management of the trading part of the concern, in which case I think I can pledge myself to double their capital in four or five years. Turn back with me, young man; for though you will never meet with my good luck, you can hardly escape my bad."

"I will not turn back for this," replied Josiah, calmly, "any more than for the advice of the varsemaker, between whom and thee, friend, I see a sort of likeness, though I can't justly say where it lies. But Miriam and I can earn our daily bread among the world's people as well as in the Shaker village. And do we want anything more, Miriam?"

"Nothing more, Josiah," said the girl, quietly.

"Yea, Miriam, and daily bread for some other little mouths, if God send them," observed the simple Shaker lad.

Miriam did not reply, but looked down into the spring, where she encountered the image of her own pretty face, blushing within the prim little bonnet. The third pilgrim now took up the conversation. He was a sunburnt countryman, of tall frame and bony strength, on whose rude and manly face there appeared a darker, more sullen and obstinate despondency, than on those of either the poet or the merchant.

"Well, now, youngster," he began, "these folks have had their say, so I'll take my turn. My story will cut but a poor figure by the side of theirs; for I never supposed that I could have a right to meat and drink, and great praise besides, only for tagging rhymes together, as it seems this man does; nor ever tried to get the substance of hundreds into my own hands, like the trader there. When I was about of your years, I married me a wife, — just such a neat and pretty young woman as Miriam, if that's her name, — and all I asked of Providence was an ordinary blessing on the sweat of my brow, so that we might be decent and comfortable, and have daily bread for ourselves, and for some other little mouths that we soon had to feed. We had no very great prospects before us; but I never wanted to be idle; and I thought it a matter of course that the Lord would help me, because I was willing to help myself."

"And didn't He help thee, friend?" demanded Josiah, with some eagerness.

"No," said the yeoman, sullenly; "for then you would not have seen me here. I have labored hard for years; and my means have been growing narrower, and my living poorer, and my heart colder and heavier, all the time; till at last I could bear it no longer. I set myself down to calculate whether I had best go on the Oregon expedition, or come here to the Shaker village; but I had not hope enough left in me to begin the world over again; and, to make my story short, here I am. And now, youngster, take my advice, and turn back; or else, some few years hence, you'll have to climb this hill, with as heavy a heart as mine."

This simple story had a strong effect on the young fugitives. The misfortunes of the poet and merchant had won little sympathy from their plain good sense and unworldly feelings, qualities which made them such unprejudiced and inflexible judges, that few men would have chosen to take the opinion of this youth and maiden as to the wisdom or folly of their pursuits. But here was one whose simple wishes had resembled their own, and who, after efforts which almost gave him a right to claim success from fate, had failed in accomplishing them.

"But thy wife, friend?" exclaimed the young man. "What became of the pretty girl, like Miriam? Oh, I am afraid she is dead!"

"Yea, poor man, she must be dead, — she and the children, too," sobbed Miriam.

The female pilgrim had been leaning over the spring, wherein latterly a tear or two might have been seen to fall, and form its little circle on the surface of the water. She now looked up, disclosing features still comely, but which had acquired an expression of fretfulness, in the same long course of evil fortune that had thrown a sullen gloom over the temper of the unprosperous yeoman.

"I am his wife," said she, a shade of irritability just perceptible in the sadness of her tone. "These poor little things, asleep on the ground, are two of our children. We had two more, but God has provided better for them than we could, by taking them to Himself."

"And what would thee advise Josiah and me to

do ?" asked Miriam, this being the first question which she had put to either of the strangers.

"'T is a thing almost against nature for a woman to try to part true lovers," answered the yeoman's wife, after a pause ; " but I 'll speak as truly to you as if these were my dying words. Though my husband told you some of our troubles, he did n't mention the greatest, and that which makes all the rest so hard to bear. If you and your sweetheart marry, you 'll be kind and pleasant to each other for a year or two, and while that 's the case, you never will repent; but, by and by, he 'll grow gloomy, rough, and hard to please, and you 'll be peevish, and full of little angry fits, and apt to be complaining by the fireside, when he comes to rest himself from his troubles out of doors ; so your love will wear away by little and little, and leave you miserable at last. It has been so with us ; and yet my husband and I were true lovers once, if ever two young folks were."

As she ceased, the yeoman and his wife exchanged a glance, in which there was more and warmer affection than they had supposed to have escaped the frost of a wintry fate, in either of their breasts. At that moment, when they stood on the utmost verge of married life, one word fitly spoken, or perhaps one peculiar look, had they had mutual confidence enough to reciprocate it, might have renewed all their old feelings, and sent them back, resolved to sustain each other amid the struggles of the world. But the crisis passed and never came again. Just then, also, the children, roused by their mother's voice, looked up, and added their wailing accents to the testimony borne by all the Canterbury pilgrims against the world from which they fled.

"We are tired and hungry!" cried they. "Is it far to the Shaker village?"

The Shaker youth and maiden looked mournfully into each other's eyes. They had but stepped across the threshold of their homes, when lo! the dark array of cares and sorrows that rose up to warn them back. The varied narratives of the strangers had arranged themselves into a parable; they seemed not merely instances of woful fate that had befallen others, but shadowy omens of disappointed hope and unavailing toil, domestic grief and estranged affection, that would cloud the onward path of these poor fugitives. But after one instant's hesitation, they opened their arms, and sealed their resolve with as pure and fond an embrace as ever youthful love had hallowed.

"We will not go back," said they. "The world never can be dark to us, for we will always love one another."

Then the Canterbury pilgrims went up the hill, while the poet chanted a drear and desperate stanza of the Farewell to his Harp, fitting music for that melancholy band. They sought a home where all former ties of nature or society would be sundered, and all old distinctions levelled, and a cold and passionless security be substituted for mortal hope and fear, as in that other refuge of the world's weary outcasts, the grave. The lovers drank at the Shaker spring, and then, with chastened hopes, but more confiding affections, went on to mingle in an untried life.

OLD NEWS.

I.

HERE is a volume of what were once newspapers, each on a small half-sheet, yellow and time-stained, of a coarse fabric, and imprinted with a rude old type. Their aspect conveys a singular impression of antiquity, in a species of literature which we are accustomed to consider as connected only with the present moment. Ephemeral as they were intended and supposed to be, they have long outlived the printer and his whole subscription-list, and have proved more durable, as to their physical existence, than most of the timber, bricks, and stone of the town where they were issued. These are but the least of their triumphs. The government, the interests, the opinions, in short, all the moral circumstances that were contemporary with their publication, have passed away, and left no better record of what they were than may be found in these frail leaves. Happy are the editors of newspapers ! Their productions excel all others in immediate popularity, and are certain to acquire another sort of value with the lapse of time. They scatter their leaves to the wind, as the sibyl did, and posterity collects them, to be treasured up among the best materials of its wisdom. With hasty pens they write for immortality.

It is pleasant to take one of these little dingy half-sheets between the thumb and finger, and picture forth the personage who, above ninety years ago, held it, wet from the press, and steaming, before the fire. Many of the numbers bear the name of an old colonial dignitary. There he sits, a major, a member of the council, and a weighty merchant, in his high-backed armchair, wearing a solemn wig and grave attire, such as befits his imposing gravity of mien, and displaying but little finery, except a huge pair of silver shoe-buckles, curiously carved. Observe the awful reverence of his visage, as he reads his Majesty's most gracious speech; and the deliberate wisdom with which he ponders over some paragraph of provincial politics, and the keener intelligence with which he glances at the ship-news and commercial advertisements. Observe, and smile! He may have been a wise man in his day; but, to us, the wisdom of the politician appears like folly, because we can compare its prognostics with actual results; and the old merchant seems to have busied himself about vanities, because we know that the expected ships have been lost at sea, or mouldered at the wharves; that his imported broadcloths were long ago worn to tatters, and his cargoes of wine quaffed to the lees; and that the most precious leaves of his ledger have become waste-paper. Yet, his avocations were not so vain as our philosophic moralizing. In this world we are the things of a moment, and are made to pursue momentary things, with here and there a thought that stretches mistily towards eternity, and perhaps may endure as long. All philosophy that would abstract mankind from the present is no more than words.

The first pages of most of these old papers are as soporific as a bed of poppies. Here we have an erudite clergyman, or perhaps a Cambridge professor, occupying several successive weeks with a criticism on Tate and Brady, as compared with the New England ver-

sion of the Psalms. Of course, the preference is given
to the native article. Here are doctors disagreeing
about the treatment of a putrid fever then prevalent,
and blackguarding each other with a characteristic
virulence that renders the controversy not altogether
unreadable. Here are President Wigglesworth and
the Rev. Dr. Colman, endeavoring to raise a fund for
the support of missionaries among the Indians of
Massachusetts Bay. Easy would be the duties of
such a mission now! Here — for there is nothing
new under the sun — are frequent complaints of the
disordered state of the currency, and the project of a
bank with a capital of five hundred thousand pounds,
secured on lands. Here are literary essays, from the
Gentleman's Magazine; and squibs against the Pre-
tender, from the London newspapers. And here, occasionally, are specimens of New England humor, la-
boriously light and lamentably mirthful, as if some
very sober person, in his zeal to be merry, were dancing a jig to the tune of a funeral-psalm. All this is
wearisome, and we must turn the leaf.

There is a good deal of amusement, and some profit,
in the perusal of those little items which characterize
the manners and circumstances of the country. New
England was then in a state incomparably more picturesque than at present, or than it has been within the
memory of man; there being, as yet, only a narrow
strip of civilization along the edge of a vast forest,
peopled with enough of its original race to contrast
the savage life with the old customs of another world.
The white population, also, was diversified by the influx
of all sorts of expatriated vagabonds, and by the continual importation of bond-servants from Ireland and
elsewhere, so that there was a wild and unsettled mul-

titude, forming a strong minority to the sober descendants of the Puritans. Then, there were the slaves,
contributing their dark shade to the picture of society.
The consequence of all this was a great variety and
singularity of action and incident, many instances of
which might be selected from these columns, where
they are told with a simplicity and quaintness of style
that bring the striking points into very strong relief.
It is natural to suppose, too, that these circumstances
affected the body of the people, and made their course
of life generally less regular than that of their descendants. There is no evidence that the moral standard
was higher then than now; or, indeed, that morality
was so well defined as it has since become. There
seem to have been quite as many frauds and robberies,
in proportion to the number of honest deeds; there
were murders, in hot-blood and in malice; and bloody
quarrels over liquor. Some of our fathers also appear
to have been yoked to unfaithful wives, if we may
trust the frequent notices of elopements from bed and
board. The pillory, the whipping-post, the prison, and
the gallows, each had their use in those old times; and,
in short, as often as our imagination lives in the past,
we find it a ruder and rougher age than our own, with
hardly any perceptible advantages, and much that gave
life a gloomier tinge.

In vain we endeavor to throw a sunny and joyous
air over our picture of this period; nothing passes before our fancy but a crowd of sad-visaged people, moving duskily through a dull gray atmosphere. It is
certain that winter rushed upon them with fiercer storms
than now, blocking up the narrow forest-paths, and
overwhelming the roads along the sea-coast with mountain snow-drifts; so that weeks elapsed before the news

paper could announce how many travellers had perished, or what wrecks had strewn the shore. The cold
was more piercing then, and lingered further into the
spring, making the chimney-corner a comfortable seat
till long past May Day. By the number of such ac-
cidents on record, we might suppose that the thunder-
stone, as they termed it, fell oftener and deadlier on
steeples, dwellings, and unsheltered wretches. In fine,
our fathers bore the brunt of more raging and pitiless
elements than we. There were forebodings, also, of a
more fearful tempest than those of the elements. At
two or three dates, we have stories of drums, trumpets,
and all sorts of martial music, passing athwart the
midnight sky, accompanied with the roar of cannon
and rattle of musketry, prophetic echoes of the sounds
that were soon to shake the land. Besides these airy
prognostics, there were rumors of French fleets on the
coast, and of the march of French and Indians through
the wilderness, along the borders of the settlements.
The country was saddened, moreover, with grievous
sicknesses. The small-pox raged in many of the towns,
and seems, though so familiar a scourge, to have been
regarded with as much affright as that which drove
the throng from Wall Street and Broadway at the approach of a new pestilence. There were autumnal fe-
vers too, and a contagious and destructive throat-dis-
temper, — diseases unwritten in medical books. The
dark superstition of former days had not yet been
so far dispelled as not to heighten the gloom of the
present time. There is an advertisement, indeed, by a
committee of the Legislature, calling for information
as to the circumstances of sufferers in the " late calamity of 1692," with a view to reparation for their losses
and misfortunes. But the tenderness with which, after

above forty years, it was thought expedient to allude to the witchcraft delusion, indicates a good deal of lingering error, as well as the advance of more enlightened opinions. The rigid hand of Puritanism might yet be felt upon the reins of government, while some of the ordinances intimate a disorderly spirit on the part of the people. The Suffolk justices, after a preamble that great disturbances have been committed by persons entering town and leaving it in coaches, chaises, calashes, and other wheel-carriages, on the evening before the Sabbath, give notice that a watch will hereafter be set at the "fortification-gate," to prevent these outrages. It is amusing to see Boston assuming the aspect of a walled city, guarded, probably, by a detachment of church-members, with a deacon at their head. Governor Belcher makes proclamation against certain "loose and dissolute people" who have been wont to stop passengers in the streets on the Fifth of November, "otherwise called Pope's Day," and levy contributions for the building of bonfires. In this instance, the populace are more puritanic than the magistrate.

The elaborate solemnities of funerals were in accordance with the sombre character of the times. In cases of ordinary death, the printer seldom fails to notice that the corpse was "very decently interred." But when some mightier mortal has yielded to his fate, the decease of the "worshipful" such-a-one is announced, with all his titles of deacon, justice, councillor, and colonel; then follows an heraldic sketch of his honorable ancestors, and lastly an account of the black pomp of his funeral, and the liberal expenditure of scarfs, gloves, and mourning-rings. The burial train glides slowly before us, as we have seen it represented

In the woodcuts of that day, the coffin, and the bearers, and the lamentable friends, trailing their long black garments, while grim Death, a most misshapen skeleton, with all kinds of doleful emblems, stalks hideously in front. There was a coachmaker at this period, one John Lucas, who seems to have gained the chief of his living by letting out a sable coach to funerals.

It would not be fair, however, to leave quite so dismal an impression on the reader's mind; nor should it be forgotten that happiness may walk soberly in dark attire, as well as dance lightsomely in a gala-dress. And this reminds us that there is an incidental notice of the " dancing-school near the Orange-Tree," whence we may infer that the saltatory art was occasionally practised, though perhaps chastened into a characteristic gravity of movement. This pastime was probably confined to the aristocratic circle, of which the royal governor was the centre. But we are scandalized at the attempt of Jonathan Furness to introduce a more reprehensible amusement: he challenges the whole country to match his black gelding in a race for a hundred pounds, to be decided on Menotomy Common or Chelsea Beach. Nothing as to the manners of the times can be inferred from this freak of an individual. There were no daily and continual opportunities of being merry; but sometimes the people rejoiced, in their own peculiar fashion, oftener with a calm, religious smile than with a broad laugh, as when they feasted, like one great family, at Thanksgiving time, or indulged a livelier mirth throughout the pleasant days of Election Week. This latter was the true holiday season of New England. Military musters were too seriously important in that warlike time to be classed among amusements; but they stirred up and enlivened the public mind, and were occasions of solemn festival to the governor and great men of the province, at the expense of the field-officers. The Revolution blotted a feast-day out of our calendar; for the anniversary of the king's birth appears to have been celebrated with most imposing pomp, by salutes from Castle William, a military parade, a grand dinner at the town-house, and a brilliant illumination in the evening. There was nothing forced nor feigned in these testimonials of loyalty to George the Second. So long as they dreaded the reëstablishment of a popish dynasty, the people were fervent for the house of Hanover; and, besides, the immediate magistracy of the country was a barrier between the monarch and the occasional discontents of the colonies; the waves of faction sometimes reached the governor's chair, but never swelled against the throne. Thus, until oppression was felt to proceed from the king's own hand, New England rejoiced with her whole heart on his Majesty's birthday.

But the slaves, we suspect, were the merriest part of the population, since it was their gift to be merry in the worst of circumstances; and they endured, comparatively, few hardships, under the domestic sway of our fathers. There seems to have been a great trade in these human commodities. No advertisements are more frequent than those of "a negro fellow, fit for almost any household work"; "a negro woman, honest, healthy, and capable"; "a negro wench of many desirable qualities"; "a negro man, very fit for a taylor." We know not in what this natural fitness for a tailor consisted, unless it were some peculiarity of conformation that enabled him to sit cross-legged. When the slaves of a family were inconveniently prolific, —

it being not quite orthodox to drown the superfluous offspring, like a litter of kittens, — notice was promulgated of " a negro child to be given away." Sometimes the slaves assumed the property of their own persons, and made their escape ; among many such instances, the governor raises a hue-and-cry after his negro Juba. But, without venturing a word in extenuation of the general system, we confess our opinion that Cæsar, Pompey, Scipio, and all such great Roman namesakes, would have been better advised had they stayed at home, foddering the cattle, cleaning dishes, — in fine, performing their moderate share of the labors of life, without being harassed by its cares. The sable inmates of the mansion were not excluded from the domestic affections : in families of middling rank, they had their places at the board ; and when the circle closed round the evening hearth, its blaze glowed on their dark shining faces, intermixed familiarly with their master's children. It must have contributed to reconcile them to their lot, that they saw white men and women imported from Europe as they had been from Africa, and sold, though only for a term of years, yet as actual slaves, to the highest bidder. Slave labor being but a small part of the industry of the country, it did not change the character of the people ; the latter, on the contrary, modified and softened the institution, making it a patriarchal, and almost a beautiful, peculiarity of the times.

Ah! We had forgotten the good old merchant, over whose shoulder we were peeping, while he read the newspaper. Let us now suppose him putting on his three-cornered gold-laced hat, grasping his cane, with a head inlaid of ebony and mother-of-pearl, and setting forth, through the crooked streets of Boston,

on various errands, suggested by the advertisements
of the day.　Thus he communes with himself: I must
be mindful, says he, to call at Captain Scut's in Creek
Lane, and examine his rich velvet, whether it be fit
for my apparel on Election Day, — that I may wear
a stately aspect in presence of the governor and my
brethren of the council.　I will look in, also, at the
shop of Michael Cario, the jeweller: he has silver
buckles of a new fashion; and mine have lasted me
some half-score years.　My fair daughter Miriam
shall have an apron of gold brocade, and a velvet
mask, — though it would be a pity the wench should
hide her comely visage; and also a French cap, from
Robert Jenkins's, on the north side of the town-house.
He hath beads, too, and ear-rings, and necklaces, of
all sorts; these are but vanities, nevertheless, they
would please the silly maiden well.　My dame de-
sireth another female in the kitchen; wherefore, I
must inspect the lot of Irish lasses, for sale by Sam-
uel Waldo, aboard the schooner Endeavor; as also
the likely negro wench at Captain Bulfinch's.　It were
not amiss that I took my daughter Miriam to see the
royal wax-work, near the town-dock, that she may
learn to honor our most gracious King and Queen, and
their royal progeny, even in their waxen images; not
that I would approve of image-worship.　The camel,
too, that strange beast from Africa, with two great
humps, to be seen near the Common; methinks I
would fain go thither, and see how the old patriarchs
were wont to ride.　I will tarry awhile in Queen
Street, at the bookstore of my good friends Kneeland
& Green, and purchase Dr. Colman's new sermon,
and the volume of discourses by Mr. Henry Flynt;
and look over the controversy on baptism, between

the Rev. Peter Clarke and an unknown adversary; and see whether this George Whitefield be as great in print as he is famed to be in the pulpit. By that time, the auction will have commenced at the Royal Exchange, in King Street. Moreover I must look to the disposal of my last cargo of West India rum and muscovado sugar; and also the lot of choice Cheshire cheese, lest it grow mouldy. It were well that I ordered a cask of good English beer, at the lower end of Milk Street. Then am I to speak with certain dealers about the lot of stout old Vidonia, rich Canary, and Oporto wines, which I have now lying in the cellar of the Old South meeting-house. But, a pipe or two of the rich Canary shall be reserved, that it may grow mellow in mine own wine-cellar, and gladden my heart when it begins to droop with old age.

Provident old gentleman! But, was he mindful of his sepulchre? Did he bethink him to call at the workshop of Timothy Sheaffe, in Cold Lane, and select such a gravestone as would best please him? There wrought the man whose handiwork, or that of his fellow-craftsmen, was ultimately in demand by all the busy multitude who have left a record of their earthly toil in these old time-stained papers. And now, as we turn over the volume, we seem to be wandering among the mossy stones of a burial-ground.

II. THE OLD FRENCH WAR.

At a period about twenty years subsequent to that of our former sketch, we again attempt a delineation of some of the characteristics of life and manners in New England. Our text-book, as before, is a file of

antique newspapers. The volume which serves us for
a writing-desk is a folio of larger dimensions than the
one before described; and the papers are generally
printed on a whole sheet, sometimes with a supple-
mental leaf of news and advertisements. They have
a venerable appearance, being overspread with a duskiness of more than seventy years, and discolored, here
and there, with the deeper stains of some liquid, as if
the contents of a wineglass had long since been splashed
upon the page. Still, the old book conveys an impression that, when the separate numbers were flying about
town, in the first day or two of their respective exist-
ences, they might have been fit reading for very sty-
lish people. Such newspapers could have been issued
nowhere but in a metropolis, the centre, not only of
public and private affairs, but of fashion and gayety.
Without any discredit to the colonial press, these
might have been, and probably were, spread out on
the tables of the British Coffee-house, in King Street,
for the perusal of the throng of officers who then
drank their wine at that celebrated establishment. To
interest these military gentlemen, there were bulletins
of the war between Prussia and Austria; between England and France, on the old battle-plains of Flanders;
and between the same antagonists, in the newer fields
of the East Indies, — and in our own trackless woods,
where white men never trod until they came to fight
there. Or, the travelled American, the petit-maître
of the colonies, — the ape of London foppery, as the
newspaper was the semblance of the London journals,
— he with his gray powdered periwig, his embroidered
coat, lace ruffles, and glossy silk stockings, golden-
clocked, — his buckles of glittering paste, at knee-band
and shoe-strap, — his scented handkerchief, and chap

eau beneath his arm, — even such a dainty figure need not have disdained to glance at these old yellow pages, while they were the mirror of passing times. For his amusement, there were essays of wit and humor, the light literature of the day, which, for breadth and license, might have proceeded from the pen of Fielding or Smollet; while, in other columns, he would delight his imagination with the enumerated items of all sorts of finery, and with the rival advertisements of half a dozen peruke-makers. In short, newer manners and customs had almost entirely superseded those of the Puritans, even in their own city of refuge.

It was natural that, with the lapse of time and increase of wealth and population, the peculiarities of the early settlers should have waxed fainter and fainter through the generations of their descendants, who also had been alloyed by a continual accession of emigrants from many countries and of all characters. It tended to assimilate the colonial manners to those of the mother-country, that the commercial intercourse was great, and that the merchants often went thither in their own ships. Indeed, almost every man of adequate fortune felt a yearning desire, and even judged it a filial duty, at least once in his life, to visit the home of his ancestors. They still called it their own home, as if New England were to them, what many of the old Puritans had considered it, not a permanent abiding-place, but merely a lodge in the wilderness, until the trouble of the times should be passed. The example of the royal governors must have had much influence on the manners of the colonists; for these rulers assumed a degree of state and splendor which had never been practised by their predecessors, who differed in nothing from republican chief-magistrates,

under the old charter. The officers of the crown, th
public characters in the interest of the administration
and the gentlemen of wealth and good descent, genei
ally noted for their loyalty, would constitute a digni
fied circle, with the governor in the centre, bearing
very passable resemblance to a court. Their ideas
their habits, their code of courtesy, and their dress
would have all the fresh glitter of fashions immedi
ately derived from the fountain-head in England. To
prevent their modes of life from becoming the stand
ard with all who had the ability to imitate them, there
was no longer an undue severity of religion, nor as
yet any disaffection to British supremacy, nor demo
cratic prejudices against pomp. Thus, while the colo
nies were attaining that strength which was soon to
render them an independent republic, it might have
been supposed that the wealthier classes were growing
into an aristocracy, and ripening for hereditary rank.
while the poor were to be stationary in their abase
ment, and the country, perhaps, to be a sister mor
archy with England. Such, doubtless, were the plausi
ble conjectures deduced from the superficial phenom
ena of our connection with a monarchical government
until the prospective nobility were levelled with the
mob, by the mere gathering of winds that preceded
the storm of the Revolution. The portents of that
storm were not yet visible in the air. A true picture
of society, therefore, would have the rich effect produced by distinctions of rank that seemed permanent,
and by appropriate habits of splendor on the part of
the gentry.

The people at large had been somewhat changed in
character, since the period of our last sketch, by their
great exploit, the conquest of Louisburg. After that

event, the New Englanders never settled into precisely the same quiet race which all the world had imagined them to be. They had done a deed of history, and were anxious to add new ones to the record. They had proved themselves powerful enough to influence the result of a war, and were thenceforth called upon, and willingly consented, to join their strength against the enemies of England; on those fields, at least, where victory would redound to their peculiar advantage. And now, in the heat of the Old French War, they might well be termed a martial people. Every man was a soldier, or the father or brother of a soldier; and the whole land literally echoed with the roll of the drum, either beating up for recruits among the towns and villages, or striking the march towards the frontiers. Besides the provincial troops, there were twenty-three British regiments in the northern colonies. The country has never known a period of such excitement and warlike life, except during the Revolution, — perhaps scarcely then; for that was a lingering war, and this a stirring and eventful one.

One would think that no very wonderful talent was requisite for an historical novel, when the rough and hurried paragraphs of these newspapers can recall the past so magically. We seem to be waiting in the street for the arrival of the post-rider — who is seldom more than twelve hours beyond his time — with letters, by way of Albany, from the various departments of the army. Or, we may fancy ourselves in the circle of listeners, all with necks stretched out towards an old gentleman in the centre, who deliberately puts on his spectacles, unfolds the wet newspaper, and gives us the details of the broken and contradictory reports which have been flying from mouth to mouth, ever since the courier alighted at Secretary Oliver's office. Sometimes we have an account of the Indian skirmishes near Lake George, and how a ranging party of provincials were so closely pursued, that they threw away their arms, and eke their shoes, stockings, and breeches, barely reaching the camp in their shirts, which also were terribly tattered by the bushes. Then there is a journal of the siege of Fort Niagara, so minute that it almost numbers the cannon-shot and bombs, and describes the effect of the latter missiles on the French commandant's stone mansion, within the fortress. In the letters of the provincial officers, it is amusing to observe how some of them endeavor to catch the careless and jovial turn of old campaigners. One gentleman tells us that he holds a brimming glass in his hand, intending to drink the health of his correspondent, unless a cannon-ball should dash the liquor from his lips; in the midst of his letter he hears the bells of the French churches ringing, in Quebec, and recollects that it is Sunday; whereupon, like a good Protestant, he resolves to disturb the Catholic worship by a few thirty-two pound shot. While this wicked man of war was thus making a jest of religion, his pious mother had probably put up a note, that very Sabbath-day, desiring the " prayers of the congregation for a son gone a soldiering." We trust, however, that there were some stout old worthies who were not ashamed to do as their fathers did, but went to prayer, with their soldiers, before leading them to battle; and doubtless fought none the worse for that. If we had enlisted in the Old French War, it should have been under such a captain; for we love to see a man keep the characteristics of his country.[1]

[1] The contemptuous jealousy of the British army, from the gen

These letters, and other intelligence from the army, are pleasant and lively reading, and stir up the mind like the music of a drum and fife. It is less agreeable to meet with accounts of women slain and scalped, and infants dashed against trees, by the Indians on the frontiers. It is a striking circumstance that innumerable bears, driven from the woods by the uproar of contending armies in their accustomed haunts, broke into the settlements, and committed great ravages among children, as well as sheep and swine. Some of them prowled where bears had never been for a century, penetrating within a mile or two of Boston; a fact that gives a strong and gloomy impression of something very terrific going on in the forest, since these savage beasts fled townward to avoid it. But it is impossible to moralize about such trifles, when every newspaper contains tales of military enterprise, and often a huzza for victory; as, for instance, the taking of Ticonderoga, long a place of awe to the provincials, and one of the bloodiest spots in the present war. Nor is it unpleasant, among whole pages of exultation, to find a note of sorrow for the fall of some brave officer; it comes wailing in, like a funeral strain amidst a peal of triumph, itself triumphant too. Such was the lamentation over Wolfe. Somewhere, in this volume of newspapers, though we cannot now lay our finger upon the passage, we recollect a report that General Wolfe

---

eral downwards, was very galling to the provincial troops. In one of the newspapers, there is an admirable letter of a New England man, copied from the London Chronicle, defending the provincials with an ability worthy of Franklin, and somewhat in his style. The letter is remarkable, also, because it takes up the cause of the whole range of colonies, as if the writer looked upon them all as constituting one country, and that his own. Colonial patriotism had not hitherto been so broad a sentiment.

was slain, not by the enemy, but by a shot from his own soldiers.

In the advertising columns, also, we are continually reminded that the country was in a state of war. Governor Pownall makes proclamation for the enlisting of soldiers, and directs the militia colonels to attend to the discipline of their regiments, and the selectmen of every town to replenish their stocks of ammunition. The magazine, by the way, was generally kept in the upper loft of the village meeting-house. The provincial captains are drumming up for soldiers, in every newspaper. Sir Jeffrey Amherst advertises for batteaux-men, to be employed on the lakes; and gives notice to the officers of seven British regiments, dispersed on the recruiting service, to rendezvous in Boston. Captain Hallowell, of the province ship-of-war King George, invites able-bodied seamen to serve his Majesty, for fifteen pounds, old tenor, per month. By the rewards offered, there would appear to have been frequent desertions from the New England forces: we applaud their wisdom, if not their valor or integrity. Cannon of all calibres, gunpowder and balls, firelocks, pistols, swords, and hangers, were common articles of merchandise. Daniel Jones, at the sign of the hat and helmet, offers to supply officers with scarlet broadcloth, gold-lace for hats and waistcoats, cockades, and other military foppery, allowing credit until the payrolls shall be made up. This advertisement gives us quite a gorgeous idea of a provincial captain in full dress.

At the commencement of the campaign of 1759, the British general informs the farmers of New England that a regular market will be established at Lake George, whither they are invited to bring provisions and refreshments of all sorts, for the use of the army. Hence we may form a singular picture of petty traffic, far away from any permanent settlements, among the hills which border that romantic lake, with the solemn woods overshadowing the scene. Carcasses of bullocks and fat porkers are placed upright against the huge trunks of the trees; fowls hang from the lower branches, bobbing against the heads of those beneath; butter - firkins, great cheeses, and brown loaves of household bread, baked in distant ovens, are collected under temporary shelters or pine-boughs, with ginger-bread, and pumpkin-pies, perhaps, and other toothsome dainties. Barrels of cider and spruce-beer are running freely into the wooden canteens of the soldiers. Imagine such a scene, beneath the dark forest canopy, with here and there a few struggling sunbeams, to dissipate the gloom. See the shrewd yeomen, haggling with their scarlet-coated customers, abating somewhat in their prices, but still dealing at monstrous profit; and then complete the picture with circumstances that bespeak war and danger. A cannon shall be seen to belch its smoke from among the trees, against some distant canoes on the lake; the traffickers shall pause, and seem to hearken, at intervals, as if they heard the rattle of musketry or the shout of Indians; a scouting-party shall be driven in, with two or three faint and bloody men among them. And, in spite of these disturbances, business goes on briskly in the market of the wilderness.

It must not be supposed that the martial character of the times interrupted all pursuits except those connected with war. On the contrary, there appears to have been a general vigor and vivacity diffused into the whole round of colonial life. During the winter of 1759, it was computed that about a thousand sled-loads of country produce were daily brought into Boston market. It was a symptom of an irregular and unquiet course of affairs, that innumerable lotteries were projected, ostensibly for the purpose of public improvements, such as roads and bridges. Many females seized the opportunity to engage in business: as, among others, Alice Quick, who dealt in crockery and hosiery, next door to Deacon Beautineau's; Mary Jackson, who sold butter, at the Brazen-Head, in Cornhill; Abigail Hiller, who taught ornamental work, near the Orange-Tree, where also were to be seen the King and Queen, in wax-work; Sarah Morehead, an instructor in glass-painting, drawing, and japanning; Mary Salmon, who shod horses, at the South End; Harriet Pain, at the Buck and Glove, and Mrs. Henrietta Maria Caine, at the Golden Fan, both fashionable milliners; Anna Adams, who advertises Quebec and Garrick bonnets, Prussian cloaks, and scarlet cardinals, opposite the old brick meeting-house; besides a lady at the head of a wine and spirit establishment. Little did these good dames expect to reappear before the public, so long after they had made their last courtesies behind the counter. Our great-grandmothers were a stirring sisterhood, and seem not to have been utterly despised by the gentlemen at the British Coffee-house; at least, some gracious bachelor, there resident, gives public notice of his willingness to take a wife, provided she be not above twenty-three, and possess brown hair, regular features, a brisk eye, and a fortune. Now, this was great condescension towards the ladies of Massachusetts Bay, in a threadbare lieutenant of foot.

Polite literature was beginning to make its appearance. Few native works were advertised, it is true, except sermons and treatises of controversial divinity ; nor were the English authors of the day much known on this side of the Atlantic. But catalogues were frequently offered at auction or private sale, comprising the standard English books, history, essays, and poetry, of Queen Anne's age, and the preceding century. We see nothing in the nature of a novel, unless it be " The Two Mothers, price four coppers." There was an American poet, however, of whom Mr. Kettell has preserved no specimen, — the author of " War, an Heroic Poem " ; he publishes by subscription, and threatens to prosecute his patrons for not taking their books. We have discovered a periodical, also, and one that has a peculiar claim to be recorded here, since it bore the title of " THE NEW ENGLAND MAGAZINE," a forgotten predecessor, for which we should have a filial respect, and take its excellence on trust. The fine arts, too, were budding into existence. At the " old glass and picture shop," in Cornhill, various maps, plates, and views are advertised, and among them a " Prospect of Boston," a copperplate engraving of Quebec, and the effigies of all the New England ministers ever done in mezzotinto. All these must have been very salable articles. Other ornamental wares were to be found at the same shop ; such as violins, flutes, hautboys, musical books, English and Dutch toys, and London babies. About this period, Mr. Dipper gives notice of a concert of vocal and instrumental music. There had already been an attempt at theatrical exhibitions.

There are tokens, in every newspaper, of a style of luxury and magnificence which we do not usually associate with our ideas of the times. When the property of a deceased person was to be sold, we find, among the household furniture, silk beds and hangings, damask table-cloths, Turkey carpets, pictures, pier-glasses, massive plate, and all things proper for a noble mansion. Wine was more generally drunk than now, though by no means to the neglect of ardent spirits. For the apparel of both sexes, the mercers and milliners imported good store of fine broadcloths, especially scarlet, crimson, and sky-blue, silks, satins, lawns, and velvets, gold brocade, and gold and silver lace, and silver tassels, and silver spangles, until Cornhill shone and sparkled with their merchandise. The gaudiest dress permissible by modern taste fades into a Quaker-like sobriety, compared with the deep, rich, glowing splendor of our ancestors. Such figures were almost too fine to go about town on foot; accordingly, carriages were so numerous as to require a tax; and it is recorded that, when Governor Bernard came to the province, he was met between Dedham and Boston by a multitude of gentlemen in their coaches and chariots.

Take my arm, gentle reader, and come with me into some street, perhaps trodden by your daily footsteps, but which now has such an aspect of half-familiar strangeness, that you suspect yourself to be walking abroad in a dream. True, there are some brick edifices which you remember from childhood, and which your father and grandfather remembered as well; but you are perplexed by the absence of many that were here only an hour or two since; and still more amazing is the presence of whole rows of wooden and plastered houses, projecting over the sidewalks, and bearing iron figures on their fronts, which prove them to have stood on the same sites above a century. Where have your eyes been that you never saw them before?

Along the ghostly street, — for, at length, you conclude that all is unsubstantial, though it be so good
a mockery of an antique town, — along the ghostly
street, there are ghostly people too. Every gentleman
has his three-cornered hat, either on his head or un-
.der his arm ; and all wear wigs in infinite variety, —
the Tie, the Brigadier, the Spencer, the Albemarle,
the Major, the Ramillies, the grave Full-bottom, or
the giddy Feather-top. Look at the elaborate lace-
ruffles, and the square-skirted coats of gorgeous hues,
bedizened with silver and gold ! Make way for the
phantom-ladies, whose hoops require such breadth of
passage, as they pace majestically along, in silken
gowns, blue, green, or yellow, brilliantly embroidered,
and with small satin hats surmounting their powdered
hair. Make way ; for the whole spectral show will
vanish, if your earthly garments brush against their
robes. Now that the scene is brightest, and the whole
street glitters with imaginary sunshine, — now hark to
the bells of the Old South and the Old North, ringing
out with a sudden and merry peal, while the cannon
of Castle William thunder below the town, and those
of the Diana frigate repeat the sound, and the Charles-
town batteries reply with a nearer roar ! You see the
crowd toss up their hats in visionary joy. You hear
of illuminations and fire-works, and of bonfires, built
on scaffolds, raised several stories above the ground,
that are to blaze all night in King Street and on Bea-
con Hill. And here come the trumpets and kettle-
drums, and the tramping hoofs of the Boston troop of
horse-guards, escorting the governor to King's Chapel,
where he is to return solemn thanks for the surrender
of Quebec. March on, thou shadowy troop ! and vanish, ghostly crowd ! and change again old street ! for
those stirring times are gone.

Opportunely for the conclusion of our sketch, a fire broke out, on the twentieth of March, 1760, at the Brazen-Head, in Cornhill, and consumed nearly four hundred buildings. Similar disasters have always been epochs in the chronology of Boston. That of 1711 had hitherto been termed the Great Fire, but now resigned its baleful dignity to one which has ever since retained it. Did we desire to move the reader's sympathies on this subject, we would not be grandiloquent about the sea of billowy flame, the glowing and crumbling streets, the broad, black, firmament of smoke, and the blast of wind that sprang up with the conflagration and roared behind it. It would be more effective to mark out a single family at the moment when the flames caught upon an angle of their dwelling : then would ensue the removal of the bedridden grandmother, the cradle with the sleeping infant, and, most dismal of all, the dying man just at the extremity of a lingering disease. Do but imagine the confused agony of one thus awfully disturbed in his last hour , his fearful glance behind at the consuming fire raging after him, from house to house, as its devoted victim ; and, finally, the almost eagerness with which he would seize some calmer interval to die! The Great Fire must have realized many such a scene.

Doubtless posterity has acquired a better city by the calamity of that generation. None will be inclined to lament it at this late day, except the lover of antiquity, who would have been glad to walk among those streets of venerable houses, fancying the old inhabitants still there, that he might commune with their shadows, and paint a more vivid picture of their times.

III. THE OLD TORY.

Again we take a leap of about twenty years, and alight in the midst of the Revolution. Indeed, having just closed a volume of colonial newspapers, 'which represented the period when monarchical and aristocratic sentiments were at the highest, — and now opening another volume printed in the same metropolis, after such sentiments had long been deemed a sin and shame, — we feel as if the leap were more than figurative. Our late course of reading has tinctured us, for the moment, with antique prejudices ; and we shrink from the strangely contrasted times into which we emerge, like one of those immutable old Tories, who acknowledge no oppression in the Stamp Act. It may be the most effective method of going through the present file of papers, to follow out this idea, and transform ourself, perchance, from a modern Tory into such a sturdy King-man as once wore that pliable nickname.

Well, then, here we sit, an old, gray, withered, sour-visaged, threadbare sort of gentleman, erect enough, here in our solitude, but marked out by a depressed and distrustful mien abroad, as one conscious of a stigma upon his forehead, though for no crime. We were already in the decline of life when the first tremors of the earthquake that has convulsed the continent were felt. Our mind had grown too rigid to change any of its opinions, when the voice of the people demanded that all should be changed. We are an Episcopalian, and sat under the High-Church doctrines of Dr. Caner ; we have been a captain of the provincial forces, and love our king the better for the blood that we shed in his cause on the Plains of Abraham. Among all the refugees, there is not one more loyal to the backbone than we. Still we lingered behind when the British army evacuated Boston, sweeping in its train most of those with whom we held 'communion; the old, loyal gentlemen, the aristocracy of the colonies, the hereditary Englishman, imbued with more than native zeal and admiration for the glorious island and its monarch, because the far-intervening ocean threw a dim reverence around them. When our brethren departed, we could not tear our aged roots out of the soil. We have remained, therefore, enduring to be outwardly a freeman, but idolizing King George in secrecy and silence, — one true old heart amongst a host of enemies. We watch, with a weary hope, for the moment when all this turmoil shall subside, and the impious novelty that has distracted our latter years, like a wild dream, give place to the blessed quietude of royal sway, with the king's name in every ordinance, his prayer in the church, his health at the board, and his love in the people's heart. Meantime, our old age finds little honor. Hustled have we been, till driven from town-meetings; dirty water has been cast upon our ruffles by a Whig chambermaid; John Hancock's coachman seizes every opportunity to bespatter us with mud; daily are we hooted by the unbreeched rebel brats; and narrowly, once, did our gray hairs escape the ignominy of tar and feathers. Alas! only that we cannot bear to die till the next royal governor comes over, we would fain be in our quiet grave.

Such an old man among new things are we who now hold at arm's-length the rebel newspaper of the day. The very figure-head, for the thousandth time, elicits a groan of spiteful lamentation. Where are the united heart and crown, the loyal emblem, that used to hallow the sheet on which it was impressed in our younger days? In its stead we find a continental officer, with the Declaration of Independence in one hand, a drawn sword in the other, and above his head a scroll, bearing the motto, " WE APPEAL TO HEAVEN." Then say we, with a prospective triumph, let Heaven judge, in its own good time! The material of the sheet attracts our scorn. It is a fair specimen of rebel manufacture, thick and coarse, like wrapping - paper, all overspread with little knobs; and of such a deep, dingy blue color, that we wipe our spectacles thrice before we can distinguish a letter of the wretched print. Thus, in all points, the newspaper is a type of the times, far more fit for the rough hands of a democratic mob than for our own delicate, though bony fingers. Nay; we will not handle it without our gloves!

Glancing down the page, our eyes are greeted everywhere by the offer of lands at auction, for sale or to be leased, not by the rightful owners, but a rebel committee; notices of the town constable, that he is authorized to receive the taxes on such an estate, in default of which, that also is to be knocked down to the highest bidder; and notifications of complaints filed by the attorney-general against certain traitorous absentees, and of confiscations that are to ensue. And who are these traitors? Our own best friends; names as old, once as honored, as any in the land where they are no longer to have a patrimony, nor to be remembered as good men who have passed away. We are ashamed of not relinquishing our little property, too; but comfort ourselves because we still keep our princi-

ples, without gratifying the rebels with our plunder.
Plunder, indeed, they are seizing everywhere, — by
the strong hand at sea, as well as by legal forms on
shore. Here are prize-vessels for sale; no French
nor Spanish merchantmen, whose wealth is the birth-
right of British subjects, but hulls of British oak,
from Liverpool, Bristol, and the Thames, laden with
the king's own stores, for his army in New York.
And what a fleet of privateers — pirates, say we —
are fitting out for new ravages, with rebellion in their
very names! The Free Yankee, the General Greene,
the Saratoga, the Lafayette, and the Grand Monarch!
Yes, the Grand Monarch; so is a French king styled
by the sons of Englishmen. And here we have an ordinance from the Court of Versailles, with the Bourbon's own signature affixed, as if New England were
already a French province. Everything is French,
— French soldiers, French sailors, French surgeons,
and French diseases too, I trow; besides French
dancing-masters and French milliners, to debauch our
daughters with French fashions! Everything in
America is French, except the Canadas, the loyal
Canadas, which we helped to wrest from France.
And to that old French province the Englishman of
the colonies must go to find his country!

Oh, the misery of seeing the whole system of things
changed in my old days, when I would be loath to
change even a pair of buckles! The British Coffee-
house, where oft we sat, brimful of wine and loyalty,
with the gallant gentlemen of Amherst's army, when
we wore a red coat too, — the British Coffee-house, forsooth, must now be styled the American, with a golden
eagle instead of the royal arms above the door. Even
the street it stands in is no longer King Street!

Nothing is the king's, except this heavy heart in my old bosom. Wherever I glance my eyes, they meet something that pricks them like a needle. This soap-maker, for instance, this Robert Hewes, has conspired against my peace, by notifying that his shop is situated near Liberty Stump. But when will their misnamed liberty have its true emblem in that Stump, hewn down by British steel?

Where shall we buy our next year's almanac? Not this of Weatherwise's, certainly; for it contains a likeness of George Washington, the upright rebel, whom we most hate, though reverentially, as a fallen angel, with his heavenly brightness undiminished, evincing pure fame in an unhallowed cause. And here is a new book for my evening's recreation, — a History of the War till the close of the year 1779, with the heads of thirteen distinguished officers, engraved on copperplate. A plague upon their heads! We desire not to see them till they grin at us from the balcony before the town-house, fixed on spikes, as the heads of traitors. How bloody-minded the villains make a peaceable old man! What next? An Oration, on the Horrid Massacre of 1770. When that blood was shed, — the first that the British soldier ever drew from the bosoms of our countrymen, — we turned sick at heart, and do so still, as often as they make it reek anew from among the stones in King Street. The pool that we saw that night has swelled into a lake, — English blood and American, — no! all British, all blood of my brethren. And here come down tears. Shame on me, since half of them are shed for rebels! Who are not rebels now! Even the women are thrusting their white hands into the war, and come out in this very paper with proposals to form a society — the lady of George Washington at their head — for clothing the continental troops. They will strip off their stiff petticoats to cover the ragged rascals, and then enlist in the ranks themselves.

What have we here? Burgoyne's proclamation turned into Hudibrastic rhyme! And here, some verses against the king, in which the scribbler leaves a blank for the name of George, as if his doggerel might yet exalt him to the pillory. Such, after years of rebellion, is the heart's unconquerable reverence for the Lord's anointed! In the next column, we have Scripture parodied in a squib against his sacred Majesty. What would our Puritan great-grandsires have said to that? They never laughed at God's word though they cut off a king's head.

Yes, it was for us to prove how disloyalty goes hand in hand with irreligion, and all other vices come trooping in the train. Nowadays men commit robbery and sacrilege for the mere luxury of wickedness, as this advertisement testifies. Three hundred pounds reward for the detection of the villains who stole and destroyed the cushions and pulpit drapery of the Brattle Street and Old South churches. Was it a crime? I can scarcely think our temples hallowed since the king ceased to be prayed for. But it is not temples only that they rob. Here a man offers a thousand dollars — a thousand dollars in Continental rags! — for the recovery of his stolen cloak and other articles of clothing. Horse-thieves are innumerable. Now is the day when every beggar gets on horseback. And is not the whole land like a beggar on horseback riding post to the Devil? Ha! here is a murder, too. A woman slain at midnight, by an unknown ruffian, and found cold, stiff, and bloody, in her violated bed! Let the hue-and-cry follow hard after the man in the uniform of blue and buff who last went by that way. My life on it, he is the blood-stained ravisher! These deserters whom we see proclaimed in every column, — proof that the banditti are as false to their Stars and Stripes as to the Holy Red Cross, — they bring the crimes of a rebel camp into a soil well suited to them; the bosom of a people, without the heart that kept them virtuous, — their king!

Here, flaunting down a whole column, with official seal and signature, here comes a proclamation. By whose authority? Ah! the United States, — these thirteen little anarchies, assembled in that one grand anarchy, their Congress. And what the import? A general Fast. By Heaven! for once the traitorous blockheads have legislated wisely! Yea; let a misguided people kneel down in sackcloth and ashes, from end to end, from border to border, of their wasted country. Well may they fast where there is no food, and cry aloud for whatever remnant of God's mercy their sins may not have exhausted. We too will fast, even at a rebel summons. Pray others as they will, there shall be at least an old man kneeling for the righteous cause. Lord, put down the rebels! God save the king!

Peace to the good old Tory! One of our objects has been to exemplify, without softening a single prejudice proper to the character which we assumed, that the Americans who clung to the losing side in the Revolution were men greatly to be pitied and often worthy of our sympathy. It would be difficult to say whose lot was most lamentable, that of the active Tories, who gave up their patrimonies for a pittance

from the British pension-roll, and their native land for
a cold reception in their miscalled home, or the passive
ones who remained behind to endure the coldness of
former friends, and the public opprobrium, as despised
citizens, under a government which they abhorred.
In justice to the old gentleman who has favored us
with his discontented musings, we must remark that
the state of the country, so far as can be gathered
from these papers, was of dismal augury for the tendencies of democratic rule. It was pardonable in the
conservative of that day to mistake the temporary
evils of a change for permanent diseases of the system which that change was to establish. A revolution,
or anything that interrupts social order, may afford
opportunities for the individual display of eminent
virtues; but its effects are pernicious to general morality. Most people are so constituted that they can
be virtuous only in a certain routine, and an irregular
course of public affairs demoralizes them. One great
source of disorder was the multitude of disbanded
troops, who were continually returning home, after
terms of service just long enough to give them a distaste to peaceable occupations; neither citizens nor
soldiers, they were very liable to become ruffians.
Almost all our impressions in regard to this period are
unpleasant, whether referring to the state of civil society, or to the character of the contest, which, especially, where native Americans were opposed to each
other, was waged with the deadly hatred of fraternal
enemies. It is the beauty of war, for men to commit
mutual havoc with undisturbed good-humor.

The present volume of newspapers contains fewer
characteristic traits than any which we have looked
over. Except for the peculiarities attendant on the

passing struggle, manners seem to have taken a modern cast. Whatever antique fashions lingered into the War of the Revolution, or beyond it, they were not so strongly marked as to leave their traces in the public journals. Moreover, the old newspapers had an indescribable picturesqueness, not to be found in the later ones. Whether it be something in the literary execution, or the ancient print and paper, and the idea that those same musty pages have been handled by people once alive and bustling amid the scenes there recorded, yet now in their graves beyond the memory of man ; so it is, that in those elder volumes we seem to find the life of a past age preserved between the leaves, like a dry specimen of foliage. It is so difficult to discover what touches are really picturesque, that we doubt whether our attempts have produced any similar effect.

THE MAN OF ADAMANT:

AN APOLOGUE.

IN the old times of religious gloom and intolerance
lived Richard Digby, the gloomiest and most intolerant of a stern brotherhood. His plan of salvation was
so narrow, that, like a plank in a tempestuous sea, it
could avail no sinner but himself, who bestrode it tri-
umphantly, and hurled anathemas against the wretches
whom he saw struggling with the billows of eternal
death. In his view of the matter, it was a most abominable crime — as, indeed, it is a great folly — for men
to trust to their own strength, or even to grapple to
any other fragment of the wreck, save this narrow
plank, which, moreover, he took special care to keep
out of their reach. In other words, as his creed was
like no man's else, and being well pleased that Providence had intrusted him alone, of mortals, with the
treasure of a true faith, Richard Digby determined to
seclude himself to the sole and constant enjoyment of
his happy fortune.

"And verily," thought he, "I deem it a chief condition of Heaven's mercy to myself, that I hold no
communion with those abominable myriads which it
hath cast off to perish. Peradventure, were I to tarry
longer in the tents of Kedar, the gracious boon would
be revoked, and I also be swallowed up in the deluge
of wrath, or consumed in the storm of fire and brimstone, or involved in whatever new kind of ruin is ordained for the horrible perversity of this generation."

So Richard Digby took an axe, to hew space enough for a tabernacle in the wilderness, and some few other necessaries, especially a sword and gun, to smite and slay any intruder upon his hallowed seclusion, and plunged into the dreariest depths of the forest. On ts verge, however, he paused a moment, to shake off the dust of his feet against the village where he had dwelt, and to invoke a curse on the meeting-house, which he regarded as a temple of heathen idolatry. He felt a curiosity, also, to see whether the fire and brimstone would not rush down from heaven at once, now that the one righteous man had provided for his own safety. But, as the sunshine continued to fall peacefully on the cottages and fields, and the husband-men labored and children played, and as there were many tokens of present happiness, and nothing omi-nous of a speedy judgment, he turned away, somewhat disappointed. The farther he went, however, and the lonelier he felt himself, and the thicker the trees stood along his path, and the darker the shadow overhead, so much the more did Richard Digby exult. He talked to himself as he strode onward; he read his Bible to himself as he sat beneath the trees; and, as the gloom of the forest hid the blessed sky, I had almost added, that, at morning, noon, and eventide, he prayed to him-self. So congenial was this mode of life to his dispo-sition, that he often laughed to himself, but was dis-pleased when an echo tossed him back the long loud roar.

In this manner he journeyed onward three days and two nights, and came, on the third evening, to the mouth of a cave, which, at first sight, reminded him of Elijah's cave at Horeb, though perhaps it more re-sembled Abraham's sepulchral cave at Machpelah. It entered into the heart of a rocky hill. There was so dense a veil of tangled foliage about it, that none but a sworn lover of gloomy recesses would have discovered the low arch of its entrance, or have dared to step within its vaulted chamber, where the burning eyes of a panther might encounter him. If Nature meant this remote and dismal cavern for the use of man, it could only be to bury in its gloom the victims of a pestilence, and then to block up its mouth with stones, and avoid the spot forever after. There was nothing bright nor cheerful near it, except a bubbling fountain, some twenty paces off, at which Richard Digby hardly threw away a glance. But he thrust his head into the cave, shivered, and congratulated himself.

"The finger of Providence hath pointed my way!" cried he, aloud, while the tomb-like den returned a strange echo, as if some one within were mocking him. "Here my soul will be at peace; for the wicked will not find me. Here I can read the Scriptures, and be no more provoked with lying interpretations. Here I can offer up acceptable prayers, because my voice will not be mingled with the sinful supplications of the multitude. Of a truth, the only way to heaven leadeth through the narrow entrance of this cave, — and I alone have found it!"

In regard to this cave it was observable that the roof, so far as the imperfect light permitted it to be seen, was hung with substances resembling opaque icicles; for the damps of unknown centuries, dripping down continually, had become as hard as adamant; and wherever that moisture fell, it seemed to possess the power of converting what it bathed to stone. The fallen leaves and sprigs of foliage, which the wind had swept into the cave, and the little feathery shrubs,

rooted near the threshold, were not wet with a natural
dew, but had been embalmed by this wondrous process.
And here I am put in mind that Richard Digby, before he withdrew himself from the world, was supposed by skilful physicians to have contracted a disease for which no remedy was written in their medical books. It was a deposition of calculous particles
within his heart, caused by an obstructed circulation
of the blood ; and, unless a miracle should be wrought
for him, there was danger that the malady might act
on the entire substance of the organ, and change his
fleshy heart to stone. Many, indeed, affirmed that the
process was already near its consummation. Richard
Digby, however, could never be convinced that any
such direful work was going on within him ; nor when
he saw the sprigs of marble foliage, did his heart even
throb the quicker, at the similitude suggested by these
once tender herbs. It may be that this same insensibility was a symptom of the disease.

Be that as it might, Richard Digby was well contented with his sepulchral cave. So dearly did he love
this congenial spot, that, instead of going a few paces
to the bubbling spring for water, he allayed his thirst
with now and then a drop of moisture from the roof,
which, had it fallen anywhere but on his tongue, would
have been congealed into a pebble. For a man pre-
disposed to stoniness of the heart, this surely was unwholesome liquor. But there he dwelt for three days
more, eating herbs and roots, drinking his own destruction, sleeping, as it were, in a tomb, and awaking to
the solitude of death, yet esteeming this horrible mode
of life as hardly inferior to celestial bliss. Perhaps
superior ; for above the sky, there would be angels to
disturb him. At the close of the third day, he sat in

the portal of his mansion, reading the Bible aloud, because no other ear could profit by it, and reading it amiss, because the rays of the setting sun did not penetrate the dismal depth of shadow round about him, nor fall upon the sacred page. Suddenly, however, a faint gleam of light was thrown over the volume, and raising his eyes, Richard Digby saw that a young woman stood before the mouth of the cave, and that the sunbeams bathed her white garment, which thus seemed to possess a radiance of its own.

"Good evening, Richard," said the girl; "I have come from afar to find thee."

The slender grace and gentle loveliness of this young woman were at once recognized by Richard Digby. Her name was Mary Goffe. She had been a convert to his preaching of the word in England, before he yielded himself to that exclusive bigotry which now enfolded him with such an iron grasp that no other sentiment could reach his bosom. When he came a pilgrim to America, she had remained in her father's hall; but now, as it appeared, had crossed the ocean after him, impelled by the same faith that led other exiles hither, and perhaps by love almost as holy. What else but faith and love united could have sustained so delicate a creature, wandering thus far into the forest, with her golden hair dishevelled by the boughs, and her feet wounded by the thorns? Yet, weary and faint though she must have been, and affrighted at the dreariness of the cave, she looked on the lonely man with a mild and pitying expression, such as might beam from an angel's eyes, towards an afflicted mortal. But the recluse, frowning sternly upon her, and keeping his finger between the leaves of his half-closed Bible, motioned her away with his hand.

"Off!" cried he. "I am sanctified, and thou art sinful. Away!"

"O Richard," said she, earnestly, "I have come this weary way because I heard that a grievous distemper had seized upon thy heart; and a great Physician hath given me the skill to cure it. There is no other remedy than this which I have brought thee. Turn me not away, therefore, nor refuse my medicine; for then must this dismal cave be thy sepulchre."

"Away!" replied Richard Digby, still with a dark frown. "My heart is in better condition than thine own. Leave me, earthly one; for the sun is almost set; and when no light reaches the door of the cave, then is my prayer-time."

Now, great as was her need, Mary Goffe did not plead with this stony-hearted man for shelter and protection, nor ask anything whatever for her own sake. All her zeal was for his welfare.

"Come back with me!" she exclaimed, clasping her hands, — "come back to thy fellow-men; for they need thee, Richard, and thou hast tenfold need of them. Stay not in this evil den; for the air is chill, and the damps are fatal; nor will any that perish within it ever find the path to heaven. Hasten hence, I entreat thee, for thine own soul's sake; for either the roof will fall upon thy head, or some other speedy destruction is at hand."

"Perverse woman!" answered Richard Digby, laughing aloud, — for he was moved to bitter mirth by her foolish vehemence, — "I tell thee that the path to heaven leadeth straight through this narrow portal where I sit. And, moreover, the destruction thou speakest of is ordained, not for this blessed cave, but for all other habitations of mankind, throughout the earth. Get thee hence speedily, that thou mayst have thy share!"

So saying, he opened his Bible again, and fixed his eyes intently on the page, being resolved to withdraw his thoughts from this child of sin and wrath, and to waste no more of his holy breath upon her. The shadow had now grown so deep, where he was sitting, that he made continual mistakes in what he read, converting all that was gracious and merciful to denunciations of vengence and unutterable woe on every created being but himself. Mary Goffe, meanwhile, was leaning against a tree, beside the sepulchral cave, very sad, yet with something heavenly and ethereal in her unselfish sorrow. The light from the setting sun still glorified her form, and was reflected a little way within the darksome den, discovering so terrible a gloom that the maiden shuddered for its self-doomed inhabitant. Espying the bright fountain near at hand, she hastened thither, and scooped up a portion of its water in a cup of birchen bark. A few tears mingled with the draught, and perhaps gave it all its efficacy. She then returned to the mouth of the cave, and knelt down at Richard Digby's feet.

"Richard," she said, with passionate fervor, yet a gentleness in all her passion, "I pray thee, by thy hope of heaven, and as thou wouldst not dwell in this tomb forever, drink of this hallowed water, be it but a single drop! Then, make room for me by thy side, and let us read together one page of that blessed volume; and, lastly, kneel down with me and pray! Do this, and thy stony heart shall become softer than a babe's and all be well."

But Richard Digby, in utter abhorrence of the proposal, cast the Bible at his feet, and eyed her with such a fixed and evil frown, that he looked less like a living man than a marble statue, wrought by some dark-imagined sculptor to express the most repulsive mood that human features could assume. And, as his look grew even devilish, so, with an equal change did Mary Goffe become more sad, more mild, more pitiful, more like a sorrowing angel. But, the more heavenly she was, the more hateful did she seem to Richard Digby, who at length raised his hand, and smote down the cup of hallowed water upon the threshold of the cave, thus rejecting the only medicine that could have cured his stony heart. A sweet perfume lingered in the air for a moment, and then was gone.

"Tempt me no more, accursed woman," exclaimed he, still with his marble frown, "lest I smite thee down also! What hast thou to do with my Bible? — what with my prayers? — what with my heaven?"

No sooner had he spoken these dreadful words, than Richard Digby's heart ceased to beat; while — so the legend says — the form of Mary Goffe melted into the last sunbeams, and returned from the sepulchral cave to heaven. For Mary Goffe had been buried in an English churchyard, months before; and either it was her ghost that haunted the wild forest, or else a dream-like spirit, typifying pure Religion.

Above a century afterwards, when the trackless forest of Richard Digby's day had long been interspersed with settlements, the children of a neighboring farmer were playing at the foot of a hill. The trees, on account of the rude and broken surface of this acclivity, had never been felled, and were crowded so densely together as to hide all but a few rocky prominences, wherever their roots could grapple with the soil. A little boy and girl, to conceal themselves from their playmates, had crept into the deepest shade, where not only the darksome pines, but a thick veil of creeping plants suspended from an overhanging rock, combined to make a twilight at noonday, and almost a midnight at all other seasons. There the children hid themselves, and shouted, repeating the cry at intervals, till the whole party of pursuers were drawn thither, and, pulling aside the matted foliage, let in a doubtful glimpse of daylight. But scarcely was this accomplished, when the little group uttered a simultaneous shriek, and tumbled headlong down the hill, making the best of their way homeward, without a second glance into the gloomy recess. Their father, unable to comprehend what had so startled them, took his axe, and, by felling one or two trees, and tearing away the creeping plants, laid the mystery open to the day. He had discovered the entrance of a cave, closely resembling the mouth of a sepulchre, within which sat the figure of a man, whose gesture and attitude warned the father and children to stand back, while his visage wore a most forbidding frown. This repulsive personage seemed to have been carved in the same gray stone that formed the walls and portal of the cave. On minuter inspection, indeed, such blemishes were observed as made it doubtful whether the figure were really a statue, chiselled by human art, and somewhat worn and defaced by the lapse of ages, or a freak of Nature, who might have chosen to imitate, in stone, her usual handiwork of flesh. Perhaps it was the least unreasonable idea, suggested by this strange spectacle, that the moisture of the cave possessed a petrifying quality, which had thus awfully embalmed a human corpse.

There was something so frightful in the aspect of this Man of Adamant, that the farmer, the moment that he recovered from the fascination of his first gaze, began to heap stones into the mouth of the cavern. His wife, who had followed him to the hill, assisted her husband's efforts. The children, also, approached as near as they durst, with their little hands full of pebbles, and cast them on the pile. Earth was then thrown into the crevices, and the whole fabric overlaid with sods. Thus all traces of the discovery were obliterated, leaving only a marvellous legend, which grew wilder from one generation to another, as the children told it to their grandchildren, and they to their posterity, till few believed that there had ever been a cavern or a statue, where now they saw but a grassy patch on the shadowy hill-side. Yet grown people avoid the spot, nor do children play there. Friendship, and Love, and Piety, all human and celestial sympathies, should keep aloof from that hidden cave ; for there still sits, and, unless an earthquake crumble down the roof upon his head, shall sit forever, the shape of Richard Digby, in the attitude of repelling the whole race of mortals, — not from heaven, — but from the horrible loneliness of his dark, cold sepulchre !

THE DEVIL IN MANUSCRIPT.

On a bitter evening of December, I arrived by mail in a large town, which was then the residence of an intimate friend, one of those gifted youths who cultivate poetry and the belles-lettres, and call themselves students at law. My first business, after supper, was to visit him at the office of his distinguished instructor. As I have said, it was a bitter night, clear starlight, but cold as Nova Zembla, — the shop-windows along the street being frosted, so as almost to hide the lights, while the wheels of coaches thundered equally loud over frozen earth and pavements of stone. There was no snow, either on the ground or the roofs of the houses. The wind blew so violently, that I had but to spread my cloak like a main-sail, and scud along the street at the rate of ten knots, greatly envied by other navigators, who were beating slowly up, with the gale right in their teeth. One of these I capsized, but was gone on the wings of the wind before he could even vociferate an oath.

After this picture of an inclement night, behold us seated by a great blazing fire, which looked so comfortable and delicious that I felt inclined to lie down and roll among the hot coals. The usual furniture of a lawyer's office was around us, — rows of volumes in sheepskin, and a multitude of writs, summonses, and other legal papers, scattered over the desks and tables. But there were certain objects which seemed to intimate that we had little dread of the intrusion of clients, or of the learned counsellor himself, who, indeed, was attending court in a distant town. A tall, decanter-shaped bottle stood on the table, between two tumblers, and beside a pile of blotted manuscripts, altogether dissimilar to any law documents recognized in our courts. My friend, whom I shall call Oberon, — it was a name of fancy and friendship between him and me, — my friend Oberon looked at these papers with a peculiar expression of disquietude.

"I do believe," said he, soberly, " or, at least, I could believe, if I chose, that there is a devil in this pile of blotted papers. You have read them, and know what I mean, — that conception in which I endeavored to embody the character of a fiend, as represented in our traditions and the written records of witchcraft. Oh, I have a horror of what was created in my own brain, and shudder at the manuscripts in which I gave that dark idea a sort of material existence ! Would they were out of my sight ! "

" And of mine, too," thought I.

" You remember," continued Oberon, " how the hellish thing used to suck away the happiness of those who, by a simple concession that seemed almost innocent, subjected themselves to his power. Just so my peace is gone, and all by these accursed manuscripts. Have you felt nothing of the same influence ? "

" Nothing," replied I, " unless the spell be hid in a desire to turn novelist, after reading your delightful tales."

" Novelist ! " exclaimed Oberon, half seriously. " Then, indeed, my devil has his claw on you ! You are gone ! You cannot even pray for deliverance ! But we will be the last and only victims ; for this night I mean to burn the manuscripts, and commit the fiend to his retribution in the flames."

"Burn your tales!" repeated I, startled at the desperation of the idea.

"Even so," said the author, despondingly. "You cannot conceive what an effect the composition of these tales has had on me. I have become ambitious of a bubble, and careless of solid reputation. I am surrounding myself with shadows, which bewilder me, by aping the realities of life. They have drawn me aside from the beaten path of the world, and led me into a strange sort of solitude, — a solitude in the midst of men, — where nobody wishes for what I do, nor thinks nor feels as I do. The tales have done all this. When they are ashes, perhaps I shall be as I was before they had existence. Moreover, the sacrifice is less than you may suppose, since nobody will publish them."

"That does make a difference, indeed," said I.

"They have been offered, by letter," continued Oberon, reddening with vexation, "to some seventeen booksellers. It would make you stare to read their answers; and read them you should, only that I burnt them as fast as they arrived. One man publishes nothing but school-books; another has five novels already under examination."

"What a voluminous mass the unpublished literature of America must be!" cried I.

"Oh, the Alexandrian manuscripts were nothing to it!" said my friend. "Well, another gentleman is just giving up business, on purpose, I verily believe, to escape publishing my book. Several, however, would not absolutely decline the agency, on my advancing half the cost of an edition, and giving bonds for the remainder, besides a high percentage to themselves, whether the book sells or not. Another advises a subscription."

" The villain ! " exclaimed I.

" A fact ! " said Oberon. " In short, of all the seventeen booksellers, only one has vouchsafed even to read my tales ; and he — a literary dabbler himself, I should judge — has the impertinence to criticise them, proposing what he calls vast improvements, and concluding, after a general sentence of condemnation, with the definitive assurance that he will not be concerned on any terms."

" It might not be amiss to pull that fellow's nose," remarked I.

" If the whole ' trade ' had one common nose, there would be some satisfaction in pulling it," answered the author. " But, there does seem to be one honest man among these seventeen unrighteous ones ; and he tells me fairly, that no American publisher will meddle with an American work, — seldom if by a known writer, and never if by a new one, — unless at the writer's risk."

" The paltry rogues ! " cried I. " Will they live by literature, and yet risk nothing for its sake ? But, after all, you might publish on your own account."

" And so I might," replied Oberon. " But the devil of the business is this. These people have put me so out of conceit with the tales, that I loathe the very thought of them, and actually experience a physical sickness of the stomach, whenever I glance at them on the table. I tell you there is a demon in them ! I anticipate a wild enjoyment in seeing them in the blaze ; such as I should feel in taking vengeance on an enemy, or destroying something noxious."

I did not very strenuously oppose this determination, being privately of opinion, in spite of my partiality for the author, that his tales would make a more brilliant appearance in the fire than anywhere else. Before proceeding to execution, we broached the bottle of champagne, which Oberon had provided for keeping up his spirits in this doleful business. We swallowed each a tumblerful, in sparkling commotion; it went bubbling down our throats, and brightened my eyes at once, but left my friend sad and heavy as before. He drew the tales towards him, with a mixture of natural affection and natural disgust, like a father taking a deformed infant into his arms.

"Pooh! Pish! Pshaw!" exclaimed he, holding them at arm's-length. " It was Gray's idea of heaven, to lounge on a sofa and read new novels. Now, what more appropriate torture would Dante himself have contrived, for the sinner who perpetrates a bad book, than to be continually turning over the manuscript?"

" It would fail of effect," said I, " because a bad author is always his own great admirer."

" I lack that one characteristic of my tribe, — the only desirable one," observed Oberon. " But how many recollections throng upon me, as I turn over these leaves! This scene came into my fancy as I walked along a hilly road, on a starlight October evening; in the pure and bracing air, I became all soul, and felt as if I could climb the sky, and run a race along the Milky-Way. Here is another tale, in which I wrapt myself during a dark and dreary night-ride in the month of March, till the rattling of the wheels and the voices of my companions seemed like faint sounds of a dream, and my visions a bright reality. That scribbled page describes shadows which I summoned to my bedside at midnight: they would not depart when I bade them; the gray dawn came, and found me wide awake and feverish, the victim of my own enchantments!"

"There must have been a sort of happiness in all this," said I, smitten with a strange longing to make proof of it.

"There may be happiness in a fever fit," replied the author. "And then the various moods in which I wrote! Sometimes my ideas were like precious stones under the earth, requiring toil to dig them up, and care to polish and brighten them; but often a delicious stream of thought would gush out upon the page at once, like water sparkling up suddenly in the desert; and when it had passed, I gnawed my pen hopelessly, or blundered on with cold and miserable toil, as if there were a wall of ice between me and my subject."

"Do you now perceive a corresponding difference," inquired I, "between the passages which you wrote so coldly, and those fervid flashes of the mind?"

"No," said Oberon, tossing the manuscripts on the table. "I find no traces of the golden pen with which I wrote in characters of fire. My treasure of fairy coin is changed to worthless dross. My picture, painted in what seemed the loveliest hues, presents nothing but a faded and indistinguishable surface. I have been eloquent and poetical and humorous in a dream, — and behold! it is all nonsense, now that I am awake."

My friend now threw sticks of wood and dry chips upon the fire, and seeing it blaze like Nebuchadnezzar's furnace, seized the champagne-bottle, and drank two or three brimming bumpers, successively. The heady liquor combined with his agitation to throw him into a species of rage. He laid violent hands on the tales. In one instant more, their faults and beauties would alike have vanished in a glowing purgatory. But, all at once, I remembered passages of high imagination, deep pathos, original thoughts, and points of such varied excellence, that the vastness of the sacrifice struck me most forcibly.   I caught his arm.

"Surely, you do not mean to burn them!" I exclaimed.

"Let me alone!" cried Oberon, his eyes flashing fire. "I will burn them! Not a scorched syllable shall escape! Would you have me a damned author? — To undergo sneers, taunts, abuse, and cold neglect, and faint praise, bestowed, for pity's sake, against the giver's conscience! A hissing and a laughing-stock to my own traitorous thoughts! An outlaw from the protection of the grave, — one whose ashes every careless foot might spurn, unhonored in life, and remembered scornfully in death! Am I to bear all this, when yonder fire will insure me from the whole? No! There go the tales! May my hand wither when it would write another!"

The deed was done. He had thrown the manuscripts into the hottest of the fire, which at first seemed to shrink away, but soon curled around them, and made them a part of its own fervent brightness. Oberon stood gazing at the conflagration, and shortly began to soliloquize, in the wildest strain, as if Fancy resisted and became riotous, at the moment when he would have compelled her to ascend that funeral pile. His words described objects which he appeared to discern in the fire, fed by his own precious thoughts; perhaps the thousand visions which the writer's magic had incorporated with these pages became visible to him in the dissolving heat, brightening forth ere they vanished forever; while the smoke, the vivid sheets of flame, the ruddy and whitening coals, caught the aspect of a varied scenery.

" They blaze," said he, " as if I had steeped them in
the intensest spirit of genius.   There I see my lovers
clasped in each other's arms.   How pure the flame
that bursts from their glowing hearts !   And yonder
the features of a villain writhing in the fire that shall
torment him to eternity.   My holy men, my pious and
angelic women, stand like martyrs amid the flames,
their mild eyes lifted heavenward.   Ring out the bells !
A city is on fire.   See ! — destruction roars through
my dark forests, while the lakes boil up in steaming
billows, and the mountains are volcanoes, and the sky
kindles with a lurid brightness !   All elements are but
one pervading flame !   Ha !   The fiend ! "

I was somewhat startled by this latter exclamation.
The tales were almost consumed, but just then threw
forth a broad sheet of fire, which flickered as with
laughter, making the whole room dance in its brightness, and then roared portentously up the chimney.

" You saw him ?   You must have seen him ! " cried
Oberon.   " How he glared at me and laughed, in that
last sheet of flame, with just the features that I imagined for him !   Well !   The tales are gone."

The papers were indeed reduced to a heap of black
cinders, with a multitude of sparks hurrying confus-
edly among them, the traces of the pen being now
represented by white lines, and the whole mass fluttering to and fro in the draughts of air.   The destroyer
knelt down to look at them.

" What is more potent than fire ! " said he, in his
gloomiest tone.   " Even thought, invisible and incor-
poreal as it is, cannot escape it.   In this little time, it
has annihilated the creations of long nights and days,
which I could no more reproduce, in their first glow
and freshness, than cause ashes and whitened bones

to rise up and live. There, too, I sacrificed the unborn children of my mind. All that I had accomplished — all that I planned for future years — has perished by one common ruin, and left only this heap of embers! The deed has been my fate. And what remains? A weary and aimless life, — a long repentance of this hour, — and at last an obscure grave, where they will bury and forget me!"

As the author concluded his dolorous moan, the extinguished embers arose and settled down and arose again, and finally flew up the chimney, like a demon with sable wings. Just as they disappeared, there was a loud and solitary cry in the street below us. "Fire!" Fire! Other voices caught up that terrible word, and it speedily became the shout of a multitude. Oberon started to his feet, in fresh excitement.

"A fire on such a night!" cried he. "The wind blows a gale, and wherever it whirls the flames, the roofs will flash up like gunpowder. Every pump is frozen up, and boiling water would turn to ice the moment it was flung from the engine. In an hour, this wooden town will be one great bonfire! What a glorious scene for my next — Pshaw!"

The street was now all alive with footsteps, and the air full of voices. We heard one engine thundering round a corner, and another rattling from a distance over the pavements. The bells of three steeples clanged out at once, spreading the alarm to many a neighboring town, and expressing hurry, confusion, and terror, so inimitably that I could almost distinguish in their peal the burden of the universal cry, — "Fire! Fire! Fire!"

"What is so eloquent as their iron tongues!" exclaimed Oberon. "My heart leaps and trembles, but not with fear. And that other sound, too, — deep and awful as a mighty organ, — the roar and thunder of the multitude on the pavement below! Come! We are losing time. I will cry out in the loudest of the uproar, and mingle my spirit with the wildest of the confusion, and be a bubble on the top of the ferment!"

From the first outcry, my forebodings had warned me of the true object and centre of alarm. There was nothing now but uproar, above, beneath, and around us; footsteps stumbling pell-mell up the public staircase, eager shouts and heavy thumps at the door, the whiz and dash of water from the engines, and the crash of furniture thrown upon the pavement. At once, the truth flashed upon my friend. His frenzy took the hue of joy, and, with a wild gesture of exultation, he leaped almost to the ceiling of the chamber.

"My tales!" cried Oberon. "The chimney! The roof! The Fiend has gone forth by night, and startled thousands in fear and wonder from their beds! Here I stand, — a triumphant author! Huzza! Huzza! My brain has set the town on fire! Huzza!"

JOHN INGLEFIELD'S THANKSGIVING.

On the evening of Thanksgiving Day, John Inglefield, the blacksmith, sat in his elbow-chair, among
those who had been keeping festival at his board. Being the central figure of the domestic circle, the fire
threw its strongest light on his massive and sturdy
frame, reddening his rough visage, so that it looked
like the head of an iron statue, all aglow from his own
forge, and with its features rudely fashioned on his
own anvil. At John Inglefield's right hand was an
empty chair. The other places round the hearth were
filled by the members of the family, who all sat quietly,
while, with a semblance of fantastic merriment, their
shadows danced on the wall behind them. One of the
group was John Inglefield's son, who had been bred
at college, and was now a student of theology at An-
dover. There was also a daughter of sixteen, whom
nobody could look at without thinking of a rose-bud
almost blossomed. The only other person at the fireside was Robert Moore, formerly an apprentice of the
blacksmith, but now his journeyman, and who seemed
more like an own son of John Inglefield than did the
pale and slender student.

Only these four had kept New England's festival
beneath that roof. The vacant chair at John Inglefield's right hand was in memory of his wife, whom
death had snatched from him since the previous
Thanksgiving. With a feeling that few would have
looked for in his rough nature, the bereaved husband

had himself set the chair in its place next his own; and often did his eye glance thitherward, as if he deemed it possible that the cold grave might send back its tenant to the cheerful fireside, at least for that one evening. Thus did he cherish the grief that was dear to him. But there was another grief which he would fain have torn from his heart; or, since that could never be, have buried it too deep for others to behold, or for his own remembrance. Within the past year another member of his household had gone from him, but not to the grave. Yet they kept no vacant chair for her.

While John Inglefield and his family were sitting round the hearth with the shadows dancing behind them on the wall, the outer door was opened, and a light footstep came along the passage. The latch of the inner door was lifted by some familiar hand, and a young girl came in, wearing a cloak and hood, which she took off, and laid on the table beneath the looking-glass. Then, after gazing a moment at the fireside circle, she approached, and took the seat at John Inglefield's right hand, as if it had been reserved on purpose for her.

"Here I am, at last, father," said she. "You ate your Thanksgiving dinner without me, but I have come back to spend the evening with you."

Yes, it was Prudence Inglefield. She wore the same neat and maidenly attire which she had been accustomed to put on when the household work was over for the day, and her hair was parted from her brow, in the simple and modest fashion that became her best of all. If her cheek might otherwise have been pale, yet the glow of the fire suffused it with a healthful bloom. If she had spent the many months of her absence in guilt and infamy, yet they seemed to have left no traces on her gentle aspect. She could not have looked less altered, had she merely stepped away from her father's fireside for half an hour, and returned while the blaze was quivering upwards from the same brands that were burning at her departure. And to John Inglefield she was the very image of his buried wife, such as he remembered her on the first Thanksgiving which they had passed under their own roof. Therefore, though naturally a stern and rugged man, he could not speak unkindly to his sinful child, nor yet could he take her to his bosom.

"You are welcome home, Prudence," said he, glancing sideways at her, and his voice faltered. "Your mother would have rejoiced to see you, but she has been gone from us these four months."

"I know it, father, I know it," replied Prudence, quickly. "And yet, when I first came in, my eyes were so dazzled by the firelight, that she seemed to be sitting in this very chair!"

By this time the other members of the family had begun to recover from their surprise, and became sensible that it was no ghost from the grave, nor vision of their vivid recollections, but Prudence, her own self. Her brother was the next that greeted her. He advanced and held out his hand affectionately, as a brother should; yet not entirely like a brother, for, with all his kindness, he was still a clergyman, and speaking to a child of sin.

"Sister Prudence," said he, earnestly, "I rejoice that a merciful Providence hath turned your steps homeward, in time for me to bid you a last farewell. In a few weeks, sister, I am to sail as a missionary to the far islands of the Pacific. There is not one of these beloved faces that I shall ever hope to behold again on this earth. Oh, may I see all of them — yours and all — beyond the grave ! "

A shadow flitted across the girl's countenance.

" The grave is very dark, brother," answered she, withdrawing her hand somewhat hastily from his grasp. "You must look your last at me by the light of this fire."

While this was passing, the twin-girl — the rose-bud that had grown on the same stem with the castaway — stood gazing at her sister, longing to fling herself upon her bosom, so that the tendrils of their hearts might intertwine again. At first she was restrained by mingled grief and shame, and by a dread that Prudence was too much changed to respond to her affection, or that her own purity would be felt as a reproach by the lost one. But, as she listened to the familiar voice, while the face grew more and more familiar, she forgot everything save that Prudence had come back. Springing forward, she would have clasped her in a close embrace. At that very instant, however, Prudence started from her chair, and held out both her hands, with a warning gesture.

" No, Mary, — no, my sister," cried she, " do not you touch me. Your bosom must not be pressed to mine ! "

Mary shuddered and stood still, for she felt that something darker than the grave was between Prudence and herself, though they seemed so near each other in the light of their father's hearth, where they had grown up together. Meanwhile Prudence threw her eyes around the room, in search of one who had not yet bidden her welcome. He had withdrawn from his seat by the fireside, and was standing near the door,

with his face averted, so that his features could be discerned only by the flickering shadow of the profile
upon the wall. But Prudence called to him, in a
cheerful and kindly tone : —

"Come, Robert," said she, "won't you shake hands
with your old friend?"

Robert Moore held back for a moment, but affection struggled powerfully, and overcame his pride and
resentment; he rushed towards Prudence, seized her
hand, and pressed it to his bosom.

"There, there, Robert!" said she, smiling sadly, as
she withdrew her hand, "you must not give me too
warm a welcome."

And now, having exchanged greetings with each
member of the family, Prudence again seated herself
in the chair at John Inglefield's right hand. She was
naturally a girl of quick and tender sensibilities, glad-
some in her general mood, but with a bewitching
pathos interfused among her merriest words and
deeds. It was remarked of her, too, that she had a
faculty, even from childhood, of throwing her own
feelings, like a spell, over her companions. Such as
she had been in her days of innocence, so did she appear this evening. Her friends, in the surprise and
bewilderment of her return, almost forgot that she had
ever left them, or that she had forfeited any of her
claims to their affection. In the morning, perhaps,
they might have looked at her with altered eyes, but
by the Thanksgiving fireside they felt only that their
own Prudence had come back to them, and were
thankful. John Inglefield's rough visage brightened
with the glow of his heart, as it grew warm and merry
within him; once or twice, even, he laughed till the
room rang again, yet seemed startled by the echo of

his own mirth. The grave young minister became as frolicksome as a school-boy. Mary, too, the rose-bud, forgot that her twin-blossom had ever been torn from the stem, and trampled in the dust. And as for Robert Moore, he gazed at Prudence with the bashful earnestness of love new-born, while she, with sweet maiden coquetry, half smiled upon and half discouraged him.

In short, it was one of those intervals when sorrow vanishes in its own depth of shadow, and joy starts forth in transitory brightness. When the clock struck eight, Prudence poured out her father's customary draught of herb-tea, which had been steeping by the fireside ever since twilight.

"God bless you, child!" said John Inglefield, as he took the cup from her hand; "you have made your old father happy again. But we miss your mother sadly, Prudence, sadly. It seems as if she ought to be here now."

"Now, father, or never," replied Prudence.

It was now the hour for domestic worship. But while the family were making preparations for this duty, they suddenly perceived that Prudence had put on her cloak and hood, and was lifting the latch of the door.

"Prudence, Prudence! where are you going?" cried they all, with one voice.

As Prudence passed out of the door she turned towards them, and flung back her hand with a gesture of farewell. But her face was so changed that they hardly recognized it. Sin and evil passions glowed through its comeliness, and wrought a horrible deformity; a smile gleamed in her eyes, as of triumphant mockery, at their surprise and grief.

"Daughter," cried John Inglefield, between wrath and sorrow, "stay and be your father's blessing, or take his curse with you!"

For an instant Prudence lingered and looked back into the fire-lighted room, while her countenance wore almost the expression as if she were struggling with a fiend, who had power to seize his victim even within the hallowed precincts of her father's hearth. The fiend prevailed; and Prudence vanished into the outer darkness. When the family rushed to the door, they could see nothing, but heard the sound of wheels rattling over the frozen ground.

That same night, among the painted beauties at the theatre of a neighboring city, there was one whose dissolute mirth seemed inconsistent with any sympathy for pure affections, and for the joys and griefs which are hallowed by them. Yet this was Prudence Inglefield. Her visit to the Thanksgiving fireside was the realization of one of those waking dreams in which the guilty soul will sometimes stray back to its innocence. But Sin, alas! is careful of her bond-slaves; they hear her voice, perhaps, at the holiest moment, and are constrained to go whither she summons them. The same dark power that drew Prudence Inglefield from her father's hearth — the same in its nature, though heightened then to a dread necessity — would snatch a guilty soul from the gate of heaven, and make its sin and its punishment alike eternal.

OLD TICONDEROGA:

A PICTURE OF THE PAST.

THE greatest attraction, in this vicinity, is the famous old fortress of Ticonderoga, the remains of which are visible from the piazza of the tavern, on a swell of land that shuts in the prospect of the lake. Those celebrated heights, Mount Defiance and Mount Independence, familiar to all Americans in history, stand too prominent not to be recognized, though neither of them precisely corresponds to the images excited by their names. In truth, the whole scene, except the interior of the fortress, disappointed me. Mount Defiance, which one pictures as a steep, lofty, and rugged hill, of most formidable aspect, frowning down with the grim visage of a precipice on old Ticonderoga, is merely a long and wooded ridge; and bore, at some former period, the gentle name of Sugar Hill. The brow is certainly difficult to climb, and high enough to look into every corner of the fortress. St. Clair's most probable reason, however, for neglecting to occupy it, was the deficiency of troops to man the works already constructed, rather than the supposed inaccessibility of Mount Defiance. It is singular that the French never fortified this height, standing, as it does, in the quarter whence they must have looked for the advance of a British army.

In my first view of the ruins, I was favored with the scientific guidance of a young lieutenant of engineers, recently from West Point, where he had gained credit for great military genius. I saw nothing but confusion in what chiefly interested him; straight lines and zigzags, defence within defence, wall opposed to wall, and ditch intersecting ditch; oblong squares of masonry below the surface of the earth, and huge mounds, or turf-covered hills of stone, above it. On one of these artificial hillocks, a pine-tree has rooted itself, and grown tall and strong, since the banner-staff was levelled. But where my unmilitary glance could trace no regularity, the young lieutenant was perfectly at home. He fathomed the meaning of every ditch, and formed an entire plan of the fortress from its half-obliterated lines. His description of Ticonderoga would be as accurate as a geometrical theorem, and as barren of the poetry that has clustered round its decay. I viewed Ticonderoga as a place of ancient strength, in ruins for half a century: where the flags of three nations had successively waved, and none waved now; where armies had struggled, so long ago that the bones of the slain were mouldered; where Peace had found a heritage in the forsaken haunts of War. Now the young West-Pointer, with his lectures on ravelins, counterscarps, angles, and covered ways, made it an affair of brick and mortar and hewn stone, arranged on certain regular principles, having a good deal to do with mathematics, but nothing at all with poetry.

I should have been glad of a hoary veteran to totter by my side, and tell me, perhaps, of the French garrisons and their Indian allies, — of Abercrombie, Lord Howe, and Amherst, — of Ethan Allen's triumph and St. Clair's surrender. The old soldier and the old fortress would be emblems of each other. His reminiscences, though vivid as the image of Ticonderoga in the lake, would harmonize with the gray influence of the scene. A survivor of the long-disbanded garrisons, though but a private soldier, might have mustered his dead chiefs and comrades, — some from Westminster Abbey, and English churchyards, and battle - fields in Europe, — others from their graves here in America, — others, not a few, who lie sleeping round the fortress ; he might have mustered them all, and bid them march through the ruined gateway, turning their old historic faces on me, as they passed. Next to such a companion, the best is one's own fancy.

At another visit I was alone, and, after rambling all over the ramparts, sat down to rest myself in one of the roofless barracks. These are old French structures, and appear to have occupied three sides of a large area, now overgrown with grass, nettles, and thistles. The one in which I sat was long and narrow, as all the rest had been, with peaked gables. The exterior walls were nearly entire, constructed of gray, flat, unpicked stones, the aged strength of which promised long to resist the elements, if no other violence should precipitate their fall. The roof, floors, partitions, and the rest of the wood-work had probably been burnt, except some bars of staunch old oak, which were blackened with fire, but still remained imbedded into the window-sills and over the doors. There were a few particles of plastering near the chimney, scratched with rude figures, perhaps by a soldier's hand. A most luxuriant crop of weeds had sprung up within the edifice, and hid the scattered fragments of the wall. Grass and weeds grew in the windows, and in all the crevices of the stone, climbing, step by step, till a tuft of yellow flowers was waving on the highest peak of the gable. Some spicy herb diffused pleasant odor through the ruin. A verdant heap of vegetation had covered the hearth of the second floor, clustering on the very spot where the huge logs had mouldered to glowing coals, and flourished beneath the broad flue, which had so often puffed the smoke over a circle of French or English soldiers. I felt that there was no other token of decay so impressive as that bed of weeds in the place of the backlog.

Here I sat, with those roofless walls about me, the clear sky over my head, and the afternoon sunshine falling gently bright through the window-frames and doorway. I heard the tinkling of a cow-bell, the twittering of birds, and the pleasant hum of insects. Once a gay butterfly, with four gold-speckled wings, came and fluttered about my head, then flew up and lighted on the highest tuft of yellow flowers, and at last took wing across the lake. Next a bee buzzed through the sunshine, and found much sweetness among the weeds. After watching him till he went off to his distant hive, I closed my eyes on Ticonderoga in ruins, and cast a dream-like glance over pictures of the past, and scenes of which this spot had been the theatre.

At first, my fancy saw only the stern hills, lonely lakes, and venerable woods. Not a tree, since their seeds were first scattered over the infant soil, had felt the axe, but had grown up and flourished through its long generation, had fallen beneath the weight of years, been buried in green moss, and nourished the roots of others as gigantic. Hark! A light paddle dips into the lake, a birch canoe glides round the point, and an Indian chief has passed, painted and feather-crested, armed with a bow of hickory, a stone tomahawk, and flint-headed arrows. But the ripple had hardly vanished from the water, when a white flag caught the breeze, over a castle in the wilderness, with frowning ramparts and a hundred cannon. There stood a French chevalier, commandant of the fortress, paying court to a copper-colored lady, the princess of the land, and winning her wild love by the arts which had been successful with Parisian dames. A war-party of French and Indians were issuing from the gate to lay waste some village of New England. Near the fortress there was a group of dancers. The merry soldiers footing it with the swart savage maids; deeper in the wood, some red men were growing frantic around a keg of the fire-water; and elsewhere a Jesuit preached the faith of high cathedrals beneath a canopy of forest boughs, and distributed crucifixes to be worn beside English scalps.

I tried to make a series of pictures from the Old French War, when fleets were on the lake and armies in the woods, and especially of Abercrombie's disastrous repulse, where thousands of lives were utterly thrown away; but, being at a loss how to order the battle, I chose an evening scene in the barracks, after the fortress had surrendered to Sir Jeffrey Amherst. What an immense fire blazes on that hearth, gleaming on swords, bayonets, and musket-barrels, and blending with the hue of the scarlet coats till the whole barrack-room is quivering with ruddy light! One soldier has thrown himself down to rest, after a deer-hunt, or perhaps a long run through the woods with Indians on his trail. Two stand up to wrestle, and are on the point of coming to blows. A fifer plays a shrill accompaniment to a drummer's song, — a strain of light love and bloody war, with a chorus thundered forth by twenty voices. Meantime, a veteran in the corner is prosing about Dettingen and Fontenoy, and relates camp-traditions of Marlborough's battles, till his pipe, having been roguishly charged with gunpowder, makes a terrible explosion under his nose. And now they all vanish in a puff of smoke from the chimney.

I merely glanced at the ensuing twenty years, which glided peacefully over the frontier fortress, till Ethan Allen's shout was heard, summoning it to surrender " in the name of the great Jehovah and of the Continental Congress." Strange allies! thought the British captain. Next came the hurried muster of the soldiers of liberty, when the cannon of Burgoyne, pointing down upon their stronghold from the brow of Mount Defiance, announced a new conqueror of Ticonderoga. No virgin fortress, this! Forth rushed the motley throng from the barracks, one man wearing the blue and buff of the Union, another the red coat of Britain, a third a dragoon's jacket, and a fourth a cotton frock ; here was a pair of leather breeches, and striped trousers there ; a grenadier's cap on one head, and a broad-brimmed hat, with a tall feather, on the next ; this fellow shouldering a king's arm, that might throw a bullet to Crown Point, and his comrade a long fowling-piece, admirable to shoot ducks on the lake. In the midst of the bustle, when the fortress was all alive with its last warlike scene, the ringing of a bell on the lake made me suddenly unclose my eyes, and behold only the gray and weed-grown ruins. They were as peaceful in the sun as a warrior's grave.

Hastening to the rampart, I perceived that the signal had been given by the steamboat Franklin, which landed a passenger from Whitehall at the tavern, and resumed its progress northward, to reach Canada the next morning. A sloop was pursuing the same track ; a little skiff had just crossed the ferry ; while a scow, laden with lumber, spread its huge square sail, and went up the lake. The whole country was a cultivated farm. Within musket-shot of the ramparts lay the neat villa of Mr. Pell, who, since the Revolution, has become proprietor of a spot for which France, England, and America have so often struggled. How forcibly the lapse of time and change of circumstances came home to my apprehension ! Banner would never wave again, nor cannon roar, nor blood be shed, nor trumpet stir up a soldier's heart, in this old fort of Ticonderoga. Tall trees have grown upon its ramparts, since the last garrison marched out, to return no more, or only at some dreamer's summons, gliding from the twilight past to vanish among realities.

THE WIVES OF THE DEAD.

THE following story, the simple and domestic incidents of which may be deemed scarcely worth relating, after such a lapse of time, awakened some degree of interest, a hundred years ago, in a principal seaport of the Bay Province. The rainy twilight of an autumn day, — a parlor on the second floor of a small house, plainly furnished, as beseemed the middling circumstances of its inhabitants, yet decorated with little curiosities from beyond the sea, and a few delicate specimens of Indian manufacture, — these are the only particulars to be premised in regard to scene and season. Two young and comely women sat together by the fireside, nursing their mutual and peculiar sorrows. They were the recent brides of two brothers, a sailor and a landsman, and two successive days had brought tidings of the death of each, by the chances of Canadian warfare and the tempestuous Atlantic. The universal sympathy excited by this bereavement drew numerous condoling guests to the habitation of the widowed sisters. Several, among whom was the minister, had remained till the verge of evening, when, one by one, whispering many comfortable passages of Scripture that were answered by more abundant tears, they took their leave, and departed to their own happier homes. The mourners, though not insensible to the kindness of their friends, had yearned to be left alone. United, as they had been, by the relationship of the living, and now more closely so by that of the dead, each felt as if whatever consolation her grief admitted were to be found in the bosom of the other. They joined their hearts, and wept together silently. But after an hour of such indulgence, one of the sisters, all of whose emotions were influenced by her mild, quiet, yet not feeble character, began to recollect the precepts of resignation and endurance which piety had taught her, when she did not think to need them. Her misfortune, besides, as earliest known, should earliest cease to interfere with her regular course of duties ; accordingly, having placed the table before the fire, and arranged a frugal meal, she took the hand of her companion.

" Come, dearest sister ; you have eaten not a morsel to-day," she said. " Arise, I pray you, and let us ask a blessing on that which is provided for us."

Her sister-in-law was of a lively and irritable temperament, and the first pangs of her sorrow had been expressed by shrieks and passionate lamentation. She now shrunk from Mary's words, like a wounded sufferer from a hand that revives the throb.

" There is no blessing left for me, neither will I ask it ! " cried Margaret, with a fresh burst of tears. " Would it were His will that I might never taste food more ! "

Yet she trembled at these rebellious expressions, almost as soon as they were uttered, and, by degrees, Mary succeeded in bringing her sister's mind nearer to the situation of her own. Time went on, and their usual hour of repose arrived. The brothers and their brides, entering the married state with no more than the slender means which then sanctioned such a step, had confederated themselves in one household, with equal rights to the parlor, and claiming exclusive privileges in two sleeping-rooms contiguous to it. Thither the widowed ones retired, after heaping ashes upon the dying embers of their fire, and placing a lighted lamp upon the hearth. The doors of both chambers were left open, so that a part of the interior of each, and the beds, with their unclosed curtains, were reciprocally visible. Sleep did not steal upon the sisters at one and the same time. Mary experienced the effect often consequent upon grief quietly borne, and soon sunk into temporary forgetfulness; while Margaret became more disturbed and feverish, in proportion as the night advanced with its deepest and stillest hours. She lay listening to the drops of rain that came down in monotonous succession, unswayed by a breath of wind; and a nervous impulse continually caused her to lift her head from the pillow, and gaze into Mary's chamber and the intermediate apartment. The cold light of the lamp threw the shadows of the furniture up against the wall, stamping them immovably there, except when they were shaken by a sudden flicker of the flame. Two vacant arm-chairs were in their old positions on opposite sides of the hearth, where the brothers had been wont to sit in young and laughing dignity, as heads of families; two humbler seats were near them, the true thrones of that little empire, where Mary and herself had exercised in love a power that love had won. The cheerful radiance of the fire had shone upon the happy circle, and the dead glimmer of the lamp might have befitted their reunion now. While Margaret groaned in bitterness, she heard a knock at the street-door.

"How would my heart have leapt at that sound but yesterday!" thought she, remembering the anxiety with which she had long awaited tidings from her hus-

band. "I care not for it now ; let them begone, for
I will not arise."

But even while a sort of childish fretfulness made
her thus resolve, she was breathing hurriedly, and
straining her ears to catch a repetition of the summons. It is difficult to be convinced of the death of
one whom we have deemed another self. The knocking was now renewed in slow and regular strokes, apparently given with the soft end of a doubled fist, and
was accompanied by words, faintly heard through several thicknesses of wall. Margaret looked to her sister's chamber, and beheld her still lying in the depths
of sleep. She arose, placed her foot upon the floor,
and slightly arrayed herself, trembling between fear
and eagerness as she did so.

"Heaven help me !" sighed she. "I have nothing
left to fear, and methinks I am ten times more a cow-
ard than ever."

Seizing the lamp from the hearth, she hastened to
the window that overlooked the street-door. It was a
lattice, turning upon hinges ; and having thrown it
back, she stretched her head a little way into the moist
atmosphere. A lantern was reddening the front of
the house, and melting its light in the neighboring
puddles, while a deluge of darkness overwhelmed every
other object. As the window grated on its hinges, a
man in a broad-brimmed hat and blanket-coat stepped
from under the shelter of the projecting story, and
looked upward to discover whom his application had
aroused. Margaret knew him as a friendly innkeeper
of the town.

"What would you have, Goodman Parker ?" cried
the widow.

"Lackaday, is it you, Mistress Margaret ?" replied

the innkeeper. "I was afraid it might be your sister Mary; for I hate to see a young woman in trouble, when I have n't a word of comfort to whisper her."

"For Heaven's sake, what news do you bring?" screamed Margaret.

"Why, there has been an express through the town within this half-hour," said Goodman Parker, "travelling from the eastern jurisdiction with letters from the governor and council. He tarried at my house to refresh himself with a drop and a morsel, and I asked him what tidings on the frontiers. He tells me we had the better in the skirmish you wot of, and that thirteen men reported slain are well and sound, and your husband among them. Besides, he is appointed of the escort to bring the captivated Frenchers and Indians home to the province jail. I judged you would n't mind being broke of your rest, and so I stepped over to tell you. Good night."

So saying, the honest man departed; and his lantern gleamed along the street, bringing to view indistinct shapes of things, and the fragments of a world, like order glimmering through chaos, or memory roaming over the past. But Margaret stayed not to watch these picturesque effects. Joy flashed into her heart, and lighted it up at once; and breathless, and with winged steps, she flew to the bedside of her sister. She paused, however, at the door of the chamber, while a thought of pain broke in upon her.

"Poor Mary!" said she to herself. "Shall I waken her, to feel her sorrow sharpened by my happiness? No; I will keep it within my own bosom till the morrow."

She approached the bed, to discover if Mary's sleep were peaceful. Her face was turned partly inward to the pillow, and had been hidden there to weep; but a look of motionless contentment was now visible upon it, as if her heart, like a deep lake, had grown calm because its dead had sunk down so far within. Happy is it, and strange, that the lighter sorrows are those from which dreams are chiefly fabricated. Margaret shrunk from disturbing her sister-in-law, and felt as if her own better fortune had rendered her involuntarily unfaithful, and as if altered and diminished affection must be the consequence of the disclosure she had to make. With a sudden step she turned away. But joy could not long be repressed, even by circumstances that would have excited heavy grief at another moment. Her mind was thronged with delightful thoughts, till sleep stole on, and transformed them to visions, more delightful and more wild, like the breath of winter (but what a cold comparison!) working fantastic tracery upon a window.

When the night was far advanced, Mary awoke with a sudden start. A vivid dream had latterly involved her in its unreal life, of which, however, she could only remember that it had been broken in upon at the most interesting point. For a little time, slumber hung about her like a morning mist, hindering her from perceiving the distinct outline of her situation. She listened with imperfect consciousness to two or three volleys of a rapid and eager knocking; and first she deemed the noise a matter of course, like the breath she drew; next, it appeared a thing in which she had no concern; and lastly, she became aware that it was a summons necessary to be obeyed. At the same moment, the pang of recollection darted into her mind; the pall of sleep was thrown back from the face of grief; the dim light of the chamber, and the

objects therein revealed, had retained all her suspended ideas, and restored them as soon as she unclosed her eyes. Again there was a quick peal upon
the street-door. Fearing that her sister would also
be disturbed, Mary wrapped herself in a cloak and
hood, took the lamp from the hearth, and hastened to
the window. By some accident, it had been left un-
hasped, and yielded easily to her hand.

"Who's there?" asked Mary, trembling as she
looked forth.

The storm was over, and the moon was up; it shone
upon broken clouds above, and below upon houses
black with moisture, and upon little lakes of the fallen
rain, curling into silver beneath the quick enchantment
of a breeze. A young man in a sailor's dress, wet as
if he had come out of the depths of the sea, stood
alone under the window. Mary recognized him as one
whose livelihood was gained by short voyages along
the coast; nor did she forget that, previous to her
marriage, he had been an unsuccessful wooer of her
own.

"What do you seek here, Stephen?" said she.

"Cheer up, Mary, for I seek to comfort you," answered the rejected lover. "You must know I got
home not ten minutes ago, and the first thing my good
mother told me was the news about your husband. So,
without saying a word to the old woman, I clapped on
my hat, and ran out of the house. I could n't have
slept a wink before speaking to you, Mary, for the
sake of old times."

"Stephen, I thought better of you!" exclaimed the
widow, with gushing tears and preparing to close the
lattice; for she was no whit inclined to imitate the
first wife of Zadig.

"But stop, and hear my story out," cried the young sailor. "I tell you we spoke a brig yesterday afternoon, bound in from Old England. And whom do you think I saw standing on deck, well and hearty, only a bit thinner than he was five months ago?"

Mary leaned from the window, but could not speak.

"Why, it was your husband himself," continued the generous seaman. "He and three others saved themselves on a spar, when the Blessing turned bottom upwards. The brig will beat into the bay by daylight, with this wind, and you'll see him here to-morrow. There's the comfort I bring you, Mary, and so good night."

He hurried away, while Mary watched him with a doubt of waking reality, that seemed stronger or weaker as he alternately entered the shade of the houses, or emerged into the broad streaks of moonlight. Gradually, however, a blessed flood of conviction swelled into her heart, in strength enough to overwhelm her, had its increase been more abrupt. Her first impulse was to rouse her sister-in-law, and communicate the new-born-gladness. She opened the chamber-door, which had been closed in the course of the night, though not latched, advanced to the bedside, and was about to lay her hand upon the slumberer's shoulder. But then she remembered that Margaret would awake to thoughts of death and woe, rendered not the less bitter by their contrast with her own felicity. She suffered the rays of the lamp to fall upon the unconscious form of the bereaved one. Margaret lay in unquiet sleep, and the drapery was displaced around her; her young cheek was rosy-tinted, and her lips half opened in a vivid smile; an expression of joy, debarred its passage by her sealed eyelids, struggled forth like incense from the whole countenance.

"My poor sister! you will waken too soon from that happy dream," thought Mary.

Before retiring, she set down the lamp, and endeavored to arrange the bedclothes so that the chill air might not do harm to the feverish slumberer. But her hand trembled against Margaret's neck, a tear also fell upon her cheek, and she suddenly awoke.

LITTLE DAFFYDOWNDILLY.

DAFFYDOWNDILLY was so called because in his nature he resembled a flower, and loved to do only what
was beautiful and agreeable, and took no delight in
labor of any kind. But while Daffydowndilly was yet
a little boy, his mother sent him away from his pleasant home, and put him under the care of a very strict
schoolmaster, who went by the name of Mr. Toil.
Those who knew him best affirmed that this Mr. Toil
was a very worthy character; and that he had done
more good, both to children and grown people, than
anybody else in the world. Certainly he had lived
long enough to do a great deal of good; for, if all
stories be true, he had dwelt upon earth ever since
Adam was driven from the garden of Eden.

Nevertheless, Mr. Toil had a severe and ugly countenance, especially for such little boys or big men as
were inclined to be idle; his voice, too, was harsh;
and all his ways and customs seemed very disagreeable to our friend Daffydowndilly. The whole day
long, this terrible old schoolmaster sat at his desk
overlooking the scholars, or stalked about the school-
room with a certain awful birch rod in his hand. Now
came a rap over the shoulders of a boy whom Mr.
Toil had caught at play; now he punished a whole
class who were behindhand with their lessons; and, in
short, unless a lad chose to attend quietly and constantly to his book, he had no chance of enjoying a
quiet moment in the school-room of Mr. Toil.

"This will never do for me," thought Daffydown dilly.

Now, the whole of Daffydowndilly's life had hitherto been passed with his dear mother, who had a much sweeter face than old Mr. Toil and who had always been very indulgent to her little boy. No wonder, therefore, that poor Daffydowndilly found it a woful change, to be sent away from the good lady's side, and put under the care of this ugly-visaged schoolmaster, who never gave him any apples or cakes, and seemed to think that little boys were created only to get lessons.

"I can't bear it any longer," said Daffydowndilly to himself, when he had been at school about a week. "I'll run away, and try to find my dear mother; and, at any rate, I shall never find anybody half so disagreeable as this old Mr. Toil!"

So, the very next morning, off started poor Daffydowndilly, and began his rambles about the world, with only some bread and cheese for his breakfast, and very little pocket-money to pay his expenses. But he had gone only a short distance when he overtook a man of grave and sedate appearance, who was trudging at a moderate pace along the road.

"Good morning, my fine lad," said the stranger; and his voice seemed hard and severe, but yet had a sort of kindness in it; "whence do you come so early, and whither are you going?"

Little Daffydowndilly was a boy of very ingenuous disposition, and had never been known to tell a lie in all his life. Nor did he tell one now. He hesitated a moment or two, but finally confessed that he had run away from school, on account of his great dislike to Mr. Toil; and that he was resolved to find some place in the world where he should never see or hear of the old schoolmaster again.

"Oh, very well, my little friend!" answered the stranger. "Then we will go together; for I, likewise, have had a good deal to do with Mr. Toil, and should be glad to find some place where he was never heard of."

Our friend Daffydowndilly would have been better pleased with a companion of his own age, with whom he might have gathered flowers along the roadside, or have chased butterflies, or have done many other things to make the journey pleasant. But he had wisdom enough to understand that he should get along through the world much easier by having a man of experience to show him the way. So he accepted the stranger's proposal, and they walked on very sociably together.

They had not gone far, when the road passed by a field where some haymakers were at work, mowing down the tall grass, and spreading it out in the sun to dry. Daffydowndilly was delighted with the sweet smell of the new-mown grass, and thought how much pleasanter it must be to make hay in the sunshine, under the blue sky, and with the birds singing sweetly in the neighboring trees and bushes, than to be shut up in a dismal school-room, learning lessons all day long, and continually scolded by old Mr. Toil. But, in the midst of these thoughts, while he was stopping to peep over the stone wall, he started back and caught hold of his companion's hand.

"Quick, quick!" cried he. "Let us run away, or he will catch us!"

"Who will catch us?" asked the stranger.

"Mr. Toil, the old schoolmaster!" answered Daffy

downdilly. "Don't you see him amongst the hay makers?"

And Daffydowndilly pointed to an elderly man, who seemed to be the owner of the field, and the employer of the men at work there. He had stripped off his coat and waistcoat, and was busily at work in his shirt-sleeves. The drops of sweat stood upon his brow; but he gave himself not a moment's rest, and kept crying out to the haymakers to make hay while the sun shone. Now, strange to say, the figure and features of this old farmer were precisely the same as those of old Mr. Toil, who, at that very moment, must have been just entering his school-room.

"Don't be afraid," said the stranger. "This is not Mr. Toil the schoolmaster, but a brother of his, who was bred a farmer; and people say he is the most disagreeable man of the two. However, he won't trouble you, unless you become a laborer on the farm."

Little Daffydowndilly believed what his companion said, but was very glad, nevertheless, when they were out of sight of the old farmer, who bore such a singular resemblance to Mr. Toil. The two travellers had gone but little farther, when they came to a spot where some carpenters were erecting a house. Daffydowndilly begged his companion to stop a moment; for it was a very pretty sight to see how neatly the carpenters did their work, with their broad-axes, and saws, and planes, and hammers, shaping out the doors, and putting in the window-sashes, and nailing on the clapboards; and he could not help thinking that he should like to take a broad-axe, a saw, a plane, and a hammer, and build a little house for himself. And then, when he should have a house of his own, old Mr. Toil would never dare to molest him.

But, just while he was delighting himself with this idea, little Daffydowndilly beheld something that made him catch hold of his companion's hand, all in a fright.

"Make haste. Quick, quick!" cried he. "There he is again!"

"Who?" asked the stranger, very quietly.

"Old Mr. Toil," said Daffydowndilly, trembling. "There! he that is overseeing the carpenters. 'T is my old schoolmaster, as sure as I 'm alive!"

The stranger cast his eyes where Daffydowndilly pointed his finger; and he saw an elderly man, with a carpenter's rule and compasses in his hand. This person went to and fro about the unfinished house, measuring pieces of timber, and marking out the work that was to be done, and continually exhorting the other carpenters to be diligent. And wherever he turned his hard and wrinkled visage, the men seemed to feel that they had a task-master over them, and sawed, and hammered, and planed, as if for dear life.

"Oh no! this is not Mr. Toil, the schoolmaster," said the stranger. "It is another brother of his, who follows the trade of carpenter."

"I am very glad to hear it," quoth Daffydowndilly; "but if you please, sir, I should like to get out of his way as soon as possible."

Then they went on a little farther, and soon heard the sound of a drum and fife. Daffydowndilly pricked up his ears at this, and besought his companion to hurry forward, that they might not miss seeing the soldiers. Accordingly, they made what haste they could, and soon met a company of soldiers, gayly dressed, with beautiful feathers in their caps, and bright muskets on their shoulders. In front marched two drummers and two fifers, beating on their drums and playing on their fifes with might and main, and making such lively music that little Daffydowndilly would gladly have followed them to the end of the world. And if he was only a soldier, then, he said to himself, old Mr. Toil would never venture to look him in the face.

"Quick step! Forward march!" shouted a gruff voice.

Little Daffydowndilly started, in great dismay; for this voice which had spoken to the soldiers sounded precisely the same as that which he had heard every day in Mr. Toil's school-room, out of Mr. Toil's own mouth. And, turning his eyes to the captain of the company, what should he see but the very image of old Mr. Toil himself, with a smart cap and feather on his head, a pair of gold epaulets on his shoulders, a laced coat on his back, a purple sash round his waist, and a long sword, instead of a birch rod, in his hand. And though he held his head so high, and strutted like a turkey-cock, still he looked quite as ugly and disagreeable as when he was hearing lessons in the school-room.

"This is certainly old Mr. Toil," said Daffydowndilly, in a trembling voice. "Let us run away, for fear he should make us enlist in his company!"

"You are mistaken again, my little friend," replied the stranger, very composedly. "This is not Mr. Toil, the schoolmaster, but a brother of his, who has served in the army all his life. People say he's a terribly severe fellow; but you and I need not be afraid of him."

"Well, well," said little Daffydowndilly, "but, if

you please, sir, I don't want to see the soldiers any more."

So the child and the stranger resumed their journey; and, by and by, they came to a house by the roadside, where a number of people were making merry. Young men and rosy-cheeked girls, with smiles on their faces, were dancing to the sound of a fiddle. It was the pleasantest sight that Daffydowndilly had yet met with, and it comforted him for all his disappointments.

"Oh, let us stop here," cried he to his companion; "for Mr. Toil will never dare to show his face where there 's a fiddler, and where people are dancing and making merry. We shall be quite safe here!"

But these last words died away upon Daffydowndilly's tongue; for, happening to cast his eyes on the fiddler, whom should he behold again but the likeness of Mr. Toil, holding a fiddle-bow instead of a birch rod, and flourishing it with as much ease and dexterity as if he had been a fiddler all his life! He had somewhat the air of a Frenchman, but still looked exactly like the old schoolmaster; and Daffydowndilly even fancied that he nodded and winked at him, and made signs for him to join in the dance.

"Oh dear me!" whispered he, turning pale, "It seems as if there was nobody but Mr. Toil in the world. Who could have thought of his playing on a fiddle!"

"This is not your old schoolmaster," observed the stranger, "but another brother of his, who was bred in France, where he learned the profession of a fiddler. He is ashamed of his family, and generally calls himself Monsieur le Plaisir; but his real name is Toil, and those who have known him best think him still more disagreeable than his brothers."

"Pray let us go a little farther," said Daffydowndilly. "I don't like the looks of this fiddler at all."

Well, thus the stranger and little Daffydowndilly went wandering along the highway, and in shady lanes, and through pleasant villages; and whithersoever they went, behold! there was the image of old Mr. Toil. He stood like a scarecrow in the cornfields. If they entered a house, he sat in the parlor; if they peeped into the kitchen, he was there. He made himself at home in every cottage, and stole, under one disguise or another, into the most splendid mansions. Everywhere there was sure to be somebody wearing the likeness of Mr. Toil, and who, as the stranger affirmed, was one of the old schoolmaster's innumerable brethren.

Little Daffydowndilly was almost tired to death, when he perceived some people reclining lazily in a shady place, by the side of the road. The poor child entreated his companion that they might sit down there, and take some repose.

"Old Mr. Toil will never come here," said he; "for he hates to see people taking their ease."

But, even while he spoke, Daffydowndilly's eyes fell upon a person who seemed the laziest, and heaviest, and most torpid of all those lazy and heavy and torpid people who had lain down to sleep in the shade. Who should it be, again, but the very image of Mr. Toil!

"There is a large family of these Toils," remarked the stranger. "This is another of the old schoolmaster's brothers, who was bred in Italy, where he acquired very idle habits, and goes by the name of Signor Far Niente. He pretends to lead an easy life, but is really the most miserable fellow in the family."

"Oh take me back! — take me back!" cried poor little Daffydowndilly, bursting into tears. "If there is nothing but Toil all the world over, I may just as well go back to the school-house!"

"Yonder it is, — there is the school-house!" said the stranger; for though he and little Daffydowndilly had taken a great many steps, they had travelled in a circle instead of a straight line. "Come; we will go back to school together."

There was something in his companion's voice that little Daffydowndilly now remembered, and it is strange that he had not remembered it sooner. Looking up into his face, behold! there again was the likeness of old Mr. Toil; so that the poor child had been in company with Toil all day, even while he was doing his best to run away from him. Some people, to whom I have told little Daffydowndilly's story, are of opinion that old Mr. Toil was a magician, and possessed the power of multiplying himself into as many shapes as he saw fit.

Be this as it may, little Daffydowndilly had learned a good lesson, and from that time forward was diligent at his task, because he knew that diligence is not a whit more toilsome than sport or idleness. And when he became better acquainted with Mr. Toil, he began to think that his ways were not so very disagreeable, and that the old schoolmaster's smile of approbation made his face almost as pleasant as even that of Daffydowndilly's mother.

MY KINSMAN, MAJOR MOLINEUX.

AFTER the kings of Great Britain had assumed the right of appointing the colonial governors, the measures of the latter seldom met with the ready and general approbation which had been paid to those of their predecessors, under the original charters. The people looked with most jealous scrutiny to the exercise of power which did not emanate from themselves, and they usually rewarded their rulers with slender gratitude for the compliances by which, in softening their instructions from beyond the sea, they had incurred the reprehension of those who gave them. The annals of Massachusetts Bay will inform us, that of six governors in the space of about forty years from the surrender of the old charter, under James II., two were imprisoned by a popular insurrection; a third, as Hutchinson inclines to believe, was driven from the province by the whizzing of a musket-ball; a fourth, in the opinion of the same historian, was hastened to his grave by continual bickerings with the House of Representatives; and the remaining two, as well as their successors, till the Revolution, were favored with few and brief intervals of peaceful sway. The inferior members of the court party, in times of high political excitement, led scarcely a more desirable life. These remarks may serve as a preface to the following adventures, which chanced upon a summer night, not far from a hundred years ago. The reader, in order to avoid a long and dry detail of colonial affairs, is requested to dispense with an account of the train of circumstances that had caused much temporary inflammation of the popular mind.

It was near nine o'clock of a moonlight evening, when a boat crossed the ferry with a single passenger, who had obtained his conveyance at that unusual hour by the promise of an extra fare. While he stood on the landing-place, searching in either pocket for the means of fulfilling his agreement, the ferryman lifted a lantern, by the aid of which, and the newly risen moon, he took a very accurate survey of the stranger's figure. He was a youth of barely eighteen years, evidently country-bred, and now, as it should seem, upon his first visit to town. He was clad in a coarse gray coat, well worn, but in excellent repair; his under garments were durably constructed of leather, and fitted tight to a pair of serviceable and well-shaped limbs; his stockings of blue yarn were the incontrovertible work of a mother or a sister; and on his head was a three-cornered hat, which in its better days had perhaps sheltered the graver brow of the lad's father. Under his left arm was a heavy cudgel formed of an oak sapling, and retaining a part of the hardened root; and his equipment was completed by a wallet, not so abundantly stocked as to incommode the vigorous shoulders on which it hung. Brown, curly hair, well-shaped features, and bright, cheerful eyes were nature's gifts, and worth all that art could have done for his adornment.

The youth, one of whose names was Robin, finally drew from his pocket the half of a little province bill of five shillings, which, in the depreciation in that sort of currency, did but satisfy the ferryman's demand, with the surplus of a sexangular piece of parchment,

valued at three pence. He then walked forward into
the town, with as light a step as if his day's journey
had not already exceeded thirty miles, and with as
eager an eye as if he were entering London city, instead of the little metropolis of a New England colony. Before Robin had proceeded far, however, it occurred to him that he knew not whither to direct his
steps ; so he paused, and looked up and down the narrow street, scrutinizing the small and mean wooden
buildings that were scattered on either side.

"This low hovel cannot be my kinsman's dwelling,"
thought he, "nor yonder old house, where the moonlight
enters at the broken casement ; and truly I see none
hereabouts that might be worthy of him. It would
have been wise to inquire my way of the ferryman,
and doubtless he would have gone with me, and earned
a shilling from the Major for his pains. But the next
man I meet will do as well."

He resumed his walk, and was glad to perceive that
the street now became wider, and the houses more respectable in their appearance. He soon discerned a
figure moving on moderately in advance, and hastened
his steps to overtake it. As Robin drew nigh, he saw
that the passenger was a man in years, with a full periwig of gray hair, a wide-skirted coat of dark cloth,
and silk stockings rolled above his knees. He carried
a long and polished cane, which he struck down perpendicularly before him at every step ; and at regular intervals he uttered two successive hems, of a pe-
culiarly solemn and sepulchral intonation. Having
made these observations, Robin laid hold of the skirt
of the old man's coat, just when the light from the
open door and windows of a barber's shop fell upon
both their figures.

" Good evening to you," honored sir, said he, making a low bow, and still retaining his hold of the skirt. " I pray you tell me whereabouts is the dwelling of my kinsman, Major Molineux."

The youth's question was uttered very loudly; and one of the barbers, whose razor was descending on a well-soaped chin, and another who was dressing a Ramillies wig, left their occupations, and came to the door. The citizen, in the mean time, turned a long-favored countenance upon Robin, and answered him in a tone of excessive anger and annoyance. His two sepulchral hems, however, broke into the very centre of his rebuke, with most singular effect, like a thought of the cold grave obtruding among wrathful passions.

" Let go my garment, fellow! I tell you, I know not the man you speak of. What! I have authority, I have — hem, hem — authority; and if this be the respect you show for your betters, your feet shall be brought acquainted with the stocks by daylight, tomorrow morning ! "

Robin released the old man's skirt, and hastened away, pursued by an ill-mannered roar of laughter from the barber's shop. He was at first considerably surprised by the result of his question, but, being a shrewd youth, soon thought himself able to account for the mystery.

" This is some country representative," was his conclusion, " who has never seen the inside of my kinsman's door, and lacks the breeding to answer a stranger civilly. The man is old, or verily — I might be tempted to turn back and smite him on the nose. Ah, Robin, Robin! even the barber's boys laugh at you for choosing such a guide! You will be wiser in time, friend Robin."

He now became entangled in a succession of crooked and narrow streets, which crossed each other, and meandered at no great distance from the water-side. The smell of tar was obvious to his nostrils, the masts of vessels pierced the moonlight above the tops of the buildings, and the numerous signs, which Robin paused to read, informed him that he was near the centre of business. But the streets were empty, the shops were closed, and lights were visible only in the second stories of a few dwelling-houses. At length, on the corner of a narrow lane, through which he was passing, he beheld the broad countenance of a British hero swinging before the door of an inn, whence proceeded the voices of many guests. The casement of one of the lower windows was thrown back, and a very thin curtain permitted Robin to distinguish a party at supper, round a well-furnished table. The fragrance of the good cheer steamed forth into the outer air, and the youth could not fail to recollect that the last remnant of his travelling stock of provision had yielded to his morning appetite, and that noon had found and left him dinnerless.

"Oh, that a parchment three-penny might give me a right to sit down at yonder table!" said Robin, with a sigh. "But the Major will make me welcome to the best of his victuals; so I will even step boldly in, and inquire my way to his dwelling."

He entered the tavern, and was guided by the murmur of voices and the fumes of tobacco to the public-room. It was a long and low apartment, with oaken walls, grown dark in the continual smoke, and a floor which was thickly sanded, but of no immaculate purity. A number of persons — the larger part of whom appeared to be mariners, or in some way connected with the sea — occupied the wooden benches, or leather-bottomed chairs, conversing on various matters, and occasionally lending their attention to some topic of general interest. Three or four little groups were draining as many bowls of punch, which the West India trade had long since made a familiar drink in the colony. Others, who had the appearance of men who lived by regular and laborious handicraft, preferred the insulated bliss of an unshared potation, and became more taciturn under its influence. Nearly all, in short, evinced a predilection for the Good Creature in some of its various shapes, for this is a vice to which, as Fast Day sermons of a hundred years ago will testify, we have a long hereditary claim. The only guests to whom Robin's sympathies inclined him were two or three sheepish countrymen, who were using the inn somewhat after the fashion of a Turkish caravansary; they had gotten themselves into the darkest corner of the room, and heedless of the Nicotian atmosphere, were supping on the bread of their own ovens, and the bacon cured in their own chimney-smoke. But though Robin felt a sort of brotherhood with these strangers, his eyes were attracted from them to a person who stood near the door, holding whispered conversation with a group of ill-dressed associates. His features were separately striking almost to grotesqueness, and the whole face left a deep impression on the memory. The forehead bulged out into a double prominence, with a vale between; the nose came boldly forth in an irregular curve, and its bridge was of more than a finger's breadth; the eyebrows were deep and shaggy, and the eyes glowed beneath them like fire in a cave.

While Robin deliberated of whom to inquire respecting his kinsman's dwelling, he was accosted by the innkeeper, a little man in a stained white apron, who had come to pay his professional welcome to the stranger. Being in the second generation from a French Protestant, he seemed to have inherited the courtesy of his parent nation ; but no variety of circumstances was ever known to change his voice from the one shrill note in which he now addressed Robin.

"From the country, I presume, sir ? " said he, with a profound bow. " Beg leave to congratulate you on your arrival, and trust you intend a long stay with us. Fine town here, sir, beautiful buildings, and much that may interest a stranger. May I hope for the honor of your commands in respect to supper? "

"The man sees a family likeness ! the rogue has guessed that I am related to the Major !" thought Robin, who had hitherto experienced little superfluous civility.

All eyes were now turned on the country lad, standing at the door, in his worn three-cornered hat, gray coat, leather breeches, and blue yarn stockings, leaning on an oaken cudgel, and bearing a wallet on his back.

Robin replied to the courteous innkeeper, with such an assumption of confidence as befitted the Major's relative. " My honest friend," he said, "I shall make it a point to patronize your house on some occasion, when " — here he could not help lowering his voice — " when I may have more than a parchment three-pence in my pocket. My present business," continued he, speaking with lofty confidence, " is merely to inquire my way to the dwelling of my kinsman, Major Molineux."

There was a sudden and general movement in the room, which Robin interpreted as expressing the eagerness of each individual to become his guide. But the innkeeper turned his eyes to a written paper on the wall, which he read, or seemed to read, with occasional recurrences to the young man's figure.

"What have we here?" said he, breaking his speech into little dry fragments. "'Left the house of the subscriber, bounden servant, Hezekiah Mudge, — had on, when he went away, gray coat, leather breeches, master's third-best hat. One pound currency reward to whosoever shall lodge him in any jail of the province.' Better trudge, boy; better trudge!"

Robin had begun to draw his hand towards the lighter end of the oak cudgel, but a strange hostility in every countenance induced him to relinquish his purpose of breaking the courteous innkeeper's head. As he turned to leave the room, he encountered a sneering glance from the bold-featured personage whom he had before noticed; and no sooner was he beyond the door, than he heard a general laugh, in which the innkeeper's voice might be distinguished, like the dropping of small stones into a kettle.

"Now, is it not strange," thought Robin, with his usual shrewdness, — "is it not strange that the confession of an empty pocket should outweigh the name of my kinsman, Major Molineux? Oh, if I had one of those grinning rascals in the woods, where I and my oak sapling grew up together, I would teach him that my arm is heavy though my purse be light!"

On turning the corner of the narrow lane, Robin found himself in a spacious street, with an unbroken line of lofty houses on each side, and a steepled building at the upper end, whence the ringing of a bell announced the hour of nine. The light of the moon, and the lamps from the numerous shop-windows, discovered people promenading on the pavement, and amongst them Robin hoped to recognize his hitherto inscrutable relative. The result of his former inquiries made him unwilling to hazard another, in a scene of such publicity, and he determined to walk slowly and silently up the street, thrusting his face close to that of every elderly gentleman, in search of the Major's lineaments. In his progress, Robin encountered many gay and gallant figures. Embroidered garments of showy colors, enormous periwigs, gold-laced hats, and silver-hilted swords glided past him and dazzled his optics. Travelled youths, imitators of the European fine gentlemen of the period, trod jauntily along, half dancing to the fashionable tunes which they hummed, and, making poor Robin ashamed of his quiet and natural gait. At length, after many pauses to examine the gorgeous display of goods in the shop-windows, and after suffering some rebukes for the impertinence of his scrutiny into people's faces, the Major's kinsman found himself near the steepled building, still unsuccessful in his search. As yet, however, he had seen only one side of the thronged street; so Robin crossed, and continued the same sort of inquisition down the opposite pavement, with stronger hopes than the philosopher seeking an honest man, but with no better fortune. He had arrived about midway towards the lower end, from which his course began, when he overheard the approach of some one who struck down a cane on the flag-stones at every step, uttering, at regular intervals, two sepulchral hems.

"Mercy on us!" quoth Robin, recognizing the sound.

Turning a corner, which chanced to be close at his right hand, he hastened to pursue his researches in some other part of the town. His patience now was wearing low, and he seemed to feel more fatigue from his rambles since he crossed the ferry, than from his journey of several days on the other side. Hunger also pleaded loudly within him, and Robin began to balance the propriety of demanding, violently, and with lifted cudgel, the necessary guidance from the first solitary passenger whom he should meet. While a resolution to this effect was gaining strength, he entered a street of mean appearance, on either side of which a row of ill-built houses was straggling towards the harbor. The moonlight fell upon no passenger along the whole extent, but in the third domicile which Robin passed there was a half-opened door, and his keen glance detected a woman's garment within.

" My luck may be better here," said he to himself.

Accordingly, he approached the door, and beheld it shut closer as he did so ; yet an open space remained, sufficing for the fair occupant to observe the stranger, without a corresponding display on her part. All that Robin could discern was a strip of scarlet petticoat, and the occasional sparkle of an eye, as if the moonbeams were trembling on some bright thing.

" Pretty mistress," for I may call her so with a good conscience, thought the shrewd youth, since I know nothing to the contrary, — " my sweet pretty mistress, will you be kind enough to tell me whereabouts I must seek the dwelling of my kinsman, Major Molineux ? "

Robin's voice was plaintive and winning, and the female, seeing nothing to be shunned in the handsome country youth, thrust open the door, and came forth into the moonlight. She was a dainty little figure, with a white neck, round arms, and a slender waist, at the extremity of which her scarlet petticoat jutted out over a hoop, as if she were standing in a balloon. Moreover, her face was oval and pretty, her hair dark beneath the little cap, and her bright eyes possessed a sly freedom, which triumphed over those of Robin.

"Major Molineux dwells here," said this fair woman.

Now, her voice was the sweetest Robin had heard that night, the airy counterpart of a stream of melted silver; yet he could not help doubting whether that sweet voice spoke Gospel truth. He looked up and down the mean street, and then surveyed the house before which they stood. It was a small, dark edifice of two stories, the second of which projected over the lower floor, and the front apartment had the aspect of a shop for petty commodities.

"Now, truly, I am in luck," replied Robin, cunningly, "and so indeed is my kinsman, the Major, in having so pretty a housekeeper. But I prithee trouble him to step to the door; I will deliver him a message from his friends in the country, and then go back to my lodgings at the inn."

"Nay, the Major has been abed this hour or more," said the lady of the scarlet petticoat; "and it would be to little purpose to disturb him to-night, seeing his evening draught was of the strongest. But he is a kind-hearted man, and it would be as much as my life's worth to let a kinsman of his turn away from the door. You are the good old gentleman's very picture, and I could swear that was his rainy-weather hat. Also he has garments very much resembling those leather small-clothes. But come in, I pray, for I bid you hearty welcome in his name."

So saying, the fair and hospitable dame took our

hero by the hand; and the touch was light, and the force was gentleness, and though Robin read in her eyes what he did not hear in her words, yet the slender-waisted woman in the scarlet petticoat proved stronger than the athletic country youth. She had drawn his half-willing footsteps nearly to the threshold, when the opening of a door in the neighborhood startled the Major's housekeeper, and, leaving the Major's kinsman, she vanished speedily into her own domicile. A heavy yawn preceded the appearance of a man, who, like the Moonshine of Pyramus and Thisbe, carried a lantern, needlessly aiding his sister luminary in the heavens. As he walked sleepily up the street, he turned his broad, dull face on Robin, and displayed a long staff, spiked at the end.

"Home, vagabond, home!" said the watchman, in accents that seemed to fall asleep as soon as they were uttered. "Home, or we'll set you in the stocks by peep of day!"

"This is the second hint of the kind," thought Robin. "I wish they would end my difficulties, by setting me there to-night."

Nevertheless, the youth felt an instinctive antipathy towards the guardian of midnight order, which at first prevented him from asking his usual question. But just when the man was about to vanish behind the corner, Robin resolved not to lose the opportunity, and shouted lustily after him, —

"I say, friend! will you guide me to the house of my kinsman, Major Molineux?"

The watchman made no reply, but turned the corner and was gone; yet Robin seemed to hear the sound of drowsy laughter stealing along the solitary street. At that moment, also, a pleasant titter saluted him from the open window above his head; he looked up, and caught the sparkle of a saucy eye; a round arm beckoned to him, and next he heard light footsteps descending the staircase within. But Robin, being of the household of a New England clergyman, was a good youth, as well as a shrewd one; so he resisted temptation, and fled away.

He now roamed desperately, and at random, through the town, almost ready to believe that a spell was on him, like that by which a wizard of his country had once kept three pursuers wandering, a whole winter night, within twenty paces of the cottage which they sought. The streets lay before him, strange and desolate, and the lights were extinguished in almost every house. Twice, however, little parties of men, among whom Robin distinguished individuals in outlandish attire, came hurrying along; but, though on both occasions they paused to address him, such intercourse did not at all enlighten his perplexity. They did but utter a few words in some language of which Robin knew nothing, and perceiving his inability to answer, bestowed a curse upon him in plain English and hastened away. Finally, the lad determined to knock at the door of every mansion that might appear worthy to be occupied by his kinsman, trusting that perseverance would overcome the fatality that had hitherto thwarted him. Firm in this resolve, he was passing beneath the walls of a church, which formed the corner of two streets, when, as he turned into the shade of its steeple, he encountered a bulky stranger, muffled in a cloak. The man was proceeding with the speed of earnest business, but Robin planted himself full before him, holding the oak cudgel with both hands across his body as a bar to further passage.

"Halt, honest man, and answer me a question," said he, very resolutely. "Tell me, this instant, whereabouts is the dwelling of my kinsman, Major Molineux!"

"Keep your tongue between your teeth, fool, and let me pass!" said a deep, gruff voice, which Robin partly remembered. "Let me pass, I say, or I'll strike you to the earth!"

"No, no, neighbor!" cried Robin, flourishing his cudgel, and then thrusting its larger end close to the man's muffled face. "No, no, I'm not the fool you take me for, nor do you pass till I have an answer to my question. Whereabouts is the dwelling of my kinsman, Major Molineux?"

The stranger, instead of attempting to force his passage, stepped back into the moonlight, unmuffled his face, and stared full into that of Robin.

"Watch here an hour, and Major Molineux will pass by," said he.

Robin gazed with dismay and astonishment on the unprecedented physiognomy of the speaker. The forehead with its double prominence, the broad hooked nose, the shaggy eyebrows, and fiery eyes were those which he had noticed at the inn, but the man's complexion had undergone a singular, or, more properly, a twofold change. One side of the face blazed an intense red, while the other was black as midnight, the division line being in the broad bridge of the nose; and a mouth which seemed to extend from ear to ear was black or red, in contrast to the color of the cheek. The effect was as if two individual devils, a fiend of fire and a fiend of darkness, had united themselves to form this infernal visage. The stranger grinned in Robin's face, muffled his party-colored features, and was out of sight in a moment.

"Strange things we travellers see!" ejaculated Robin.

He seated himself, however, upon the steps of the church-door, resolving to wait the appointed time for his kinsman. A few moments were consumed in philosophical speculations upon the species of man who had just left him; but having settled this point shrewdly, rationally, and satisfactorily, he was compelled to look elsewhere for his amusement. And first he threw his eyes along the street. It was of more respectable appearance than most of those into which he had wandered; and the moon, creating, like the imaginative power, a beautiful strangeness in familiar objects, gave something of romance to a scene that might not have possessed it in the light of day. The irregular and often quaint architecture of the houses, some of whose roofs were broken into numerous little peaks, while others ascended, steep and narrow, into a single point, and others again were square; the pure snow-white of some of their complexions, the aged darkness of others, and the thousand sparklings, reflected from bright substances in the walls of many; these matters engaged Robin's attention for a while, and then began to grow wearisome. Next he endeavored to define the forms of distant objects, starting away, with almost ghostly indistinctness, just as his eye appeared to grasp them; and finally he took a minute survey of an edifice which stood on the opposite side of the street, directly in front of the church-door, where he was stationed. It was a large, square mansion, distinguished from its neighbors by a balcony, which rested on tall pillars, and by an elaborate Gothic window, communicating therewith.

"Perhaps this is the very house I have been seeking," thought Robin.

Then he strove to speed away the time, by listening to a murmur which swept continually along the street, yet was scarcely audible, except to an unaccustomed ear like his; it was a low, dull, dreamy sound, compounded of many noises, each of which was at too great a distance to be separately heard. Robin marvelled at this snore of a sleeping town, and marvelled more whenever its continuity was broken by now and then a distant shout, apparently loud where it originated. But altogether it was a sleep-inspiring sound, and, to shake off its drowsy influence, Robin arose, and climbed a window-frame, that he might view the interior of the church. There the moonbeams came trembling in, and fell down upon the deserted pews, and extended along the quiet aisles. A fainter yet more awful radiance was hovering around the pulpit, and one solitary ray had dared to rest upon the open page of the great Bible. Had nature, in that deep hour, become a worshipper in the house which man had builded? Or was that heavenly light the visible sanctity of the place, — visible because no earthly and impure feet were within the walls? The scene made Robin's heart shiver with a sensation of loneliness stronger than he had ever felt in the remotest depths of his native woods; so he turned away and sat down again before the door. There were graves around the church, and now an uneasy thought obtruded into Robin's breast. What if the object of his search, which had been so often and so strangely thwarted, were all the time mouldering in his shroud? What if his kinsman should glide through yonder gate, and nod and smile to him in dimly passing by?

"Oh that any breathing thing were here with me!" said Robin.

Recalling his thoughts from this uncomfortable track, he sent them over forest, hill, and stream, and attempted to imagine how that evening of ambiguity and weariness had been spent by his father's household. He pictured them assembled at the door, beneath the tree, the great old tree, which had been spared for its huge twisted trunk and venerable shade, when a thousand leafy brethren fell. There, at the going down of the summer sun, it was his father's custom to perform domestic worship, that the neighbors might come and join with him like brothers of the family, and that the wayfaring man might pause to drink at that fountain, and keep his heart pure by freshening the memory of home. Robin distinguished the seat of every individual of the little audience; he saw the good man in the midst, holding the Scriptures in the golden light that fell from the western clouds; he beheld him close the book and all rise up to pray. He heard the old thanksgivings for daily mercies, the old supplications for their continuance, to which he had so often listened in weariness, but which were now among his dear remembrances. He perceived the slight inequality of his father's voice when he came to speak of the absent one; he noted how his mother turned her face to the broad and knotted trunk; how his elder brother scorned, because the beard was rough upon his upper lip, to permit his features to be moved; how the younger sister drew down a low hanging branch before her eyes; and how the little one of all, whose sports had hitherto broken the decorum of the scene, understood the prayer for her playmate, and burst into clamorous grief. Then he saw them go in at the door; and when Robin would have entered also, the latch tinkled into its place, and he was excluded from his home.

"Am I here, or there?" cried Robin, starting; for all at once, when his thoughts had become visible and audible in a dream, the long, wide, solitary street shone out before him.

He aroused himself, and endeavored to fix his attention steadily upon the large edifice which he had surveyed before. But still his mind kept vibrating between fancy and reality; by turns, the pillars of the balcony lengthened into the tall, bare stems of pines, dwindled down to human figures, settled again into their true shape and size, and then commenced a new succession of changes. For a single moment, when he deemed himself awake, he could have sworn that a visage — one which he seemed to remember, yet could not absolutely name as his kinsman's — was looking towards him from the Gothic window. A deeper sleep wrestled with and nearly overcame him, but fled at the sound of footsteps along the opposite pavement. Robin rubbed his eyes, discerned a man passing at the foot of the balcony, and addressed him in a loud, peevish, and lamentable cry.

"Hallo, friend! must I wait here all night for my kinsman, Major Molineux?"

The sleeping echoes awoke, and answered the voice; and the passenger, barely able to discern a figure sitting in the oblique shade of the steeple, traversed the street to obtain a nearer view. He was himself a gentleman in his prime, of open, intelligent, cheerful, and altogether prepossessing countenance. Perceiving a country youth, apparently homeless and without friends, he accosted him in a tone of real kindness, which had become strange to Robin's ears.

"Well, my good lad, why are you sitting here?" inquired he. "Can I be of service to you in any way?"

"I am afraid not, sir," replied Robin, despond-ingly; "yet I shall take it kindly, if you 'll answer me a single question. I 've been searching, half the night, for one Major Molineux; now, sir, is there really such a person in these parts, or am I dream-ing?"

"Major Molineux! The name is not altogether strange to me," said the gentleman, smiling. "Have you any objection to telling me the nature of your business with him?"

Then Robin briefly related that his father was a clergyman, settled on a small salary, at a long dis-tance back in the country, and that he and Major Mol-ineux were brothers' children. The Major, having in-herited riches, and acquired civil and military rank, had visited his cousin, in great pomp, a year or two before; had manifested much interest in Robin and an elder brother, and, being childless himself, had thrown out hints respecting the future establishment of one of them in life. The elder brother was des-tined to succeed to the farm which his father culti-vated in the interval of sacred duties; it was therefore determined that Robin should profit by his kinsman's generous intentions, especially as he seemed to be rather the favorite, and was thought to possess other necessary endowments.

"For I have the name of being a shrewd youth," observed Robin, in this part of his story.

"I doubt not you deserve it," replied his new friend, good-naturedly; "but pray proceed."

"Well, sir, being nearly eighteen years old, and well grown, as you see," continued Robin, drawing himself up to his full height, "I thought it high time to begin the world. So my mother and sister put me in handsome trim, and my father gave me half the remnant of his last year's salary, and five days ago I started for this place, to pay the Major a visit. But, would you believe it, sir! I crossed the ferry a little after dark, and have yet found nobody that would show me the way to his dwelling; only, an hour or two since, I was told to wait here, and Major Molineux would pass by."

"Can you describe the man who told you this?" inquired the gentleman.

"Oh, he was a very ill-favored fellow, sir," replied Robin, "with two great bumps on his forehead, a hook nose, fiery eyes; and, what struck me as the strangest, his face was of two different colors. Do you happen to know such a man, sir?"

"Not intimately," answered the stranger, "but I chanced to meet him a little time previous to your stopping me. I believe you may trust his word, and that the Major will very shortly pass through this street. In the mean time, as I have a singular curiosity to witness your meeting, I will sit down here upon the steps and bear you company."

He seated himself accordingly, and soon engaged his companion in animated discourse. It was but of brief continuance, however, for a noise of shouting, which had long been remotely audible, drew so much nearer that Robin inquired its cause.

"What may be the meaning of this uproar?" asked he. "Truly, if your town be always as noisy, I shall find little sleep while I am an inhabitant."

"Why, indeed, friend Robin, there do appear to be three or four riotous fellows abroad to-night," replied the gentleman. "You must not expect all the stillness of your native woods here in our streets. But the watch will shortly be at the heels of these lads and " —

"Ay, and set them in the stocks by peep of day," interrupted Robin, recollecting his own encounter with the drowsy lantern-bearer. "But, dear sir, if I may trust my ears, an army of watchmen would never make head against such a multitude of rioters. There were at least a thousand voices went up to make that one shout."

"May not a man have several voices, Robin, as well as two complexions?" said his friend.

"Perhaps a man may; but Heaven forbid that a woman should!" responded the shrewd youth, thinking of the seductive tones of the Major's housekeeper.

The sounds of a trumpet in some neighboring street now became so evident and continual, that Robin's curiosity was strongly excited. In addition to the shouts, he heard frequent bursts from many instruments of discord, and a wild and confused laughter filled up the intervals. Robin rose from the steps, and looked wistfully towards a point whither people seemed to be hastening.

"Surely some prodigious merry-making is going on," exclaimed he. "I have laughed very little since I left home, sir, and should be sorry to lose an opportunity. Shall we step round the corner by that darkish house, and take our share of the fun?"

"Sit down again, sit down, good Robin," replied the gentleman, laying his hand on the skirt of the gray coat. "You forget that we must wait here for your kinsman; and there is reason to believe that he will pass by, in the course of a very few moments."

The near approach of the uproar had now disturbed the neighborhood: windows flew open on all sides;

and many heads, in the attire of the pillow, and confused by sleep suddenly broken, were protruded to the gaze of whoever had leisure to observe them. Eager voices hailed each other from house to house, all demanding the explanation, which not a soul could give. Half-dressed men hurried towards the unknown commotion, stumbling as they went over the stone steps that thrust themselves into the narrow foot-walk. The shouts, the laughter, and the tuneless bray, the antipodes of music, came onwards with increasing din, till scattered individuals, and then denser bodies, began to appear round a corner at the distance of a hundred yards.

" Will you recognize your kinsman, if he passes in this crowd ? " inquired the gentleman.

" Indeed, I can't warrant it, sir; but I 'll take my stand here, and keep a bright lookout," answered Robin, descending to the outer edge of the pavement.

A mighty stream of people now emptied into the street, and came rolling slowly towards the church. A single horseman wheeled the corner in the midst of them, and close behind him came a band of fearful wind-instruments, sending forth a fresher discord now that no intervening buildings kept it from the ear. Then a redder light disturbed the moonbeams, and a dense multitude of torches shone along the street, concealing, by their glare, whatever object they illuminated. The single horseman, clad in a military dress, and bearing a drawn sword, rode onward as the leader, and, by his fierce and variegated countenance, appeared like war personified ; the red of one cheek was an emblem of fire and sword ; the blackness of the other betokened the mourning that attends them. In his train were wild figures in the Indian dress, and many fantastic shapes without a model, giving the whole march a visionary air, as if a dream had broken forth from some feverish brain, and were sweeping visibly through the midnight streets. A mass of people, inactive, except as applauding spectators, hemmed the procession in ; and several women ran along the sidewalk, piercing the confusion of heavier sounds with their shrill voices of mirth or terror.

"The double-faced fellow has his eye upon me," muttered Robin, with an indefinite but an uncomfortable idea that he was himself to bear a part in the pageantry.

The leader turned himself in the saddle, and fixed his glance full upon the country youth, as the steed went slowly by. When Robin had freed his eyes from those fiery ones, the musicians were passing before him, and the torches were close at hand ; but the unsteady brightness of the latter formed a veil which he could not penetrate. The rattling of wheels over the stones sometimes found its way to his ear, and confused traces of a human form appeared at intervals, and then melted into the vivid light. A moment more, and the leader thundered a command to halt : the trumpets vomited a horrid breath, and then held their peace ; the shouts and laughter of the people died away, and there remained only a universal hum, allied to silence. Right before Robin's eyes was an uncovered cart. There the torches blazed the brightest, there the moon shone out like day, and there, in tar-and-feathery dignity, sat his kinsman, Major Molineux !

He was an elderly man, of large and majestic person, and strong, square features, betokening a steady soul ; but steady as it was, his enemies had found means to shake it. His face was pale as death, and far more ghastly; the broad forehead was contracted in his agony, so that his eyebrows formed one grizzled line; his eyes were red and wild, and the foam hung white upon his quivering lip. His whole frame was agitated by a quick and continual tremor, which his pride strove to quell, even in those circumstances of overwhelming humiliation. But perhaps the bitterest pang of all was when his eyes met those of Robin; for he evidently knew him on the instant, as the youth stood witnessing the foul disgrace of a head grown gray in honor. They stared at each other in silence, and Robin's knees shook, and his hair bristled, with a mixture of pity and terror. Soon, however, a bewildering excitement began to seize upon his mind; the preceding adventures of the night, the unexpected appearance of the crowd, the torches, the confused din and the hush that followed, the spectre of his kinsman reviled by that great multitude, — all this, and, more than all, a perception of tremendous ridicule in the whole scene, affected him with a sort of mental inebriety. At that moment a voice of sluggish merriment saluted Robin's ears; he turned instinctively, and just behind the corner of the church stood the lantern-bearer, rubbing his eyes, and drowsily enjoying the lad's amazement. Then he heard a peal of laughter like the ringing of silvery bells; a woman twitched his arm, a saucy eye met his, and he saw the lady of the scarlet petticoat. A sharp, dry cachinnation appealed to his memory, and, standing on tiptoe in the crowd, with his white apron over his head, he beheld the courteous little innkeeper. And lastly, there sailed over the heads of the multitude a great, broad laugh, broken in the midst by two sepulchral hems; thus,

" Haw, haw, haw, — hem, hem, — haw, haw, haw, haw ! "

The sound proceeded from the balcony of the opposite edifice, and thither Robin turned his eyes. In front of the Gothic window stood the old citizen, wrapped in a wide gown, his gray periwig exchanged for a nightcap, which was thrust back from his forehead, and his silk stockings hanging about his legs. He supported himself on his polished cane in a fit of convulsive merriment, which manifested itself on his solemn old features like a funny inscription on a tombstone. Then Robin seemed to hear the voices of the barbers, of the guests of the inn, and of all who had made sport of him that night. The contagion was spreading among the multitude, when all at once, it seized upon Robin, and he sent forth a shout of laughter that echoed through the street, — every man shook his sides, every man emptied his lungs, but Robin's shout was the loudest there. The cloud-spirits peeped from their silvery islands, as the congregated mirth went roaring up the sky! The Man in the Moon heard the far bellow. "Oho," quoth he, " the old earth is frolicsome to-night ! "

When there was a momentary calm in that tempestuous sea of sound, the leader gave the sign, the procession resumed its march. On they went, like fiends that throng in mockery around some dead potentate, mighty no more, but majestic still in his agony. On they went, in counterfeited pomp, in senseless uproar, in frenzied merriment, trampling all on an old man's heart. On swept the tumult, and left a silent street behind.

.   .   .   .

" Well, Robin, are you dreaming?" inquired the gentleman, laying his hand on the youth's shoulder.

Robin started, and withdrew his arm from the stone post to which he had instinctively clung, as the living stream rolled by him. His cheek was somewhat pale, and his eye not quite as lively as in the earlier part of the evening.

"Will you be kind enough to show me the way to the ferry?" said he, after a moment's pause.

"You have, then, adopted a new subject of inquiry?" observed his companion, with a smile.

"Why, yes, sir," replied Robin, rather dryly. "Thanks to you, and to my other friends, I have at last met my kinsman, and he will scarce desire to see my face again. I begin to grow weary of a town life, sir. Will you show me the way to the ferry?"

"No, my good friend Robin, — not to-night, at least," said the gentleman. "Some few days hence, if you wish it, I will speed you on your journey. Or, if you prefer to remain with us, perhaps, as you are a shrewd youth, you may rise in the world without the help of your kinsman, Major Molineux."

Lightning Source UK Ltd.
Milton Keynes UK
UKOW011851270112

186201UK00006B/282/P